WITCHY EYE

Flight of the Serpent's Daughter

D.J. BUTLER

Witchy Eye

This is a work of fiction. All the characters and events portrayed in this book are fictional, and any resemblance to real people or incidents is purely coincidental.

A Baen Books Original

Baen Publishing Enterprises
P.O. Box 1403
Riverdale, NY 10471
www.baen.com

ISBN: 978-1-4767-8211-9

Cover art by Daniel Dos Santos
Map by Rhys Davies

First printing, March 2017

Distributed by Simon & Schuster
1230 Avenue of the Americas
New York, NY 10020

10 9 8 7 6 5 4 3 2 1

Pages by Joy Freeman (www.pagesbyjoy.com)
Printed in the United States of America

For Katelyn Westergard,
who was an early reader.

And for David Young,
who knew my mad ambitions years ago.

"Everybody hide your fairies!"

CHAPTER ONE

It was red, puffy, shiny and swollen. Like some obscene overripe fruit from Jamaica, her eye bulged in its socket, useless, sealed shut, and glinting with a hint of pus. Was it twitching at him? Obadiah shuddered.

"Witchy eye," he muttered. "'Erne's 'orn, that's a blighted phiz, poor chick."

The gnarled Appalachee crawled like a pot of fire ants, boiling out of their secret holes in the hills and trickling down their winding trails to the Tobacco Fair. They never quite managed to form up into lines until they got to Nashville's gates and the solid Imperial stone forced them to.

With them had come the rickety mule-pulled cart, the gaggle of whipcord-thin waifs jangling about it, and this ugly, smash-faced girl pulling the lead rope.

Even without the eye, she would have been no great beauty. Her hair was thin, black, and ragged, her skin so pale it was almost white, and she was filthy. Obadiah knew it was a trick of the mind, but he thought he could smell her stink cutting through the fetid miasma of the crowd from fifty feet away. She had a wool shawl over her shoulders—purple, with smiling golden suns woven into it—but it covered nothing. The shawl was more a defiant spit in the eye of the coming winter than an actual garment. Under the wool she wore the tight shirt—forearms

1

bare—and slatternly high skirt of Appalachee, clothing that would have been scandalous in Philadelphia or in New Amsterdam.

Not that Obadiah would have minded seeing a little flesh; on the contrary, he enjoyed looking at a woman, as long as she had meat on her bones.

And two good eyes. He looked again at the Appalachee's swollen face and cringed.

Around Obadiah, Market Street—the wide, stone-cobbled way that led from the Charlotte Pike Gate to the Cumberland River— teemed with life. The emperor's Revenue Men guarded the heavy iron portcullises of the gate, dour-faced but shining with their breastplates, steel bonnets and long Brown Bess muskets. On the towers, Pitchers watched the road outside town and polished their big guns. The gate was of recent construction, like the walls. It was only—Obadiah scratched his belly and did the math—thirty-odd years ago that the Philadelphia Compact had set aside the Imperial Towns as revenue sources for the emperor. Thirty-one years, this being the Year of Our Lord eighteen hundred fifteen. Old John Penn, no fool he, had got right down to building walls and gates and, of course, setting taxes.

The Revenue Men couldn't do much off Imperial land, so they did as much as they could where they were allowed. Today they assessed on each entering vehicle the lawful Fair Toll, thrupp-ence per wheel, payable in whatever coin the party could scrape together. Louisianan sols, Ferdinandian pesos, German thalers, and copper duits from the Hudson Valley rattled around in the Revenue Men's iron box alongside the more familiar pennies struck in the Philadelphia Mint or the Tower of London. Obadiah had a similar chaos of currency in his wallet, as did any traveling man, but mostly he carried the Imperial and Ohio Company coins in which he was paid.

The bustle of activity on Market Street clustered around the canvas tents of the great tobacco buyers. The tents and stalls varied wildly in appearance, and Obadiah knew that each look was carefully cultivated. A white, washed canvas, stiff and upright with the pennant of its merchant house flying was a signal to sellers that this was a prosperous buyer, who would likely pay the best rates. A tent that sagged and was gray with the history of the road told the Appalachee the buyer might be somewhat down on his luck, and not to get too demanding on price. A disordered stall was a trick, a feint that pretended that the stall's owner was distracted or inattentive, and was a ready victim for sharp haggling. It was all show.

The bulk of the buyers spoke with the soft drawl of the southern Crown Lands, Georgia and Carolina, but Obadiah recognized the nasal twang of dour-faced Roundheads, the bouncing verbal roll of tall, blond Dutchmen and the crisp, happy tones of brown-skinned Igbo Free City men in the chuckling Babel around him. There were Geechees in the market crowd, too, and Haudenosaunee, and Frenchmen. No beastfolk that Obadiah had seen (not that he would have been troubled to see beastkind—a woman with a bitch's head, or a nanny's legs and tail, was still a perfectly serviceable woman), only one or two of the Soulless and a single Jew of Araby, looking ready to freeze to death in his bright silks and turban.

A stream of wagons oozed down the street from the gate. The canny hillfolk drove two-wheeled vehicles if they could manage to cram their piles of cured brown leaves into a cart that small (the poorest of the poor growers carried their leaf on their backs to avoid the toll entirely), and four-wheeled only if absolutely necessary. Every cart or wagon was overburdened almost to the point of collapse, in the interest of minimizing the taxes paid to Obadiah's master's master, the Emperor Thomas Penn. The tobacco growers crouched on their conveyances with ears cocked, listening to queries and bids whooped at them on every side until they heard one they would accept, at least as a basis for beginning negotiations. Obadiah heard snatches of Castilian, Dutch, and French, but the business of Nashville was mostly conducted in English.

"Two pounds, I'll give ye!"

"What'll you take for it by the hank, sir?"

"Is that Brightleaf, son, or Fire-Cured?"

Nashville's Tobacco Fair, like any market day, was doubled in size by the addition of swarms of people who neither bought nor sold pipeweed but sought instead to profit by catering to the needs of the tobacco traffickers. Apart from doing his job, this was the part of the fair that interested Obadiah. Less savory entertainments (quite savory enough, to Obadiah's taste) would be offered later, but even this early in the morning every scrap of cobblestone not occupied by a buyer's tent or a seller's wagon was home to a juggling act, an ale-seller, a puppeteer, a shifty-eyed poet, a bellowing news-paperman, or a hawker of rolled cigarettes.

Obadiah disliked trade; his father had been a cooper in London, more or less successful, and it was a damned life. Too much getting up early, too much risk of failure, too much counting of pennies and scrimping to buy more stock and tools for the business. His was not the life Obadiah wanted.

Obadiah wanted steady money, drink, and women.

When he'd left his father's shop he hadn't gone far, at first— he'd just walked down to the marshes of Woolwich, to train for the cannon. That had seemed promising at the time. The coat of arms of the House of Spencer sprang into Obadiah's mind's eye, a griffin rampant over the Cross of St. George, horn sinister and hammer dexter. Only later...later he'd decided he needed to leave England entirely. Obadiah's own tongue tasted bitter to him and he grimaced.

He dismissed the train of thought from his mind. Suffice it to say, Obadiah was no bazaar tentman, and he was more interested in the entertainment than in the buying and selling going on about him. Also, he suffered from a fierce thirst for a mug of good ale. Herne's hoofs, even *bad* ale would do. He just needed to get a little work done first.

He finished the circuit of Market Street with his gaze and came again to the witchy-eyed girl. She had stopped and stood still, glaring at him. He glared back, willing her to move along. Her one good eye squinted in his direction, looking devious and infernal alongside its slick, monstrous mate.

No, he was no merchant, Obadiah told himself, even if he too had come with his master to meet the needs of participants in the Tobacco Fair. His employer was no merchant, either, though he shared a high-pitched nasal accent with the Roundhead traders, what Obadiah in his youth would have called a *Norfolk whine*. The Right Reverend Father Ezekiel Angleton would take money, but he took it as offerings from a collection plate, and he took it, Obadiah recited as if it were a table of numbers learned by rote, because taking it allowed the givers to have the blessing of a voluntary act of sacrifice.

Obadiah snorted to himself. A man said what he had to say to earn a living, and Ezekiel Angleton had to earn a living the same as anyone else. Obadiah didn't care. There might or might not be a Heaven, just like there might or might not be a Herne the Hunter or a Wayland Smith. In any case, this life and its pleasures were enough for Obadiah, and if there were a Hell, Obadiah calculated that working for a priest covered his bets. In any case, Father Angleton didn't charge listeners a fee for his sermonizing. He had a stipend from the emperor, and Obadiah had his room and board and a silver shilling a week from Father Angleton, which was good money for being man of all business to a priest, and none of the worry and hassle of being a tradesman. The travel meant that Obadiah's women always had new faces.

It was a little strange they had come here, though. They'd been to Imperial Towns before—Providence was fine, good pies and plenty of available womanflesh, and Youngstown hadn't been too bad, though that was awfully close to the Eldritch King-doms and Angleton got antsy if he saw too many of their pasty faces—but they had never been as far south as Nashville. For that matter, it was strange that they would travel at all, without the Blues. He didn't know why they had left Philadelphia and come all the way to this forsaken place. Oh, even these stunted cracker goblins were children of God, he knew Father Angleton would say if asked, but there were plenty of children of God to minister to in Pennsland. The Right Reverend Father still held, he had assured Obadiah several times on their journey south and east, his very worthy and useful post as chaplain to the emperor's House Light Dragoons, the famous Philadelphia Blues—so why not stay with the dragoons, then? Obadiah thought he would prefer a trip with those hard-riding soldiers to any festering pit in the empire to spending any more time with these cross-eyed, gap-toothed wretches.

Cross-eyed—at least Witchy Eye (as Obadiah began to name her in his mind) had been spared *that* blight. He chuckled. She might be gap-toothed, though—he looked at her again, still not moving, her stare growing angrier and more intense by the minute. Did she think he was staring at her? The girl's mule was skin and bones and her two-wheeled cart was piled high with cured brown leaf. Half a dozen red- and black-haired beggar-looking wretches surrounded the cart, dirty, unkempt, and wild. Obadiah wrinkled his nose.

Not that Obadiah would object to a few minutes behind a tent flap with one of their older, plumper sisters later in the day, if the occasion offered. A few minutes behind a tent flap, and then get quit of Appalachee.

Obadiah cleared his throat. "Ladies an' gents," he croaked. His voice was rough and loud; it was his greatest professional asset. At Woolwich, he'd been told he might make sergeant on the strength of his voice alone, and now he imagined he was mustering a line of pikemen into formation to stand against the Caliph's hordes. A few heads turned, including the ugly girl's. "Ladies an' gents, 'ark all, this be a great day in the 'istory of Nashville Town!" He raised his hands high above his head, but most of the spectators looked away again and went about their business.

He'd already gotten it wrong, and he scratched himself in mild frustration. Habit. He cleared his throat once more and did it the way the Right Reverend Father had told him to. "Children of the New Light, 'ark ye! A mighty preacher be come amonk ye!" Heads were turning back his way. He reminded himself to make no mention of the Right Reverend Father's being a priest. New Lighters hated the Old Gods, the *pagan* gods they called them, but they had no real affection for priests of any kind, even Christian ones. "Ezekiel Angleton be 'is name," he bellowed, "an' 'e'll be preachink free times today! First sermon to start in one hour's time! Preachink *an'* prophesyink!"

"Where?" shouted one of the buyers, and Obadiah knew he had his hook in.

"By the Town 'All." Obadiah pointed with one arm, and enough heads turned that he calculated his work was done—he'd move on and make his announcement again elsewhere. Might be time for a pint before the first sermon.

"You don't mean that old codger from over Bum Tickle Crick way, do you?" yelled Witchy Eye in a shrill and surprisingly loud voice. "Iffen that's the one, I done heard him preach and prophesy once already, and it weren't worth a coon's bark." There was scattered laughter in the crowd.

Obadiah forced himself to squeeze out a merry rolling laugh and a smile. He didn't care much for Father Angleton's dignity—the priest could fend for himself—but he didn't like feeling personally attacked. "Nay, my wee lass, I don't intend no old codger. Why don't you come alonk an' 'ear 'im? You brink your wee friends, an' you'll 'ear preachink you'll tell your own whelps about." There, that should do it. He turned to go.

"I'm pretty sure Zeke Angleton was his name, though," the ugly girl insisted loudly. "Runtiest lookin' feller you e'er laid eyes on? Talks to hisself a lot, dribbles out the mouth? You sure that ain't him?"

"The Right Reverend Father does not dribble out 'is mouff!" Obadiah wheeled on the pustule-faced girl, and when he saw the triumphant gleam in her one good eye he knew he'd made a mistake.

"The Right Reverend Father, huh?" she repeated slowly, balling her free hand into a fist on her hip. "Well, if you's talkin' about a *churched* man, that's another kettle of fish *al*together. I guess they's two Zeke Angletons in this ol' world, who'd a thunk it?" She kept her face straight, but her eye was laughing at him. Many in the crowd snickered, and some openly guffawed.

Obadiah's cheeks burned. He was used to yelling out announcements to large gatherings, and he was not accustomed to being heckled in the process. "Do you 'old then that if a man be a priest, 'is opinions be wrong, no matter what?" That should recover some of the ground he'd lost.

"Oh, I ain't no swoonin' Barton Stone enthusiast," she shot back. "I reckon a priest's as good a man as many, and maybe even better'n most, when it comes to the business of preachin'. I'm jest interested in honest advertisement, seein' as how we're at the Fair."

"Aye, 'e be churched," Obadiah admitted, because in effect he had already said as much. He needed to win the crowd back. He needed a little theater. "But that don't mean 'e ben't a mighty preacher. I've 'eard 'im shake the very walls with the righteous sound of 'is voice alone!" Obadiah churned the air with his fist for emphasis. "I've seen *soldiers* weep to 'ear 'im preach!"

"Soldiers? Is the Right Reverend Father Zeke Angleton an *army* preacher, then?" The girl's face mocked innocence. "Who e'er heard of a chaplain takin' to the tent?" Most of the crowd was laughing now, and the ugly girl's comrades were laughing hardest of all. In a flash in his mind's eye Obadiah saw himself seizing the tallest of them, a lanky, unhandsome lad with long red hair, and smashing his head into his own cart, over and over again, bloodying the brown tobacco leaves and throwing the body under the wheels on Market Street.

Obadiah tried to focus, but he was flailing. In his building anger, he had a hard time concentrating, and he groped for a dramatic, inspiring image, something to get him out of being ridiculed and to again excite the mob to hear the Right Reverend Father. Not that he gave a tinker's damn whether any of them listened to the priest, much less were saved by his preaching, but Obadiah wanted to keep his job.

He fell back on a polished pitch he'd made in many a street of Boston and Philadelphia. It was a good pitch, full of high drama, and it had never failed him. "Not since St. Martin Luther nailed the skin of the Eldritch 'eretic Cetes to the church door in Wittenberk an' cried ''ere I stand!' 'as such powerful preachink been 'eard by Christian ears, I trow!"

He saw immediately that he had made another misstep.

"Oh, he's a *Martinite*!" The girl's visible eye danced with glee. "Everybody hide your fairies!" The crowd roared.

Obadiah struggled to remember Father Angleton's instructions. He was to have kept it simple, addressed the crowd as the Children of the New Light, invited them to hear preaching and prophesying, and make no mention of the Church, Father Angleton's titles, or the fact he was a member of the Order of St. Martin Luther. That was the path Obadiah had started down—how had he gone so far wrong?

It was the girl with the bad eye. She was malicious, maybe even evil. She was still keeping a straight face, but the loud laughter all around him seemed to Obadiah to be *her* laughter, and it humiliated him.

His instructions didn't tell him what to do now. Obadiah wanted an incisive remark, something that would stamp out the wicked spark in the ugly girl and show the crowd he was master. His mouth gaped and his jaw worked, but before he could form any words, the girl shrugged and walked on, leading the mule and cart and the sharp-elbowed, snickering gaggle of Appalachee runts behind her.

Calvin Calhoun was laughing pretty hard inside, but he didn't let it show—that would have ruined Sarah's joke. Of course, he knew in some sense the joke was on her, and it was an ironic one.

The hillfolk around Nashville would walk twenty miles and stand up to their knees in mud under a lightning storm to hear a New Light preacher, or at least the Christians would. There were plenty of people in the hills, decent folks even, who followed after the strange old gods of wood and creek, worshipping in the high places and the groves, and those were the ones who most agitated the really enthusiastic New Lighters. There were also more than a few residents of Free Imperial Nashville who'd come from the Crown Lands, and called on John Churchill's English Gods, Woden, Wayland, and Herne.

But precious few people of any persuasion in Appalachee would spit in the mouth of an ordained Christian cleric, even if he was dying of thirst. It wasn't that he was a follower of St. Martin Luther—in general, people around Nashville didn't care one way or the other whether the Firstborn had souls or not, had no opinion on the Serpents War in the Old World or the Moundbuilder Kingdoms in the New—it was just that he was a priest.

Sarah had exposed the Right Reverend Father Ezekiel Angleton as an outsider and a priest, which was good fun and he was fair game, having set up as a public preacher. Rightfully her mockery should have dried his listening audience—of hillfolk, anyhow—right to zero...except that now people would expect *her* to come to the tent and engage the preacher as she had engaged his hard-faced herald. Baiting preachers, especially foreign preachers, was popular sport, and she had probably just increased the Right Reverend Father's audience. Did she plan to show them she was up to the challenge? Knowing Sarah, she probably did.

Young Andy broke into sing-song. "Twelve Electors, nary a crown," he sang, "one from each Imperial town."

"Good as far as it goes," Cal judged, "and you jest about hit the melody perfect. Of course, the hard part's the list."

"Andy never gits past Chattanooga," one of the other youn-guns said.

"How far do *you* git?" Cal took all music seriously, but in particular he reverenced the Elector Songs. It was important to know how the emperor was chosen, because that was how he was kept under control, too. And the Elector Songs were new, just a little older than Cal himself, so they weren't stuck deep down in everyone's memory like most of the best songs were.

"Asheville," she admitted, and looked at her feet.

Cal cleared his throat and sang.

Youngstown, Chattanooga, Trenton
Blacksburg, Akron, Scranton
Knoxville, Johnson City, Asheville
Cleveland, Providence, Nashville
Twelve Electors, nary a crown
One from each Imperial Town

It wasn't a great song, more of a chant, really, with no real melody despite what he'd said to Young Andy, but it told the tale it was supposed to tell. There were lots of Elector Songs, all of them written by John Penn's old minstrel Walter Fitzroy, because the empire was made up of lots of different powers, so it was best to learn them young.

"Trenton," Young Andy sighed in exasperation. "Why can't I ever remember Trenton?"

"Keep tryin'," Cal encouraged him.

"Cal!" Sarah jerked her thumb at a buyer over her shoulder, "I b'lieve I heard a shillin' two per hank from that skinny meneer back there. Whyn't you go have a jawin' session with him?" Sarah's eye was hideous, but Cal had known her all his life and thought nothing of it. She was his auntie, and when they were in town to trade she was the leader.

Cal would handle the coins. He was tallest, and oldest—notwithstanding that Sarah was technically his aunt, the very late and youngest daughter of his grandfather—and he was nearly always sober, which was more unusual than one might imagine. Everyone liked to hear the New Light preached. Tear down the high places, burn the groves, and stay away from all their ungodly trappings: the fornicating, the liquor, the wild dancing, and the priests. Prayer and faith and the Bible, that's what a man needed to get through the strait and narrow gate. Everyone liked it as preaching, but not very many people took it as seriously as Cal did. He had no use for priests at all, and no use for liquor. Well, almost no use. Lord hates a man as can't make merry once in a while, and didn't David dance before the Ark?

But no *wild* dancing, and no drunkenness. Drunkenness got Noah into trouble.

Sarah herself would have done a fine job with the cash, of course, but she tried to handle money as little as she possibly could. Cal didn't really know why—Sarah was much better at adding and subtracting than he was. She could read, write, and cipher even with big numbers, and she knew languages; Calvin could rope, brand, shoot a rifle, and throw a tomahawk. His learning was a man's, but hers wasn't a woman's, not exactly. It was something extraordinary, and it was a mark of the fact that her father, Cal's grandfather, the Elector Calhoun, doted on her.

"Aunt Sarah," Young Andy Calhoun called, peeling himself out of the bubbling knot of the Calhoun younguns. Young Andy was David Calhoun's oldest boy, and David was Sarah's oldest brother. Young Andy was almost Sarah's age, but he was *Young Andy* because her father the Elector was also Andy Calhoun. Not that you would ever call her father *Old Andy* or *Old Man Calhoun* to his face, nossiree, Cal had made that mistake once years ago and the cheeks of his buttocks still stung him just to think about it. He was Elector Calhoun or, if you knew his military exploits in the Spanish War and the Pontiac Uprising and even as far back as the Ohio Forks War, and you were a friend, you might call him *Iron Andy*. Behind his back, you might call him a lot of things, and people did. The Elector knew it and laughed.

"What is it, Andy?" she asked.

"You see this?" Young Andy held up a dirty, creased sheet of paper.

Sarah took the sheet from her nephew and Calvin crowded to look over his shoulder. "Why, this ain't nothin' but a newspaper," she explained. Young Andy knew his letters well enough, but the only combination he knew how to put them into was A-N-D-R-E-W-C-A-L-H-O-U-N. If pushed by someone with real willpower, he was sometimes willing to admit also to knowing A-N-D-Y. He resisted all attempts at further education on the grounds that those letters were sufficient to identify either him or his grandpa, that was right powerful and to the purpose, thank you very much, and he didn't see no point in learning any more. Cal was sympathetic. "I hope you didn't let no slick-talkin' Nashville news-paper-man trick you out of a penny, Andy Calhoun."

Cal squinted to see the words—he was a workaday reader at best, but while Sarah and Andy were joshing around, he managed to puzzle out the head-line and the main story. The scrap was indeed a news-paper, the *Nashville Town Imperial Intelligencer*, and it was today's issue:

EMPEROR'S SISTER DIES! POWERS MOURN

<u>Philadelphia</u>. *Sing*, ye Mournful *Seraphs*!!! Our former Empress Hannah, beloved of her Family, every Pennslander & *every Heart Beating* in the <u>Empire of the New World East of the Mississippi</u>, has *Succumbed!* after fifteen Long Years of Struggle, to her *Broken Heart*. HIS IMPERIAL MAJESTY, THE EMPEROR THOMAS PENN Has Laid her to Rest in Franklin's Lightning Cathedral, gathered to the Dust of her <u>Illustrious Ancestors</u>!! Ambassadors from every Power of the Empire & from the Great Kingdoms of the Old World, England, Spain, the Low Country Protectorates, the Caliphate of the West, &cetera, Attended to DO HIM HONOR & *Sang her to her Eternal Sleep.*

People and places so far away, they might as well be fairy tales. Cal didn't have much of an emotional reaction to the news of Mad Hannah's death, except a vague feeling that it was probably a mercy; she'd been locked up since her husband died, and that was as long as Calvin could remember.

"No I did not. I jest saw this here paper on the ground and reckoned as you might like it. Knowin' you was sweet on paper, and all." Young Andy grinned at her. "You're as sweet on paper as Calvin is sweet on you!"

"You jackass." Sarah took a good-natured swipe at her nephew. "Well?" she prompted Calvin.

"Jumpin' Jerusalem, Sarah!" he cursed, smiling. "I ain't forgot the Dutchman, I's jest readin' me a little news. Can't a feller try to elevate hisself a bit without you gittin' mad at him?"

She smiled. If he'd been younger, she might have put him in his place for that bit of wise-assery, but he was one of the oldest grandchildren, several years older than she was, and they were peers. Peers and friends, to Calvin's great delight.

Cal took a hank of the cured tobacco from the Calhoun cart and loped over through the jostling crowd to confirm the price Sarah had heard from the meneer, whistling. He wished he had his tomahawk with him, but walking into town with a war axe dangling from your belt wasn't civilized behavior, so he consoled himself by running his fingertips along the braided leather lariat that hung tied beside where the tomahawk would usually be. Like every man living on Calhoun Mountain, Cal was a cow thief, and he happened to be a good one. He was quiet, he had a sense for animals, and he could throw a rope as accurately as any man. In a pinch, the lariat would do for a weapon, as would the knife in Cal's moccasin boot.

"Graag," Calvin said to the Dutchman, trying to gargle his Gs like the Hudson River Republicans did. It was the only Dutch he knew, but that hardly mattered. He hadn't met a Dutchman yet whose English wasn't at least as good as Cal's, though they sounded funny. The Dutch were famous traders (and sometimes smugglers, like the Catalans and the Hansa), and wherever they went, they spoke the language—the traders of the Dutch Ohio Company probably did their haggling in Ophidian. Cal's *Graag* was meant to show polite interest and respect.

"Graag to you, dank u wel," the Dutchman said. He was a skinny fellow like Cal, but shorter and older, with hair that had gone totally gray and eyebrows that were black.

Cal hefted the leaves in his hand. "One shillin', tuppence a hank, I reckon I heard you call out?"

The Dutchman nodded and pulled out a leather wallet, finely tooled with an image of a spouting whale and held shut with ivory snaps. "Ye-e-es," he said, in that round fashion the Dutch had. "How much do you have?"

Cal grinned. "I got me a fair pile. 'Course, I ain't surprised you ain't payin' but one-and-two, seein' the sickly lookin' leaf you got stacked here. Let me show you a leaf that'll git you wantin' to pay me a shillin' *five*, on account of the price you'll be able to get outta your own customers." He sniffed the leaves and smiled.

Sarah and the other Calhoun younguns kept an eye on the cart while Cal finished his conversation with the Dutchman, and Cal watched them. People who knew the Calhouns—and locally, that was a lot of folks—nodded without ceremony as they passed. She nodded back. Townspeople (who saw her only rarely) and outsiders looked at her face and almost all of them reacted. It was her eye that got their attention, her eye that had never opened and never healed. Sometimes it got a small, controlled response, a slight raising of the brows and then a turning of the head away as if the person looking had been pinched. Sometimes it earned a look of revulsion or fear. Calvin had seen pure disgust all over the face of that preacher's hawker, and he had no doubt that was why Sarah had stopped to harass him. Well, to hell with the Englishman.

To hell with all of them. Calvin would stand with Sarah. She was so stubborn she embarrassed the mules, but she stuck up for her own, and she was funny.

Cal closed with the Dutchman and returned to the cart, smiling just enough for Sarah to know he'd gotten a good deal for Old Man Calhoun's tobacco. He jingled his purse as a further signal, then tucked it into the pocket of his breeches. Unlooping the two rawhide thongs that hung the gate of the cart vertical on the cart's rear posts, he dropped the gate open. Then he grabbed an armload of crinkling, aromatic tobacco leaves as an example for the other boys.

"Pardon me," said a man's voice, so gentle Cal almost took it for a girl's, "may I ask for your assistance?"

Cal turned and saw Sarah facing the questioner with a face full of hostility and just a hint of surprise. The man addressing her stood very close, so close *Calvin* felt uncomfortable, but what surprised him more was that he was smiling at Sarah, looking her full in the eyes with an expression that was unspeakably... *kind*. Cal reckoned Sarah had never received such a look from anyone who wasn't kin, and precious few such looks from those that were.

"What you want?" Sarah stepped back from the stranger.

"Pardon me again," the man said. "I've been told many times that I stand too close for others' comfort. Please forgive me." He was of middling-to-short height, thin, with very pale skin and expressive eyebrows under his mop of dark hair. His eyes wrinkled deeply as he spoke, but otherwise his age was hard for Cal to guess. Over his shoulder he had slung a leather satchel. He wore a simple gray robe, belted with rope, and a crescent moon-shaped brooch of white stone on his breast. Calvin knew a lot of the monastic orders had adopted insignia to mark their folks, but he didn't remember who used the moon. It wasn't the Rangers or the Circulators, he was sure of that. And the man didn't seem to be carrying any books, so he wasn't a Wandering Johnny.

Then again, it needn't be a monastic order. The fellow could be a knight, or in the service of some Power. The Elector songs told you who voted for emperor, but, like it or not, they didn't list flags and coats of arms, and that was the kind of thing Cal didn't have a very good grasp of.

Sarah would know.

"I don't recognize your accent," she said to the stranger. "But you ain't from these parts." Cal watched intently. He was aware that the other Calhoun younguns, though they pretended they were still jostling each other and playing at having an adventure in the big town, were watching her conversation closely, too. Sarah was oldest, and she was leader, so it was on her to show the younguns how to act in town, and around foreigners. Calvin had the same obligation, for that matter, and he was proud he'd wrangled the meneer's price up a couple of pennies, more for the principle than for the sum. Take advantage of foreigners before they take advantage of you, that was a basic precept of Calhoun family schooling.

"I'm not. I'm from the Ohio. My names is Thalanes, and I'm a priest." The little man smiled and bowed, and Cal noted that a bald circle—was it called a *tonsure?*—had been shaved into the top of his head. He said his name *THAH-lah-nace*, and it was very foreign-sounding, even more so than *Ezekiel Angleton.* "I was hoping I could ask you directions."

"Where you wanna git to?" Sarah asked.

"I'm looking for Andrew Calhoun." Thalanes still smiled. "The Elector."

"You of the Craft?" Sarah asked. "Iffen you're lookin' for a lodge, I reckon they's one right here in town as'd be easier to find."

"I'm not a Freemason," the little man said. "I'm a priest."

"You can be both." Sarah shrugged. "Freemason's got to believe in God, don't he?"

"I know where Calhoun's cabin used to be, years ago, but I've been up there early this morning and it's gone." The little man peered closely into her face, searching, and Calvin wondered whether Sarah felt uncomfortable. He considered intervening, but held himself back—she wouldn't appreciate his coming to her rescue unless she really needed it.

Cal rested his fingers on his lariat and wished again he'd brought his tomahawk. He wondered about the Elector's cabin—it hadn't moved in Calvin's memory. Did that make this man a liar, or a friend who hadn't been to visit in the last decade or more? As for that, the Elector wasn't hardcore New Light, but he was New Light enough that it was odd to think of him being friendly with a monk. Of course, two decades ago, nobody was

New Light. Maybe this monk was someone the Elector knew from the Spanish War.

"Oh yeah?"

"I was hoping you might be going that way, now that you've sold your leaf, and that I might be able to follow."

"That's jest the thing about a cabin," she told him. "You git uncomfortable where you are, you jest up sticks and move. Best home is a mobile home. Youins might oughtta give it a try out there in the Ohio, instead of them big dirt piles." Calvin let himself chuckle out loud. Score a point for the Appalachee girl—tell the foreigner nothing, and mock him at every opportunity. He looked at the younguns, and saw they were drinking it up. This was a more entertaining lesson than trying to remember the names of the twelve Free Imperial Towns.

"The Mounds. Yes, they would take more than a couple of hours to rebuild." The monk laughed gently, and Cal felt puzzled. Sarah was trying to drive the outsider away with hostility and ignorance, but the man kept grinning as if he was her favorite uncle and they were enjoying a private joke. Whatever Sarah felt, she kept it inside, more credit to her. "So, can you take me to where the Elector lives?"

"Not exactly," she lied. "I ain't no kin of his." Another lie. "Besides, we ain't goin' home right now, we'll be around town for a few hours." That at least might be true; they often lingered in Nashville after a market day, and Sarah may well have resolved that she would heckle the Martinite preacher, or do worse to him. She might feel her honor depended on it. She might reckon the Elector Calhoun's honor was at stake.

"I see," the monk nodded, still smiling as if he were enjoying a secret jest.

"What you wanna do, though," Sarah told him, "is head down thataway, cross the river, and then git on out through the Jefferson Pike Gate on the other side of town. I heard Old Man Calhoun has moved about thirty-forty miles on up the hills, so you'll wanna jest keep goin' and ask directions on the way."

Cal was very careful not to laugh this time, which was hard. He buried his face in his armload of tobacco to smother any chuckling that got through. Sarah had just coolly directed the foreigner out the wrong side of town. Well, if he was going to act like there was some kind of secret joke going on, he couldn't complain when he got one.

"Thank you," Thalanes said, still smiling. "You haven't told me your name."

"Sarah Jackson," she lied. Cal didn't think he could lie so easily. Of course, if he had to pick an Appalachee name to pretend was his own, Jackson was the one every foreigner had heard of, thanks to Andrew Jackson and his crazy bid to make himself king.

"Thank you, Sarah Jackson. I believe I'll enjoy some of Nashville's entertainments before I go find my friend the Elector. I understand there's a preacher in town."

He smiled, bowed again, and then walked off toward the river in the direction Sarah had indicated.

The cart was empty now, and Cal jingled the purse again to get the others' attention. "A shillin' four."

Young Andy whooped. "Small beer with lunch!"

The tobacco was all unloaded and on the Dutchman's table. Cal closed up the back of the cart and looped it into place.

"Small beer it is!" Sarah agreed. "Was he wearin' them wooden shoes like they do?"

"I b'lieve you jest sent that there foreigner off to the Kentuck." Cal laughed. "And to my grave disappointment, no, that ol' Dutchman's boots were leather. No wooden shoes, and not even buckles. I graaged him good and hard, though, like you taught me."

"He graag you back?"

Cal nodded. "Maybe next time it'll be an Acadian and I'll git to practice my *bonjour*."

Sarah watched the little man walking away and shrugged. "If that fool gits all the way to the Kentuck afore he turns around, he deserves it. You reckon we made enough off that baccy so's we can buy a little keg of whisky?"

"As if I's the kind of feller as'd know the price of whisky." Cal put on a fake look of reproach and winked.

"Calvin Calhoun," she shot back, "you may not know the price of whisky, but I expect when it comes time to buy some, you'll get it for half price. You're tight as a Catalan, and you know it."

"Why, Auntie Sarah," he said, "I do my best. But ain't the small beer enough for you? You plannin' on gettin' plastered already and it ain't yet noon?"

"Not I," she answered. "I'm fixin' to go to church."

✧   ✧   ✧

Serve Your Emperor...
!! SUPPORT THE PACIFICATION OF THE OHIO !!
~ Join the Imperial Army Today ~
Dragoons : Musketeers : Grenadiers : Pikemen : Artillerymen
Bonuses Paid for Friends Recruited

Above the text was a striking woodcut of His Imperial Majesty Thomas Penn, tall, bold and handsome, slicing at a curtain of wriggling snakes surrounding him. Thalanes knew the emperor personally, had known him since he was a nervous eighteen-year-old boy rushing into the Spanish War with a commission purchased by his father, eager to prove himself, and the likeness was a good one. Thomas was dressed like the officer he had been, in a long coat, with a sash from shoulder to hip to hold a cavalry saber, but he wore an ornate crown. The crown had three tall points like the façade of Franklin's Cathedral and had the Imperial horses, ship, and eagle carved into it in tiny detail. The image was nothing like any real crown Thalanes had ever seen, but it clearly communicated the emperor's identity. More subtly worked into the crown was the seal of the planet Mars.

Mars for war.

Thalanes would have laughed at the recruiting sign, pinned with a heavy iron nail to the side of a cobbler's shop, if it didn't make him want to despair. He looked away and continued his amble down Market Street.

The little Cetean monk enjoyed walking through the Tobacco Fair crowd. He had come south and west from Philadelphia over eight hundred miles in a little over three weeks, on foot all the way. He was a good walker, and he had judiciously supplemented his natural speed with a little gramarye. He'd taken the Old Road West, through the Ohio, which had had the double advantage of being less traveled and lying along a strong ley line, but avoiding the Imperial Highways had added many miles to his journey and confined him to a rougher track.

Also, it had taken him through the Ohio, and he had seen the Pacification firsthand. He had been away from his homeland for years, tending to Hannah in her immurement, and he didn't like seeing it again with Imperial garrisons at every town and crossroads, the Imperial hand in every pocket and the Imperial boot in every face.

Hannah would never have stood for such bald-faced evil, nor certainly Kyres. Nor would the young Thomas Penn, the aspiring military hero. But ambition, greed, and power had changed Thomas. He had the will, the means, and a pretext, and the Ohio was under his heel.

Never mind, Thalanes told himself. His errand was secret, of the *utmost* secrecy, and he had sped as quickly and as invisibly as he'd been able. Penn's pet Martinite Angleton was in Nashville, but he didn't yet have the girl. And he *wouldn't* get her.

Thalanes would not fail his empress again.

You didn't fail her before, he lied to himself. *It wasn't your fault. She insisted on knowing, and you only respected her will. Your position as her father confessor bound you to do that, to say nothing of the Rule of St. Cetes.*

Thalanes enjoyed the crowd. Birdsong and rain had done very nicely for companions on his rushed march, but he was happy to smell again the thick, warm, sometimes sour aroma of mankind, the filthy stink of the rich Imperial Town, and the charred air of woodsmoke from its chimneys. He loved the burbling voices, the thump of the wagon wheels, the whinny of horses, and the clink of money changing hands.

He read the signboards of Nashville's taverns as he walked. He saw the *Heron King*, a bird-faced man with an iron crown; the *Benedict Arnold*, with an image of the war hero, undaunted in the moment of having his horse killed under him by New Spanish lances; and the *Oliver Cromwell*, with a country gentleman's face on one side of the board and a helmeted death's head on the other. Thalanes crossed himself. Some of the children of Eve still adored the Lord Protector of the Eternal Commonwealth as a hero through John Churchill had unmasked him as the Necromancer and driven him from England. Oliver Cromwell had been particularly evil to the Firstborn, but he had killed plenty of ordinary Frenchmen, Dutchmen, and Germans.

And Nashville didn't seem to have any taverns named the *Wallenstein* or the *Queen Adela Podebradas*, at least not on Market Street. Thalanes sighed. There was a *Franklin*, though, which was auspicious. The bishop's famous seal, three letters around a bolt of lightning, was nailed into the frame of the tavern door on either side, in matching iron plates.

Thalanes spotted another Firstborn, a tobacco buyer with

a string of sturdy ponies. He was a fellow Ohioan, Thalanes guessed from his long cloak, knee-high boots and tunic that came halfway down his thigh, but the nod he gave the other man was no greater and no less than the salute he gave everyone else. Thalanes loved all Adam's children, in their colors and their smells and their busy motion and their relentless creative buzz of choice and free will.

He stopped at a board-built box, roofless but painted on its front with a rough image of a teacup full of black liquid. The man standing inside the stall wore a short-brimmed, boxy beaver hat, a doeskin vest over a yellow silk blouse, and red corte-du-roi trousers. He looked as stern as the sign, even inhospitable with his thin-bridged nose ending in broad flared nostrils, his high, bony cheeks and his nearly invisible upper lip, but his inhospitality was overpowered by the magnetic smell coming from his simmering pots.

Algonk of some kind. "Boozhoo!" Thalanes tried a greeting in Ojibwe, rubbing his hands together in anticipation.

"I savvy English, Padre," the Algonk shot back. "You want to parley? To ballet? You want to chanty and hold hands and share feelings, or you want a cuppa?"

"Yes, please," Thalanes said, chastened, "coffee. Black. And I'll buy roasted beans, too, if you have them."

Thalanes paid with a few Philadelphia pennies and tucked the little sack of beans into his satchel with his tiny pot. He stood by the coffee stall and smiled at its Algonk proprietor, sipping the hot restorative into his chest one life-instilling blow at a time. Soon he would feel himself again.

He noted that the Imperial Town had its peace kept by a substantial blue-uniformed watch, the presence of which was very visible. They were probably all on duty for the fair, he judged. The stone walls surrounding the small town were built like a castle's, high and thick, with protection for defending musketeers and numerous mounting-poles for anchoring arquebuses in conflict. Big guns spaced along the walls were staffed by leather-caped cannoneers, many of whom were female; the Pitchers were famous for being the only Imperial military service to admit women.

All of Nashville gave the impression of thriving life and solid security, but Thalanes felt uneasy.

It was not your fault, he said to himself for the thousandth time. *Let no will be coerced. Even the empress had to be allowed to choose.*

He gave the empty cup back, thanked the coffee-man and ambled on his way down the street.

The Town Hall was a stone building of three stories, a chimney puffing merrily at each end on this busy day. The street was cobbled with small square stones right down to the river and the wide bridge spanning it, but across the street from the Town Hall was a grassy field, not quite shaped into a park and not quite left wild as a meadow, either. In the field stood the promised tent, large and dirty-white, and before the tent glowered Angleton's servant, the scruffy Englishman.

Obadiah Dogsbody was thick about the head, neck, shoulders, chest and belly, and thin through the hips and legs. He was unshaven, his three-cornered hat, black coat and knee-length breeches were travel-stained, and he stank with an odor Thalanes didn't enjoy—hard liquor, hard riding, and a hard heart. He stood in the tent door with one hand on the crosspiece of a broadsword and his other around the neck of a bottle of cheap rum. Tucked into his wide leather belt he also carried a new—and expensive—flintlock pistol.

Thalanes knew Obadiah from Philadelphia and wondered whether the factotum would recognize him. Best to take precautions. "*Faciem muto,*" he murmured, touching one finger to his brooch and one to his cheek. He felt the *thrum* of pulsating power within the brooch as he cast the spell, his own soul's power, carefully hoarded and stored a bit at a time. Not a powerful spell, especially without any physical components, but a good one, and it should be enough to keep Obadiah or his master from recognizing the Cetean monk. The best spell was the one that accomplished its purpose without exhausting the caster, wrecking his body, or killing him.

Thalanes nodded at Obadiah, got an indifferent grunt in return, and ducked under the tent flap.

The stained tent canvas hung down from a horizontal pole like a roofbeam and was propped on further poles at each corner and along the walls. The inside of the tent was empty of furnishings other than a cask of water by the door, a low wooden platform with a barrel set up on its end as a pulpit, and a couple of dirty spittoons. Thalanes savored the fading taste of coffee while he looked at the crowd. Some of the people were residents of Nashville itself, dressed in the nicer shoes and newer clothes of the farmers and merchants who lived down in the valley, but many of the waiting spectators wore the short skirts and long hunting shirts that gave away a true Appalachee highlander. These people grinned with anticipation and the monk inferred that they knew very well that there would be no Barton Stone-style preaching. They had heard young Sarah harangue Obadiah and were here to see more of the show.

It promised to be quite a display. The girl had her mother's wit, her father's courage, and all the stubborn will of her adopted people. How ironic, to race nearly a thousand miles against Angleton to be the first to reach Sarah, and to arrive only to find her, as if by some unerring instinct attracted to self-destruction, harassing the Right Reverend Father.

Thalanes stationed himself beside the door. He didn't think Obadiah would recognize her or else he would simply have grabbed her when they met on Market Street. Angleton must not trust his man much—still, better safe than sorry. Thalanes watched the door and the spectators flowing in, looking for the black-haired girl with the bad eye.

Why was Angleton preaching from a tent? He could think of only one reason, and it made him uncomfortable. Maybe he should have talked to Sarah more openly in the street, told her his purpose, rather than risking that Angleton might get to her first. He considered, and decided he had made the right move. He thought it was only fair to talk to the Elector first, for all he had done. And the girl was still safe and free, he was watching. Angleton's mission surely could not be to *kill* her. Gentle persuasion was not his style, either, but he must be here to find the child, or at most capture her.

Of course, once in Philadelphia they would kill her, as they had finally killed her mother.

Still, Thalanes preferred to give her time, so she could learn to trust him. Every child of God chooses his or her own path. Let no will be coerced.

And it was not your fault.

"Whisky!" someone said behind him, and Thalanes turned in surprise. There they were, Sarah and the lanky young man with long red hair tied behind his neck—now without his cattleman's lariat. They had entered the tent and evaded Obadiah, and Thalanes almost laughed out loud at the simplicity of their means; they had pulled up a stake and crawled under the tent wall. Apparently they had rolled a small keg with them, and now they were setting it up beside the water barrel and prying off the lid.

While an appreciative highlander took the first sip from the whisky, Thalanes kept his eye keenly trained on Sarah. Very discreetly and, he was sure, unseen by anyone in the tent other than himself, she nicked her finger with a small belt knife and squeezed a little of her own blood—one...two...three drops—into the water barrel. At the same time, her lips moved slightly.

She's hexing it, the monk realized, and again almost laughed out loud. *O Kyres, my heroic, my tragic friend, what a daughter you have!* Everyone entering the tent drank from either the whisky or the water, and some circled back to drink again; for the Right Reverend Ezekiel Angleton's sermon they would all be either tipsy or hexed by Sarah Elytharias Penn.

Sarah Calhoun, he reminded himself sternly. *Sarah Calhoun.* And what would the hex do?

The tent was full. Sarah lurked carefully behind a pair of burly wagoneers, keeping her face averted and her telltale eye tucked down toward her shoulder as she bled her finger into the water cask.

"He loves me, he loves me not, he loves me, he loves me not, he loves me, he loves me not." She chanted the child's mantra once with each drop, and she could feel energy flowing out of her and into the water, through the blood but also through the words. She could hex without words if she had to, was counted a talented hexer by the few people on Calhoun Mountain who knew enough to judge, but putting the hex into words got it out of her and into the world easier.

She felt tired when the hex was done. She'd have laid down and gone right to sleep, if she hadn't had more important things to do.

A flap in the tent wall behind the platform opened and the Right Reverend Father Ezekiel Angleton, Martinite, stepped in. Around the wagoneers impeding her view Sarah could see that he was long and straight in limb and face, cold blue eyes fixed close beside a hawkish nose beneath a high forehead. The tonsure he must have cut out of the top of his long hair, Sarah reckoned, was hidden by a tall black steeple hat, Yankee-style. He wasn't wearing the black tabard of his order (the Martinites had something of a history as a military society, since they had begun as the thugs who went around Wittenberg enforcing Martin Luther's commands and stealing all the property of the German Eldritch), but a simple white shirt and brown breeches. The Hammer and Nail of St. Martin Luther—the Elector had made her learn the insignia of all the common orders, preaching and otherwise—were nowhere in evidence.

Well, damn him if he thought he could come down here and treat Sarah and her family like fools. She didn't care one way or the other about St. Martin Luther and his followers' grudge against the Firstborn, and who in hell cared whether they had a soul or not, she never could understand. Still, a Yankee preacher within a few miles of her home constituted a foreign invasion. What was he doing here, anyway? Nashville didn't have an Eldritch population any more than it had beastkind—just townsfolk and hillfolk, and everybody more or less Appalachee but the traders passing through.

The Martinite's disappointment and boredom shone from his face like twin beacons of gloom. He looked once around the gathered crowd and his face became even further crestfallen. In his hand he held a heavy Bible, and he opened it as he stepped to the barrel pulpit and looked down at the printed pages.

"As you all may have learned by now," he began, in a pinched drone that Sarah knew would never excite this congregation, "the Empress Hannah has been gathered to the angels." What was this fool preacher playing at? Had he traveled to Appalachee just to preach a funeral sermon? Did he not care about the crowd? Then why had he summoned them here?

He continued. "Yaas, all Pennsland grieves, and we of Appalachee must grieve with them." Angleton delivered his words in a dull monotone with the nasal twang of the Covenant Tract man he was.

We of Appalachee... Sarah almost laughed. Ezekiel Angleton could scarcely have looked more out of place had he lacked a head and been speaking from a face in his belly.

"My text this morning is from Isaiah fifty-eight." The priest mumbled now, face-down in the Bible. Mutters of dissatisfaction were beginning to be voiced in the crowd. "Is not this the fast that I have chosen? To loose the bands of wickedness, to undo the heavy burdens, and to let the oppressed go free, and that ye break every yoke?"

Here we go. Sarah would mock the sanctimonious Yankee a bit, and then bring down the house like Samson. Only she'd try not to get crushed. "I might could suggest a different text!" she yelled.

"Hush!" Angleton barked, peering at the crowd. Sarah crouched low behind the wagoneers.

"How about Psalm thirty-nine?" Sarah continued. This was not her first preacher-baiting, and she had verses to hand. "'I was dumb, I opened not my mouth'?" The crowd broke into laughter, but she kept a straight, pious face for the benefit of those that could see her.

"Who's that causing a disturbance?" the preacher demanded in his sour Yankee whistle.

Someone grabbed at her arm, but missed, and Sarah didn't see who it had been before she pushed through the wagoneers to reveal herself. "Whoo-wee, you're purty!" someone shouted, but other spectators gasped in alarm. Well, they could go to hell right alongside the Right Reverend Father. She hoped one of the tentpoles fell on top of them.

Angleton dropped his jaw and his Bible, the latter slithering off the corner of the barrel and thudding hard to the floor.

"Or maybe Numbers twenty-five?" Sarah continued coyly. "'Am I not thine ass'?" The audience erupted into a fit of laughter that did not die down when the Right Reverend Father Ezekiel Angleton flapped his arms in an attempt to calm it.

Time to end the show and get out, before the preacher or his fat servant came after her. She raised her voice, though the tent walls were thin enough that Young Andy ought to be able to hear her already. "Mebbe Genesis nine: 'he was uncovered within his tent'?" Sarah stood bold and proud, feet planted apart and hands on her hips as she faced the preacher. Just disrupting this foreigner's show wouldn't be satisfying; she wanted him to see who had done it. She only wished the fat Englishman could see too, serve him right for the pig-eyed stares he'd given her.

Angleton's lip curled into a sneer. "What's your name, girl? And what's wrong with that eye?" He squinted. "Are you fey?"

Come on, Andy, she thought. *You missed your call.* "I *said*," she yelled louder, "'*uncovered within his tent*'!"

Still nothing.

"Come here, child," Angleton said quietly. "I want to talk to you."

Sarah started to back away.

The Martinite preacher put his hand onto the top of the improvised pulpit and picked up something that had been lying there, invisible to the crowd, all along. It was a fine flintlock pistol, matching the one the Englishman carried, and he leveled its deadly mouth at her.

"Child," Angleton repeated. "I said *come here*."

"You know, I expect, what His Grace will do,
if he is not repaid tomorrow?"

CHAPTER TWO

Bad Bill glared at himself in the mirror shard he'd fixed to the crumbling yellow plaster with scavenged nails. "Hell's Bells, suh, are you still alive?"

His green eyes, once lively and commanding and the fascination of many a fine-looking young woman, stared dully through bloodshot whites out of a face of hammered stone. The hair on his skull was short white stubble, cropped close to lie under his perruque; at least the long mustache still had some iron in it.

Was Charles shaving? He immediately clamped down on the oft-repeated thought, forcing it from his mind. Bill had never seen it, but of course his son had been shaving for a decade now. Bill hoped Charles wore a handsome, manly mustache.

He fumbled for his battered tin shaving basin and found it full of clean, warm water. Madame Beaulieu cared for him beyond her duty, and in return he was a bad lodger, frequently behind in the rent. He was behind in the rent today, though he couldn't have named a figure.

He'd have to rectify that ignorance.

Fifteen years! Fifteen years he'd been out of the dragoons, fifteen years he'd been banished from Johnsland, fifteen years of this life worrying about rent and daily bread, and still he couldn't bring himself to concentrate when it came to matters of accounting and numbers. He still felt that he was a gentleman and that money was beneath him. At least, *keeping track* of money was beneath him—he was acutely aware that he needed cash to live.

He took the boar bristle brush to the brown bar of soap and began to whip up lather for his face, enjoying the ritual of it and the pungent stink of the soap as it dissolved into foam. At least he was sober and awake enough to tell the washbasin from the chamberpot—*that* was a mistake he didn't care to repeat.

What did he have to do today, besides figure out how much rent he owed Madame Beaulieu? He searched his memory as it crept back to him through the fading smoky tendrils of whisky. A duel. Not in his own interest, of course; no one ever had occasion to challenge Bad Bill in an *affaire d'honneur*, and if anyone ever did, surely his reputation as dangerous bodyguard, bouncer, bounty hunter, ruffian for hire, and general violent man of the frontier would be enough to make all but the most deeply affronted think twice.

Bill sighed.

No, this was a duel for money. He was to act as champion for an offended client. A cuckolded hidalgo merchant, he remembered, without caring very much. The details didn't matter. Only the time and place mattered, and that information he had stamped clearly in his memory: sunset, under the north side of the Bishop de Bienville Bridge. Some of his pay he'd had in advance, and he wondered as he finished scraping the little hairs off his jaw and chin how much, if any, still lurked in his pocket. The remainder, the lion's share, he'd have after the duel.

He had challenged the doomed lover the night before, in a glittering salon on the edge of the Quarter. Light from a thousand genuine wax candles had sparkled in crystals hanging from the ceiling and in glass windows and in the polished brass buttons of all the servants. It had been a grand house and a very wealthy set of young people in attendance. Bill had gained admittance by handing the last of his gold coins over to a footman at the kitchen door.

In small, red-brick Richmond and the surrounding plantations a letter, delivered by a second, would have been traditional. If there were to be a personal confrontation, the blow would have been a symbolic one with an empty glove. Here in New Orleans, duels were commenced with rather less ceremony. Bill had spotted his man in a cluster of made-up dandies giggling around a sofa and chattering in French. He had tapped him on the shoulder, enjoyed the look of surprise on his face and then punched the young fop in the jaw. Standing over the stunned man in a sea of the rouged cheeks and grease-penciled facial hair of his gawking friends, he had then announced his errand.

"I'm William Johnston Lee, and you, suh, have offended me, for which I shall have satisfaction of your body tomorrow night at dusk."

Bill's client, Don Luis Maria Salvador Sandoval de Burgos—he thought that was the name, or at least close, though it didn't seem right to him that the man should be named *Maria*—had insisted that Bill claim to be offended in his own right. He'd promised to pay extra for it. Bill needed the money badly enough that he hadn't scrupled.

The young man had only stared.

"You are the challenged, suh," Bill had reminded him. "Will it be swords or pistols?"

The lover, who apparently spoke no English, had taken advice in a flurry of monsieur-jabber from his witnessing friends, and then advised Bill he would prefer "le pistolet," and no wonder, as Bill was at least a head taller and more heavily muscled. They had fixed time and place, Bill agreeing as a matter of course to the challenged's suggestion of Smuggler's Shelf. Exchange Alley, or the dirt square behind the cathedral, were more convenient sites as they involved much less walking and Bill was without a horse, but Bishopsbridge was not extraordinary. Perhaps the young fellow had some reason to wish to keep his duel as discreet as possible. Not that very much discretion was possible, after the highly public challenge.

Bill had tipped his hat and stalked from the salon.

He pulled the hat on now, over the black perruque tied neatly at the nape of his neck with a little black ribbon. It was the same hat he'd worn as captain of the Blues, broad-brimmed and black. He'd worn it with a peacock's feather then, for elegance and dash; now, after years of sweat and rain, he just tried to keep it approximately in its original shape. The broad brim distinguished it from the tricorner hat that was the uniform of the Blues, almost to the point of making it resemble a Pennslander's hat. Bill had worn it anyway, with permission from the Imperial Consort; it was Bill's lucky hat. No star, no medallion, no rabbit's foot, no lady's kiss—not even Sally's—had ever brought him as much luck as this hat, and he had no intention of ever buying another, fashion be damned.

He belted on his heavy cavalry saber, inlaid with gold and silver on the basket guard—that, at least, was as sharp and gleaming as ever, all along its forward edge and the tip sharp as well and good for thrusting.

Next the waistcoat; not his ornate Blues waistcoat, long ago pawned for cash, but a simpler red one, cut for his now-larger paunch. He buttoned it up and then shrugged into the long scarlet coat, torn and weatherbeaten but still serviceable. Its inner pocket jingled, but his brief hopes were shattered when he pulled the coins out and saw that they amounted to a few drinks at most. He didn't remember spending the rest, but the dry roughness of his mouth and the fog receding from his brain corroborated the likely explanation that it had gone for liquor. And of course, the Louis he had paid the footman as a bribe to get into the salon.

After the coat, the accouterments of a gunman: powder horn, priming horn, and the leather pouch containing rags, mink oil, vent pick, brush, and bone powder measures.

Finally, he picked up his two long horse pistols, also painstakingly maintained. Bill checked that they were both loaded and primed (New Orleans was the sort of town where a man might meet enemies unexpectedly), then tucked one into his belt and the other into the long right-hand outside pocket of the red coat.

He looked at the long-barreled Kentucky rifle leaning in the corner. He couldn't think of any reason he'd need it today, so he left it. No one ever broke into Madame Beaulieu's boarding house—there were far too many rough men about, and far too little worth stealing—so it would be safe.

Bill locked the door and headed downstairs.

His room faced the interior of the building, opening onto the balcony running around the unroofed courtyard at the center of the boarding house. The air was no cooler here, but it smelled better and that refreshed Bill, if only a little bit. He was getting old and he was heavier than he'd ever been as a soldier, but he still moved easily as he padded down the hard steps into the jungle of ferns that his landlady made of the open space.

At the bottom of the creaking stairs, Madame Beaulieu herself waited in the greenery, smiling.

"Monsieur Bill," she addressed him cheerfully. "Avez-vous le loyer? Le . . . rent?"

Bill winced, then shook his head. "I must again throw myself upon your much-infringed patience, ma'am. I have an expectation of coming into funds this evening. How many months do I owe you? Quant, er . . ." he fumbled, "months?"

"Trois," she said, holding up fingers. "Three."

Embarrassed, Bill realized that he had asked the wrong question. "Yes, ma'am, so I owe you . . ."

"Trois," she said, holding up the same fingers. "Three Louis d'or."

Ah, yes. "Thank you for your forbearance, Madame Beaulieu," he tipped his hat to her and left the building, passing several fellow-lodgers smoking or just lounging on wrought iron chairs among the plants. They all looked away to avoid making eye contact with Bad Bill.

Three looeys, fine, he'd make that tonight and to spare.

The October afternoon was mild for New Orleans, but humid and warm as Bad Bill stepped out of the Pension de Madame Beaulieu and onto the creaking wood of the boardwalk.

A few steps away lay the tree-lined Esplanade Avenue and beyond that the cesspit of the Faubourg Marigny. The Faubourg was dirtier than the Quarter, smashed up against the eastern wall of the city, and more impoverished, but what mattered to Bill was that it afforded him little opportunity of employment, full as it was of poor drunk Creoles, Irishmen, Portugee, and Catalans. The Faubourg was dangerous. Its inhabitants fought all the time, maybe even more than the people of the Quarter, but they were poorer, so they did their own fighting, with knives and sticks and teeth.

Bill turned his back on the Faubourg's stink and headed deeper into the Quarter. He stuck to the boardwalk for the shade it afforded. The packed-dirt streets weren't empty, but afternoon was a slow time for the Quarter, with only actual residents and local tradesman drifting about. The action would heat up when the sun went down and people came from elsewhere into the Quarter to drink, dance, sport, and generally live loud. Those were the people who provided Bill with his livelihood, either as clients or as targets.

What foot traffic there was in the warm afternoon saw Bad

Bill coming and steered well clear, other than a wizened, coffee-colored crone, head tightly wrapped in bright silk and shawl bouncing wildly about her shoulders. She trotted up to Bill and pressed him with assorted objects.

"Luck, sir?" She shoved a pink string-doll into his face. "Love? Protection?" She fanned a handful of the little poppets in his direction, wound together of different-colored yarn but each with pins for eyes and tucked into a tiny shift of rough cotton fabric.

"No, ma'am." Bill tried in vain to step around her. Vodun was not his brand of superstition.

"Beybey?" she changed propositions, scooping all the dolls into one gnarled hand and using the other to show a strand of leather on her shoulder bearing a series of brass medallions, like a thin belt threaded with multiple buckles. The medallions were elaborately cut with the loops and lines that Bill recognized as the holy symbols of various loa. "Legba, he bring you luck. Agwé for a sea journey, or if you a fisherman."

"I am not a fisherman, ma'am," Bill objected mildly, "and I try very hard to avoid ever setting foot on any ship."

She looked him up and down, spying his pistols and his saber. "You a fighter, ah? A fightin' man? Fine, you want Ogoun, he swing the big machete, he watch over fightin' men!" She showed him the beybey of Ogoun, a web of triangles and asterisks framed by scrollwork. "You want? Ogoun, he a real bargain, big mojo loa!"

"Jesus is my loa." Bill was vaguely Christian, but what he really meant was *leave me alone*.

"Read you a fortune?" the gypsy squeaked at him in a final effort. Bill saw the backs of the cards and recognized a cheap New Orleans printing of Franklin's Tarock.

"No, thank you, ma'am." He pushed definitively past her. It wasn't that he didn't believe she could read his future in the cards—rather, he didn't want to know what the future held. He gripped his hat and pulled it securely down over his ears, trying to block out the sound of her spitting and cursing him.

Bill squinted against the sun at the lattice-railed balconies and the hanging green jasmine, not yet blooming as the weather had just begun to turn cool. He had the afternoon ahead of him and nothing in his schedule, so he went where he always did when he had no plan.

Grissot's—which Bill could not bring himself to pronounce

other than as *GRISS-uts*, though the proprietor said his name *grease-OH*—was a public house that at night featured musical entertainments, frequently including Igbo banjo-pickers and Bantu fiddlers from east and north of the city, and girls calling invitations from the iron-railed balconies above to passersby in the street.

In the afternoon, *Grissot's* featured strong drink and Long Cathy.

At the door, Bill bumped into two plain-robed people, faces so deeply shrouded in hoods that he could see no features. They held their fingers steepled before them, and the sight made Bill sigh. *Priests.* The empire was lousy with them. They seemed to exist just to disagree with each other; these priests liked the Eldritch, those ones didn't; these priests ordained women, those objected; these ones over here in red robes taught wizards, and their rivals in green burned witches; some printed books, some preached to the Indians, some fought the Turk. Bill had a hard time caring—he just wanted someone to baptize and marry his children and say the occasional Mass when he was in the mood. Too much priest-talk, and Bill started to wish he burned a Yule log and sang at the solstice with his pagan neighbors in Johnsland.

The priests bobbled slightly, as if anxious about something. Bill wasn't interested, so he tipped his hat, smiled politely and turned inside.

Cathy was at the bar. She didn't sit on the stools, she wasn't leaning, and she didn't seem to Bill to be floating...she just *was*. Bill knew very well the worn, smoke-stained, and knife-scarred wood that made up the interior of *Grissot's*, but somehow, around Cathy, it became something else, something fine. Something like... a ballroom, maybe, or a salon, though it felt more like Cavalier Richmond to him than French New Orleans. He bowed and swept his hat to her, careful not to dislodge the perruque—nothing was less impressive than a fat old man who was also bald.

"My knight," she smiled at him, "Sir William."

More than once, he had taken it upon himself to rid her of some unpleasant client. "Mrs. Filmer," returned Captain Sir William Johnston Lee. "It's an unspeakable pleasure to see you again. Might I be permitted the honor of buying you a drink?"

Catherine Filmer was tall and graceful, with dark brown hair to her shoulders and dancing blue eyes. She was born

Catherine Howard (like King Henry's wife, a rose without a thorn), a Virginian, from a small town not far over the border from William's own ancestral lands. She had grown up a gentleman farmer's daughter, had been educated by the Sisters of St. William Harvey, had married a bright young schoolteacher with no prospects, had moved west with her husband to allow him to teach at an academy in the Memphis of Menelik V, and had buried him upon arrival, flat dead of the pox.

Trash floats downstream, the Memphites sniffed and the residents of New Orleans agreed in cheerful self-mockery, but in this case, after a stint with a cloister of beguines that Bill vaguely thought had ended in scandal, the mighty Mississippi had brought tumbling down a diamond. Long Cathy had arrived shortly before William and had been brightening his dark days since the first.

"Why, Sir William, you always have my permission to buy me a drink, and I live in hope that you will avail yourself of it." She smiled and the back of William's neck tingled.

"I hope you know that if ever you are in need of companionship for a libation, I am most certainly at your service."

"Would that it were not merely a libation." She smiled again, and William shivered. He was hopeless before Mrs. Catherine Filmer, he was her votary.

"Two whiskies!" Sir William Lee called to the hunchbacked Irishman behind the bar. He kissed Long Cathy's knuckles and sat, elbow on the dark wood. "I cannot regret, ma'am, my inability to pay you more personal attentions, as I remain a faithfully married man. In another life, however..." The whisky had arrived, prompt because the public house was otherwise empty, and he raised his glass. "Honor," he began the toast.

"In defense of innocence," she finished it, then joined him, sipping like a lady. "In another life, Sir William," she agreed, "and perhaps yet in this one."

"Have you heard, ma'am?" he chatted breezily. "The chevalier has promised a stronger gendarmerie to police the Quarter. Apparently some citizens are concerned that there are low characters to be found in this part of New Orleans."

"No!"

He nodded ruefully. "Ruffians, they say."

She smiled bells and sunshine at him, dazzling him with her

white teeth, shining eyes, and glittering Harvite locket. St. William Harvey had been an English medical doctor. Now his Sisters, sometimes called the Harvites or the Circulators, were physicians and apothecaries, with a special mission to help the needy.

"The poor honest gentlefolk must be trembling in their beds." She sighed. "Perhaps they could consider hiring protection when they come to the Quarter, if the chevalier cannot provide an adequate number of gendarmes."

"Perhaps they could at that, ma'am," he agreed. "Perhaps some enterprising person will undertake to offer them the service of watching their bodies."

"I fear I am somewhat a-quiver, myself," Long Cathy said. "Might *you* do me the service of watching *my* body?"

"I'm your humble servant," William replied. "Until the day they row me out into the Pontchartrain Sea and throw me into the Hulks."

A second whisky came for each, a few more precious minutes of ironic civilized pleasantries passed and then William guessed he was likely out of money and should leave. He thought she would have allowed him to stay and talk longer even without a drink, but he knew that his bearlike presence on the stool could only frighten away potential customers, and he wished her too well to cause her such harm.

"I must bid you a good evening, Mrs. Filmer," he saluted her, rising to his feet and executing another bow-and-sweep. He emptied his coins onto the counter, relieved to find he had enough to pay for the drinks and also leave a small gratuity for the Irishman. "I fear that I have business to attend to."

"A good evening to you, too, Sir William," she replied, "but surely it is your *business* that fears *you*."

Another kiss to her unscarred hand and Bad Bill was out the door again, warmed inside by the two whiskies and by the few priceless minutes of having been permitted to be Sir William.

Fifteen years. He sighed.

For fifteen years it had been only the shared polite moments like this with Long Cathy that had kept him still wishing to live.

The genteel company of Long Cathy and the thought of home, of course, he corrected himself. Sally and the children. The children . . . Heaven's beard, they'd be grown now. Images flashed into his mind of stick-fencing with young Charles, and playing at battle with toy soldiers, and he wondered whether the boy was now grown into a military man. He must be; Bill's family had always produced military men.

Whump!

The club took him by surprise, thumping hard into his belly as he stepped around the corner of *Grissot's*. Bill went down, losing his hat. A second blow of the cudgel hit him across the back of the head and turned his vision starry and spinning. Tumbling on the hard boardwalk, Bill groped for his sword hilt but froze when he felt a pistol shoved against his nose.

He eased over slowly, hands held away from his weapons, breath creeping back while his head still swam. His attackers let him roll, and when he lay on his back Bill saw that there were five of them, two armed with clubs, one with a brace of pistols, and one with a bell-mouthed blunderbuss, all scrutinizing him closely.

The four armed men were the usual New Orleans mongrels, killers of any race and country, all with desperation blazing in hungry eye sockets and all wearing simple black waistcoats. Bill ignored them and looked at the fifth man, their leader, whose broad, brown face was smiling in an incongruously kindly way. He wore an expensive coat, polished riding boots and fistfuls of gold rings. He was not visibly armed, and he held a smoldering cigarette. His waistcoat was black like his followers', but was elaborately stitched with silver thread, a web of triangles and asterisks framed by scrollwork. Beneath it his waist was wrapped in a red silk sash, knotted on his right hip.

"Etienne," Bill acknowledged the smiling man. "Ubosi oma." He meant it as a friendly greeting—it was the only Igbo he knew. Or was it Amharic? His head hurt.

"Shut your mouth, you ignorant piece of filth." Etienne still smiled.

"May I sit up?" Bill asked in his most polite tones.

"I prefer you to lie where you are, you fat old man. It might help you remember this meeting better."

Bill acquiesced, but did at least reach out and pick his hat up off the boardwalk. His head had stopped spinning and he assessed his chances. They were not good. Even if he managed to distract the thugs' attention and knock out one of the shooters in a surprise attack, the other would surely get him, and that didn't take into account the toughs with cudgels. Nor could Bill expect any help from the city's blue-and-gold-coated gendarmes or any passersby; this was the Quarter, and an attack by one set of thugs on another would raise not a single eyebrow.

He hoped this meeting would prove just to be a reminder. He would try to hasten the conversation to its climax.

"I will be able to repay your father tomorrow, Etienne." Bill tried to look as trustworthy as he could. He meant it—he would duel the frog lover of his dago employer's mistress tonight, and then he'd be able to pay back the loan. Even the interest, he hoped, though he had no idea how much that would be.

How interest really worked he had never understood very well, and it struck Bill as likely being somehow part of the curse brought on by Original Sin. *Sums of money become larger if you wait* was the only summary he could have given of the principle. That was a fine thing if you owned the money or you were a lending banker and a significant inconvenience, Bill had found, when you owed it.

"His Grace," Etienne corrected him.

"I will be able to repay *His Grace* tomorrow," Bill hastily agreed.

Etienne took a long drag. "I am very glad to hear it."

"I have some work arranged for tonight, and I'll make good money." Bill was talking too much. *Shut up now.*

"Repayment tomorrow would be completely acceptable." Etienne's continued happy smiling was beginning to take on an insane cast. "This conversation is a peaceful one, in the nature of a reminder to a friend. An *urgent* reminder, to a friend who might be about to make a terrible mistake."

"Thank you," Bill said.

"With interest, your debt is now a large one, at eight Louis d'or. You know, I expect, what His Grace will do if he is not repaid tomorrow?"

"Excommunication?" Bill tried to squeeze all the charm he had into a roguish grin.

"Last rites." Etienne stepped back and his two toughs with cudgels closed in. They beat Bill half a dozen strokes each while the bishop's son laughed heartily at his appropriation of Bill's jest.

They left him on the boardwalk, battered but conscious and still clutching his lucky hat. Bill let himself lie still and recover, but only for a few moments—his reputation as a man of arms would suffer if any potential client saw him lying there. When he stood he stood tall, for the same reason, willing himself to straighten his aching back and not hunch over or fuss at the bruises he knew were forming on his arms and thighs. He blocked his hat into the best shape he could with his fists and perched it atop his perruque.

If only he weren't a drinking man. If he'd saved his cash for fifteen years instead of throwing it away on various kinds of rotgut (whisky, whenever possible, but there was a surprising variety of distilled substances that would do in a pinch), he'd own his own house in the Garden District by now. And a business—maybe a stage coach, with drivers and guards in his employ. And he'd never have had to borrow money from that bloodthirsty usurer, the Bishop of New Orleans.

His head hurt, and he almost stepped back into *Grissot's* to buy another drink. Abrupt recollection of his completely empty purse, together with a sudden wave of shame at the thought that Long Cathy might see him in this defeated state, stopped him at the door.

He staggered down the street, collecting his thoughts. He would win his duel tonight—he always won, and this hapless frenchie looked more likely to grab the wrong end of the pistol and shoot himself than to be any danger to Bill—and that would let him pay his rent and repay his loan. What had Madame Beaulieu said about the size of his debt? Three looeys? And another eight to the bishop? That should work out just fine. He had ten looeys coming to him from Don Sandoval, and the hidalgo had promised Bill a bonus if the offending Frenchman actually died.

And if he had to owe Madame Beaulieu just one Louis d'or for a few more days, she'd still have to see that as an improvement.

Bill realized he was passing Hackett's, the pawnbroker, and he stopped to look in the window at the glorious jumble that was the treasure of other people's lives, sold cheap. Behind iron bars, among jewelry, tools, books, furniture, and even pairs of boots, he saw weapons that other desperate men had pawned, none as nice as Bill's. He had borrowed money on his guns before—he'd gotten into debt with the bishop the last time he'd needed his pistols out of hock for a job. He hadn't borrowed eight looeys, either—he wasn't sure, but it seemed to him he might have borrowed four. Or even three. Someday he would master this concept of interest.

In any case, he wasn't going to pawn his weapons now; he needed them. His own lengthening shadow reminded him he had an appointment at the river, and he turned and let himself drift out of the French Quarter west, toward the city walls and beyond them the bridge named after Bishop Chinwe Philippe Ukwu's famous predecessor, Bishop Henri de Bienville.

Bill arrived at the bridge first, as he'd intended, and breathing through his mouth to keep out the stink.

He took extra care, moving outside of the city after dark. Close as it was to the wild no man's lands of Texia and the Great Green Wood, New Orleans saw plenty of beastkind even within city limits. Outside city limits, and across the river, they were even more common, and some of them were feral. Not that Louisiana needed wild beastkind to be dangerous—bandits, pirates, robbers, drunk Texians, war bands of the free horse people, and alligators were all possible, even likely, encounters. Bill walked with his hands always on his pistols and his eyes never resting, darting from one Spanish moss-draped oak to the next.

Bishop Henri de Bienville Bridge, or Bishopsbridge, was only a couple of miles west of the city, and crossed the low end of the Mississippi River to connect the highway out of New Orleans with the large Westwego sugar plantations on the south bank of the river. One of the plantations belonged to the bishopric, so it was not pure public-spiritedness alone that had driven Bishop de Bienville to construct his famous crossing.

The Bishops of New Orleans had always been men of wealth and power, from the very beginning. The first Bishop de Bienville was a younger son of the Le Moyne family, and brother to the Chevalier Le Moyne in his day, whenever exactly that was. Perhaps as long as two hundred years. Bishops had owned businesses and land and farms and had servants throughout New Orleans's history, and Henri de Bienville had been the richest of them all, a major landowner and benefactor in the city and the surrounding country. Bill knew this about the bishopric and about St. Henri because everyone in New Orleans knew it.

But not until the bishopric had passed into the hands of the Igbo Bishop Ukwu had the Bishop of New Orleans ever before been a crime lord and a moneylender. Bill looked at the Bridge and wondered whether he ought to think about actually attending church some time. It might convince the bishop to give him better interest rates.

The bridge was enormous, a span of seven great stone arches shooting across the wide river and creating a passage that could accommodate four large wagons abreast. Local oral history was emphatic that Bishop de Bienville had engaged a team of thauma-turgical engineers to build the bridge, and the sheer size of the thing made Bill believe the tale. The same oral history was also convinced that the effort of constructing the bridge had been so huge that it had actually killed the engineers, and de Bienville had buried their bodies inside the bridge's foundations.

Around Bishopsbridge, the Mississippi River created shallow muddy stinking wetlands that provided good pickings for fishing birds but fouled the air. The bridge's first arch began back from the river's edge and at a low bluff, to keep the bridge above the swamp and the river itself, even during high flood. This created a plain of sand under the stone that was surrounded by mud and water but was itself exposed and firm, if not exactly dry, most of the year. It was also hidden from casual observation. This concealed sandbar, known as Smuggler's Shelf, saw a steady stream of traffic for a variety of purposes, none of them completely innocent and many of them downright nefarious.

Croaking frogs and *wharooooping* river birds cheered Bill on as he scrambled down the slope onto the shelf.

Bang!

Bill drove the inevitable clutch of lovers too poor to afford a room from the sandbar with the unanswerable argument of a single pistol shot, fired out over the river. That stopped the birds and frogs, too. He reloaded and checked his other pistol as well while the couples scattered and the river creatures regained the courage to begin singing to him again—loaded and primed. He didn't fear being reported—even if any of the lovers felt confident enough to do so, he'd be gone by the time any gendarme could get here from the city.

And no gendarme would waste his time, anyway. Men killed each other on Smuggler's Shelf—that was a simple fact, and the law didn't very much care. Pistols checked, Bill leaned against the stone to wait.

His client Don Sandoval arrived next, with two bodyguards, on horseback. All three had long rich black perruques and they wore yellow coats and breeches, but only the don wore make-up, his cheeks carefully rouged and a neat moustache penciled onto his upper lip. *Mutton dressed as lamb.* Bill snorted, but he didn't say anything. The two bodyguards were scarred and hard-faced, with misshapen noses and notched ears, and they carried two pistols and a long rifle each. One of them was old enough that he might be a veteran of the Spanish War, like Bill, only on the opposite side of the conflict. The other was a relative pup, but in Texia, New Spain, and New Orleans, pups learned to bite at a young age.

The don was a ship-owning trader, soft and weak, and Bill didn't wonder that he would hire someone else to avenge the insult inflicted by the young frog who had climbed between his mistress's sheets. He was a bit perplexed that Don Sandoval hadn't simply had one of his own bodyguards do the job, but maybe the Don overestimated the Frenchman's skill and preferred not to risk his own man. Maybe the Don didn't want his men to bear the brunt of any repercussions, if some gendarme decided to take offense to the killing. In any case, Bill needed the cash.

"Will you watch, then, suh?" Bill bowed slightly as the Spaniards dismounted.

"She is a good night for a duel. We will watch from over there," Don Sandoval told him, indicating a deep patch of shadow beside the bridge.

"Very good, suh." Bill noted the spot mentally. Odd creature, this dago, with odd notions. He seemed to want to redeem his honor anonymously, which did not at all accord with Bill's ideas of how things should be done, but the Spaniard would get what he wanted, as long as the Spaniard was paying gold. Bill had learned long ago not to care too much about the strange notions of other men, so long as he got paid.

"Ten looeys after the shots are fired?" Bill willed his employer to remember the bonus he had offered.

Don Sandoval nodded. "And a further ten, señor, if you kill the young man."

Bill nodded too, keeping his comportment professional. Twenty looeys would see him out of debt and nicely in cash for a while—too bad for the young Frenchman. Maybe his friends would learn a valuable lesson about rich men's mistresses, and then the boy's death wouldn't be a total waste.

The Spaniards took their horses with them and hid.

The sun sank. Bill paced the Shelf in the gloom and waited, listening to the placid gurgle of the river around the stanchions of Bishopsbridge and the harmonies of the frogs and the birds.

The night air was getting colder, and it smelled bad.

Bill's mind wandered to thoughts of Long Cathy and a wish he wasn't still bound to a family in Johnsland he hadn't seen in fifteen years. He felt bad for that wish, and focused his mind on Sally. Sally was a good woman, worth far more to him even than the very good dowry she had brought to the marriage. She'd given him two sons and two daughters, and of those only the one boy had died in infancy, too small and weak to even get a name before he expired in her arms, mewling like a cat.

The girls had both lived, and Charles. Hell, Charles might even have his commission by now. Bill hoped it was in the service of the Earl of Johnsland. However insane the Earl might be, he was better than Thomas Penn.

And he had sworn he would not vent his anger at Bill upon Bill's family.

Three Frenchman arrived. They clattered down the slope, crashed through a brake of river reeds, and waded into the darkness under Bishopsbridge in the tight yellow embrace of a lantern.

"Ribbit," Bill called in greeting.

The Frenchmen were young and rich. None of them was wearing the makeup that seemed mandatory in salon society, and that they had been wearing the night before. Bill's opponent—he knew him by his jaw, bruised and puffy—looked the richest of all, in a silk shirt and elaborately brocaded waistcoat and jacket, but all three dressed like dandies, with plain black cloaks thrown over the top.

"Mistair Lee!" cried the young lover. "I yam 'ere!" His English was ridiculous, but it struck Bill suddenly and painfully that this young man whom he was about to murder was probably the same age as Bill's own son.

Forget *fallen*, he thought. It's a *damned* world.

Bill swallowed back thoughts of his boy, nodded a salute and approached the foreign dandies. "You are here, indeed, Monsieur le Frog. Shall we mark off ten paces?"

The three men conferred in French, and then one of the friends, shorter and with a round, plump face, spoke. His English was clear, though notably accented. "We believe ze Code Duello entitles my master . . . er, my friend, to know his offense, and to apologize, if he wishes. We acknowledge zat we have taken ze ground, which in principle precludes any apology until shots have been fired, but my friend informs me zat he does not understand why he has been challenged."

Bill wasn't accustomed anymore to transacting violence with gentlemen, and suddenly he wished he had employed more regular process. Well, this was New Orleans, not Richmond or Philadelphia or Paris, and the young monsieur didn't seem to be standing too unreasonably on his rights.

"Tell your friend, suh, that his offense was to make free with Miss Lefevre." That much was true. "Miss Lefevre is my mistress." Bill regretted the lie, but he needed the looeys.

Miss Lefevre was a young actress, well known in New Orleans, particularly for her work in stage comedies. Bill had seen her in something called *L'École des femmes*, which he understood to mean *The School for Wives*. The play had been all in French, and considerably less exciting than Bill had been led by the title to believe.

She was also the mistress of Bill's dago employer.

Bill's claim to be the actress's beau occasioned another three-sided flurry of French, and then the plump-faced man spoke again. "My master is surprised that you are so intimate with Miss Lefevre. He acknowledges ze insult and regrets zat it places him at odds with you. Neverzeless, he cannot apologize, as he is in love with ze lady."

Bill sighed. He needed to kill the Frenchman quickly; he was starting to like the lad, and that would throw off his aim. "Ten paces, then. Your *friend* fires first, as I expect you know." The reek of the swamp was even thicker than usual.

The third Frenchman, the lantern-holder, sallow-complected and small, rushed forward. "Please, sir, I beg you! Zis is not just any young man. His fazer—"

"Arrêtez-vous!" shouted the challenged young man. Bill thought that meant *stop*. The sallow-faced friend fell silent and both he and the interpreter looked at their feet.

Bill hesitated, then decided the brave young man deserved fair warning. "Tell your friend that I'll be shooting to kill."

If it were Charles in such a duel rather than the Frenchman, Bill would want the other fellow to warn his son.

Bill laid his coat on the ground carefully and took both his long pistols in hand; the challenged Frenchman armed himself similarly, and Bill noticed that his pistols were a pair of very expensive flint-locks, reflecting the lantern's light with elaborate gold and silver inlays. The guns were long and light, the pistols of a marksman. Sallow took the lantern off to the side and held it high.

Both men checked their weapons; Bill's were dry, loaded, and primed.

"Commêncez-vous," Sallow said, then started counting. "Une... deux... trois."

Bill marched. He heard the young man's boots behind him as they paced off ten crunching steps each in the wet sand. Might the young Frenchman be more dangerous than Bill had imagined? He had impressive pistols, and he seemed to know the Code Duello, or at least Plump Face did.

Bill glanced as he paced at the shadows where the Spaniards were hiding, and saw nothing. Even those yellow coats they wore were concealed by the deep darkness under Bishopsbridge.

Bill reached his ten paces and turned. He let both hands hang at his side. Maybe the Frenchman would kill him. Would that really be so bad? Death would come for him somewhere, and Bill had always expected it to be violent when it came. He'd lived through four years of the Spanish War, with battles all over Texia and the Cotton League and of course the Siege of Mobile. He'd been young then, just a boy. He'd lived through ten years of riding with the Imperial Consort, putting down road-agents, Comanche slavers, beastkind riots, and rapacious banks. He'd lived by the sword, so he expected to die by it, too, just as Shakespeare said... or was it Jesus? Why couldn't the French-man be the one to pull the trigger? Would Bill really miss this dishonorable ruffian's life?

And even if he won, if he killed this Frenchman, repaid his debts and lived, would he ever return to Johnsland? That he might return on the earl's death had been a constant prayer for fifteen years. He hoped the old man would finally die and the new earl would revoke his sentence of banishment. But the old man seemed to continue unnaturally, as if he had decided to live forever, just to spite William Lee.

If Bill died, though, he would never have the chance to see his son Charles as a grown man.

The Frenchman raised his pistol to take aim, and Bill saw that death would not come for him tonight. The young man's arm wobbled as he pointed his gun. He might know how to shoot, might even be a good shot, but he had never before shot at a living man. Bill sighed. He hoped that if his son were in such a duel, he would at least be able to aim straight.

Bang!

The sound of the explosion echoed across the river and bounced back from the underside of the bridge, and the Frenchman lowered his gun. As bad a shot as the Frenchman was, Bill thought, his willingness to engage in the duel to defend his lady's honor was that much more courageous. And courage was a dangerous, dangerous virtue to possess.

"Goodbye, suh," Bill murmured inaudibly to the young Frenchman. "I'd be proud to be your father." Then he took steady aim, pulled the trigger of his long pistol, and blew the young man to kingdom come.

The sound of Bill's shot echoed for a long time in his ears, while he picked up and put on his coat, replaced his pistols in his belt and his pocket, and then approached the Frenchmen again, his feet surprisingly heavy in the sand. Sallow and Plump Face stood jabbering over the body; he needed them to leave, so he could meet with his principal and collect his evening's payment.

"May I help you with the body, gentlemen?" he offered, and after some more wild-eyed French chattering between the two of them they agreed that he could. Bill quailed momentarily when he saw the gallant young man's face, still, serene and unfairly dead, but he forced himself to hoist the deceased man by his shoulders. This was not the first young man he'd ever killed. Why should this one bother him more than any of the others? He'd shot Spanish soldiers in Texia who weren't old enough to shave and who were barely able to hold up a rifle, and it hadn't bothered him, because it had been necessary. Bill shook his head to clear it.

Each friend took a leg, Sallow still struggling with the lantern as well, and they huffed and puffed the corpse back up the slope to the highway, where a large coach-and-four waited. The blue-and-gold-uniformed coachman crossed himself repeatedly, nearly losing hold of his short, neat wig as he stumbled down from his high seat to open the carriage door.

The three men shoved the body inside the coach onto the floor and Bill stepped back, brushing off his hands. "This is an impressive conveyance," he observed, examining the blue paint, the gold trim, and above all the gold fleur-de-lis that decorated its door, glimmering in the light of the lantern. "I don't have occasion often to mingle with French-speaking society, but I've seen the chevalier once or twice, and I have to say, this looks every bit as fine as *his* coaches."

"I tried to tell you," Sallow muttered.

"I take it you gentlemen are of good family?" Bill hadn't worked much for the city's rich French families, but he wouldn't object to doing so, and it occurred to him that at least these young men knew he was an accurate shot, and willing to do the job. Even if they couldn't give him work themselves, they might be able to provide a reference.

"No," Plump Face said sadly. "We were his friends and servants."

"I tried to tell you," Sallow repeated.

"Yes," Bill acknowledged, remembering the dead man silencing his friend. "What did you try to tell me?"

"The man you killed tonight, monsieur," Sallow said, "is no ordinary fellow."

"Yes, suh." Bill was losing his patience. "You said that part before. And you mentioned his father. What's the part that you *didn't* already tell me?"

Sallow began to weep. Plump Face looked terrified. Bill resisted the impulse to pull out the horse pistol that was still loaded and shoot another frog.

"What is it?" he coaxed them gently.

Finally, Plump Face spoke. "Our master," he said slowly, "was ze youngest son of ze chevalier."

"He might a wept, but He ain't sent no Electors."

⟫⟩◦⟨⟪

CHAPTER THREE

Calvin Calhoun wasn't frightened by guns. He'd been around guns every day of his life and was a good shot with the long rifle—but the sight of the pistol in the preacher's hand made him freeze.

He was afraid for Sarah, from his long red hair to his big, bony feet. Sarah Calhoun was stubborn enough to go and get herself shot by some Yankee preacher just for the sport of it, and he didn't want her getting hurt.

After all, she was his aunt.

Most of the crowd gasped or ducked when the gun came up, but a man beside Cal muttered instead—"*pallottolam averto*," Cal thought he heard—and brushed his hand as if swatting a fly. Cal recognized the sound of Latin from the many hours he'd heard the Elector marching Sarah through her *amo-amas-amat*.

Cal turned to look, and was startled by what he saw: beside him the man's face, unfamiliar and instantly forgettable, slipped off him like shadows in a changing light and revealed underneath the fair complexion and dark hair of the little foreign monk who had wanted to see the Elector.

The Ohioan priest was a wizard. Wizards were rare—even honest-to-God hexers like Sarah were rare enough, though plenty of folk pretended they could hex and were happy to take your copper bits in trade for a bit of pointless mumbo jumbo when

47

you were in love. It wasn't a coincidence that the man Sarah had taunted in Market Street was now here in the tent.

He was following her.

"You're sure enough a stranger to these parts," Sarah called out to the preacher, and Cal snapped his head back around to focus again on the gun. "'Round here, boredom ain't a mortal sin. And our preachers ain't so much in the habit of shootin' their congregations."

The crowd tried to back away, to the edges of the tent and even out the door—none of these folks saw the drama playing out as any of their business. There were too many people for anyone to easily get away, however, and the throng milled about, poised to explode.

"Mister, we's jest funnin' you," Cal said, raising his voice and stepping forward to try to defuse the situation. That put the wizard into his peripheral vision and almost out of sight entirely, which made him nervous, but you have to pick your battles and the Martinite had a gun.

The Yankee stared at him from the pulpit.

"It's a kind of a game we play," Cal tried to explain, "funnin' priests. No need to get fussed, you can jest consider it your welcome to Appalachee and be grateful ain't nobody stole your horse yet."

"Step aside." The tall priest's voice was cold. "I'm taking that girl with me."

"Whyn't we go across the road to the Town Hall?" Sarah suggested. "It's tall enough, we could re-enact the Defenestration of Prague, help you relive the glorious roots of your order using the streets of Nashville and your Martinite buttocks."

"That isn't funny, child."

Cal thought it was, and he almost laughed despite his fear.

"Oh, it's funny, all right," Sarah disagreed, "only it might not be fair. I heard as the two fellers those Bohemians threw out the window in 1618 were the Martinite Jaroslav and Ferdinand's tax collector. Anyone as has read the Bible knows how partial Jesus is to tax collectors, and you gotta wonder if mebbe, on his own, that old Martinite might not a bounced quite so well."

"Silence!" The Martinite stepped to the edge of the platform, his pistol trembling.

The pale monk moved up quietly, joining Cal in the line of fire. "You make very bold, Ezekiel." His voice was calm. "But you aren't in the Covenant Tract, or in Thomas Penn's Philadelphia, and there are many people here. Why don't you put the pistol down?"

Cal thought the gun-wielding priest's eyes glazed over for a moment, but then he squinted hard and shook his head. Cal heard cursing behind him as the priest's heavy announcer struggled with the crowd, trying to get into the tent.

"You're a traitor, monk," Angleton replied. "You should have stuck to saying prayers over your dead mistress. But my errand isn't to deal with you. I'm here for the girl, and I'm wiling to take her with me as a corpse."

Sarah pushed past Calvin and planted herself squarely in front of the Right Reverend Father, hands on her skinny hips.

"Sarah—" Cal tried in vain to stop her. *Fool girl!*

"Shoot me, then, you filthy Yankee!" She spat.

"Hold on," Cal said. The priest wouldn't possibly really try to kill anyone in front of a crowd in broad daylight. Surely someone would step in, or the threat of the town watch's involvement would stop things before they went any further.

Angleton aimed at Sarah's chest, his face a dispassionate mask, and squeezed the trigger.

Bang!

"No!" Cal threw himself forward into the acrid blue jet of gunpowder smoke.

The preacher couldn't possibly miss at that range, but somehow, incredibly, he did. Cal heard a soft *thump!* over his head as the bullet went high and wide—*yards* high and wide—and buried itself in the pole that served the preaching tent as ceiling beam.

There was a moment's pause, during which Cal noted the look of disbelief and irritation on Father Angleton's face.

And then the tent fell sideways.

Young Andy must have missed his cue, but yanked the lariat when he heard the gunshot. The poles on the left side of the tent all had their bottoms jerked out from under them and slid away beyond the white canvas.

The congregation stampeded, pulling down the tent supports with them.

The Yankee, wide-eyed in surprise, lurched around his pulpit and staggered to the attack. He raised his pistol over his head like a club—

and Calvin Calhoun cold-cocked him with a hard ball of

knuckles to the jaw. The blow sent the tall priest sprawling into the upright barrel and across his preaching stage. "Can't take a punch any more'n he can take a joke," Cal muttered, and then the sky fell.

Cal batted at the descending canvas to keep it away from his face, but it was a losing battle and soon he couldn't see at all for the dirty white shroud over his entire body. He fought to where he thought Sarah had stood, knocking knees and elbows with the hollering crowd, and found her gone.

"Sarah!" No answer. "Grandpa's gonna kill me," he muttered, and waded as quickly as he could, pushing and kicking and cursing when he had to, to climb out from under the tent.

"Not one word outta you, d'you 'ear me?" Cal heard as he emerged. The priest's burly Englishman had one hand tangled in Sarah's hair and the other covering her mouth while he pinned her arm with his elbow. He was easily three times her size, and though Sarah struggled, red-faced and wiggling, she was pinned. "You bide 'ere wiff me until I've sorted this out wiff the Right Reverend Father, you ill-faced wee witch."

"Let her go, muttonhead!" Cal wished he had brought his rifle to town this morning. He thought of his boot knife, but it was too far to reach in the short instant he had.

The Englishman's eyes widened. "You be the one what 'it 'im!"

Cal charged.

The Englishman reached for his pistol, freeing Sarah's mouth and arms—

"Damned limey!" Sarah yelled as she elbowed the Englishman in the belly—

and Cal grabbed the pistol, still on the belt, with both his hands to the Englishman's one. They struggled, grunting and spitting, for control of the weapon, but the heavier man had the fingers of one hand still entwined in Sarah's hair, pulling her neck back at an uncomfortable angle, and Calvin slowly gained the advantage, wrapping the fingers of one hand around the trigger guard and the thumb of the other onto the pistol's hammer.

Sarah twisted and tore herself free, leaving a clump of black hair in the heavy man's mitt. She punched the big man's side. Unfazed, the Englishman turned his freed hand to Calvin—he gripped the entire right side of Calvin's face in his greasy paw and pushed his thumb into the skin under Cal's left eye.

Cal had a sudden vision of losing his eye. He pulled back the pistol's hammer and squeezed the trigger.

Bang!

"Aaarrawaaargh!" The fat man tumbled back and to the ground. Blood spattered his gray stocking and welled out a neat little hole in his scuffed black shoe.

Cal threw the pistol away and became aware that the paved street was a sea of yelling faces. Had the little monk made it out of the tent? He'd almost seemed like an ally during the confrontation, though Cal couldn't figure out why he would be. Maybe because he was the Elector's friend? But Sarah had told him that she was a Jackson.

"Sarah, you all right?" he called.

She kicked the yelping Englishman and spat on him. "Lost me a little hair is all." Cal saw blood in her scalp.

The heavy man stumbled to his feet and staggered away, leaving bloody tracks.

Calvin looked past the Englishman up Market Street toward the Charlotte Pike Gate, a quarter mile away. Half a dozen men in blue and gold uniforms ran toward them, long Brown Besses in their hands, the Imperial ship, shield, and eagle, with horses on each side on their chests marking them as the town watch.

The preacher's man ran right toward the Imperials, yelling, "officers! officers!"

"Jerusalem," Cal muttered. Young Andy and the other Calhoun younguns were beyond the Watch, pulling the Elector's cart away toward the gate at a measured pace, but Andy watched the commotion around the tent over the braided leather looped on his shoulder. Andy had bungled the timing, but at least he hadn't lost Cal's lariat.

"It ain't obvious to me how we're a-gittin' outta here," Sarah said.

Cal looked the other way, toward the Jonathan Edwards Bridge, and saw four more men of the Watch. They were having a heated conversation with the pair of tall wagoneers from the tent, and the wagoneers repeatedly pointed in Sarah's direction. He looked up again, met Andy's gaze and shook his head.

"It ain't obvious to me, either," he admitted. Andy nodded and turned away, continuing his innocent plod up Market Street. "But I'd sure feel a sight better iffen I'd brought my tomahawk to town."

"Shh," urged a gentle voice, and suddenly the monk was standing with them. "Back under the tent with me."

Calvin stared dumbly, and Sarah looked plain obstinate.

"Please," he added. "I can help."

Cal lifted up a piece of the canvas—a knot of former spectators still struggled under the heavy cloth, some trying to get out and some simply attempting to stand—and tented it up over the three of them as they pushed into hiding.

"Thank goodness you're so tall," the monk observed. "If I had to play tentpole, you'd both be blind."

"Who are you?" Sarah jutted out a suspicious jaw.

"No more tricks." Cal kept his eye fixed squarely on the little man.

"No more tricks," the monk agreed, and for once he wasn't smiling. "As I told you, I'm a friend of your . . . father's. We have no time." Reaching up with both hands, he touched each Calhoun on the cheek simultaneously and spoke again in Latin. "*Facies muto.*"

"What are you doin'?" Then Cal turned to look at Sarah and nearly jumped out of his skin. Where Sarah had been standing, and wearing her purple-and-suns shawl, was a pudgy woman with graying hair and two good eyes. "Jerusalem!"

Wizardry, indeed. That explained the Latin.

And the Right Reverend Father's impossible miss.

And whatever spell the little man had cast on himself before to change his own face, he had now cast on Sarah.

"What you lookin' at, beanpole?" the graying woman demanded sternly in Sarah's voice. Then she looked doubtful. "Cal? Is that you?"

"What do I look like?" he asked.

"You look handsome," Sarah told him. "I can't hardly b'lieve it's you!"

"No one will recognize either of you." The little monk suddenly seemed tired. "Now we should leave the tent separately, one at a time, and make our way up the street. We'll meet by the stall of the Dutchman who bought your leaf."

Calvin ambled out first, hands in the pockets of his breeches, feet held to a steady, scuffing gait. He'd had plenty of experience walking innocent, but none quite this brazen; he strolled straight at the gaggle of Watchmen and the limping preacher's assistant, nodding a lazy salute in complete reliance on the monk's spellcraft. Cal didn't know any of the Watchmen's names—they were townsfolk—but he recognized their faces and he wondered what they saw when they looked at him. Apparently, a handsome man. He chuckled softly at Sarah's barbed wit.

"Old man," one of them barked, "we're lookin' for a couple hillfolk kids, a tall redheaded feller and a girl with a real bad eye."

Cal almost walked past before he realized the Watchman was talking to him. He clattered to an awkward stop. "What? Sorry, I . . . I ain't deef yet, but I'm a-gittin' there."

"'E can't 'elp us, let 'im go." The Englishman smiled sourly at Cal as Cal continued past and on up Market Street.

Old ghosts troubled him, and Captain Sir Daniel Berkeley badly wanted to cast his Tarock. He'd foregone his customary morning casting along with breakfast; they were within a day's ride of Free Imperial Nashville, and he wanted to catch up to his chaplain.

He was irked that Father Angleton had left Philadelphia ahead of him, and more than a little impressed that, for all their hard riding on the best-kept roads in the empire, Berkeley and his men had been unable to overtake the priest before reaching Nashville. It must be Angleton's gramarye. He knew from experience the Martinite wasn't a strong enough wizard to speed up the entire corps of the Philadelphia Blues, or ease their fatigue, or make them fly. Angleton was a priest, first and foremost, and only secondarily a magician.

Angleton accompanied the dragoons for the purpose of hearing confessions, administering last rites and saying prayers when the occasion required. Funeral prayers, for instance, might theoretically be important to a combat unit like the Blues, though it had been several years since any of them died in active duty. If from time to time he managed a small, moderately helpful bit of magic, so much the better.

Tomorrow Berkeley would overtake him. Him and the girl with the bad eye old Iron Andy Calhoun was hiding.

If it had been Berkeley alone in pursuit, on his Virginia-bred gray Andalusian, he would have overtaken the parson days ago.

The girl was a ghost, a tattered remaining shred of a banner Berkeley had believed torn down and destroyed. He had served the King of Cahokia, in his day, but Berkeley's lord and master was His Imperial Majesty Thomas Penn now, and no fondness for men long dead, nor ghostlike daughterly apparitions, would sway him from his course. Berkeley would do his duty.

Subject, as everything was, to the capricious whims of fate.

Berkeley was not a superstitious man. His mother had obsessed over her stars, as did the emperor, and his father had spent long hours in young Daniel's hearing debating the numerological secrets of the Apocalypse of St. John, but Daniel Berkeley had grown up convinced that he was free.

War, though, changes one's perspective. Before his first battle, a border skirmish with a regiment of Virginia volunteers against some cracker encroachers, he had scoffed to see the older men polishing lucky medals, saying prayers and tucking rabbit's feet and crosses into secret pockets. After the battle, after young Daniel had watched the cloud of musketballs capriciously take one man here and another there, with no apparent rhyme or reason, no respect for skill, age or wisdom, he hadn't been so sure.

Before his second battle, Daniel Berkeley had cast the Tarock for the first time.

The Blues now cantered over the crest of a hill, and Berkeley saw down another length of stone-paved Imperial pike, surrounded by the piled orange and brown detritus of autumn. "Break! Check arms!" Berkeley called, and while they stopped to rest their horses and confirm that their pistols and Paget carbines were loaded and primed, he discreetly slipped his Tarock into his hand. It was a costly set, sturdy cards, and on the back of each they bore an elaborate scrolled portrayal of Franklin's Shield, the letters TCB with a lightning bolt crashing through them.

He drew the top three cards.

The first card was the Priest. The painting on Berkeley's deck was of a tonsured fat man in a long friar's robe and sandals. He carried a walking staff on his shoulder that finished in a cross on top, and he held a bag or a wallet in his other hand. Encircling the Priest, as on every card of the Tarock, was a flowing frame of interlaced knots. The Priest meant consecration and commitment. Was that Angleton? The Martinite wasn't fat and he wore boots, but he was a priest and he wore his hair in a tonsure. The picture on the card rather resembled a Spaniard, one of the Conquistador Fathers who had razed the Aztecs' spiritual empire as Cortés had toppled the political one. What was the cross, then ... a burden to bear? A holy mission? A grudge? And the bag could be anything. It could be money, a collection for the poor. It could be Aztec loot. Judas had held the bag, hadn't he, among the disciples? Did Ezekiel Angleton plan some betrayal? Or maybe the bag was a thing obtained or a mission achieved . . . maybe it signified that Angleton had accomplished his task, and already had the girl in his possession.

Berkeley needed more information.

He turned the next card up: the Drunkard. The Drunkard on this card was a thin man with red eyes, unshaven. He guzzled from a horn like a Viking, and was captured in the moment of tripping over his own toes and falling forward onto his face. Angleton was no drinker. Berkeley drank, as a gentleman did, but he was not a drunk. Angleton's servant Dogsbody drank to the point of being ridiculous. The Tarock's image didn't resemble the Englishman, though. If anything, it looked like it might be meant to portray an Appalachee, in one of their long shirts. On the other hand, the Englishman was a pagan, and the drinking horn painted onto the card looked as pagan as you could get. Didn't the vitkis of the Mississippi Germans use a horn along with their sacred knives in making magic? There was something in the background that resembled a barrel, too, and another object. Those didn't look particularly English or pagan. Could the object be a copper pot? Was the Drunkard a moonshiner? The Drunkard indicated accident, catastrophe, failure. Had Angleton, the consecrated man, had the girl in his hands, and then tripped and lost her?

The third card was Simon Sword.

Simon Sword was always painted as a child, and in this picture he held an enormous blade in both his hands, one of those long crushing and slicing weapons the Scots called *claymores*. He had floppy blond hair and a childlike grin, and his giant sword sliced off the heads of three men simultaneously.

Blazes. Simon Sword was a portentous card to draw at any time, indicating violence, trial, change, war, and judgment. Berkeley shook his head. He didn't think the Priest could refer to him, and the Drunkard was not much more likely. Nor could either of them mean the girl, unless the cracker habit of corn whisky had gotten to her earlier than usual. The cards didn't seem to be telling *his* story at all.

Who, then, was to be on trial?

✧　　✧　　✧

Once past the watch, Sarah picked up her pace. Calvin was ahead of her, though she'd lost track of him in the press of people, and she wanted to catch him and get out of town before the monk found them again. The little man had helped them out of a tight spot, but she still preferred to let him find his own way to Calhoun land, even if he really was the Elector's friend.

And if he wasn't the Elector's friend, she preferred that he disappear.

She was disappointed, therefore, to reach the Dutchman's stall and find Calvin standing beside it, chatting with the little monk. Cal had his own face back, so she assumed she did, too. When had it returned? Calvin looked uncomfortable, but that might just be because the monk stood closer to him than any human being had any business standing to another person, unless they had love on their minds, or knives in their hands.

"Welcome, Sarah," Thalanes said to her. "Calvin was just telling me you know Latin."

"Calvin's got a big mouth sometimes," she said grimly, "and you got surprisingly quick feet, monk." She kept walking, toward the gate, looking for Young Andy and the cart. Cal and Thalanes followed.

"You have some education. I expect you know the Elector Songs pretty well," the monk speculated.

"Oh, that's too easy for Sarah," Cal said. "Jerusalem, *I* can sing you *those* iffen that's all it takes to impress you."

"Any child knows one or two," Sarah conceded. Why was it any of this man's business that she knew Latin, or whether she could recite the Electors?

"Sing me one," he asked. "Please."

She squinted at him with her one good eye and chanted out a rhyme in nasal Appalachee sing-song. "Louisiana sends two Electors, that's clear: the Bishop of New Orleans and the chevalier."

Calvin laughed.

Thalanes laughed too, merrily, making the wrinkles around his eyes jump and dance. "Jesus wept," he said.

"He might a wept," Sarah said with a scowl, "but He ain't sent no Electors."

"Of course." The monk smiled. They were in sight of the Charlotte Pike Gate now and Sarah saw the Calhoun younguns and their mule-cart, creeping out through the gate and onto the Imperial

Highway. "Many years ago, when I first became a novice, my preceptor, a gruff old warhorse named Palindres, insisted I memorize a verse of Scripture every day. 'Jesus wept' was my first day's work."

"John eleven," Sarah told him. Might as well let the monk know she was no gump.

"Yes, I saw that you know Scripture." He never stopped smiling. "I expect you know *all* the Elector Songs, don't you?"

"I expect it ain't really your business, Father Thalanes of the Order of St. Cetes!" she snapped. "You Eldritch, Father?"

His smile faded slightly; now she had him back on his heels, the nosy little foreigner. She knew all about St. Cetes, the Mayor of Wittenberg who was too sanctified even to stand up for himself when Martin Luther plotted against him, and she wasn't impressed. Firstborn or not, any fool knew enough to take his own side in a fight.

They passed through the gate and onto the broad, hard-packed Charlotte Pike, the monk looking thoughtful and the blue-and-gold-wrapped guards waving them through. The pike marched south and west through smallhold farms and fields belonging to townsfolk of Nashville and was already carrying away some of the traders at the fair. The first Toll Gate wasn't for miles, so the hillfolk happily used the short stretch of the pike closest in to town.

"Yes." The monk's voice was quiet and submissive. "I'm Firstborn. Are you?"

Sarah Calhoun snorted. "Hell, no! My pa is the Elector Calhoun."

"I see." The Eldritch monk contemplated her gravely. "Is he allergic to silver, like you?"

Sara felt her bad eye might pop open from sheer surprise. "You peepin' into my thoughts, wizard? I'm allergic to silver 'cause my mamma was an Injun woman. Everybody knows a lot of Injuns are allergic." She saw Cal staring at her and the monk both, bewildered.

"They are," Thalanes agreed. "There's Eldritch blood in most tribes, and a few tribes have quite a bit of it. Such as the Lenni Lenape. And of course, some people have gifts and vulnerabilities that defy explanation."

"Huh," Sarah said.

"Do you know your mother, then?" the Cetean priest asked. "Is she Shawnee?"

"I reckon that's personal, monk," she rebuffed him. "Lessen you want to tell me about *your* mother first."

"Did your mother also give you your lily white complexion, as white as mine, as white as any Moundbuilder's?"

Sarah was stunned. She wished she could shut the monk's mouth, but a part of her—more than a small part—found him making sense. She never *had* met her mother, and had just taken it on faith from her father that she was an Indian. And silver *did* blister her skin on prolonged contact. Sarah deepened her scowl.

"I know what comes after twelve," she said stubbornly.

The barb only made him chuckle. "And did your manifest talent at hexing come from your Indian mother, too?"

"My pa's the Elector," Sarah insisted, and then she decided to shut the monk up with a lie. "My mamma's Shawnee, lives a ways down on the Cumberland."

He shook his head patiently, his smile looking like an amused frown. "Why do you feel you must dissemble, Sarah?"

"Don't know what you mean," she dissembled.

He laughed out loud and then fell silent.

They had passed the farms now, and Sarah relaxed slightly. The highway was Imperial territory, of course, but fifty feet off it to either side was now Calhoun land. She expected His Imperial Majesty Thomas Penn probably did have officers somewhere who would be willing to try to exert their authority in Calhoun territory—his Foresters, maybe—but it wouldn't be any of the boys in Nashville. She looked at Cal, expecting to see him looking calmer, too, but he had an expression on his face that combined astonishment, wariness, fear, and . . . something else. Hope, maybe, though that seemed an odd emotion for the circumstances.

They overtook Young Andy with the cart and the younguns, and he delivered his report. "I never did hear you give the signal, Aunt Sarah, there was so much noise. I heard the gunshot, all right, and I reckoned it was time to pull that ol' tent down, so we done it. One pull."

He handed Cal the lariat and grinned, looking for Sarah's approval.

She gave it to him. "Well done, Andy. You done fine."

"You decide to bring this feller home?" Andy pointed at Thalanes. "I reckoned him for a foreigner."

"He *is* a foreigner." Sarah glared at the monk. "He's from a country called Grinland, where they ain't got but the one facial expression and everybody dies of boredom."

"You a Wanderin' Johnny?" Andy asked the monk.

"The Poor Disciples of St. John Gutenberg do an important work," Thalanes said, smiling again. Damn fool. "I'm not one of them. I'm a storyteller. May I tell you a story?"

"How about a song?" Young Andy suggested instead.

"Do you know your Elector Songs?" Thalanes asked with a smile.

"He loves those Elector Songs," Sarah grumbled.

Young Andy shot a sidelong glance at Cal and blushed. "How about Cal sings something?"

"I think I've had jest about enough of the Elector Songs for the day, though," Cal said. "What iffen I sing 'O Listen, Ye Fathers'?"

A couple of the younguns hooted. "That's a song about the emperor," Andy told the foreigner.

"Believe me, I know," the monk said, his mouth a flat line.

Cal unleashed his fine tenor voice and sang:

> *The first time I saw him was in eighty-one*
> *We rode the Ohio, with sword and with gun*
> *The Serpents would see him, they'd turn and they'd run*
> *One flash of his saber, the battle was won*
>
> > *O listen, ye fathers, from far and from near*
> > *Ye'd best hide your daughters, Lord Thomas is here*
>
> *There never was fairer a lord among men*
> *He was stout with his saber and bold with his pen*
> *And the ladies would follow, o'er moor and through fen*
> *For one look at the locks of fair Thomas Penn*
>
> > *O listen, ye fathers, from far and from near*
> > *Best lock up your daughters, Lord Thomas is here*

Cal stopped, a bashful look on his face. "It's got a nice tune. And it's kind of a love song."

"It ain't a love song," Sarah disagreed.

"Kind of," he repeated.

"I love history," Young Andy said.

"Is that what that song is?" Thalanes asked. "History?"

Sarah wondered whether he might be offended. "Sorry," she said. Thalanes waved off her concern.

Young Andy was undeterred. "And I might could tell *you* a story. Do you know the tale about how the archwizard Sir Isaac Newton defeated the Necromancer"—he spit over his left shoulder—"at the Second Battle of Putney? Not to mention Black Tom Fairfax, the Sorcerer Hooke and their legions of marching dead?"

Calvin knuckled Andy gently on the arm. "Don't spit."

Young Andy was showing off for the other younguns, but none of them acknowledged his excellence—they continued to rattle and gripe at each other in a hubbub just a few notches short of an outright brawl.

"I do," the monk said, and Sarah warmed to him a little for taking Young Andy seriously. "He worked mighty weather gramarye and flooded the Thames, washing out his pontoons and splitting Cromwell's New Model Army in two. Make no mistake, though, it was John Churchill's mixed pikemen and musketeers that then smashed Cromwell's forces in Kensington, including the Lazars, and forced the Lord Protector to surrender. Wizards can't do everything all by themselves, even powerful ones."

"And everyone knows John Churchill had to git help from dark powers, hisself," Young Andy supplied cheerfully. "His men were the Unbaptized. He turned England back pagan."

"Exceptin' the Duchy of Monmouth," Sarah pointed out.

"Yeah, But the rest of it went back to blood sacrifice and druids, to beat the Necromancer." Young Andy spit over his shoulder again.

This time Cal knuckled him hard. "I said stop it, Andy!"

"You want the Crooked Man to git me?" Young Andy asked.

"The Crooked Man ain't gonna come git you jest on account of you mentionin' some evil power," Cal explained. "And iffen he was, I don't reckon spittin' at him would help you much."

Andy hung his head.

"Now *that* tale is history," Thalanes said to Young Andy. "Your knowledge is impressive. May I tell my story now?" The compliment was generally jeered at by the younguns.

Andy, both proud and abashed, agreed that he could and settled into a comfortable listening lope. Sarah watched the monk's face closely as he gathered his thoughts; his expression was both remote, as if he were trying to remember the tale, and at the same time deeply mournful, as if it were a story the pain of which he could never forget.

"Once upon a time..." Andy prompted him.

"No," Thalanes contradicted him. "No, not once upon a time. 'Once upon a time' means fairies under mushroom caps and trolls in the hills, and this story happened in a time of gunpowder and three-masted sailing ships. It took place...let us say for now that it took place a few years ago.

"A few years ago, a powerful king rode his bounds. A king must travel, you know, to be seen by his people and to see them, and in particular a king must travel the border of his kingdom, to maintain its integrity, to know his lands and to pray for their blessing.

"This king was a wizard also." The monk met Sarah's gaze. "He was Firstborn, and the lord of one of the Ohio kingdoms. And he was married to a queen of another land, an empress, and together they were wealthy and powerful and loved, but they had no children.

"They were loved by most, but not by all. The empress had a brother, who thought the empire should be his, and so he hated his sister and even more he hated her husband, because he was a stranger and he was Eldritch and because he sat upon the imperial throne as the empress's consort. Do you know what a 'consort' is?"

The question was directed at Young Andy, but Sarah intervened. "It means he was the empress's husband, but he wasn't the emperor. She stayed in charge."

"Very good," Thalanes murmured. "So the king rode the bounds of his kingdom, away in the west, with a few chosen companions and his personal troop of soldiers for his defense. And one terrible night, there was a grave accident, and the king was left wounded and dying.

"The king couldn't be saved by all the art of his companions—his wounds were too terrible—but he didn't die immediately. As he lay bleeding, he saw that he was sheltered under an oak tree, and he asked that three acorns be brought to him. He instructed his companions to take the acorns to his wife the empress, and then with his own blood and his dying breath he anointed them and pronounced upon them his blessing."

"Ewww," Andy said.

"His companions buried him and they returned to the empress. She grieved, tearing her dress and shattering her crown upon the floor. Her brother shut her away her and pronounced her mad. An election was called, and her brother came to sit upon the Imperial Throne."

"Mad Hannah," Sarah said, almost whispering. For the first time, she felt sad for the broken empress whose death notice she had read that morning. "And so the king must have been her husband, the Imperial Consort Kyres Elytharias."

"Who's that?" Young Andy asked.

"He was a sort of knight, I reckon," Calvin offered.

"Like a Teutonic Knight?" Andy asked. "Like a Savoyard, fighting the Turk?"

"King of Cahokia," Thalanes said. "The Lion of Missouri. He belonged to an order called the Swords of Wisdom. Some of them fight the Turk, but they fight many enemies."

"Well, that explains all the crazy acorn nonsense." Even as he thoughtfully digested this story, Andy shifted from one foot to the other and couldn't stop moving. "I always heard the Kings of Cahokia was wizards, and they don't know how to count to eleven."

"Thirteen, you mean," Sarah told him.

"Do I?" Young Andy was confused. "All I recollect is as they count in twelves, not in tens."

"That don't seem right," Calvin said. "A man's got ten fingers, in Nashville and in the Ohio both."

"True," Thalanes admitted. "The question is, because man has ten fingers, should he look around him and force everything else into systems counted by ten? Or should he look for order in the world around him, and number things as God has numbered them in the cosmos...for instance, by twelves?"

"It's man as has dominion over the beasts," Sarah grumbled. "If horses could count, I reckon maybe they'd do it by fours."

"Twelve houses of the zodiac," the monk pointed out. "Twelve points of the compass. Twelve months of the year."

"Months are made up," Sarah said. "They could jest as easily be ten, or thirty, or two, or no months at all. Same for points of the compass."

"Twelve cycles of the moon to each cycle of the sun, then."

"Not exactly."

"Anyway, that ain't the way I heard the story," Cal observed.

"No," the monk agreed, "it is not. You heard that the Empress Hannah went insane and was immured for her own good. By her brother, Thomas Penn, who rides the Ohio with his flashing sword and his irresistibility to women."

Cal looked embarrassed. "Yeah, I guess that's jest about what I heard of the matter. And I heard Cahokia ain't had a king since. It's been under the Pacification."

"Also at the hand of the Emperor Thomas Penn."

"Bonuses paid for friend recruited!" one of the younguns chimed in, and Young Andy elbowed him aside.

"Crown's lost and all," Cal added more soberly.

"The crown and the other regalia of the kingdom. Things of power." Thalanes let a silence settle for a few moments before he continued. "The consort's companions delivered the acorns to the empress. Alone with a few trusted servants in her Philadelphia cage, she treasured those seeds of the mighty oak. She carried them about on her person, she caressed them, spoke and sang to them as if to children, and even gave them names."

"And then, one day, she ate them."

"So she really *was* mad." Sarah felt both revulsion and compassion.

Thalanes ignored her. "The empress conceived. Do you know what 'conceived' means, Andy?"

Andy snickered. "It means a sow and a boar make shoats. 'Round these parts, conceivin' is one thing we know all about. I'm from a litter of seven myself, and Calvin there is the oldest of nine. Sarah, what are you, the Elector's *thirteenth*, ain't you? Some folks reckon thirteen's a bad luck number, and that explains Sarah's eye."

Thalanes shook his head and laughed. "I don't think the number thirteen explains Sarah's eye at all. Nor do I think she's bad luck. Nor do you, the way you take her lead."

"I reckon not," Andy agreed affably.

Sarah found herself warming to the little priest again. She steeled her heart.

"The empress conceived," the monk went on. "And in time, she bore three children—triplets."

"Conceived of who?" Andy asked. "I know it's the woman as conceives, but she conceives *of* somebody, most generally a man, or she don't conceive at all. The king was dead, right?"

"It's just a story," Sarah objected.

"She conceived of the acorns, apparently," Thalanes explained.

Cal whistled low. "Are you tellin' us this is a true tale?"

"The children were born . . . marked. Disfigured, some would say. They were taken at birth by loyal servants. They were ridden to far corners of the empire and hidden, and nothing was said of their birth to the new emperor."

"It figures an oak whelp couldn't e'er be normal," Andy reasoned. "Did they have little barky caps with stems on their heads? Hard, shiny faces?" His grin made it clear he had decided not to take this story seriously.

Thalanes walked in silence.

"Then what?" Cal asked. "Is that the end? That don't sound like the end of no story to me."

"Years passed. The empress believed she was dying, and longed to know more of her children," the monk continued slowly. "Of the three loyal servants, only one had returned, her dead husband's chaplain and father confessor and now her confessor also, and she importuned him for information. In his weakness, he finally succumbed. He told her only about one child, the oldest, the one he had hidden. He told the empress where he had placed the child, and he told her about the baby's mark. The empress's oldest child was born with one eye swollen shut and inflamed, and in all the time the father confessor had traveled with the baby, that eye had never healed or opened."

"She had a witchy eye, then. Was it much like Sarah's?" Young Andy wanted to know.

"Yes," Thalanes replied. "It was just like Sarah's."

There was a terrible, terrible silence.

"That still ain't the end of any story," Cal repeated.

"No, it ain't," Sarah jumped in, "but it'll have to do for now. Time to leave the emperor's road."

Turning the cart was no complicated operation and didn't particularly require special attention, but Sarah wanted to end the story. The rest of the Calhouns took her lead and didn't press Thalanes for any more of the tale. She felt the monk's eyes resting heavy on her as she took the mule's lead rope and walked it off the Pike onto a narrow dirt track.

"Sorry," Calvin said to the little monk. "I didn't mean any offense, I's jest singin'."

"You have nothing to apologize for." Thalanes put his hand on Calvin's arm. "I like the song, too. Many great songs have words that are pure nonsense."

They followed the trail into the woods, beginning to turn orange and yellow, and then up as the land rose beneath them and the path became the knife edge of a steep, forested ridge. The track was wide enough for the cart, but only barely.

The younguns resumed their jostling and Sarah wondered about Calvin, and about the monk. Cal was not a man of many words at any time, but he was normally conversational, and now he was sunk in a thoughtful silence. Was he feeling rueful, or embarrassed at his song choice? She smiled at him to show her support. When she caught his eye, he smiled back at her, but shyly.

That look made Sarah feel queer and uncertain of herself.

As for the monk . . . he seemed kind, but he was a foreigner and a painfully nosy one at that. He cared way too much about Sarah's personal affairs, and the whole deformed-acorn princess story struck her as a ridiculous lie aimed to make her feel self-conscious.

Which she refused to do.

The ridge ended where the crown of the hill began; the track ahead rose up through a narrow stone canyon, leading up to the forested cap of the mountain.

Cal whistled, loud, *hyoo-hyoo-hyoo-whee-up*, a sort of birdcall that belonged to no bird but served as a recognition sign, and three young Calhoun men appeared, each casually carrying a long rifle. One slipped into view out a crack in the canyon wall ahead and two faded from the woods. They all wore the hunting shirts and breeches of Appalachee men.

"What you got there, Auntie Sarah?" one of them called, strolling from the trees. "That feller don't look like no Calhoun to me." He spat a squirt of brown tobacco juice into the leaves.

"I'm a friend," Thalanes said immediately.

Young Andy took the lead rope and continued to drag the mule and cart uphill, younguns bouncing all around him like kernels of popping corn, while Sarah and Calvin stopped with the monk.

"He's a priest, Shadrach," Sarah added. "Claims he's a friend of the Elector."

"I don't know if I can let him up, bein' a priest." Shadrach eyed Thalanes with suspicion.

"I'm unarmed." The monk spread his arms wide.

"Arms ain't the issue. I'm New Light," Shadrach explained, a mocking edge to his voice, "and so's the Elector. So's James over there, and especially Red Charlie, that feller up the canyon, he's *really* New Light."

"I admire New Light Christians." Thalanes was far too soft, too gentle. These rough Calhoun boys would tear the monk to bits like a tissue paper doll. Sarah had mixed feelings about that prospect. "I respect the choices of all God's children, and I especially respect any choice of spiritual commitment."

"I thank you, Father," Shadrach said, executing an ironic little bow, "but our commitment ain't the issue. The issue is that we like hard preachers up here in the hills, and we don't much care for churches and priests."

"I see," the monk said.

"So I might could let you up the mountain, but only if you can convince me that you're a hard preacher . . ." Shadrach raised his eyebrows, "who just *happens* to be a priest."

"You want a sermon?" Thalanes clarified doubtfully. He was so mild in his manner, Sarah thought it had to be a trick. She half-expected him to raise his hand at any second and turn Shadrach into a toad.

"Hellfire and brimstone, Father." The Calhoun sentinel spat a third time into the carpet of fallen leaves. "You give us a hellfire and brimstone sermon, and I'll send you up. Otherwise, I don't see as I can let you past, and I certainly can't be responsible for the actions of Red Charlie. I consider myself a man of principle, but he has *strong* feelin's."

Thalanes smiled at Charlie and James. Sarah thought it was about even odds between the monk's getting turned away and his getting outright shot. Either way, she'd be rid of him.

"Are you listening, Charlie?" Thalanes called up the canyon in a voice that surprised Sarah with its booming volume. "Here's my sermon. 'Then one of them, which was a lawyer, asked him a question, tempting him, and saying, master, which is the great commandment in the law? Jesus said unto him, thou shalt love the Lord thy God with all thy heart, and with all thy soul, and with all thy mind. This is the first and great commandment. And the second is like unto it, thou shalt love thy neighbour as thyself.'"

Shadrach seemed caught off-guard and puzzled. "I told you hellfire and brimstone, monk."

"Or else *you go to hell*." The Ohioan snarled the last few words, then brushed past Shadrach and started up the canyon.

The Calhoun guards looked at each other, at a loss. Red Charlie Calhoun, face colored like a lobster and his copper hair down to his shoulders, took a half-hearted step to block the priest's way.

"Did—did you jest tell me to go to hell, old man?" Shadrach hollered.

"Let him up!" yelled a voice from the top of the draw, and Charlie backed away. The Elector, Andrew Calhoun himself, towered at the end of the track, collar to toe in his customary black, waving with his one arm to call off the guards. Sarah and Cal stared from the bottom of the canyon.

"This absolutely has to be the strangest Tobacco Fair day I ever seen, Sarah," Cal said to her as Father Thalanes disappeared up the top of the canyon. "What's goin' on?"

"I dunno," she said, "but I think I jest saw my pa invite a priest up onto Calhoun Mountain. I b'lieve the whole world is about to turn upside down."

"I'd be happy to abduct you."

—➤◆◄—

CHAPTER FOUR

Whunk!

The chunk of wood split open as Cal brought it down on the chopping stump, pulling apart neatly into two halves and falling to the grass. He scooped them up and laid them on the pile. When Cal was a boy, his grandfather had warned him over and over against idle hands, and if you ever run out of useful things to do and you haven't got a stick to whittle, boy, you can always chop wood for the pile.

Before he could pick up the next piece to split, he heard a familiar sharp whistle.

"Yessir," he greeted his grandfather with surprise, burying the blade of the wood-chopping axe in the stump.

"Walk with me, boy." Andrew Calhoun grabbed his much taller grandson by the elbow with his one arm and steered him into a stroll about the top of Calhoun Mountain.

Cal nodded and went along happily. They walked together along a broad dirt path beaten into the wiry grass among clusters of log cabins and small orange and yellow groves by generations of Calhoun feet.

"The Fair went well enough, I reckon," Cal volunteered—he hadn't had a chance yet to report on the outcome of the morning's trip, and nor had any of its other participants, since the Elector had been holed up since their return with the little Cahokian monk.

"I heard." The Elector's tone of voice both praised Calvin and told him the Tobacco Fair was not to be the subject of this conversation. "I need you to do somethin' for me, boy."

"Sure." Cal wondered what that might be. "Jest name it, and it's done already."

"Sarah's a-goin' on a journey," the Elector told him as they passed beyond the cabins into a meadow of tall dry autumn grass. "She don't know it yet, but she don't really have a choice."

"Has it got somethin' to do with this monk?" Cal couldn't think of any other reason why Sarah would need to go on a journey anywhere. Cal had traveled, stealing cattle more or less locally and driving the ones the family didn't eat to markets as far away as possible, but Sarah had always stuck very close to Calhoun Mountain. They were alone now, and stopped walking. "That little feller tells strange stories, but they got a ring to 'em as makes 'em sound like they jest might be true. Sarah ain't really my auntie, is she?"

"It has," his grandfather confirmed, looking Cal in the face from the impenetrably deep wells of his eyes, "and she ain't. This ain't gonna be a safe journey for Sarah, you understand me?"

Cal's heart jumped at the possibilities. "I reckon someone oughtta go with her, then, don't you? Someone as has traveled and knows his way around."

"Someone as can hunt and track and trap and trade and make shelter and git water and provide food," Iron Andy Calhoun agreed. "Someone as can find his path in any weather and fight his way outta any scrape. Someone as is set to become a real hell of a feller, and someone I can trust."

Cal blushed. "Jerusalem, grandpa. Mebbe you oughtta go yourself."

"Damn straight I would, too," the Elector said, "iffen I had two arms and I's jest ten years younger. As it is, will you go in my place?" He gripped Calvin by the elbow and stared into his grandson's soul.

"Yes, I will," Cal said, as if he was swearing a solemn oath.

"Jest because she ain't your aunt," the Elector added with a hint of menace in his voice, "don't mean I don't feel about her like about my own daughters."

"I'll do right by her." Cal blushed again and looked at his feet.

"I know you will," his grandfather agreed. "That's why I'm a-sendin' you." He tugged Cal's elbow and turned them both back toward the cabins. "You got good morals, a good reputation. You're sound in body and in mind, and ain't nobody on this here mountain don't love you. You ain't e'er killed a man, I know. But I'm countin' on you to do it iffen you have to."

Cal nodded, flattered but also daunted. "When does this journey start?"

"Soon," the Elector told him. "Stick close to Sarah, son. Stick real close. I got a feelin' she might want to start even sooner'n I intend, and iffen she does, I don't want her goin' alone."

"I'll keep her close," Cal promised.

"Do you believe in God?"

Cal hesitated. Did his grandfather want him to *pray* for Sarah? "You know I do, grandpa," he finally said, with an awkward shrug. "I believe in God. I'm New Light, you know that. I'm as New Light as a man can be as ain't plain crazy."

The old man nodded. "You remember that. You and I are gonna be talking again tonight, Calvin. Jest remember the answer to the next question you git asked is 'I do.'"

Calvin thought of wedding vows, and he gulped.

He needed to let her decide, Thalanes reminded himself. Sarah was a child of Adam like anyone else, and he had to respect her right to choose, no matter what.

Young Andy let her in from the dogtrot.

Thalanes sat in the Elector's Whittlin' House, or, as some of his family referred to it, the Thinkin' Shed. Though he was long a widower and his children other than his daughter Sarah (foster daughter, Thalanes reminded himself—she seemed so at home here that even the monk had begun to think of her as a Calhoun) had all grown and moved out, the Elector was important enough to merit two rooms (and his own outhouse behind, discreetly veiled by stands of dogwood and maple), at the top of the long meadow on Calhoun Mountain, with a splendid view looking north upon Nashville and an infinity of green forested hills. The two rooms were two separate mud-chinked log cabins sharing one wide plank porch and a peaked roof. The roofed passage between the cabins was called a dogtrot. Sarah and the Elector shared one cabin as living quarters; in the other, the Elector whittled and thought, conducted serious interviews, planned battles, and handed down private judgment.

The Thinkin' Shed was full of carved animals, handmade chairs and stools, and above all, walking sticks. The Elector sat with his back to the low fire in a wood chair of his own manufacture, horn-handled clasp knife in his hand, shaping a six-foot length of ash into a staff. His eyes, set deep in the shadows of a craggy, weathered face under a shock of snow white hair, didn't focus on the stick at all, but stared into a corner as the knife worked its magic without direction. Thalanes knew Andrew Calhoun well enough to recognize that he was distracted and troubled by the news the monk had brought and the errand on which he had come, but he carved wood effortlessly, the stick cradled against his neck as he turned it from a rough branch into a polished staff, with its top cut into the shape of a horse's head, like a large wooden chess piece.

Sarah came in from the dogtrot and shut the door.

"Did I do right bringin' this Unsouled monk up the mountain, then, Pa?" She settled into another of the Elector's chairs.

"You did right to let him up, daughter," Calhoun assured her, and then he grinned, his deep eyes twinkling. "You did right to make him work for it, too."

She laughed. "I'd a brung him direct if I'd a knew he was tellin' the truth about bein' your friend."

"Penn's English, child," the old man said to her, and his shoulders slumped a little. "Yes, he's my friend. He's your friend, too, and he's come on an important mission, which I need to discuss with you."

He deftly shut the locking knife with one hand, then slipped it into a pocket in his breeches and laid the staff aside.

"I'm here, Father," Sarah said, and she sat on the edge of her seat to take the Elector's gnarled and suntanned paw in her two smooth ivory hands. *Poor girl. Can she handle my news? Will she make the right decisions on her hard road?*

"Dear sweet child," the Elector began after a pause. "I've kept something from you all your life. I've told you a lie, and I don't regret it, because it was a necessary lie and a lie that saved your life, but I fear you'll be hurt and angry with me. Before I tell you the truth, I want you to understand I love you very much, and I hope you'll be able to forgive me."

The tender words were incongruous coming from a face so cragged and careworn. Sarah's lip trembled and her good eye looked a little glassy.

"Sarah, my child," Elector Calhoun continued, and he squeezed her hands so tight his knuckles whitened. "I'm not your father."

She sobbed, once, and then regained control. Thalanes bowed his head out of respect for her emotion.

There was a brief silence, and then Sarah spoke again, in a tremulous voice. "Who are my parents?"

Calhoun nodded. "Your parents were good friends of mine, friends and allies. I shed blood on the sands of Texia with your father in the Spanish War, and I served under your great-grandfather, your mother's father, in the Ohio Forks War. I took you in, as my own child, out of love for all of them."

He looked her in the eye. "I *raised* you out of love for *you*."

"Who were they?" she repeated. "Were they Appalachee? *Are* they Appalachee? Are they dead?" *She must know the answers to these questions*, Thalanes thought, *I've practically already told her.* He would have liked to comfort her, but that was not his role now.

"Your father fought alongside me in the Spanish War," the Elector repeated. "He was captain of the Cahokia volunteers, and he was only a prince at the time. Prince and not even heir."

"Kyres Elytharias," Sarah whispered. "The dead King of Cahokia."

"Not just dead, child," Thalanes said, "but murdered. You are his oldest child, and heir to his throne. You are the rightful Queen of Cahokia."

"You're the heir to two kingdoms, my dear daughter," Calhoun told her. "Pennsland is also yours by right of inheritance."

"Pennsland ain't a kingdom," Sarah said. She seemed to have an innate reflex that made her kick back against everyone and everything, even her foster father. "It's private land, all owned by the Penn landholder in the name of the Penn family."

"Yes," Calhoun agreed calmly. "By right, you're the Penn landholder."

"Your fairy tale is true, then," Sarah said to Thalanes. "At least, some of it is. I'm the daughter of Mad Hannah. But what do you mean, 'murdered'? You said before that the Imperial Consort died in an accident."

"She was never mad," Thalanes murmured, remembering the fiery, willful empress. "She was wise and good and strong, and she suffered greatly at the hands of designing men." He paused, his memories of the terrible night fifteen years earlier heavy on his soul. "It has generally been told that Kyres Elytharias died of a fall from his horse. That story is a lie; your father was murdered by one of his own guard, by one of the Philadelphia Blues, while they stood watch together."

There was silence for a time.

"This changes nothing," Sarah finally said, and her voice was fierce and a little bitter. "Why did you come, monk? Did you want to tell me my mother is dead? I read that in the Nashville Imperial Intelligencer this morning."

"He came to take you with him," Calhoun told her, "and, like it or not, you have to go."

She sobbed again, sudden and hard, and her accent flooded back. "You're gonna cast me out?"

Calhoun pulled his foster daughter into a crushing one-armed embrace, kissing her cheek and whispering into her ear. "You *always* have a place here. I would give *anything* to protect you. But I don't have the strength to resist the emperor."

She pulled away from her foster father and turned to face Thalanes, tears streaked down her face, her emotion-reddened complexion softening the stark horror of her bad eye. "The emperor wants me?"

The monk nodded. "The Right Reverend Father Ezekiel Angleton is the emperor's man. He is chaplain to the emperor's own Imperial House Light Dragoons, the Philadelphia Blues, but their relationship goes far back, and he has always been your uncle's servant."

"My uncle," Sarah whispered thoughtfully. "But you said he didn't know about Hannah's children. You said someone told him."

With an effort, Thalanes forced the words out, nodding in acknowledgement of his shame. "He didn't know. But I was your mother's confessor in her confinement, as I had been your father's before that. I was the servant who brought you here, a newborn infant, and hid you with the Elector and his family, and I was the fool who allowed your mother to talk me into telling her about you. What you were like, and where I had hidden you."

Tears flowed down Sarah's cheeks now, but her voice was firm. "So what?"

Thalanes steeled himself with a deep breath. "Two weeks ago, your uncle learned his sister had given birth to triplets, fifteen years earlier. He had her tortured. Put her on the rack like some medieval heretic, pulled her fingernails out, and did worse. He tortured her until she told him everything she knew about the children. Tortured her to death."

Sarah was silent, stunned.

"I don't believe your uncle learned where your brother and sister are located, because I don't believe the Empress Hannah knew that information. I don't know it, myself. I don't think the empress knew who had hidden her other two children; I certainly didn't tell her, though I could have. But I know that Thomas Penn learned where to find you. And I know he learned of my role . . . my treachery, as he and his servants have called it."

"That's what Angleton was talking about," Sarah realized.

He nodded, wretched. And Angleton was right, too. Thalanes had committed treason against the emperor, and a jury of twelve good Pennslanders and true might very well sentence him to hang for it, if it ever came to a trial. Only his betrayal of the Empress Hannah had been much worse—he never should have told her about Sarah, no matter how much she had importuned. And he had betrayed Sarah's father, too, in his turn—he never should have let the king take a turn standing watch, that dark night when he had been murdered.

"I narrowly escaped Philadelphia with my life," he said. "I came here to take you with me, and to hide you again where Thomas cannot find you."

"You must go with him, my daughter," Calhoun urged her.

"What if I don't want to go?" she asked.

Could she possibly be so stubborn? "Please," Thalanes said, "I beg you, you must. Angleton had to have raced out of Philadelphia on my heels to have gotten here so soon, but the emperor has more powerful servants, and they'll be after you soon, if they aren't already on their way. And you saw that even the priest was willing to kill you."

Thalanes felt a pang of guilt, realizing he was manipulating her, but he knew it was necessary. This girl was so strong-willed and rash, she might get it into her head to run off alone to try to inflict vengeance on the Martinite.

"I saw he was a terrible shot." Sarah's accent returned. "Pa, let me stay. I won't go back to town, at least not for a spell, and that fool preacher'll ne'er find his way up here."

The Elector looked racked by guilt and fear. "It isn't wise, Sarah."

"Please," Thalanes whispered.

"I won't do it." She stood.

"You *must!*" Thalanes yelled, leaping to his feet and closing in on her. His own voice sounded far away, and he tried to calm down, to keep his distance, to employ gentle persuasion, but he roared into the child's face. "I will *not* have the blood of another Penn on my hands! You *will* come with me! You *must!* I *order* you!"

She took one step back and looked at him, nostrils flared and the eyebrow over her good eye arched high and proud. "*Must* I?"

He stopped himself. What had he done? *Let no will be coerced*, the first precept. It was so important that Thomas Penn not capture and kill this child. But could Thalanes coerce her will, even if he tried? "Please," he said again simply.

Sarah spun on her heel and left by the dogtrot door.

He forgave Obadiah for letting the girl go. It wasn't easy, because she was such an abomination, but Ezekiel Angleton's Savior had forgiven him his debts, so Ezekiel in turn forgave his own debtors.

Even hard-hearted, unbelieving Obadiah.

Besides, he hadn't trusted Obadiah enough to tell him what they were after; if he had, Obadiah might have delivered the child to him, neat and tidy, earlier that morning. Ezekiel had reaped, and Ezekiel had sown. Perhaps he had erred because he was too tired—Ezekiel had not slept well on the journey down to Nashville, dreaming often, disturbed dreams of running through the forest.

He considered the possibility that it might have been a mistake, also, not to have strengthened himself with magic before he had ever entered the tent. He dismissed that self-criticism immediately; he hadn't the power to maintain decent battle magic even for a very long skirmish, much less employ it repeatedly throughout a single day, and he had had no idea when, or if at all, he might encounter the child. Entering the tent that morning, he had expected at most to get a glimpse of the girl, or get information about her.

Besides, even to think that he could *strengthen himself with magic* was a childish and ridiculous contradiction in terms. Any physical strength he piled upon himself by means of gramarye would be torn from him in the form of exhaustion or sickness after. If he had cast combat magic, his favored *ani gibbor* incantation, for instance, and Thalanes had still managed to help the girl escape, Ezekiel would now be empty-handed still, and also drained.

Magic was best in tiny, shaped applications. Combat spells were best reserved for actual battle.

He also forced out of his mind the smug thought—the *suggestion* of a thought—that it served Obadiah right to get shot in the foot. The thought was not Christian. Ezekiel had already cast some simple magic to speed along the healing of Obadiah's injured foot.

Ezekiel didn't like the fact that he himself had pointed a gun at the girl and pulled the trigger; he had been angry to have missed so badly, but also relieved. Killing the girl like that, unarmed, unjudged, wasn't his intention. He was a man of God, he was a Christian knight, and he would do what he must do, absolutely anything that he must do, in order to remedy the blasphemy the girl represented, remove it from the face of the earth, but simply killing her was the crudest possible solution.

He much preferred to capture her and take her back to Philadelphia, where the emperor himself, and the emperor's magistrates, could judge her.

"I fink this'll do the trick, won't it?" Obadiah asked. "Can't you, er, wot you...? Wiff 'er 'air? An' then it ben't a total loss."

Ezekiel looked down again at the black hairs in the palm of his hand. "I'm pleased with your work, Obadiah." He forced himself to smile. "It would have been very convenient if you had managed to keep hold of the child this morning, but you're correct, this will do the trick very nicely. We've been blessed."

Obadiah grinned, like a stupid, vicious dog that fears a beating and is scratched behind the ears instead.

They sat at a table in the low-ceilinged common room of a run-down Nashville inn, the *John Paul Jones*, its signboard featuring a chipped painting of the famous sea captain in his blue bicorn hat. Ezekiel had unstrapped his sword, a long, straight weapon inherited from his father (who had been a soldier in the Order of the Friends in Christ of Eugene of Savoy, and who had died in the dungeons of Turkish Vienna), from his belt and laid it across his lap. His black steeple hat sat beside him on the bench.

Light streamed into the tavern's common room, tinted green and amber, through rough bottle-glass windows. The noon crowd had come and gone while Ezekiel dealt with the town watch and the mess of the tent, and now he and his servant had the privacy of a corner booth. The tobacco smoke cloud left by the midday diners had mostly dissipated, but all the sour smells lingered.

Ezekiel hated the Appalachee. He didn't care much for their food (he ached for a bowl of pease porridge and a good hot huckleberry pie), or their lewd clothing with its exuberant colors, or their ceaseless liquor and tobacco, but what really bothered him was their constant mewling about *freedom*. About their *liberties*.

As if the only true freedom were not the freedom to follow the will of God, to show your election by living his covenant. And by the grace of God, Ezekiel Angleton knew, the elect would find freedom also from death.

"Get me your bowl, would you, Mr. Dogsbody?" Ezekiel ordered.

He untied his purse and set it aside, as far away from himself on the table as he could, and then considered the hairs while Obadiah stumped upstairs for his kit. A minor lodestone-finding sort of spell should suffice, and wouldn't exhaust him.

He had aided and entertained his friend Thomas—*His Imperial Majesty*, he reminded himself—at Harvard many times with such trivial gramarye. He'd cast wakefulness cantrips on nights before examinations and sobering hexes on mornings after revelry for his gentleman room-mate, young Colonel Lord Thomas Penn. Thomas was older than Ezekiel, and was already then a veteran of the Spanish War, but, other than with respect to the minutia of ascendants and triplicities, and the bloody details of military history, he was an absent-minded student. Thomas perpetually lost books and needed Ezekiel's help to find them. All those little magics, and Ezekiel had spent most of his time with Thomas at Harvard feeling sick and wasted.

He'd had the hangover, without the drunken riot.

Thomas had always been needy and always a drain, until the night when Ezekiel's Lucy had died, young Lucy Winthrop. Ezekiel's eyes swam in sudden hot tears as he thought of the lost love of his youth. He remembered whispering professions of faithfulness to her through the double-bell-ended courting stick across the great hearth of the Winthrop family home. He'd been a penniless young theology student, but the great man, Samuel Winthrop, had accepted Ezekiel's love for his daughter. They had slept together in her parents' home, separated by the bundling board and her feet bound together for chastity's sake but holding hands and sharing dreams through the night, they had planned a home and children, they had published the banns in Boston's Old North Church.

Then Lucy had fallen from her mother's calash on a bright Sunday morning in spring, on her way to a lecture on the Prophets by the great Bishop Franklin, one of Franklin's very last.

She had died suddenly and alone.

Ezekiel had lain drunk in a Boston gutter for weeks, time he had never been able clearly to remember, other than that he recalled begging for pennies with which to buy liquor.

Her family, the Winthrops, rejected him. His own family had never been any use, too few and, with his father gone, always too poor to help, so their failure in his moment of crisis had come as no surprise and cost him no pain.

But Thomas had taken him in. Thomas had drunk with Ezekiel until the beasts within were well and truly insensate, and then dried him out. Thomas had ordered the deans of Harvard—*ordered* them—not to expel Ezekiel, and had similarly instructed Ezekiel's professors. Thomas had been the one to recommend Ezekiel to the Father-General of the Order of St. Martin (and had that also been phrased as a command?), and among the Martinites Ezekiel had thrived. Later, after Ezekiel had graduated from Harvard, Thomas had found him a series of posts and preferments, including, finally, the coveted position of chaplain to the emperor's own Philadelphia Blues.

Thomas had pulled Ezekiel up with him.

So Ezekiel was glad that he had been able to help Thomas find lost objects now and then as a student, and for every assistance he had been able to render his master. He would retrieve this girl and return her to Thomas, just like any lost object, and then, somehow, he would learn where the other two were hidden.

He was more than happy to serve—when he had heard Mad Hannah's confession, and the location and description of the oldest child, he had sprinted from Penn's Slate Roof House to run to Nashville and find the girl, stopping only long enough to get his warrant sworn out before a Philadelphia magistrate.

He looked at the dried blood and the wiry black strands. Not a beautiful child. Cursed by its Serpentborn blood, or she would have been handsome, like her mother.

He remembered Mad Hannah—mad to have taken a soulless Eldritch king as a lover—as she had been at the end. She had had blood in her hair, too, and on her ruined fingers and on her face, but she hadn't confessed or asked forgiveness. Ezekiel had given her absolution, anyway. It was in his power, and it was the Christian thing to do, even though she was a heretic and an Ophidian, and even though at his master's bidding Ezekiel had participated in the interrogation that had ended in her death.

Thomas had prepared the announcement to the news-papers of her death in advance. He had shown them to his sister after she had broken.

Obadiah returned with his simple wooden bowl.

"Let us contrive a tool." Ezekiel laid the hairs into the bottom of the bowl and then poured some of his drink, a little light-colored beer, over them. From his pocket he produced a vial of quicksilver and let a small drop fall into the bowl. It rolled to the bottom, coming to rest on the thick hairs.

Obadiah looked as if he was holding his breath.

Ezekiel cleared his mind and then let it fill with an image of the girl, as he had seen her that morning. Pasty white skin, angry red eye, ragged black hair, sluttish dress. He thought of her essence, of the blasphemy that she was, the Unsouled blood staining the holy escutcheon of the House of Penn, and he willed all those images into the bowl, into the beer, into the hair and mercury.

He took the wooden bowl in his two hands and leaned in close, the exhalations from his nostrils on the beer like the breath of God on the waters of the First Day. He felt his will gathering in his throat, and, closing his eyes, he formed it into words.

"*Ani mechapes yaldah,*" he muttered in Hebrew, and he felt his power moving through the words of the ancient, sacred language into the bowl, "*ani mechapes yaldah.*"

As he finished speaking, he opened his eyes. The drop of quicksilver trembled, rolled steadily up through the beer, moving along the hairs and turning them with it, and then stopped, quivering, dragging the tail of hairs out behind it like a comet.

Ezekiel sagged in his seat, weary.

"Wayland's 'ammer," Obadiah muttered.

"This will take you straight to her tonight," Ezekiel said. "Go to the market and gather three or four big men; I'll wait here for you. Take my purse, offer them a crown each for a few hours' work. If they're reluctant, go as high as a pound. Take the warrant to show them, in case any of them worries about law."

Obadiah stood gingerly, adjusting his belt under his paunch. "Aye, Father."

"If any of them worries about *sin*," Ezekiel told his servant, "assure them that I'll give them absolution, in advance." He smiled, an expression that he meant to be wise, calm and fatherly. "After all, this is the Lord's work."

Obadiah trundled out the door on his errand, and Ezekiel raised a hand to get the attention of the tavern's girl. He couldn't get the huckleberry pie he wanted, but he'd make do with another beer.

"I'd be happy to abduct you," Cal offered around a mouthful of boiled pork and griddle cake. "We could move right away from here. There's plenty of empty land in Appalachee, and you know I can hunt, skin, trade, and build a cabin. And the Elector has always said he'd set me up with my own herd—I reckon he'd do that even if I abducted you. Or I could rustle someone else's. Those Donelsons up Knoxville way've always got more cows'n they know how to count."

"You're sweet, Calvin," Sarah told him, "but then you'd have to be married to me, and that'd jest be me out the fryin' pan, you in the fire."

Cal sipped water from his jar and scuffed the dirt with his feet. "Aw, Sarah, you ain't all that bad."

"I reckon not," Sarah agreed bitterly, "to a stone drunk feller, so long as he could only see the one half of my face." She set her tin plate aside, food untouched, and drew her knees up under her chin.

They sat on a wooden bench of the Elector's making in the late afternoon. The long meadow, copses of trees and scattered cabins on top of Calhoun Mountain were accented all around with benches and seats like this one—Andrew Calhoun had been a carver and improver all his life.

Sarah had needed to talk to someone, someone who was neither the Elector nor the odd little monk. And she needed someone who was old enough to understand, but she didn't want to discuss her day's revelations with any of her brothers and sisters. Calvin was the natural choice.

Sarah couldn't hate the Elector, because she looked into his eyes and saw that he loved her and had only done what he thought he'd had to. Besides, he still felt like her father . . . more or less. The Eldritch warrior of the Ohio, the musketeer swordsman hero of both Battles of the Ouachita and also of the Siege of Mobile, was a figure of history to her, and not someone she could understand. She didn't really feel like she had a father at all—the one had rejected her and the other felt cold and foreign.

With poor Mad Hannah, on the other hand, she had instantly felt a kinship. Loathed and feared by everyone, locked away by her brother, the Empress Hannah fascinated Sarah. She felt close to the cloistered and betrayed woman.

Betrayed, that was how Sarah felt.

"A pretty face ain't the only thing a man values in a wife," Cal offered.

"Which is to say I ain't pretty, but don't worry my ugly little head about it. Thank you very much, Calvin Calhoun, I shan't forget it. I shall feel mightily comforted in my dark hours knowin' that you're the kind of feller's willin' to marry hisself a deformed woman."

"Sarah Calhoun," Cal objected, "that ain't fair!"

"No," she conceded, "it ain't fair. And I ain't Sarah Calhoun, neither. I'm . . ." She trailed off as she realized she wasn't sure just what her name was. "Well, you can call me Sarah for the time bein'. Jest plain Sarah, iffen you please."

"Old Andy don't *want* you to leave," Cal insisted. "You're his favorite, Sarah."

"I ain't even *his*," she muttered.

"You can't really mean that," Cal pressed. "When all his natural-born granddaughters were out plowin' and cookin' and stitchin' shirts, he never let you leave his side, and it was always 'remember me the year of the Peace of Augsberg,' and 'by what hilarious name did the Emperor Ferdinand call the execution of his wife Queen Adela Podebradas' and 'gimme your *amo-amas-amat* backward this time,' like he wanted you to be ready to go be a schoolmarm, like he thought you needed to be as smart as *him*. That old man *loves* you!"

"Not a schoolmarm," Sarah said, thinking out loud. "He wanted me ready to be a queen." She felt lonely and tired.

"The Elector wouldn't cast you out for love or money, Sarah," Cal finished his pitch. "He must b'lieve it ain't safe here for you."

Sarah thought of the cruel-eyed Roundhead preacher who had shot at her. She shook her head, embarrassed to think how foolish she had been, standing to face that man and daring him to shoot her. "I reckon he's right, too, Cal. I gotta leave tonight."

Calvin looked uncertain. "You're gonna go with the little priest."

Sarah sighed. She didn't yet trust the monk. Her feelings about the Elector, her father...her *foster* father...had become unexpectedly complicated. This morning, she had loved him devotedly. Now she felt tricked and rejected, but at the same time she still loved him as the only father she had ever known, and didn't wish him hurt in any way.

"No, Cal," she said slowly. "I b'lieve I gotta escape from him, too." She turned her face to Calvin and smiled.

"Jest don't go escapin' without me," Cal said. "I wouldn't regard that as fair."

"Iffen I did, Calvin Calhoun," she said, "who'd sing me to sleep on the road?"

"Nobody, and you'd be thankful." He laughed. "Besides, I know how to get off the mountain."

"How's that then, *fall?* I reckon I'll just do a bit of hexin', trick my way out the door without Red Charlie or Caleb e'er bein' the wiser."

"I can save you the trouble," he offered, "iffen you know how to climb a tree."

"I can climb," she hesitated. "I jest don't know iffen it's such a good idea for you to come along, Calvin."

"It's easy enough," Cal persisted. "Black Charlie and Abe and a couple of those fellers got a cave on the west slope where they like to get drunk and dance to the Crooked Man. I caught 'em sneakin' back in once, when I's out doin' a bit of rustlin'. Nothin' to it, they's this tree as grows close to the cliff on the west side, and any halfway decent climber can use it jest like a ladder, up and down. We could even sleep the night in their cave, if we wanted, get a start walkin' in the mornin'."

Sarah feigned astonishment. "Calvin Calhoun, are you tellin' me that they's folks on this mountain still worship the Crooked Man, and you don't have principles as make you put a stop to it?"

Cal shrugged. "Sure, I got principles. And I also got friends. And while I reckon that fillin' their bellies with corn liquor, strippin' off their clothes and howlin' at the moon in the name of some crazy old hill god makes 'em gone gumps, I don't reckon it means they're goin' to Hell for it. Besides, I think it's mostly a place they keep for takin' girls to."

"Shockin'."

"That's life, I reckon."

"Tree sure sounds easier." Sarah considered. "All right."

She didn't really think Cal would show up, and if he did, he could be helpful to her in making an escape without actually marrying her. And if he insisted, well...no, he wouldn't persist with this foolish notion of marrying Sarah. It was pure Appalachee gallantry, and she loved him for it, but it would pass.

"It's a plan, then," he said. "In the cattle market we might spit and shake hands, but I know you're as good as your word."

"I won't hold you to your offer, Calvin Calhoun," Sarah said, "and I won't think less of you iffen you change your mind. But iffen you still want to abduct me, I reckon I'll be out here on this bench tonight with a bundle of necessaries, as soon as the Elector falls asleep."

Cal was on his way to put together a pack.

He stepped around the corner of Azariah Calhoun's cabin, nodding to old Granny Clay. Granny sat sucking her gums on the porch in a rocking chair the Elector had made for her twenty years earlier and which she had scarcely left since. She wore the same red shawl, year in and year out, and only ever looked any different if she had a plate of food on her lap, or if it was winter and one of her grandchildren had spread a blanket over her.

Granny Clay smiled at Cal, toothless and slow, and he smiled back.

Then someone threw a sack over his head.

He was caught by surprise, but Lord hates a man as leaves his pants down after he's been walked in on, so Cal laid about him with his fists. He pounded his knuckles into flesh and bone more than once before he heard the voice of his grandfather whisper in his ear, "be still, Calvin."

"Yessir," he answered, and obeyed.

His moccasined feet felt solid earth under their soles and he heard breathing around him for several minutes, but the winding route he was led along defied his sense of direction, and when his captors finally stopped, Cal had no idea where he was. He could feel the heat on his skin and smell the burning wood of a fire, but the bag was too thick to let through any light stronger than glimmers.

A voice spoke. Cal recognized it as belonging to his Uncle David.

"Calvin Calhoun," David intoned gravely, "do you declare, upon your honor afore these here gentlemen, as how you freely and voluntarily offer yourself a candidate for the mysteries of Masonry?"

Masonry?

Then Cal remembered what his grandpa had told him. He'd half expected a wedding, and was more than a little disappointed to find out his grandfather had something different in mind.

Still, he knew what to say. "I do."

"Do you sincerely declare, upon your honor afore these here gentlemen, as how you solicit the privileges of Masonry because of a favorable opinion conceived of the institution, a desire of knowledge, and a sincere wish of bein' serviceable to your fellow-creatures?" Still David.

"I do." Cal gulped. What did this have to do with Sarah?

"Do you sincerely declare, upon your honor afore these here gentlemen, as how you will cheerfully conform to all the ancient established usages and customs of the fraternity?"

"I do." He had no idea what those usages and customs might be.

The bag was yanked off Cal's head. He stood in a clearing, and around him in a circle ranged roughly twenty of the senior men of his family, uncles, older cousins, and of course his grandfather. His uncle David held an open Bible. A third of the men held burning torches. Before Calvin on the ground lay a white sheet embroidered with many colors of thread. In his quick look at the patterns, Calvin spotted two stylized pillars, a cross and a square and compass. There was a boxy shape that might have been an altar, and above it, dominating the scene, a capital letter G.

Two of his older cousins started to pull off Calvin's clothes. Following a nod from the Elector, he helped them, and stripped down to just his long hunting shirt. The night was chilly, even with the torches and the trees to break the wind.

David spoke again. "Brethren, at the request of Mr. Andrew Calhoun, Mr. Calvin Calhoun has been proposed and accepted in the regular form. I therefore recommend him as a proper candidate for the Mysteries of Masonry, and worthy to partake of the privileges of the fraternity."

"Amen," rumbled Cal's assembled male relatives.

One of his cousins handed Cal an unfamiliar pair of breeches, and he stepped into them. His cousins put one of his feet in a slipper, pulled one arm out of its sleeve, and the last thing they did before wrapping a blindfold over his eyes was hang a knotted noose and short rope around his neck.

Cal resisted the urge to laugh as a means to calm his nerves; the Calhoun men around him didn't look to be in a jovial mood.

Blind and shivering, Calvin heard a noise like rapping at a door. *Knock, knock, knock.*

"Who comes there?" The voice was his cousin Shadrach's. "Who comes there? Who comes there?"

It was very important not to drink the compass. This was harder than it sounded, because Obadiah was thirsty.

He'd done as the Right Reverend Father had directed him, and it had been easy. Four men, heavy and scarred, had been happy to join up with Obadiah for the promised crown. None of them had asked to see the warrant, and two of them had laughed out loud when Obadiah mentioned the promised absolution of their sins. Fair enough; he would have done the same.

Father Angleton had ridden with Obadiah and the four hired men out of town—in the afternoon, before the sun had set and Nashville's town watch had dropped the portcullis—but he'd waited behind, in a forest clearing in the valley, not far from the Charlotte Pike, while Obadiah had taken his *posse comitatus*, duly authorized if not particularly interested in its own authority, and crept up the hill in the dark.

The clear night sky gave enough glow that Obadiah could look into the bowl by its light and see the mercury blob. He couldn't walk and read the compass, but he trod carefully through the autumnal leaf fall from one clearing to the next (extra carefully, as, even with the accelerating effects of the Right Reverend Father's spell upon its healing process, his foot was still sore), stopping whenever he was under open sky to check his bearing.

The men didn't complain, and Obadiah wondered what sort of men they must be, to follow around a foreigner with his face in a bowl in the hills at night. Desperate men, no doubt. Might they be desperate enough to cut Obadiah's throat for whatever might be in his purse?

Obadiah loosened his pistols in his belt and checked that his sword was still on his hip.

They had come across a path, early, that seemed to lead up the hill where the compass was directing them, but Obadiah had eschewed it in favor of creeping through the trees. His mission was to make a lawful arrest, if convenient, but he had heard enough stories about the crazed bushwhacker clans of Appalachee that he preferred to make this lawful arrest as quietly and as secretly as he possibly could. Preferably the inbred mountain men would all be drunk and snuggling their sisters, and Obadiah could sneak in unnoticed, grab the witchy-eyed girl the Right Reverend Father was so interested in, and get out again.

Obadiah found the thought of the drunk cracker varmints cuddling up to their filthy sisters so distracting he almost walked headlong into a stone wall, and kept from spilling the beer compass only by a combination of fierce concentration and good luck.

His posse laughed.

"Shut it, ye!" Obadiah hissed.

He looked up. The wall was a natural cliff of stone, a sudden rise creating a gray limestone crown on the top of the mountain. He looked closely at the rock—it was pocked and dimpled and cut through with crevices such that a smaller, more limber man might have been tempted to climb it.

Not Obadiah.

He considered his options. The trail he had foregone would hit this wall to his left, if it didn't circle around it entirely, but, again, he didn't want to try formally to serve notice of his Warrant on some gap-toothed, hatchet-wielding Appalachee brawler at the gate. He needed a hidden way up this stone, so he decided to turn right and follow the cliff around.

He was about to inform his crew when he chanced to look down and saw, in the silvery-amber puddle of moon-illuminated beer, a moving shadow. He put his eye closer to the compass and squinted. The quicksilver was moving visibly. It was moving fast.

Obadiah was no surveyor, but he knew enough about direction and distance to realize that if the girl was moving rapidly enough to make the compass needle move with her, visibly to his unaided eye, then either she was moving very quickly indeed, or she was very close.

The quicksilver rolled around the rim of the bowl and stopped, pointing right.

"This direction," Obadiah whispered. "Guns ready, she ben't far now."

He pulled his pistol and led the way, beer compass now a little more precarious in his left hand alone, but it shouldn't matter if he spilled it, once he had the little witch. He fought his way through a wiry octopus of briar and followed the limestone cliff around a sharp corner, and then stopped abruptly when he saw the boy.

The wheezing, tiptoeing ruffian immediately behind Obadiah did not stop, and when he bumped Obadiah it wasn't hard, but it was enough to knock the bowl compass from his grasp, spilling the beer, hair, and mercury into the dirt. Obadiah muttered a curse and pushed the man back with his elbow, but the boy hadn't reacted, and Obadiah could see the girl now, too.

Obadiah looked over his shoulder. For just a moment, in the shadow of the cliff, he thought he saw not four, but *six* men following him, six hulking silhouettes with their faces hidden in the darkness. *Bloody grifting freeloaders, some Nashville scum heard there was easy money to be had and decided to tag along.* But then he blinked, and the number of men in the posse returned to the expected four. Trick of the light, and Obadiah looked forward again to focus on his quarry.

A skeletal maple tree climbed up the limestone, all its branches growing out away in the other direction, right where the cliff dipped in a little notch. At the foot of the tree stood the tall, gangly lad from the Fair, long red hair tied behind his neck and hanging over a much-patched wool coat. Two packs lay on the ground by his feet, as well as a musket—an ancient matchlock, fitting for these impoverished dirt-scratchers—and a tomahawk hung from his belt. He stood with his back to Obadiah, looking up into the maple and coaxing along the girl.

She wore a similar heavy coat, no doubt over the revealing clothing Obadiah remembered from the Fair (he smiled, remembering the purple shawl with the golden suns on it, and in his memory he plumped the witch up to a more reasonable and ripe womanhood), and she picked her way from branch to branch, slowly clambering down the natural ladder of the tree's limbs. How could this route be unguarded by the bushwhackers? But they probably had a guard at the top, death to any attacker fool enough to climb a tree in the face of defending gunfire.

Fine. They were coming down the mountain on their own, so he didn't need to go creeping into the Appalachee stronghold. It was good to have luck on his side.

He turned back and whispered to the nearest hired man. "If you see anyffink movink at the top of that tree, shoot it."

The thug nodded.

The boy's back was turned and the girl was concentrating on her hands and feet, so Obadiah crept up easily. When the girl had almost reached the ground, he smashed the boy across the back of the head with a pistol butt. The young man fell like a slaughtered pig, hit the leaves, and lay still.

"No!" the girl shrieked. She looked up and saw that there was a twenty-foot climb between her and the notch in the cliff, but only inches between her and Obadiah Dogsbody.

"Mind the clifftop, lads." Obadiah thumbed back the hammer of his pistol and pointed it at the boy. "My name be Obadiah Dogsbody, poppet. Pleased to make your acquaintance."

"What do you want from me?" the scrawny thing asked, pulling herself back up a branch.

"Me? 'Erne's 'oofs, I don't want nuffink," Obadiah said truthfully. "My master, the Right Reverend Father Ezekiel Angleton, would mickle like to 'ave a conversation wiff you. I regret that I didn't wot that this mornink, or I'd 'ave nicked you then, an' saved us all this bother."

She hitched herself up another branch. "Your master tried to shoot me!" Her bad eye was goblin purple in the moonlight.

"Now see 'ere, I trow that was a misunderstandink," Obadiah lied. "But do not misunderstand me now, you filffy wee beggar. I'm goink to start countink, an' when I 'it five, I'm goink to blow your friend's brains out into the autumn leaves. I ought to warn you that I 'ad but little schoolink as a child, an' I 'ave been known to skip numbers. *One!*"

"Stop, that's murder!" she begged, and he ground his teeth. "*Four!*"

Witchy Eye jumped to the ground, suddenly docile. Grunting in satisfaction, Obadiah gripped her by the arm and aimed his pistol at her belly.

"As of right now, your life ain't worth a chewed plug."

———◆———

CHAPTER FIVE

Sarah was having a hard time counting. The moonlight was dim, and that didn't help; nor did the fact that she was slung over the scratchy, bony shoulder of an ill-smelling Nashville tough, bouncing with every rough spot on the slope; nor still did the fact that, to begin with, she only had the one good eye.

Still, she knew Obadiah was in front, leading his gang down the hill in a rolling limp. Back to Nashville? But the Imperial Town shut its gates at dusk and didn't open them again until dawn, out of fear of things that might go bump in the night, including the rowdier members of the Calhoun family. The brute manhandling her down the slope was second in line, which she was sure of because Obadiah periodically pinched her bum or slapped her thighs and made a *tut-tut-tut* of disapproval.

She yanked her imagination away from thoughts of cutting Obadiah's throat. She needed to be working on her escape.

Following Sarah—and, because she faced backward over the man's shoulder, in her line of sight—marched three more ruffians. They were dirty, tough, and armed, the kind of men who were too dangerous and too lazy to make an honest living. Nashville was full of such desperadoes; the Imperial Highways were sufficiently well patrolled to make banditry risky, but there was still plenty of traffic on the Natchez Trace and other old ways, or on the rivers, and travelers in town were often easy prey. A few of Nashville's criminals even got desperate or bold enough to take to road-agenting on the Imperial Pikes, or interfering with Thomas Penn's tax collectors. Their depredations were why the Imperial Foresters existed, and if the armed men in Imperial Blue sneaking through the forest discouraged attempts to evade the Toll Gates, so much the better for the Penn family coffers.

Sarah forced herself to laugh out loud, though it hurt her belly. "The Elector's gonna kill you boys, sure enough," she muttered, just loud enough for the toughs nearest her to hear.

"Shut up," the thug immediately in her line of sight said. He huffed and puffed under the combined weight of the packs she and Calvin had brought. Hers wasn't all that heavy, but knowing Calvin, he'd probably packed half the contents of his tidy little half-dogtrot in that bag.

"That fool Englishman tell you that I'm Old Andy Calhoun's daughter?" she asked.

The ruffian looked surprised for a moment, but then hardened his face. "You're lyin'," he said. "I know you're a foreigner. Pennslander, the Englishman told us all about you. Besides, the Elector ain't gonna find out."

"Do I sound like a Pennslander to you, gump?" she snapped.

He shrugged.

She would have spit on him, had she been able. Beyond him, the last two thugs carried Calvin, one lugging him by the feet and the other with arms looped under his shoulders. His hands and feet were tied with rope, as were Sarah's. Sarah assumed the only reason they hadn't killed poor Calvin was to be able to motivate her with the threat of violence. They'd stripped him of his weapons and he still languished unconscious. Calvin was tough, but Sarah had seen men die from lesser blows to the head.

Nobody carried Cal's old musket—the Englishman had smashed it on the limestone cliffs. Obadiah himself only carried the alcohol. He had rifled through their packs and found two full skins of wine, which he had promptly appropriated. He had been suckling at one of them all along, and as they trudged down the side of the mountain, he broke into a song, surprisingly loud in the night, of climbing and plunging melody.

To Anacreon in 'eav'n, where 'e sat in full glee
A few sons of 'armony, sent a petition!

"Really?" Sarah tried again to get under the thug's skin. "That's the feller you believe when he tells you I'm a Philadelphia belle? You think *that* fool's gonna be able to keep his mouth shut?"

"Shut up!" he hissed back.

There they were again, as she looked up to try to make eye contact with the pack carrier. Over his shoulder, out of the corner of her eye, she would have *sworn* she saw two more men, not carrying anything and trailing along behind the others in silence. When she focused on them, they disappeared. When she had first noticed them, as she was being carried away from the maple tree where she'd been caught, she thought she had seen one of them bend down and pick something off the ground; otherwise, they did nothing but follow mutely.

Obadiah kept singing:

> *That 'e their inspirer an' patron would be*
> *When this answer arrived from the jolly old Grecian!*

"Iffen you're lucky enough to git out alive," she advised the ruffian, "you might should beat it outta Nashville and ne'er look back. By the time my pa finishes with you, you'll wish you'd turned into a pillar of salt. You'll wish you'd been tore into twelve pieces and rode to the wind by Imperial couriers, like that old Levite concubine, rather than have to stand afore the righteous wrath and judgment of my pa."

Sarah didn't have a plan. She was antagonizing this man in the hope that if she managed to create a little chaos, she might find a way to escape. And if she couldn't escape, any delay she created would give the Calhoun boys more time to come after them. The Calhouns and even the odd little Cetean; she wouldn't turn up her nose at his help.

"Stop it, you little witch!"

> *Voice, fiddle an' flute, no longer be mute*
> *I'll lend you my name an' inspire you to boot!*

Obadiah was hit and miss at best on the tune, but he had enthusiasm.

There they were again, the two shadow figures, and then they were gone.

Cal stirred.

"As of right now, your life ain't worth a chewed plug." Sarah lowered her face, expecting a blow and hoping to duck it.

The fist pounded her in her shoulder and neck, and also thumped the man carrying her.

"Hey!" he shouted, and threw her to the ground.

Sarah landed hard; the ground was grassy and carpeted with fallen leaves, but she was stunned, and lay still to collect her breath.

The man following also dropped his burden.

"The *hell* you hittin' me for, Angus?" demanded the injured thug.

Cal moaned piteously as the men carrying him tossed him to the ground, too.

"Shut up, Bob, I weren't hittin' you, but the little tricksy-mouthed vixen!"

Obadiah had stopped singing. "Shut it, the lot of ye! You, what be your name, Angus? Did I 'ear you say you 'it the girl?"

"She won't shut up!" Angus snarled. "She keeps goin' on 'bout how the Elector's gonna kill me!"

Bob clucked like a chicken. "Po' little Angus, gittin' scairt by a girl!"

"To hell with the girl!" Angus barked. "I'd chop her to pieces right here and now and eat her heart raw and not miss a wink of sleep over it. But iffen she really *is* Iron Andy's daughter? Damn right, I'm a mite nervous! Ain't *you?*"

Bob spat in the leaves. "Don't be such a goddamned coward."

"I ain't afraid. I jest don't relish gittin' my tongue cut out, and havin' my fingernails torn off, and bein' hung from a tree by my own guts. They say he *crucified* people in the Ohio Forks War. They say he took *scalps*. They say he's the one as killed George Washington, stabbed him in the heart in his sleep with Washington's own sword."

"All that shit you heard about the Elector jest ain't true," Bob said. "The Calhouns spread those notions around to make folks scairt of 'em. Besides, didn't nobody kill George Washington; John Penn bought him off with a bunch of land somewhere and he jest up and quit. Pontiac's the one they killed, and it was hangin', not no midnight assassination. And iffen any of it *is* true, it happened a long time ago. He's jest an old feller now with a lot of rough cracker grandsons who live out in the woods, stealin' cattle, drinkin' home-made corn likker, and sportin' with their own sisters."

"You ain't from around here," Angus muttered. "You don't know."

Obadiah laughed and sucked at the wineskin again. "Don't ye worry, lads, I wot what'll fix 'er." Kneeling in the blanket of leaves, he looked Sarah in the eye. "I'd tell you that this'll 'urt me worse than it'll 'urt you," he said to her, "but it'd be a lie."

He punched her in her good eye.

Her field of vision filled with stars. Her head spun. *Very clever maneuvering, Sarah*, she told herself. *Well done.*

Blood ran down around her eye and onto her cheek.

The men laughed. Sarah had to yank her imagination away from thinking about slitting all their throats but Angus, and leaving him hanging from a tree by his own guts.

Her vision cleared, she saw Obadiah still looming over her, and she found she had a plan.

"Get that devil drink away from me!" she snapped. She hoped he was stupid enough—or drunk enough—not to wonder why she would have wine in her pack, if she hated it so much. Maybe he'd think it was Cal's, that would be ironic. Maybe he'd think it was medicinal.

"New Light, eh?" Obadiah had another swig. "One of Barton's Children, eh? Followers of the *former* Bishop Stone?"

Sarah put her face down, doing her best to look sulky and defiant. With her chin tucked against her collarbone her face was in shadow, and she took the opportunity to tear her own lower lip with her teeth. She was rewarded with the warm metallic tang of blood on her tongue.

"'Im, too?" The Englishman gestured at Calvin. Cal was stirring into wakefulness, and two of the thugs kept pistols trained on him. "'E goes in for the tent-preachink an' the speakink in tongues?"

Sarah nodded sulkily. She wondered about the other two men, the shadowed ones she had such a hard time pinning down in her field of vision. Well, seven to one against wasn't much worse than five to one. She'd have to try to get Obadiah moving in the right direction, and hope all the others would all follow.

"Right, drink up!" Yanking her to a sitting position, Obadiah shoved the wineskin to her lips.

Sarah spluttered and coughed to look convincing, and carefully, with her tongue and teeth, forced blood into the wineskin. Three pulses with her tongue should make three drops. As she bled her own lip into the wineskin, she focused her mind, hexing the wine with blood and will. She trembled, feeling energy flow from her into the wineskin. If her mouth had been free, she would have chanted a rhyme, but she'd have to do without. It was taking a long time to get three drops squeezed out, and she hoped Obadiah wouldn't notice her eagerness to keep her mouth on the wineskin's opening.

Obadiah did notice, but misunderstood. "Look at that, the wee squaw likes it mickle well after all!" he laughed raucously. "Let's try it on 'er brave!"

He threw Sarah back into the leaves.

Cal looked groggy but his eyes were open. He must have seen Sarah resist the drink, because he played along, shying away and whimpering before allowing wine to be poured down his throat. She was proud of him for focusing and trying to help her, even not knowing what she was up to. Of course, now he'd be hexed, too, and that might complicate things.

She would just have to deal with that later.

The men all laughed and one of them kicked Calvin in the chest.

"I don't see as any of this is gonna make the Elector any happier," Angus muttered, "iffen he catches us."

Obadiah resumed his song, louder and merrier than before.

> And besides, I'll instruct you, like me, to entwine
> The myrtle of Venus wiff Bacchus's vine!

He took a long swig.

Her captors all roared with laughter and Sarah held her breath. Angus reached for the wine but Obadiah rebuffed him with an elbow, and then drank deeply, finishing off the skin, tossing it aside, and finally relieving pressure from his chest with a long, loud belch.

Immediately, he reached for the second wineskin.

"Obadiah, my dear," Sarah called in her sweetest, clearest Penn's English. "These ropes are uncomfortable."

The Nashville thugs laughed again, but Obadiah Dogsbody

looked merely puzzled. He scratched his head. "Aye, poppet." He pulled a clasp knife from his pocket, snapping the blade open.

"Hell, no!" Angus snapped. "Don't kill her, and if you're gonna do it, don't do it right here under the old man's nose!"

The other ruffians laughed again. "Give it to her!" one of them shouted as Obadiah trudged back to Sarah's side and knelt. Then carefully, even gently, Obadiah slipped his blade between her wrists and cut away the ropes. He also cut the rope from her ankles.

The men from Nashville stopped laughing.

Sarah stood. She had him, the fat bully. "Would you help my nephew Calvin?"

Obadiah cut Calvin loose, and he staggered to his feet too, staring at Sarah just a little too intently. *Uh oh.* A brawl between the two of them would do her no good.

Obadiah put away his knife and took Sarah's hand, stroking her arm. "My master the Right Reverend Father mickle wishes to see you, my pet," he whispered. He stank of wine and sweat and horses, but she forced herself to smile lovingly at her captor.

"Of course," she said. "I am very honored to go see him. Please take me there directly."

Obadiah grinned and turned to go, still holding her hand. She threw a quick glance at Cal; he was balling up his fists and flaring his nostrils.

"Dear Obadiah, wait a moment," she said. It wasn't a strong enough hex to control the man, it just infatuated him, and maybe confused him a little bit where she was concerned, so she needed to be careful. And subtle, like the serpent.

The big man stopped and listened.

"Did the Right Reverend Father ask to see my nephew Calvin, as well?"

"Nay." Obadiah frowned.

"His mamma will be so worried." She knitted her brows. "If you would be so kind, I would like to take my nephew home. I'll go with him, because I'm not sure he knows the way. If you tell me where I can find you, I'll come join you later this evening, and we'll speak to the Right Reverend Father together."

Obadiah shot Calvin a suspicious look. "Your nephew?"

Sarah nodded. "He's my brother's son." It was a lie she herself would have believed a day earlier. "He's a good boy."

Obadiah smiled. "Very well, my pet. I'll tell Father Angleton to expect you, shall I?"

The Nashville ruffians stood with their jaws open, blinking in disbelief.

"The *hell's* goin' on *here*?" Bob demanded.

Obadiah spun and struck Bob in the mouth, then drew his pistol. Bob dropped to the ground and held his jaw.

"Anyone else got a question, lads?" Obadiah menaced his men.

"We just don't wanna git ourselves shot," Angus said, raising trembling hands in surrender. "Or worse."

"She be comink back straight away," Obadiah grunted. "Ben't you, poppet?"

"Of course, my love," she told him.

"Very good." He smiled placidly.

Calvin Calhoun loved Sarah.

He had always loved Sarah, he knew that. Even when they had both been children, and she was his dear little auntie, his father's sister though she was younger than Calvin himself, he had adored her.

He loved her because she was funny. He loved her because she was smart, smarter than anyone, even as smart as Old Man Calhoun, maybe. He loved her because she was tough, and proud, and a leader. He even thought she was pretty, though it was hard to say that about a girl with such an unfortunate eye, but then his own face had more than once been compared to the head of his tomahawk. He was in no position to go casting stones at the homely.

He could never say anything about his feelings because she had been his aunt, which was too close. You could marry a cousin, but not your father's sister, that was bad and if you tried it, they wouldn't let you marry in church or even in public and nobody would acknowledge that you even *were* married, much less recognize your kids. And everybody knew your children would be sickly and deformed. The Elector himself had reinforced this point when Cal was a boy, dragging all his grandchildren down to Nashville with pennies in their fists to see a traveling circus that featured a two-headed bull calf, stuffed and mounted, and warning them in dark whispers that the calf's sire and dam had been brother and sister. Cal had often wondered if that was the real story behind Sarah's eye, that her mother hadn't been some

Shawnee concubine warming his bed in his old age, like the Elector'd put about, but some close kin of the Old Man's.

It turned out neither was true. Sarah was somebody else entirely, a Penn or an Ohioan, if Cal had understood correctly.

Sarah was not a Calhoun, and he could marry her.

He had proposed already, she had accepted, and he had abducted her almost in the traditional fashion (without notice to kin, though that was due to the circumstances and could be remedied later). Lord hates a man as can't recognize the sound of opportunity knocking at his door. She hadn't seemed too thrilled about it, but she had accepted him, and she'd come around, especially if he could prove himself as a protector and provider.

Then something had happened, he wasn't sure what, but he had been knocked out. His head still throbbed.

When he'd woken up, it had been to watch Sarah pretend she was New Light and resist a drink of Calvin's wine. Cal had played along, and then somehow—he wasn't quite sure how, he had still been groggy from whatever blow he'd suffered—she had talked the fat Englishman into letting them both go.

The love for her in his heart had exploded then, into a million flowers and singing birds. He felt tingly all over, and lightheaded, and he knew in some corner of his mind that he was overreacting, that she had saved his life from the ruffians and his natural gratitude was being blown all out of proportion by his love.

He knew that, but still his lips wanted to sing and his feet wanted to dance, to stomp out a bright rhythm of courtship for Sarah Calhoun. Sarah Penn.

The sudden riot of love in his head was so powerful, it almost made him forget the evening's other strange event. This was a night on which Cal had perpetrated one abduction and had himself been kidnapped twice. His first kidnapping had been at the hands of his grandfather, whom he now knew as Grand Master of the Calhoun Mountain Lodge, and under the direction of the Grand Master, Cal had been inducted into the Craft as an Entered Apprentice, and then promptly raised to the degree of Fellow Craft, and then raised to Master Mason.

This was not normal procedure, his grandfather had explained, and it might be seen as rushed, but it was something he had done in order to give Cal all the help he could in preparation for his upcoming journey.

Calvin Calhoun's head spun with signs, tokens, and passwords almost as much as it spun with love.

He wasn't entirely sure why his grandfather had inducted him into the Craft. The old man had only said, as he'd walked Cal back to his cabin through the woods, that a Mason was obligated to help another Mason in need, and that the signs and tokens and passwords could be used to call for that help.

Cal wondered how that would work. If Sarah hadn't rescued them from the Nashville men, could he have used the passwords to find out if any of them were Masons, and ask them to let him go?

Maybe. In the meantime, his head spun.

He stumbled along, haggard and weary and Cupid-smitten, humping one pack on his shoulder and dragging the other under his arm. He wished the Englishman hadn't shattered his pa's old gun, but at least it made one less thing for him to carry.

"Sarah," he gasped, "you're pretty as a picture from any angle, but iffen you'd slow down, I might could look at your face once in a while!"

She didn't answer and she didn't slow down.

He noticed something that surprised him, then, cutting through the fog. "Sarah, are we goin' the right way? It seems to me we ain't got off Calhoun Mountain yet, so we should be goin' *down*hill."

"I can't say for sure how long that hex'll hold him," she shot back over her shoulder, "or how long he can keep his hired men in check. And the gun's gone, and you been hit on the head and need lookin' at. We can leave tomorrow, iffen you're still fixin' to come with me."

"Hold who?" Where did she get all her energy? Cal wanted to stop, catch his breath, maybe lie down. Touch her hair softly and say kind things.

"Obadiah Dogsbody. The Englishman."

Cal laughed. "You hexed that muttonhead? No wonder I couldn't make out why he's lettin' us go!" He slapped his knee and stopped walking. "How about we celebrate your cleverness with a kiss, girl?"

She kept walking.

"Come on, Sarah!" he called after her.

Still walking.

"My head's jest fine!" he yelled.

Calvin heard a rustle on the slope behind him. He was in love, but he was neither deaf nor stupid, and the senses he'd trained in a lifetime of hunting deer and sneaking other men's cattle out of their pastures had not deserted him. He spun on the balls of his feet, whipping out his tomahawk with his free hand.

Something manlike—and *not a man*—stood in a clearing among the trees on the slope below him. Cal saw it clear as could be, with the moon shining full down on the not-a-man. The near-human thing had no features and no clothing. It was like a statue of the humanoid form, unfinished. It didn't shine or glow or reflect light; in the moonlight, it looked like it might be brown or gray, top to bottom.

As Cal turned, the not-a-man froze. Cal got a good hard look at it, and then it bolted into the trees. Cal thought he saw a second... *thing*...behind the first, disappearing into the night. He waited a moment, staring holes into the forest, but nothing stirred.

Cal whipped back around and trotted up the slope again after Sarah. He strained his ears to listen, conscious of eyes, or at least vision, on his back as whatever it was he had seen watched him from behind. The hair on his neck stood, and he shivered. He kept a tight grip on his war axe, brandishing it to the side occasionally so the unseen watchers would know he was armed.

Sarah paused to look down at him, panting. "Come on, you danged slowpoke!"

Then her eye widened. "Run, Cal, run!" she yelled. "Run like the Devil hisself is after you!"

Cal ran, his moccasin-clad feet slamming ball-first into the soft dirt of the hillside as he tore up it, as fast as he could make himself go. He threw a quick look over his shoulder, and almost tripped.

There were two of them, and they were gray. They looked soft, or muddy, slippery and half-formed. They looked like nothing so much as clay men, faceless, featureless, naked, terrifying, like something a child might mold out of riverbank dirt and play with, only six feet tall and running. Their breath hissed out of ragged, flapping mouths as they came, and their bare gray feet thumped and rustled on the hillside.

They were right behind him and running faster than he was. He was doomed.

At least he could protect Sarah. If he died but she escaped, that would be a noble sacrifice and a fair trade. He'd do it for love, and the Elector would be proud of him. He might call Cal a hell of a fellow at Cal's funeral and bury Cal in his own lambskin Mason's apron.

Cal swung his head back around downhill and then let the motion carry him into a turn of his whole body, shoulders first, arms swinging around, feet planted. He whipped the pack in his left hand up like a comet—

and then down—

and released it, hurling it straight into the chest of the first not-a-man.

It whooshed breath out but made no other noise as it staggered and fell back, entangling the legs of its companion and buying Calvin enough time to shrug off the other pack and free up his tomahawk arm. As the second not-a-man stumbled over its companion and lunged at him, Cal struck as hard as he could with the war axe, burying it deep in the clay thing's head.

The clay creature didn't stop. It didn't even slow down.

It landed on Calvin with its elbows, pounding him in the chest and wrapping its cold wet hands around his neck. The creature wrenched the tomahawk handle from his grip. The not-a-man's fingers were long and clammy, and Cal struggled to breathe as he fell.

The stink of mud and clay clogged his nostrils. He was being attacked by a river bottom.

Cal pushed, but the monster was stronger than him and it bore down, crushing his windpipe with its cold fingers. He stared up into the eyeless space where a face should be and saw only blank, merciless nothing. The mouth opened, showing only darkness, and hissing the vegetable stink of a swamp into Cal's face. His own fingers dug into the moist clay of the not-a-man's chest, scrabbling large slippery furrows but gaining no grip. He felt his lungs emptying and the skin of his neck beginning to tear.

He thought of his lariat, looped on his hip, but he couldn't imagine it would hurt this enemy. Cal had no weapons that could do any damage to this thing.

He was going to die.

He heard Sarah running down the slope and he tried to call her off, but could only wave and gasp out useless choking sounds.

He wanted her to run, to escape, Sarah his love, Sarah whom he could marry after all, because she wasn't a Calhoun, she was a Penn, and Eldritch, to boot.

Sarah whom he would never marry because he was going to die under an avalanche of fighting mud-man.

Sarah, who was allergic to silver.

Silver and magic didn't mix.

Cal's head started to spin as he fumbled for his belt, and knew the rest of his life might be measured in moments. He dug into the purse, grateful that Obadiah Dogsbody hadn't found it, and even more grateful for his own thrifty habit of saving.

His fist closed around several coins—at least one of them had to be silver. He pulled the fistful of change from his purse, and slapped it into the thing's face.

Aaaaaaaaoooooowwwarrragh!

The creature arched its back and howled, its humid, earthy exhalations filling Calvin's lungs as it let him go and he was able to suck in air. His neck stung; he was bleeding.

The thing had eyes now, one in its forehead and one in its cheek, each formed by a dull silver Pennsland shilling and each spluttering and emitting a foul yellow smoke as the silver burned its way into the clay. Cal saw his blood on its fingers and shuddered at the nearness of his escape. The not-a-man reared back, clawing and slapping at its own head, and tumbled away down the hill.

Rraaagraaaaaaaooggh!

Calvin swallowed cold night air into his chest and dragged himself to his feet. The second not-a-man, its balance recovered from tripping over Cal's pack, hesitated. Cal scrounged another shilling from his purse and raised it over his head like a weapon. He just needed a sling, and he'd be King David Calhoun, shooting mudmen Philistines in the face with money.

"Git back, you . . . *thing!*" Sarah reached his side, and he was foolishly proud.

"Cal, what did you do?" she panted.

Waaaraaawraaaagh!

His vision firmed up and he stepped forward, threatening with his shilling. The wounded not-a-man disappeared into the trees, still bellowing in pain and scratching at its own head, and its companion hissed and then retreated, disappearing into the shadow.

Calvin grinned weakly and checked his purse. "Don't be vexed with me, dear. I jest spent half our savings."

Obadiah whistled a drinking song as he approached the camp: "To Anacreon in Heaven."

Even just whistling the bawdy parts reminded him of his sweet poppet and brought a smile to his face. She'd rejoin him in camp soon, and he looked forward to it. He'd dawdled on his return path, in part because his foot still troubled him but also to give her more time and in the hope that they might arrive at camp together. He imagined holding her, being kind to her, giving her gifts, and receiving her tender smiles.

He'd released the Nashville men. They had protested strongly, especially the one named Angus, who had cursed a lot and threatened to go retake the girl. Obadiah had a hard time understanding their objections, but he had been firm, and pointed out that they'd already been paid, and their services were no longer needed.

Eventually they had given up trying and left. Angus, in particular, had fled in a full sprint.

Obadiah finished the verse verbally as he strolled into the firelight, "the myrtle of Venus wiff Bacchus's vine!" In Obadiah's absence, the Right Reverend Father had lit a small fire, but he had pitched no tent, and he sat on a fallen log in his tall black hat and his cloak, looking expectantly at his servant.

"Well?" Father Angleton asked in his high-pitched nasal whine.

Obadiah wanted to ward off any grumpiness on the priest's part, and offered the last of the second wineskin to the priest. "Drink, Father?"

Angleton rose to his feet, brows knitted. "Obadiah, have I dreamed true? Have you failed me again?"

There was a dangerous edge to his employer's voice, and Obadiah willed himself to be sober as he tamped the stopper back into the skin. "Nay, sir, I've 'ad mickle great success tonight." He cleared his throat and spat into the leaves.

"You're drunk, Obadiah Dogsbody, and you're alone. Explain to me this great success you believe you've had."

"Ah, aye." Angleton would be happy once Obadiah had explained the matter to him. "I trow this must look a mite surprisink to you." He straightened his back and collected himself.

"I sent the men off, you see. An' the wine—" he looked at it cheerfully, "I took it from the girl."

"I don't care about the men!" Angleton roared.

Obadiah shuffled back a step.

Angleton pressed forward, spittle flying out of his mouth with every word. "And I *certainly* don't care where you got your wine! Where's the *girl?* You remember the girl, don't you? The girl with the deformed eye? The girl whose hair I bound into a lodestone so even *you* could find her? You took her drink apparently, so you must have seen her—where is she?"

"She be comink, she be comink," Obadiah hastened to reassure his master. "I did see 'er, as you well wot was the plan, an' she be comink 'ere. She'll be 'ere by and by." He smiled to put the Right Reverend Father's mind at ease.

Angleton backed away from Obadiah, doubt in his eyes. "Is someone bringing her? Did you send your Nashville men to get her?"

That might have been a good idea. Obadiah could have gone with her, and then the Right Reverend Father wouldn't be so nervous. "Nay, she be comink 'ere on 'er own." He widened his grin. "Released wiffout bond, as a magistrate might say it."

Angleton's look of confusion faded and was replaced by a suspicious stare. He reached into his purse and pulled out a silver coin.

"Be that a gift, Father?" Obadiah was flattered. "You needn't, sir." Still, he held out his hand, rough palm up. It was starting to feel to Obadiah as if Yuletide had come early this year. He half expected to hear the firing of celebratory guns.

But Father Angleton reached up and pressed the money against Obadiah's forehead. Obadiah was startled, but submitted. He felt nothing, other than the coolness of the coin on his face and the slight humiliation of being touched by his master in this fashion.

"Where's the *girl?*" Angleton asked him.

"Blast an' confound it!" Obadiah roared, surprising himself. "Wayland's blood, but that scab-eyed wee witch hexed me!"

"Yaas." Angleton's teeth ground together. "The fault is mine. After your first failure, I should have gone myself. She defeated you completely, Obadiah."

"That she did," drawled a lazy mountain voice from outside the circle of the fire. Its owner was a tall Appalachee youth with a long Kentucky rifle crooked in his arm, its muzzle aimed not at Obadiah and his master, but near enough that it could be immediately brought to bear. "And I reckon she done a powerful job of it, too, from the gump look on your face as you was traipsin' about the woods tonight." The cracker spat into the brush.

Obadiah growled and reached for his the hilt of his broadsword—the man would only get one shot off with that rifle, and Obadiah calculated he'd likely miss, in the dark and the excitement, and then Obadiah would cut him down. Then Obadiah noticed several other long-bodied mountaineers lurking in the shadows, all armed with rifles, and he paused.

"'Erne's teef," he said, "but you be a right coward. Aye, ye be all a bunch of cowards, the lot of ye."

"Says the armed desperado as goes about kidnappin' girls," rejoined the mountaineer. "But we ain't here for no ruckus."

"Be ye not?" Obadiah felt a curious hollowness inside, and it seemed to him Father Angleton's hex-dispelling coin had taken something from him. Life was flatter, duller, harder than it had been ten minutes earlier.

"What do you want?" Father Angleton spoke up.

"Name's Calhoun," the rifleman said. "Shadrach Calhoun."

"You won't shoot me," the priest told him. "I am chaplain to the Philadelphia Blues, and the personal confessor of the emperor." He sounded as wary as Obadiah felt.

"We ain't gonna shoot you," Shadrach agreed. "You're on Calhoun land, and we come to welcome you."

"We'll leave," Angleton offered, his voice smoldering, and turned to go, but Shadrach swung his rifle up and stopped the man.

"No, you won't," he contradicted the priest. "Not yet. Every priest has e'er come onto Calhoun land, we ain't let him leave without he preached us a sermon first. I reckon a half hour ought to do, so long as it's a half hour of solid noisy hellfire and brimstone. Approximate, as I ain't got no hourglass."

"I can certainly preach to you about the Day of *Judgment*," Angleton said sharply. Obadiah saw the fire in his master's eyes and was a little nervous, even though the Right Reverend Father was snapping at the Appalachee. "The great and terrible day when all will stand *naked before the Lord* to be judged for our sins."

"I reckon that'd be perfect." Shadrach Calhoun he raised his rifle, pointing it at Obadiah, and his shadow-hidden companions all took aim as well, surrounding the strangers with a bristling hedge of firearms. "I reckon I'd git a great deal of benefit out of a noisy hellfire and brimstone sermon 'bout how we appear afore the Lord on Judgment Day. And I reckon it'd be especially effective iffen the preacher and the congregation—" he nodded at Angleton and Obadiah, "both demonstrated the finer theological points in dramatic form."

Obadiah didn't understand, but he had a sneaking suspicion that his evening was about to get even worse. "What do you intend?"

"Ain't it obvious?" Shadrach drawled slowly, and then spat a great brown squirt at Obadiah's feet. "I mean I want to hear this sermon, and I want you and the preacher both to be like the man said. *Nekkid afore the Lord.*"

"I only regret that you are not emissaries
of Father Christmas instead, ma'am."

<hr />

CHAPTER SIX

Bill drifted back down the bluff and onto Smuggler's Shelf feeling shaken. He had been troubled enough about the young frog's
death when the lad was a gallant nobody, and only reminded Bill
of his own Charles; knowing he was the chevalier's son made Bill
downright uncomfortable.

He thrashed his way with both arms through a thicket of brittle
reeds, boots splashing in thin mud, and emerged onto the sand.

Well, Bill would pay off his debts in the morning—later
tonight, if he could find Etienne Ukwu—and then figure out what
to do about the chevalier. Maybe nothing, maybe the chevalier
wouldn't know who had killed his son.

No, that was unlikely, given how publicly Bill had challenged
the young man, and how he'd told the onlookers and the seconds
that *he, personally*, William Lee, was affronted by the Frenchman's
attentions to *his* actress lover. That was more than unlikely, it
was delusional.

Was this why Don Sandoval had insisted that Bill challenge
his romantic rival in Bill's own name?

Was Bill being set up?

Bill reached into the pocket of his coat and wrapped his hand
around the grip of the pistol that was still loaded and primed,
just in case.

He could simply apologize to the chevalier.

But dueling was a hanging offense, no matter how generally it was tolerated, and the chevalier was New Orleans's chief officer of the law. Even if the chevalier himself didn't come after Bill, how many of his gendarmes would get the notion they could curry favor with their master for the low price of a single bullet?

He could run. To the Ohio, or the upper Mississippi, or across the river to the lands of the free horse people.

But first he had to deal with the Spaniards.

Under Bishopsbridge, Don Sandoval and his two bodyguards waited in their yellow coats. In the moonlight and shadow, the yellow looked like sickness. They looked like three men covered in pus and vomit.

Don Sandoval sat on his horse and in front of him, blocking Bill's path to his employer, stood the two bodyguards, hands on their belts. Bill sized up the two toughs and chose the one he'd kill first—the older one, the one who had probably seen more action and looked calmer.

"Twenty looeys, suh!" Bill called, keeping his voice as jocular as he could. He bowed slightly, sweeping his hat off with his left hand but keeping his eyes on the three men.

Don Sandoval raised a white handkerchief and dabbed at the corner of one eye with a mock tragic air. "Good-bye, Señor Dollar Bill."

His men grabbed for their guns.

Bill didn't bother to pull the horse pistol from his coat; he simply swung it up, still in the long pocket, and fired right through the fabric.

Bang!

The older bodyguard dropped in a fountain of blood, one gun snagged in his belt and the other leaping from his dead fingers into the night.

As Bill fired, he charged, and the world about him slowed. Don Sandoval yelled something in Castilian, struggling to keep mastery over his suddenly bucking mount. The surviving bodyguard, surprise registering on his face at the unexpected annihilation of his comrade, pulled his guns from his belt—

and Bill flung his broad brimmed hat, spinning it like a skipped rock, into the bodyguard's eyes.

Bang! Bang!

Both the bodyguard's pistols went off. His aim was spoiled by the hat in his face, but one of the bullets hit Bill anyway; he felt it punch into his left shoulder and push him a little off-center, but Bill was a large man and his forward charge was not slowed. He crashed into the bodyguard with all his weight and all the strength in his legs pounding down behind his big, bony knuckles.

Bill's aim was put off by the bullet, so he missed the man's nose and pounded his jaw instead, and the Spaniard's strangled cry of pain and the satisfying *crack!* made by the bone as he connected told Bill his attack had hit home.

Lucky hat.

The merchant's mount got the better of him and bolted. The other horses followed, ripping out tethering stakes and galloping away.

"Damn you!" Bill whirled away from the flailing bodyguard. He hated to turn his back on an enemy who could still fight, but rage at his betrayal boiled within him, overwhelming cool trained fighting habits.

He threw himself at the body of the dead bodyguard, landing fully prone on the man with a jar that sent lightning bolts of pain from his own shoulder into his chest and arm. He gritted his teeth against the agony and jerked the pistol from the Spaniard's belt. Resting his elbows on the dead man's chest to steady his aim, he squinted at the retreating horseman, and shot the horse.

Bill was rewarded with a whinny of surprised pain and the sight of Don Sandoval hurtling from the animal's back onto the sand, and then he heard the steel rasp of a blade being drawn behind him.

Bill threw himself sideways and the attacker's knife slashed down into the corpse with a meaty *thunk!* The bodyguard shouted incoherently, spitting syrupy blood from his dangling mouth, and Bill spun on his shoulder blades to kick at the man with both his feet. The Spaniard was stooping low to free his knife, so one heavy boot smashed his jaw and the other caught him in the belly, sending him staggering away.

Bill risked a glance over his shoulder as he climbed to his feet; Don Sandoval was struggling to get up. Perfect. Bill drew his sword and faced the Don's bodyguard, bloodied and unsteady on his feet.

If only he had reloaded his other pistol.

But the Spaniard might not realize he hadn't.

Bill jerked the empty pistol from his pocket and pointed it at his antagonist. "*Entrénase!*" he barked. Didn't that mean *surrender* in Castilian?

The man blinked and swayed on his feet. Bill noted that he was losing a lot of blood out his mouth and down the front of his chest. Bill's own shoulder felt as if a drill was chewing its way through it and he bit back a powerful urge to vomit.

"Give up, you dago bastard!" Bill repeated himself. "You've nothing worth dying for here! *Entrénase*, dog on you!" The man made no move to attack, but also didn't raise his hands, drop his knife, or otherwise indicate surrender. He just stood where he was, shifting back and forth a bit on the balls of his feet as if he were a green tree swaying in a strong breeze. In the darkness Bill couldn't see the man's eyes.

Bill looked over his shoulder again. Don Sandoval had risen to his feet and was limping in a meandering line across the Shelf toward the bluff.

No more time for fooling around.

Bill took a step forward, raising his saber . . . and the hidalgo ruffian collapsed, falling sideways without bending, like a felled tree trunk.

Bill shoved his pistol back into his pocket, his sword into its scabbard, and his victorious hat onto his head. Taking a deep breath, he scanned the mud and sand and quickly found the only unfired pistol on Smuggler's Shelf, the one that had been dropped to the ground when Bill had blasted the first man to oblivion. He blew off the sand and checked its firing pan, then stomped across the Shelf toward his former employer.

Don Luis Maria Salvador Sandoval de Burgos was beginning to clamber on all fours up the scrub grass, still groggy and whimpering, when Bill grabbed his black coat by the shoulders and pulled the merchant down, throwing him into the mud with a soggy *splash*.

"Twenty looeys!" Bill raged.

Don Sandoval looked up trembling and Bill shoved the borrowed pistol into his cheek, just below one eye, irreparably smearing the Don's rouge. Should he be demanding more? Something held him back. Bill shook his head to clear it, and for a moment he thought he saw, out of the corner of his eye, the dead young frog.

He shuddered.

"I-I d-do not have it, Señor." Tears furrowed the wrecked make-up on the merchant's cheeks.

"Show me your purse," Bill snarled. Don Sandoval fumbled at his waist and then handed over a black silk purse that was, to Bill's disappointment and mounting sense of fury, empty. Bill had more than half a mind to shoot the dago, regardless of his observation by dead Frenchmen.

"D-d-do not kill me! I have treated you ill, it is true, but please, do not kill me! Please, I...I have a son!"

Damn the man! "Just because you're named Maria, suh, doesn't mean you have to cry."

"I am s-sorry, and you are right. Please, I d-do not have the money."

"Twenty looeys—how soon can you get it?" These fat merchants lived off the poor planting Cavaliers, and Don Sandoval must have chests of cash. Bill tried to remember what the Don traded in. Sugar? Wheat? Bantu cotton? He glanced discreetly to his side to make sure the chevalier's son was not looking over his shoulder.

"Soon!" the Spaniard's eyes brightened and he clasped his hands together as if in prayer. "Ten days, maybe she is a week only!"

"What!?" Bill yelled. "You're rich as Croesus, suh, rich as William Penn, rich as John Hancock and just as much a thief! Don't lie to me!" He was furious at the betrayal, at the lancing pain in his shoulder, and at the thought that if the Bishop of New Orleans didn't kill him tomorrow, the chevalier surely would.

"I am no smuggler," the merchant protested. "My money, she is in bales of cotton, and notes, and bills of exchange. I have no cash, I would have to borrow from my partners, and she will take time. I am sorry, my cotton is all stamped by the chevalier's customs men, and my cash, she is all spent."

"Spent on what?" Bill asked.

"Some of it you have already had," Don Sandoval told him. "The remainder is all gone...on Miss Lefevre, mostly." His eyes teared up and he looked away.

Bill snorted. "Don't weep on Miss Lefevre's account. She's had other affections before yours, and she'll have others after."

"I weep for myself," the Spaniard said. "And for the young Frenchman. And maybe for you, too. Please, Señor D-Dollar Bill, do not kill me."

Bill pulled back the hammer on the gun and carefully considered his future. There was nothing Don Sandoval could do to save him from the chevalier—Bill had publicly called out the nobleman's son, and killed him, and now Bill would pay the price. Apparently, the merchant couldn't help him with the bishop, either, at least not tomorrow. Should he hold Don Sandoval for ransom? How much would the hidalgo's partners or his family pay to free the fellow?

On the other hand, Bill was tempted by the idea of justice. One squeeze of his finger and at least the Spaniard would never trouble him again. Bill's finger twitched, but in his mind's eye he saw the chevalier's son, bravely and uselessly waving his pistol at Bill, and above the young man's shoulders he saw the face of his own son Charles.

The Frenchman would not have approved of this vindictive killing, and that thought strangely shamed Bill. The frog would have disapproved, Charles would have been ashamed, and once, he acknowledged to himself, feeling sick to his stomach, such a murder would have been anathema to Sir William Lee as well.

The Spaniard was beaten. It was enough.

"My name, *suh*," he squeezed out through clenched teeth, "is not *Dollar Bill*. My name is *Captain Sir William Johnston Lee*." With an effort of will, he eased the hammer back into place and then tossed the gun aside. "You owe me twenty looeys, suh. You should anticipate that I shall come collecting *soon*, and thank God that I am no great friend of the concept of *interest*."

Bill marched up the bluff without looking back. He tried to take dignified steps, imagining that at least one, and maybe two hidalgos were watching his departure, but between the pain of his shoulder and the weight of his gut he found it impossible to do better than a rolling uphill lurch. He hoped he'd find one of the Spaniards' horses at the top of the hill—he didn't feel up to hobbling all the way back to New Orleans.

Bill stumbled onto the highway groaning. Every heartbeat pounded in his shoulder and a fair amount of blood ran through his sleeve and his shirt, puddling sticky at his belt and dripping down his fingers to the ground.

At least the air got a little easier to breathe as he rose up away from the river.

On the highway waited two figures, standing like puppets

against a curtain of Spanish moss, dark and gloomy and silvery-green in the moonlight. They were robed and hooded in dark cloth, so he could not see their faces or tell whether they were armed. They seemed dimly familiar, and then he realized where he'd seen them before—standing in front of *Grissot's* that afternoon.

"This is becoming an eventful evening." He stopped in his tracks.

"We are messengers," creaked one of the figures in a dry, slow voice.

"Just tell me that you monks aren't servants of the chevalier."

"No," the same figure said. It peeled back its hood to reveal the forward-curling, leathery head of a tortoise, gray in the moonlight, bullet-shaped eyes glittering black and silver.

"We are not servants of the chevalier."

The other figure pulled back its hood—*her* hood—as well, revealing a woman's face that was strikingly beautiful in all respects but one. She had a waterfall of golden hair, slender eyebrows, fair skin, high cheekbones, shimmering blue eyes... and where her nose and mouth should have been, there protruded from her face the long yellow beak of a duck.

"Moreover, we are not monks," she said. "We serve the Heron King." Her voice tinkled like tiny silver bells. As he looked at it, Bill began to think that her beak wasn't ugly, after all. It was strangely feminine and alluring.

"Beastkind," Bill muttered. That he found the duck-billed woman beautiful only made him mistrust her more. He kicked himself for not reloading the pistols. He rested his hand on the hilt of his saber, but left it in its scabbard. "If you are road-agents, you have chosen the wrong man. I'm penniless."

"We are not outlaws." The woman's duck-smile troubled Bill.

"If you're hungry, I'm armed." Bill felt his strength ebbing with his blood loss.

"We are not here to hurt thee, Captain Sir William Johnston Lee," the tortoise-headed man croaked, twisting its beak into something approaching a smile. The night had already been so strange that Court Speech coming out of the mouth of this turtle-headed man barely struck Bill as incongruous. "Thou art not an enemy and we are not feral."

"If you truly wish me no harm, suh," Bill quipped, refusing to be drawn into the Jacobean thees and thous that had once been second nature to him, "that fact may make you unique in the entire territory of Louisiana."

"We have come looking for thee, Sir William," fluted the beautiful duck.

Bill wondered whether her body was feathered underneath the robe she wore. He wondered...he snapped his mind back from pointless speculation. "I don't suppose I'm so fortunate that you might be moneylenders, anxious to lend me twenty gold looeys? Preferably not subject to the terrible Adamic curse of interest? If not, and if you're not offering me a ride back to New Orleans in your invisible carriage, then I must be on my way."

They ignored his jokes. Blasted beastkind—no sense of humor. Bill felt faint.

"We are emissaries of the Heron King," the duck-bill tinkled again. "We bear thee a message."

Bill snorted. He'd heard stories of the Heron King, growing up in Johnsland, but they weren't stories of the sort you took very seriously once you were out of short pants. "I only regret that you are not emissaries of Father Christmas instead, ma'am," he rejoined, "bearing me gifts of frankincense, myrrh, and twenty gold looeys."

It must be the blood loss. Bill was lightheaded; he must be hallucinating. This whole encounter was all in his head. There was no Turtle Head, no Duck-Faced Woman. He was probably lying unconscious on the Shelf while Don Sandoval hacked him to pieces with a dagger and put rouge on his cheeks.

At least he couldn't feel it.

"Thou shalt see the queen soon," Tortoise-head told him. "Tell her Peter Plowshare is dead. The Heron King conveys his congratulations upon the occasion of her return, he supports her in her claims to her thrones, and he hopes she will entertain his suit for a close alliance between his kingdom and hers...a close alliance, and also marriage."

Bill sucked in cool air through his teeth. Peter Plowshare? The queen? This hallucination got odder as it was prolonged. He could just manage to keep the beastfolk's faces in view, but the world around them spun in crazy smears of silvery-moonlit color.

"The difficulty you face, suh," he tried to tell the tortoise-headed man, "isn't my memory, which is passing adequate to the herald's task, but the fact that I don't expect in the proximate future to be seeing any queens...or any other gentlefolk at all... unless, you understand, they happen to reside in the bottom of potter's field."

He wasn't sure how much of his message he got out coherently.

He began losing consciousness in the middle of it, and when he reached the end, Bill passed out and fell.

"Someone on the boardwalk wants to talk to you," Petit Jacques the stable boy told Cathy, speaking French, the only language he knew.

Petit Jacques was out of place in the smoke-clouded common room of *Grissot's*, where he was not generally allowed at night. His breeches and shapeless cap were battered and dirty, but the horse smell wasn't strong enough to cut through the odors of woodsmoke, tobacco, and sweat, and he wasn't trailing straw or manure behind him, so Cathy didn't mind, whatever Grand Jacques said.

Over the *bum-ditty* of the banjo picker in the corner and the *click-and-roll* of the man beside him, shuffling his hard-soled shoes and snapping a pair of rib bones in each hand to keep time, no one but Cathy could hear Petit Jacques, anyway. The musicians were dark-skinned Igbo men in long, embroidered tunics, and while the banjo-picker hummed a wordless basso drone, the bones player sang a folk tune. Cathy knew it well, though it was not a song she'd ever heard in her native Virginia; she'd been catching snatches of it on and off for over fifteen years, since she'd first come to the Mississippi.

> *Peter Plowshare's a farming man*
> *King of maize and bean and gourd*
> *Who takes your crop whene'er he can?*
> *The rascal, Simon Sword!*

"I don't entertain gentlemen in the street," she told the boy softly in his tongue, and smiled at him. *Charm everyone.* "That simply wouldn't do." *Maintain your standards. Let people come to you.*

"I don't think they're gentlemen, and I don't think they want to be entertained," Petit Jacques insisted. "They might be priests."

"How very interesting," Cathy said. "Well, I do hope they

decide to come in and see me, then." *Patience in all things.* She scanned the room, disappointed that the potential clientele was so scarce and poor tonight. She prided herself on giving men more than some of her fellow entertainers did: class and sophistication. She could converse, she had read widely, she could sing, and some men came to her for those things. They paid more for it, and that was important, as it almost made up for the fact that many men found her simply over-priced.

Petit Jacques fished something from his pocket. "This was their tip to *me*."

> *Peter Plowshare's a builder fair*
> *Log and chink and stone and board*
> *Who tears down buildings everywhere?*
> *The villain, Simon Sword!*

It was a gold coin, one that Cathy did not recognize, stamped simply with a plow on one side and a sword on the other, no letters or numbers at all. Her eyebrows arched involuntarily, and she beat them down with a will of iron. *Grace at all times.* She smiled. "How fortunate, Jacky. Be careful how you spend it, now." *Restraint.*

Cultivate an impression of mastery and mystery.

Petit Jacques shook his head. "Very well, Madame, you do whatever you want to. I told them you would not come out, but they asked me to try. It has something to do with Monsieur Bad Bill, they said. I think he may be in danger." He eyed Grand Jacques at the bar, then skipped out.

> *Peter Plowshare shapes the land*
> *Road and fence and bridge and ford*
> *Who smashes all with a hateful hand?*
> *The reaver, Simon Sword!*

Cathy mastered her surprise. Bad Bill! Captain Sir William Johnston Lee, once an Imperial officer of some renown. He didn't know it, but she owed Bill a great debt—two debts, really.

In the first place, his daily visits to her and his reputation as a dangerous man had freed her of the need to work for a procurer, since most of the Quarter assumed she worked for

Bill, and they feared him too much to harm Cathy. It helped that Bill had more than once intervened when a client of hers had become troublesome, throwing men into horse troughs or frightening them away simply by resting his hand on a pistol grip. Having no pander and working out of a tavern rather than a true bawdy house meant Cathy kept all her earnings, which was an enormous gain. Some working women she knew gave up more than half their take for the 'protection' of a gold-toothed cutthroat who beat them, or worse.

In the second place, and on a less mercenary plane, Sir William's visits kept her sane. She thought they might serve the same function for him—a daily moment of deliberate refinement and gentility to keep the stinking, fleshy, oil-lit barbarism of New Orleans at bay—and she loved him for it. She flirted with him knowing it was in vain, on account of William's dogged faithfulness to a wife whom he believed might still be true to him.

Paradoxically, his insistent loyalty to the family—and wife—he hadn't seen for years made him more attractive to Cathy. She admired his stubborn attachment, she found it reassuring. The fact that that family included children, that Sir William was a father, made her think of her own child, the child she had never told Sir William about, and in her fancy she liked to imagine that Sir William was the child's father.

In some secret chamber of her inner heart into which even she could not see clearly, Cathy Filmer suspected, she was in love with Bill. She loved him almost enough to be completely honest with him.

Almost, but not quite.

She rose to her feet gracefully. The clients, the diners and the drinkers in the room didn't notice, but as she headed to the door she looked to the bar and saw Grand Jacques's tiny-eyed, heavy-jowled face staring at her. He knew Cathy did not leave her position while she was at work—she let the men come to *her*—and he knew she was too professional to quit work early. He said nothing, though, and went back to refilling tumblers.

> Peter Plowshare's an even judge
> Fair to farmer, and mighty lord
> Who hates us all with an even grudge?
> The waster, Simon Sword!

The street outside roiled, fumed, and belched with the midnight traffic of the Quarter, all sins bought and sold in the cool night air, which at least had the virtue of reeking less of tobacco smoke than did the air inside. Among the loungers on the walk stood a solitary robed and hooded figure, rather than the two Petit Jacques had described. This was not an atmosphere that attracted many clerics, so the figure must be one of the priests in question.

"Good evening," she said, "bon soir." This commonplace New Orleans maneuver gave the other party the choice of language in which to proceed.

"Good even," the figure replied, and pulled back its hood slightly. Cathy nearly jumped at finding that beneath the hood was a woman's face with long yellow hair and a duck's beak. *Grace*.

"I am Mrs. Catherine Filmer." Cathy nodded slightly.

"Thou mayest call me Picaw." *Picaw* wasn't so much a name as a sound like a bird's cry, *picaw!*

"A pleasure." Cathy nodded again. "Are you one of the persons who sent me young Jacques? He indicated that you might have business concerning my friend, Sir William Lee."

"If thou art a friend of the man Lee," the duck-faced woman said in musical, lilting tones, "come now. He lieth at death's door."

Picaw got several steps' head start as Cathy recovered from the surprise. *Mastery*, she told herself. *Mastery and grace.* She followed the beastwife down the boardwalk to the alley running up the side of *Grissot's*. The narrow street stank of boozy piss. There, shadowed from the flickering torch- and oil-light of the street, Bill lay unconscious, with a tortoise-headed beastman crouching over him. Bill's waistcoat was gone and his shirt and neckcloth were dark with his own blood, oozing through a rude bandage around his left shoulder.

"We have no healing magics to help him," creaked the beastman.

"Carry him," Cathy heard herself saying, her instincts of control taking over even as the perceiving part of her retreated into a distant, stunned shell, "and come with me."

She smiled with all the force of her charm to the smoky common room as she entered, but it was not enough to prevent a stunned hush. Even the banjo and bones fell silent at the sight of the beastfolk following her, Tortoise-head hoisting Bad Bill slung over his shoulder. How far had they carried Bill? Who were they? What was their connection with William Lee?

Grand Jacques's eyes bulged, but she pushed past him into the kitchen. The beastfolk followed, Tortoise-head shrugging Bill to the floor in front of the fire.

Jacques trailed them into the kitchen, protesting. "Monsieur Grissot will not like this." He was right.

Cathy sighed. "I have to stop the bleeding, and the fire in my room isn't lit. Now get me a bottle of whisky. I'll pay for it and I'll handle Monsieur Grissot."

The bartender stood undecided.

Cathy sighed. She pulled one of Bill's pistols from his coat pocket and pointed it at Grand Jacques's forehead.

"*Don't* get me the whisky," she snarled, "and I will *shoot* you!" Her own ferocity surprised even her, but it worked. By the time she had Bill's shoulder stripped and a couple of kitchen knives lying to be sterilized in the hot coals, a square bottle of whisky had appeared.

Thankfully, the bullet had passed through Bill's upper arm without hitting a bone—she could see the entrance and exit wounds clearly. Still, this would hurt, even if she did everything right. It was a good thing Bill was unconscious. She began with a prayer she hadn't said in years: "St. William Harvey, guide now my knife. As I have faith and seek to follow thee, restore thou health to this suffering child of Adam. Amen."

Wrapping its handle in a dishtowel, she picked up a knife.

Bill opened his eyes to pain. He lay in an unfamiliar bed that smelled of flowers and stared at a white plaster ceiling illuminated dimly by cracks of light creeping between heavy velvet curtains.

His arm was killing him.

His head hurt, too, but his head generally hurt when he woke up.

"Franklin's teeth," he said. "Where am I?"

"Why, Sir William," drawled a familiar woman's voice. "I finally have you where I have always wanted you."

Bill tried to prop himself up on his elbow and collapsed immediately as a jagged shard of agony ripped through his shoulder. He remembered killing the young Frenchman, being double-crossed by his dago employer and shot by the man's bodyguards, and then, he thought he recalled, meeting some queer figures on the highway. Had he been delirious? He shook his head to clear away the fog.

He must be in Cathy's bed; he felt an illicit thrill.

She sat on a wooden chair beside him. She wore a straight blue frock and no makeup. Perhaps it was the elation and relief of finding himself still alive, but Bill thought he had never seen her look more beautiful.

Incongruously, for a moment he imagined that she might be covered with fine golden feathers all over her body.

And then he realized that he was naked.

"Whatever adventures may have brought me here last night," Bill commented wryly, "I am saddened to discover that I've forgotten the pleasing part. I do note, however, that I appear to be entirely disrobed."

"Mrs. Lee need not fear, I'm afraid," she said, smiling at him. "Although I've pierced the veil of your modesty quite ruthlessly, Sir William, and I confess that I've made free with your shoulder, I haven't otherwise abused your person."

Bill probed at his wounded shoulder and found both an entry and an exit wound from the bullet, each puckered, cauterized, and tender. "I find myself regretting not having been abused, ma'am. Sin without guilt has always been the secret goal of the Christian man. Someone has very neatly treated my wounds."

"Simple Circulator training." She shrugged.

"Other than your failure to take advantage of me in the night, I see that I've been extraordinarily fortunate."

She nodded seriously. "Your beastmen...*friends* brought me to you. They left once I had stopped the bleeding."

So it hadn't been a hallucination. Bill puffed his cheeks and exhaled slowly. "I wouldn't have called them my *friends*. I met them by chance on the highway, and it's my pure good fortune and much to my surprise that they turned out to be benevolent beastkind, and not maneaters. Did they tell you their names?"

"The woman is called Picaw," she said. "The tortoise never told me his name."

"I found the woman with the duck face disturbingly attractive," Bill remembered. He winked at Cathy. "I'll be grateful to you, Mrs. Filmer, if you can help me forget her."

"I don't know that I can, Sir William." Cathy arched a suggestive eyebrow in Bill's direction. "I found her troubling, myself."

Bill chuckled and fell to rumination.

He had no money. He owed the Bishop of New Orleans, what was it, eight looeys? He owed eight looeys today. And he owed Madame Beaulieu another three. He would prefer to lie here in Long Cathy's bed and enjoy tantalizing conversation, but he needed to get going.

He sat up, pulling himself with the strength of his good arm and trying to protect his punctured modesty with the bedsheet. The effort made him lightheaded, and he breathed deeply to recover.

"Mrs. Filmer," he asked, "does God smile so much upon me this morning that my clothing has been salvaged?"

"He does," she told him, "although apparently He hated your shirt, which could not be saved, and which I've replaced out of the impeccable wardrobe of Grand Jacques. I've cleaned your clothes and darned a large hole in the bottom of your coat pocket."

She stepped out to let him dress, which he accomplished with gingerness and muttered oaths, leaving his waistcoat unbuttoned to avoid putting too much pressure on his injury. He found his weapons and he armed himself, though he didn't bother to load the pistols. There was no need now.

He took extra care fist-blocking out his hat. It had served him well.

Grissot's creaked and hummed with the soft sounds of a tavern's daily routine in the absence of customers. It all smelled of old wood, and too many people. The hall and stairs were dark, but Bill managed to grope his way through by instinct.

He saw Long Cathy again in the common room, composed and calm, alone at a small table with a bottle of whisky. Sunlight poured in through the glass windows like an army of avenging angels, burning Bill's eyes into a squint. "Thank you, ma'am," he said to her, sweeping his hat. "I find that I must add you to my list of creditors, for laundry, clothing, hospitality, and medical services."

"And drink," she added, pouring him a glass.

"And drink. Honor," he said, belting the whisky back. The throbbing in his head and his shoulder both eased slightly. He would have liked to take the whole bottle.

"In defense of innocence." She drank.

"Thank you, ma'am," Bill said, beginning to feel like himself again. "As it happens, I'll be visiting Mr. Hackett's in an attempt to resolve some of my outstanding debts this very day, but I expect that I'll find you eternally in my ledger on the creditor side."

"Bill." Cathy looked as earnest, as direct, as uncomposed as he had ever seen her. "Sir William. I don't know what you're involved in that has you trafficking with beastfolk and being shot, but I urge you to be careful. There is at least one heart in New Orleans that would grieve for you."

It took Bill a moment to recover his balance.

"The beasts are terrifying and strange," he managed to agree, and he winked at her, "but in my experience, Mrs. Filmer, the Spaniards are much, *much* worse."

He didn't allow himself to linger—Etienne Ukwu would be up and looking for Bill soon, if he wasn't already. He kissed her hand, bowed, and squinted out into the warm, bright afternoon.

No sign of the bishop's collectors on the street. For that matter, no sign of the gendarmes, or any other of the chevalier's men. And no sign of the thugs who worked for Don Luis Maria Salvador Sandoval de Burgos. Just the iron grillwork of the Quarter's balconies, the walls of jasmine and wisteria, and a token population of residents getting ready for the evening.

Bill headed straight for Hackett's.

It was noon, and the pawnbroker's shop was open. The boardwalk creaked under his boots and a tiny bell above the door jingled as Bill entered. Hackett himself manned the counter, with his fine silver hair, his jolly lined face and the leaping gleam in his slitted eyes. Around the other three walls of the shop were shelves groaning with all manner of pawned objects.

"Captain Bill." Hackett dealt with old soldiers on a regular basis, and was known for treating them with sympathy.

With a heavy heart, Bill laid both his pistols and the scabbarded sword on Hackett's thick countertop. "Mister Hackett," he pleaded, "you know I'm not good at figures. I beg you to treat me generously."

With very little discussion—Bill could not bear to negotiate when money was at issue—Hackett loaned him six Louis d'or and gave Bill the ticket that would let him redeem the weapons for nine looeys if presented within a month.

Interest again, dammitall.

Bill looked at the six gold coins in his hand with ashes in his mouth. It wasn't even enough to pay off the bishop.

He'd go get his rifle and pawn that, too. Then pay off Bishop Ukwu and . . . and what? He hated to be without weapons; Bill had enemies. He needed to find work to let him buy back his weapons and pay Madame Beaulieu. Maybe he could force Don Sandoval to pay what he owed in a week, though how he would persuade the dago to do that without guns, Bill couldn't imagine. Pure bluster, maybe. If he was lucky, maybe he could find someone else to loan him the money to buy back his weapons from Hackett, and then recover his twenty looeys from Don Sandoval and pay off the new loan. Thinking about money made his head hurt.

Bill squinted as he stepped onto the boardwalk.

He made it onto the street.

He made it to the Pension de Madame Beaulieu. Madame Beaulieu stood in the ferns and seemed a bit nervous as she nodded to him, passing through the door on his way up to retrieve the long Kentucky rifle for pawning.

Her nerves disquieted him. No doubt she was anxious to be paid, but she had never seemed uncomfortable around him before.

Bill hesitated.

Best not go upstairs—Etienne might be waiting, or the chevalier's men. Bill retreated from the courtyard and stepped back out the front door.

A heavy cudgel cracked down on the back of his skull. He staggered off the boardwalk onto the dirt and fell face up, seeing nothing but the merciless blare of the sun until Etienne Ukwu's smiling brown face poked into one corner of his whirling field of vision.

"Ubosi oma," Etienne greeted him. "Your time is up. You owe His Grace eight Louis d'or."

Bill had lost his hat. His head hurt, and his shoulder, and his pride. He still clutched the six looeys in his hand, and he tried to hold them out to Etienne, fumbling them onto the dirt in an attack of vertigo.

Etienne's thugs crowded around as Etienne picked up the coins and counted them. "I know you are not very good at mathematics, Bill." Blasted iggy accent made him sound cheerful all the time. "But even you must realize that eight is greater than six."

Bill gaped like a fish as he tried to form words of explanation, tell Etienne that he had been on his way to resolve the debt at this very moment, but no sound came out. His shoulder felt as if a mule had just kicked him. He pulled the claim ticket from his pocket and tried to show it to Etienne, but he was overwhelmed by vertigo and nausea and he dropped the paper.

"We have taken your rifle from your lodgings and will sell that to achieve final satisfaction of your outstanding debt to His Grace," Etienne said. "Which means that I, to my regret, will not be killing you today." He stooped and picked up Bill's dropped claim ticket, looked at it and tucked it into the pocket of his waistcoat. "Perhaps Mr. Hackett will wish to purchase it."

Mercy from the bishop's son seemed impossible, and the mere hint of it made Bill nervous. What was going on? Was Etienne about to take off his arm, or torture him?

But Etienne and his red sash and his men simply walked away, leaving Bill lying on the earth with his head running around him in circles. Bill took a deep breath, managed to sit up—

and found himself surrounded by blue-and-gold coated gendarmes.

The chevalier's men.

Hell's Bells.

"You're forgettin' the bears."

⎯⎯➤◦⬱⎯⎯

CHAPTER SEVEN

Ezekiel Angleton had slept poorly.

Even before that whistling pagan oaf Obadiah Dogsbody had blundered back empty-handed, Ezekiel's evening had been haunted by strange visions. It had been a long, hard ride from Philadelphia, sharing stale beds with Obadiah in ordinaries along the way, so he'd curled up in his cloak on a bed of leaves and dozed off. He'd slept fitfully, but he'd been interrupted by strange dreams.

He had dreamed he was someone else, or perhaps some*thing* else, and that thing was locked in a body that was as unfamiliar to it as it was to Ezekiel. This was just like the dreams that had trampled through his restless nights on the hard ride south.

On those previous nights he had dreamed he ran over hills and through forests, encountering no one. Ezekiel had told himself the strange fluidity of the movement and the constant slapping of branches on his dream-face were reflections of his state of mind, dream-mirrors of the uncertain wilderness in which his soul wandered, until he could capture the witchy-eyed girl and end her blasphemy against the Penn family name.

Last night, dozing beside his fire in the forest and waiting for Obadiah to bring him the girl, the dreams had returned. Moreover, they had become prophetic. In fragmented images split up by his surfacing to the waking world for air he had seemed to follow his servant Obadiah Dogsbody upon the slopes of Calhoun Mountain. There he'd seen Obadiah drink himself stupid and then release the girl, so Ezekiel had not truly been surprised when Obadiah had returned to camp alone.

It had been a harsh disappointment, but a hurt that brought its own balm. Knowing his dreams had been the vehicle of prophecy thrilled Ezekiel Angleton, and he thought of the next part of his evening's visions, in which he'd found the Penn girl and her Appalachee beau and had attacked them, wrestling the man to the ground with his bare hands. Surely, this was a great portent for this morning's venture: as Obadiah had lost the girl, Ezekiel would find her again.

But what did it mean that in his dream the cracker lad had arisen with a handful of fire like the cherub sealing off the gate of Eden, and had struck Ezekiel in his dream-face, wounding him gravely? Ezekiel rubbed his cheek at the memory of the dream-pain, searing and intense, and of the smoke that poured out of his burning dream-flesh.

Was the Appalachee lad Ezekiel's death? Did his hand hold for Ezekiel the fires of Hell? Did God have no grace to pour down on him?

At the least, the dream contained both a promise and a warning, and Ezekiel would take great care.

The Philadelphia Blues had found him early this morning; they, too, had ridden hard from Philadelphia, and only Ezekiel's earlier start had gotten him to Nashville one day ahead. He had been deep in prayer and the Psalms in the small canvas tent he had made Obadiah pitch for him when a drumming of hooves had preceded the arrival of men on horseback.

Ezekiel had emerged from the tent, feeling the pleasant stretching burn of legs unkinking after spiritual exercise. His heart struggled with a more puzzled feeling. Wrestling through the strange images of his dreams, he had hounded on their trail through verse after verse, in Isaiah and Daniel and Zephaniah, and finally he had struck upon the eighty-second Psalm.

Captain Sir Daniel Berkeley had pounded into view at the head of the Blues astride his enormous gray horse. "You're fast, Parson." He swung easily to the ground.

Captain Berkeley was tall and muscular, with a high forehead and aquiline nose framed dramatically by his glossy black perruque. Berkeley must be in his mid-forties, Ezekiel guessed. His

Imperial Majesty Thomas Penn had elevated him to the captaincy of the Blues immediately following his own coronation nearly fifteen years earlier, at the same time he had elevated Ezekiel.

The years since then had mostly been spent in the saddle, either traveling with Thomas or riding on his errand. Berkeley didn't show the years or the miles. He was lean and hard, he breathed through flared nostrils, and his eyes stared everywhere they looked.

The captain rode behind Ezekiel now on the huge gray horse of which he was so proud, Obadiah following him, and then the Philadelphia Blues, in Indian file.

The Imperial House Light Dragoons were the emperor's personal troops; they were his bodyguard in war and on long journeys, and his special agents at other times. They were mounted gunmen, and each was armed with a brace of long horse pistols, large-bored and designed to kill men in single, accurate shots, as well as the longer Paget carbine. Strapped behind his saddle, each man carried a box of paper cartridges, prepared in advance to speed reloading time. In addition, they carried swords. By tradition, they rode under the emperor's banner when in his company, and otherwise had no insignia, being recognizable only by their blue uniforms, simple and sturdy for the road, with a dress set embroidered elaborately in gold and buttoned with ivory disks. Even their captain wore no special marker of rank; his men knew who he was. The Blues wore tricorner hats against the rain and long riding coats against the October chill.

I have said, Ye are gods, said the Psalmist.

Was that a message for Ezekiel, too, as his dreams were? Was it as a god that Ezekiel ran through the forests of the New World in his dream, battling Appalachee angels of fire? *All of you are children of the Most High. But ye shall die like men, and fall like one of the princes.* Surely, a god need not fear death. Nor need a god fear failure; perhaps the Psalmist only congratulated Ezekiel on his work in the service of God, and promised success. And yet the Psalmist warned the gods that they should die like men.

What gods were these?

No, Ezekiel thought. *Ye shall be as the gods, knowing good and evil.* That was in the Bible too, but it was a lie in the mouth of the serpent, it was false Ophidian doctrine. God was god and man was man and the only bridge between them was God's grace, which was not for all of the children of Eve and which could not be had by any of the Soulless, the Children of the Serpent.

Ezekiel frowned. Whatever it was he had dreamed of being in his forest-running, Appalachee-battling dreams, it wasn't a god.

On the highway they had ridden two abreast, out the Charlotte Pike Gate in a light drizzle of cold rain. At the turn-off to Calhoun Mountain—a faint path indicated to them by an old man passing by with two oxen yoked to a dilapidated wagon, but only after payment of a gold sovereign—they had been forced by the narrower path to collapse into a single file.

Ezekiel no longer had his compass of the day before, nor all the materials to recreate it—he bit back his tongue from cursing Obadiah again—but he knew the way to Calhoun Mountain now, and he knew the Elector was hiding Mad Hannah's Hell-spawned, Ophidian child.

The Elector would be made to give her up.

Ezekiel rode first, and he abandoned his anonymity of the day before in favor of the black and white tabard with the hammer and nail emblazoned on its chest. The insignia marked him as a priest, or, as he preferred to think of himself, a knight, riding to holy war under the banner of St. Martin. Martin Luther himself had given it its military character. After he dethroned the tyrant Cetes from the Lord Mayoralty of Wittenberg, he had created the Order, appointed its first Father-General, and directed it to act in defense of the children of Eve.

God had given dominion over the earth to Adam and Eve and therefore to their children, the Book of Genesis clearly taught. That meant, as St. Martin had clarified in his *Ninety-Five Theses*, that it was an unnatural and unholy inversion of God's design for any child of Eve to be ruled by any creature other than another child of Eve. The Soulless could not be allowed to rule over the Souled, and so the first and irrevocable mandate of every member of the Order everywhere was to remove the so-called Firstborn from positions of dominion. St. Martin would not have them rule, in the church or in the palace.

Even when Penn blood coursed in their veins.

Especially when they were Penns.

Ezekiel had the blight-faced little abomination holed up now, and he felt great satisfaction at the prospect of her imminent capture. And if she moved again, his dreams would tell him.

They rode up the ridge through the soft rustle of drifting leaves, Obadiah occasionally bursting into snatches of whistled tune and then each time cutting himself off; Ezekiel recognized the songs as lewd ones. Obadiah was a brute and an infidel pagan, but he was useful—he ran errands and he was dependable muscle when force was called for.

He also stood as constant evidence to Ezekiel of the Fall, and of the imperfection of the children of Eve. He fought for them not because they were more virtuous or more noble than the Eldritch, but because that was the commandment of Ezekiel's God.

Also, Obadiah's presence reminded Ezekiel that even Christendom held many souls yet to come to Christ.

The Blues were more disciplined than Obadiah; they knew they were in territory that was in hostile hands, if not in the hands of outright enemies, and they rode in silence, watching the woods.

At the top of the ridge, they reached the mouth of a narrow canyon that cut up through the crown of the hill and led, the ox-driver had said, to the homes on the top of Calhoun Mountain; Ezekiel reined in his horse.

Ten Appalachee men in long hunting shirts, fringed jackets, and floppy hats lounged about the mouth of the canyon. More stood in the canyon and others likely lurked at the top. Ezekiel searched for the faces of Shadrach Calhoun and the other men who had ambushed him in the woods, laughing as they forced him to recite scripture and undress, but didn't see them.

He shook his head; he was not here to avenge his own harms, however egregious they were. Ezekiel closed his eyes and tried to remember last night's dreams—he didn't think he'd seen this place. Presumably the spot where he would catch the girl was further up.

Captain Berkeley eased up to Ezekiel's side. "Be wary of these highlanders, Parson. They dress themselves like vagrants, but they are famous shots, and they are not arranged so casually as they may appear."

It irritated Ezekiel to be called *parson*, which was not his title, since he was not a parish priest, and which was instead a deliberately barbed reminder that Berkeley was indifferent to his authority. Still, he looked again and saw Berkeley was right; each of the Appalachee men held a long rifle and many had a second close to hand, or a pistol tucked into a belt. All appeared to lie casually and relaxed, but each sat on or beside some boulder, stump, or crack that could provide cover from return fire.

"I see," he murmured. The heretic traitor Thalanes had done a despicable thing in concealing Mad Hannah's child, but he had hidden her well and in a place that was stoutly defended. Ezekiel was duly impressed. Impressed, but not daunted.

He was a paladin, and he rode under the banner of a crusade.

Ezekiel moved forward a few feet, to try to give the Blues behind him room to come up, but there was no clearing at the foot of the canyon, and most of the dragoons continued to sit in the saddle in single file. This also left them in a tactical position that was less than ideal, since it would force them to attack the defile one at a time, if this meeting came to blows.

"Be wary," Captain Berkeley repeated. "God's will no doubt shall come to pass, but there's no need for us to tempt fate with imprudence."

Ezekiel nodded, then cleared his throat and politely removed his tall black hat to address the Calhouns.

"Git the hell off my land!" one of the Calhouns snapped.

Ezekiel focused on the speaker. He was an old man, standing about halfway up the draw, with a cragged face under a blaze of snow-white hair. He wore all black and had just one arm. He was the only one of the Appalachee men who appeared to be without a weapon.

"Pardon me?" Ezekiel called.

"Youins are foreigners, armed and trespassin'! I repeat myself, git the hell off my land afore I decide to exercise my natural liberties and eject you by the seat of your too-tight britches!"

Ezekiel wasn't surprised to find that the crackers weren't predisposed to cooperate. That was fine with him; he had come prepared to cajole and bully.

"You must be the Elector Calhoun!" Ezekiel called. "I'm Father Ezekiel Angleton of the Order of St. Martin, confessor to His Imperial Majesty Thomas Penn. This is Captain Sir Daniel Berkeley of the Imperial House Light Dragoons, and those are the dragoons themselves on the trail behind me."

"The only man I e'er called 'father' is buried on this here mountain, you jackanapes!" Calhoun shouted back. "Your precious St. Martin was a robber, a lecher, and a drunk, and as far that poltroon's rank goes, I am, as it happens, Lieutenant Colonel Andrew Calhoun of the First Appalachee Volunteers.

"I stood tall against Wallenstein's Germans and Algonks in fifty-five and sixty, when I don't reckon either one of you was even born! Hell, for that matter, I don't reckon you's born when I fought Washington and Pontiac in sixty-three, and if you's alive when I personally drove the Spanish out of Natchez in seventy-nine, then you must a been tiny little shits, still wipin' your noses and your asses on your mammas' frilly skirts!"

Ezekiel realized he'd backed his horse away a step under the verbal onslaught. He urged the beast forward again.

"I have an Imperial Warrant," he called, "for the arrest of a girl name Sarah Penn. You may know her as Sarah Calhoun. We aren't actively seeking trouble, and expect to receive your assistance in locating Miss Calhoun."

"Iffen you reckon I'm fixin' to surrender to you fellers anybody at all as goes by the last name of Calhoun, you can jest piss right off and die!"

"Even if the girl isn't really a Calhoun?" Ezekiel called.

The Elector ignored his question. "As to your havin' an imperial warrant, I b'lieve you'll find you left the highway several miles back—this is Calhoun land, and your warrant ain't worth the breath it'd take you to read it!"

Ezekiel frowned. This wasn't how it was supposed to go. He knew he was in no position to mount an actual attack here, but he'd expected the Blues to have more weight as a threat than they appeared to have.

"Easy, Father," Berkeley warned him, and it almost warmed Ezekiel's heart to hear his proper form of address in the captain's mouth. "If we are to fight these men, we must choose a better battleground. This is terrible positioning, and the cards do not favor us today."

The cards? Ezekiel sighed.

"Technically the warrant is, of course, only executable on Imperial land, you're correct, and the emperor respects your liberties," he called to the Elector, trying to mollify him before the hammer blow. He was lying; the emperor acted off Imperial land as often as he could get away with it. That was what the Imperial Foresters were for, and the Philadelphia Blues, and that didn't even begin to take into account the Pacification of the

Ohio. "Of course, he's also your emperor, and he expects that in return for his acknowledgement of your liberties, you'll cooperate with the exercise of his power. Give us the child Sarah, and there's no need for any violence."

The craggy face broke open in wild, high-pitched laughter that drew hearty chuckles from the other Calhoun men and went on too long, leaving Ezekiel feeling nervous. Abruptly, the laughter stopped—

the Elector raised his one arm above his head—

every Calhoun rifleman suddenly pulled up his gun, and a bristling briar patch of firearms stared down at Ezekiel Angleton and the Blues.

"You forget yourself, Angleton!" the Elector shouted. "I don't need no civics instruction from a whelp like you, I was there in eighty-four! I signed the Compact myself with the one arm George Washington left me, and I know good and damn well exactly what the Imperial nonsense is all about!"

"Blazes, Parson," Captain Berkeley muttered. "What are you thinking?"

"I didn't sign the Compact to take John Penn as my king, you ignoramus! I signed it to tell him iffen he ever got too big for his britches, we'd throw him on out and elect us someone new! As for *Thomas* Penn, Hell, I voted *against* that Chaldee numbskull!"

"Are you repudiating your emperor?" The constitutional talk left Ezekiel irritated, especially in light of the assault he'd suffered the night before. "Are you telling me you plan to invoke an election?"

"As to expectations," Calhoun shouted again, "yours *and* little Tommy Penn's, you can expect that when I lower my arm, every one of my boys is gonna shoot you. You can expect that some of youins'll escape, and you can expect that some of us'll likely die in the return fire. But you can be damned sure that St. Martin Luther'll end the day down one father, and the emperor down one cap'n."

Ezekiel gnashed his teeth. His horse fretted beneath him and he jammed his hat back onto his head.

"Take all the time you want to chew it over," the Elector called. "Only recognize that I ain't got no Aaron up here to prop my one arm up, and these wild-eyed sons of Jacob'd be more'n happy to shoot themselves a few Amalekites!"

"About face!" Captain Berkeley called. "We're finished here!" he snapped, and pushed past Obadiah to lead his men back down the ridge.

Ezekiel took one long look at the Calhoun riflemen and the mountain above them. He felt anger, but he wasn't discouraged. Somewhere up there, he knew he would encounter Sarah Calhoun and her young highland friend, and he expected to defeat them. He only needed to understand what the dream-fire was, and then he would be prepared for battle.

Laughter from the ravine followed him down as he pushed his horse to catch up to Captain Berkeley.

"Captain," he began, attracting the man's attention by calling over his shoulder, "thank you for your wise counsel and support. Let's discuss the possibilities of laying siege to this mountain."

Cal held the spoonful of moonshine with a pinch of gunpowder in it in his left hand. In his right he held the Elector's rifle, primed and cocked but not loaded. He brought the firing pan of the rifle close to the spoon and angled the gun to direct the sparks.

"What are you doing?" Thalanes leaned over Cal's shoulder.

Sarah was content to sit a couple of paces away and not too close to the still, in case anything exploded.

Cal squeezed the trigger.

Poomf!

The sparks lit the gunpowder and the moonshine both, and Cal was suddenly holding a spoonful of blue flame. "I'm jest proofin' the moonshine." He held up the burning spoon. "See? Burnin' blue, moonshine's true."

He shook the blazing alcohol out onto the cave floor and toed sand over it to snuff out the flame.

"I thought you were New Light, like your cousins," the little monk said.

Cal put the spoon away. "Jest 'cause I'm New Light don't mean I can't know how to proof moonshine."

The three of them were in the Crooked Man's Cave, where they had spent the last hours of the night. It was a shallow depression in the limestone, no more than five or six of Calvin's paces deep. There were dirty blankets in the corner, some obscene chalk sketches on the stone, and a rough bit of wood sculpture in the back that looked vaguely like an ugly old man with a hunched back and twisted legs. Under the sculpture lay bits of tobacco ash and shattered glass that might be the remains of sacrifices.

And there was a still, consisting mostly of a copper pot and a wooden barrel, with a couple of glass bottles' worth of genuine corn likker that Cal had just judged to be good.

"So I guess you'll bring along the moonshine," Thalanes concluded.

"Yeah, I reckon I will." Cal tapped the cork back into the bottle and slid the bottle into his pack. "Iffen we don't want to drink it ourselves, somebody else will, and we can always trade. Lessen you've got a problem with that."

"Don't you feel like it's theft?" Thalanes asked.

Cal shook his head. "This cave is on Calhoun land, and this still is a Calhoun still, and besides, I done these boys plenty of favors when they needed them. Now I reckon they can do me one."

"Ain't you gonna tell us where we're a-goin'?" Sarah asked. "I don't reckon you're fixin' to live the rest of your life in some cracker pagan temple cave."

"*Aren't.* You should practice your Penn's English," Thalanes advised her. "Not only will people take you more seriously, outside of Appalachee, but you'll be less conspicuous."

"*Ain't* that somethin' of a contradiction?" Sarah defied him.

"Nothin' wrong with the word *ain't*," Calvin grumbled.

Thalanes hummed cheerfully.

The three of them had slipped down Calhoun Mountain in the rainy night, carrying packs of necessaries, wrapped in wool coats (even the monk had borrowed one), and shod in walking shoes—moccasins, in fact, Indian-style but stitched by the nimble fingers of Calhoun women.

There had been Imperial soldiers on the track, on the highway and in the woods, men with long blue cloaks and blue tricorner hats, but after rubbing a little dirt on each of their cheeks the monk had whispered "*oculos obscuro*" and advised them to walk casually and quietly past. None of the soldiers batted an eyelash. Sarah felt like laughing out loud as she passed within five feet of two guards standing on the edge of the Charlotte Pike, directly in front of them, and they continued their empty men's talk about horses and women the entire time.

The men were the Philadelphia Blues, Thalanes had explained as they walked, the Imperial House Light Dragoons. The emperor's personal elite military unit, his bodyguard, the men who undertook his most sensitive errands. When her father had been the Imperial Consort, they had ridden with him. Sarah had felt uneasy just thinking about it.

Calvin had brought the three of them to the Crooked Man's Cave, where they'd gotten a few hours of sleep and acquired some moonshine. Now, in the gray of the morning, they shouldered their packs again.

"Farewell, cave," Thalanes said as they stepped out. "You've been good to us, despite your occupant."

Cal shrugged. "In these hills, the line between a haint and a saint can git so fine you don't even see it."

Sarah's pack held a little clothing and a bedroll, and she carried a gift from the Elector in the shape of a new walking staff, with a crisp, delicate horse's head carved into the top of it. "White ash," he had said to her in his gruffest voice at their parting. "It's good against evil spirits."

"The horse for fast travel?" she had asked.

He'd nodded. "And for the knight on the chessboard, who jumps o'er his enemies without stoppin'."

"You might could a jest carved me a bird," she had teased him. "Then I'd a flew."

"I would a done so, child," his eyes had twinkled at her, "only I worried the short-legged priest wouldn't e'er a kept up."

Cal was burdened with the bulk of their camp gear: canvas sheets that could be made easily into a tent, Calvin's bedroll, a pot, some rope, flint and steel, a little dry tinder. They each had a waterskin, but they carried very little food: a bag of bonny clabber, a wrapped parcel of griddle cakes, and some strips of air-dried beef. And now two bottles of moonshine liquor.

Cal also carried his tomahawk and lariat, strapped to his belt with thin rawhide ties, his boot knife, and a gift from the Elector that Sarah knew he had found extravagant: the Elector's own Kentucky rifle, shiny and worn but perfect in its fringed buckskin sheath slung over Calvin's shoulder. Iron Andy had taken it down from over the fireplace himself and pressed it into Calvin's hands, whispering something to Cal that Sarah hadn't heard, but that had resulted in him blushing. Along with the rifle, the Elector had given his grandson the related tools, powder and bullets, and a bag that clinked mysteriously before disappearing into Calvin's pack.

Other than the borrowed coat, the monk had left as he had arrived, carrying nothing but a worn old satchel, of the contents of which Sarah was completely ignorant.

She was also ignorant of their destination. This left her at the mercy of the meddling little priest, but this morning the Elector had insisted, and she had given in, feeling she was doing her duty to the man who had raised her. The night before last Calvin had fended off the clay-men, but not without some injury, and she no longer felt safe on Calhoun Mountain. Also, she doubted her own ability to escape the forces that pursued her without assistance, or with Cal's help alone. The little monk was a clever wizard, and she resolved to get him to teach her how he did it. She could always slip away later, if she found an opportunity.

As long as Thalanes was holding out on her, though, she felt no obligation to be forthcoming with him. She hadn't told him, and, at her urging, Cal had also kept silent, about the claylike faceless men that had attacked them. She couldn't put her finger on a good reason why she should withhold this information, only that it pleased her to do so. Pride, maybe—she didn't want it known that she had put herself and Calvin in as much danger as she had. Sheer mule-headed stubbornness. And a will to pay the monk back, tit for tat, for his close mouth. They had told him about Obadiah Dogsbody and his men, and the hectoring that afforded him seemed to satisfy his yearning to indulge in I-told-you-so, at least for the present.

The best thing about being on the road was that, as long as they were walking, the monk couldn't crowd too close.

They pushed over the top of a low ridge, feet plowing furrows in the drifts of fallen leaves, and Sarah realized where they were headed. "You're takin' us to the Trace, ain't you?" When Thalanes continued his introspective humming, she tried again. "You're taking us to the Natchez Trace, *aren't* you?"

"Yes," he said brightly. "The Imperial Highways are quicker, and so are the rivers, but on the old roads you attract less attention."

"You attract bandits," Cal observed doubtfully, "and bears."

"I'll be counting on your help against both," Thalanes said. "The Elector spoke very highly of your shooting."

"I most gen'rally hit what I aim at," Cal allowed.

"He's even better with the tomahawk," Sarah boasted for him. Cal had been subdued since his failed effort to abduct her and she worried about his morale. "And he's hell on wheels with the lasso."

"No wonder the Elector insisted that he accompany us," the monk said. "Though I suspect it may also have to do with Calvin's own repeatedly expressed preference."

Cal just blushed. "It ain't jest my druthers. The Elector wanted me to keep Sarah safe."

"*Calvin* is an interesting name," Thalanes continued. "You're named for the French lawyer, I guess? The man who defended John Dee and Giordano Bruno against blasphemy charges?"

"He didn't reckon a man ought to be killed for disagreein' with his priest," Cal muttered. "It's a common enough name in Appalachee."

"It's a fine name," Thalanes concurred.

"It ain't... it *isn't* just the attention, though, is it?" Sarah pressed. "I mean, in the one day I've known you, you've changed my face, stared down Shadrach Calhoun, and turned me invisible, so I don't think you're worried you might run into that Martinite again on the highway." She had an idea as to what drove the little man's thinking, but she wanted him to admit it. "I mean, you're a wizard."

"There are darker things on the road than Ezekiel Angleton," Thalanes replied, and Sarah felt a momentary twitch of guilt wondering whether he already knew, somehow, about their clay attackers, "though you shouldn't underestimate the Right Reverend Father, either. But you're right, there are other reasons to be on the old paths."

Sarah waited, but the monk was silent.

"I'm not a child, you know," she told him.

He looked startled. "Do you feel that I'm treating you like a child?"

"Like a *stupid* child." Her face was hot. "You want me to follow you around, but you won't tell me why or where, and you hide even the little answers, like why you want to travel on the Natchez Trace, even though it's lousy with outlaws and we only have the one rifle among the three of us! You can say *let no will be coerced* until the cows come home, *Father*, but dragging me around in ignorance and fear is the same thing as telling me what to do."

The monk stopped mid-stride and they all came to a halt in the leaves; his face looked as if he had been slapped. Sarah had a momentary impulse to apologize, but bit her tongue and defied him with her eyebrows instead.

"You don't need to fear nothin', long as I'm here," Calvin offered. "I got the tomahawk as well as the gun."

Thalanes shook his head as if he was emerging from under water. "I forget how smart you are. And how well Andrew Calhoun has taught you." He laughed and shook his head again. "You're just like your mother."

"A crazy woman," Sarah said pointedly. "I see you've been attending the Calvin Calhoun school of compliments and gallantry."

"Hey!" Cal objected.

"The Empress Hannah was never mad." Thalanes sobered suddenly, and was silent for a moment. "You're right, of course. Demanding that you act without information and in fear for your lives is no better than coercion. My only defense is that I, too, act out of great fear. Tonight... when I am comfortable that we are well away from prying eyes and curious ears...I'll tell you where I would like you to go with me." He sighed wistfully and his eyes twinkled. "I fear Palindres would be disappointed with me. The free will of others is such a fragile thing."

Sarah felt slightly mollified. "I reckon...I *think* he'd be proud of you for trying so hard."

The little monk smiled. "I hope so." He resumed walking. "As to why I wish to travel on the Trace, I assume you must be baiting me for some reason, since you are an accomplished hexer yourself. Nevertheless, as a sign of good faith, I'll stick my foot in the trap.

"The Imperial Highways are fast, efficient roads. They're fast and efficient because they're made by surveyors, geographers, and engineers, men who take square and compass to a map and plot the shortest distance between two points. The pikes are geometric, abstract and rational, and if you wish to walk from Nashville to Philadelphia taking the smallest possible number of steps, it would be hard to do better than the Imperial Highways.

"The old roads are different. Most of them were old before man saw them."

"By 'man,' do you mean just the sons and daughters of Eve, or are you including the Firstborn?" Sarah asked, mostly to show him that she was paying attention, and that she knew very well what he was talking about.

Thalanes nodded. "I mean the Eldritch, too. All of the children of Adam. The old roads were made by animals, by spirits, by the lines of the land itself, and those movements and those shapes had power in them, and they imbued power into the roads. Adam's children, coming later, marked the old ways with cairns and standing stones, and celebrated their intersections with henges and temples . . . and they found that there was power in the roads."

"Ley lines," Cal jumped to the point. "They's a ley line runnin' down the Trace?"

"Yes," the monk said. "Sarah, have you ever had occasion to use a ley line? Are you able?"

"I've done my fair share of hexing," she admitted, "but all little things. I've never tried to do anything you'd call wizardry, or gramarye, nothing so big that I didn't have enough power to do it myself. I don't know if I'm able or not. Besides, you've got to be careful. Too much hexing'll dry your fluids right up."

"That why all the good hexers are shriveled old women?" Cal asked. "I mean, other'n you, Sarah? Not that they's so many good hexers, 'cause they ain't."

"Magic doesn't dry up your fluids," Thalanes said.

"Sure, it does," Sarah disagreed. "Cal's right, I ain't the only hexer on Calhoun Mountain, but the others're broken old women. Granny Clay used to hex, when she was a girl. I heard she used to turn heads from Louisville to Chattanooga."

"Then she got old," Cal said. "And not in a good way."

The monk nodded. "I don't disagree that magic is hard on your body, it definitely is. I'm just saying that it doesn't 'dry up' your 'fluids.' You see, any magical act takes energy. Really, it's more basic than that—any act at all, physical, magical, mental, or spiritual, requires some kind of energy. Every person—every animal too, every living thing—has its own supply of magical energy. Call it power, or mana, or chi, or orenda. Ordinary, everyday sorts of spells, like cantrips to mend a pot, or soothe the pain of a burn, or find your way home, can be cast using your own personal reserve. For a lot of magicians, of course, that's all the magic they can do."

"And most folks can't do any magic at all," Cal observed. "Not for lack of puttin' pins into dolls or drops of blood into beer, it jest don't work for lots of people."

Thalanes nodded agreement. "A wizard's reserve of energy then recovers with rest and food, just like physical energy. Not *just like* physical energy, it *is* physical energy, and casting spells can make you tired and sick. I'm sure you've noticed that, haven't you, Sarah?"

It was Sarah's turn to nod.

"Pushing yourself too hard magically can age you, too," the monk said. "And if you wanted to cast a more powerful spell than your own body can power, you would need to use another energy source."

"Like a ley line," Cal said. "Seems easy enough."

"Many things in the natural world generate energy. The tides, the motions of heavenly bodies, births, even some deaths. Some of this energy dissipates, or is consumed, and some of it gets trapped in the ley lines. They are reservoirs of magical power, shaped by the face of the land and the patterns of life upon it. Not just anyone can use them, though. It takes training, and a natural gift, to be able to sense and draw energy from the lines."

"Not even wizards?" Cal asked. "Not even all wizards can use a ley line?"

"Not even all wizards," Thalanes agreed. "And those who can, use them with caution. Too much energy running through a wizard is like too much water in a riverbed—it will do damage."

"Make you tired and sick and old," Cal inferred.

"And dead," Thalanes added. "Magical power can kill you as easily as a bolt of lightning. It's not much different from a bolt of lightning, in fact."

"So you want to travel on the Natchez Trace because, being a wizard, you'll have access to magical power," Sarah concluded.

"And therefore I'm not so very worried about bandits," Thalanes agreed. "Which is a little foolish of me, because a gang of bandits in any reasonable size would be a serious threat to us. And even a single bandit could take us by surprise and kill one of us before we could stop him, if he wanted. But still."

"And you're forgettin' the bears," Cal reminded him cheerfully. "And what if they was magical bears, as could use ley lines to find their way home, and mend their bear pots? I still reckon they's reason to be afeared."

"There always is," said the monk. "There always is."

"The regalia of Cahokia," Sarah said, drawing her thought out as it occurred to her. "You said they were things of power. What kind of power? The same kind of power as ley lines? Magical power?"

Thalanes looked thoughtful. "I don't really know," he eventually told her, and Sarah thought his answer was at least half an evasion.

✧   ✧   ✧

"I reckon I should beg your pardon . . . Father, for somethin' I'm fixin' to do," Cal said, and then his eyes widened. "I reckon I should beg both your pardons."

It was night, and Calvin had settled them into a sheltered glade far enough from the road to be hidden. He'd lit a fire, laid out bedrolls (no tent necessary, because rain was a stark improbability) and then built the fire while he and Sarah nibbled on griddle cakes (Thalanes had declined) until it had a solid bed of coals.

Sarah lay back on her bedroll, looking at the bright stars of Orion through the leafless branches of the maples, ashes, and dogwoods surrounding them. Her feet hurt. She was accustomed to walking everywhere she went, but she wasn't accustomed to walking nearly as much as she had this day. The stars gave her some comfort—she'd lost her home and changed her identity, but the stars stayed the same.

What did Calvin have in mind?

"You can call me Thalanes," the priest said, "though I appreciate the gesture. What is it you intend to do?"

Cal held up a little bag—the pouch the Elector had so discreetly given him—and unknotted its strings, showing his companions that its contents were dully gleaming silver, in the shape of a few rings and coins. "The Elector said he wished he had some silver bullets to give me, but he didn't, so he made me promise I'd make a few, first fire we laid. Does this . . . ? I don't wanna hurt you."

"Then don't shoot me." Thalanes smiled. "I'm Firstborn, Calvin Calhoun, not a hobgoblin. Silver irritates my skin, and it may undo my magic, but it won't burn me at the touch or poison me."

Cal looked at Sarah expectantly; he wanted her permission, too. "Cal, I've been around silver all my life. You think all of the sudden it's going to kill me from ten feet away?"

Calvin shook his head sheepishly and set to work, filling a small long-handled iron cup with the odd bits of silver and resting it in the coals.

"Well, then, Thalanes," Sarah called out, "Calvin's shown us what's in his secret magical bag. Is it your turn now?" She began her question lightheartedly, but found she really wanted to know. The monk knew all her secrets and she didn't know his, and she found that hard to bear.

"I wondered why you were lighting such a large fire," Thalanes said, settling down with his back against a tree trunk. He had no bedroll, and showed no sign at all that he thought he needed one. "You're a good man, Calvin. Dependable and capable."

"Hear, hear," Sarah added, teasing absently. "Calvin for king!"

Calvin blushed furiously. "What's it like? I mean, to be . . . ?"

"Eldritch? Ophidian? One of Wisdom's Children? Firstborn? Of the Elder Folk? Serpentspawn? Serpentborn? Snakes? Wigglies? Fey? Elves? Fairies?" Thalanes smiled. "We're all children of Adam, Cal, and I suspect being me is much like being you, except perhaps for the fact that there are some people in this world who really, really don't like me just because I'm Firstborn."

"I been to Raleigh sellin' cattle and I seen the lights of Atlanta," Calvin responded. "Turns out they's folks in this world as really, really don't like me jest for bein' Appalachee."

"Touché," Thalanes said. "Adam's children are all hewn rough from the mountain stone. We must crash against each other until we become smooth."

"I reckon so," Cal agreed.

"It's too bad you're New Light, Cal," Thalanes said. "Your strong common sense and feel for the reality of people would have made you a good priest. Have you thought about being a lay preacher, at least?"

"A tent and cookies man?" Cal chuckled. "I reckon not." He poured molten silver into the grip-mold he had and set the cup back in the heat. A few moments later he plunked out a hot silver bullet onto the leather of his pack, and then carefully clipped away the sprue, dropping it gently back in the cup to melt again.

"Cal's already had a ministry of sorts," Sarah said.

"No I ain't."

"Now you're jest bein' modest." Sarah turned to the monk to explain. "Calvin here was a corn reader."

"*Was*," Cal said immediately. "*Was* a corn reader. I got the New Light now."

Thalanes furrowed his brow, then smiled. "You mean . . . you read to people's crops?"

"No harm in it, I reckon. I ain't sayin' I drove away evil spirits or nothing'. Jest readin' a little Gospel of John o'er a planted field, and if the farmer wanted to give me a little something for it, who's the worse?"

"No one's the worse," Thalanes agreed. "But you have the New Light now."

"I reckon I might could make eight bullets, all told," Cal said, veering back to the subject of the silver, "so let's be careful about what kind of critter we challenge to a firefight. Also, I'll keep the rifle loaded with lead, for now, jest in case we see somethin' worth eatin'."

"Eight silver musket balls is a lot," Thalanes said.

"The Elector ain't a poor man," Cal answered. "Lord hates a feller as don't know when to spend his money."

"As to my bag," the monk turned to Sarah's question, "like any wizard worth his salt, I carry a potion when I travel. Or at least, as you might say in Appalachee, I carry the fixin's."

"Show us," Sarah demanded.

"It's in the nature of a travel potion." The priest smiled. "I'll do better than show you—tomorrow morning, before we go, I'll share it with you. I'd have done it this morning, but I was drained already, from lack of sleep and all the hiding spells through the night."

"Where are we going?" Sarah asked. It was interesting to see Cal making bullets, but only because he was doing it with silver. Why did the Elector think he would need silver bullets? Had Cal told the Elector about their faceless claylike attackers? "You said you'd tell us."

"New Orleans," Thalanes answered immediately. "I am sorry I didn't tell you sooner, but I had the sensation, back at the mountain, that there were eyes upon us. I think we've left our pursuers behind, now, at least for the moment."

"What's in New Orleans?" she pressed.

"*Who* is in New Orleans, is the right question," the monk said. "When I took you, as a newborn baby, to hide you with the Elector and his family, two other trusted servants of your mother took your two siblings—your brother and your sister—and hid them elsewhere."

"You think one of them is in Louisiana?" Talk of Sarah's new identity made her jumpy.

"I don't know where they might be." Suddenly Thalanes seemed tired. "Wherever they are, they must be in danger, as you're in danger. I wish to find them, and take all three of you and hide you some place where you'll be safe from the ruthless ambition of your uncle, at least for a few more years."

"Well, who's in New Orleans, then?" Cal plunked out another bullet.

"The man who hid Sarah's brother was a soldier," the little priest said, "a good friend to your father, as I was, and present at your father's death...as was I. He's not the sort of man who readily disappears for very long, and after he hid your brother, he resurfaced in New Orleans. He's been there, I believe, these last fifteen years. He can help us find your brother and sister."

A shiver ran down Sarah's back, and she leaned back to focus on the night sky. That her mysterious unknown siblings were a brother and a sister made them begin to become real. She felt cheated that she had not been able to know her mother, Mad Hannah. And her father, too—Andrew Calhoun had been as good to her as any father could be, but knowing she was tied to some other man, a man she could never know or even see, made her feel bitter. Her sister and brother lived, though—*might* be alive—and she longed to know them.

"You described the regalia as 'things of power,'" she said. "If I had them, maybe I could use that power to protect my brother and sister. Maybe I could take back my father's throne."

Thalanes made no comment.

"What are their names?" she asked.

There was a brief silence, interrupted by the *plunk!* of another silver bullet falling onto the leather.

"Nathaniel Kyres Penn is the name your mother gave your brother," Thalanes said. "As she gave your sister the name Margaret Elytharias Penn. And, of course, you're Sarah Elytharias Penn."

"Calhoun," Sarah muttered, retreating from a sudden surge of hot emotion. "I like the name *Calhoun*."

"*Sarah Calhoun* sounds jest fine to me, too," Cal allowed, cutting away more silver sprue. She looked at him, on the verge of tears, and was grateful for the shy, slightly flirtatious eye he cast in her direction. The gratitude came with a pang of guilt—she'd hexed Cal with the same love charm she'd put on Obadiah, and clearly he hadn't yet recovered.

"I like it, too," Thalanes agreed, "but not for now. For now neither one of you can be a Calhoun, in case your uncle's agents are using that name to search for you."

"We could be called Carpenter," Cal suggested with a mischievous grin. "Like the Holy Family, fleein' your uncle King Herod, goin' down to the fleshpots of New Orleans."

Sarah laughed out loud and it felt good. "Only I ain't pregnant,

Calvin Calhoun, and iffen I was, no child of mine'd e'er turn out to be the Baby Jesus."

"I don't intend no comment on neither the pregnancy nor the virginity of any party," Cal said. "Likewise, though I do carry an axe, you shouldn't ought to imagine that I have any great skill at carpenterin'. I remain at best, like my father afore me, a halfway decent cattle rustler."

They all laughed. Sarah thought for a moment that she might tell Thalanes about the clay creatures, but she didn't. After all, they were a thing of the past, and the monk had said he thought they'd left their pursuers behind. Besides, a silver bullet should make short work of such creatures.

Instead, she asked a question. "You told me yesterday my father was killed by one of his own dragoons. What can you tell me about that man, the killer?"

Thalanes looked into the fire in silence for long moments. "Bayard Prideux," he named the traitor softly, and Sarah's heart felt a sharp pinch. "He was a young soldier. Not a very good one; he was undisciplined and lazy. I never understood why he did it. He killed your father in a terrible storm. We tried to catch him, but failed."

"Who's 'we'?" Sarah asked. "Were you there, then?"

"I was there," Thalanes said. "I was your father's confessor, and chaplain to the Philadelphia Blues. 'We' is the rest of the dragoons, the men who stayed faithful to your father. All old men now, if not dead."

"What's the name of the man we're going to find, then? The soldier who hid my brother, I mean?"

"Will," the monk said. "He was Captain of the Dragoons at the time and a minor hero of the Spanish War. He fell from grace. Rather, Thomas threw him from grace, immediately upon his rise to power."

"Will what?" Sarah insisted, "or is his name a secret, too?"

"William," Thalanes told her. "Captain Sir William Johnston Lee."

"I had hoped for at least a chicken gizzard,
or some John the Conqueror Root."

CHAPTER EIGHT

They took Bill's hat away.

They were rough about it, punching him, smashing him down with heavy boots, and shouting in French. They also took his coat.

Bill had never been arrested before, and had only the vaguest idea of what to expect next—and that was nothing good. The gendarmes of New Orleans didn't generally bother to arrest people, at least not in the Quarter. They weren't part of any judicial process, they were rabble control, and their job was to arrive after the commission of a crime, rough up a few people on the scene—ideally, but not necessarily, the guilty parties—and leave everyone duly admonished to stay on the chevalier's good side and stick to the Quarter.

For crimes committed elsewhere in New Orleans, people got arrested. Bill understood there were actual investigations, and even trials, though he'd never seen anything of either. He knew prisoners sat and rotted in the Hulks on the Pontchartrain Sea while they were being investigated and tried and he knew that most prisoners were found guilty.

Bill also he knew that there were essentially two punishments: payment of a large fine (the Chevalier's Ransom, *la rançon du Chevalier*, as some thought such payments had created the chevalier's proverbial wealth) and death by hanging (commonly called the Bishop's Penny, *le sou de l'évêque*, after the amount that the executed paid for the privilege of being buried in the potter's fields owned by the bishopric).

Bill half expected the gendarmes simply to shoot him on the boardwalk. Instead, they bound his hands together, tied them to a short lead rope behind one of their horses, and led him stumbling through the Quarter. Somewhere along the way a knotted noose was thrown around his head, and Bill struggled to keep from tripping over the length of line that dangled down his chest.

A good portion of that run was nothing but a blur of mocking faces to Bill, which was merciful. With great clarity, though, he observed *Grissot's* as he was made to trot past. He watched Cathy come out the door to join the jeering crowd on the boardwalk, and he saw her turn her head and look away.

Bill thought the shame might kill him.

They rode him right out of the Quarter and tossed him into the back of a cramped two-wheeled cart. Bill had never seen New Orleans from quite this vantage point, sky rattling over his face, teeth rattling against his jaw, the tops of tall buildings rattling past, and the warped wooden sides of a cart rattling in a frame around it all. Bouncing under the befouled and lichen-begrimed stones of one of the city's gates, Bill recognized it as the St. Louis, between the cemeteries.

They were bound for the Pontchartrain Docks, one of New Orleans's two commercial ports.

That meant the Hulks.

The gendarmes jerked him from the cart at the docks and kicked him into a splintering rowboat. In his still-oscillating vision, Bill saw the rows of tall warehouses, the wagons, the ships, the crowds of merchants and their servants, all staring. Two gendarmes climbed into the boat, before Bill and behind, and then the filthy boatman began to row.

"Merci," Bill managed to force through his teeth, with a smashed purple grin.

The boatman nodded.

"I must warn you, suh. I have no cash with which to offer a gratuity."

The gendarme Bill faced pulled two pistols, cocked their hammers and trained them both on Bill. Bill assumed the man behind him was similarly armed and occupied, and four guns were enough to keep Bill in line. He was battered and broken, his head swam, he could barely see, he felt like retching, and his hands were tied. It took a Herculean effort on Bill's part to sit up; that, and the tiniest amount of repartee, were all he could manage.

He focused on the small details of the gendarme's uniform to keep from vomiting. They wore blue and gold, which were also the Imperial colors, so the gendarme looked like a constabulary version of a member of Bill's old unit, the Philadelphia Blues. The fleur-de-lis was not nearly as handsome as the Penns' ship-and-eagle, but he would have been willing to wear it, in better circumstances.

Bill had in fact tried, shortly after his arrival in New Orleans fifteen years earlier, to get a post as a gendarme, or in the cheva-lier's house. He had thought that the combination of his military experience in the area and his Imperial credentials would make his acceptance inevitable, but he'd been mistaken. The recruit-ers had spoken only French, and had laughed at him until he'd given up and left.

The whole city was the same—no French, no Castilian, no work. Even the smugglers wouldn't take him on, without a little Igbo or some Catalan. And so Bill had found himself at the arse end of the empire, hiding from Thomas Penn's wrathful eye, unable to get work consistent with his station and forced to turn for his daily bread to low violence.

If only he'd been a Frenchman, it would have gone so much better for him. He would certainly be free now, and he might even be rich.

On the other hand, then he'd be a frog.

Bill's vision began to calm down and he looked past the gendarme before him to the front of the boat, at the French-man rowing. He was big-chested and long-armed, with the large, knuckly hands of a fighter. His visage was a fighter's too; he lacked one ear and the opposite side of his face had been badly burned.

Damn me. He probably couldn't even get work rowing the boat out to the Hulks, with his tiny smattering of French. How had he lived so long in this town and not learned the language?

The Frenchman eyed Bill, and Bill felt himself blush. Making a show of bravado, Bill sneered back at the man, eyes lingering deliberately on his burns and scars.

A gendarme cuffed him on the shoulder and the pain nearly knocked Bill to the bottom of the boat.

They were approaching the Hulks, and Bill squinted to get a better look. There were six of them, large sailing ships that had once prowled the seas against New Spain, or up the river after those Bantu who hadn't surrendered their ancestral occupation of piracy and settled down to the raising of cotton, or east along the coast of the Caribbean after Igbo and Catalan smugglers. Louisiana was a small territory, but its Chevalier was a wealthy and powerful man, and he cast a large shadow in the region.

After their years of service, the ships had been brought through the deeper-dredged channels of the sea and run aground here, then demasted and ballasted with rock to keep them permanently anchored. Bill saw shattered timbers in the forecastle and aftcastle of some of them, well above the waterline; those must be scars of the ships' final engagements, not worth repairing at the end of the great beasts' lives. They were green-ribbed and moldy, necrotic leviathans of wood breaching the surface of the water to feed.

The boatman directed the vessel toward one of the hulks, and Bill peered at its hull to try to read the gold-lettered name through the caked green: *Incroyable.* That sounded good, whatever it meant. It sounded tough. If Bill was going to be imprisoned on a ship, he preferred it to have a good, soldierly name. No *Queen Henrietta* for him, thank you, or *Adela Podebradas*, however much he admired the lady's verve.

On their slowly-rotting decks walked men in simpler blue uniforms, consisting of mere waistcoats—not gendarmes, but prison guards, still in the service of the chevalier but with much less dignity.

Bill wished he had a coin with which to tip the boatman, and tried to think of some other gesture of gallantry. Hatless and with hands tied, he couldn't even execute a proper bow. Well, he would do his best. He concentrated, summoning his most polished French phrases.

The boat bumped against a ladder on the side of the *Incroyable* and the boatman steadied it with one hand. Bill stood and bowed to the boatman.

"Merci beaucoup, Monsieur," he said, and he was pretty sure that this far, he was on solid ground. "Je me presente. Je suis le célèbre Bad Bill, Mauvais Guillaume, du Vieux Carré." He was reasonably sure that those were his name and the name of the Quarter in French.

The frog seemed to appreciate Bill's gesture. He stood and turned to Bill, still holding the ladder with one hand, and then he, too, made an uncomfortable bow, after which he jabbered some French. Bill tried to smile, and then submitted to the goading of his captors and went up the ladder.

Bill made it to the deck of the hulk with great effort and pain. He hauled his weight with his one good arm, the injured one flapping uselessly tied to it. All his strength and will would not have sufficed regardless, but for the constant pushing of a gendarme's shoulder below him.

When he staggered onto the deck he felt sick, tired, and weak, and his shoulder was howling at him. He leaned over to rest his elbows on his knees, panting and staring up close at the boards under his feet, the cloth and caulking between them fraying frighteningly. How old was this ship?

Bill stood upright, still breathing heavy, to face three prison guards in blue vests, hefting cudgels, and their leader, an ill-looking man Bill knew, but hadn't seen for fifteen years.

Was it possible, after all this time?

And here?

The man was thin and curved, with eyes too close together and lips too large for his face. Lank, greasy black hair fell to his shoulders. He wore the blue vest of his fellow guards, but, in what looked like an indication of superior rank, he also wore a blue cap and blue trousers, one leg of which ran down to a canvas shoe, while the other was knotted in a slovenly fashion around a wooden dowel.

"*Captain* William Lee," the peg-legged man sneered. "'Ow I would like to say zat I 'ave missed you."

Anger and lust for revenge welled up in Bill like a river in flash flood, but he forced himself to be cool. "I'm surprised to see you looking like this, Bayard," he said, pointedly addressing the other man familiarly. "I thought reptiles' legs grew back."

"You should not imagine zat it was you zat wounded my leg so," the Frenchman responded. "I broke it in ze fall."

Bill shrugged.

"God moves in mysterious ways, Bayard," he said. "Perhaps someday you'll fall again, and break the rest of you."

Bayard Prideux.

It had been fifteen years, and Bill's mind flowed with images.

Kyres Elytharias, the Lion of Missouri, king of the great Ohioan kingdom Cahokia and Imperial Consort, dead of multiple stabbing wounds among the red oak trees, Prideux standing over him, a chase in the rain, a sword battle. Bill had wounded the traitor, but he had disappeared in the lightning and the trees. Escaped, flown over the cliff as if he were a bird. They'd never found a body, and Bill had always hoped the man had drowned in the Ohio.

How long had he been in New Orleans? Had the two of them been in the same town all this time? Hell's Bells.

Bill really needed to learn French.

"You will not enjoy your new life, Captain Lee," Prideux informed him gleefully. "I am ze warden 'ere."

"I'm glad you've found your station," Bill snarled. "I have long thought you belonged among condemned men."

"I am a personal friend of ze chevalier." Prideux's haughty tone clashed with his grubby uniform. He said *chevalier* the Frog way, *shuh-VOL-yay*. "It is no accident 'e 'as given you to me."

Could that possibly be true? "I suppose that means that you're going up in the world, Bayard," Bill drawled. "Shame you aren't smelling any better."

"'E 'as made me promise not to kill you," Prideux told Bill.

"The chevalier is a gentleman."

"Of course, 'e 'as also insisted zat I make you suffer as much as I possibly can."

Something hard smashed onto the back of Bill's skull and he collapsed.

In the morning, Thalanes unveiled to Sarah and Calvin the mystery of his satchel, which turned out to contain a sack of roasted coffee beans and a small pot. When they awoke, they found the monk already up and a handful of the beans smashed between two rocks and boiling in water.

"I'm disappointed," Sarah admitted. "I'd hoped for at least a chicken gizzard, or some John the Conqueror Root."

"This will do us much more good," Thalanes assured her. "The potion will be ready momentarily and then we should go."

"You look tired." Cal unfolded himself out of his bedroll. "You sleep at all?"

"I couldn't," the monk admitted. "I believe there is something out there in these hills hunting us."

"They found us already?" Sarah snapped, getting up, alarmed.

"Not Angleton and his lackeys," Thalanes said. "Something else. Whatever it is, it hasn't found us yet, and I'm doing what I can to throw it off our trail. Still, we need to drink this and get going."

"You sure it ain't *found* us?" Cal asked. "Mebbe it jest ain't *attacked* us yet."

Sarah's own natural nerves took the baton from the monk, and she began looking over her shoulder and through the skeletal trees, wondering what could have been stalking them in the night. The clay things, maybe? Something worse?

They packed quickly, then poured the hot brown brew into three cups, and Thalanes muttered a little Latin over it: "*pedes accelero crures augeoque.*"

That seemed easy enough; was the Latin more effective than the songs and rhymes Sarah hexed with? Was that all there was to gramarye? Just Latin? She drank the plain black coffee and felt warmth and strength flow into her legs and feet.

"New Orleans is this way, boys," she said to them, and turned back toward the Trace.

They sped all that day at a fast walking pace, and Sarah's legs never tired. Thalanes's spell was a good one, then. Her feet hurt less than expected, too.

"I reckon we could swap stories," Calvin suggested, a few minutes out of their camp. "It'd make the walkin' easier. Lessen you think there's somethin' so close on our trail we shouldn't ought to talk at all."

"I've told my story," the monk said. "Does that make it your turn, or Sarah's?"

"Mine," Sarah jumped in, and she didn't wait for agreement. "Once upon a time there lived a barber. I say *once upon a time*, because I think this is a made-up story, but old Bishop Franklin made it up, so it's probably a good one. This barber lived in a small town, it might have been in Pennsland or the Covenant Tract, and I guess he was a good barber, because he got rich."

"How rich can a barber git?" Calvin asked.

"Rich enough," she explained, "that he traded under the sign of the silver shears. Sometimes he even cut with them, too. And one night his son comes into the shop and says 'give me my inheritance early, for I've found a lass and I wish to marry and set up in business as a brewer and the thing I can't do without in this world is money.'"

"This story is a little dark," Thalanes said softly. "Could we hear a happier tale?"

Sarah pushed ahead. She was glad to make the monk uncomfortable. "But the barber couldn't do without his money either. So the barber and his son fought like cats in a sack, and the son jumped on his horse and ran away. In the dark, the barber's son rode too fast, his horse stumbled, he was thrown from its back and he broke his neck. Folks ran to the barber for help, but when he arrived his son was dead."

"I reckon I heard this one afore," Calvin said. "It's one of the Poor Richard Sermons, ain't it?" Sarah shot him a stern glance and he wilted. "Well go on, I didn't say stop, I love to hear Poor Richard."

Thalanes looked at the ground and said nothing.

Sarah pressed on. "The son's fiancée was a witch and possessed of a dark and vengeful mind. Three days after his burial, in the dark of night, the barber heard clawing at the door. He tried to ignore it, but the clawing continued and then turned into howling, too, and finally he answered.

"And there was his son. Dead."

"But walkin'," Cal pointed out.

"'What do you want, my son?' asked the barber, who was a brave fellow.

"The son said nothing. He just whined and groaned and rumbled."

"Grumpy feller," Calvin observed. "I guess he would be, when he was about to git hisself married and jest up and died instead."

"'I see you're still anxious to marry and become a brewer,' the barber said. 'Come with me to the shop. In three days, your hair and nails have grown long enough to need trimming, and at the shop I'll give you your inheritance, my most prized possession.' Then the father led his son to his shop, and sat him in the chair, and took out his famous silver shears."

"Stab him!" Cal whispered, trying to give advice to the barber.

"The son couldn't talk, but groaned like he was full of complaints the whole time. The barber listened attentively and trimmed his dead son's nails, first one foot, then the other, now the left hand and at last the right. Finally, after the barber's son had told his bellyaches to his father, the father said, 'yes, son, I understand you, and I am very sorry to have caused you grief.' Then the barber cut his son's hair, kissed his son on the cheek and laid him back in his grave. And the dead man never returned again to trouble his parents."

She ended the story. Leaves fell gently around her as she walked.

Thalanes looked thoroughly disquieted. "I'm with Calvin. He should have stabbed the son with the shears."

"Aw, but you left out the best part," Cal protested. "It's a Poor Richard Sermon, you gotta have a moral."

"I don't care about the moral," Sarah said. "I just want to tell a story. Stick your own damn moral on it if you want, Calvin Calhoun."

"A soft ear turns away wrath," Thalanes suggested.

"No, you gotta say 'Poor Richard Says,' and it's somethin' stranger than that," Cal said. "Don't remember me, I think I can git it . . . somethin' like 'Poor Richard Says: family love survives the grave. So does a family quarrel.' That sound right?"

"If it makes you happy," Sarah conceded, "I bless your moral."

"Thank you." Cal grinned.

Calvin was smiling, but Sarah felt a pall over the party. She didn't know exactly what had caused it, but she felt she was to blame.

"I have another story I'd like to share after all," Thalanes said. "It's a little different in tone."

"You mean *happy*?" Cal asked.

"It's Scripture," Thalanes said. "Though not in the Bible as you probably know it."

"What does that mean?" Sarah found that she'd put herself out as much as she'd put out the monk with her story, and now she was relieved the others were talking. "Like those strange books that are read by Christians in the lands of the Turk?"

"Yes," the monk agreed, "like the *Book of Enoch*, or *Jubilees*, or the *Shepherd of Hermas*. I'm impressed you know about those. They're not your usual pulpit fare in Appalachee."

"I *don't* know about 'em." Cal squinted sidelong at Sarah, but his feigned suspicion dissolved into a grin. "Ain't no accounting for foreigners, I reckon."

"Think of it as a book like the Bible," Thalanes explained, "to be read along with the Bible. Only this is a book of Scripture that belongs to the Firstborn. It's not the only one, but it's one of my favorites, because it talks about the Creation, and is beautiful."

"Shoot," Cal told him.

"It's called *The Song of Etyles the Preacher*," Thalanes started. "'And God spake, and said, Shall we not give unto Man a companion? And God said, Yea. And God made for Man a companion, of starlight and river rock and foam of the sea. And God named her Wisdom, for she was more subtle than any beast of the field, and breathed upon her, and she arose and shone. And she bare unto Man daughters and sons, and the starlight was within them all the days of their lives.

"'And when the days of Wisdom were fulfilled and the light left her, her daughters and sons digged the earth and raised stones and built for her a place of vision and light that would be forever.

"'And God spake, and said, Shall Man be alone in his age? And God said, Nay. And God made for Man a new companion, of the rib of Man, for she would bear him up under his shoulder in his infirmity. And God named her Life, for her strength was new life to Man, and breathed upon her, and she arose and lived. And she bare unto Man sons and daughters, and they began from the first to slay each other.'"

Thalanes finished, and they kept walking.

Cal whistled. "Well," he admitted, "that's pretty. It ain't clear to me as it's any happier'n Sarah's Poor Richard Sermon, and I don't claim to understand it, but I reckon I like it anyway. Is it about Eve?"

"The Firstborn believe that Eve was Adam's second wife," Thalanes said. "His first was a great lady whose name is only spoken in secret, but who is sometimes called Wisdom, and who is known by many signs, including the Tree and the Serpent. This is a short account of her marriage to Adam, the great progenitor of all the human race."

Neither Sarah nor Calvin had anything to say to that, and they fell again to walking in silence.

To Sarah's relief, the pall was gone.

Late in the morning they stopped and ate bonny clabber. Sarah had been looking forward to watching the little foreigner try to eat the sour congealed milk; the monk made a displeased face as he chewed it, but it wasn't displeased enough, and she suspected it was an act for her benefit, which only put her in a grumpy mood. He knew the Elector, she realized, so he'd probably eaten clabber before. For all she knew, he loved bonny clabber.

Irritated, she made a point of starting first every time they set out after that and never calling for a stop, letting Thalanes or, more often, Calvin ask to be allowed to rest. She wanted to talk to the monk about magic, but she could wait—even at their accelerated pace, it would be two weeks or more before they reached New Orleans.

They were moving fast, though. They passed travelers on the road going both directions. Most of the travelers were either Appalachee hunters or long-shirted Igbo traders, but there were Bantu from the Cotton League (Sarah was disappointed that they didn't dress like pirates), Spaniards from Ferdinandia (who sort of *did* look like pirates, with floppy hats, earrings and pointed beards), four beguines who claimed they'd come all the way from Pennsland on business to a sister cloister in the Free Cities, Crown Land Cavaliers who rode fast and didn't look back, caramel-colored Memphites in layers of silk (whose trundling wagons, pulled by multiple yokes of sweating and cursing Draft Men, were so slow Sarah wondered how it could possibly be worth it to be pulled by slaves), a scrawny Wandering Johnny from Youngstown with his bundle of primers strapped to the back of a jenny mule heading to the frontier, a pair of Sons of St. Robert Rogers coming back the other way in their buffalo robes (their walking sticks notched to record baptisms of Texians, Comanche and, they claimed, New Muscovites), several genuine Texian leatherstockings, and even a small gaggle of Firstborn, traveling from the Ohio.

With these last in particular, Sarah watched them and the monk closely, half-expecting to see some coded exchange between them, but Thalanes simply offered a cheerful greeting and returned to his walking.

They passed stands every five or ten miles as they walked, little ordinaries on the side of the road, usually built of stone for safety, but often enough mere log cabins, horses tethered in barns or stables and almost invariably a dog sleeping on the porch.

They bought bread and pork stew for lunch from a humorless skillet-faced innkeeper in such a stand, and Sarah expected they would stop for the night in one of them. As Thalanes gave no indication, however, and she was in no mood to make any concessions, Sarah herself kept them marching past dark, and when the monk's spell had faded and she was dead on her feet, there were no lights in view, so she simply led them off the road into a thick knot of pine and crashed into sleep.

She was vaguely aware, as she sank into oblivion, of someone draping a bedroll over her and covering her with fallen leaves.

In the morning, Calvin and Thalanes both looked tired; they must have alternated watches. It was coffee-and-gramarye again, and the rest of the bonny clabber, and this time Thalanes looked genuinely disgusted. Sarah let Cal set the pace.

They continued to pass travelers throughout the day, marching in their beeline among the skeletons of deciduous trees and a sprinkling of piney woods toward Louisiana. After a lunch of apples stolen from the corner of an orchard, Sarah broached the subject of gramarye with the monk: "Why Latin?"

He knit his brows and considered. "Why Latin *what*? Why Latin diplomacy? Why Latin scholarship? Why the Republic of Rome?"

"I mean, when you work gramarye, you do it in Latin?"

"Ah." He smiled. "Gramarye is simple. It's no different from hexing. They're the same kind of magic."

"What do you mean, other kinds of folk do different kinds of magic?" Sarah asked. "Like what, like beastkind, you mean?"

"That's exactly what I mean," he agreed. "Or Lullian alchemy. Cabala. Runes. Shamanism. Angel summoning. Brauchers' prayers. At a fundamental level, they may all be identical—opinions differ—but hexing and gramarye are definitely the same art."

"You're wrong," she begged to differ. "They aren't the same. Hexing is easy."

"Is it?" he asked. "That's an extraordinary opinion. Tell me what you mean."

"It ain't easy," Calvin contradicted her, too. "I can't do it a lick, and it ain't for lack of tryin'. Nor can most folks do it, neither. And the ones as can, it leaves 'em broken and twisted. Sarah's got a special gift, she jest ain't comfortable admittin' it."

Sarah shrugged. "Not everybody has the talent for hexing, but folks that do have it to different degrees. It comes easy to me, so lucky me, I guess."

"Tell me about it," Thalanes encouraged her.

"It's like this," she said. "I sing a song. The older the song, the stronger the hex. If I can, I use a bit of something solid to make the hex stick. Dirty things, body things, are better than others—blood is best of all, but spit or hair, or sometimes other stuff, depending on the hex. Eggs, or twigs, or . . . you know, it depends."

"Can you hex without using any material thing to make the hex stick?" Thalanes asked.

"Sure," she said, "everyone knows that, only it's a lot harder."

"Can you hex without words?"

"Yes," she allowed slowly, remembering her love-hexing of Obadiah. She couldn't bring herself to look at Calvin. "And that makes it harder, too."

"So what are you really doing when you hex?" he pressed her. "What's the part you can't hex without?"

"Why Latin?" Cal asked. "Why rhymes and songs?" Sarah was grateful for the interruption, because she didn't know how to answer the monk's question. "I ain't no hexer, never had the gift, so this might could be jack-assery on my part, but iffen you gotta say somethin', why not jest say it in English? Why not 'hey, boulder, git outta my way' instead of 'o thou boulder, *amo-amas-amat*'?"

Thalanes laughed. "It isn't jack-assery at all, Calvin. In fact, you *could* use everyday English. Everyday English would be more powerful in magic-making than saying nothing at all, because it's helpful to have a medium, a channel to get the power out of you and realized as a spell, but it turns out words from old languages, especially dead ones, or words that are ritualized, that have had their meaning killed by being fixed into, for instance, a song, carry more power. That makes them better channels for transferring magic from within the magician to the outside world."

Cal considered. "Remembers me of what you said about ley lines. It's like how a lot of use leaves a trail of power in the ground, and likewise, a lot of use leaves a trail of power in a language. So I reckon mebbe someday, when enough folks have spoke it for a long enough time, English'll be a language of power too."

"Excellent!" Thalanes beamed. "Are you sure you don't have the gift for it yourself, Calvin? You did corn readings, after all."

"Tolerable sure," Cal affirmed.

"Perhaps you just need to try. If you have the gift for wizardry, it would be a shame to miss out on the calling."

"A corn reader ain't nothin' but a body as knows how to read.

Besides, yesterday you were worried as I might miss out on my callin' to be a preacher," Calvin said. "Tomorrow I reckon you'll want me to go into politickin'."

Thalanes laughed. "Whatever you do, Calvin Calhoun, don't go into politicking. When Aristotle told us that man is a political animal, it was a warning, with the proper emphasis on the word *animal*."

"Will," Sarah said. "Mind. Wish. Choice. I don't know what to call it. The part of the hex I can't do without is the part where I focus and try to bring to pass the thing I want."

"Very good." The monk nodded enthusiastically. "Hexing and gramarye are the same—at their heart they are simply the application of will by a person with the rare talent for it. The wizard, the hexer, the thaumaturge, burns energy from some source, most often himself, and exerts the force of his mind. Words help, words of power, because they're a good channel through which to move energy, from yourself or from some other source into your spell. Stuff, or, as a formally trained wizard might say, *material components*, serves the same function—and it works better, the more connection or similarity your components have to the subject of your spell—and so do gestures with your hands, for some of us. But at bottom, it's always a question of talent, will, and power."

"What Latin?" Sarah asked. "I never learned any Latin nursery rhymes."

"Any Latin is pretty effective," the wizard said. "I try to stick to very basic indicative sentences myself, and maybe once in a while a command. I just describe in simple Latin what I want to happen. Short and simple means easy to use in a pinch."

"Short and simple is better than the alternative," Sarah agreed.

"The advantage of using a dead language over songs and nursery rhymes," Thalanes said, "is flexibility. I find it's usually easier to say a simple sentence that suits my spell than to think of a rhyme that matches it."

Sarah nodded. It seemed obvious, as he explained it. "I admit I'm disappointed. I'd thought the only bright side to leaving home like this was no more drills from my father . . . from the Elector. Now it sounds like I have a lifetime of Latin ahead of me."

"What a blessing!" Thalanes grinned.

They stayed again in the woods that night, in a twisted ditch that hid them from prying eyes. Sarah took a four-hour watch, over the objections of both her companions, and she sat awake, listening to a hoot owl at the top of the hill and watching the Pleiades and then the Twins march westward.

She couldn't be sure in the shadows, but she thought, more than once, that she saw Thalanes watching her.

On the third day they bought cheese and potatoes at a stand operated by two Igbo brothers and in the evening Cal shot a turkey that had had the temerity to squat on a moldering log in full view and gobble. Over roasted fowl and tuber and a few sips of the Crooked Man's moonshine, Cal asked a question that Sarah realized he'd been holding back for days.

"Why do the Martinites care?" he asked. "Why did Martin Luther raise such a big ruckus about baptizin' the Firstborn, and why does he still have followers today? What do they want? I ain't no theologian, but it jest seems like such a silly thing to do, goin' around tellin' folks not to baptize the Eldritch."

Thalanes finished his last mouthful of potato thoughtfully, looking across the fire at Calvin and considering his answer. "Do you remember, when I said there is a burst of energy, of magical energy, when any creature is born?"

"Sure do," Calvin said. "It gits into the ley lines, jest like energy from the tides and the sunrise and such, you said."

"Good memory. Do you know what happens when a First-born dies?"

Cal shrugged. "Heaven or hell, I guess, dependin'."

Thalanes laughed. "Very good. And you may be right. But Martin Luther was convinced the Firstborn had no souls at all and therefore couldn't go to either heaven or hell, but merely ceased to exist on death. You've heard the term *Unsouled*, I know—he coined it. Which is why he taught that it was no sin to kill one of the Firstborn, and in fact he killed a great many himself. He also preached that it was a grave error to baptize any Eldritch, much less ordain or marry them, in the same way that it would be a grave error, a sort of blasphemy, to baptize a jug of whisky or a rocking chair."

Sarah felt embarrassed. She had used the term *Unsouled* before, even when talking with the Elector in front of Thalanes. She'd meant it jokingly, without thinking about what it meant. It had seemed a funny oddity; now it seemed deeply personal, both to Thalanes and to her.

"I'm sorry," she whispered.

He paused to smile at her, and then continued. "But Martin Luther's basic starting point was exegesis, it was how he read a certain verse in the Book of Genesis. In chapter one of Genesis, God creates man in His image, male and female, and then Genesis reports that 'God blessed them, and God said unto them, Be fruitful, and multiply, and replenish the earth, and subdue it: and have dominion over the fish of the sea, and over the fowl of the air, and over every living thing that moveth upon the earth.'"

"Sounds familiar," Cal said. "I don't git it."

"Luther believed," Thalanes explained, "that in this verse we see the Creator giving Adam and Eve and their children dominion over all other living things."

"Including giving them dominion over the children of Adam and Adam's first wife," Sarah said, putting the pieces together. "The lady of the Serpent and the Tree. Wisdom."

"Correct. So Luther saw any situation in which one of the Firstborn exercised 'dominion' over any child of Eve as an abomination. His personal mission, and the quest of the Order he founded, has been to remove the Firstborn from all positions of authority, in the church or out of it. Everything else followed after that, all the other theology and all of the killing."

"Does that mean Luther believed Adam had a first wife, and you . . . *we* are descended from her?" Sarah asked.

Thalanes shrugged. "He believed it, or he knew that we believed it and he held our belief against us. Does it matter?"

"To him, I guess it might," Sarah realized, "but not to me."

"Well that jest seems stupid," Cal objected.

"It gets stupider the more you think about it," Sarah mused, digging deep into her memory and thinking about the Bible passages Thalanes was quoting. "Genesis one doesn't name the people 'Adam' and 'Eve,' does it?"

"No," Thalanes agreed with a faint smile, "it doesn't. In Genesis chapter one, God creates 'man,' 'male and female.' In Genesis chapter two, God seems to create 'man' again, names him Adam, and then pulls a woman from his side. In Genesis chapter three, Adam finally names his female companion . . . possibly his *second* female companion . . . 'Eve.'"

Sarah had always realized that the Bible was a complicated affair. It was seeming more complicated by the moment.

"I reckon I'm missin' the point," Cal said.

"The point," Sarah explained, "is that you could read Genesis differently from Martin Luther. You could read it exactly opposite to him, in fact. You could think that Genesis chapter one is about Adam and his *first* wife, and that they were the ones that were given dominion. And then Eve only comes on the scene later, in Genesis chapter two."

"You're as smart as your mother ever was." Thalanes sounded sad. "Be careful."

"So remember me again what's the name of your feller? Cetes? I guess Cetes must a been someone as read Genesis the other way?"

Sarah shook her head. "He wasn't a theologian at all, was he?" Her words had the form of a question, but really she wanted Thalanes to know she was listening, and she understood, and she knew her history. "He was Lord Mayor of Wittenberg. And he refused to fight back when Martin Luther and his men came after him with pitchforks."

Thalanes's facial expression fell somewhere between *pained* and *amused*. "The Order would say he let Luther's will be uncoerced."

Sarah laughed. "The First Precept. Yeah, I bet they would. And I bet when the Order talks about the fact that none of Cetes's people ever tried to bring Luther to justice, they'd cite the Second Precept. Only God can judge, or something like that, right?"

Thalanes looked away. "Later, there were the Swords of Wisdom."

"Look," Cal said, shaking his head. "In the first place, all of that Genesis one, Genesis two stuff ain't a good enough reason to kill folks, with pitchforks or otherwise. A verse in the Bible, one danged verse? And in the second, what in Jerusalem gave him the idea the Firstborn ain't got souls? You walk and talk and smile jest like anybody else. What'm I missin'?"

"You're a good man, Calvin Calhoun," Thalanes said. "That makes it hard for you to understand the evil of others. But even you kill the food you hunt, and I think if you had to, you would find that you could kill a man, for the right reasons. To defend your family, for instance, or your home. Or Sarah. But from Eve's first sons on down, there have been men willing to kill each other for more trivial reasons. For differences of religion. Or for different politics. Different calendars, even. Envy of a successful sacrifice. And I think many of St. Martin's followers act out of strict devotion to a principle in which they firmly believe."

Thalanes walked in silence for a long time.

"As to why Martin Luther became convinced the Firstborn had no souls, well, he knew what I am about to tell you. When any child of Adam is born, it is born in a burst of magical energy. This is a good thing, as a midwife or someone else in a position to help can use that energy to ease the birth, heal the mother, console the child, and so on."

"That's true," Sarah confirmed. "I've hexed many a newborn Calhoun into a happy smile and a mild first feed."

Thalanes nodded. "When a daughter or son of Wisdom, one of the Firstborn, dies, there is a similar burst of energy, that is not present at the death of a son or daughter of Eve." He paused to let that information sink in.

"Nope," said Calvin, "I still ain't seein' it. So what?"

"Martin Luther became convinced, and convinced many other people, that that burst of energy represents the escape of the power that animates the Firstborn during their life. He taught that the Firstborn do not have immortal souls, but are creatures created by magic and destroyed at death. As such, their baptism is a blasphemy and their ordination is an insult to God."

"Yeah, I recall that bit. So the Martinites ain't so much angry at the Firstborn," Cal summarized, "as opposed to the folks as let the Firstborn get baptized, be priests, or hold public office. Is that about the size of it?"

"At least on paper, yes," the monk agreed. "In practice...well, the sons and daughters of Eve are accomplished haters."

"Just the sons and daughters of *Eve*?" Sarah asked pointedly.

Thalanes laughed. "No. Of course not."

Cal shook his head. "Well, then what is it? I mean, if Luther's wrong, then what is the 'burst of energy' that pops outta the Firstborn when they die?"

Thalanes shrugged. "I don't know. I don't think anyone really does."

"The Memphites think a person has five parts." Sarah was happy for every opportunity to show that she knew what she was talking about. "There's the body, and the shadow, and the name, and two things that don't make a lot of sense from a Christian perspective, the *ka* and the *ba*."

"Crows and sheep," Cal muttered. "What's a *ka* and a *ba*?"

"It's hard to say." Sarah hid her ignorance behind an evasion. "They're both kind of like the soul, as we know it."

"Two souls?" Cal asked. "You're right, that don't sound Christian."

"No?" Thalanes pushed. "But Paul says to the Thessalonians 'I pray God your whole spirit and soul and body be preserved blameless.' That's *psyche* and *pneuma* in Greek, two different things. He uses the same words again in chapter four of the Epistle to the Hebrews, *psyche* and *pneuma*, 'the dividing asunder of soul and spirit, and of the joints and marrow.' St. Jerome translates them as *spiritus* and *anima*. Doesn't that sound to you like a person has two invisible parts, a soul and a spirit? Do you think Paul wasn't a good Christian?"

"You're askin' the wrong feller." Calvin retreated into a shrug. "I'm jest a poor cattle rustler, and I don't have the answers."

"I'm just a poor monk," Thalanes said, "and I don't have any of the answers, either. But I hope that St. Paul is right, and that you're right, too, Cal. I hope when I die, my *ka* or my *pneuma* will explode in a burst of energy, and my *psyche* or my *ba* will go to Heaven."

"What if you're wrong?" Sarah asked him. "Aren't you kind of gambling your salvation on a guess?"

"Don't we all do that, all the time?" Thalanes countered. "Do we have any other choice?"

It was in the afternoon of their fourth day on the Natchez Trace that Sarah finally put her foot down.

"Tonight," she said, "I am going to have a bath."

Cal wasn't going to argue, but he thought for a moment the little monk might object. Thalanes hesitated, nodded, and finally said, "I think that's an excellent idea. Do you want to choose an ordinary for us?"

Sarah selected a stand just on the other side of the next river, which turned out to be a long, low building, peppered with chimneys along its length, with walls of stone halfway up to the wooden roof and then timbers to finish. There was a well in the front yard, a two-doored outhouse behind, a stable, and a long sagging porch with scattered benches and chairs. Sarah walked up to a man in denim britches and a gray flannel shirt drawing water from the well and asked where she could find the innkeeper.

"This here's Crowder's Stand." He heaved the wooden bucket out onto the lip of the well and spat tobacco juice in the dirt. "I'm Crowder." He was paunchy and thick-legged, with a greasy forehead underneath a shiny bald pate, and he stared Sarah right in her bad eye. Calvin flinched, expecting a storm.

"I'm Sarah Carpenter," Sarah lied smooth as butter. "We want us a room for the night, and a bath." Cal could see that her fists were knotted tight and he knew that in her heart Sarah wanted to haul back and pop Crowder one right in his glossy face. "Payin' in Imperial."

"Sixpence," Crowder said. "A shilling'll get food for the three of you as well, clapbread and bacon for breakfast and whate'er you can git outta the missus for your supper, iffen you ain't already et. I'll bring a tub and a heatin' pot around to your room and youins can warm the water yourselves."

Calvin produced a shilling, which Crowder bit suspiciously and then pocketed before pointing out to them an empty room and the way to kitchen. A big-eared Bassett lazing on the porch lifted one droopy eyelid as they stepped over him into their room. They laid down their packs and then Thalanes suggested Calvin go to the kitchen for food.

"Just in case Angleton or others are trying to find us on the Trace," he explained. "Sarah is distinctive, and I'm obviously a foreigner."

"I could eat a horse," Sarah said.

Cal patted his tomahawk and lariat, both hanging on his belt. "I jest about hope I *do* run into that Martinite again."

He went to the kitchen. Mrs. Crowder was no more friendly than her husband, but she acknowledged in surprisingly expressive grunts that Cal and his companions were paying guests, and she reckoned as how he could help himself from the pantry and the icehouse. He chose a loaf of brown bread and a glazed clay bowl full of cold fried chicken and then shuffled back toward the room.

Sarah met him on the porch. "Come with me," she said urgently. "I need to discuss something with you." The Bassett hound crouched behind her on the porch, tail between its legs, whining.

Cal didn't say anything, but now that the prospect of a bath was in view, he did think she smelled rather ... earthy. Something about that bothered him, but he couldn't put his finger on it. The bath would fix it. Jerusalem, he was sure he smelled worse.

Baths all around, it would have to be.

"Sure," he said. "Jest let me go put this food in the room."

"No!" She gripped his arm with surprising strength. "I need to talk to you now, and I don't want the priest to overhear."

Cal's heart skipped a beat. Had Sarah tired of the monk, and was she now interested again in the original plan of running away with Calvin to be married? He followed her.

The melt-faced hound barked once, short and sharp, as Calvin left the porch.

"Want some chicken?" He bit into a modest-sized piece himself. "No."

"Thalanes say somethin' put you off your appetite?" Cal asked, following her out of the inn's yard and back through the woods toward the river they'd just crossed. He tossed the chicken bone, not caring too much this deep in the woods whether he might attract a raccoon, or an opossum, or even a black bear. "You was ravenous afore."

Sarah crossed the narrow, rutted Trace and turned downstream at the large water-rounded rocks of the river's edge. She looked determined. Her fire intimidated a lot of men, but Cal liked it. That indomitable will would help her survive, whatever life did to her, and if they were about to go off and set up a homestead somewhere, it would be a valuable asset to both of them.

He looked back over his shoulder and couldn't see Crowder's through the trees. "I reckon we're far enough now the monk can't hear you," he told her. "Unless you Firstborn have magic hearin' powers you ain't told me about."

She stopped at the riverbank, picked up a fist-sized rock and squared her shoulders to him, grim-visaged as a harpy.

"Sorry," he apologized, feeling abashed and crestfallen. "I didn't mean to sound insultin', I's jest funnin' a bit. You shouldn't ought to think I b'lieve anythin' bad about you at all, Sarah. I think it's jest terrific that you're... you know ... a Penn, and a Firstborn, and a daughter of Wisdom and all. Or part Firstborn, anyway. You know ... well, I *reckon* you know how I feel."

She crooked a finger at him. "Come here."

He blushed. For the four days they'd been on the Trace, he'd

spent the entire time hoping there was still a chance this journey would end in his marrying Sarah, and imagining their life
together. He could take care of her, he could give her a life in
which she'd be happy, and he figured Appalachee was big enough
that the two of them could disappear and no Martinite would
ever find them. Now it looked as if his dreaming was about to
become sweet, thrilling fact.

He leaned in to hear what she had to say.

Sarah swung the rock at his head.

"Do you not believe in judgment, Parson?"

———◦———

CHAPTER NINE

Cal's height saved him.

A shorter man would have taken the rock in the temple. Calvin Calhoun, though he had been leaning forward in anticipation of hearing some sweet confession from Sarah, jerked backward as she swung at him, and the rock only struck him on the shoulder.

Still, it hurt.

"Jumpin' Jerusalem!" He staggered sideways. "What in tarnation has got into you?"

She swung again, backhand with the rock, and thumped him in the breast. A little higher, and his collarbone would have been broken.

"Iffen you're mad, Sarah, go ahead and slap me!" He stumbled back. "Jest put down the rock afore one of us gits hurt!"

She jumped at him, clawing for his eyes with her left hand. He twisted away, feeling her nails rake down his cheek and draw blood.

He smelled her earthy odor again. *Dirty person* was a smell Calvin knew well from his years on Calhoun Mountain, where bathing was permitted but not enthusiastically encouraged, and Sarah's reek didn't quite fit that description. She smelled like wet earth, or clay. Somewhere in his head Cal heard a dim warning bell.

He tried to push her away gently, but she was too strong, and he ended up just pressing the bread and the fried chicken against her chest. She swung the rock again, catching him this time in the ribs. Cal felt something snap in his side.

"Dang it, Sarah!" he barked, and then he realized where he had smelled that riverbank smell before.

This wasn't Sarah.

It was one of those clay-not-a-man things he'd struggled with on the slopes of Calhoun Mountain. But how? He narrowly avoided another swipe at his face. How did this monster get a face and a voice at all, and especially how did it come to look and sound exactly like Sarah?

Well, in any case, he knew how to deal with them.

Lord hates a man as can't throw an honest punch when it's called for. He winced with both the emotional and the physical pain of it, but hauled off and slammed not-Sarah as hard as he could with his knuckles, right in the face. Its nose flattened and completely disappeared into its Sarah-face, without the faintest hint of blood. It rocked back from the force of Cal's blow, and he grabbed for his purse, yanking it from underneath his belt and jerking at the drawstrings to open it and get at the silver inside.

Not-Sarah slapped his hands, stinging his fingers with the violence of the blow. He lost his grip on the purse, bobbled it, and then not-Sarah smacked his hands up and the bag went sailing away—in a high arc that dropped it, *splash!*, into the middle of the river.

Jerusalem! He thought of the silver bullets he'd cast ... but his pouch of bullets was with his powderhorns and the Elector's rifle, back at Crowder's. He didn't relish the thought of sprinting through the woods with this beast slashing at his back. There had to be another way.

Cal dropped a shoulder and punched it into not-Sarah's chest, grabbing it by the shoulders as if to wrassle, and then heaving with all his might. It punched at him, landing blows on his chest and back that would show as bruises the next day, and then he threw the clay monster into the air and—

whumph!—

hard on the ground onto its back. The sound it made as it hit the river rocks was wet and squishy. It sounded boneless. It sounded like a sack of wet corn mush slapping onto a hardwood floor. He turned to face not-Sarah and backed away, grunting from the pain in his ribs and slipping the tomahawk into his hand.

The tomahawk hadn't worked very well against these things on Calhoun Mountain; he had gone for the creature's head, and the axe had just sunk in harmlessly. This time, he'd go for a different target.

Not-Sarah pulled itself off the ground with a sucking sound, rolling sideways, and Cal got a glimpse of its back. It was dimpled with large indentations now, cratered and pocked like one of the fancy cheeses Cal had tried once in an overpriced tavern in Raleigh, and its spine, if it had one, now bent sideways. Landing on the stones had smashed the creature all out of its Sarah-shape.

Calvin hesitated and not-Sarah launched itself at him again, hands extended and arms growing longer.

Was that even possible?

Cal stepped aside and swung the tomahawk down in a swift overhand blow. The sharp, heavy head of the war axe sliced cleanly through not-Sarah's wrist, completely severing the hand. No bone. The blow felt like cutting through rich, rock-free soil with a spade or a mattock, and the severed stump was gray and bloodless.

What unearthly thing was this? He didn't think any of the Poor Richard Sermons mentioned shapechanging clay people, and nothing on the subject came to Cal's mind out of his considerable repertoire of songs, either.

The hand dropped to the leaves and not-Sarah spun away and fell to its knees, roaring in rage. It no longer had Sarah's voice, but that deep, ragged howl Cal had drawn out of it on Calhoun Mountain. *Good*, Cal thought. *I hurt the blasted thing.*

He stepped forward, grunting in pain as he raised the tomahawk.

Something caught his foot and Cal stumbled. He looked down; not-Sarah's severed hand was stuck to the sole of his moccasin, fingers gripping his foot tightly.

"Jumpin' Jerusalem!" Calvin swore, shaking his foot but not freeing it from the tenacious white fingers.

Not-Sarah lumbered to its feet and turned to face him. The severed stump of not-Sarah's wrist writhed and bubbled as it stepped forward. Gray knobs popped out of it, and then elongated into tendrils, and the tendrils hardened into fingers that sprouted nails and then webbing among the fingers thickened into a palm.

It grew another hand to replace the lost one.

The hair on the back of Calvin's neck stood up. Part of his brain screamed at him, telling him to run, to get back to Sarah and warn her. But he couldn't run, he couldn't take the risk that this thing would get past him.

There had been two of these things before—where was the other one? Maybe Thalanes had been tricked out of position and was already dead, and Cal was the last line of defense. Calvin had promised the Elector he'd take care of her.

Dread filled him, and resolve. His tomahawk hand trembled with the will to strike.

He wished he still had his purse, but his precious silver shillings were at the bottom of the river.

He needed to chop off bigger pieces.

Calvin lurched forward, off-balance because of the hand that clawed at his foot and ankle, and smashed down with the war axe. He aimed for the creature's bicep, but it saw the attack coming, and rather than move aside, it stepped closer to Calvin.

The tomahawk bit into not-Sarah's shoulder and sank deep into its torso, releasing more clay-stink but no blood or gore.

Not-Sarah punched Cal in the stomach, pushing his breath out of him in a painful gasp.

Cal wrenched at the axe handle in vain, crying out from the effort and the sharp stabbing pain in his ribs.

Not-Sarah dove forward, wrapping its arms around Cal's chest in a bear hug, burying its face in his shoulder and squeezing. "Aaaaaaaggh!" Cal yelled, tears whipping from his eyes. He flailed at the axe and knocked it free, but with the same motion sent it flying out of his reach.

The creature squeezed again, and Cal howled. He scrabbled at not-Sarah's face and wrapped both his hands around it, pushing. He felt its skin sliding around under his fingers, like the loose peel of a grape.

With a desperate sob, he snapped its head back.

Nothing broke, nothing cracked, but not-Sarah's neck bent at a sharp angle, and its head twisted back to touch its own shoulder blades. And stayed. Cal stared in shock and horror down into the noseless face of the creature, smelling the reek of the river rising from its orifices and stretched and torn skin.

"What are you?" Cal demanded.

"My name is Legion!" not-Sarah growled in a deep, rotting

voice, and then laughed like a maniac, eyes staring up past Cal at the late afternoon sky.

It squeezed him again, and Cal wept from the pain.

Obadiah Dogsbody slapped the mule's hindquarters. "Get on, ye!" he shouted at the balky string of animals.

The hindmost beast rooted its hoofs in the ground and brayed.

"'Ark ye, I said to move!"

Once, he would have diverted himself by imagining the rump he was spanking belonged to something other than a foot-planting, cantankerous jenny, and idled away time on the trail looking forward to his next visit to a town large enough to have a significant complement of generously proportioned women. But Nashville had such women, he'd seen them hanging out of second-story windows and whispering to him from the darkened doorways of the seediest taverns, and their lush, juicy blandishments had left Obadiah completely cold.

The pleasure of rough sport had dried up for him, as had all his others. Beer was sour, tobacco turned his mouth bitter, food he ate only because he needed to live. Obadiah was losing weight, enough that his jacket and breeches began to hang off him in an unseemly fashion, and he was preoccupied.

He kept thinking about her.

He was so appalled with his own behavior, he could barely bring himself to even identify the *her* in question, but it was the little Appalachee minx, Witchy Eye, Sarah Calhoun, as the other Appalachee called her.

He remembered his first glimpse of her, replayed it over and over again in his mind, her standing in the bubbling crowd of the Fair, purple shawl with gold suns proud and queenlike around her shoulders, eye flashing, back straight and strong. Obadiah had seen proud Queen Caroline once, on his first day at the Royal Military Academy in Woolwich. That was before the officers had told him he didn't have the makings of an artilleryman or an engineer after all, and begun drilling him with a pike, and Obadiah had stood proudly in line in his scarlet brushed wool coat, black tricorner, and white sash.

He'd heard the chanters and the drums and smelled the estuary on the breeze as the queen rose under a slate-gray sheet of English sky to the great menhir, straight-backed in her silk dress to pour out a libation of strong ale to Wayland Smith before the academy's ranking godi dragged the first of his sheep onto the unhewn stones.

The queen had been glorious and indomitable in English red and white and she'd touched Obadiah's heart. He'd been a little bit in love with her, and in that moment he'd been proud to be a soldier. He'd have given his life for Queen Caroline, much more readily than for her husband, King George Spencer.

Witchy Eye touched his heart, too. Not in quite the same fashion.

It wasn't that he thought of her in a...in a fleshy way. He wished that was it—lust was something he was familiar with, lust he could understand, and he could gratify it or distract it with the satisfaction of some other desire. This was different. He didn't think of her with physical feeling at all, but with something sweeter, something that might have been kindness and tenderness.

He was beginning to think of himself as weak, as Obadiah-who-had-gone-soft. By the Hammer, sometimes he caught himself wondering what he needed to do to be a better man for Witchy Eye.

He disgusted himself.

It had all started with her curse. She'd hexed him, and he remembered that during her hex, he'd felt tingly from his head to his toes. His ears had echoed full of birdsong and his every step had been cushioned by soft, sweet grass. Then the Right Reverend Father had undone the spell with a bit of silver—and Obadiah wasn't interested in being hexed again—but the world hadn't gone back to normal.

Instead, it had become a cold, dead thing, a dry husk, a mouthful of parched corn that Obadiah chewed because he had to, when what he really wanted to do was to spit it all out and sink what teeth remained to him into something sweet, bite into the fruit of the tree of life, juicy and cool and perfect.

He wanted the feeling back, and he hated himself for wanting it, but he didn't think he could live any longer in such a flat, tasteless, unsalted world. He had lived a life with meaning for those precious minutes while he had been hexed, and he wanted that back. He wanted Queen Caroline at the menhir.

He wanted to be in love again.

It had been so long.

It was afternoon, crisp and cool, and Obadiah was returning from Nashville. The mules loped into the Blues' camp, a little further up the slopes of Calhoun Mountain than Obadiah would have liked, but he understood that they needed to be this close to keep their cordon around the Elector's people. The Blues stood twelve-hour shifts at key points around the mountain, watching to make sure Witchy Eye (as she was coming to be generally called among the Imperials) didn't escape.

The Calhouns took no notice and hid nothing, walking in and out through the blockade as bold as mice, spitting at the soldiers and mocking them. Faces grew harder on both sides and the mountain bristled with rifles, but nothing had yet come to blows. When they weren't standing watch, the Blues slept in camp or drilled, riding, moving in and out of formation on foot and on horseback, and especially shooting. For hours at a time, Calhoun Mountain was covered in a shroud of blue gunpowder smoke from their obsessive practice.

Obadiah assumed that one purpose of the drilling was to menace the besieged Calhouns, but the Appalachee didn't seem intimidated. They just watched with disdainful grins, and once in a while one of the dragoons would find his notched bark target snatched out of his sight by the shout of a distant rifle, generally followed by gleeful hollering from the limestone redoubt.

Responsibility for keeping the whole operation fed and watered had devolved upon Obadiah. That was fine with him. He'd driven the wagon for his father's cooperage many hard miles around southern England; he'd done it again for the Royal Pikemen in the Academy; and more than once, his duties for the Right Reverend Father Ezekiel Angleton had included acting as mule-skinner or teamster.

He tied the mules and checked the regiment's heavy iron cauldron that he kept bubbling over the fire on a tripod of lashed logs. Someone had eaten—that made it time to throw in more ingredients.

Obadiah set about unloading the mules' packs and organizing himself to tend to the perpetually-cooking stew, picking his way among Blues dozing in their little two-man tents. He occasionally kicked at an arm or leg flopped in sleep across his trail, but doing it made him think of his Witchy Eye and feel guilty, so he tried to restrain himself.

Obadiah set a scarred cutting plank and piles of meat and vegetables on a camp table beside the cooking fire and began to cut.

"I'm not soft in the head, and what I'm telling you is no mere whimsy," Father Angleton was saying. He and Captain Berkeley sat at the light wooden folding table under the high-walled tent that served as the camp's headquarters. "My mind is as clear as it's ever been, and I'm an honest and a God-fearing man."

"But are you a prophet, Parson?" Berkeley asked in a cold and insolent drawl. He had his ever-present deck of Franklin's Tarock, and was dealing cards out face up in front of himself, in the simple triplet that he favored.

The Tarock was a New World obsession, something the old Lightning Bishop had borrowed from the Florentines or the French (before Bonaparte imposed his Caliphate and ended such occult frivolities) and fiddled with to fit it to the land of the Chesapeake Bay and the Mississippi River. It was effeminate, the kind of thing women did for entertainment behind closed doors. No self-respecting Englishman could take seriously any purported attempt at divination that didn't involve the death of at least one animal.

"I endeavor to be sensitive to the things of the spirit, myself," Berkeley continued. "See—again I draw Simon Sword. Simon Sword, the wild child, the berserker, the forces of the natural world unhinged, the bringer of trial, and above all the harbinger of judgment. Always judgment, everywhere I see. Judgment and the Horseman. Judgment and the Emperor. Judgment and the Priest. Judgment and the Lovers."

Obadiah chopped turnips and tried to hide his interest. The Lovers—could that mean him? Was his love to be judged? Or what did the Lovers card signify—relationships and choices, he guessed, wishing for once that he had been behind more fortune-tellers' curtains in his life. Sacrifice, maybe. Permanence. Sharing, intimacy, giving, love.

It had been a long time since Obadiah had thought of such things.

"You cannot pretend to equate such parlor games with the word of the Lord." The Right Reverend Father's disdain was clear in his voice.

"Do you mean the word of the Lord in the Bible?" Berkeley

spoke slowly, which made his speech sound insulting. "Or do you mean the word of the Lord to you *personally*?"

"Both!" Angleton snapped. "The disciples didn't sneer upon the writings of the prophets just because they had the Lord Himself with them."

"Oh, I had misunderstood." Berkeley smiled devilishly. "I had thought you were merely a prophet, but now I see that you consider yourself the Lord God of Heaven."

Angleton's face stiffened and his voice grew cold. "Do not insult me and do not blaspheme. And do not pretend that a man who believes in God must believe in any other manner of foolishness that happens along."

"Blazes, Parson, do you not believe in judgment?" Berkeley asked, teasing. "Or do you not believe in Simon Sword?"

Obadiah cut pork into strips and threw them into the stew.

"I believe in judgment." Angleton set his jaw in a straight line. "Judgment comes for every man, as surely as death."

"And taxes, Parson," Berkeley finished the saying for him.

"As for Simon Sword and other such bogeys," the Right Reverend Father continued, "a man may believe in many powers and yet not serve them, nor approve their service."

"Judgment is but change," the captain observed. Obadiah realized he'd stopped working on the stew and was staring. "We all change, we're all judged. The Horseman, the Priest, the Emperor…" He considered the cards. "It's the damnedest thing, Parson."

"Yaas. And yet you play with it constantly."

"I don't mean that. I mean that I haven't drawn one of the Minor Arcana since I came to Nashville. Not one key, not one coin, not one cup, not one bolt of lightning. I've been turning the cards for days, and all I ever find are the Major Arcana." Berkeley drew another card, smiled at it, and then held it up for Father Angleton to see. "I had hoped speaking of it might break the spell, but here again I have drawn the Drunkard." He turned and waved the card in Obadiah's direction before slapping it down on the table.

Obadiah's ears burned and he went back to work, stowing casks of beans and flour under an oiled cloth. It wasn't fair. He drank, but he didn't drink more than any of the dragoons. Or not much more, anyhow.

And besides, since he last saw Witchy Eye, he hadn't been drunk once.

"My Lord has given me a vision," Angleton insisted quietly. "Your belief or lack of it, and your endless mooning over a deck of cards, are utterly irrelevant. The one to be judged will be the girl with the bad eye. And I shall preside over her trial."

Sarah surveyed the room's contents in a single glance: half a dozen pallets, wool blankets, rough stone fireplace, stack of split wood.

She leaned her white ash staff into a corner. "It isn't homey, but it'll do. At least we don't have to sleep three to a bed."

Thalanes hitched up his gray robe and knelt. He swept aside a carpet of ash with a log and stacked several thick pieces of wood in the fireplace. "Let's get the fire going. We don't want to delay your bath."

"Calvin's got flint and steel," Sarah said.

"Why don't you just hex it? Or as they might say in Philadelphia, why don't you use a little gramarye?" Thalanes's eyes twinkled; Sarah felt like she was in on the joke this time, so she laughed along. "Ordinarily, I'd say it probably wasn't worth the effort to do something by gramarye that you could as easily do by hand, but I'd like to see you practice."

"I don't know a fire hex." She furrowed her brow and thought a moment. "I guess I could try something with 'ladybug, ladybug, fly away home.'"

Thalanes squatted beside the stacked firewood. "I want you to try three things, Sarah."

The little monk was teaching Sarah to do gramarye the way he did it, and she hadn't even had to ask. "Sure."

"First, I want you to try to form the spell with Latin. Just basic words, no need for a song or a rhyme. Just think of a simple sentence that tells what you want to happen, and use those words to vocalize your magic."

Sarah nodded. "I think I can do that. I suppose that's the difference between hexing and gramarye, then—hexing is nursery rhymes in the hills, and gramarye is dead languages in the city? I guess that kind of thing must make a good impression on the fancy folk."

"Well, yes." Thalanes smiled. "And some magicians go in for

big dramatic gestures and trappings. You know what I mean: candles, colored powders, and smokes. But my purpose isn't to impress the fancy folk. Being able to cast spells using Latin—or some other dead tongue, if you know another one—frees you from the necessity of having to know a nursery rhyme for every piece of magic you want to do. It gives you flexibility and power."

"I see that." Sarah had always protested against the Latin, telling the Elector she didn't plan to become a barrister or a land conveyancer or a priest. Now she was grateful for it. She sat down beside the fireplace. "Latin it is. What's the second thing?"

Thalanes dug into Calvin's pack and pulled out his powder-horn. He shook a pinch of the gunpowder into the palm of one hand. "I want you to use this gunpowder as a material component of the gramarye. I doubt you'd find it necessary—will and word suffice for many purposes—but a material component helps. Just like you used three drops of blood back in Nashville, in your love-charm in Father Angleton's tent."

Sarah blushed, thinking of poor Calvin, still smitten. "I think I can do that."

"The gunpowder serves the same function as the words," Thalanes explained. "They both build a bridge, to get power from you into the fire."

"Of course." Sarah felt slightly offended. "Like the blood in my love-charm."

"Forgive my lecturing," Thalanes said. "I am, after all, a priest. Sir Isaac Newton, you probably know, was a great wizard."

"Everyone knows that."

"He was a great practicing magician and an even greater theoretical one."

"What's a theoretical magician?"

"I mean a scholar of magic, and how magic works."

"You mean that Sir Isaac wrote the *Philosophiae Naturalis Principia Magica* just the year before he joined John Churchill's Glorious Revolution against the Necromancer's Eternal Commonwealth. Everyone knows that, too."

Thalanes smiled. "Perhaps not everyone."

"Fine, but I know it."

"Have you read the book?"

Sarah shook her head. "The Elector's got a library, but it isn't that good."

"Read it when you can. Newton formulated two laws to explain the efficacy of a material component in any work of gramarye."

"This I don't know."

"I'm glad to hear I am finally able to teach you something." Thalanes laughed. "Newton's Law of Sympathy states that things that appear to be connected, are in fact connected. And his Law of Contagion states that things that have once been together, are always together."

Sarah tried to apply Newton's laws to the lighting of the fire and the little pile of gunpowder in Thalanes's palm. "So Sir Isaac would say that the gunpowder is an efficacious material component," she said slowly, "because gunpowder and fire appear to be connected, so they really are."

"Very good."

She considered further. "I suppose if I hold the gunpowder in my hand and then throw it into the fire when I cast, then I also catch up the Law of Contagion. Me, the gunpowder, and the fire will always be together, because we were once together."

"Excellent," Thalanes said. "You would have run circles even around old Palindres." He poured the gunpowder into her hand, carefully dusting all of the grains off his fingers into the neat little pile.

"Colored powder and smoke. What's the third thing?" Sarah tried not to show her pride.

"The third thing I want you do," he said, "is the trickiest of all, and there's no guarantee you'll be able to do it."

"I reckon I'll be able." Sarah lapsed into her Calhoun Mountain accent.

"Instead of using the words to bring magic power out from inside you to light the fire, I want you to use the ley line."

She felt daunted, but tried not to show it. "Wouldn't it work better if there was a bridge between me and the ley line, something like the Latin words and the gunpowder? Or maybe if I went and stood in the ley line directly."

"Yes," he said, smiling, "proximity matters. You can't just stand anywhere in the world and tap into a ley line anywhere else. But I think we're close enough that you'll be able to do it, using the same words you use to the light the fire. Will you try?"

"How do I go about it?"

"Close your eyes," he instructed her. "Can you feel your own energy?"

"Inside me," she told him. "Like burning. Not like a fire, like a tiny sun."

"Very good. Now, keep your eyes closed and feel around you. With your heart, if that makes sense. Try to find my energy."

Sarah concentrated. It was like sitting in the darkness by a bright flame, turning away to look beyond the comforting radius of her own light to see if there were others.

And there were. She could feel him, suddenly, in the same room. "There you are!"

"Here I am," he agreed. "That's very good. Most people aren't able to detect the mana of others, at least not so easily, not without a spell. If you can sense me, you're probably able to perceive and use ley lines. Keep your eyes closed. Try to find the ley line. It's close."

She let her feelings drift further out into the darkness. She sensed a pool of magical energy nearby that wasn't human, but was warm and friendly to her. It was also uneasy.

"I think I found the dog," she told Thalanes. "He's nervous."

"That's what makes him a good guard dog," the monk said. He was quiet for a moment. "It's interesting that you can sense his feelings. I can't do that much. Now search out beyond the dog."

And there it was. Like a huge river of flame, not far from where she sat, like a roaring bonfire that she had been unable to see before because she had been blinded by the candle in her own hand.

"I have it," she informed him.

"Use your words to make yourself a bridge between the line and the fireplace. The bridge will have to come through you. Light the fire."

Sarah took a deep breath and opened her soul to the shining light of the ley line. "*Ignem facio,*" she uttered, and she tossed the gunpowder into the fire.

Light and heat poured through her. It was what she thought it must feel like to be hit by lightning, her whole body crackled and hurt and then she felt drained . . . and fire sprang from the wood.

"It turns out that you're able to use ley lines," Thalanes said as she opened her eyes. His face looked gentle and proud in the flickering yellow light of the fire, and on impulse, Sarah leaped forward and hugged him. He patted her back awkwardly at first, but then wrapped his arms around her and hugged her back.

The hug hurt a little; her skin felt strangely tender.

The dog barked outside and the door opened. Calvin stood in the doorway, his lanky body framed and his features hidden by the cold sunlight behind him.

"Cal!" she called, disentangling herself from the monk and scooting aside to give Calvin a clear view of the flames. "Look, I lit the fire! I mean, using hexing...gramarye...Latin and a bit of your gunpowder and the ley line!"

"Very good." Cal sounded distracted, but he came and crouched down beside her and looked close at the flames. He needed a bath, too—he smelled like wet riverbank.

Cal reached into the fireplace and grabbed one end of a burning log. He shifted it around, adjusting the pile of wood.

"I thought you were going to get food," Sarah pressed him, seeing he had returned empty-handed.

"Careful," Thalanes said to him. "You don't want to put the fire out."

"No," Cal answered, "I don't." He swung the blazing log out of the fire and cracked it against the monk's head, striking him to the floor in a shower of sparks.

Calvin felt himself starting to swoon and he figured he had just one chance left.

Not-Sarah's head was still bent back to touch its own shoulderblades as it squeezed Cal. He staggered back, gasping from the pain, until he could feel a tree behind him, and dug his heels into its lower trunk. His ribs ached and breath barely squeaked in and out of him as the thing crushed his chest. It was now or never; he covered both of not-Sarah's eyes with his hands, ignoring the muddy stench that rose from its face—

and kicked himself forward with both legs.

He rode not-Sarah down with his chest, feeling its wet head and body thumping horribly into the rocks, cushioning his fall as they hit.

Calvin rolled away and scrambled to his feet, sucking cool air into his lungs. He was tempted to turn and run up to Crowder's and get help, but a blow to the back of his head with a stone would kill him and put paid to any thought that he might rescue—much less marry—Sarah.

Besides, he had a plan.

Not-Sarah sprang to its feet with a limberness that was horrible when matched with the creature's deformity. It slid partly out of its Sarah-hide like a rabbit halfway skinned for the pot. Its head poked backward and down from its shoulders, and its skull and back were punched up like a ball of kneaded bread dough.

The monster charged.

Cal was ready.

He slipped the lariat off his belt and threw the loop over not-Sarah's shoulders. Its head, knocked askew as it was, made a perfect hook for the braided leather, and Cal's long-practiced muscles overcame his exhaustion and pain. He neatly lassoed not-Sarah's head as it charged him, pulled it hard in his direction and then jumped aside, turning the lariat around a tree trunk behind him as he moved. Not-Sarah fell to its side, lariat tightened around its neck. Cal heaved with all his weight against the heavy dragging clay. He looped the other end of the rope around its leg and then pulled it tight to the tree trunk, finishing it with a quick hitch.

Not-Sarah lay twisted around the trunk of the tree, tied bent head to pelvis like some hideously mutilated calf. It glared at Cal with banked fire in its open eye. It rattled once, and then was still.

"I reckon that'll hold you." Cal picked up his tomahawk, wiping greasy clay residue from its sharp head in the leaves and replacing it on his belt.

Not-Sarah grunted, and Cal peered at it again. It was straining, as if by the strength of its broken, boneless neck it could pull the tree down.

"That ain't gonna work," Calvin sneered, but he took a closer look.

The lariat was beginning to dig into the clay of the creature's neck. That would have been an excruciating—and very bloody—wound in a man, but not-Sarah grunted and snuffled and continued to pull, sawing the braided leather of the lariat loop deeper into its neck.

It was going to cut its own head off to escape.

"Dammit!" Cal shouted. "Don't you ever give up?"

Not-Sarah laughed, deep and hollow.

Cal splashed out into the river, searching among the stones.

Not-Sarah continued to pull. The lariat was halfway through its neck now, and the head hung free at a gruesome angle, like the loose stopper of a wineskin or a tent flap in the wind.

Where was his money pouch? Calvin cursed the stones for being the same brown-leather color as his wallet. He wasn't sure exactly where in the river the purse had fallen. He splashed to his knees, shivering, and felt his way across the stones.

Plop! Calvin looked over and saw that not-Sarah's head had fallen completely off. It lay in the leaves on one cheek, staring at him. Not-Sarah kicked and fumbled to dislodge itself from his rope.

He searched more urgently. The water was chilled by the season and his fingers quickly lost all capacity for subtle discernment— they had barely enough sensation in them to check each stone for slime before moving on to the next half-seen, submerged object. Where was that purse? He felt his heart hammer in his chest and the twinge in his ribcage became a spear in his lungs.

Not-Sarah jerked itself free and jumped to its feet.

Waaaaraaagh!

It rushed at him.

Cal's hand found the leather of his purse and plucked it from the freezing torrent. "Jumpin' Jerusalem!" He stumbled up and away from the charging monster.

He tugged at the drawstrings and found them swollen and sticking.

Cal nearly tripped over the rocks as he exited the river on the far side and kicked through leaf drifts. The wet clay smell and the squish-splash of the heavy feet warned him that not-Sarah was upon him. He ducked and spun away, cutting upstream at a sharp angle. The creature lunged past him, then turned on his trail.

His hands were as numb as the rest of him was seared and screaming, but Calvin managed to yank open the drawstrings and jam his fingers down inside. His hands closed around a fistful of coins just as not-Sarah plowed into him from behind, knocking him sprawling.

Stunned, reeling, battered, he held on to the money.

Its arms were wrapped around his neck, and he felt the wet, squishy clay of them as they screwed tight, crushing the air out of his body.

With one eye pressed down against a cold, damp river rock, Cal managed to peer into his gnarled claw of a fist with the other. Three silver shillings.

He clamped his open palm down on not-Sarah's forearm.

Graaaawraagh!

He was rewarded instantly with a howl. Eerily, the howl came not from the body clinging to his back and neck but from the disconnected head, still across the river.

Cal shuddered in disgust.

The thing jerked spastically and tried to disengage. Cal's head spun with pain and lack of oxygen, but he refused to let not-Sarah go, wrapping his own arms around its bicep, choking through the cloud of yellow sulfur that billowed out from the three coins.

It dragged him and they rolled, thrashing on the rocks.

Grwaaaaaagh! the head cried, like a pint-sized wailing goblin.

Not-Sarah heaved him off and they both scrambled to their feet. Swaying, Calvin gouged for a handful of clay flesh under the yellow fumes and came away with the coins in a gobbet of muck. Not-Sarah whimpered for a moment, and turned as if to run.

Cal tackled it. His body screamed as they went down again onto the rocks together, this time with the headless not-Sarah facing forward and Calvin on top, his fist free and armed. He rose up above his attacker, fist held high, and punched his hand full of vengeful silver down into its chest with a loud wet *plop*.

Aaaghaaaghaaaaaarahghg! not-Sarah wailed. Cal looked across the river, and saw the disembodied head twitching.

"Shut up!" he roared, and swished his hand around inside the muddy mess. The creature's chest was liquefying as the sulfur jetted out. It quivered and thrashed under him.

Nghaagh! Nghaagh! Nooooo!

Suddenly, sulfur erupted from the bad eye of not-Sarah's head and its body's thrashing became a wild bucking, like a horse in need of being broken.

Cal held on. His body ached, his eyes stung, his tongue tasted of brimstone, but he knew he'd won. He rode out at the last few seconds of flailing, then found himself kneeling in a puddle of wet clay, his clothing soaked, muddy and rimed in yellow, the fingers of his fist closed around his three precious silver coins.

He lurched to his feet, urgently aware that there had been two of these things before, and that the other might at any moment attack him or, worse, might now be attacking Sarah. He hobbled to retrieve his clay-smeared lariat. Looping it, he took the opportunity to spit on the gray and yellow lump where not-Sarah's head had burned itself out like a firework on the emperor's birthday.

"You should a stuck to pigs."

He turned his face uphill and stumbled as fast as he could toward Crowder's stand. Sarah might need him.

"If I'd a knew it'd be such a blessin' to you,
I'd a beat you years ago."

———•◦◄———

CHAPTER TEN

Sarah stumbled away from Calvin, her body crackling with fear.

"Calvin Calhoun!" she snapped. "What are you doin'?"

Calvin said nothing and swung the flaming log at her head. Sarah slipped on a straw pallet and fell as the great arc of fire *whooshed* over her. She hit the dirt floor hard, landing enough on her hands and backside that she was stung, but didn't lose her breath.

She rolled away and he swung a second time, overhand, smashing his flaming club into the straw-stuffed pallet. Sparks showered from it, and the pallet, old and dry and oily, promptly began to smolder.

"Calvin, stop it!" she yelled.

He attacked again, she ducked, and he plowed a furrow of sparks out of the timber wall. Many of them fell glittering onto a second pallet, which also took flame.

She had to put the fire out. Cal raised his arm to swat at her again—

Sarah opened herself to the ley line and shouted, "*ignem exstinguo!*"

Her body tingled painfully as the energy of the ley roared through her. She had no time to direct her will precisely, and all the fires in the room—fireplace, pallets, club—were snuffed out. Calvin hesitated, looking in surprise at the charred wood in his hand.

189

Sarah dove for the corner. Her knees wobbled, and she felt like vomiting. Too much, she realized, she hadn't been careful enough, she had put out too many fires at once and poured out too much of her body's own energy.

She grabbed the Elector's staff, wheeling to keep Calvin at bay. Good against evil spirits, white ash, and Calvin stepped back warily, eyes impassive and searching.

Was he possessed?

Sarah's hands shook, holding a staff that she had walked with all the way from Calhoun Mountain but that now felt like lead in her grip. She couldn't fight him off, ash staff or not; he was bigger and heavier and had a longer reach. She groped into her mental drawer of Latin and tried to put together an attack spell. She didn't have much strength left, but she figured it was all right if her spell knocked her unconscious, as long as it got Calvin, too.

"*Corporem*—" she began, and Calvin threw his log weapon— slamming her in the chest.

"Whooomph!" she gasped, and she lost the spell along with the air in her lungs.

She rocked back, slamming into the cabin wall.

"*Corporem*—" she squeaked.

Calvin fell on her like a hammer on an anvil, pounding her in the mouth, in the cheek, knocking her to the ground. She couldn't bring her will to bear under the onslaught, couldn't think of a way to fight back, didn't think she had the power to muster a decent magical counterattack, anyway.

Terror and pain gripped her, but she wouldn't give in. Gripping the ash staff, she raised it to try to ward him off.

He punched her in her bad eye.

A flash of scorching agony and light flooded her mind and she rolled forward, facedown onto the hard dirt. She dropped the staff and buried her face in her hands.

Too much, too much pain, in her skin, in her chest, and especially in her head.

She felt something loose and moving inside her eye socket, the one that had never opened.

Was her skull shattered? Calvin punched her again in the back, and then stopped. She realized from the sound of his footsteps and the scrape of wood on packed earth that he was picking up his club again.

She was too hurt to care anymore. She touched her battered eye tenderly, wincing at the fresh pain. Something moved behind the always-closed eyelid, which then opened, and in a soft dribble of warm fluid, a small, hard object fell into her fingers.

Had she lost her eye?

She almost laughed at herself for caring. Any second now, Calvin—the thing that *looked like* Calvin—would bash her brains out with a hunk of firewood, and here she lay, worrying about whether she had lost, of all things, her bad eye.

Through split lips, she laughed defiantly.

Calvin yelled without words. She didn't brace herself, just relaxed, closed her eyes, and prepared for her death.

But the blow didn't fall on her.

Sarah heard a scuffle and looked up.

The world was different, wildly different from anything she had ever seen before, and she almost vomited at the suddenness and extremeness of the change. Two figures struggled in the center of the room, wrestling with arms on shoulders, and through her good eye they looked like two identical Calvin Calhouns.

Nearly identical, because one of them looked beat all to hell, was caked in yellow grime, and had a tomahawk and lariat on his belt.

Hammered yellow Calvin seemed to be attempting to slap a clenched fist to the other Calvin's face, and the other Calvin, bad Calvin, the Calvin who had been attacking her moments earlier, fought to get his hands around battered Calvin's neck.

What made the room suddenly alien, though, what disoriented her, were the images coming through her other eye, the eye through which she had never before seen. She saw two figures still, but neither one of them looked exactly like the Calvin Calhoun she was accustomed to seeing.

One of them was a column of warm, white light.

The other was a smoking, black, cold fire, sucking brilliance and heat out of the room.

With her witchy eye, too, she saw the light of the dog, barking madly from the doorway, and the wan light of Thalanes, slumped on the floor, and out the door, coursing through the stand's yard like the Mississippi, a giant river of multicolored light.

The ley line of the Natchez Trace.

If she could see out her witchy eye, though, what was she holding in her hand?

"Git outta here! Sarah, git up and git on outta here!" It was column-of-light Calvin, hammered yellow Calvin...real Calvin.

The ash staff lay on the floor. Looking at it through her witchy eye Sarah saw that it, too, was a thin, hot line of light. She picked it up and levered herself to her feet, moving slowly and feeling that the wrestling Calvins moved even more slowly, lumbering back and forth across the room, each fighting to get at the other's head and neck.

She took a deep breath. Then she readied the staff, rotating it to point its butt end at the struggling columns of light and darkness. She kept wrapped in her fingers, and held tight to the staff, the hard, rounded thing that had fallen out of her eye socket.

"*Diabolum expello,*" she muttered, running her fingers over the staff and channeling into it the energy torrent of the ley line outside the door. Her skin burned and she couldn't breathe.

Light-Calvin was gaining the upper hand, pushing dark-Calvin's throat with one forearm; he was within inches of clapping his balled fist to dark-Calvin's face.

"Run, Sarah!" he shouted again. His expression was harrowed. How must she look, with her bad eye smashed open? Something awful.

Then dark-Calvin jerked light-Calvin sideways bodily—

light-Calvin gasped in pain—

and dark-Calvin grabbed his foe by the throat. The real Calvin Calhoun tried to shout again, but only choked and gagged.

"*Diabolum expello,*" Sarah murmured again.

Stepping forward, she jammed the Elector's white ash staff into the chest of dark-Calvin. The bruises on her chest and arms flared painfully and she gasped, but still she shoved with all her might, and the staff sank into the creature's flesh, piercing it like a spear.

Sarah's body exploded in heat and pain and she fell.

Immediately, dark-Calvin released his grip on light-Calvin's neck. Light-Calvin—just plain *Calvin*—stepped back unsteadily, rocking on the balls of his feet.

The *thing* impaled on her walking stick howled and began to convulse. She watched it from the floor, wishing she'd been able to hold on to the staff, to keep the creature pinned. Instead, it jerked and spun wildly about with the wood sticking out of its body.

The black fire she saw through her witchy eye popped and jumped like water on a hot skillet, sometimes seeming to pull right out of the physical body that held it, only to snap back. Finally the black column gripped the staff to pull it out—

and Calvin slapped his open hand onto the thing's chest.

Graaaaraaaraaaarghhhhh!

The scream pierced her brain, the convulsions redoubled, and bitter yellow brimstone filled the air in long plumes firing from the creature's body. Calvin kept his fist pressed against the monster and grabbed Sarah's ash staff with his other hand to pin it in place. It jerked, it tumbled, it spun like a pinwheel, throwing off yellow smoke thick mud. It shrank and melted as it spun, and then finally the ash staff fell through empty air to clatter on the hard floor and the black fire was gone.

Calvin fell to his knees. "Jerusalem, Sarah. Lord hates a whiner, but I b'lieved we'd had it for a minute there, you and I."

Sarah closed her witchy eye, and found she could thereby shut out the strange images of Calvin as a figure of white light and Thalanes as a glowing blue puddle. "I b'lieve Iron Andy sent the right man on this here journey," she said.

"Iffen he'd a knew about these mud fellers, I expect he might a sent more'n one." His cheerfulness, weak and wry as it was, was almost shocking to her. She felt as if she'd been trampled by a herd of flaming mustangs. "You're a sight, Sarah."

She laughed. "I reckon I might prefer you not see me at this moment, Calvin Calhoun, iffen I look half as bad as you do."

"Iffen you *feel* half as bad," he replied, "you could use a barrel of cold beer and a week's sleep. Mebbe we should ought to tell Thalanes about these here clay things now, do you reckon?"

"For that bump on his noggin, he deserves to know. And I still need a bath."

She kept her witchy eye firmly shut so Calvin couldn't see it—she wanted to examine herself in a mirror before she let anyone else look at her—and climbed gingerly to her feet. He helped her limp to the light of the doorway, where she shook him off.

She stood on the stand's porch looking down at her clenched fingers. Did she dare open them?

"Sarah, what's wrong?" Cal called over her shoulder. "Don't be shy, you look jest fine in yeller!"

She slowly uncurled her fingers.

Lying in her palm, now caked in soggy yellow brimstone, was an acorn.

Through her good eye, Sarah saw it plain, brown, and ordinary, but through her witchy eye it burned with the brilliance and power of a lighthouse, blue and white.

Ezekiel Angleton dreamed, as he'd dreamed every night for weeks, of running through the forest. He was a tireless creature that followed its quarry along a narrow track through deciduous skeletons and clumps of bristling pine.

In the dreams, he ran south and west. He knew that from the sun that rose on his left shoulder and set before him by day, and by the sinking end of the zodiac into which he charged through the night.

His quarry ran ahead of him, and though he could not see it, he sensed it. He could *taste* it on the wind.

Since his dream of attacking Sarah . . . Sarah . . . he couldn't bring himself to attach a surname to her anymore, connecting her either with the Imperial family or with these obstinate sniping hill-rat Calhouns . . . since he had dreamed of attacking *Witchy Eye* and battling the strange youth with fire in his hand, he'd passed all his sleeping moments running. He had not dreamed again of Calhoun Mountain, and though he didn't doubt his God, or God's servant St. Martin, he began to wonder whether, after all, he'd been correct to judge his dream a prophecy.

This time, again, he dreamed that he fought.

He dreamed of racing along the narrow track, following the scent—the *taste*—of his prey, a wet river crossing, a large stone- and timber-built waystation, a courtyard, a well, a long-eared dog that growled and yapped at him.

Suddenly he was looking at *her*, inside a chamber red with fire. The Witchy Eye, the abomination.

Also the traitor monk, Thalanes. He saw them tall and liquid in his dream, flowing before his eyes in flickering light, but he could not mistake their identities. They welcomed him; they didn't know he was their enemy.

Ezekiel rejoiced in his heart when his dream-self struck down the priest with a sword of fire. He thrilled towering over the abomination, forcing her to cower as he prepared a killing blow.

But he was shaken by the dream's end. He was surprised

again, and the abomination was spared, by the appearance of the tall young man, the demonic angel with his fistful of fire. They fought, and Ezekiel struggled mightily to keep that fire from his face, and to wrestle down the young man, and he was on the cusp of winning, had his strong fingers wrapped around the fire-thrower's throat—

when a spear was shoved into his side.

Even as my Lord, he thought as he collapsed, shuddering, in his dream and awoke, shivering, in his tent. *My cross alone is not enough, my enemies must pierce my side with the spear as well.*

He lay still, recollecting where he was. It was late afternoon, and he sprawled on a blanket in his tent on the slopes of Calhoun Mountain. Lazy Appalachee birds chirruped their defiance and the air was just beginning to turn cold.

He had been dreaming.

It wasn't a dream of his death. Not did it seem prophecy. But if not prophecy, what was it? The Lord helped his servants, and Ezekiel believed this dream must be of God, it must be telling him something.

But what?

The dreams ended in defeat. Not *his* defeat, though, if they were not prophetic, but the defeat of something else, some unknown ally. Some creature through whose eyes Ezekiel could see in his sleep. Not prophecy, but still a divine gift of vision.

Where his ally had failed, Ezekiel would triumph.

What were the dreams telling him?

They gave him a direction. South and west. In the dreams, some ally followed the Witchy Eye south and west on a narrow track through the wilderness. It was no Imperial road, it was some other trail, some well-traveled backcountry highway.

South and west.

He ruminated as he pulled on his boots and rolled to his feet. "Captain Berkeley!"

"In the tent, Mr. Angleton," Berkeley drawled.

Ezekiel found Berkeley sitting at the table, laying out his cards. God curse the Crown Land Cavaliers! Either they were outright pagans or they were verminous with silly superstitions, always blathering on about horoscopes and fortune telling.

"Captain Berkeley," he started again, "am I right to think that the north end of the Natchez Trace is near here? It's a narrow road, isn't it, cutting through the forest?" Ezekiel had traveled in the empire, but hadn't often been this far south and west, and he generally rode on the emperor's highways.

"I believe you're correct," Berkeley agreed, "though I've always had a preference for the speed of the Imperial Pikes."

"That goes south and west, doesn't it? Where does it end up?"

Berkeley raised his eyebrows in surprise. "Blazes."

"What's wrong with you, man?" Ezekiel snapped, in no mood for the captain's pettishness.

Berkeley pointed at the table, where he had laid out three cards: the Highway, the River, and the City. "You'll notice that my luck continues. I turn up the Major Arcana."

"Damn your superstition, man," Ezekiel growled. "Tell me about the Natchez Trace."

"Damn *yours*, Parson," Berkeley snapped back.

Ezekiel wanted to hit the man. "Is that what I must tell His Imperial Majesty, then? That the Captain of his dragoons damned the Lord God and refused to answer a simple question put to him by the emperor's confessor?"

Berkeley sighed and looked down.

"The Natchez Trace does go south and west." He picked up the Tarock identified as the Highway and showed it to Ezekiel. The painting was not of an Imperial Pike, of course, since Franklin had designed his Tarock before the signing of the Compact, but of an older, narrower highway, barely more than a dirt track, winding away from the viewer toward a distant river, between wooded hills.

Berkeley set aside the Highway and continued. "It runs from Nashville and it carries traffic toward the city of New Orleans." He showed Ezekiel the City, a horizon of spires and a busy marketplace underneath.

"That's the Lightning Cathedral," Ezekiel said.

"Or the Cathedral of St. Louis on the Place d'Armes."

"That's a painting of Philadelphia," Ezekiel snapped. "Stop imagining things. The cards do not talk to you, Captain."

Berkeley shrugged and traded it for the River, the card showing a muddy brown expanse so wide it might have been a sea. Thick green forest bordered the river on the left side of the card, and the lights of houses twinkled in the darkness on the right. "New Orleans, of course, being the city at the mouth of the Mississippi River."

✧   ✧   ✧

"If I'd a knew it'd be such a blessin' to you," Calvin said, "I'd a beat you years ago."

Sarah had not, after all, had a bath. When Thalanes had awakened, Calvin and Sarah had recounted to him their previous encounter with the clay not-men, and their battles with the ersatz Sarah by the riverside and Calvin in the cabin.

"Mockers," he had said, holding his injured head. "There may be others with them, or something worse. We must flee."

They had quickly tended wounds—Thalanes pronounced Calvin's rib probably bruised, possibly cracked, but definitely not broken—and had gathered their packs again. Calvin had gone back to Mrs. Crowder's pantry for a loaf of oat-flour bread and salt ham, and then they'd resumed their march, all three dusted yellow from crown to toe. They moved slowly, and Sarah knew it was because of her, but she didn't object. She felt stretched and burned.

Thalanes led them under cover of trees off the road but parallel to it, keeping the Trace in sight and stopping to scrutinize every group of travelers they saw.

He had said nothing since they had left Crowder's stand.

Sarah had torn a strip of fabric from her skirt and wrapped it around her head, covering her witchy eye with a makeshift patch—the visions of light and power made ordinary movement nauseating, so she shut them out.

She leaned on her staff, scorched and stained yellow but unbroken. After a couple of hours of silence from Thalanes, she had tried to draw him out of his shell by telling them both about her revelations of the afternoon. Sarah recounted that she'd been hit in the head by the not-Calvin Mocker, that it had opened her eye and that through her witchy eye she saw living things as columns of light, and that she could see the ley line through it.

She didn't mention the acorn, which she had tucked hidden away inside her dress.

Thalanes hadn't taken the bait, but Calvin had been impressed. Every few minutes, for the rest of the afternoon, he whistled in inarticulate amazement.

"I guess you've got a right to be grumpy," she said to the monk.

Thalanes sighed. "I'm not grumpy." He paused for several long seconds. "I'm a little grumpy. But much more than that, I'm terrified. Also, I'm trying to concentrate, to be sure that we're not being followed by further Mockers, or by other foes. The effort drains me."

"I find it a mite unsettlin' that the Mockers leave you feelin' scairt, too," Cal commented. "I's hopin' you'd be more...non-chalant."

"They do scare me," Thalanes admitted. "But what scares me more is that I'm quite certain that Ezekiel Angleton didn't send those things. He's a strict man, and a dangerous one, and he can work a bit of gramarye, but Mockers are black magic. I've known Angleton for years, and I'm confident that's something he would never knowingly touch."

"So I have another enemy." Sarah feigned indifference. "So what? It was the emperor, or someone in his service."

"How'd those things take our shapes?" Cal asked. "The first time, they weren't nothin' but faceless clay."

"They must have got hold of a piece of you—skin, or hair, or blood, or something similar—the first time you met them. That's also how they were following us, I expect." Thalanes considered. "As for who sent the Mockers...I wonder."

"What do you mean, black magic?" Sarah felt relief that the monk was talking to her again.

Thalanes frowned. "The Mocker's body is common clay. It's animated by a devil that is summoned and bound into it. Christian wizards argue about what kind of magic is appropriate, but this is *definitely* infernal gramarye, the sort of thing *no* Christian wizard will touch."

"Stinks of Oliver Cromwell to me," Cal said, "the New Model Army."

Sarah shivered at his mention of the Necromancer and almost turned to spit over her shoulder, to ward off the name's bad luck.

"The New Model Army were wood, weren't they?" she asked. "I always imagined them like big wooden puppets without strings, marching off to fight for the Commonwealth."

"Yes," the monk murmured, "you have it pretty much right. And yes, Cal, it does stink of Oliver Cromwell."

They walked in ominous silence for a few minutes, and then Calvin offered his considered view, "I can't see as this changes much of anything."

"It doesn't," Thalanes agreed. "We're still bound for New Orleans to find Will. This is only a reminder that we must take great care."

"Is there any chance those Mockers we left back at Crowder's might follow us?" Sarah was a hexer, but such creatures were outside her experience. "Any chance they're not destroyed after all?"

"No chance," the monk said. "I doubt the demons are destroyed, but the bodies are, and you cast the demons out quite nicely. I wish you'd told me about them sooner, but I congratulate both of you for handling them as you did. Mockers have dragged many a watchful man down to an early death. You did very well."

"Thank you." Cal accepted the compliment with good humor. "I do feel as I'm collectin' some interestin' stories to tell my grandkids one day... iffen I survive to have any."

Thalanes lapsed again into silence. They walked into the night, until the monk declared himself satisfied they had not been followed, whereupon Cal located a spring in a sheltered hollow masked by a stand of pine, and made camp.

"I'll take the first watch. After all, I had a nap this afternoon." Thalanes grinned and rubbed the contusion on his head. "Sarah, will you join me for a few minutes?"

Calvin looked as if he might object, but Sarah shot pleading eyes at him and he shut his mouth, bundling himself into his bedroll and falling quickly into regular snores. Sarah followed the monk to the top of the hollow and they sat, shaded from the light of the half moon by a pair of bent old pine trees.

He sat very close, but she found it didn't bother her as much as it used to.

"Let me look at your eye," he said to her gently.

She balked, but loosed her eye patch and turned her face to him. He no longer trembled, but glowed a bright white, with a tinge of blue. She found, looking at him directly, that she could make out his features with her witchy eye's sight, and they were not quite the same. He was recognizably Thalanes, but he looked younger, and nobler, and less worn.

"The eye is open," Thalanes said. Sarah bit back the impulse to congratulate him on stating the obvious. "Is this the first time it's ever opened?" She nodded, and he continued his inspection. "It doesn't look infected," the monk told her. "It looks like whatever was bothering it has gone away. The tissue is inflamed, but it should heal now."

Sarah thought of the acorn and felt she had to say something. She owed it to the little monk.

"Your irises are not the same color," he observed. "This eye's iris looks white, or perhaps very pale blue. And the pupil is much larger."

"Like I said, I see different out of this one." She again explained seeing the ley line, and the Mocker, and the dog, and her companions.

"What do I look like?" he asked her.

"White. Kind of blue. Shiny. Handsome."

He chuckled gently. "That's a change. And can you see the ley line still?"

She pointed down into the valley below them. "It follows the road pretty close, though not exactly. It's huge. It's a big river of fire, white and blue and all sorts of colors."

"What about other creatures? What can you see around us now?"

Sarah looked around. In the moonlight, her natural eye strained to see anything, but living, moving things jumped out at her in blazes of light through her witchy eye. "Owl," she said. "Mockingbird. Woodpecker. Two deer, down along the ridge—one's a fawn. Raccoon." She saw several large bright smudges, further away but moving closer, hugging the ley line. "Two people, both mounted."

"Do they seem out of the ordinary?" he asked her.

"That's a stupid question," she snapped, and immediately regretted it. "Sorry. I mean, everything seems out of the ordinary. I ain't used...I'm not used to seeing people glow like this. But those folks glow just like Calvin does, just plain white."

"Just like Calvin, but not like me?" he clarified.

"Exactly," she said. "You're sort of blue."

"You're seeing the life energies of things. Their *auras*, a practitioner of gramarye should say. *Our* auras. Fascinating."

Sarah huddled deeper into her coat. She didn't feel fascinating, she felt like a monster. Like a monster that had been very stupid, several times, and was now extremely lucky even to be alive.

What did her own aura look like? As discreetly as she could, she gazed down through her witchy eye at her bare hands. She shouldn't have been, but in the moment, she was shocked to see that her own aura was blue-tinged, more like Thalanes's than Calvin's.

Like the acorn that had fallen from her eye.

She pulled the acorn from its hiding place and held it out to Thalanes with a trembling hand.

He looked puzzled. "What's that?"

"This is what was troubling my eye," she said quietly. "This was *inside* my eye, under my eyelid."

"I'm not sure I understand," he said.

She tried again. "It's *always* been inside my eye, without my knowing it, and today it popped out."

He was quiet for several long moments. "Thank you," he said. His voice sounded almost reverent. "I suggest you put that away, and keep it a secret."

"What is it?" she asked him.

The monk shook his head slowly. "I don't know, beyond what I've already told you. Your father blessed three acorns with his dying breath, your mother ate them, she conceived and bore three children who were all born wounded. Now it turns out your wound held an acorn all along." He shrugged. "I don't know what it means, but keep the acorn, and keep it secret. It may turn out to be a thing of power."

"Like the Cahokian regalia?"

"Yes." He chuckled. "And I see I owe you more explanation. Here again, I regret that I don't know much. The origins and uses of the regalia are unknown to me, and would have been given to you in the right time and place by your father." He looked down into the hollow where Calvin lay. "I can tell you that the regalia consist of three things, and each bears a different sort of power."

"The crown, the orb, and the sword," Sarah said. "Those are famous."

"Correct. The iron crown of Cahokia, called the Sevenfold Crown for its seven iron points, is its ultimate symbol of *political* power. The nobles of Cahokia swear all their important oaths upon it and its presence provides the legitimate seal of any occasion of royal action. Without it, the king or queen of Cahokia is no ruler. Its absence is one reason the nobles of Cahokia have been unable to unite behind any one candidate for the throne for the last fifteen years."

"If there's no Sevenfold Crown, there's no monarchy and no kingdom," she said meditatively. "The decision to choose a king without the crown would be a decision to remake the kingdom entirely from scratch, to throw away all tradition and heritage."

"Yes," the monk said, surprise in his face. "That's a very perceptive comment."

"I tried to make sure Iron Andy wasn't wasting his time." She felt shy.

"The iron orb," Thalanes continued, "is named the Orb of Etyles, and it's a thing of *magical* power. I don't know any more than that, except to say that in my years with your father, he never allowed himself to be without the Orb of Etyles, and he cast all his mightiest spells with it in his hand."

"Etyles was a prophet," she said. "You were quoting him to us the other day, about Adam's first wife."

Thalanes nodded. "The sword is the only item of the regalia not made of iron. The metal of which it's forged is unknown, at least to me, but it has the appearance of gold. It is a weapon for heroes, and I understand from your father that it bestows great *martial* prowess. Your father carried it into the Spanish War, and against highwaymen and beastkind in the borders of the Ohio, and was a renowned warrior."

"The Lion of Missouri." She'd heard the songs.

"I'm afraid I don't know the sword's name," Thalanes continued, "but that doesn't mean it doesn't have one. I was your father's confessor, but I wasn't privy to all his secrets, especially to his royal secrets."

"What do you mean, royal secrets?"

"I mean that the Kings of Cahokia passed down things to their heirs besides the regalia. Information, secrets, ancient alliances, and obligations. I am ignorant of all of it."

Sarah let the information sink in. She was glad she'd come from Calhoun Mountain with Thalanes, and she was beginning to trust him, but she didn't understand the man at all.

"Why are you helping me, Father?" she asked.

"Once you raise your banner," he said slowly, "you'll find that many people will flock to it. Even, I think, without the Sevenfold Crown. You're the rightful Queen of Cahokia, *my* queen, as you are rightfully the head of the Penn family, and those things make you very special."

"That ain't it, though, is it? I mean, that *isn't* it."

"In part, it is." He was quiet for a long time. "I've served your father and your mother for many years. They were my earthly lord and lady as they were my friends, and I serve you now because I remain in their service. All I can do for you, I will."

"Can you tell me how to be queen?" she asked. "I don't know anything about being a leader."

"Don't you?"

She considered. "I suppose a leader should be a really good person," she said after a few moments. "I mean, like Jesus. Noble and self-sacrificing."

Thalanes laughed. "That's an answer for Sunday School." She thought he was mocking her. "But really, Sarah, I'm the wrong person to ask. I've never been a leader—I'm a solitary person and I belong to an order of solitary people. All I know of leadership is that the leader is the person who has to make all the hard choices. That will be one of your roles as queen, the maker of difficult decisions. I don't envy you; no sane person would."

She was disappointed. "Can't you tell me anything more helpful than that?"

"I can tell you men will follow a leader who is good to them," he said, frowning slightly, "whether that leader is personally righteous or not."

"Thank you," Sarah said. "That gives me a lot to work on."

"Is that sarcasm?" he asked after a moment.

"It was meant to be humility."

He patted her shoulder. "It's good that you're improving your gramarye and learning to use the leys. You must be very careful with that, of course—if you open up your soul too far to a ley line, it can suck you dry or burn you to a cinder. You should also accustom yourself to the new vision your eye is giving you, learn to understand and use it."

"Any particular advice to give me on that?"

"None." He shook his head. "I don't have that gift myself, though I've heard of it. Some call it 'Second Sight.' Do you know how to speak in Court Speech? If not, you should learn."

"I think I'll manage with Court Speech," she said. "I've read my Bible, and a fair amount of Shakespeare. I wouldn't want to have to talk like that all the time, though."

"No," he agreed, "well, you won't have to. The beauty of Court Speech is that every Power determines how it's used in its own court. Usually, nobles and Electors speak to each other without it, and save the Court Speech for when they address inferiors and ambassadors. It serves them as a sort of insulation against familiarity."

He paused.

"What is it?" she asked. "Is something wrong?"

"I'm talking a lot." Thalanes buried his face in his hands

a moment. "Sarah, you shouldn't lean on me more than you absolutely have to—not on anyone, really, but especially not on me—I am a broken reed, at best."

Sarah laughed out loud. "If you're a broken reed, Father, I'm stubble."

"I've already failed you. I told your mother about you, and when she was tortured, she told the emperor." Thalanes's face was flat, but his voice quivered.

Sarah felt sick. She had known, more or less, that something of that nature must have happened, but it hurt her to hear the events recounted so baldly. She should have been there; she felt *she* had failed her mother, which she knew was a completely unreasonable response, and then she saw what the monk must be feeling. "You told her at her request."

"Yes," he agreed. "I should have been wiser. Also, I should have been wiser than to leave your father alone with the man who betrayed him."

"Did you know he was going to be betrayed?"

"No." Thalanes shook his head. "But I knew the storms of envy and hatred that surrounded him. I should have been stronger than my friendships, and wiser than my precepts."

The quiet sorrow in his voice corresponded with a changed tone to the color she saw in him through her witchy eye, nothing she could describe, but a nuance that pierced Sarah's heart. She could *see* his emotional turmoil. She felt like weeping; with an effort, she restrained herself. She needed this man's help, and he was one of her greatest protectors. "Didn't you also take the acorns that my father blessed with his dying breath to my mother?"

He nodded, slightly.

"And you hid me with Elector Calhoun?"

He nodded again.

"And you raced from Philadelphia ahead of the emperor's chaplain, to rescue me from a mortal threat."

"So I haven't led a completely useless life," he said wryly.

"I owe you my very existence," she said to him. "Three times, at least. As your queen, I order you to remember that."

Fearing that if she stayed any longer she would do something to undercut the authority she'd just assumed, Sarah stood and descended into the hollow. She crawled into the bedroll Cal had arranged and stretched herself out gratefully for sleep.

Her body ached. Bread must feel like this, kneaded and baked. It eased her pain a little bit to hear Cal's regular breathing in the darkness. It reminded her of Calhoun Mountain and the Elector and home, and she smiled.

Before replacing the patch over her eye, she looked up at the little monk, still sitting his vigil on the hill above them. She could tell by the subtle shift in the tone of his aura that he was less grieved, calmer.

He felt better.

That made her happy, and she let herself fall asleep.

In the morning they washed in the spring and beat the dust out of their clothing. It wasn't perfect—they all looked jaundiced—but it would do.

Sarah still ached, but as the morning progressed she began to unkink. Her skin was still too warm to the touch and felt like old paper, and she was exhausted, but that was an improvement.

That afternoon, Thalanes and Cal left her in a grove of trees and went down together to a creek flowing across the main path of the Trace to fill their waterskins. Sarah sat, grateful to rest her legs and feet, and closed her eye to try to catch a few minutes' nap.

Click.

"Come along quick and quiet, miss, and don't nobody have to git her brains blowed out today."

Sarah opened her eyes.

The man standing before her was of middling height and heavy, with a slack face not too different from the Crowder's Bassett, and he wore the dirtiest orange cape Sarah had ever seen, over a ragged brown shirt and reddish corte-du-roi trousers. In any other season, the outfit would have been a beacon that made him impossible to miss. In the autumn, it just might make him invisible.

He pointed a pistol at Sarah, with the hammer cocked.

"Poacher?" she asked.

"Git up and let's go," he ordered her.

She stood.

"Smuggler?" she guessed again.

"Yer friends're too far away to hear you even iffen you shout," the heavy man snarled. "So don't try it." He waggled his pistol.

"Besides, Mr. Bullet here'd git to you afore them fellers could git back."

"What do you want?" Sarah needed to buy a minute or two, to think of what to do or maybe to give Cal and Thalanes time to return.

She felt so tired.

"Shut yer mouth and git on that mule." Orange Cape gestured with his pistol. Sarah saw a lean gray horse tethered in the trees and behind it a pack mule, saddled with a ragged blanket.

"You gonna kill me?" She took slow steps toward the pack animal.

"If yer dead, I won't git any money outta you from the Memphites." He grinned, showing yellow teeth with big gaps.

Sarah was to be sold into slavery. She'd pull a wagon, or worse.

"You won't git nothing for me," she warned him. "I'm ugly."

"You'll do jest fine." Orange Cape ran a shivering gaze up and down Sarah's body. "Don't you worry, I'll teach you everythin' you need to know to make the Memphites happy."

Sarah spat. She wanted to cast a spell, but she was weak and tired. She had to do something quick, easy, and effective.

"Git movin'," he ground out through his rotting teeth, and gestured again with the pistol.

Sarah walked slowly toward the mule. "My husband and my father git back here and catch you," she said, "you're a dead man. On the other hand, I got a bit of cash in my pack, and iffen you want it, you can jest take it and go."

She stopped, standing deliberately a couple of paces to the side of the pack mule.

"Like Hell," Orange Cape said. "But you got somethin' else I'd like to have very much, and I reckon I'll jest go ahead and take it from you, soon as we get safely outta here and away from your menfolk. And when I'm finished, I reckon they'll be enough left over to sell to the Memphites." His face hardened. "Now git on my damn mule—"

He gestured with his pistol again, pointing at the mule.

"*Ignem mitto*," Sarah muttered, and she sent a tiny spark into the firing pan of his pistol.

Bang! Orange Cape's gun fired—

the horse and mule both jumped, jerking the tether away—

and Sarah ran.

"Damn you!" Orange Cape shouted.

Sarah didn't look back. She heard the whinnying of the man's horse and the braying of his mule and the crashing sounds of both animals plunging into the thick trees, but she couldn't tell whether Orange Cape was dealing with his animals or chasing her.

She'd had a head start, but she was exhausted and the few extra yards would never be enough to save her. She counted on him to need the horse more than he wanted her, and to be afraid of tangling with Calvin and Thalanes.

She staggered and fell into a crinkling bed of leaves. When a man's hands picked her up moments later, she was enormously relieved to find they belonged to Calvin.

They continued to follow the ley line south and west. They stayed away from inns except when they all went into a stand or a village together to buy food. They stayed off the Trace, though parallel to it, and avoided people. When they could, they ate off the land—berries, apples, hickory nuts, birds, small game.

The little monk was uncomplaining, could walk forever, slept on the ground and ate anything, but it was Calvin who had the skills that fed and sheltered them, building lean-tos tight under the bases of large pines when it rained, shooting and preparing game, and keeping them out of sight of the Trace but always close. He was even more than usually solicitous of Sarah's comfort, which made her feel ill at ease. On the one hand, it made her think it might be nice to be married to Calvin Calhoun. On the other, she felt guilty for having hexed him.

At least she ought to let him in on some of her secrets.

Sarah didn't feel comfortable showing Cal her eye directly, but she let him see it, as if casually, while she had her patch off and was using her Second Sight—she didn't want him to feel as if she was hiding from him. She practiced her Second Sight several times a day, and found that if she tried to use it more than that, she became exhausted and her head hurt. She learned to see increasingly subtle changes in the aural tones of Thalanes and Calvin, and found she could guess their feelings very well, along with such things as, for instance, whether they were lying.

She also found, over the course of a couple of days, that she could read the ley line. The energy flowing through it was disrupted by things traveling on it, and she found that she could thereby predict the size of an approaching party miles before it rolled into view.

Sitting up during her turn at watch through the night, Sarah watched the ley line and wondered whether she'd be able to tell from the disturbance of the line that an approaching party was, for instance, a Mocker—could the line somehow tell her that?

As she felt better, she practiced her gramarye, trying to make it second nature to undertake such simple tasks as firestarting and locating plants. With practice, the short Latin sentences came easier. Sentences and gestures she practiced a lot almost became rote spells, like wizards in stories cast.

She also took guidance from the little monk on tending to the wounds they had each received, gathering herbs and binding them by gramarye into healing compounds that were ingested or made into poultices. After a few days, all their bruises had disappeared, Calvin declared he felt as whole as new, and even her eye had lost the soreness, redness, and inflammation she'd lived with her entire life.

She worked all this magic using the energy of the Natchez Trace ley in carefully controlled amounts. She could only channel a small amount of it through herself at once, and when she took in too much it burned her; also, the ley resisted, it wanted to give her only a little bit of itself, and she had to wrestle with it to draw power from it for larger spells. Could the ley be depleted, say, by a natural disaster? And if it were, would it then draw the life energy out of people and other creatures along its length to replenish itself?

She also learned and practiced various kinds of arcane concealment. She erased their physical tracks from time to time, and made them personally invisible, and cloaked their auras, and created illusions of them walking the other way up the Trace to Nashville just in time to pass New Orleans-bound travelers, and cast spells to lay blankets of forgetfulness on the creatures watching them as they passed. It was too much of an effort to cast any of the spells together, or to sustain any of them for very long, but the hope driving the strategy, devised by the three of them together over a campfire on the second day out from Crowder's stand, was that constant rotation through the various tricks would baffle anyone tracking them.

On the third night after the encounter at Crowder's stand,

Sarah sat watch, alternately chanting her way through Latin paradigms and talking to herself in the Biblical-Shakespearean cadences of Court Speech, as Thalanes had hinted she should. They camped without a fire in a small hollow above the Trace, and she gazed on the multicolored strand of power flow beneath her. The moon was nearing full and the sky was clear, so out her normal eye she had a ghostly-silver view of the valley, with its skeletal trees and occasional rail fences. Out the other she saw a landscape alive with crawling, creeping, and hopping things.

She watched the Trace, and she also watched the two travelers.

They had trudged to a halt and laid down their bedrolls late, after Calvin and Thalanes had fallen asleep. They made their camp at the bottom of the hill on the other side of the Trace, by a spring of fresh water that also been the reason Calvin had settled on the campsite he'd chosen. Sarah knew they were First-born by the blue of their auras—through her normal eye, they were undistinguished, just a couple of men with broad-brimmed hats and long coats.

She had seen Eldritch before, in Nashville with some frequency and more occasionally traveling through the countryside on the Imperial Pikes, about perfectly ordinary business. But she had not before had occasion to watch the Firstborn secretly, knowing she herself was one of them.

After the excitement of watching people with blue auras wore off, Sarah realized that once again she was watching the Eldritch do completely mundane things: they ate bread, they drank water, they stashed their food in a tree away from their bedrolls, they lay down and—she could tell by the tone of their glow—went to sleep. She felt kinship for them the warmth of which surprised her. Was that despite their ordinariness, or because of it?

When the six riders appeared, coming from the direction of Nashville, Sarah thought nothing of them. There were dressed in long blue coats and blue tricorner hats, reminding Sarah of the soldiers who had besieged Calhoun Mountain, but their auras were white.

They were riding very fast, for such a small road at night.

The riders saw the Eldritch travelers and stopped. Sarah couldn't hear what was said, but there was some conversation, and the riders lingered. What were they talking about? The tones of both parties' auras changed.

The riders looked angrier.

The Eldritch looked fearful.

Pop!

She heard the gunshot like the explosion of a toy gun's cork, perfectly audible in the still night air. And suddenly there answered a volley of *pops* that sounded enormous in the small valley, but that could not have lasted more than a dozen shots. She couldn't see the guns or the smoke or even, with her good eye, the physical bodies of any of the people, but she saw the Eldritch die.

One moment, their auras glowed healthy blue, with a fear-tinged note to them, and the next, almost simultaneously, the auras exploded, dissipating into rings of light that washed Sarah, the voiceless, fear-clenched witness on the hill above, with a wave of energy.

She felt their deaths in a way she had never before felt any death. Sarah knew that if she had wanted to, if she had been sufficiently self-possessed, she could have harnessed that energy. She felt sick at the thought, it was vile to imagine someone could do such a thing, but Sarah knew that with her Second Sight, she'd be able to see and feel when the rings of such energy struck her, and that the energy could be used just like the power in any ley line.

The battle was over, and Calvin and Thalanes were up. She couldn't talk, stunned by the violence as well as by the strangeness of experiencing the Ophidians' deaths, but she gestured down at the valley, and her companions saw the horsemen ride away.

Five days of magic-coffee-fueled marching after they left Crowder's stand, in the silver light of a moon that was just shy of full, they arrived at Natchez.

Natchez proper sat on a bluff, huddled behind a palisade of sharpened logs like the fierce wooden teeth of some guard dog set to fend off the forest and the river. It looked like a trading town of maybe a thousand people in houses mostly made of rough logs, squatting at the great junction of the long highway and the Mississippi River, fiercely trying to mind its own business and jealously guarding its privileges.

The forest gave way to planted fields a few miles outside the town walls, and they found themselves compelled to travel again directly on the Natchez Trace. Sarah felt exposed as she walked under the most open sky she'd seen in nearly two weeks. She slipped off her patch to sneak a glimpse of the ley line and was reassured that the traffic behind them seemed ordinarily sparse and showed no signs of being . . . unusual.

Thalanes cloaked their faces with his gramarye.

They followed the Trace to the gates of Natchez, which were shut and watched by four helmet- and cuirass-clad guardsmen. The Trace continued around the town and steeply down to the base of the bluff, where Sarah saw in yellow torchlight a long line of wooden wharves insulating the impossibly wide river from its bank, and jammed up against the wharves a wide planked road and an even longer line of ramshackle buildings. The place swarmed with traffic, humans and boats, carts and dogs alike.

It was as if the town of Natchez above had let down its hair, and that hair jumped and crawled with vermin.

"Natchez-under-the-Hill," Cal said to them. "I been here once or twice to sell cattle, and I's always glad to escape with my skin."

"We can get a boat ride from here to New Orleans," Thalanes asserted blandly.

"Likely," Cal agreed. "Also, we can git knifed or shot. These Hansa towns are tough iffen you ain't Hansa yourself."

Sarah stared at the river as they descended into Natchez-under-the-Hill. It was like a sea, it was so far to the other side. She could see the opposite shore—it lay thick with tangled forest, and there were no lights. On an impulse, she slipped her patch up and turned her Second Sight upon the Mississippi River.

It almost blinded her. It pulsed and throbbed like a sleeping dragon, a gigantic strand of energy dwarfing the Natchez Trace ley as the river itself physically dwarfed the Trace. An immense ley line coursed up and down the Mississippi, in the water and above it, and she wondered what mighty spells could be cast using its power, and how powerful a magician would have to be to draw from it, and what a cinder that vast channel of power would reduce her to if the entire thing were turned to flow through her body. Its color, too, was distinctive. It was multicolored like the Natchez Trace ley line, but the Trace ley was predominantly white, whereas the river ley luxuriated in shimmering deep green. Was that . . . river energy? The spiritual tracks of thousands of years of catfish?

Sarah looked down at the wharf town before replacing her patch, and was reassured by the more human glow of white, like a phosphorescent anthill swarming on the riverbank. Between them and the town, though, stood two figures.

Two figures whose auras were green, like the Mississippi's.

She snapped her patch back into place and they stopped.

"Evenin'," Cal said affably. "We ain't lookin' for trouble."

Looking through her good eye—not her *good* eye, Sarah reminded herself, but her *normal* eye, her *mundane* eye—she saw that the two figures both wore hooded robes, and had their faces deep in shadow. The figures both pulled back the hoods and Sarah was shocked to see emerge from those shadows a tortoise's head and the head of a lovely woman with a duck's bill incongruously sprouting out of the middle of her face.

Beastmen! No, beast*kind*, since at least one of them seemed to be a female. She had never seen one close up before, and only rarely from a distance, in Nashville.

"Your Majesty," they said together, the tortoise's bass croak undergirding the melodious flute-like voice of the duckfaced woman. They bowed low.

They were bowing to *her*.

"Please," she said, "that's enough." She scrambled to regain her composure and protect her dignity. Had anyone else noticed? "Please rise."

They straightened out of their bows.

"Your Majesty," Tortoise-Head repeated in its (his?) low, throaty rumble. "Peter Plowshare is dead."

"I see I've gone mad.
Was it the whippings, or the whisky?"

⟶⬥⟵

CHAPTER ELEVEN

Bill awoke in near-complete darkness, his head pounding and his throat dry, tongue swollen like a wad of cotton. He needed whisky.

He rolled around, discovering that he was chained, wrists and ankles. He had a bump on the back of his head the size of an egg and tender to the touch, but the real pain was inside his skull.

Whisky.

He groped with trembling fingers and found water in a metal bucket. He forced himself to drink it, though the taste was stale. He felt like throwing up, and he was dimly relieved that Charles would never be able to see him in this wretched state.

Surely, he would die here.

He could smell the Pontchartrain's salty tang and feel the curving of one wall; he was still on the hulk. The back left part of the ship, or aft and port, as he thought sailors would say—he'd never been on anything bigger than a riverboat, himself. Bill had always fought on land and ridden to his battles on a horse.

Bill explored his chains and found them anchored to the ribs of the ship. He heard breathing in the darkness, and Bill called out "hello!" in the hope of initiating a conversation.

Nothing.

"Bonjour!" he tried, in vain.

"Buenos días," he tried again, "como está? Están? Quantos... er..."

Bayard heard him.

The traitorous weasel came stumping through the belly of the ship with an oil lantern in one hand and a cat o' nine tails looped in the other. In the yellow puddle of light Bayard dragged with him, Bill briefly saw his fellow prisoners: emaciated, broken creatures, chained in their own filth and barely breathing, only a few of them conscious enough to even raise their heads.

Were these men awaiting trial, or just the final mercy of death? Or did the chevalier keep this hulk in the Pontchartrain for the permanent detention of prisoners, like a medieval dungeon, an oubliette-on-the-sea?

Beelzebub's bedpan, this is a dark place.

Bayard brought with him three guards in blue vests. Two of them were bulky men who spoke French with the former Philadelphia Blue. Their voices were thick and their eyes dull— simpletons. Still dangerous, but it gave Bill hope to see that Bayard was assisted by idiots. Hope, and curiosity.

At first it seemed to Bill that the third guard spoke no French, as Bayard continually tapped him on the shoulder and told him what he wanted done with a great deal of exaggerated pointing and gesturing and pantomiming of actions. Then, however, Bayard uncoiled and cracked his whip—

Snap!

Though the third man stood just a few feet away with his back turned to his master, he didn't flinch at the sound.

The man was a deaf-mute. He dressed like a Dutchman, in knee-length brown trousers, white stockings and a brown coat of a very simple cut over his blue uniform waistcoat. His shoes shone dully in the lamplight with large brass buckles.

"Have you brought me whisky, gentlemen?" Bill asked.

The frog simpletons ripped his shirt from his back and Bill offered no struggle. They snagged his manacles onto hooks that hung from the ceiling and Bayard flogged him, cursing in French. Bill didn't count the blows, focusing his will on not crying out, on showing no weakness.

He was almost successful.

When they laid Bill again on the floor, on his side, Bayard and his idiots looked smug, but the deaf-mute appeared troubled. Or at least, not triumphant.

He slept again. When he next awoke, he still wanted whisky,

the craving so strong it made his hands shake. It must have been daytime, because white light blazed through chinks in the hulk's hull like shafts of lightning.

He crawled to his water pail, begging God to repeat and even outdo the miracle of the feast of Cana, but unable in his utter weakness to curse his luck when God saw fit not to change the water into Kentucky bourbon. If only he had more faith and said his prayers a little more often. Still, he sucked the metallic-tasting liquid down and felt better. This time, at least, he didn't want to vomit.

After drinking, he lay a while and tried to feel nothing. He failed, and found to his surprise that of all his feelings—despair, rage, impotence, and all the others—the one that swelled his heart to bursting was that he missed Charles. Shooting the chevalier's son, he felt as if he'd shot his own.

Don Sandoval had said he had a son, too; what was the Spaniard's boy like?

With the filtered daylight Bill resolved to explore his surroundings. This turned out to be a quick project—he was able to see in slightly more detail the rows of insensate wretches stretching away down the length of the ship, chained each a few feet from the next. The extra detail he saw (weeping sores, scaled skin, puddles of urine) only told him the prisoners suffered. Bill did see that he had many more square feet than the others, almost a room to himself—the better to whip him, likely.

He checked his person and made an inventory of his possessions. It was a short list: one pair of breeches, one tattered pair of stockings. The gendarmes had relieved him of his hat. His belt and boots he had lost, he did not know when. Grand Jacques's shirt had been torn to shreds. Even the claim ticket with which he might repurchase his saber and pistols from Hackett was gone.

Bayard came belowdecks to flog Bill again, once more with a pair of idiots and the unhappy-looking deaf-mute. They again dangled Bill from the ceiling like butcher's meat, and Bill had enough strength to taunt his tormentor.

"Bored, Bayard?" he called over his shoulder. "Or are you out of sorts because you're still losing at cards to the geniuses with whom you surround yourself these days?"

The answer came in nine tails, and hurt.

Bill lost track of time. He was fed once or twice, crusts of bread and rough, sticky porridge with unidentifiable clots of gristly protein. His hands stopped shaking, but he still awoke craving whisky every time.

Bayard came to whip him a third time. The idiots hung Bill from his hooks and took the opportunity to handle him roughly, plucking and scratching at the torn skin of his back. The extra insult and injury annoyed Bill, and in turn he goaded Bayard more than before.

"Hell's Bells, Bayard! You can whip me to death if it'll impress your imbecile friends, I don't care! You'll still be a worm and a murderer and a foresworn man!"

Bayard beat him into unconsciousness.

More than once, in his first few days in the hold of the hulk *Incroyable*, Bill dreamed Bayard sat beside him in the darkness, drinking, talking nonsense, and weeping.

When he awoke next, it was to find his cheek pressed against the rough, foul-stinking planks of the floor and a flickering light overhead shining into one eye. As sleep crept from his skull, he saw a shoe standing before him, a brass-buckled black shoe, and a stocking within it, and baggy brown knickerbockers above.

It was the deaf-mute.

"Sweet Bayard," Bill called out mockingly, "is it my whipping time again already?"

The Dutchman set a square bottle of brown liquid on the floor in front of Bill's face, so that Bill could read the black paper label.

Elijah Pepper's
Finest Kentucky Bourbon
Straight ~ 96 Proof

Bill lurched to a sitting position, groaning as scabs on his back tore. His hands again shook as he fumbled out the cork and slurped like a dog at the bottle's mouth.

The deaf-mute stood watching him for a moment, and then sat down crosslegged. He set his light source, a short candle, to one side on the floor, and looked at Bill intently. His face was open and fair, nearly beardless although it didn't look particularly boyish, with blue eyes under a mop of straight blond hair.

"Honor," Bill croaked reflexively, "in defense of innocence."

Bayard was not to be seen.

The sudden burning in his throat and belly pushed back Bill's demon thirst, and he offered the bottle to his benefactor. "I gather you're a deaf-mute, suh, so it can matter but little what I say to you or even what language I say it in. I find this strangely liberating. Thank you very much. Would you care for a drink?"

"I am not a deaf-mute today." The blond man's accent was not Dutch. It wasn't anything else that Bill recognized, either, just a pleasant voice, clear and foreign-sounding in no identifiable way.

Maybe a little reminiscent of the many Ohioans he had known.

Bill considered this while he took another swig. "I see I've gone mad." He felt quite calm. "Was it the whippings, or the whisky?"

"You have not had whisky for several days," the man observed.

"I see," Bill agreed. "It was the sobriety that did it."

"You are William Lee," said the foreigner.

"Yes, suh, I am." Bill held out his hand. The stranger took it briefly, looking amused, as if he enjoyed the novelty of a handshake. "I'm more commonly known in New Orleans as Bad Bill."

"You are not the man I expected," the blond man said.

"I don't understand enough of your meaning to know whether I should be flattered or offended, and I don't care enough to make the inquiry. I accept the fact that you expected something other than a fat old drunkard lying half-naked and crusted in his own gore. Since *I* expected a deaf-mute, perhaps we're even."

"Perhaps." The non-deaf-mute looked delighted.

Bill took another swallow and realized he was drinking it too fast. The level of the whisky was getting low, and he pounded the cork in with the heel of his hand to try to save some for later, though he didn't know where he would hide it.

Inside the water pail?

"But you haven't introduced yourself, suh," he observed.

"Forgive me," said the blond man, "I am not yet accustomed to your ways, and sometimes I forget that you do not know who I am." He was silent for a moment, as if thinking.

"My ways." Bill chuckled. The whisky helped.

"My name is Jacob Hop." He said it *YAH-cobe HOPE*, and he sounded like a Dutchman when he said it.

"Your name sounds pure Hudson River," Bill noted, "if you'll pardon an observation. Your accent, however, I cannot identify."

"I have no doubt my accent is strange," Hop said. "I am an insatiable traveler."

"And yet here you are, aboard a ship incapable of taking you anywhere." Bill laughed. "What an ironic sense of humor the gods must have."

"What do you want, William Lee?" Hop abruptly asked.

Bill was taken aback by the directness of the question. "What do *I* want? Mr. Hop, what do *you* want? I'm in chains, and you've come to me. *My* desires seem beside the point."

"Yes, of course," Hop replied. "It is a strange question. And of course you want to be free. But if you were free this moment, William Lee, what would you want? What would you do?"

Bill looked around him warily. He didn't think anyone else was listening in the dark hold of the ship. It seemed to be night. Then he shrugged. Hell's Bells, he was most likely hallucinating in any case, and what if Bayard *were* listening?

What did he care?

"Justice, suh," he said. "I would avenge myself upon my keeper, Bayard Prideux. He owes me a life. His death, however painful and prolonged, cannot possibly be enough to extinguish the debt of his crime against me, and against all this land. But it will be a start. If I were free, Mr. Hop, Bayard Prideux would be a dead man."

Hop nodded, his face solemn but his eyes sparkling in the candlelight. "It is a good start."

Bill chuckled. "I'm glad you approve. The whisky, the encouragement, even your very name cause me to take heart, Mr. Hop. Is it possible that you're about to hand me the key to my chains?"

"I am not, William Lee." Hop smiled. "But take courage. I will help you any way I can, though I am far away, and am not powerful upon the sea. And then, the queen is nearer than you know."

"In what sense are you far away, suh?" Bill asked. "Are you not here before me?"

"Yes," agreed Jacob Hop. "Yes, I am."

Then he picked up his candle and was gone.

"What queen?" Bill asked the darkness, but there was no answer. It was the same damned thing the beastkind had said to him, standing beside Bishopsbridge in the middle of the night. It had made no sense then, and it still made none.

"What queen?"

Obadiah grabbed four stones and spread them out around the rectangular board counterclockwise, one stone per scooped-out hole. He tried to do it quickly, like the iggy bastard across the board did, but he felt big and awkward.

The board and stones were nothing special, just a plank with its edges smoothed and depressions scooped out of it and a fistful of polished pebbles from the river. It was the speed at which the Igbo played that made the game impressive, a whirl of sparkling color and nimble brown hands.

Except when Obadiah played.

"Take." Obadiah snatched three stones off his opponent's side off the board.

The Igbo grinned under his little cap, rounded and brimless and embroidered with a wreath of interlocking green leaves. He might have been fifty, but his curly hair didn't show the slightest trace of gray and only a few deep lines around his smile gave him away. Obadiah thought his name was Udo, but he insisted on being called Michael. He was a cacao trader, he said, which probably meant he was a smuggler.

Most of the Igbo were smugglers. If they weren't evading the emperor's men, they were sneaking past the chevalier or the Dons of Ferdinandia or New Spain. They were old hands at it, as a people; it was said that the great John Hancock himself learned the arts of forged custom stamps, fraudulent bills of lading, and systematic graft from the Igbo. This traditional occupation didn't make the Igbo too different from the Dutch, really, except that the Igbo seemed to do everything in organized families or towns, whereas the Dutch were every man for himself.

The Igbo apparently gambled in families, too. Obadiah wouldn't have minded so much the circle of brown faces around him staring at the game and cheering on the plays, except he couldn't shake a deep-seated feeling that he was about to lose. Again.

Michael's long-fingered hand scooped up stones and whizzed around the board. "Take!" he rejoined, and then frowned deeply. "But woe, I take a mere two stones. Are you sure, Mr. Dogsbody, that you did not grow up in England playing Okwe as a boy?"

There was scattered clapping and cheering among the spectators.

Michael dropped his two taken stones into his pile. His pile and Obadiah's seemed to be the same size, but Obadiah knew Michael was still one ahead, because he kept track in his head. When he wasn't drunk, Obadiah was a good gambler.

He just wasn't good at *this* game. He'd only barely learned it.

They sat at a table in a large, one-story building with a high-peaked roof thatched with fronds and no walls at all. The roof rested on four round pillars that might have been tree trunks growing right out of the ground, with the floor built around them. The sturdy wood floor was scattered with reeds, just like the biggest buildings of the Academy had always been.

The platform might be some sort of market building or town hall; Obadiah had seen similar constructions in the other Igbo communities, and such buildings were always in the center of town, beside a large open square with a wide road leading to the pike. It seemed to Obadiah that all the Igbo towns were laid out identically, and they had all been planned by traders.

Obadiah didn't like the Igbo. He didn't like their thatched houses in their tidy little villages just off the highway—fifty feet off the highway, no doubt, and therefore not subject to direct Imperial taxation. He was unimpressed by the nudity of their children, by their little round hats, and by the knee-length tunics their men and women alike wore, no matter how ornately embroidered they were. He was positively irritated by the constant chatter of buying and selling and of a bustling daily life that assailed him among them—it gave him the strong and unpleasant impression the Igbo were determined to be happy. He hated banjo-picking, and he couldn't bear the taste of rice and yams. He disliked the unfailingly happy sound of their accent—how could an entire people sound happy all the time? It was impious.

He had agreed to sit down at the Okwe table because he thought he could still get a little entertainment from a game of chance, even if it meant he had to learn to play something he'd never played before. He was sorely disappointed.

Like everything else, Obadiah found Okwe hollow. Also, he couldn't quite see how, but he had the distinct impression that he was about to lose. He eyed the pile of coins to the side of the board: Michael's Ferdinandian pesos against his own Imperial shillings, a decent sum.

"Shall I point out to you your legal moves at this juncture?" Michael's polite and cheerful voice made Obadiah want to punch him.

Some of the crowd made less polite noises that sounded a lot like jeering.

Obadiah growled and spun stones around the board.

Michael moved; neither of them had taken. A player took when he ended his turn on the other man's side with two or three stones in the hole, and the game would end when there were four stones or fewer on the board in total.

Obadiah squinted, saw his opportunity, moved. "Take." Two. He was up one.

"Oooooooh," groaned the spectators in suspense.

Michael moved. "Take, and to my joy it is three." He grinned. Applause.

The leftmost depression in front of Michael held one stone, and the third from the left held two. Obadiah's side of the board was empty except for three stones at his right.

Obadiah grinned.

He only had one legal move, but it was a winner. He picked up his three stones and plunked them, one, two, three, in front of Michael.

"Take," he rumbled, and snatched away the three stones, tossing them into his pile. "Four stones left means that the game be over, Udo." He used the man's Igbo name on purpose and said it with a bit of a sneer. He reached for the pile of winnings—"oooooooooh," said the crowd—and Michael grabbed his hand.

"'Ere now, Michael," Obadiah said slowly. "The game be over."

"Yes, the game is over, friend Obadiah," Michael said, the smile not leaving his face. "But we must calculate our scores."

"I've *been* calculatink," Obadiah growled. "I win by one point."

Michael nodded at the board. "You are forgetting the stones still on the board," he suggested.

Obadiah looked at the board. Michael was right. Stones left on the board went to the player whose side they were on. That was three more points for Michael, and that meant that he won by two.

"'Erne's bloody 'orn!" Obadiah spat, and staggered to his feet.

Michael's family and neighbors cheered and laughed. Obadiah rushed away but Michael's laughter followed him, and the sound of Michael scraping coins into his purse. Served Obadiah right. He should have stuck to games he knew.

It was time to go, anyway. The Blues were saddling up.

This was Obadiah's first journey this far south in the New World, and he rode with the Blues—at the rear of the troop, leading baggage horses and mules—along the Imperial Highway between Birmingham and Jackson. Beyond Jackson lay New Orleans, whither they were bound and where Obadiah's heart lay.

He didn't understand why they were going to New Orleans— sometimes it seemed it was because Father Angleton had had a vision, and sometimes it seemed it was because Captain Berkeley had read his Tarock, and often the two men quarreled over which was the important reason—but they all agreed that Sarah was on her way to New Orleans. Obadiah didn't trouble himself too much about the decision-making process. At least Obadiah was with the main force of the Blues, traveling along the highway, and not one of the handful whose task had been to rush down the Natchez Trace at breakneck speed.

The road he traveled, the Jackson Pike, ran through the heart of the Free Cities territory, where the Igbo dominated. Obadiah had distrusted them even before his first footstep into their territory, and his Okwe losses had made him dislike them more.

The Blues were lining up to leave the little village where they'd quartered for the night, four to a bed in an ordinary called the *King Stephen Nzekwu* at what the Igbo proprietor assured Captain Berkeley were special rates for Imperial officers. Obadiah scrambled into his saddle and took the mule string's lead rope in hand in time to see the Right Reverend Father riding in his direction.

"Here," Angleton said. "You're so fond of reading now, read this. See what's at stake here." Then he turned back and rode to rejoin Captain Berkeley.

While the men ahead of him coiled slowly onto the Pike, Obadiah uncrumpled the sheet of paper and looked at it. It was a news-paper.

SERPENTSPAWN DEPREDATIONS

~ *The Pacification of the Ohio Continues* ~

Cahokia. *Good men and true* in the service of HIS IMPE-RIAL MAJESTY, THE EMPEROR THOMAS PENN, are murdered! *Honest men* have died with their throats cut in their sleep!! their bodies torn as if by Animals!! Insurgents ~ such as the Much Despised Ophidian Knights ~ claim that the crimes are the acts of feral Beast-Kind, who have recently been very Agitated, but *loyal citizens* are not fooled,

& HIS IMPERIAL MAJESTY is said to be sending further *troops from Free Imperial Youngstown & from Pittsburgh* to Reinforce the Forces of *order & good administration.*

Obadiah frowned. Why was this at stake? They pursued Sarah because she was some relative of Thomas Penn, and maybe intended to make a play for the throne. That was what the Blues whispered around the campfire, anyway, and it made sense of the journey so far.

Was she an Ophidian?

And what did that say about the emperor if she was?

Obadiah's horse clopped onto the Pike. The next Toll Gate was miles away—the emperor's men would be waved through, but others would be charged a toll for any traffic other than those traveling strictly on foot—so Obadiah had time to think.

He missed Sarah. He thought of his night on Calhoun Mountain, when he'd kidnapped her and then fallen in love. He knew he'd been hexed, but the effects of the spell had long since ended.

What remained, what haunted his journey along the Jackson Pike and kept him awake at night, was love. It had to be love. Obadiah's heart was cold and rusty in love's ways, but he knew how he had felt with her. He knew he wanted that feeling back. He cringed inside, thinking she must hate him, but he dared to dream he could persuade her of his worth. And even if he couldn't, now his life had meaning. For the first time in years, Obadiah cared about something beyond his appetites.

For the first time, really, since Peg had broken his heart.

He drank less, limiting himself mostly to water. He ate less, too, though that was mostly a matter of his being distracted by thoughts of Sarah. He was becoming thinner. He wanted some other method of self-improvement and found he had none to hand, so he turned to his Bible.

It was an old book, and unread. Obadiah's father had been a Christian from his youth in the Duchy of Monmouth, one of the dwindling and secretive minority in England under the Spencers. He'd wordlessly given Obadiah the book as a gift, the day Obadiah had gone off to Woolwich. Obadiah had opened it twice at the Academy, and hadn't read it since, carrying it around in his personal belongings like a talisman. Obadiah furtively read his father's Bible now, though he found he had to separate some pages with his knife. He read in the mornings, while the Blues struck camp, and in the evenings, while he stirred the pot. He tried to be discreet, but in a camp this small, others were bound to notice and talk, and they did.

Even Father Angleton had noticed, he now knew.

Obadiah read the Psalms and the Gospels, because Father Angleton quoted from them a lot. He tried to read the Old Testament, too, which was much harder. Genesis was interesting, with lots of women in tents, and Obadiah lay in his own small tent, when he wasn't in some flea-bitten ordinary's cot, and shivered at the thoughts that came to him. Exodus was full of storm and drama, with its plagues and God appearing in the mountains, but then there were long hard stretches Obadiah couldn't bring himself to look at.

The part Obadiah found with astonishment and then kept coming back to was the Canticles. *Her eyes are as the eyes of doves by the rivers of waters,* he read, *washed with milk, and fitly set,* and he thought of Sarah.

Turn away thine eyes from me, for they have overcome me, he read, and he remembered her standing by the Charlotte Pike Gate in Nashville wearing her purple shawl with gold suns, looking at him with her blessed eye, challenging him to open his heart.

Who is she that looketh forth as the morning, fair as the moon, clear as the sun, and terrible as an army with banners?

"May we see it, Your Majesty?" Duckface's voice was hushed, almost reverential.

They sat in a corner booth in the nicest tavern in Natchez-under-the-Hill, the *Fitzroy.* Unlike most of its local competitors, the *Fitzroy* actually had a signboard, painted to depict the great herald and jongleur with his long dark hair and his lips in the rounded O of emitting some ineffable golden note. He strummed a long-necked lute.

Walter Fitzroy had written over four hundred songs. The tunes in his Elector Song Cycle were the best known, not because they were the best songs, but because they were pounded into children all over the empire to teach them who voted to select a new emperor, or a remove a bad one. Calvin had seen the signboard and immediately broken into song, his voice sweet and melodic. Sarah had great affection for Calvin Calhoun, but, objectively speaking, it was astonishing that such a sweet voice could come out of such an ugly face.

> *The Free Cities of the Igbo*
> *Have one Elector each, no more*
> *Birmingham, Montgomery, Jackson*
> *And Mobile on the shore*

"Calvin," she'd whispered, "we ain't in Igbo territory."

"Give a feller a little credit," he'd agreed, ducking under the low, heavy wooden door frame, "I been here afore, and I ain't forgot that Natchez is in the Cotton League. Only I ain't ever cared much for that melody."

The same image of John Penn's court troubadour hung in an oil-painted canvas behind the *Fitzroy's* bar, or rather, *almost* the same image. Sarah looked with curiosity at the lute in the painting—on its fretboard, partly obscured behind its many strings, were inlaid distinct images: a key at the fifth fret, a cup at the seventh and two coins at the ninth. At the twelfth fret was inlaid a lightning bolt. Sarah had seen a few instruments in her time, but never one with decoration that fancy. Was the signboard painted in a simpler fashion because it hung outside, and required more frequent repainting?

The *Fitzroy* was the nicest tavern in town because it reeked of tobacco smoke and ale more than of urine, and also because it had actual booths around the walls of its common room, permitting some semblance of privacy.

Sarah sat on one side of such a booth and the beastkind sat opposite her, giving the three of them the most concealment from prying eyes. She still had seen no sign of the Philadelphia Blues in Natchez-under-the-Hill, but there was no sense being anything less than cautious. Cal sat in the corner, warily watching the common room with his tomahawk cradled in his lap. Thalanes sat quietly beside Calvin, seeming to concentrate on something other than the table conversation. Was he cloaking them with gramarye? Watching for enemies? The little man generally looked tired, and Sarah now understood why—it had been weeks since he'd had any respite from constant spell-casting.

She took a sip of her small beer, slightly darkened with molasses.

"Why?" she asked.

She refrained from saying all that was on her mind, such as: *my eye ain't none your business, I'll take off my patch when youins take off your robes*, and *what in tarnation you want from me, you foreign, animal-headed freaks?* She had adopted a sort of regal position with respect to Thalanes, and acting too paranoid or standoffish now might weaken her authority.

Also, she felt she had to at least *try* to be a good queen.

"Forgive us if we ask too great a boon, Your Majesty," Tortoise-Head rumbled, dipping his wrinkled cranium in submission. "We know thou art the queen we seek, and we do not ask for a sign. It is only that our master has prophesied much of thee and thy great silver eye. We would see it, if we may. We would be witnesses to thine advent."

Advent? That didn't even sound like queen-talk anymore, it sounded like prophecy and religion. Sarah hated hearing herself talked of like this, and she wasn't even sure she preferred worship to fear and revulsion. Part of her longed to push the beastfolk away, beat them down.

"Jerusalem, Sarah." Cal snorted. "They make you sound like a regular King Andy Jackson. Keep your eye out for them Lafittes."

"Hush," Thalanes urged him, snapping out of his reverie. "If you had seen how Jackson ended, you wouldn't compare him to Sarah even in jest."

Sarah shared Cal's instinct to puncture all the high-toned flimflam the beastkind were throwing at her. Still, she wanted to play the part of queen, so she slipped the patch off over the top of her head and gazed upon the beastkind. Again she saw them as shimmering mud-green clouds. She looked closely at their features with her witchy eye, and was intrigued to find that with her Second Sight they appeared both as completely human and simultaneously as completely animal. She couldn't have said whether she was looking at a woman and a man or a tortoise and a duck.

"Whyn't youins tell me your names?" she suggested to them, and then cringed at the Appalachee sounds coming out of her own mouth. So much for her Court Speech.

"Grungle." The beastman bowed until his forehead grazed the scarred tabletop.

"Picaw." The beastwife stooped similarly.

"Picaw and Grungle," Sarah said slowly, ironing her words into something more eloquent than their natural state. "Witness, then. Tell your master what ye have seen here."

She replaced her patch. Calvin smiled at her warmly. Thalanes once again had his attention elsewhere.

"Your Majesty," Picaw said in her flute-like voice. "Peter Plowshare is dead."

"I understand," Sarah lied. No need to show any weakness to the beastkind.

"Our master, the Heron King, conveys his congratulations upon the occasion of thy return," Picaw continued. "He supports thy claims, and he would be thine ally."

"Thank you." This was was getting stranger by the minute, and Sarah felt as if she were acting in a play to which everyone but her knew the script, while these queer ultra-Mississippians were in deadly earnest. Wasn't the Heron King a character of folklore? And yet here were two emissaries claiming to be in his service and bringing her messages. She had stepped with one foot into a fairy tale, while the other remained in solid, rough and tumble Natchez-under-the-Hill.

"He would even," Grungle continued, "enter into discussions with thee about the prospects of a dynastic alliance. About the possibility, Your Majesty, of marriage."

"What!?" Calvin spat out the word in astonishment, and Thalanes, too, snapped abruptly to attention.

Sarah felt all eyes on her and blushed. Suddenly, the fairy tale she had stepped into became a yawning chasm beneath her feet.

"Thank your master for the message of support," she said, "and for the invitation to discuss. I expect we shall be conversing of many things over the coming years. I am young, yet, to contract a marriage, and I ain't yet...I *am not* yet come into my throne." She tried and failed to let herself be drawn naturally into the cadences of Court Speech.

Her discomfort with the whole situation made it difficult.

Sarah wanted to avoid angering the beastkind, and from their smiles and nods, she thought she had succeeded, but she also wanted to avoid crushing Calvin by promising them too much. She looked at him closely, and he looked away. He thought he loved her still, then. He would get over it someday.

He was gallant and brave, and he would get over it.

Thalanes smiled at her.

"Your Majesty," Picaw said tentatively, "we were sent with a message to New Orleans, which we delivered. We have come to find thee here as an act beyond our errand, because Simon Sword despises a slothful servant, and because it appeared that the recipient of our message had been detained, and might not meet thee on the road."

Simon Sword? The fairy tale yawned beneath Sarah's feet again. "I see." Who had the recipient of the beastfolk's message been? And why had they expected that person to meet her?

"We would go still further beyond our errand," the beastwife continued. "We beseech thee to come with us, across the great river, into the forest, to the hall of our master. It is not many days from here. We would bring thee to meet him, to treat with him, and to seek his aid."

Sarah felt all eyes on her again, and especially the eyes of the little monk. She met his gaze, and saw therein gentle pleading as well as nervousness. She knew his plan was to find Sarah's siblings—Nathaniel and Margaret—and hide them again, at least for the time being, to keep them all safe from her uncle. She knew he wanted her to continue with his plan; she resisted the impulse to tear her patch from her head and stare into his aura, to try to gauge the depth of his feelings.

But the beastmen were promising her aid. Assistance from magical, legendary figures—it was as if the Three Wise Men or the Pharaoh of Egypt had appeared and promised to help her. What if they could make good on their promises?

Cahokia had no king, and had had no king since the death of her father. Her father via the acorn he had strangely blessed, and the acorn she had hidden away in her dress pulled at her with the heavy weight of destiny. If there was a Heron King, and he was the mighty wizard of folklore, might he not help her fill the empty throne? Might he not help her recover the lost Cahokian regalia, the things of power Thalanes had told her about?

If Sarah found Nathaniel and Margaret now, weak as she was, she might only draw misfortune upon their heads—shouldn't she do everything she could to become powerful, so she could take her siblings under her protective wing?

And as Queen of Cahokia, possessor of things of power, couldn't she also contest for her inheritance of the Penn wealth? Could she not have justice for her father and her mother?

Might she not, in fact, become empress?

But she didn't know whether she could trust the beastkind. They didn't have the sorcerous black auras of the Mockers, but their souls looked alien enough that she was unsure how to read them. She could as soon tell the mood of the Mississippi as discern whether Picaw and Grungle were lying. They might, after all, be agents of the emperor.

Or they might be insane.

Or the Heron King might not be the powerful figure about whom she'd heard so many whispered campfire tales, so many moralistic sermon-stories.

Or the Heron King might decide he didn't want to help her after all, or he might demand too high a price. She couldn't really see herself, in the end, married to a fairy tale creature.

And Thalanes... Thalanes had a plan, and it didn't include thrones, regalia, or fairy tale alliances. Not yet, anyway.

Surely he was right. The safest course was the simplest, and the humblest.

She smiled at all the staring eyes. "I am on an errand of grave import to me and to my family that draws me to Louisiana. I thank you again and I ask you to thank your lord. When I have resolved my errand, I shall come see him in his hall. Or he may come see me in mine."

Calvin and Thalanes both looked happy with her words, and the beastfolk looked at least unperturbed. Maybe even satisfied.

She didn't like being queen. At least, she didn't like the decisions part.

"We thank thee, Your Majesty." Grungle bowed his head.

Picaw also nodded. "May we assist thee in resolving thy current errand, then?"

"I do not see how," Sarah answered evasively. She still had no wish to trust or rely on the alien beastkind.

"Perhaps we may, in ways thou canst not yet see," Picaw suggested. "Dost thou seek the man William Lee?"

Sarah felt a cold stone in the pit of her stomach. "Pardon me?" She looked at her companions; Thalanes arched his eyebrows at her to indicate that he shared her surprise, and Calvin held his face in a carefully motionless expression, as he did when he played cards.

"Captain Sir William Johnston Lee," Grungle joined in, slowly enunciating the name, as if he found it a difficult one to say. "He is in New Orleans. The Heron King sent us to him with our message. We know where he is."

The beastkind knew way too much. "How'd youins find me?"

"The Heron King is a great prophet," Picaw fluted. "Some of his servants bear a humbler touch of his gift."

"We could not be certain that we would find thee in Natchez," Grungle explained, "but we dreamed of thee here. From our dreams, we knew how to recognize thee."

"The eye?" Sarah asked.

"Your Majesty is unmistakable for many reasons," Picaw demurred gently.

Sarah's head reeled. "Captain Lee was the recipient of your message?" She struggled to get back control of her dialect. "The one who was detained?"

"Yes, Your Majesty," both beastfolk said.

"Where is he?"

"We do not know exactly where he is held," Grungle amended his earlier statement. "He was taken by other men. But we know someone who will be able to help thee find him."

"Tell me," Sarah said.

The beastkind looked at each other. "Her name is Filmer," Picaw said. "We cannot describe to thee the place where she is, but we can take thee there."

Sarah met Thalanes's gaze with her own and saw in his eyes the same cheerless resignation she felt in her own heart. She was going to have to trust the beastkind, after all.

"Hell's Bells, suh, stop winking at me."

———❖———

CHAPTER TWELVE

Bayard Prideux's wooden leg drilled through Bill's stupor and pried his eyelids apart.

He wanted the whisky so bad he almost crawled immediately over to his water pail, where he'd hidden the remaining quarter bottle of Elijah Pepper's aqua vitae. He checked himself in time and instead trundled his carcass up into a sitting position. *Time to be whipped.*

The hold of the hulk was mired in the pitch black of night on the Pontchartrain. Bayard came alone. He lit his stomping path with the yellow wash from a stinking taper held high in his right hand; something heavier swung in shadow, clutched in the fingers of his left.

A pistol?

"Have you come to kill me, suh?" Bill called gamely.

Bayard stopped in his tracks. "You are awake." His voice was slurred. The yellow light drew out his nose and made him look like a bird of prey, perched in a high eyrie from which it considered diving for Bill the hare.

Bayard sniffed.

He swayed, slightly, his eyes pools of shadow beneath his streaked and greasy forehead. He bent over and set the candle on the floor to one side. He shifted from foot to foot, hawked, and spat into the darkness.

He thrust his left hand forward, the thing he clutched sparkling amber in the candlelight. Bill flinched, expecting a shot or a blow—and instead, Bayard fell over.

By pure good luck, the candle landed upright, its flame still burning. The Frenchman smelled strongly of liquor and lay still. Bill lunged forward, gratifying images filling his mind, visions of tearing Bayard's head from his shoulders, of strangling him with Bill's chains, of beating his jailor to death—

the shackles pulled him up short.

He strained and pushed, but the chains stayed firmly anchored and Bayard remained safely out of his reach, snoring through a stupor of precious alcohol.

Bill wept. He shrank back against the curved belly of the whale that had swallowed him and shed hot tears of anguish and anger.

When the weeping washed the last of the sleep-fog from Bill's brain, he assessed his situation. Bayard breathed deeply and raggedly, the phlegm in his nose and throat making a noise like several forests being simultaneously sawed to the ground. The candle was out of Bill's reach. The thing Bayard had been carrying, though, lay in shadow beside Bayard's body, on the near side of him. If it was a pistol, or even a long enough knife, Bill might still have his justice. He crawled forward and stretched as far as he could, grabbing the object with the tips of his fingers and caressing it to himself.

He found he had requisitioned a bottle. A full bottle. A tall, square, full bottle of Kentucky bourbon. Bill took it in his trembling hands and retreated to the wall. "Honor in defense of innocence," he murmured.

He drank, and considered.

The bottle was not long enough to strike Bayard with it. It was too heavy to conveniently turn into a bladed weapon by smashing it. But Bill could throw it. Bill was weak and his arms were chained, but Bayard was still, and would never be an easier target.

Bill drank some more, not to stiffen his resolve but because he hated to waste good whisky. Even on killing a varmint like Bayard. It wouldn't do to totally empty the bottle though, so he cut himself off after a few long sips, and tamped the cork back into place.

Bill was a pistol man, really, but a soldier fights with the weapons he has to hand. Bill attempted a few positions and decided that his best shot was to rest the weight of the long chain over his shoulder. This forced him a couple of steps further back from his target, but it took most of the burden off his throwing hand.

Bill practiced a couple of dry casts; each time he swung the sloshing missile, he imagined it hurtling down in a straight line, a comet of high-proof justice, cracking Bayard's traitorous skull open. Maybe then the talking deaf-mute Hop would find Bill a key, and he would escape. And if Bill wasted away and died in the belly of the *Incroyable*, he would die satisfied.

He was ready. He checked the other prisoners; but for the recurring moans, they might be dead.

One more practice cast, and then Bill threw the bottle.

Thunk.

The bottle hit Bayard on the shoulder and back, missing his head entirely, and dropping with a *slosh* to the floor.

"Damn me."

If only he'd been wearing his lucky hat, Bayard Prideux would be a dead man right now.

He considered grabbing the other bottle, the one hidden in the water pail, and throwing it, too, but he didn't have the heart.

He sat and might have wept again, except that Bayard stirred. "Ah . . . eh . . . ." The French former Blue tumbled over, away from Bill and further out of his reach. He rubbed his shoulder and rolled up, stiffly and woozily. The two men sat facing each other.

"I regret, Bill," Bayard said blearily.

"To hell with your regrets, *suh*!" Bill spat.

Bayard took this calmly through his stupor. "I mean, I am sorry."

"To hell with your sorry, too."

"Do you not feel remorse? Do you not ever sorrow for ze wrong choices you 'ave made?"

Bill said nothing. His remorse was none of Bayard's damned affair.

"*I* do," Bayard confessed.

Bill bit his tongue. How could he get Bayard to come close enough so that Bill could strangle him?

"I am so lonely," Bayard said. "'E surrounds me with deaf-mutes and idiots, I speak to no one. Even ze 'ore he sends me once a month is a tongueless Choctaw. All my communication with 'er is animal, and degraded."

Bayard was as much a prisoner as Bill was.

"I am not ze man I once was. I am not a man at all anymore, Bill. Captain Lee. I am not permitted to even be a man, I am nothing. 'E leaves me nothing. I gave 'im wealth, and 'e gives me only isolation and darkness."

"Who, Bayard?" Bill just wanted to keep Bayard talking, get his guard down, and draw him close enough to murder him. "Who gives you nothing?"

"Ze chevalier, of course." Bayard moped, and Bill sneered inside at the other man's misery.

"I thought the chevalier was your friend."

"'E should be. I made 'im a rich man."

Bill's brain caught on this statement in surprise. Bayard had been a penniless soldier, a failed poet, some bankrupt Louisiana planter's youngest scion sent off to make his unhappy career as a soldier. He had treated the military mostly as an opportunity to raise hell. He had gotten into the Blues by some family influence, Bill remembered, and not because of wealth. None of that made Bayard particularly unusual, and neither did it suggest any way in which he might have brought the Chevalier of New Orleans wealth.

"What are you talking about?" Bill asked. "The Chevaliers Le Moyne have always been rich."

Bayard shook his head and patted the floor about him in the darkness. "Ze Chevaliers 'ave always 'ad ze 'ead of ze New Orleans government," he said, "and land. Generally, zey 'ave 'ad no cash."

Bill nodded; he knew how that was. "And taxes. The chevalier collects taxes and tariffs and tolls of all kinds."

"Yes," Bayard agreed. "But zen 'e must pay for many things with zis money. Ze gendarmes, and ze magistrates, ze public buildings, and so on. Zis is ze curse of ze great man. Taxes do not make 'im rich."

Bayard continued to grope in the dark.

"What are you doing?" Bill asked.

"I 'ad a bottle. Where's my bottle?"

Bill gritted his teeth and said nothing.

"Zere it is." Bayard found the whisky and took a long drink, wincing visibly. "I seem to have 'urt my shoulder."

"You fell," Bill told him.

"We all fall," Bayard said.

"Some farther than others, suh," Bill muttered, his heart dark.

"I told ze chevalier, you know." The Frenchman took a drink.

"Told him what?"

"I told ze chevalier I was a murderer. 'Ow did you say it? Zat I was a foresworn man." Drink. "Of course, I was obeying orders. And I did not tell 'im everything." Bayard winked.

"No, suh? What treachery, tell me, did you conceal from the chevalier?"

"No, Bill." Bayard clucked his tongue. "I did not conceal ze treachery. I told ze chevalier zat I stole ze king's regalia. But I did not tell 'im where I 'id it." He winked again.

"You hid the regalia?" Bill and the other House Light Dragoons had never found Kyres's sword, orb and crown.

"Oui. Yes. Anyway, I wrote down in ze letter where I 'id zem, but in a riddle, in a way ze chevalier will never understand." Bayard winked again several times, exaggeratedly, his eye a fluttering yellow-black butterfly in the candlelight.

"Hell's Bells, suh, stop winking at me. I am not your beau. What orders? Who gave you orders?" Surely Thomas Penn had been behind the murder of his brother-in-law Kyres Elytharias, but Bill had had no proof—only Thomas's immuring of his sister and his own rise to the head of the Penn family and election to the Imperial Throne.

"A great man. A great man 'oo zen turned on me."

"Thomas, I suppose. And your exile to this rotting pile of planks was your punishment?"

Bayard laughed and drank again. "Zis was my *reward*. I came 'ere to New Orleans fifteen years ago fearing for my life, and I asked to enter ze chevalier's service. I told 'im everything, I wrote down everything in a letter zat 'e 'olds, and 'e took me into 'is service and protected me."

"Here? On this hulk?" Bill was incredulous.

Bayard nodded.

"You've been here for *fifteen years*?"

"Most of zat time, yes, on zis ship. Occasionally, 'e permits me to go ashore. Only occasionally. I do not miss it so very much, you know." Bayard spat. "Zis city is full of witches and crazy people, always Papa Legba zis and Grande Al-Zan zat, cut me off ze 'ead of a chicken to 'ex my neighbor and make me a doll for good mojo at ze races."

"And he surrounds you with the deaf and the stupid," Bill said thoughtfully.

"It keeps me protected," Bayard said.

"It keeps you imprisoned, suh." Suddenly and painfully, Bill felt a twinge of sympathy for the other man. "What did the chevalier do with your confession?"

Bayard hesitated, and took another drink.

"How did you make him rich? You didn't give him the regalia, did you, Bayard?"

"No, zat would 'ave been foolish."

"More foolish than writing him a letter with the location in a riddle?"

"'E will never decipher it," Bayard sneered. "Ze regalia are safe from 'im."

"He told somebody, didn't he?" Bill probed. "About the murder."

Bayard nodded.

Bill snorted with surprised laughter at sudden insight. "You told him that Thomas Penn put you up to it, didn't you?"

Bayard took another slug of the bottle.

"You came down here to New Orleans with this sordid tale of treachery and murder, you blamed the new emperor, and the chevalier has been blackmailing His Imperial Majesty Thomas Penn ever since!"

"'E won't get rid of me," Bayard said. "I am in 'is service."

"He won't get rid of you because you're his witness. And he keeps you chained up here with the deaf, the stupid, and the damned to keep safe his very precious, very profitable secret!" Bill laughed out loud. He now had a weapon to use against Bayard.

The Frenchman drank again.

"Bayard, I'm surprised at you." Bill spoke softly, to try to insinuate himself into Bayard's sodden brain as the voice of sagacity—the wise serpent, the enemy offering advice that is nevertheless not to be ignored.

"What do you mean?"

"I don't know how a weasel like you can hold such a powerful moneymaking opportunity in his hand and not see it," Bill said.

"What, blackmail ze emperor?" Bayard shuddered. "I would not dare. Ze chevalier can do it because 'e 'as men and land to keep 'im safe. 'E is 'ere in New Orleans, far from Philadelphia."

Bill harrumphed. "Not the emperor. Give me the bottle, you coward. You don't deserve whisky."

Bayard corked the whisky bottle and slid it across the floor to Bill. "I am no coward, and I am also no fool."

Bill suppressed the urge to hurl the bottle again. Instead, he took a long drink—the whisky was almost gone. "Blackmail the chevalier," he said, slowly and distinctly. "Tell him you want money, or you will publish his crime. You could get better lodgings than this, suh, even in isolation. You don't have to live like a condemned man."

Bayard was silent, considering.

"Come on, man! He could get you a whore with a tongue, at least!"

"Ze 'ore is not so bad," Bayard protested. "She 'as culture, she is from a good family. 'Er brozer is ze right hand man of ze chevalier 'imself, du Plessis."

"I am no expert in what passes for a good family in New Orleans or among the French," Bill admitted. "But none of *my* sisters was ever heard to be called a whore."

"It would never work," Bayard said faintly.

Bill shrugged, letting his suggestion play out in Bayard's head.

Bayard's eyebrows shot up. "'E would kill me."

"He needs you. Just write him a letter and tell him that you want your fair share of the riches he's getting from Thomas Penn."

Bayard looked very serious. Bill laughed inside in anticipation of the little worm threatening the chevalier and getting crushed for his trouble.

But then Bayard lurched to his feet. "No! Don't you understand? 'E doesn't need me, I wrote 'im a letter fifteen years ago, and I told 'im everything! Don't you see? I told 'im my guilt in writing, and if I make trouble now, 'e doesn't need me! If I demand money, ze chevalier will kill me! Or even if 'e does not kill me, 'e may simply not protect me, and I will be in danger!"

"From Penn?" Bill snorted. "The emperor is very far away."

"And ze ozer!" Bayard shrieked. "In danger from Penn and ze ozer!"

"Zee Uzzah?" Was Bayard shrieking the name of some Biblically-minded Dutchman? "Do you mean *the other*?" he asked, but Bayard was already staggering away; his flight was so precipitous, he left behind the candle.

The conversation hadn't gone quite as Bill had hoped, but all was not lost. Bill swallowed the last of the whisky and grinned. Maybe he could get Jacob Hop to bring him paper, ink, and a quill, and he would write the chevalier himself...on Bayard's behalf. If he could provoke the little French viper's master to action against him, he might be able to see a little justice. That would be something to be proud of, something Charles would be proud of, even if Bill ended his days as a rotting carcass in the belly of the *Incroyable*.

But who was the *other* of whom Bayard Prideux was so afraid?

"Prepare yourself," Sarah said. "I think the schnitzels are about to kill another cat."

"Aw, the melodies ain't that bad," Cal said. "I only wish I knew what the words meant."

"I think I'm just as happy not having any idea," Sarah disagreed. "If I knew they was going on and on about the Serpents War and Albrecht von Wallenstein, with Queen Adela Podebradas divorcin' the Holy Roman Emperor by choppin' the head off his emissary and him divorcin' her back by chopping off her very own head, and so forth, I believe I'd still find it tiresome."

"I dunno," Cal mused. "If they's a song about them fellers as got themselves threw out a window, that might could be hilarious."

They lay wrapped in their bedrolls on the keelboat cabin's roof, looking up at the bright blue sky of an early morning. The boat was long and thin, bowed up fore and aft to sharp points, and filled in the middle with a long cabin consisting of a single room.

Fore, the keelboat's prow was carved into the shape of a horse's head, which Cal had commented at least half a dozen times must be a sign for them of good luck, since the Elector had carved Sarah a walking stick with the same shape. He'd even mentioned the coincidence to the Germans in Natchez-under-the-Hill, when he was trying to talk down their suggested price—in the end, the last of Crooked Man's moonshine had gone a long way to alleviating the cash burden of their fare—and the blond men had seemed duly impressed.

Aft, it ended in a thin pole, from which snapped the flag of the Duchy of Chicago, seven horizontal stripes, yellow and black. Over a hundred fifty years now, the descendants of old Albrecht von Wallenstein had ruled in Chicago. That made their arms safe colors for a Mississippi riverboat to fly.

The half-dozen Germans who poled them downriver (supplementing the money they planned to make selling their cargo of carefully-packed cheese and beer) sang as they worked. Since there were always at least two of them at the poles, Sarah had been hearing volksmusik belted out by iron lungs for twenty-four hours straight, and expected to hear it for another solid forty-eight. It was already pounded so deeply into her brain that when the Germans' dog, a big, indolent wolfish-looking creature, opened its mouth to yawn or stretch its jaws, she imagined it singing *o Wandern, o Wandern, du freie Burschenlust,* whatever that meant.

Thalanes sat upright nearby; the beastfolk were elsewhere on the boat, lurking quietly in some corner. They had paid for their own passage, with gold coins Sarah didn't recognize.

"I would have liked to sleep in," the monk said. He still looked better than he had on the Natchez Trace. Maybe he was less worried about pursuit. Or maybe he felt better because he didn't start every morning with tiring gramarye.

"I reckon they sing so's other boats can hear 'em," Cal volunteered. "In the fog, for instance, and at night."

There were plenty of other boats. Keelboats were common, but Sarah had seen many flatboats too, and a few Memphite barges. Sails and multiple banks of chained rowers combined pushed the sharp-prowed Memphite ships with staring hawks' eyes painted on either side of the keel at speeds that surprised Sarah, even against the current.

"They did sing all night," Thalanes confirmed with a weary smile, "though they had the decency to lower the volume. Ever so slightly."

"Why don't we see big ships?" Sarah asked. "The river's so wide, it's like a sea. Why all the small boats, and no big ships?"

"It's wide, all right," Cal agreed, "but it ain't deep. Some places you can practically walk across on foot, I heard."

"That's true." Thalanes yawned. "Now, who's going to make me some coffee?"

"Don't go wearing yourself out with gramarye when we don't need it," Sarah admonished the monk.

"I want the coffee," Thalanes said, "precisely so I won't feel worn out. But I promise, I don't plan to do anything with it but drink it."

"I wouldn't half mind some myself." Calvin rolled out of his blanket. "I'll go tell Hans and Franz and Dieter we're gonna use a corner of their stovetop."

He rattled down off the cabin roof, scooting the singing dog out of his way with a friendly push, and tried to find one of the Germans who spoke English. That was a surprisingly difficult task, in part because the six Germans were all family and looked, to Sarah's eyes, identical.

Dieter alone stood out for the fact that he dressed all in black and never smiled—Sarah had initially assumed it was for some profoundly German reason, like a family curse or a broken vow or a murdered love. At sunrise and sunup, though, Dieter stood in the water beside the prow, cut the palm of his hand, and rubbed small amounts of his own blood into certain angles of the horse's head.

A runemaster, then. A vitki. Ohio River Germans were Christians and their wizards were called brauchers, but Sarah had read that their Mississippi cousins were mostly pagan, and consulted wise men who carved runes. And here was an apparent vitki in the flesh.

"You could pass on the little brown devil bean this morning and try some sleep instead," Sarah told Thalanes. She tried to sound wise rather than fretful.

Thalanes looked to be sure that Calvin wasn't too close and spoke softly. "Something is following us."

"You haven't *seen* anything...it isn't *that* close," Sarah half-asserted, half-asked.

Thalanes shook his head. "I can sense it. I don't know what it is, but I know it seeks you and it stinks of death."

Sarah shuddered. "Can you tell where it is? Help me see."

Thalanes nodded at the Mississippi. "Upstream. A couple of days behind us is my best guess, but I could be wrong. There's no need to panic."

Sarah turned her face upstream. A lone German stood in the stern of the keelboat, intent on working his pole against the river bottom and pushing away drifting objects that threatened the vessel and its sweet cargo. She had carefully kept the patch over her eye since Natchez-under-the-Hill, not wanting to be blinded by the proximity of the river, but now she slipped it off her head and looked upstream.

She plunged into a green-stained, multicolored glow that surrounded the boat. Sarah was disoriented for a moment, and then realized that she had expected to see the ley line, and instead she was standing *inside* it, seeing everything else *through* it.

"Are you all right?" the monk asked her.

Sarah brushed him away with her hands, trying to concentrate.

She shaped her will. She formed an intention to see upriver, along the Mississippi ley, and she poured her perception into the intent. She wished she had something material she could use—a crystal, a seeing stone, a spyglass—but she didn't. She was actually touching the ley, standing inside it, that was something. Or was it? Was the ley material, like a physical object? But whether or not it was, she knew it could conduct magical energy.

Sarah considered using the acorn in her dress, which had, after all, spent fifteen years tucked against her eyeball, but that didn't seem quite right. Then, without knowing exactly what she was doing, she focused her intention through her witchy eye itself, willing the spell through it in the same way she would have through a bit of blood or skin she might use in a hex.

"*Hostem video.*" She touched her witchy eye and drew the smallest trickle of green-tinged power from the Mississippi. Even that tiny sip jolted through her like lightning.

She sucked in cool morning air as her vision raced along the ley. Faster than falling, faster than flight, her eye rocketed up the river in a tunnel of green, trees and buildings and bluffs and swamps and stockades streaming by in a whirl. She passed Natchez, and the staggering pyramids and necropolises of Memphis, and a high hill towering over the junction of two mighty rivers.

Suddenly, she was there.

She saw a keelboat. Its crew worked with frowns and furrowed brows, and the cabinless boat carried no cargo other than a circle of men huddled in the center. The banner on the back of the boat, a pair of standing sheaves and a rising sun, tickled her memory, but she wasn't sure whose it was.

Imperial Youngstown, maybe.

"I see them," she said. Black-evil-murder-smoke wisped off the men, similar to the auras of the Mockers.

"Tell me what you see," the little monk urged her.

"There are five . . . six men," she counted. She absorbed their faces, which were dirty, pale and impassive. Two of the men sat apart, and might have been commanders or leaders of some sort. They all had long hair. "They don't talk. There's something wrong

with their auras, they're not natural. They have...their eyes...
they're white. They just sit there. They are all armed, knives and
some pistols. They're on a boat. I don't recognize any of them.
Their clothing is torn up pretty bad. The boatmen are afraid of
them." She paused, focusing to be sure before she said anything.
"They seem to be moving much faster than we are, though I
don't know how that's possible."

She felt Thalanes touching her arm, as if it were something
happening very far away. "Let me see," he told her, and she nodded.

"*Visionem condivido,*" she heard him say, and then she felt
the monk inside her head. He was there as a weight, a presence
that tired her, but only slightly. He gasped. "Sarah," he murmured
appreciatively, "your vision is so...clear...so powerful."

"Tell me what you think of these men." Sarah was too nervous to feel proud.

Thalanes spoke slowly. "Look at their hair and their nails.
See how long they are? And their skin is so pallid. And their
clothing isn't tattered, it's rotten."

"Yeah," Sarah agreed, "they got a real deficit of fashion sense.
What are they?"

"Can't you guess? They're Lazars. Dead men," Thalanes whispered, and Sarah felt a chill in her bones.

"Do you mean they're like Black Tom Fairfax?" she asked.
"And the sorcerer Hooke?"

"They aren't like them," Thalanes said. "They *are* them."

Sarah's mind revolted at the thought and she started to
panic...the vision blurred...

"Calm down." Thalanes squeezed her forearm. "Breathe."

Sarah took a deep breath and re-inserted herself into her vision.

"We have a great advantage," she heard the monk say. "You
have an extraordinary natural talent, a seer's gift. They're far
away, and we can see them."

"They're coming fast," Sarah objected in a whisper. "Lazars."

"True," Thalanes agreed, "but the river's long, and they're
still a couple of days behind us. We know they're coming, we
can keep track of them and maybe throw them off the scent."

"What else do we need to look at?" she asked.

"I've seen enough," he said, and as he let go of her arm, she
felt his mind withdraw.

She released the vision and it disappeared, leaving her again on the roof of the keelboat in cheerful autumn morning sun. She looked north into the green ley energy and realized now that she could see flecks of black filtering to her witchy eye. Those were hints of the band of dead men on her trail, hundreds of miles upriver.

"I can see so much," she whispered, and she slipped the patch back down over her eye. "But I know so little."

"You can." Thalanes lay down on the roof of the cabin. "And you know much more than you think you do. It gives me comfort to know that I'm traveling with such a visionary. So much comfort that I'm not afraid of a couple of old Englishmen, just because they have a bit of grave-mold on them."

"I thought Lucky John's men killed them in Putney," Sarah said. "Wasn't that the whole point of the Silver Lancers, John Churchill's special squad? I read that equipping those men sucked the coffers of William of Orange dry. All that, and they failed?"

"All that and they *won*," the monk reminded her. "They drove the Necromancer out of England, along with Tom Long-Knife and the Sorcerer Hooke."

"And sent 'em on over here to the New World so's they could chase after me. I jest git luckier by the day."

Thalanes waited a moment. "Are you frightened?"

"Hell yes," Sarah shot back. She could feel her pulse racing and her breath was short.

"Would it help you to think of them as tragic figures?" Thalanes asked.

"I don't reckon it would," she guessed.

"Tom Fairfax was a rebel," Thalanes said, as if he was bound and determined to make his point anyway. "He rose up against his king, and then when he realized Cromwell was worse than what he'd replaced, he rebelled against Cromwell, too. Cromwell crushed the Rising of York, and his punishment for poor Black Tom was cruel."

"Black Tom killed a lot of people with his knife, afore and after he was dead. I reckon that was cruel, too."

"Yes," Thalanes agreed. "And then his old friend Cromwell killed him with his own knife, and bound Tom into Cromwell's service, forcing him to wield that same knife in the service of the man he hated, eternally."

"Cry me a river." Sarah gestured beyond the boat. "Cry me the damn Mississippi."

"And Hooke *asked* to become what Cromwell made him."

"What?" Sarah was startled. "Why in Hell would anybody ever want to become a walking corpse?"

"To live forever," Thalanes explained. "Hooke was a great wizard, practical and theoretical, much like Sir Isaac. When the only thing that drives you is *curiosity*, the thing you want most is *time*."

"And then what? They all jest came to the New World and hid for a hundred years, waitin' to jump out and grab me?"

"No one knows quite what happened to Cromwell," Thalanes said. "There are persistent rumors that William Penn sheltered him."

"My grandfather?" In context it was only a minor surprise. Sarah was beginning to regain control of herself and her accent. "Why would he have done anything so stupid?"

"Great-great-grandfather. Cromwell gave him his original land grant. That's where your family estates come from, Sarah . . . they were bestowed by the Necromancer. And after he'd been driven out, the Penns were established and King John had his hands full of other matters and no one was in any position to do much about it. Besides, people *liked* William Penn. He was a good man."

"Who made a deal with Hell."

"Maybe. Or maybe he didn't shelter Cromwell, and those rumors are just the baseless gossip of your family's enemies."

"Dammit," Sarah complained, "life is complicated."

"Many atrocities committed along the banks of the Mississippi over the years have been attributed to the Lazars," Thalanes continued. "Your father hunted them, though without much success."

"Oliver Cromwell is my enemy, then," Sarah said.

"The Lazars are, at least," Thalanes yawned again, "but we have a head start and we can see them. I'm sorry that you feel disquieted; your vision has put *my* mind at ease." He lay flat on the cabin roof and laced his fingers together over his breast. "So much so, that I'm now going to take a nap, and you'll have to drink my share of the coffee."

He shut his eyes and instantly he was breathing the soft, deep rhythms of sleep.

Calvin clambered back up onto the cabin roof. "I put water on the stove," he said, and then he saw the monk dozing. "I reckon it's jest coffee for two, then."

"Cal," Sarah told him, feeling shaky, "best keep the Elector's gun loaded with silver from now on. We got trouble a-comin'."

✧   ✧   ✧

The talkative deaf-mute returned the next night. At Bill's politest request, he disappeared again for a few minutes and came back with writing materials.

Bill lay on his belly and spread the sheet of paper out before him. He dipped the quill into the pot of black ink and considered carefully.

"Hell," he said.

"What vexes you, William Lee?" Hop sat cross-legged across the sheet from Bill, and he looked amused.

"For starters, Mr. Hop, you might consider calling me *Bill*. When you call me *William Lee* every time, it sounds as if you're reading an obituary."

Hop looked delighted. "Very good, Bill. I do not know what an obituary is, but perhaps you could call me Jake."

"Excellent, suh," Bill agreed. "Don't be offended at my provincialism, but *YAH-cobe* is difficult for me to remember, and *Mr. Hope* makes you sound like a fairy."

Hop laughed.

"An obituary, Jake," Bill continued, "is a printed notice, in a news-paper or similar publication, of a person's death. I'm surprised to learn the Dutch don't publish them. I've been to New Amsterdam, and it seemed a civilized enough place."

Hop shrugged.

"Secondly, although you've promoted my scheme in a most excellent and prompt manner, Jake, procuring these writing implements as you have, I find myself realizing that there are at least two tremendous weaknesses in my plan."

"What weaknesses? Perhaps I can help," Hop said.

"I can write well enough," Bill said, "to my grandfather's shame, who thought it beneath a gentleman, but I can't write Frog, and I don't expect that the chevalier will read a letter in English and believe it comes from Bayard Prideux. In addition, I find that I have no way to get a letter to the chevalier. My plan is ill-thought out and I am thwarted."

Hop clapped his hands together once. "I can solve both those problems, friend Bill!" He leaned forward, touched the inkpot, and muttered some jibber-jabber that didn't sound Dutch to Bill—or French, or Castilian, or Latin, or anything else remotely familiar.

The quill Bill was holding tingled to the touch.

"Why, Jake," Bill was surprised. "Have you been holding out on me? Are you a knickerbocker wizard, my good meneer?"

"I have some talent," Hop conceded, smiling.

"Heaven be praised," Bill said. "I may get out of here yet." He held up the quill and admired it in the candlelight. "And what will this enchanted pen do?"

"Write what you will, my friend," Hop explained. "The pen will turn it into French." He furrowed his brow. "You did mean French, yes, and not actually the language of frogs?"

Bill laughed loud. "Yes I did mean French, you delightfully simple Dutchman! The language of frogs, indeed!"

Hop only raised his eyebrows and smiled.

"Very good, Jake!" Bill shook his elbow out of habit, as if shaking a sleeve out of the way, though he was naked to the waist. He dipped the quill into the inkpot again and attacked the blank sheet. "My dearest Gaspard," he said aloud as he laboriously wrote. "Gaspard is the chevalier's Christian name. A touch of insolence will help provoke the desired reaction," he explained in an aside to Jacob Hop.

You, sir, he continued, *owe me. I have shared my secret with you, and it has made you great wealth. The source of your new riches, in turn, I have told no man, but I find that the recompense for service to you is miserable. You treat me as a prisoner, sir, as an outcast and as a disgrace. I deserve better. You should share your bounty with me, and give me place at your side. I warn you out of the warmest affection I have for you, that failure to so reward me may result in the alienation of my regard.*

He looked back at what he had written and what he saw made him laugh out loud. Not only was it all French—he could barely puzzle out the odd word, here and there—but Bill's native hand, hacked out of the page like fire-cleared brush, had been transformed in the act of writing into something elegant, letters curling and twisting on the paper like dancing sprites.

"This is the first time I've ever *written* a French letter." He winked. "You're a genius, Jake!" He signed the letter with the initials *B.P.*

"Very good, Bill," Hop said, beaming. "Shall I see to the delivery as well?"

Bill folded the letter, printing *to the Chevalier* on the outside in his accustomed blocky letters and marveling again that it came out as *au Chevalier*, in lovely script. "Can you? Will you give the letter wings?"

Hop laughed. "No, I cannot do that. Not here. I told you before, friend Bill, my power is weak upon the sea. There are other powers here, and they contest me, and then I am not yet come into my full strength. It is hard enough for me to be here at all, and to accomplish small magics, like putting words into your pen. I do not have the strength to manipulate physical objects on this ship—if I did, I would simply remove your manacles and we could swim away. It would be another matter entirely, you understand, if you were imprisoned upon the Mississippi."

Bill was disappointed. "You will find someone, though, to deliver it."

"Yes," Hop said. "Yes, Bill, I will. Besides, what madman would take delivery of a letter that arrived flapping its own wings?"

Kinta Jane Embry pitied the Frenchman on the hulk. She pitied most of the men she knew, and all of the men she served. They were lonely, they were needy, they were sad. Whatever it was they paid her to do, however much of her time and body they bought, what they really wanted was someone to pay them attention.

And most importantly, the men who hired Kinta Jane were usually men who wanted a woman who wouldn't talk back. They got what they wanted; for years, Kinta Jane had been an expert in keeping her mouth shut.

The Conventicle had equipped her for that.

The saddest of them all, though, was the Frenchman on the hulk. He talked so much. She understood him and she let him speak, but she tried to ignore everything he said and hold him, and she did what he wanted when he was ready.

His talk was insane, drunk talk, the grand scheming of every failed criminal, with constant hints at dark secrets and at his importance to the chevalier. He was pathetic, he was lonely, he was eager, he was desperate. And if he was so important to the chevalier, why was he a guard on a rotting prison ship? Her half-brother René was important to the chevalier, and he lived in the Palais.

Not that the chevalier's motives mattered to her. She served René and the Conventicle, René and the Conventicle wanted the

Frenchman watched, and Kinta Jane was the one to do it. She took the Conventicle's orders—when the Conventicle gave her orders, which was a rare event—but it was the chevalier, or at least, René, who was the chevalier's seneschal, who paid her every month to visit the *Incroyable*. Paid her, and gave her money to pay the scarred boatman who rowed her out.

Kinta Jane did her duty by the sad Frenchman, and when she could she made a little extra cash by letting the Frenchman's idiot assistants grope her or kiss her for whatever copper coins they had scavenged. Visiting the sad Frenchman did not bring Kinta Jane much money, but she had other clients.

She needed those other clients—the Conventicle didn't pay. One joined the Conventicle and did its work for the greater good, in order to protect Adam's children from the coming storm, because one believed in Franklin's vision. Kinta Jane believed in Franklin's vision. She also believed in René, who had recruited her and who was her cell leader. To this day she only knew two other people in the Conventicle—the other members of her cell. That, and she had an address in Philadelphia to which she could send a message, if something happened and René, her cell leader, was disabled.

She finished with the Frenchman and held him while he fell asleep. Then she dressed, first pulling the cluster of beybey medallions over her head and laying them on her breast, then covering them with her tight blouse and stepping into her wide-flounced skirt.

René couldn't protect her from everything, and Pritchard didn't protect her from anything at all, so Kinta Jane Embry walked the streets with Papa Legba. New Orleans was the meeting place of two armies of gods, as she saw it. Jesus and His saints came down to it from the heavens, and Papa Legba and his mystères crawled up to it out of the ground and the forests and the cemeteries and the swamps.

Where Kinta Jane worked and lived, she was closer to the swamps.

She took her lantern and went back out onto the creaking deck of the hulk. The idiots were nowhere in sight—it was late, they were likely all asleep, and the only one who had been interested in any of Kinta Jane's ministrations had already had his petty favors and paid for them—but the blond man, the deaf-mute, stood by the side of the ship's ladder.

Kinta Jane shrugged deeper into her shawl against the night's chill. She smiled and nodded at the deaf-mute; he had always seemed oblivious to her, though he nodded and waved politely enough.

He smiled back and she moved to pass him.

"May I ask a service of you?" the deaf-mute said in an unfamiliar lyrical accent.

She could say nothing in return—she had voluntarily had her tongue removed, when the Conventicle judged that it was necessary—but she had grown up speaking and still had verbal reflexes. Out of sheer surprise she grunted, a sound of which she was immediately embarrassed.

She touched the beybey through the thin material of her blouse and nodded.

The deaf-mute held up two folded letters. "Will you please deliver these for me?" Then he produced a coin.

Kinta Jane took the letters and examined them. They were clearly addressed, in French, in the same elegant hand, to the chevalier and to the bishop. This was an easy commission, so she nodded. The deaf-mute handed her the coin, spun on his heel and walked away into the darkness.

She climbed down the ladder and got in the boat. As the boatman pulled at his oars to drag them from the hulk to the shore, Kinta Jane opened her hand discreetly and looked down at the coin she had just taken.

The letters were strange enough; the coin was positively exotic. In the light of the full moon it glowed large and gold, like a Louis d'or, but it bore no letters or numbers. She had never seen its like. On its obverse was stamped the clear image of a plow, and on the reverse a sword.

She knew who minted coins like these, and the sight of it chilled her. The time had come, she mused, looking back for another glimpse of the deaf-mute as the lights of shore drew nearer.

Franklin's terrifying vision was coming true again.

Peter Plowshare must be dead.

Another god had come to New Orleans.

"Lord hates a man as can't laugh."

———◆———

CHAPTER THIRTEEN

"I thought they's river pirates," Cal said. "What's with the horses?"

He stood with Sarah and Thalanes in the Place d'Armes, a broad cobbled square in the center of the Quarter, staring up at an enormous bronze statue. They had been deposited by the melodious Germans at the Mississippi docks at midday, hearing the deep ringing of church bells even as they walked up the long wharf, and had made their way here; Thalanes was familiar with the city, and the distance between the Mississippi River and the Place d'Armes was short.

The two beastkind had held back at the gate to the Place d'Armes.

"We will await you outside," Picaw had sung.

Cal had never been to a city as large as Louisiana's metropolis—there were lucrative cattle markets much closer to Calhoun Mountain. He found New Orleans fascinating, with its iron balconies, its hanging greenery, its boardwalks, and its motley population. He'd only heard three or four snatches of English spoken since they'd arrived, and they'd been wading constantly through a bubbling sea of humanity.

Sarah had seemed not to be paying attention to any of it, as if her mind were elsewhere. She would periodically take the improvised patch off her face and gaze upriver, and doing so always left her looking troubled and tired.

Cal was not enthusiastic about the idea that they were being stalked by dead men—Sarah had told him of her vision—but he stayed calm. He kept his eyes open, and the Elector's gun loaded with a silver ball.

The Place d'Armes roiled with people. Tarock readers with thumb-worn wooden folding tables, a turban-wearing hedge witch clutching a chicken under one arm and offering curses and love charms at cut rates, jugglers with batons and glass balls, a sword-swallower with a two-edged serpentine appetizer halfway down his gullet, and a ragged, shuffling band comprised of banjo, horn, lute, and three battered copper pots competed against two gesticulating friars and a university man publicly declaiming his thesis on the inevitable cycles of history, all to the jeers, catcalls and hoorahs of a shifting Babel. Cal even caught a glimpse of beastkind, a couple of shuffling anteater-headed things dragging their long snouts close to the ground.

The statue around which all this sweating, exerting, exhorting humanity swarmed was colossal. Rising from a square marble platform, it depicted two mustachioed men on horseback, each armed with a long pistol. One horse reared as its rider sighted and fired into the distance, west and upriver; the other plunged forward at a right angle toward Decatur Street and the Mississippi, its rider spurring its flanks and waving his gun in the air.

"I'm not surprised that in Appalachee they're known as pirates," Thalanes said. "But of course the people here are *happy* that Andrew Jackson's ambitions were thwarted by Jean and Pierre Lafitte. Louisiana thinks of the Lafitte brothers as respectable militiamen and heroes. I believe Pierre owns a blacksmith shop, and Jean is still, as they say, on the account."

"You mean he's a pirate," Sarah interpreted.

"But a respectable one," Cal added.

"Well," Thalanes said, "as I hear it, he mostly steals from the Spanish."

"The Calhouns and plenty of other Appalachee folk are perfectly content that the Lafittes stopped Andy Jackson from crowning himself king of the Mississippi," Sarah pointed out. "We're mostly opposed to people declaring themselves kings."

"I imagine that's true," Thalanes conceded. "Mostly."

"Lord hates a man as gets too big for his britches," Cal said.

"Would you like to see him?" Thalanes asked. "You could look at the fit of his britches yourself."

"You mean Jackson?" Sarah frowned. "Isn't he dead?"

"Ain't they somethin' famous about their pistols, though?" Cal tried to remember. "Weren't they magic, or some such?"

"They were blessed." Sarah knew everything.

"They were consecrated by the bishop before the battle," Thalanes told them. "After the battle, the Lafittes laid the pistols on the altar in gratitude for their victory. I think they may still be in the cathedral."

They walked on, past two stump speakers, hollering at each other from three feet apart on separate barrels. The two men were a study in contrasts, one short, plump, blond, and handsome, and the other dark, long in the leg, gangly, and scowling. They yelled to be heard over the crowd, but Cal found their words surprisingly droll.

"But Your Honor speaks very harshly of Wisdom," the tall one shouted, "even, some might say, to the point of defaming Her. Was She not the serpent that Moses raised on a pole in the desert, that healed the children of Israel?"

Cal heard a few scattered hand-claps in the crowd.

"No, sir," the short man rejoined, "I have not heard that She was. I have always understood, however, that there was a serpent in the *garden*, and that our first parents—or should I say rather, *my* first parents—took great harm therefrom."

There were loud guffaws in response, and a low hissing boo when the man said '*my* first parents.'

"Damn right!" yelled a dirty man in a slouch hat, leaning on a long rifle.

The gangly fellow grinned. "Oh, that is an old chestnut." He somehow managed to shout and sound mild at the same time. "Even Paul knew to warn the Corinthians that Old Scratch may appear as an angel of light."

More subdued laughter. They were past the debaters and moving on, and Cal heard just one last retort from the smaller man.

"I might be more persuaded," he bellowed, "if the serpent's children didn't insist on filling the Ohio with their thousand Babel towers, cluttering up the place like some blighted plain of Shinar!"

Then the two men were gone and the St. Louis Cathedral stared down at Cal, its three slate steeples frowning in disapproval. The tall, thin windows of the cathedral, rounded at the tops, its stacked columns and its plain, workaday clock face gave it the appearance of the palace of a stern king in some fairyland.

The cathedral was flanked by two stone mansions. They looked identical to Cal, or nearly so, each showering two rows of stone arches upon the Place d'Armes, mounted underneath a sloping mansard roof and a-glitter with glass windows.

"It jest ain't right that a bishop'd live in such a fancy place," he grumbled. "The buildings on this square reek of money."

"The bishop shares your discomfort," the monk told him, surveying the cathedral and its companions. "That's why he only occupies a few rooms of his palace, and lets the Polites and the Gutenbergians have the rest. This way." He ambled toward the mansion on the right.

"What's in the other one?" Cal gestured left and loped easily into the monk's wake.

"Polites . . . that's St. Reginald Pole, isn't it? Aren't they alchemists, or something?" Sarah asked.

"The Polites promote Christian study of gramarye," Thalanes answered, "in all its permissible specialties."

"What's a permissible specialty?" she asked. "Healing the sick, multiplying loaves and fishes, casting out devils, that sort of thing?"

"They's a difference between magic and miracles," Cal muttered.

"Views differ," Thalanes said, "even among the Polites. But a Polite who started dabbling in necromancy or demonology, for instance, would quickly find himself expelled and probably excommunicated. Some alchemy is problematic. Summoning and binding angels or other powers of Heaven—what is sometimes called theurgy."

"And the other one?" Cal repeated. "Who's so fancy as he gets a buildin' jest as big and shiny as the Polites?"

"Government," Thalanes said. "The other palace holds the offices and meeting chambers of the City Council. The chevalier gives them impressive chambers instead of meaningful power."

"Lucky for the Polites the bishop didn't shack 'em up with a gang of Mattheans," Cal quipped.

"You won't find any followers of St. Matthew Hopkins in New Orleans." Thalanes said. "I'd be surprised to see a Witchfinder anywhere south of Philadelphia, really."

Cal grunted. Waste of a good joke. Lord hates a man as can't laugh, and didn't Abraham laugh when Sarah was with child? Come to think of it, maybe it was Sarah who laughed.

"Maybe that's too bad," Thalanes continued. "Maybe a few Mattheans would be just what we need."

"What?" Sarah snapped. "You anxious to git yourself tried for witchcraft?"

"Matthew Hopkins persecuted spellcasters of all sorts," the monk explained with a queer little smile. "Including Oliver Cromwell. Before Cromwell was ever the Necromancer, when he was just the Lord Protector of the Commonwealth of England and beginning to hunt down and kill England's Firstborn, Hopkins opposed him and tried to prosecute him for sorcery. He failed, of course, and Cromwell had him executed on Tyburn Tree, but not before Hopkins had a lot of Cromwell's minions hanged. He was demented and wicked, but he was the first rebel against an even more demented and wicked man."

"The enemy of my enemy is my friend?" Sarah suggested.

"No," Thalanes said. "They're both my enemies. But I wouldn't mind seeing them fight each other. Here we are." He looked up and pointed.

A row of tall poles held suspended a series of iron cages, each exactly the size of a man. All held scraps of cloth, leather and bone, and a few held entire skeletons. Inside the cage Thalanes indicated was a corpse, face rotted beyond recognition and collapsing in decay. Bone showed through the split, leathery skin of the corpse's face, and the hands were gone, fallen off if they hadn't been cut off in the first place. It wore a blue military uniform, with tarnished brass buttons running down the chest in parallel rows, and the hair on its head was a thick white mane.

"What in Jerusalem's *that*?" Cal felt a little uneasy at the sight.

"That," Thalanes said, "is Mr. Andrew Jackson."

"King Andy," Sarah said softly. What was she thinking?

Thalanes walked on, and Sarah and Cal followed.

They approached the palace, and Cal looked at a clutch of men and women simmering under the arches, knitted together in brow-furrowing conversation. "I seen a few Wanderin' Johnnies come through Nashville, and they ain't never dressed in red. I guess mostly they jest carried books."

"The adherents of the Humble Order of St. Reginald Pole wear red," Thalanes said. "They have no other icon. The Gutenbergians have no official icon at all, though sometimes they use the image of an open book."

"How many of them are there?" Cal asked. "That's a big buildin'."

"I suspect that most of the building is library, laboratory, and lecture hall," Thalanes said. "The Polites are a small order."

"They jest ain't that many hexers," Cal agreed.

As he neared the Polites' building the monk turned, guiding them around it and down the narrow street running along its left side, separating the palace from the cathedral. He marched up to a small, unmarked door in the palace's wall and rapped on the wood.

"Remember me again what we're a-doin' here?" Cal felt ill at ease standing on the doorstep of a bishop, no matter how humble or pious the man might be. In fact, the reputation for humility and piety made it worse—Calvin preferred his bishops arrogant, worldly, and far away. It fit his preconceptions better. Calvin had put his question to Sarah, but he shot a sidelong look at Thalanes.

"It was my decision, Cal," Sarah said, and Thalanes bowed his head.

There was an awkward pause and Cal regretted that he'd said anything. He tried to break the silence. "I don't know for fancy houses, but ain't this a servants' entrance?"

"Yes," the monk agreed with a small smile. "I rather think that's the point."

The door opened to reveal a slight, stooped man, with a deeply-lined brown face framed between the stiff white collar of his black priest's shirt and the tightly-curled growth of white heather above his forehead.

"Thalanes!" The stooped man immediately embraced the monk. The little old man looked so benign that Calvin immediately felt embarrassed. He noticed that Thalanes was pulling his old trick of standing very close to a body, closer than Calvin would have been comfortable with, but the bishop didn't object.

Priests just had no sense of personal space.

"Your Grace," Thalanes said, disentangling himself from the hug and smiling. "May I present my traveling companions? These are Sarah and Calvin Carpenter." Sarah curtseyed. Calvin made to bow, but the old man seized his arm in a tight grip and shook his hand.

"The Carpenters. Like the Holy Family." The bishop took

Sarah's face in his hands and kissed her cheeks. "But in my house, you must call me Chinwe, because if you call me *Your Grace* or *Father,* my old friend Thalanes will insist on doing the same, and I could never bear such treatment." He stepped back from the door and ushered them in. "You must forgive me if my English is rusty. We are accustomed to speaking French in this town."

The apartment they entered was small and crammed full of books. Books marched in double file on the wooden floor along the baseboards of the hallway, books tottered on high shelves nailed haphazardly onto all the walls, tall piles of books swayed on top of every piece of furniture. Just when he'd almost felt himself warming to the bishop, the old man had to go and ruin it.

"That there's a lot of books," he complained.

"They are my great treasure," the priest said, "which makes me a very poor Christian, for does not the Lord exhort us to lay up our treasures in Heaven? And yet mine are stacked upon the carpet, where the moth does indeed corrupt. Please," he smiled, "lay your burdens down here."

They dropped their gear and arms in a small room opening from the hallway.

"I am glad you are here, old friend." The bishop ushered them all into a small kitchen where a cast-iron stove squatted on slates in the corner and the smell of spiced chicken and rice punched Calvin in the stomach. The walls were egg-yolk yellow, clean but bare, other than a simple wooden cross on one wall. "It is a wonderful surprise to see you. I have an unpleasant task ahead of me, and I need my resolve strengthened. Also, you are just in time to share our food. No fried basilisk or broiled sea serpent, but there is enough for everyone!"

A younger man with the same smile rose from a seat beside the stove. He, too, wore priestly black with the white collar. "I'll set three more places, Father," he said, and quickly plated up food for the new arrivals.

"You must ignore the way this one addresses me." The bishop leaned in close to Cal conspiratorially. "His name is Chigozie, and he really *is* my son. Ha!"

They sat on mismatched stools around the small table. The five of them crowded the room to capacity; Cal ate with his elbows pinned to his sides and he ran a constant risk of bumping a shelf of crockery behind him.

"Where's your other son, Chinwe?" Thalanes asked. "Is Ofodile not pursuing the family profession?"

"My brother has chosen a different occupation." Chigozie didn't look up.

"You may find him in the Vieux Carré if you are here long," the bishop added. "We do not see him often; he is a man of business, and has much on his hands. But if you see him, you must call him *Etienne*—he goes by his second name now."

"Etienne does indeed have much on his hands." Again Chigozie kept his gaze focused on his plate.

The rice was heavy with peppers and onions and Calvin had never eaten anything with so much flavor. He wolfed it down and tried to listen.

"I've long owed you a friendly visit, Chinwe," Thalanes said, "and, sadly, this isn't it. I come to you in need and in strange circumstances, with evil at my heels. But if I can be of any assistance to you in your pastoral travails, please tell me how to do so."

The bishop chuckled. "My old friend, you cannot poke beehives with a stick and then complain when the bees come after you."

Thalanes smiled ruefully. "There may be someone in this world who can teach me the art of leaving beehives alone, but it isn't you, Chinwe. I fear, though, that you won't be pleased to see the bees I've stirred up."

"No?" the bishop asked. "Then let me tell you first about my bee."

"Only one? A solitary bee hardly seems worth the attention of a beekeeper of your prowess."

"One is enough if it is the right bee. Only one bee troubles me, but he is a very large bee, with many drones. He is a great, fat bee who feeds...from a golden lily."

Some information had passed from the bishop to the monk, but Cal had missed it. Thalanes's head snapped up from his rice and his eyebrows shot to the top of his forehead.

"Why does this bee trouble you, Chinwe?" Thalanes continued after a moment.

The bishop set down his fork and knife. "I have received a confession of one of the bee's drones," he went on. "A written confession, which in itself is strange. The content of the confession is troubling, too; it tells me the bee of the golden lily is a thief. For many years, he has been stealing honey from another beehive. A very important beehive, rich with honey and peopled by bees with mighty stings. And now, I fear, it is my duty to confront the great, fat bee, and remind him of the walls where his own hive ends."

Thalanes knotted his fingers together and raised his eyebrows. "How may I help you, Chinwe?"

"Your presence alone fortifies my will, and in the end it is not such a very large thing. Just a simple conversation between a beekeeper and a bee. Ha!" The bishop picked up his utensils again and resumed eating. "Tell me about your bees, and what an old bee-man like me can do to help."

"I have two needs, Chinwe," Thalanes said. "The first is this: I am looking for a man."

"Can you not use your gramarye to find this person?" Chigozie asked. "My father speaks often of your skill at magic."

Thalanes shook his head. "I haven't seen this man for years, I don't know where he is, and I have nothing of his to use in a scrying. Gramarye in this case would be scarcely more useful than simply walking about and using my eyes, and it would be much more tiring."

"If *your* vision is insufficient," the bishop asked, his dark eyes glittering in his lined face, "what about *hers*?"

Cal rocked back on his chair. Sarah and Thalanes both had surprised looks on their faces.

"She has a great gift, it's true," the monk said slowly, "but I believe it's beyond her to find this man."

"How did you know?" Sarah asked the bishop. "Are you a wizard, too?"

The little old man bowed his head. "I have no gift of gramarye. I am just a parish priest who sometimes dreams, when times are troubled. Recently, I have dreamed of a one-eyed queen who can see the entire Mississippi. I think I am not the only one to dream of her."

"Perhaps you've also dreamed of the man I'm looking for?" Thalanes wondered.

"I doubt it. Tell me who he is, old friend. Perhaps he is a parishioner. Perhaps I can take you directly to him."

Thalanes nodded. "I'm looking for a man I knew as Captain Sir William Johnston Lee. He was a soldier, an officer, a gentleman, a great servant to Empress Hannah and her husband. He distinguished himself in the Spanish War, in Texia, and at the Siege of Mobile. He has been in New Orleans, I believe, for a long time."

The bishop shook his head. "I think I would remember such a person."

"I believe Captain Lee has fallen on hard times. He may not be recognizable as the man he once was. And I think he may be using the name Bad Bill."

"Bad Bill? *Bad Bill*?" Chigozie's eyes widened in surprise.

"Do you know this man?" the bishop asked his son.

Chigozie shook his head. "I do not know him, but I have heard of him. He is...he is not the sort of man my father is likely to know."

"What sort of man is he?" Cal felt uneasy.

"He is the sort of man my brother would associate with," Chigozie said, after some hesitation. "You should speak with Etienne. He has...he does much business in the Vieux Carré."

"Thank you," Thalanes said.

The bishop shrugged. "What else, old friend?"

The monk hesitated. "As I seek my former comrade, Captain Lee," he finally said, his voice heavy, "so I in turn am sought, by a former enemy."

The bishop looked worried. "Who is this enemy?"

Thalanes sighed. "I fear there may be a very old enemy, indeed, behind the curtain. Our footsteps are dogged by dead men, my friend. By Black Tom Fairfax and the Sorcerer Robert Hooke."

Chigozie dropped his fork and it clattered on the table. "Did I hear you say the *Lazars* are following you? Thomas Fairfax, the Scourge of the Low Countries? And Hooke, Isaac Newton's Shadow? Were they not destroyed, more than a century ago?"

"You heard me correctly," the monk agreed. "Black Tom and the Sorcerer were not destroyed by John Churchill's Glorious Revolution, only driven out of England. And two days ago, I saw Hooke and Fairfax both in a vision. They were coming this way."

"Can you not mislead them, or hide your tracks, with your craft?" the bishop asked.

"I've done what I can," Thalanes said. "Still they come. Either they have some other way of knowing where we are, or Robert Hooke is simply a more powerful wizard than I am. Both possibilities are grim. Both are likely."

"I saw them this morning," Sarah said softly.

"In New Orleans?" the bishop asked her.

She shook her head. "Not yet. But soon. Maybe as soon as tomorrow."

There was a terrible silence. Cal was suddenly very aware of the lightness of his belt and the fact that his weapons were all in the other room.

When the bishop spoke again, his words surprised Cal. "I have seen my own death. God has shown it to me, and the face of the man who will kill me. I didn't know the face, but I saw that he wore a hat and fired a gun. He had the eyes of a doomed man, so doomed I felt compassion for him. Perhaps it was a Lazar."

The room felt very, very small.

"I'm sorry, my friend." Thalanes's voice was strained. "I knew evil was at my heels, but I didn't understand how great an evil it was."

"God's will." The bishop ruminated for a few moments. "I do not think I have any weapons I can give you."

"What about the Lafitte pistols?" Calvin asked.

The bishop smiled. "Well," he said, "they are there behind the altar, but I do not think they will help you. They are very ordinary pistols, and are not regularly maintained. Do you need pistols?" He stood, and rummaged in a drawer under the kitchen counter.

"I ain't much of a shot with a handgun, anyways." Cal shrugged. "I jest heard they's special."

The bishop turned back to face the table with a small purse in his hand. "They *are* special pistols. But they are not magical. Take this; at least I can help you purchase supplies." He handed the purse to Calvin. "I assume you are the one handling the silver in this group?"

"Yessir, I reckon I am." Cal took the money.

"Thank you," Thalanes murmured.

"Excuse me," Chigozie said. He stood up from the table and walked out.

"So how do we find Etienne?" Cal asked—it seemed like the practical question that needed answering.

"Chigozie will help you," the bishop told him. "Chigozie!" he called.

The younger priest came back into the kitchen, holding a small knife in a leather sheath. "Yes," he agreed. "I will take you to Etienne's... office. I have some duties in the cathedral this afternoon, though, and in any case, Etienne works late. May I take you tonight? Perhaps you would care to rest here for a few hours in the meantime."

"We have other errands in New Orleans," Thalanes demurred. "Maybe we can come find you here again this evening, and you could take us to find Ofodile... Etienne?"

"Of course, as you wish." Chigozie held up the little knife, and Cal saw that its sheath was elaborately tooled, and that its hilt was wrapped in leather. "I wish I had a better weapon to offer than this," he said, and he pulled it from its sheath. "It is a letter opener—the Bishop of Miami sent it to me as a gift upon my ordination—but if it were sharpened to a finer edge, I believe it would be meaningful as a weapon."

Cal was about to protest that he hadn't held a knife so tiny since he got out of short pants, but then his eye caught the dull gleam of the blade and he realized why Father Chigozie was offering them his letter opener.

The knife was made of silver.

"Thank you." He accepted the weapon.

The Heron King clubbed William Penn in the head. For the first time in many days, Obadiah laughed.

"But, sir," cried the Penn puppet in a shrill, nasal voice, "I shall have this land whether thou wilt or no. My Germans, my Englishmen, and my Lenni Lenape desire a land where they may live in peace." He wore a Pennslander's hat, round-crowned, wide-brimmed, and black, and curly white hair fell to his shoulders. He was dressed all in blue, with conspicuous gold thread.

Thump, thump. More blows on Penn's head.

"I am king here, Brother Onas," the Heron King boomed back, "undying and unchallenged, and I regard thee not!" The Heron King puppet was a long-necked bird with a three-pointed brass crown on its head. Its puppet body consisted mostly of long legs ending in more or less birdlike claws, but it also had a pair of hands that held its club. "Fie upon thee for a knave and a trespasser!"

Obadiah watched the puppets have at each other upon their tiny wooden stage and laughed harder than the show deserved. The puppets were marionettes, innocent and childlike in all their exaggerated movements, they weren't responsible for their actions. For puppets, there was indeed a higher world, and it was only two feet over their heads, pulling their strings. And no matter how much puppets pummeled each other with their little clubs, none of them was ever hurt.

The puppet show was the first thing that Obadiah had been able to find really engaging since the night he had failed to kidnap Sarah.

"An thou resist, thou spindle-shanked humbug, I shall be compelled to use main force, and shall take the land of peace from thee!"

William Penn produced a club and began thumping the Heron King back.

"Imbecile!" The Heron King dropped his club and fled off the stage.

"Booby!" Penn did a little high-kneed dance of victory, to the cheers and applause of the crowd. Obadiah patted his hands together, too.

Unexpectedly, the Heron King rushed back on stage, this time holding a much bigger club. "Varlet!" he roared, and set upon Penn with animal ferocity. He knocked away Penn's club and pounded him to the ground, shrieking and whistling.

Penn raised a supplicating arm and waved it at the audience. "Help! Help! Oh Lord, is there no help for the widow's son?"

Obadiah laughed harder.

Was this what the world was like for the gods? A cramped wooden stage, a cheap curtain, and millions upon millions of puppets on strings?

Maybe it was finally time, Obadiah thought, to get to know his father's faith as other Christians knew it. In his mind's eye a scene unfolded that had never taken place in real life—Obadiah and Father Angleton sitting at a campfire, leafing through Obadiah's Bible together and discussing weighty matters of life, death, eternity, and love.

"Obadiah!" Father Angleton barked.

Obadiah jerked about and realized that he had come to a dead stop in the middle of the street to stare at the puppets. New Orleans sizzled with energy and behind him his string of mules drifted on its line, but he had been completely absorbed in the marionettes.

He had fallen behind. The Blues were gone, and Father Angleton was hissing at him in anger and frustration because he had had to come back to find his hired man.

"Obadiah!" the Right Reverend Father snapped again.

"Aye," he said dully. "Sorry, Father. I . . ."

He had been distracted even before he had seen the puppets, thinking about Sarah, wondering when he would see her. He had forgotten he was leading the baggage train of the Philadelphia Blues, and it had been easy to let himself become entranced by the show.

"I was finkink, Father," he said, "mayhap you an' I could read some Bible together in the mornink. Discuss a wee bit of feology."

"What?" Angleton's eyes were incredulous and indignant.

"I asked the price of a pot, to replace the one what lost its 'andle," Obadiah lied, changing the subject. "I fell behind."

"I don't have time for this, Obadiah." Angleton rode away.

Obadiah held his tongue and followed his master.

With similar reluctance, the mules followed him in turn.

New Orleans was nearly as large as Philadelphia and London, though less sprawling than either of those. It looked more like a Spanish or a French city than an English one, with its continental buildings and its exotic plants. There was greenery everywhere Obadiah looked, in myriad ferns, jasmine, wisteria, and lilies that crawled up the walls, hung from balconies and clotted the street corners. Outside the city walls, the countryside was a jungle of cypress, magnolia, walnut, hickory, and those eerie oak trees dripping with moss, like green-haired crones stretching out over the pike and muttering in the breeze of the horrible fates that awaited outsiders in Louisiana. New Orleans *sounded* French or Castilian too, in its hubbub.

Obadiah missed Sarah.

The pike had ended at a ferry, by means of which they had crossed the narrow mouth of the Pontchartrain Sea. On the far side of the Pontchartrain they had rejoined the squad of Blues that had split off to ride the Natchez Trace; they had made their discreet report to Captain Berkeley and Father Angleton, and then the entire company had ridden into and across New Orleans. Obadiah was impressed by Angleton's confidence and knowledge of the city, even as he felt increasingly estranged from the Right Reverend Father.

But then, he felt increasingly estranged from himself.

They were passing out of the lively zone called the Quarter now, across a fantastically wide boulevard full of buying and selling humanity. They rode toward more genteel parts of the city on its western side, full of larger houses, iron-fenced homes with carefully manicured grass growing around them, and many edifices that looked like commercial or government buildings, still within the great stone walls that kept out pirates, Texians, and beastkind.

By force of being even more cantankerous than they were, Obadiah hauled the mules forward, brutal in his determination not to be left behind again.

Father Angleton set a brisk pace; soon they turned right around a solid brick building so large it occupied its own block, its doors guarded by men in blue and gold fleur-de-lis livery and marked with the legend *City of New Orleans*, and ran into the tail of the Philadelphia Blues. A receding column of horses' rumps was the view of the Blues to which Obadiah had become accustomed, and as a matter of habit he slowed, but this time he followed the Right Reverend Father, mule string and all, to the front of the line. The Blues paid him with looks of complete indifference as he passed. But for the first time in two weeks, Obadiah was at the front of the company, and he felt wanted, or at least visible.

Captain Berkeley raised his hand to stop the column. They had reached the chevalier's palace.

The palace brooded in its gray stone between a tall iron fence and acres of green grass, the colonnaded portico surrounding it masked by groves of magnolia and sparkling fountains. Above the portico, further rows of columns sprang skyward, support-ing tiers of balconies that piled jumbled up to the heavens, like a great stone wedding cake.

Obadiah imagined himself getting married with such a cake. A Christian wedding filled his head, rather than the sacrificial wedding feast of the followers of Herne and Wayland that he and Peg had once planned. He imagined himself, to his own surprise, as a squire, wearing a long-tailed coat with brass but-tons and a shiny black hat, shaved and greeting all the county notables, walking cane inscribing elegant circles in the air or tucked insouciantly under his arm. Peg, walking a carpet of flowers with the traditional wedding horseshoe in hand. Sarah, rather. Signing the register. Gifting the parson. Vows outside the chapel door. Cutting the cake and serving it, but not the top, not the christening cake, that would be saved for the baptism of their first child. He looked up at the chevalier's palace and tried to imagine which part of it would be the christening cake. He hoped their children got her looks.

Except for the eye.

They trotted across the street to a two-story gatehouse, wide enough for two carriages to pass through abreast. Its portcullis was up and a dozen men stood guard, again in the blue and gold, bearing the fleur-de-lis, armed with pikes and pistols.

Father Angleton reached under his tabard—he had changed into the formal hammer-and-nail suit this morning, in anticipation of reaching New Orleans—and produced a card, which he handed to the commander of the gate guard.

"I am Father Ezekiel Angleton," he said, "Chaplain to the Imperial House Light Dragoons. This is Captain Sir Daniel Berkeley, Captain of the Dragoons. We have come to pay our respects to the Chevalier of New Orleans."

The commander simply nodded and sent the card inside with one of his men. At Berkeley's gesture, the Blues brought up their line into a more compact formation and stayed mounted. Obadiah pulled the mule string in close and shushed the beasts. They all stood in silence, inspecting each other.

The man sent inside returned, and he came accompanied. The second person was not in a soldier's uniform, but wore a crisp coat, neck cloth and cravat, and had a thick gold chain on his chest. He was tall and bony, with a severe face that looked both French and Indian of some sort. He made a rolling motion with one hand and the portcullis was promptly drawn up.

"Father Angleton," he said, bowing slightly to the Right Reverend Father. "The chevalier is pleased to receive your visit. He regrets he cannot receive you personally yet, but he is engaged in business matters. I am René du Plessis, Seneschal of the Palais du Chevalier." This man was a servant like Obadiah, but a servant with standing, a man who could treat his master's guests almost as equals.

"Many thanks to the chevalier, I am sure," Captain Berkeley replied. "Mr. du Plessis, might you indicate to me some inn or hostel where I could quarter my men?"

"Certainly, Captain," the seneschal replied. "You may install them in the City Building, which you see there behind you, across the street. The Gendarme Station in the building has extra bunks. They will need to circle around the building to get in; the entrance to the station is on the Perdido Street side."

Obadiah experienced a tortured moment of indecision as Father Angleton and Captain Berkeley turned with the seneschal and entered the chevalier's Palace, while the rest of the Blues peeled away and headed back the way they had come. He wanted to follow the Right Reverend Father, but Angleton didn't look back, and as he receded across the wide courtyard, past a pair of waiting coaches and lines of footmen and guards, the lead rope of the mule string grew heavier and heavier in Obadiah's hand. Finally, the rope grew so heavy that it pulled him back, and he turned away from the master who had turned away from him, drifted listlessly back across the street and followed the Blues to their quarters.

Bill woke to a pair of shoes in his view again. He counted them; two shoes; so the feet did not belong to Bayard. And they were buckled; Jacob Hop. He rolled over and looked up into the smiling, blond-framed face.

"Just when I thought I had *lost* hope," he quipped, but didn't bother sitting up. He felt drained, as if the act of forging a letter to the chevalier had consumed the last of his vitality, and now he could only lie spent. He saw chinks of light in the walls and frowned—he was used to seeing the Dutchman, at least in his talking persona, at night. "Is evening upon us, Jake?"

"Yes, another night is almost here," Hop said.

Another night. And another, and another, and another. Bayard had not again whipped Bill, but neither had he again brought Bill liquor. Bill felt weak and tired.

"I hope you've brought me a pistol this time," he said. "Or the keys."

Hop handed Bill a bottle: rum. "The whisky is all gone."

"It's all the same, suh," Bill lied, and took a slug of the rum. If he'd wanted a sailor's drink, he'd have worn rope shoes and a ribbon in his hat. He didn't know any sailors' toasts.

"There are no guns on the ship," Hop told Bill. "And the keys are locked up. What would you do with a pistol?"

"Shoot myself." Silly Dutchman. If he had a pistol, he would kill Bayard Prideux, the next time he dared to show his face. "Keys seem like a surpassingly strange thing to keep *locked up*, don't they?"

"You can't shoot yourself now, Bill." A mischievous smile crept across Hop's face. "This is all just about to get interesting."

"It's unnatural and effeminate."

———⟫•⟪———

CHAPTER FOURTEEN

Sarah followed Thalanes back under Andrew Jackson's death-cage as the sun sank; Calvin followed her in turn. She felt like a banjo string wound to the point of snapping, and yet she knew that she would be wound tighter still before she could relax.

The Lazars were as much as a day behind her, though no more than two. It added to her tension that, away from the Mississippi and its gigantic ley, she could no longer see her walking-corpse pursuers.

Would a day be enough to find William Lee? New Orleans was a large city, one of the largest in the empire. Sarah stumbled through a vast carnival, and all the inhabitants were in costume and putting on a show.

She had tried, from the keelboat, to exercise her Second Sight to find Lee. After all, Thalanes didn't really know her limitations, and she had been able to find the Lazars. She had seen endless swarms of people, but she had no idea how to distinguish William Lee.

If she had something that belonged to Lee, or, better still, a physical piece of him, it would be easy to devise a spell that would lead her to the man, or reveal him. That was Newton's Law of Contagion. And if she had something that *looked* like him as well, or maybe something that looked like a finding device, then she'd get the benefit of the theoretical magician's Law of Sympathy, too.

269

If.

But the beastfolk claimed they could lead her to someone who knew Lee. And failing that, Father Chigozie Ukwu had already promised to take her to his brother.

The monk slowed his pace to walk with Sarah. "Before we meet Grungle and Picaw again, I would like to tell you another story."

"Can't wait," Cal said from behind.

"You'll like it," Thalanes told him over his shoulder. "It's from the Poor Richard Sermons, and I remember the moral."

"You know as I like a good moral."

"Is there something in particular on your mind?" Sarah asked the monk.

He shrugged. "I want to impart a thought before we rejoin our beastkind friends, who wish to offer their help and who say they are emissaries of the Heron King."

"You don't believe 'em?" Cal asked.

"I believe them." Thalanes cleared his throat and began. "The burgomaster and aldermen of a small town west of Chicago were meeting in council one day to discuss the draining of the local swamp, when a stranger appeared and offered to drain it for them. He was long of face and limb and would not identify himself, however he was pressed, other than to say that he was the Heron King, which the gentlemen found strange, as he was dressed in rags."

"You sound like you've memorized this," Sarah said.

"This one I know reasonably well." Thalanes nodded. "'What price will you ask of us for this feat of engineering?' the burgomaster asked the Heron King.

"'A very modest price, indeed,' the Heron King replied. 'I only ask your permission to dry out your land, and then I will do it, not for any reward from you, but for the amusement of seeing how you enjoy my gift. And I will accomplish no feat of engineering, for I am not an engineer, nor do I employ any. I shall dry out your land by magic.'"

"That's a lot of gramarye," Sarah noted.

Thalanes shook his head. "I don't think it's gramarye at all, not as you and I understand it. 'Very well,' laughed the burgomaster and all the aldermen. 'You have our permission to dry out our land.' The Heron King bowed and disappeared. The council then had a good laugh and they all went home and told their wives and children about the mad beggar who had promised to dry up their swamp. The wives and children all laughed, too, and then they all went to bed.

"In the morning they awoke to find that not only had their swamp been drained, but the moisture had been parched out of all the land for twenty miles around the town. The wells had dried up, the plants had died and the arable fields had been reduced to dust.

"The Heron King, still dressed in rags, stood in the square, and the town gathered around him. First the townspeople objected to what he had done, then they yelled in anger, and finally they pleaded, abasing themselves on the ground and weeping, for him to restore their land to what it had been.

"The Heron King listened to it all silently, a curious smile on his lips, and when every last person of the town had dried his throat begging and reddened his eyes with tears, and the whole crowd had fallen silent again, he finally spoke.

"'Thank you,' he said, 'for the amusement.' And then he was gone."

"What's the moral?" Sarah felt troubled.

"Poor Richard says: be very careful what you wish for, and beware consequences that you do not intend."

"Jest 'cause it turns out that the Heron King is real don't mean that every story e'er told about him is true," Cal pointed out.

"The Heron King is real, all right," Thalanes said. "The people of Cahokia have never been able to think any different, no matter how much he might sound like a figure of folklore elsewhere in the empire. And most stories, Calvin, have some basis in fact."

"If you know so much about the Heron King," Sarah said testily, "then who are Simon Sword and Peter Plowshare? What does it mean that Peter Plowshare is dead?"

Thalanes sighed. "I'm puzzled, myself. I had always understood that Peter Plowshare and Simon Sword were different titles of the same person, the Heron King. That's how the names are used in Cahokia. I thought they all meant the same thing."

"And now?"

"Now I'm not so sure."

Grungle and Picaw loitered beyond the gates to the Place d'Armes. As she approached, they both bowed, which made her feel conspicuous, since everyone else on the street seemed determined to ignore her presence.

"Why are you concerned to hide your faces?" she asked them. "This city is so full of different kinds of folk, it's hard to imagine anyone would care what you look like."

"Yeah," Cal added, "I saw a snout-faced feller jest over there who must a been a beastman. Didn't nobody look at him cross-eyed."

"Thou art almost certainly right, Your Majesty," Grungle answered, "but we feel it is safer to stay concealed. Just in case."

Sarah smiled. "I agree completely. Which is why you must not bow to me or address me as Your Majesty. At least, not in the open." Had she gone too far? Could she give orders to the beastkind? Probably not. Thalanes had placed himself under her command, had told her she was his queen, but Picaw and Grungle served the Heron King.

But after a moment's silence, both the beastfolk nodded their agreement.

"Please take us to the person you mentioned," Sarah added. "I believe you called her Filmer."

The Quarter was busier now. Sarah tried to take the additional traffic in stride, keeping the same casual distance between herself and Thalanes as she had before, but Calvin evidently had no concern to look nonchalant—he closed up the distance behind her until she could hear the faint puff of his breath and the padding sound of his moccasins.

God bless poor Calvin, he still thought he was in love with her.

The beastkind quickly led Sarah and her companions to a plasterwork-and-iron public house whose signboard identified it as *Grissot's*.

A row of horses hitched to rings set in iron posts impeded access to the public house's boardwalk, and as she struggled to squeeze between two of the animals behind the diminutive Father Thalanes, she heard the insistent *bum-ditty, bum-ditty* of banjo frailing.

The beastkind hesitated at the door, and Sarah waved to stand them down. "Filmer lives here?"

"Lives and works," Picaw said.

"We'll come find you afterward," Sarah said to the beastfolk.

She almost asked them to wait outside, but in fact she didn't want them to stick around. They felt strongly that she should accompany them to their mysterious and legendary and apparently very whimsical lord the Heron King. She had other things to do—family business to attend to—first, and in any case, having just found herself to be a queen, she was in no hurry to be anyone's vassal.

All in all, she thought she'd be just as happy if the beastkind disappeared.

The inside of *Grissot's* was all dark wood, dancing, smoke, and sweat. Sarah almost laughed to see how incongruous both Calvin and Thalanes looked in the drinking crowd, but she probably looked even stranger. Like a patient from some Harvites' hospital, she thought, with her eye patch. Like a refugee from a war. Like a beggar.

Like the witch she really was.

The men dangled hesitantly just inside the door, so Sarah pushed past them, slipping around a paunchy, purple-robed Memphite who swayed in a close dance grip with a golden-skinned Creole girl. She stepped up to the bar beside a tall woman with long brown hair. The woman watched Sarah with cool blue eyes as she tried to get the hunchbacked bartender's attention.

"Excuse me," she said, and then again, louder, "excuse me!"

The barkeep shuffled over, a fumble-footed mushroom of flesh. "Aye, me lass, have ye got a thirst on ye? And what'll it be, then?" You didn't see many Irish in Nashville, but of course, this close to Texia, it stood to reason there'd be plenty. They let anyone at all into Texia. "The beer's passable, but then, a lot of things go down all right, once you're willing to drink vomit."

"I'm looking for someone," Sarah said, and the cool brown-haired woman returned her gaze to the dancers.

"Oh, aye?" the Irishman inquired blandly. "I can direct you to the nearest gendarme station, if you wish. Although if you're thirsty *and* looking for someone, you've like enough come to the right place."

Sarah didn't know whether she was being taken advantage of, but she felt Thalanes and Calvin behind her now and their presence gave her confidence. "A beer, then."

The hunchback uncovered a pitcher that stood cloth-shrouded in a row of its gape-mouthed brethren and poured beer into a pewter mug. "Who're ye looking for, then, lass?" He squinted at Sarah out one eye. The gesture was likely accidental—especially, Sarah reminded herself, since her witchy eye was covered—but it still rubbed her the wrong way.

"Filmer." Sarah quashed her irritation. "I'm looking for a woman named Filmer." The tall woman raised her eyebrows slightly at the name. Sarah sipped the beer.

"Oh, aye?" The Irishman wore a curious look on his gargoyle face. "I'm not sure I know a Filmer. Why're ye looking for her? She owe you money, does she?"

Sarah felt she was being played. "No. I don't know Miss Filmer. I need her help finding a . . . a common acquaintance."

"Who's that, then?" the barkeep asked. "Is *he* the one owes you money? Maybe it's someone I know. A lot of bad debts walk in here to wet their whistles, I can tell ye."

Sarah looked briefly at Thalanes but got no indicators from the little monk. He seemed attentive. "I'm looking for a man named William Lee," she said finally. "You might know him as Bad Bill."

The elegant woman with long brown hair abruptly broke her cool silence. "Bill!"

"Are you Miss Filmer?" Sarah asked.

The tall woman flashed a wave of emotion and then visibly fought it down. "*Mrs.* Filmer. Who are *you*?"

"Sarah Carpenter," Sarah slid smoothly into the practiced fib, and then she indicated her companions. "That's my husband Calvin, and Father Thalanes." She tried not to notice the look of delight on Calvin's face. "I'm looking for William Lee, and I've been told you're his friend."

Mrs. Filmer's façade of cool self-mastery had returned. "Are *you* a friend of *William's*? I must tell you that he has never mentioned anyone named Sarah Carpenter. Your voice doesn't sound Johnslander to me. Are you . . ." She hesitated. "Are you family?"

"Mrs. Filmer." Thalanes stepped forward to the bar. "Is there somewhere more private we could speak?"

Calvin paid for the beer from the bishop's funds and Mrs. Filmer led them upstairs into a parlor. There she took a thin vase of roses from a small table beside a door and brought it inside with them, shutting the door behind them and setting the vase on a windowsill.

"Please sit," she said, gesturing to the room's three upholstered sofas. "As long as we keep the flowers in here, no one will disturb us." Sarah plunked herself down and Thalanes perched; Cal positioned himself standing in a corner, eyes wide open.

Cathy Filmer sat, composed and dignified. "Is Bill in trouble?"

Sarah's heart sank. "You don't know where he is, then, Mrs. Filmer?"

The taller woman shook her head. "Please call me Cathy. I used to see him...frequently." Did she sound wistful? "He was taken about two weeks ago."

Cal's face was cool. "Do you mean he was your lover?"

"Who took him?" Thalanes interjected.

Cathy shook her head again. "It's my regret that William and I have never been lovers," she told Calvin gently. "As to the identity of his captors, he was taken by the chevalier's men. The gendarmes."

"Where did the gendarmes take him—do you know?" Sarah didn't relish the thought of fighting the Chevalier of New Orleans to rescue William Lee.

"Can you tell us *why* he was taken?" Thalanes asked.

"I don't know why he was taken." Cathy's voice cracked. As if to camouflage the slip in her self-control, she shifted her posture, crossing her ankles gracefully, folding her hands in her lap. "They don't publish the banns when men are arrested. He was... *is*...a man who makes enemies. As far as what the gendarmes have done with him, the possibilities are all dire, and I fear for my friend Sir William. But you haven't yet told me who you are, and why you seek him."

"I'm an old friend of Sir William's," Thalanes said. "And he has a long acquaintance with Sarah's family, is a friend of her parents. We're here on family business."

"We need to find him." Sarah was a little annoyed that Thalanes kept cutting her off.

"*Carpenter* family business," Cathy said, and she gave Sarah an appraising look. "Because Captain Sir William Johnston Lee, former commander of the Imperial House Light Dragoons, is a great friend to the *Carpenter* family. As are you, a Cetean monk."

"Yes," Cal blurted out.

"A servant of the emperor may know many families," Thalanes said quietly.

"Yes, he *may*." Cathy Filmer took a deep breath. "As I said, the possibilities are dire. The most common fate of anyone snatched by the gendarmes is a thorough beating. However, as I also said, I haven't seen Bill in two weeks, which may be the longest I've gone without seeing him in nearly fifteen years. I doubt he was released."

"What are the other possibilities?" Sarah asked.

Thalanes looked worried.

"Death is the next most common. Execution on the spot, or in a convenient dark alley, or in some cold basement of a gendarme station, or in a bayou. If you're lucky—if *we* are lucky—then perhaps the gendarmes simply ran Bill out of town on a rail, though if that is the case, again, I'm surprised and disappointed not to have seen him return."

"Is there any possibility he might simply be detained?" Thalanes pressed.

"It isn't likely." Cathy shook her head. "He's not the sort of man to whom the chevalier would grant such niceties as a trial. The gendarmes would only hold him if the chevalier wished to torture William. Or, perhaps, if he had some use for him."

"If he were in prison, would you know where?" Sarah might be able to use her Second Sight or her gramarye to better advantage if she had some idea where to start the search.

Cathy shrugged, a gesture that on her shoulders was refined and feminine. "The basement of any gendarme station," she said, "or the Palais du Chevalier, or on the Pontchartrain, in the hulks."

That limited the search, though Sarah didn't know how to find any of those places. "Thank you. Do you have anything of William's? Any ... personal pledges, any clothing?"

Cathy shook her head. "I have nothing of his, I regret to say." She paused in thought. "But I know where you can find something."

St. Joan of Arc presided over the Perdido Street station, smiling benignly down from her image with a long sword in one hand and a fleur-de-lis in the other. Obadiah felt no particular warmth in his heart for members of the constabulary, not even now when the gendarmes of New Orleans were giving him his room and board, their boxy-headed hounds padding about among the cots looking for scraps.

St. Joan, though, was no constable. She was a woman, which was soothing, and, like Obadiah, she was from the Old World and a bit out of place. If the Maid of Orleans could be at home here, so could he.

Sitting in the corner of the spacious cot-furnished barracks, Obadiah ate the fish stew and brown bread given him by his gendarme hosts in slow, mechanical silence, ignoring the cigarette smoke and the *plink!* of brown spit hitting the bottoms of brass spittoons and the soldierly chatter. He gazed up at St. Joan and tried to think.

He had felt uncertain for a couple of weeks. He had been floating, he had been in love. Another reason he was pleased to look at the painting of St. Joan was that she reminded him of Sarah, a dangerous young woman. Obadiah knew very well that his feelings for Sarah had started in a magic spell.

His hexed love for her had disappeared when the spell had ended.

But then the real enchantment had taken place. To his astonishment, Obadiah had longed to be ensorcelled again. Being hexed had revealed to him a new world, an existence in which he could care about truth and beauty and love, and not just the satisfaction of his belly and his loins. Not a new world, but a world he had once lived in.

Obadiah wanted to feel that way again.

He clung stubbornly to the hope that Sarah might bring him to that world. He knew he was idealizing her, but he needed that ideal. He had tried to get closer to his employer, the Right Reverend Father Ezekiel Angleton, in the hope that some combination of theology, commitment, service, and sanctification would give him the life he craved. But the Right Reverend Father was hell-bent on distancing Obadiah.

St. Joan of Arc gazed down on Obadiah. *Come home*, the saint said to him.

Come home to what? To England? There was nothing for him there. His father was dead, the cooperage long converted into cash money and spent—much of it, and he felt for the first time a small twinge of guilt, wasted on getting him into the academy, where he'd failed at the cannon and then run away from the pike. He had no siblings, and no affection for any of his cousins or, for that matter, for King George I of England.

There was Queen Caroline, of course.

And Peg.

Obadiah's appetite was gone. He set his bowl on the floor for a snuffling hound.

England was the land of his youth, and Obadiah remembered it fondly as a green and innocent place, despite the ruins scattered across its landscape and the blood of lambs poured regularly across its standing stones. Innocent, that is, until Obadiah had come trudging up to Peg's father's door on leave from the Royal Military Academy, resplendent and proud in the polished boots and buttons of his uniform, to ask her father for permission to court Peg. He'd already had an understanding, he thought, with the cheerful young tailor's daughter, but Obadiah had wanted to do things properly, and had told Peg so in one of the many letters he had written from the academy.

He remembered the doorstep clearly, the worn brown bricks of the building's face, the warm spring air, and her father's surprised eyes. "Why, sure, an' I'd 'ave give it you," the droop-faced old man had said, "you beink such a grand lad, even if your old dad be one of them Christ-chasers. Only she's run off just the other day wiff another fellow. Still, I fink she'd 'ave you, if only you'd go an' fight 'im for 'er."

Obadiah had not chased Peg and fought for her. Instead, he'd gone to a brothel, a narrow, windowless building in the shadow of St. Mary-le-Bow, the first such visit of his life. He'd gone expecting to feel pain and guilt, wanting to feel them, wanting to make Peg feel them, too. Instead, he'd felt numb, but vaguely satisfied, as if he'd scratched an itch.

He'd stayed in the brothel three days, drunk the entire time.

Two weeks later he'd boarded a ship for the New World.

Maybe the time had arrived for him to come home. Not to Peg, of course. He hadn't fought for Peg, and now she was long gone. If she was still alive, she was married somewhere in the Midlands, and had grandchildren by now.

But he could come home to Sarah. Obadiah looked up, met St. Joan's gaze, and nodded solemnly.

He could still fight for Sarah.

The halls were lined with saints, depicted in paintings and sculptures and tile mosaics and even charcoal drawings. Ezekiel was a theologian and he recognized many of them, but there had always been too many saints to keep track of, and every time a council of bishops was convened to try to pare down the list, the princes of the church came away instead having added more.

At the brisk clip at which he followed du Plessis through the Palais, Ezekiel barely had enough time to register each image.

He could only identify a few of the holy people, but he knew from their icons they were all saints, whether he even would have recognized each saint's claim to beatification.

Du Plessis took them up wide marble stairs tropical with ferns and orchids and down a narrow side passage, ushering them into a salon furnished with sofas, a wide, gold-painted harpsichord, and a small counter in the corner with tumblers, a pitcher of ice, a bowl of cubed sugar, and multiple bottles of liquor.

"Please wait here," du Plessis urged the Imperials, and then bowed his way back out the door, shutting it behind him.

Berkeley made a beeline for the alcohol. "Are you drinking, Parson?" he asked belligerently.

Ezekiel waved the question away with a distracted hand; he was examining the images on the walls. In the salon, too, the chevalier had decorated his walls with saints, and as Ezekiel perused the paintings with a little more leisure, he realized why he had failed to recognize so many of the images in the outer halls.

These weren't just any saints, they were all French—the chevalier had turned the Palais into a home for the many and varied saints of New Orleans.

There was St. Samuel de Champlain, with his compass and his globe and his beaverskin hat. The first Governor of Acadia was more properly native to the northeast of the New World, but he had been a great explorer and ruler, and Ezekiel wasn't surprised to see his painting here. St. Henri de Bienville, once the Bishop of New Orleans, held an allegorical crowned catfish in his lap. He was a truly indigenous saint, born in New Orleans after the founders of the city had split into the Le Moyne and de Bienville branches, one providing Louisiana with its chevaliers and the other furnishing its bishops. The theologian and ideologue St. Jean-Jacques Rousseau smiled out of his painting with the unblinking eyes of a fanatic, a short-barreled musket and his two most famous theological tracts, *On Education* and *The Confessions*, held out before him.

"The chevalier has an obsession." Berkeley clinked the ice in his glass.

"He's haunted," Ezekiel said. "Haunted by God and all His saints."

"It's unnatural," Berkeley objected, "and effeminate. A man takes what fate deals him, good or bad, and doesn't whine to the dead for favors."

"It's beautiful," Ezekiel disagreed, "even if all the saints he likes are Frenchmen."

Ezekiel had spent time in New Orleans as a younger man, but he remembered this spot as exhausted, empty old plantation land, burned over by the Spanish under the command of Count Galvéz. In the opulent, unforgetting, spiritual, and obsessive quality of these chambers, the chevalier had captured the soul of the great city, never moving forward without one eye over its shoulder for the grandeur and travails of the past.

It was so different from his own upbringing, where the past was nothing, the doings of man still less, and what counted was the ineluctable will of God, as expressed in His world and in His word.

There was another aspect of this wall of the sanctified that struck a chord in Ezekiel's heart. The many images of the saints were not only a memory of past godliness, they were a standing rebuke to death. In his icon, in his continuing blessing, each saint lived eternally.

As he turned from picture to picture to the other saints' icons in the room, Ezekiel tried to imagine whose image he would find next. Each time, he more than half hoped to discover a painting of Lucy Winthrop, beautiful in a russet and orange dress, auburn hair crowned with a white lace cap over warm, lively blue eyes.

He never did.

At least he hadn't found any portraits of St. Cetes, or of any other heretical Unsouled 'saints,' such as Richelieu the Crypto-Elf, serial traitor and machinator of the Serpentwars, or the hag Adela Podebradas, who had brought so much death to the children of Eve in Bohemia and the Palatinate with her obstinate rebellion against the combined wills of God and her husband.

"Blazes." Berkeley drained his glass.

The door opened and Gaspard le Moyne, the Chevalier of New Orleans, strode through it. He was alone and armed, with a dueling sword in a glittering sheath and a brace of pistols in well-worn leather holsters. He recognized the chevalier from having seen him at the Imperial Court in Philadelphia, where most Electors of the empire made periodic appearances, but he doubted the chevalier would know him—he and Berkeley were both mere servants in the Emperor Thomas's retinue, and his sole previous personal contact with the chevalier had been to bow deeply as the man walked past across the audience chamber of Horse Hall.

"My Lord Chevalier," the emperor's men said together. They doffed hats and bowed deeply.

The chevalier returned their greeting with a nod, closing the door. The chevalier was tall and thin. His hair, trimmed short and neat above his ears, was dark but beginning to go gray.

"You're well-armed for a man at home, My Lord," Captain Berkeley observed.

"My home is New Orleans," the chevalier said with a hint of a French accent, and crossed the room to the countertop bar. He laid his pistols on the countertop where, Ezekiel couldn't help noticing, they pointed at the chevalier's guests. "Does that make you feel better?" He poured himself a drink.

Berkeley laughed. "I'm perfectly at ease, My Lord." He deliberately sat down directly in the line of fire of the guns.

Ezekiel wasn't sure where this mutual baiting was going, but he thought he should head it off. "Thank you for seeing us, My Lord."

Slowly, deliberately, the chevalier pulled a long cigar from his pocket, bit off the ends and lit it with a Lucifer match struck on a button of his waistcoat. "What does Thomas want?"

In other circumstances, Ezekiel might have thought the question *admirably* or *refreshingly* direct, but with the pistols pointed at him he did not feel either refreshed or inclined to admire. The chevalier's familiarity toward his lord, Thomas Penn, also annoyed Ezekiel. "We're on His Imperial Majesty's errand, My Lord. However, the emperor didn't send us to see you, or even specifically to New Orleans. We're tracking a fugitive."

The chevalier puffed contemplatively on his cigar. Had the chevalier relaxed at the information that Ezekiel had not specifically come to see him?

"Thank you for quartering my men," Berkeley said to the chevalier. "I don't know how long it will take us to search New Orleans."

"It may take you some time." The chevalier's voice was cool. "New Orleans is a large, grand old lady, and she doesn't always appreciate being searched."

Berkeley laughed. "Then I hope we may rely upon your hospitality for a few days, while we find out what she has tucked underneath her petticoats."

"Of course," the chevalier agreed.

"Perhaps you might also be able to lend us some of your men to assist in our search," Ezekiel suggested modestly.

The chevalier arched an eyebrow. "Tell me about your fugitive."

Ezekiel and Captain Berkeley shared a glance, and Ezekiel floundered. He had come expecting basic assistance as a matter of courtesy extended from one Power to another, or from an Elector to his emperor, but he hadn't anticipated being questioned.

What could he tell this man? How much could he trust him?

"She's a girl. A young woman," he finally said. Simple, true and innocuous.

The chevalier looked at him with amused eyes, nursing his cigar. "Thomas sent the House Light Dragoons to New Orleans to capture *a little girl*," he said, drawing out the words for emphasis.

Ezekiel nodded.

"She must be quite a girl," the chevalier said. "A Sufi assassin, perhaps. Or a troublesome reforming cleric. Some Philadelphian Queen Adela Podebradas, anxious to serve the emperor with a sanguinary Writ of Divorce."

"She's a pretender." Captain Berkeley stood and Ezekiel was grateful. "Nothing more, and nothing of interest. We had other business in the Cotton League, so the emperor has tasked us with picking her up as well. It's a minor matter, My Lord Chevalier, hardly worth raising to your attention, other than out of an abundance of courtesy and our need for a few more men."

"We have a Warrant," Ezekiel said. Penn's warrant was irrelevant if the chevalier was already willing to cooperate, and powerless if the chevalier wasn't.

The chevalier opened his mouth to speak but stopped as there was a knock at the door. René du Plessis pushed the door open and inserted his harsh face. "My Lord, His Grace is here to see you."

The chevalier grabbed one of his pistols. An involuntary reaction? He stood impassive for long seconds, breathing through his flared nostrils, before answering.

"Please have His Grace escorted to this room."

Du Plessis nodded and disappeared.

"Have you met the Bishop of New Orleans?" The chevalier released his grip on the pistol; Ezekiel couldn't help noticing that he left the guns on the countertop.

They shook their heads that they had not.

"There is nothing so generous, so giving, and so full of grace as a dead saint," the chevalier told them, "and nothing so inconvenient, so obstreperous, and so irritating as a live one."

Berkeley laughed and downed his drink. Ezekiel held his tongue. After all, Bishop Ukwu was a secular priest, not a Martinite, and Ezekiel was hardly tasked with defending the dignity of all priests everywhere—indeed, there were more than a few priests that he would like to see hanged for heresy or insurrection . . . or both.

"Indeed, Bishop Ukwu is so obstinately righteous, I've taken the liberty of spreading rumors about him." The chevalier chewed a deep puff of cigar smoke with a thoughtful expression.

"Rumors?" Ezekiel asked.

"That the bishop is a moneylender and a criminal. Easy enough to do, since former bishops plied those trades. And his son makes my task easier, by taking up the businesses his father won't. It wouldn't do to have people take the bishop too seriously, you see. And yet many of them do."

The bishop entered with a strong stride. He was short and thin, with a lined brown face and shocking white hair, but authority radiated from his black robe, red sash, and skullcap.

"Your Grace." The chevalier bowed as deeply as the bar permitted him. He and Berkeley joined their host in his bow, and Ezekiel tried to feel and express sincere respect for the episcopal office and its holder. "How may I serve the diocese this evening? Would Your Grace enjoy a cigar?"

Bishop Ukwu looked pointedly at the two Imperial officers and then back to the chevalier. "I have come to discuss a matter with you, Gaspard. It is personal to you and you may prefer to dismiss your guests before we enter into the subject."

Ezekiel felt stung by the omitted honorific and the offensive presumption of intimacy, but the chevalier smiled. "Why, Your Grace," he said unctuously, "I can't believe you could have a matter to discuss with me so arcane that it couldn't be shared with these two servants of the Emperor Thomas."

The bishop hesitated, looking a little surprised. "You would have me call you to repentance before these men?"

The chevalier nodded slowly, and leaned forward with his elbows on the countertop . . . putting his hands, Ezekiel noticed, very close to the pistols. "I would, Your Grace."

He gulped a mouthful out of his cigar and blew an indistinct ring of blue smoke into the center of the room.

"As you wish." The bishop's hesitation fell away. He raised one hand with an admonishing finger and, to Ezekiel's utter astonishment, began to yell. "Sinner! Wretch! Vile and corrupt man!" The intrinsically happy sound of his Igbo accent clashed strongly with the strident tones of his remonstrance.

"True," interrupted the chevalier smoothly, "but let us get beyond the general shortcomings of the species and focus on the details of my personal errors."

Berkeley looked amused.

"Your charm will avail you nothing, nor will your wealth and power! Fear God, who will call in your debt at the last day!"

"Yes," agreed the chevalier, "and require interest payments until then." Berkeley snorted a short laugh. "But can you please get to the point, Your Grace? I have business with these men."

The bishop's fury rose unabated in the face of the chevalier's mockery. "You are a blackmailer! I have heard from one of your servants, and I know you are a thug, a criminal, a low extortionist!"

"Yes?" the chevalier asked. "Tell me more, Your Grace."

Did he *want* the bishop to chastise him?

The bishop spun and advanced on Ezekiel, but his extended finger rotated away and continued to point at the chevalier. "Your master, Thomas Penn!" Ukwu snapped at Ezekiel. "The chevalier blackmails him for money, and accuses him of murder!"

"Is that so," Captain Berkeley said. It wasn't a question.

"Yes!" the bishop snapped. "And our emperor, I am sad to say, does not behave in this matter like an innocent man!"

Ezekiel went weak in the knees and stomach. How could this Bishop know anything of Mad Hannah's death? How could the chevalier know?

He looked over the bishop's shoulder and saw that Berkeley was white as a sheet, with his mouth hanging open and his hands near his pistols. How did Berkeley know? Perhaps the emperor had taken the Captain of the Blues into his confidence. Ezekiel ground his teeth.

"What murder, Your Grace?" the chevalier asked coolly.

The bishop wheeled back again to face the object of his scolding. "Do not play games with me! You have accused the emperor of killing the Imperial Consort Elytharias! You blackmail the emperor, and he pays! The blood money you thus steal has built the very house we stand in, and you seek to buy your way out of the guilt by plastering images of God's saints on its walls! Shame!"

Elytharias! Ezekiel felt dizzy. This was not about Mad Hannah, then, it was about her husband. But why would the chevalier think that Thomas had killed the former King of Cahokia? And the chevalier had no right to blackmail Thomas, no matter what Thomas might be guilty of. Thomas was the emperor! Though Thomas *was* guilty, and so was Ezekiel, at least of the blood of his sister, Mad Hannah.

But . . . Elytharias?

"Is that all?" the chevalier asked.

The bishop shook his head in sorrow. "I had thought to come here to urge you to repent. I had hoped you would lay aside your evil scheme. I see now that I shall have to take to the pulpit to further persuade you."

"Please, Your Grace," the chevalier protested urbanely. "It has been a long time since I've been persuaded by anything said from a pulpit."

The bishop clamped his mouth shut and then, to Ezekiel's shock, stepped out of his footwear. He bent to the leather sandals, picked them up and deliberately slapped them together, shaking the dust off their soles and onto the marble floor of the Palais du chevalier.

"I curse you," he said coldly, his calm tone at odds with the fervor of his words. "I curse you that your body will not sleep and your mind will know no rest. I curse you that you will waste and wither, that the tree you plant will bear no fruit and the field you till will lie barren, until the day of your repentance. I will unmask you all, and if I fall in the attempt, then I curse you in the name of the Lord God with a successor who will plague you even more."

Then he stepped back into his shoes, turned, and stalked out the door.

Ezekiel realized he had been holding his breath. He let the air out in a long hiss.

Berkeley collapsed onto a sofa. "I need a drink."

"The Imperial Consort!" Ezekiel exclaimed. "Captain, do you know what he's talking about?"

Berkeley didn't meet his gaze. "Damned priest," he said,

and Ezekiel felt a chill in his spine. So it was true! Thomas had murdered Kyres Elytharias, and Captain Berkeley knew. Well, he had been one of the Blues when Elytharias had died, fifteen years earlier. Ezekiel couldn't blame Thomas for removing the Unsouled stain from the escutcheon of the Penns—wasn't he about the same business, trying to capture or kill Elytharias's daughter? And the chevalier was blackmailing Thomas; Ezekiel felt anger, but if Thomas wished to pay the chevalier, it was not Ezekiel's business.

And Ezekiel needed the chevalier's help to find Witchy Eye.

Ezekiel sat down and took deep breaths.

The chevalier was eyeing Berkeley closely; *scrutinizing* him.

"Gentlemen," the chevalier finally said, setting his cigar down. "I believe I can be of assistance to you."

"You ain't exactly short of guns 'round here."

CHAPTER FIFTEEN

Cathy Filmer told them William's usual source of cash in desperation was a pawnbroker named Hackett, and then led them to his shop, but by the time they arrived the sun was setting and Hackett was gone. Thalanes thanked Cathy and then suggested that she might go home.

She stayed.

Thalanes worried the expedition was out of his control. On the other hand, it was good that Sarah was taking command. She was his queen, and if she were really going to rule a kingdom—or two powers at the same time—or the empire—she must learn to govern.

So he was challenging Sarah, and she was fighting him back as an equal. And her choices had been as good as any decisions could be, given how blind they were and the dangers that beset her. They seemed close to finding William Lee, and once they'd found Will, they'd find the other Penn children.

Thalanes would hide them further away this time. New Muscovy, or among the free horse people, or somewhere in the Old World, if he had to. The Caliphate and the Ottoman Empire had their own risks and dangers, but he was reasonably sure that their lands were beyond the reach of Oliver Cromwell.

He worried about Cathy Filmer. They didn't need her anymore, and bringing her along meant one more person's safety to worry about and one more person who might betray them. He thought Cathy's interest was in William, but that mollified him only slightly.

They returned through the Quarter and across the Place d'Armes to the Bishop's Palace. The beastkind didn't rejoin them, but Thalanes saw, from time to time, the two hooded, robed figures of the Heron King's emissaries, trailing them.

The beastkind added another unknown quantity to worry about. What did the Heron King want? Who was he, really? What was this strange announcement of the death of Peter Plowshare?

Cathy Filmer walked side by side with Sarah and engaged her in conversation, which was slightly disquieting to Thalanes but which made Calvin look simply put out, like an unwanted and grumpy hound dog.

The youth might just be the Calhoun Elector some day, despite the monk's warning to him not to go into politicking. That was possible not because Iron Andy was his grandfather—that wasn't how the Appalachee selected their leaders—but because he had the nerve, the will, and the charisma that could bring him to the top of the heap in the rough-and-tumble political elbowing that determined who was the head of any of the families of the Ascendancy.

Now, too, he was getting a strong shock of world experience that would strengthen him, and if Sarah ever came into any of her birthrights, his connection with her—whatever exactly it ended up being—could only help him. Thalanes had had many occasions to be glad Calvin was accompanying them, though he foresaw a necessary moment when Thalanes would leave the young cattle rustler behind, the better to hide Sarah.

But for now the little monk had more pressing concerns.

As promised, Chigozie put down his reading—Thomas Paine's last book, the provocative *Deistic Reflections upon the Gospel of St. John*—and shrugged into his black coat to accompany them. He chatted engagingly with Cathy and Sarah as they turned north and moved behind the cathedral.

They passed through an empty dirt yard, through which Chigozie seemed anxious to hustle them quickly. "This is a notorious dueling ground," he explained. "It is shameful that men kill each other in sight of the cathedral, but such is New Orleans."

"Looks like a cattle pen." Cal scuffed at the hard dirt with his moccasin. "Jest shy a couple fences."

"No one is here now," Chigozie admitted, "but it is in the nature of disagreements to heat up quickly, so let us not delay." Beyond the dueling yard, he led them through a couple of turns and down several long city blocks crowded with nighttime revelers, stopping in front of a large and singular-looking building.

"A fine lair for a bishop's son, is it not?" Chigozie asked. "You see what my father puts up with?"

"At least he has a sense of humor," Cathy offered in demure defense of Etienne's choice, and Thalanes had to admit she had a point.

The boxy structure was built of stone. Multicolored light streamed into the night through its many large windows, stained and patterned like the windows of a wealthy chapel, only the images here were voluptuous, comical, aggressive, and even obscene. Angels defecated onto the pages of books held open by nude women; zodiacal signs copulated dangerously; beast-headed men played at cards with man-headed beasts; it all tumbled together into an abyss filled with fire, the long tongues of which licked lasciviously at the falling bodies.

Above the chaos presided, flinging gold coins from both his hands, a dark-faced man who bore a significant resemblance, even in his stained-glass image, to Chigozie and the bishop. The building was an anti-cathedral.

The crowd around it, pushing and panting, desperate to get in through its doors, blocked traffic through the street.

"Yes," Chigozie agreed, chagrined. "His sense of humor is the one piece of our father that my brother inherited." The bells of the St. Louis Cathedral struck eight o'clock.

"It may not be the best piece," Thalanes said, "but it's a good one."

"That, and they both love tobacco." Chigozie shook his head.

"I reckon your brother's business is successful," Cal observed, "whate'er it is. This palace wasn't built by no poor man."

"I try not to ask how my brother makes his money," Chigozie said grimly, and started pushing through the crowd. "Nor what god he serves."

Two heavy men in simple black waistcoats and shirtsleeves pushed the bubbling stew of humanity away from the door with cudgels, but when they saw Chigozie, they admitted him and, following his indication, his party. Passing through the door,

Chigozie explained to Thalanes, as if apologizing, "it amuses my brother to let me in, anytime I wish to see him."

"Then you do him a sort of service," Thalanes suggested.

"Perhaps. I myself am not so amused."

"That only makes your service all the more charitable."

A short, broad entrance hall, nearly square, opened up onto a dance floor thumping with a hurricane of noise that snarled out of the unlikely combination of an array of brass kettle drums, a banjo, a fiddle, and a two-headed wooden flute. The same crowd continued inside, drinking, smoking, dancing, and playing various games of chance, and in the writhing mass of bodies Thalanes saw a reminder that he should be grateful he had become a follower of St. Cetes, and not some parish officeholder whose daily burden included the war against *this*.

Another waistcoat-clad ruffian hulked before a heavy interior door, and Chigozie nodded a wary salutation. "Mon frère Ofodile," Chigozie addressed the man in French. "Est-il en haut?"

"Oui." The ruffian showed a row of gold teeth in a smile that looked knowing and vicious, and opened the door. "Montez-vous."

Behind the door were stairs, and at the top of the stairs was an office. Two more black-waistcoated men loomed up to block their path, but Thalanes stuck close to Chigozie's shoulder and moved between the thugs easily, Sarah and the others in his wake.

The ruffians faded back into relaxed vigilance.

Ofodile Etienne Ukwu, the bishop's more entrepreneurial son, stood up from a heavy writing desk where he was reviewing a ledger with a fat, sweating Creole in the waistcoat that Thalanes by now recognized as a uniform. His office was a carefully orchestrated display. The thick carpet on the floor was Arabian or Persian. There were knives on the walls, running from the floor up to eye level. The blades were arranged, but they gleamed from meticulous care and whispered of their own razor sharpness.

Above eye level and up to the ceiling, a mural painting ran around three sides of the room. It depicted an empty plain, with few and unfamiliar stars in a night sky. Two roads converged from opposite corners and met at a crossroads, behind and above Etienne Ukwu's desk. At the crossroads stood an old man. He wore a broad-brimmed straw hat and simple coat. In his teeth he clenched a smoldering pipe, with one hand he sprinkled something on the crossroads that might have been water, and with the other he leaned on a cane.

He wore a key on a string around his neck.

Behind him came a little dog, wagging his tail and looking at the viewer.

Thalanes had the unsettling impression the dog was laughing at him. He shook it off, and tried to focus on the people in the room.

Seeing Ofodile—Etienne—Thalanes was reminded that Chigozie took after their mother, who had died when the boys were young and Chinwe had not yet been marked for the priesthood, and how much Etienne looked like a younger version of his father. His fingers, though, glittered with rings and held a jaunty cigarette, and his waistcoat flashed carved ivory buttons and silver embroidery in an elaborate pattern of elegant bow-like recurves, straight lines, stars, and leaves. Instead of a belt he wore a red silk sash, knotted on his right hip.

"Mon cher Chigozie," the younger Ukwu brother said, "tu es venu en cherchant l'emploi au moment parfait! J'ai perdu un croupier ce soir et l'être d'équipe de nuit serait tout à fait compatible avec tes devoirs à la Cathédrale." He smiled a look of intimate envy and malice at his brother.

"English, please, brother, my guests are not from Louisiana." Chigozie's words were peaceable, but Thalanes heard strain in his voice.

"I am happy to welcome your guests, brother Chigozie," Etienne said with an amicability that threw knives. He sucked smoke in from his cigarette and then stubbed it out in an ashtray.

"Thank you," Chigozie said.

"Perhaps one of *them* would like a job dealing cards?" his brother suggested. "Although the tall one looks more like a debt collector, and I can always use another good sticks and stones man. Or are they, like my righteous brother Chigozie, waiting for their fathers to die, so they can inherit thrones and wealth?"

Etienne waved at his fat bookkeeper and the Creole scuttled away downstairs.

"The bishopric is not my inheritance," Chigozie protested. "You know that is not how it works."

"Is it not? When my father dies, whom will the Synod anoint in his place? Some stranger? Some nominee of the emperor, or the despised chevalier? Some Geechee tent-worker, an aspiring Haudenosaunee prelate, or a Yonkerman savant? Or will they simply appoint the beloved son of the beloved departed bishop?" Etienne's smile never faltered. Thalanes frowned; something about the pattern on Etienne's waistcoat bothered him. It was familiar, somehow.

"The Synod will appoint whomever it wishes," Chigozie said, "and I will serve however I may."

The pattern on Etienne's waistcoat approximately matched the outline of the stars in the alien landscape of the mural.

"I expect so." Etienne's eyes glittered like a ferret's. "Perhaps you will continue to play second fiddle, and it will now be to this monk who stands at your shoulder. How about it, Father? Would you be pleased to be Bishop of New Orleans, if it were offered to you?"

"Not I," Thalanes said, broadcasting all the modesty he could summon. "I'm a Cetean, and a monk, and I like it that way. No parish for me, thank you, much less a diocese."

"St. Cetes, of course!" Etienne whistled low. "We do not see many of you this far downriver. Although, to be perfectly frank, I do not see many priests at all, myself. Other than the ones in my saintly family."

"Perhaps your décor discourages them from visiting." Thalanes smiled.

"You do not like my windows? I hired the best artists who could be had for money."

"The building is beautiful, of course," Thalanes said. "It's also a joke, of the sort that not all priests will enjoy. Some priests might even think your beautiful building is a joke of which they are the butt."

"I see." Etienne nodded. "And do you feel that I am mocking you, then?"

"No." Thalanes smiled. "I think the butt of your joke is man. And man deserves it."

Etienne laughed heartily. Thalanes shot a quick look at Chigozie and saw a puzzled expression on his face.

"And my painting, Father Cetean?" Etienne asked. "Do you like my painting, too? Is it an amusing joke?"

Thalanes looked at the painting again, the crossroads, the old man, the dog, the key. He had no idea what it meant, though a vague thought nagged him that he should.

"St. Peter has always been one of my favorites," he said evenly.

At that answer, deliberately ambiguous, Etienne stopped laughing. The bishop's son arched his eyebrows at Thalanes and pursed his lips. "Can it be true, Father Cetean, that your order has no hierarchy at all? Once ordained, you are answerable only to God?"

"My name is Thalanes. Yes, it's true. One spends one's novitiate studying under a Preceptor, but once ordained, a disciple of St. Cetes serves no ecclesiastical authority. He serves God, and his conscience. Or *her* conscience, as the case may be."

"I like it!" Etienne beamed. "No hierarchy at all, just direct responsibility! It seems very Ohioan to me, Father Thalanes, I must say."

"You are thinking of Talega, perhaps."

Etienne nodded. "The moundbuilders are not all identical. And some of them are great slavers, too. Isn't that funny, that a people who are so proud of their own liberty keep slaves? Maybe it was proximity to the Memphites that led them to it. Pyramids on one side of the Ohio, mounds on the other, eh?"

"The kings of the Ohio had been keeping slaves for hundreds of years before the Prester and his sons ever sailed up the Mississippi," Thalanes said. "And the paradox isn't all that strange; a society that sees freedom as a man's greatest good can think of no greater punishment than to take that freedom away from him."

Etienne nodded. "You are Eldritch?"

"Hey, there!" Calvin snapped. "Be polite."

Etienne waved him off. "A Firstborn, is that the polite term? Here in the Quarter we mostly use epithets—iggy, frog, dago, schnitzel, yankee, limey, cracker, bathead, minnie, serpentspawn, kraut, you understand. I know my manners are unfit for polished society. I deal with rough men and I make no apologies. The important thing is that we understand each other."

"Man's kingdoms and God's needn't have the same power structures." Thalanes felt he was undercutting Chigozie, though he hoped only slightly. The pattern on Etienne's waistcoat continued to nag at him.

Did it have some iconographic meaning? Some New Orleans saint?

"But you cannot mean no princes of the church!" Etienne gasped.

"Believe me," Chigozie said wearily, "that would make me as happy as it would make you. Probably happier."

"Etienne." Sarah pushed forward into the center of the conversation. "I was hoping you could help me."

Thalanes kicked himself mentally—he should have foreseen the possibility that Sarah would jump in and take control. How would Etienne respond? Would Thalanes lose the progress he'd made in the conversation so far? As long as she didn't slip into her Appalachee patois...

He felt nervous, and he saw an uncomfortable look on Cal's face.

By contrast, Cathy looked completely composed and self-assured.

Etienne hung paused in mid-thought while he absorbed this new development. "Excuse me, I do not know who you are."

"My name's Sarah Carpenter," she said with a defiant glint in her eye. "These men—" she indicated Calvin and Thalanes, "serve me, and your brother agreed to help me by bringing me to see you."

Etienne looked dumbfounded.

Thalanes held his breath, waiting to learn how this turned out. He willed Cal to keep his mouth shut; he would talk with the young man later, try to soothe any injured feelings he might have.

Etienne smiled. "Sarah Carpenter, Queen of Priests, with the bandaged head," he said, and then laughed out loud. "Excellent! You will fit in very well here in New Orleans, you are picaresque enough to be one of us already."

"I'm not a dancing bear," Sarah objected.

"No? Disappointing. Very well, Queen Carpenter, tell me what you believe I can do for you."

"I'm looking for another servant of mine," Sarah said. How far would she push this approach? "I been told—I *understand* you may know him."

"I know many people," Etienne agreed. "I am a sort of priest, too. I minister to all the gamblers, drunkards, and whores of New Orleans. Is your missing servant such a man?"

At the words *I am a sort of priest, too*, Thalanes knew where he had seen the image. It was a *vevé*, an icon of Vodun significance. Every loa had its *vevé*, or *beybey*, which was its beacon and which stood in for it, in certain ritual circumstances. Why was Etienne Ukwu wearing a *vevé*? And to which loa did it belong? And did the *vevé* have something to do with the old man at the crossroads?

He wished he were not so ignorant. He doubted he could ask Chinwe these questions without wounding him. And he was certain he couldn't ask Chigozie.

"She seeks Bad Bill," Chigozie said.

"*Bad Bill* is your servant?" Etienne laughed again, and Sarah nodded defiantly. "Well, I must warn you, Queen Carpenter, that I think you will find him a very poor help. Bill was once an employee of mine, but he was an unreliable drunkard, and I had to let him go."

"I'm forgiving."

"How long has he been in your service?" Etienne asked.

"Not long," Sarah said cagily. "Can you tell me where to find him?"

Etienne took something small from his waistcoat pocket and looked at it; Thalanes saw a flash of silver as he replaced the object.

Finally, the bishop's son shook his head. "I would like to help you, Queen Carpenter, because you are amusing, but I am afraid I do not know. The chevalier's men took him two weeks ago, and I have not seen him since."

Thalanes had recovered from his surprise at recognizing Etienne's decoration. He was keenly disappointed that Etienne had no information to share, but pleased Sarah had navigated the conversational shoals.

"Thank you, Etienne," he said.

"You got anything of Bill's?" Sarah continued as if Thalanes hadn't spoken. "Clothing of his, mebbe?" It was a good question, and Thalanes both kicked himself and felt proud of her, despite her slouching accent.

Etienne looked at Sarah through narrowed and calculating eyes. "Are you a witch, then, Queen Carpenter?"

"What do you care if I am, houngan?"

Chigozie hissed, and Etienne furrowed his brows.

"What do you know about houngans?" Etienne demanded.

"I read books," Sarah said. "I see an old man at a crossroads with a dog and a key, I know who he is. Jest like when I see you, I know who you are."

Thalanes almost fell over in surprise.

Etienne laughed, but a little uneasily. "What exactly is under that eye patch you wear, girl?"

Sarah stared back at him without flinching. She did look like a stage witch, with her eye patch and her horse-headed ash staff, burnt black and stained sulfur-yellow.

"An eyeball," she said.

"And what does that eyeball see in me?" he wanted to know. "Who do you think I am?"

Sarah slowly and deliberately removed her eye patch and looked Etienne in the face. He breathed in through his teeth, whistling slightly, but didn't look away.

They stayed locked in each other's gazes for long seconds.

"You're Ofodile Etienne Ukwu," she said. "You're the bishop's son."

Etienne sat down, looking suddenly heavier and older.

Sarah put her eye patch back over her face.

"Very well," said the bishop's younger son. "It is none of my affair why you want Bill. I used to have a Kentucky rifle that belonged to him, but I sold it in satisfaction of his debts."

"You have nothing, then?" Sarah pressed him.

"Nothing," he agreed, and then furrowed his brows. "Except…" He turned back to his desk and plucked a scrap of paper from between the pages of his ledger. "I have this." Sarah reached out to take the scrap, but he held it back. "It is worth money to me," he told her. "Cash."

"What is it?" she asked.

"It is a claim ticket. Before your man Bill was arrested, he pawned his sword and pistols. This is his ticket. I intend to go reclaim the weapons from the pawnbroker, at a price that is very reasonable for weapons of such quality." Etienne grinned broadly.

"How much?" Cal asked.

"Very direct, my cracker friend. Are you sure you would not like to work as a debt collector?" Cal scowled at him in answer. "Three Louis d'or would make me happy."

"I can't reckon it's even worth one looey to you," Cal disagreed. "You ain't exactly short of guns 'round here. I'll give you a shiny Philadelphia shilling."

Etienne frowned, looking at the same moment a little pleased, or at least entertained. "Yes, my men use guns and I need a good supply. Three Louis d'or."

"And yet in the two weeks you had it, you ain't turned in the claim ticket. Besides, you got better things for your men to do." Cal dug a finger into the purse at his belt and tossed a single coin to Etienne, who caught it mid-air in his free hand. "One looey, it's all I got, take it or leave it."

Etienne rapped the Louis d'or against his desk and then set the coin down. "One is not enough. I am not trying to dicker with you, my cracker friend, I am telling you that I know I can redeem these pistols, resell them and make three looeys. If you can give me three looeys directly instead, so much the better for me. Otherwise, you are out of luck. And the truth is, I do not need the money, anyway." He gestured at the office around him. "I have money."

"And I ain't bargainin' with you, either," Cal said. "I ain't got three looeys. What *do* you need? I ain't got time to work it off for you as a sticks and stones man, whate'er that may be. You need a tomahawk? A lariat? A good Kentucky rifle?"

A light flickered in Etienne's eyes and he handed the single Louis d'or back across the desk. "I would like a lock of Queen Carpenter's hair," he said.

"Go to Hell," Sarah said.

"That is hardly diplomatic, Your Majesty," he protested. "And it does not respect my faith. A lock of a pretty girl's hair brings good luck. I am in the business of gambling, Queen Carpenter... would you deny me the luck I need?"

"Yeah," she said. "Yeah, I would. So listen close, because I'll be a-makin' you one offer, and one offer only. Iffen you don't take it, I walk away and we're done."

"I am listening." Etienne's facial expression was focused.

"You give me the claim ticket." Sarah stared Etienne hard in the face. "You will also give me however much money it is that I will need to redeem the ticket. In return...I will owe you a favor."

"Bill, 'e 'as sent for you!"

A light shone in Bill's sleep-thickened eyes and something wooden thumped in his ear. His shoulder shook. Dreams clattered away, draining out of his skull, dreams of riding horseback, of drill, of barked commands and the acrid smell of black powder burning across a field of bleeding men.

"If you mean Old Scratch, suh, tell him he's too late. I've sold my soul to the army."

"Bill, it is ze chevalier's men!" Bill forced his eyes open and found Bayard Prideux standing above him with a lantern, shaking Bill by the shoulder—

within reach.

Bill grabbed Bayard by his wooden leg and rolled away, jerking Prideux off his feet.

Foot, rather.

The Frenchman executed an unplanned one-legged hop back-ward and planted himself solidly onto the deck, the air *whoosh-ing* out of his lungs and the lantern flying against the wall. Bill staggered up and found he was still holding the wooden leg, a leather strap with a shattered buckle dangling at the end of it.

"Ze chevalier!" squealed Bayard.

"Damn the chevalier!"

And any other Frenchman who stood between him and justice. Bill brought the peg leg club down hard. Bayard flung up his hands defensively, and Bill hit his forearm with a loud wet *crack!*, the leather strap whipping around to further sting the murderer.

"Bill! What are you doing?" Bayard shrieked.

Visions of his murdered friend and lord, Kyres Elytharias, flashed before Bill's eyes, and he continued to pummel the downed Frenchman.

"Do not—"

crunch!—

"mistake me—"

thwack!—

"for a friend!"

Bill found himself standing above Bayard and looking down, his chest heaving. As his blood cooled and his head cleared, he saw the lantern had shattered, spraying burning oil across the wall.

A curtain of flame rose from floor to ceiling.

Bayard trembled slightly.

"Suh!"

Smash!

Bayard lay still; justice was served.

Bill threw the peg leg aside. He'd killed many men in his career, but he'd never killed anyone whose death he'd wanted more than Bayard's. Still, looking down at the French traitor's broken body, he felt no satisfaction.

In the end, he and Bayard had been too similar—old, broken warhorses, isolated in their stables and waiting to die.

Bayard might have the key to his shackles in his pocket, but Bill couldn't bring himself to care. Sally might be alive, but he couldn't know, because she hadn't written him, not one damned time. That was hard, however much he admired the woman for keeping her promises, even when the promises were terrible threats.

Cathy . . . he thought of Long Cathy's long brown hair and gentle voice and felt a warmth inside . . . he cared for Cathy Filmer, and in other circumstances he might even have loved her.

Bill wished he had a king to serve again, a banner to ride under. But he was an exile, and a cheap killer, and those days were gone.

The fire crackled as it spread along the floor, sending up an inarticulate jangle of whimpering and moaning from the lost souls chained in the *Incroyable*'s hold. He looked into the flames to welcome them, and he fancied he could see Bayard there, already roasting on the Devil's spit. *Well, you rotten French bastard, I'll have a spit of my own soon enough.*

But there were others who belonged in Hell too, for what they had done.

His Imperial Majesty, the Emperor Thomas Penn.

And the other . . . the 'ozer' that Bayard had been afraid of. Whoever he was.

Bill couldn't let himself die—he still had justice to seek. His muscles aching, he dropped to his knees to fumble through Bayard's pockets.

Bayard had a ring of keys. Bill snatched it and began shoving keys one at a time into the lock on his shackles, trying to find the one that would set him free. The heat from the flames grew more intense.

The lost souls began to scream.

Click.

Bill unlocked himself. He crouched, rubbing the painful chafe-wounds on his wrists and ankles and looked up to find an exit.

The fire was a solid wall now, cutting him off from the ladder. Bill heard the dying screams of the other prisoners, and the choking as their lungs gave out. The air filled with bitter gray smoke. He looked around him, the fire providing the best illumination he'd had since he'd been imprisoned. There were no windows, no hatches, no other ladders, no escape.

Something was moving on the far side. A thick plank was shoved through, and then another, and a third. They fell to the deck and made a causeway across the fire. Across the flames Bill saw a man—features unrecognizable through the smoke and the dancing orange light—beckoning to Bill to come out.

"Hell's Bells."

Bill lurched across the wooden bridge. He arrived at the other side coughing, his eyes and lungs seared, and the unknown man took him by the arm and half-dragged him up the ladder. Bill couldn't see for the tears pouring from his eyes, and he cursed as his bare toes repeatedly kicked the solid wood.

The cool night air soothed his face as he stumbled onto the deck, coughing and spitting. His vision still swam, but Bill could make out enough now to help his rescuer get him to the side of the ship. Other men moved around in the night, shouting.

"The gangplank is gone." His rescuer spoke with a soft French accent. "Can you climb?"

Bill nodded. His rescuer—a tall, fit man with iron gray hair, who looked familiar—gave Bill a hand over the lip and onto the ladder, and Bill scrambled down a few rungs on his own.

Then other men grabbed him, pulling him to safety on an adjacent, smaller ship.

A yacht.

A very expensive yacht, trim and sleek. It was large for a yacht, with two masts and elaborate carving in the woodwork, the ship of someone very wealthy or very powerful or both. Bill's eyes were clear now and as his rescuer followed him down the ladder and joined him on the yacht, they opened wide in surprise.

"I see I've chosen the right man," his rescuer said. Bill could only stare, open-mouthed.

His rescuer was the Chevalier of New Orleans.

Bill said nothing. He didn't know what he could say to the man who had imprisoned him, the man who had sheltered Bayard Prideux, the man who had blackmailed the emperor.

The man whose son he'd killed.

A wool blanket was thrown around Bill's shoulders and he stared about the yacht. All of Bayard's men—the frog imbeciles and also the surprisingly verbal deaf-mute Hop—stood against the rail, watching the *Incroyable* burn. As Bill looked at him, Jake met his gaze and smiled. Men in gendarme uniforms dropped from the hulk to the yacht, and then the yacht pushed away from the burning ship and turned out onto the Pontchartrain, its sails bellying gently in the cool night breeze.

"Excuse me," the chevalier said, and stepped down a ladder in the center of the deck, disappearing into the hold.

Bang!

Bill heard a gunshot and wheeled to look. One of the French morons crumpled overboard into the water, his skull blown open by a gendarme. The other imbeciles squeaked and honked in protest as the chevalier's men raised pistols to dispose of them similarly.

Jake! Bill wanted to cry out, but didn't. But where was the little Dutchman? Bill couldn't see him anywhere. Had he been shot first, and was he already overboard, silting up the Pontchartrain with his bones?

In any case, there was nothing Bill could do.

The chevalier reappeared, holding a long bundle wrapped in cloth under one arm and a bottle in the other. "Come with me, Captain." He turned and walked toward the slightly raised back of the ship. Was that the poop deck? Bill followed, and found himself alone with the chevalier.

Before them lay a spangle of glimmering yellow that was New Orleans. What Bill saw was the Pontchartrain docks, ill-lit this late at night, but beyond them and behind the city's walls rose a more general glow where the all-night neighborhoods lay.

Bill heard further gunshots, and then the whimpering sounds stopped.

Would his head be the next one shot? Or might he be given food instead?

The chevalier uncorked the bottle and handed it to Bill. Bill couldn't read the label in the darkness, but he could smell the bourbon. "Honor," he toasted the chevalier, taking a sip and passing the bottle back. He wanted to take a bigger drink, but now wasn't the time.

"Yes, to honor." The chevalier took a drink before stoppering up the bottle.

Bill found himself frowning, though there was no reason he should—he'd survived the fire, he'd escaped imprisonment. The chevalier could not possibly have come out onto the Pontchartrain personally for the purpose of killing him, Bill reasoned. Still... best not to hide anything at this point.

"Suh," he began, unable to remember what honorific one was supposed to use to address the chevalier, "you know that I killed your son."

The chevalier set the bundle at his feet, then turned and looked at the shore, knuckles resting lightly on the polished handrail. Bill didn't dare say anything else, and just waited. What did this man want? Why did he not shoot Bill and throw him overboard with the idiots?

"Three hundred thousand," the chevalier said at last. "That we can count."

"Pardon me, suh, but I don't follow your meaning."

The chevalier turned to look at him directly, and his face was unsentimental flint. "I have three hundred thousand children," he explained, gesturing with one hand at the shore. "At least. When you add in all the uncountables—the illiterate, the homeless, the traders who identify some other place as their home, but who are here all the time—it may be five. Five hundred thousand children, not counting the loa and the rats."

"Yes, suh," Bill said, unsure where the conversation was heading.

"I can't allow myself to become too maudlin about any one of them."

Bill thought a moment.

"Your son was a brave fighter and a gentleman," he offered, and he meant it, but it didn't sound like enough. *Damn your French eyes and your cold French heart*, he wanted to shout, *I regret that I killed your son, I regret that I am the man I have become, I certainly deserve to die and you have the right to kill me!*

The chevalier nodded. "Thank you."

"My Lord Chevalier," Bill said, remembering the form of address now and wishing he had more clothing, "I don't know why you've freed me."

"My children are threatened, Captain Lee. They need you. I free you in exchange for your assistance."

Bill's mind raced. What assistance could the chevalier possibly need from him? He still half expected one of the chevalier's men to put a gun to his head and blow out his brains.

"I hope I may help, suh," he said neutrally. He almost laughed at his own reluctance—he had nothing to lose, so why did he care what the chevalier asked of him? Was there really anything he was unwilling to risk, anything he wouldn't do?

"There's an insect at the heart of New Orleans," the chevalier continued slowly, gesturing at the veiny yellow lights. "A tiny, wicked, spiderlike man, a parasite who threatens the prosperity, and therefore the safety and the very life, of my half million children. Rid me of that man, and I will not only free you, but will take you into my service and pay you handsomely."

Bill nodded. Easy enough. "What man, suh?"

The chevalier looked at him closely. "The Bishop of New Orleans."

Bill spat into the water. "Damned money-lender!"

The chevalier regarded Bill with a detached and curious look. "Yours is not the gift of tongues, I understand."

What kind of question was that? Bill shrugged. "I can Frog it up a little—I beg your pardon, suh, I mean to say that I speak some French. *Comment ça va?* for instance, and *ça va, ça va*, and the like. And I possess a similar level of mastery of a smattering of other New World dialects: Igbo and Castilian, among others." He felt like this was an unflattering portrait of himself and that he needed to say something in his defense. "As much as your predecessor, the old Count Galvéz, I understand."

The chevalier snorted an angry, derisive laugh, his disciplined façade splintering. "La Bête was in no sense my predecessor, Captain!"

"No?" The count had ruled New Orleans for several years on behalf of New Spain, and Bill had always felt kinship for the man who had governed the city without speaking a word of French. "I had heard he was the chevalier for a period, during the war. Though he spoke Dago, I expect, and not English."

The chevalier collected himself. "The Chevalier of New Orleans has been a Le Moyne as long as there has been a chevalier. The Beast was a usurper, an interloper, an affront."

"Yes, My Lord Chevalier," Bill agreed quickly. "But my true spiritual inheritance, suh, is the gift of mayhem."

The chevalier nodded solemnly. "I could use you in my service, Captain Lee. The gift of mayhem, indeed. Will you undertake this commission for me? Will you rid me of this criminal?"

Bill looked to the *Incroyable*, Bayard Prideux's outsized funeral pyre, burning down now almost to the waterline. His head was spinning, and he tried to think through his situation. He could serve a real lord again, again be Sir William. He could bring justice to the unknown 'other' man, and maybe even to the emperor.

Was this a trap?

But why would the chevalier need to do anything to trap Bill, when he could simply shoot him on the spot, or could even have left him to burn on the *Incroyable*? He considered the fact that the chevalier was blackmailing the emperor and found he didn't care. Bill had half a mind to kill the bishop anyway, for the beatings he'd received at the hands of Etienne and his thugs.

He nodded. "My Lord, as you've likely noticed, I'm unarmed."

The chevalier stooped to pick up the bundle from the deck and uncovered it. Within the cloth wrapping, the bundle contained Bill's coat, a shirt, neckcloth and cravat, belt, stockings, boots, even his black perruque, all of which gave him an unexpectedly large amount of comfort, as well as a long, sturdy saber—not his own, but it certainly looked deadly enough for the job—and one more thing.

One more thing that the chevalier took from the top of the long bundle and handed to Bill.

Bill fist-blocked it into decent shape and pulled it over his short white hair.

His lucky hat.

"Very good, suh," he said, pushing his hand firmly into the saber's basket guard. "Consider the bishop dead."

"Pray do not tell the ladies of New Orleans, suh."

CHAPTER SIXTEEN

A saber wasn't going to be enough.

Bill knew how to use a sword, and the bishop likely didn't. But the bishop had bodyguards; also, the Quarter was a dangerous place and Bill had enemies. The last time he'd walked about New Orleans without pistols, Bill had been jumped by Etienne and taken by the gendarmes. He needed to defend himself.

Bill wanted guns.

It would have been presumptuous to ask the chevalier for further weapons, especially given that the chevalier had given Bill freedom, clothing, and a sword *after* Bill had murdered his son.

Much less could he ask for anything so base and venal as *cash* from his new lord.

What to do? Take a risk he wouldn't need a gun? Steal one? He could break into Hackett's shop and take his own pistols back, but Etienne had likely already redeemed the weapons, and besides, old Hackett had always treated Bill with dignity, and it would be wrong to repay that with burglary. Plus, Hackett's shop would almost certainly be hexed to high heaven, or guarded by a spring-gun.

There was the debt—however dubious—owed him by Don Sandoval. Bill had been out of sight for a couple of weeks now, and it seemed unlikely that the hidalgo merchant would be on his guard, expecting Bill to resurface and demand payment.

Three figures stood on the pier as Bill's boat approached. Waiting for him? Unlikely—two of the three dressed like monks. Bill's boat bumped against the pier and Bill scrambled out. When he straightened up again, he looked up the dock and saw a solitary man, watching Bill.

Hand on the hilt of his newly bestowed sword, Bill sauntered up the wooden walkway to meet the stranger.

But it was no stranger. "Jake!" Bill cried on seeing his friend in captivity, and dropped his swagger. "Beelzebub's teeth, man, I was worried they might have shot you!"

Hop laughed. "No one has ever shot me, Bill."

"I wish I could say the same!" Bill's shoulder twinged. "Well, Jake, you've not been given your leaving pay in lead, at least, but as your place of work has burnt to nothing and your colleagues are all dead, can I assume you're no longer in the chevalier's service?"

"I do not serve the chevalier," Hop agreed. "I never have."

"I like your fire, Jake! As it happens, I have undertaken some service for Monsieur Le Moyne, and I have a commission to attempt tonight. But perhaps afterward, we might meet for a drink, sitting at a bar, like men. Tomorrow, I think, is more likely to be good for me than later tonight. Where are you staying?"

Hop shrugged. "I was staying on the *Incroyable.*"

Bill felt a stab of guilt. "No family in New Orleans, I suppose?"

"None," Hop said, "but I thought I might come with you, Bill. I could help you on your commission."

Bill had worked alone during his time in New Orleans, but mostly because he could never manage to work well with frogs or dagoes. And once upon a time, not really so very long ago, Bill had been a leader of men. Also, the talking deaf-mute was at least a passable wizard.

"I'd be honored to have you, friend Jake." He'd take care of the Dutchman. For a moment, he imagined Jacob Hop as his son, but then shook that thought from his mind. He already had a son. But he didn't have an aide, a protégé, and Hop might fill that role. "If it should happen, in the course of our errands, that you are able to assist me with a minor cantrip or two, I encourage you to feel free to do so."

"A minor cantrip or two," Hop agreed, and they shook hands.

✧   ✧   ✧

Sarah stepped out of Etienne's anti-cathedral and was stopped by a wall of human flesh.

"Excuse us," Father Chigozie said mildly, and was ignored by the throng. "I said excuse us. Please make way."

He was answered by jeers and indifference.

"Git outta the way." With elbows and shoulders forward Cal hammered into the crowd. Behind him a space opened up and Sarah darted into it, following him through the would-be dancers and gamblers until they reached open street. Etienne was right; Calvin would make a good ruffian, if he had the mind.

Sarah felt sick to her heart from her interaction with the Vodun priest. She regretted her promise to the man that she would owe him a favor. When she'd said it, she meant it as a trick on a stranger, like she'd have been happy to play on any foreigner around Calhoun Mountain. Like she'd tried to play on Thalanes, that day at the Tobacco Fair that now seemed an eternity ago. But when she had made her offer and met Etienne Ukwu's gaze, her words had no longer seemed like a trick to her, and she had felt a little frightened.

The man was a Vodun priest. Sarah knew enough about Papa Legba to identify the images in Etienne's mural, but that didn't make her comfortable with the idea that she was trifling with dark powers.

Papa Legba was the man at the crossroads, the great Vodun spirit of the doorway and communication, but he had another aspect, too. Maitre Carrefour. Younger than Papa Legba, a demon, a killer, associated with black magic.

Time to find William Lee and get out of New Orleans.

If she was lucky, Etienne's favor might never be called.

"Cal," she tapped him on the shoulder, "git us a quiet spot for a minute, would you? No big deal, just git us off this main street."

Cal nodded and steered down the nearest narrow alley. Light from the street pierced the narrow way, but the only occupants were two men huddling in the alley mouth, taking turns at a pipe emitting a sweet, cloying smell. They blinked slowly at Calvin and then retreated deeper into the darkness. Once the smell of their pipe faded, the alley stank like a privy.

"This all right?" Calvin's voice was strained.

"Thanks," she said.

Sarah cupped the ticket in her palms. It wasn't much. "*Ducem bellorum quaeso*," she muttered, and willed her strength into the little scrap of paper, urging it to move and show her where William Lee was.

It twitched, once, and then lay inert.

"Hell," Sarah said. It had failed. She hoped that the failure was because the claim ticket did not have a strong enough connection to Lee. She wondered how long it had been in his possession and tucked the paper safely away with her acorn.

"We'll get Sir William's guns in the morning," she announced.

"He probably didn't have the ticket very long," Thalanes said blandly, repeating her own guess.

Sarah nodded. Thinking of how to prosecute her search to find Captain Lee, she was reminded of the parties searching for her. "I need to go down to the river."

"First thing in the mornin'll likely be a sight safer," Cal pointed out.

"I need to go tonight," she insisted, a little more firmly than she meant to.

"Yes, Your Majesty," he muttered, and led the way silently back onto the street. They crossed the dueling ground, passed the cathedral, and headed across the Place d'Armes toward the Mississippi River. A trio of drunks huddled beneath the mouldering remains of Andrew Jackson, serenading him.

> *Old King Andy Jackson, he was the best of men*
> *He visited New Orleans, in eighteen hundred ten*
> *The frenchies threw old Jackson out, but he marched*
>   *back in again*
> *Doff your hat to old King Andy Jackson*
>
> *Old King Andy Jackson was thirsty for a drink*
> *The Mississippi water's wet, but it has a mighty stink*
> *Jean met him on the Pontchartrain, and there he let*
>   *him sink*
> *Raise your glass to old King Andy Jackson*
>
> *Old King Andy Jackson's a fellow no one grieves*
> *Some nameless soldier shot him, with stripes upon*
>   *his sleeves*
> *They hung him in an iron cage, between two Geechee*
>   *thieves*
> *Bow the knee to Old King Andy Jackson*

The clicking of Sarah's staff on the stones became loud in her ears, even over the drunken whistles and jeering of the makeshift choir.

On the far side of the Place d'Armes, Calvin's pace slowed and he held up a warning hand slightly to his side. At the same time he moved directly in front of Sarah and completely blocked her view.

"Calvin!" She almost raised her walking stick to hit him with it, but then she heard Thalanes speaking behind her.

"*Facies muto*," the little monk said.

He and Calvin had seen something she had missed.

She let herself drift to one side and look ahead. At the south gate of the Place d'Armes, exiting onto Decatur, she saw two men in blue uniforms. Not the gendarmes' blue-and-gold with fleur-de-lis, but a plain blue with a tricorner hat. She had seen such uniforms before, the morning she had escaped with Thalanes and Calvin from Calhoun Mountain. She had seen them again on the Natchez Trace.

The Philadelphia Blues.

Calvin kept up his long-stepped amble, walking straight for the two men. Sarah followed him, trying her best to look unconcerned while at the same time keeping an eye on the soldiers.

The two Blues stood together, scanning the Place d'Armes and Decatur Street.

Calvin kept walking. His course would have him turn within an elbow of Angleton's men, but he kept a steady pace. Sarah's heart beat wildly. She breathed deeply and controlled herself.

Calvin was ten feet from the Blues.

Five feet.

He was passing them, nodding slightly. Sarah looked at her feet.

A horse neighed, directly ahead. Sarah lifted her eyes slowly, afraid to attract any attention from the soldiers, now within arm's reach. More Blues had appeared in the gate, another half-dozen, riding up from Decatur Street—the horses were theirs, and they had nearly trampled Calvin. Calvin ducked and bowed and retreated, and as he shifted about, Sarah caught a glimpse of his disguise. She struggled to refrain from laughing at the sight of the dark-complected, bulbous-nosed face.

Then Calvin was past, and then Sarah, and they were heading along Decatur with the others in their wake. Sarah held her breath, waiting to hear yells and the thud of pursuing bootheels, but instead the nighttime crowd of the Quarter swallowed her and her companions, and the Blues disappeared.

Sarah quickened her step and caught up to Cal as they cut through the knot of gendarmes around the Mississippi Gate. His face looked sullen and withdrawn.

"Why're you actin' like a baby?" she asked. "What wrong with you?"

"Ain't nothin' wrong with me."

"Cal, don't you git mad at me. What did I do?"

"Yes, Your Majesty." His face was hard. "Don't worry about it."

"I can't stand it, Cal, not from you! Tell me what's stuck in your craw." Sarah was conscious that Thalanes, Cathy Filmer, and Chigozie were all only a step or two behind them, and afraid to have a public row with Calvin, but she was also stung by his cold shoulder.

Cal sighed. His normal easy lope had become a wooden clomp. "Nothin', I suppose. I reckon I jest wanted more'n to be your servant."

"Calvin, you *are* more," she tried to assure him.

"Thanks," he said dryly.

She knew what he wanted, or what he thought he wanted—Calvin was still fixated on the idea of marrying her. She'd turned his head with her hex, and it had never turned back. "Cal, you shouldn't ought to confuse love with love-hexin'."

"No." His voice quivered. "I reckon you shouldn't ought to do that."

The Quarter piled right up against the tall gray stone walls of the city, and, as if the city had funneled at high pressure through the Mississippi Gate, the evidence of human activity exploded again just on the other side, in a long row of wharves, piers, and warehouses, stretching a quarter mile in either direction along a hard-packed gravel street. Despite the hour, there were still ships being loaded or unloaded, and men with lights moving up and down the quay.

Cal stopped. "What you lookin' for, Sarah?"

Sarah stepped down onto an untrafficked pier. She slipped the patch from her eye and looked at the river, conscious of her companions filling in around her in a protective ring. The river pulsed green and scintillating, but it still showed the dark streaks indicating the presence on the ley of the Lazars.

The streaks were blacker now, and bigger.

"*Hostes video*," she incanted, touching her eye, and her vision again rode the mighty green current of the Mississippi upstream at lightning speed—

but only for a split second this time, and then she saw them.

They were in a sailboat now, a small one, but between the wind and the river's current it was moving at a frightening pace downstream—toward her. Rain soaked the boat and its occupants. Men worked the helm and the sails of the craft, men with frightened faces, but the Lazars all sat in a circle, unmoving and quiet, water dripping from the brims of their hats, faces hidden as they hunched down into long wool scarves.

No, not all of them.

One of them stood in the prow of the ship, hat, scarf, ornate and billowy cravat, and long, curly red hair all flapping in the wind, one hand gripping one of the small ship's many ropes and one foot grinding against a gunwale. Some sense screamed at her mutely to look away, to end the vision, to pull back, but she ignored it and examined the Lazar. He looked ahead, downstream.

He was looking at her.

Their eyes met, and his were white and blank, oozing black in their corners. Suddenly his words cut into her mind, dry and rustling. *Ophidian*, he said-thought to her, *Adam's Bastard, Egg-Hatched, Unsouled, Unclean, Serpentspawn. I sensed thee before, and now I see thee plain.*

"Robert Hooke," she whispered, sounding less resolute than she liked. "The Sorcerer." That sounded a little more respectful than she liked, so she groped for something more disparaging. "Newton's little shadow."

I know who thou art, too, child. The black in the corners of his eyes writhed. *I have known many like thee, known and devoured. Thy people are serpents, there is no throne for thee or any of thine and no refuge, not on Earth, not in Heaven and not even in the blackest pits of Hell. Ye shall feed my lord the Necromancer with your undying screams, thou and all of thine.*

The black substance in the corners of his eyes was a mass of tiny black worms, squirming as he spoke to her.

Sarah forced herself to laugh. "You ain't nothin' but rotten meat." She released her vision.

But the vision did not release her.

Robert Hooke laughed. *I have thee, soulless.* His worms thrilled like perverse little harpstrings. *Rotten meat or no.*

Sarah pulled away, yanked to rip herself out of the vision, and found she could not. She closed her witchy eye and the vision did not go away. "*Visionem termino,*" she coughed out, willing the connection to end.

It didn't.

I have not given thee leave to depart, Snakechild, the Sorcerer hissed into her mind, a sound like rustling leaves. The light seemed dimmer to Sarah, as if she were seeing it through a pall of smoke, or from underwater.

Hooke reached forward over the prow of the ship, reaching out to her face with the long, curled nails of his white hand.

Sarah couldn't move; something brushed her and she looked down. She could see her body beneath her, but below that was neither the Mississippi River nor the New Orleans wharf, but infinite murky space, falling away forever. Fingertips brushed her, and she floated in a thicket of hands that groped and caressed and pulled at her—

far away from her vision, where her body was, Sarah tightened her grip on her white ash staff—

Hooke's long, yellow nails touched her jaw and she felt cold to the marrow of her bones, knowing that she was not only about to die, but about to lose her soul to the Sorcerer Robert Hooke—

green fire flared in her vision! Sarah heard muttering and she was pulled to the ground, collapsing under Calvin's weight. Her vision was snuffed into nothing.

"Sarah! Sarah!" Cal barked into her ear. "Sarah, can you hear me?"

"You're crushin' me, Cal," she protested. "Not that it ain't thoroughly enjoyable, but iffen you git off me a minute I might jest could breathe."

Cal rolled away with a sound that was half-sob and half-laugh and Sarah sat up. The wharf about her was still untrafficked, and her companions stood in a screen, hiding her from the stevedores and gendarmes moving up and down the gravel. Thalanes looked strained, and Picaw and Grungle had joined them—the beastkind's presence probably explained the green light in her vision at the end.

She wasn't sure quite how, but the Heron King's emissaries had helped save her.

Thalanes knelt and looked at her with concern. "Are you all right?"

Sarah nodded and pulled the patch back over her seer's eye. "I saw the Lazars again."

"And the Sorcerer Hooke saw you in turn," Thalanes noted. "Did he say anything?"

"He called me names, but that ain't nothin'. I git that a *lot*."

Thalanes smiled, but didn't laugh. "How close are they?"

"Close," she said. "They'll be here tomorrow, I reckon."

"It ain't too late to git on outta here," Cal suggested. "I know you want to help your . . . your sister and brother, but you can leave me here to sniff out this Lee feller, and you and Thalanes can light out for someplace else. Someplace safer. They jest ain't no reason to take the risk. Without you here, I don't expect anybody'll care two squirts about me and Lee."

Sarah put her hand gently on Calvin's forearm and shook her head. "I'll find him faster, Cal. I'll find him first thing in the morning, and then we'll get out of here."

Chigozie looked confused. "I am not sure what has just happened here, but I am certain of one thing: my father will be very disappointed if you do not spend the night with us. Even if at this point the night consists of only a few hours."

Sarah looked to Thalanes for guidance and he nodded. "Thank you, Father," she replied to Chigozie. "We gratefully accept."

The two beastfolk looked at each other. "We shall watch the river," Grungle croaked solemnly. "When the Lazars arrive, we will do what we can to delay them, and we shall warn thee."

Sarah nodded. "Thank you," she said. "And please thank your master."

"Thou mayest thank him in person," Picaw suggested with a twist of her beak that looked like a smile.

Grungle held his hand out to Sarah. Shadowed in his palm lay a smooth, rounded, flat object, like a small tile. She took it and found it warm and slightly flexible. She held it up to catch what light she could from stray lanterns on the quay and found it reddish-brown and streaked with other colors.

"What is this?" she asked.

"A bit of my shell," he croaked. "I trust thou wilt know what to do with it, should Your Majesty have need of me."

"You have a shell?" she asked, surprised.

"I am not a tortoise, Your Majesty," the beastman said, "nor even part tortoise. But in some ways, I am very much *like* a tortoise."

"Some time, we should all git nekkid and share secrets," Cal suggested sarcastically. "But mebbe not tonight."

Sarah pocketed the bit of shell. "Thank you very much."

He nodded and executed a neat little bow. She bowed back.

Then Cal and Thalanes helped Sarah to her feet. She let them and the ash staff bear most of her weight to the landward end of the pier. There she pulled away, stepping down onto rocks dark with river water and crouching to gather mud on the tip of one finger.

"*Adventum videbo*," she muttered, and lifted her patch to daub the mud on her witchy eye. No sense relying on the tortoise shell alone, when she could have the help of the Mississippi River.

"Sarah," Cal asked, "what you reckon you're a-doin'?"

"No disrespect," she said to the beastkind as she lowered the patch over her eye, "but I intend to stand watch with you."

The two men crossed New Orleans at a rapid pace. Bill tried to pass the time in conversation with Hop.

"Are you a Dutchman, then?" he asked collegially.

"No."

"But Jacob Hop...isn't that a meneer's name?"

"Oh, yes, it is."

"Where are you from, Jake?"

"I live on the Mississippi."

"Some Hansa town, then. Is your family Dutch? Your parents?"

"No. My father lived on the Mississippi, like me. So will my son. We have always lived on the Mississippi, he and I, and we always will."

Bill tried to stay focused. "Well, how did you come by a Dutch name?"

"By the exercise of my power, of course."

Bill began to wonder if Jacob Hop were simple. Was it possible to be both an imbecile and a magician?

Kyres Elytharias had been a great man and a magician, but even he had had a bit of a mad streak, unpredictable and idiosyncratic. He'd run away to fight in the Spanish War without his father's permission, and even as king he'd ridden the bounds

of his lands in person, dealing out justice to road-agents and
Comanche slavers on the fringes of the Great Green Wood. He'd
been good, but he'd also been impulsive and wild.

Bill inquired about Hop's profession. "How long have you
been a prison guard, Jake?"

"I am not a prison guard."

"I mean, how long *were* you a prison guard? I know you
were a guard on the *Incroyable* . . . have you been a prison guard
elsewhere?"

"Friend Bill, did I give you the impression that I was trying
to keep you imprisoned?"

Bill couldn't decide whether that was a good point or not,
but it seemed to be denying the basic facts. He decided to switch
tactics and approach Jake on the universal masculine level.

"So, Jake," he said heartily, "tell me about Jacob Hop and
his women! Do you have a lady love ashore? Do we need to find
you one?"

"I do not love at all as you know it, Bill. However, I am
looking for a queen."

They had skirted the Quarter, passed under the shadow of the
Palais du Chevalier, and were now at the edges of the Garden
District, where mercantile buildings gave way to the elaborate
columned homes of New Orleans's wealthy.

The awkwardness thickened into tension and finally Bill
stopped walking.

"You're the strangest man I ever met, Jake, and that's a fact.
I can't discover where you're from, what your native language is
or what kind of man you are, and I've been trying the better
part of an hour!"

Jake stopped to consider this. "I am your friend, Bill," he
said. "Is that not enough?"

Bill reached under his perruque to scratch his itching scalp,
wondering whether he'd picked up lice in the *Incroyable*. His
head needed shaving.

"Yes, Jake," he finally admitted, "strange though I find the
fact, it is indeed enough for me. You've been good to me and
I'll not begrudge you your peculiarities. Hell's Bells, I'm an odd
enough man myself."

"Would it help you if I told you that I am the rightful king
of the great river valley in which you stand?" Hop asked with

a faint and curious smile. "That my servants have slept during my father's long reign, but that now I shall recover my power, the great might of the Mississippi will be roused again, and war and judgment will be loosed upon the land?"

Bill laughed heartily. "Heaven love you, Jake. A sense of humor is a necessary piece of a fighting man's accouterment; nothing drowns out the whistling of musketballs like a good joke. Have you ever considered becoming a soldier?"

"I have not," Jacob Hop said. "Tell me about soldiers."

It had been a long time since Bill had been a soldier. "The greatest soldier I ever knew was the Lion of Missouri."

"I have heard of the Lion."

"You've heard the songs, I expect," Bill predicted. "There are plays, also, and novels and poems and puppet shows."

"Why does this man so interest your artists, then?" Hop asked.

"Understand this, Jake. A *good* soldier is loyal. To his king, to his country, to his flag, to his captain. A man who fights for money is a *mercenary*, which is little better than being a mere *thug*."

"I understand that," the Dutchman said.

"A *great* soldier also fights for *ideals*. He serves a king and country, but he fights for freedom, for honor, for justice, for peace, for brotherhood." Bill's eyes misted over, memories flooding through his mind.

"And the Lion of Missouri was such a man."

"His toast," Bill explained. "Military men drink, Jake, and they make toasts. They make the same toasts over and over again, like a ritual, like polishing your boots or keeping your sword sharp. One man toasts and the other men toast him back. Usually, the toasts are funny, in the nature of shared jokes, like *to the girls we've left behind, and to the ones we'll leave behind tomorrow*, or they're bellicose, like *death to the Spaniard and confusion to the Turk*."

"These are things soldiers say to each other when they drink."

"Yes," Bill agreed, "exactly. The Lion of Missouri always made the same toast. After a few years with him, I found I was saying it, too. He toasted *honor in defense of innocence*, and the hell of it was, he meant it. He had a good sense of humor too, Jake, he could tell a joke and he could take one, but never once, when he made his toast, did I see him crack a smile. He was a truly unironic man."

"He fought for the innocent, then?"

Bill nodded. "I met him as a young man. We were both youths, fighting off the Viceroy of New Spain when he decided that even taking New Orleans wasn't enough for him. You're a lad yourself, but you must have heard of this, there were regiments from the Tappan Zee, fighting under one of your Stuyvesant warlords."

"I have heard of your Spanish War," Hop said.

"It was everyone's Spanish War, that's the point," Bill insisted. "It made the New World into the empire, because for once we all fought on the same side, more or less, because everyone was worried about New Spain and how far up the Mississippi they might get. Then the war ended and we were all friendly and Franklin put together his Compact to finish the job. That was when I learned my languages, in the war, because I had dago allies, and frogs, and iggies and Germans and Algonks and everything you can imagine. And I went because that's what a gentleman does, he goes to war with his lord, and the Earl of Johnsland went.

"But Kyres didn't have to fight. He was a prince, and his kingdom wasn't in jeopardy, and his father forbade him to go. But he thought the Spaniards were killing innocent people, so off he went and fought himself, sword and gun and tooth and nail. He shed a lot of his blood in Mobile, and a lot more Spanish blood on the Ouachita River."

Jacob Hop listened in silence.

"But even battling against a cruel and aggressive invader," Bill went on, "he always fought fair. He honored the rules of war, he honored his foes, he loved his men. I knew him when he was a great soldier, and then I knew him in Missouri, when he was even greater."

"What do you mean?" Jacob Hop asked.

How to explain? "They called him the Lion of Missouri," Bill started slowly, "because he rode through that country half king, half outlaw, and all legend. The Missouri territory lies across the Mississippi from Cahokia—"

"I know," Hop said.

"—and the Kings of Cahokia have always figured as major powers in the area, but the Lion made it his personal obsession. The small farmers had a hard life, squeezed by the landowners, the petty squabbling nobles, the banks, the gangs of outlaws, the beastkind, and what have you, and Kyres Elytharias took their side. He was the king, you understand? He was the Imperial Consort by then, too, and he protected these farmers, he gave them justice, he righted their wrongs. He risked life and limb for those dirt farmers, and attracted enemies like a dog attracts fleas."

Hop said nothing and Bill groped through his chest of memories for something that would illustrate the awe in which he held his old master. It hurt him to talk so much about Kyres, but it hurt in a good way. Maybe Bill was finally digging a bullet out of an old wound, and now the injury might really heal.

"Once," he said, "we came upon a small town where several barns had been burned. The burgomaster and the aldermen told us it had been an outlaw band and showed us the tracks of the bandits' horses. We followed their trail into the hills and there, in a canyon, we were ambushed. The firefight lasted two days, and it was touch and go whether we would die of thirst or be shot full of holes. In the end, we gambled on a desperate ruse and managed to turn the tables on the outlaws, killing a couple of them and capturing the rest. It cost us four good men, four dragoons dead, and when we interrogated the outlaws, it turned out they were people from the town—the burgomaster and one of the aldermen were among our prisoners."

To his astonishment, Bill felt his eyes misting slightly. Hop's expression was fixed and intent. "The whole town was in on it," Bill continued. "They burned their own barns to lure Kyres in. It turned out that some bank had put a price on Kyres's head—think about that, Jake, he was the Imperial Consort and there were banks offering reward money for his death." Bill remembered the sheet-white expressions of fear on the faces of the burgomaster and the alderman.

"So he killed them all?" Jacob Hop guessed.

Bill shook his head. "The Lion asked them what they needed the money for, and they told him they had had a drought and a bad harvest, and the town was in danger of starving to death."

"He took hostages, at least, for their good behavior?"

"He let them go," Bill said. "And he gave them his purse. All the money he had on his person, a small fortune."

Hop stared at Bill.

"Kyres Elytharias was the greatest soldier I ever knew. He was more than just a soldier, he was a knight. Literally. I am a *Cavalier*, Jake, which means that I am a man of the Chesapeake, and I am an *officer*, which means that I hold, or held, military rank, and I hope to be a *gentleman*, which has something to do with my being born to a family that owns land and rides horses and something to do with not having disgraced myself. The Imperial Consort was a *paladin*. He belonged to a chivalric order of the Firstborn, something called the Swords of Wisdom. Perhaps that was where he got his ideals, I never knew. Perhaps he got them from his father, though he defied the man."

"A man does not always share his father's ideals," Jacob Hop pointed out.

Bill thought of his son Charles and wondered what ideals the young man held, and whether he was the sort of man who would fight for them. "Come on, Jake. We have a cotton trader to meet."

Don Luis Maria Salvador Sandoval de Burgos lived in a house that climbed up its own white columns and pink stucco walls, scattering wide fern-sprouting balconies and showers of lilies, orchids and jasmines that collapsed into a hubbub of garden barely contained by a fleur-de-lis-tipped iron fence. It nestled between two similarly aristocratic abodes, and two swordsmen idled just within its tall gate, watching the wide, calm street sleep through the pre-dawn light.

The other homes on the street were similarly large, opulent, and guarded.

Bill stood in the shadows several houses away and considered the tactical situation. He doubted the Don would welcome his arrival, but his alternatives to an open approach were problematic. Stealth was definitely not his forte, and it was not obvious to him that even a stealthy man could sneak past the guards; nor could he see any other way into the yard. Attacking the guards would put an end to any possibility that he might be paid what he was owed, even if he won.

"Friend Bill," Jacob Hop said. "Is this an appropriate moment for a minor cantrip?"

"Yes, Jake, it might very well be. I don't believe, however, that a letter in French is likely to serve our present need. What else might you be able to do?"

Hop looked at Sandoval's manse. "Do you wish harm to that house? Shall I destroy it?"

Bill chuckled. "No, Jake, I merely need to speak with the house's occupant."

"That seems easy enough." Hop considered. "Shall I put those two men to sleep?"

"Can you do that?" Bill asked.

"We are close to the river," Jacob Hop explained. "Jibber jabber me honky wonk buggeroo," he added, or something that sounded very similar. The two men at Don Sandoval's gate crumpled to the ground.

Bill looked up and down the street—the other guards hadn't seen the collapse, or possibly didn't care.

"Excellent work, Jake." Bill clapped his companion on the shoulder and strolled to the Don's house.

Bill pushed the gate open, stepped over the snoring toughs, and marched up to the double-wide oak door. The little Dutchman followed, and whenever Bill turned to look at his companion, he found him grinning.

Bill revised his ambitions upward as he clanked the heavy brass knocker of the door. Jacob Hop was turning out to be a very can-do sort of wizard, and Bill might actually be in a position to demand his twenty looeys, rather than plead for them. Indeed, if his former employer didn't cooperate, Bill might be in a position to simply take the money.

And why stop there? He could rob Don Sandoval.

He instantly dismissed the thought. He was the chevalier's man, now, on the chevalier's errand—he was only stopping here because he was owed money, and he needed the cash to arm himself.

The hatch opened and through the iron grill Bill recognized Don Sandoval's face. The Don's eyes opened wide, Bill groped through his fatigued wit to find some clever way to put his demand to the old hidalgo, and then Don Sandoval shut the hatch again.

Damn.

Well, maybe Hop could knock down the door with his gobble-dygook. Bill turned to the deaf-mute to make the suggestion—

and Don Sandoval opened the door.

"Sir William!" He lunged.

Bill flinched and stepped back, reaching for the hilt of his sword, but to his utter astonishment, the Spaniard grabbed him by the face and kissed both his cheeks.

No matter how long he lived in New Orleans, Bill was never going to understand these dagoes.

"Sir William! Come in!" Don Sandoval pulled Bill in through his door, faltering only when he saw his crumpled guards. "My men, they are...?"

"They merely sleep, suh," Bill assured him. What on earth was going on?

"Ah, fine," said the merchant. Wearing only a long night-shirt, with no rouge on his face and his wizened musket-ball skull unadorned by a perruque, he looked different to Bill: fantastical, vulnerable, old. Bill shuddered, realizing that he must look the same under his own gear. "Forgive my disarray, I am awake early for doing the accounts. And this is your associate?" He shut the heavy door behind Jacob Hop.

Bill considered the Dutchman with a proud eye. "My protégé."

"You will learn much from el Capitán, from Sir William," the hidalgo advised the Dutchman, then took Bill by the arm and led them both across an unlit drawing room. "Tell me, Sir William," he said confidentially to Bill, "where have you gone? She is two weeks since I last saw you. I was become worried for you."

Hell's Bells, but the world had gotten strange. Beastkind, talking deaf-mutes, magical French letters, and now this embrace from a man who had tried to kill him.

Was this a trap?

Bill hesitated at the threshold to the next room and almost stumbled, but Don Sandoval pulled him onward and Jacob Hop pressed at his heels.

It made no sense as a trap; if the hidalgo wanted to kill him, he never would have opened the door to him and let him in, especially undressed and unarmed. Or he would have let whatever warding spells he had protecting his house, and he must surely be rich enough to have something, prevent Bill's entry.

"I had business with the chevalier, suh," he said.

The next room was a study, paneled in dark woods and furnished with a dark wood desk, broad and heavy, an immense armoire of dark wood, dark wood shelves, and a striped orange pelt on the floor that must belong to a tiger. Across the desk lay an open book of scrawled columns of numbers. The light through the window had lost the blue tinge of pre-dawn and now looked clear and yellow, but the room was also lit by a candlestick on the desktop, holding glimmering candles of fine wax on three arms. Don Sandoval stopped and clasped Bill's hand.

"I am sorry," he told Bill. "I did you a great wrong, and I see that you have suffered. You look so thin. You have been in prison, no?"

Bill dismissed the past with a wave. "Pray do not tell the ladies of New Orleans, suh, or they will be rushing to take the waters of the Pontchartrain Sea."

Don Sandoval laughed with delight. "Into the very teeth of death and hell, a true knight casts his defiant jest!"

A true knight. Bill felt tired, uncomfortable and confused. He was happy that Don Sandoval hadn't unleashed a pack of thugs against him. On the other hand, this strangely ardent welcome left him disoriented.

"Don Sandoval," he began tentatively, "I dislike to trouble you..."

"I owe you money," the hidalgo interrupted him. "I should not make a *caballero* stoop to ask for something as low as recompense." He released his grip on Bill's arm and pounced upon his desk, where a raid into a top drawer produced a small purse, tied shut, which he rushed to put into Bill's hands.

"Ten Louis d'or," he said, "as agreed. And ten further Louis d'or, your bonus, as we discussed. And yet another ten Louis d'or as interest, though, like a true gentleman, you said you would not ask for it. But I know your creditors are men without mercy, and you should not suffer because of my delay."

Thirty looeys! Bill felt guilt for killing the chevalier's son, but he had come to ask for the money owed him, because he needed it. Now, with Don Sandoval praising him relentlessly, calling him *Sir William* and referring to him as a knight, he felt worse about the young frog's death.

Hadn't Judas got thirty looeys for kissing Jesus?

He couldn't take the money, but he couldn't go into the Quarter unarmed, or armed only with the pig-sticker. He'd be eaten alive. He squeezed the purse tightly in his fingers.

He couldn't take it. Not for killing an innocent.

"I find my circumstances changed, suh," he said slowly, pressing the purse back into Don Sandoval's hand and closing the old man's fingers over it, "such that I cannot accept the money you so generously offer."

Don Sandoval looked up at Bill with eyes that were alert, sorrowful, and quizzical. "Please, Capitán Sir William, you have spared my life and I am in your debt. My son...my whole family is in your debt. Tell me how we may repay you."

"I do not consider you to be in my debt, suh," Bill said, astonishing himself.

The hidalgo looked surprised, too. "But you have come here for something, surely. Must I...shall I speak to the chevalier, and reveal to him that I was the cause of his son's death?"

Bill scratched again under his perruque. "Well, suh, as it happens, I am desperately in need of arms. I would be very pleased if you could do me a service, one gentleman to another."

"Anything."

"I would be honored," Bill said, "if you could lend me a brace of pistols."

"This jest gits worse and worse."

———◦———

CHAPTER SEVENTEEN

It had been a long time since Bill had set foot inside a church, but Jacob Hop looked about him with a bewilderment that suggested this was his very first visit ever.

"I have been deceived," Bill whispered. "I thought the Dutch were great churchgoers."

"Oh, yes?"

"Yes. I held the wall in Mobile with a crusty Dutch sergeant named Harmonszoon. He called his gun *Old Mortality*, and he sat up there on the palisade with me and talked Bible the whole time. In between shooting at the Spanish, of course."

"Of course."

"One day I told him if he was going to quote the Bible all day, at least he could quote the parts with pretty girls in them."

"Which parts are those?" Jacob Hop asked.

Bill shrugged. "Apparently, there aren't any."

They stood by the rood screen that separated the nave and the transepts from the chancel. The roof of the church resounded with an incessant hammering of rain. The cathedral's interior was faintly illuminated by Bill's dark lantern, just enough to reveal the images in the building's stained-glass windows. The seven days of creation ran up one side of the nave, the crucifixion and resurrection ran down the other, and the fall of man, with a Creole-looking Adam and Eve sharing a bright red apple, crowned the apse. More than one New Orleans voice whispered that the Creator depicted in the windows bore a suspicious resemblance to the former bishop, Henri de Bienville.

Bill had Don Sandoval's two large-bore pistols stuck in his belt; Jacob Hop wore the chevalier's sword in its scabbard, hanging down his back from a belt over his shoulder. Hop had let them into the church by "another simple cantrip," which had neatly unlocked a side door leading from the bare packed-dirt dueling yard behind the cathedral into the apse through a devotional chapel. The chapel housed the most prominent de Bienvilles, including the famous Bishop Henri, who lay in a glass coffin in his red bishop's robe and cap, marinating in honey. Bill had crossed himself and bowed his head deeply as he passed the bishop's tomb.

"This is a mighty god," Hop said. "That is the message of this building. That its god is the ruler of heaven, earth, all men, and other gods." He pointed to a gold stand, behind and above the altar, on which rested a pair of crossed small-bore pistols. "He is a vengeful god."

"Other gods?" Bill asked.

Jacob Hop pointed at various stained glass windows. "There the god destroys dragons of the earth and sea and builds creation upon their bodies. There he is accompanied in his work by all the lesser gods, the stars of the night sky. The same gods attend the birth of his son, singing the music of the spheres. And there the servitor gods are arrayed in his worship. See? The one with the key, the one with the sword, the one with the lion, and the one with compass and level?"

Bill scratched under his perruque. "I'm no theologian, Jake, but you and I don't see those pictures the same way. Those are Leviathan and Behemoth, they're monsters that God kills. And those 'lesser gods' you're talking about are the angel choir. And...what did you say, servants? Servitors? Those are Saints Peter and Paul, I believe, and Jerome is the one with the lion. And St. Jeremiah Dixon, I believe, though it's more ordinary to show St. Jerry alongside Charlie Mason, with his telescope and his loaf of bread."

"I do not see any difference," Hop said stubbornly, "between your understanding and mine."

"I suppose you may be right." Bill was getting used to the

Dutchman's oddities. He believed Jake hadn't been a deaf-mute at all, he had been taken for one on account of his madness. "Where do you think we should hide?"

Hop shrugged. "In the little room?"

Bill frowned. "I believe that might be called the vestry, Jake. It holds vestments, anyway. It's a fine suggestion, although I think the priest goes there first. We require a vantage point from which we can watch for a few minutes before we're certain of our target."

Hop grinned wide and ran his fingers through his straight blond hair. "Shall I turn us into magpies, and we can watch from the rafters for the bishop to enter?"

Bill laughed. "I'd be unable to use Don Sandoval's pistols to any advantage as a magpie," he said, joining the joke. "Unless, of course, you could turn me into a magpie with hands."

Hop frowned good-naturedly. "That would certainly be more difficult."

"I've stumped the wizard Jacob Hop!" Bill cried in mock triumph. "Well, fear not, Jake, we can secrete ourselves at the platform at the top of this stair. It's where the priest delivers the homily, and it will give us a good view of the scene. We'll see immediately, for instance, whether the bishop brings any of his bodyguards."

There came a *rattle* and a *click* in the darkness, and Bill shuffled toward the stair. "Hurry, Jake, that's likely the bishop." They sprang up the steps and hid behind the waist-high balustrade of the preacher's crenellated perch. Bill shuttered the lantern.

A new light source entered the cathedral. It came from a transept door, the one facing the bishop's palace.

Bill waited.

He listened for the door; it shut again, and he heard it lock. Then he listened to the footsteps—one man, and not in a hurry. The new arrival walked into the chancel. As Bill had predicted, he went straight to the vestry and began making preparations.

Bill had never met the Bishop of New Orleans face to face—using his son Etienne as a front man let the bishop maintain his public façade of piety—but he knew what the bishop looked like.

Now, as the priest went about dressing himself in ceremonial garb and setting out bread and wine for the morning's rite, Bill eased himself onto the winding stair, took his hat in his hand and snaked one eye up over the bannister to examine the man below.

It was not the Bishop of New Orleans.

The man dressing for mass by the light of an oil lantern looked like the bishop, but was younger. He looked something like Etienne, too, but Bill guessed it must be the bishop's other son. Bill had never had dealings with the man before, he was altogether on the priestcraft side of the family business.

"Shall we kill him?" Hop's voice had a note of mischief in it.

Bill shook his head. "It's the wrong man," he whispered. "You can't just kill anyone you like, Jake. That isn't good soldiering."

"Is it not?"

"We're not out to cause random mayhem, Jake, we have a target. If we kill this man, we've sprung our trap and the bishop will be warned. If we assassinate the wrong man *and* the bishop escapes, we've fouled it doubly."

"Shall we go find the bishop, then?" Hop asked.

"We stay hidden," Bill said. "We wait until the bishop comes."

"Are you sure he'll come?"

"No." Bill peered over the rail again to be certain they weren't heard. Their voices sounded loud to him, but the bishop's son showed no sign of having noticed—the rain on the roof and its loud echo within the cathedral must be masking their noise. "But he's the bishop, and I understand that he says Mass every day. Apparently he doesn't say the morning Mass, but it might be the midday Mass, so we need to hide ourselves and wait."

"And if he never comes into the church today?"

"I'd rather surprise him here, where he's out of his home and on the move," Bill whispered, checking the priest again and finding him still dressing, his back turned to them, "but if the bishop doesn't come to us, we'll have to make some plan for breaking into his palace. Perhaps a bribe to a footman, though there we run into the problem of my shortage of funds."

Bill shuddered at the thought of that undertaking; the bishop's palace was a huge building, and it was always full of people. Priests mostly, Polites, he thought—weren't they the ones who wore red? The thought that the bishop might have a cadre of spell-casting vicars for a bodyguard made Bill very uncomfortable.

"Can we hide in the chamber below?" Hop sounded eager. "The one full of bones?"

"I don't understand how a dead man can do magic at all," Sarah said.

Sarah had finally had her bath, in a half-barrel tub in a small tiled room in the bishop's apartment, with Cathy Filmer to keep her company; they had talked little, and Sarah had tried to stick to what they had already told the other woman—that she was here seeking her old family friend, William Lee, on family business. It had helped that Sarah was exhausted; she drifted in and out of sleep in the hot water.

Picaw and Grungle hadn't reappeared and the alarm spell Sarah had cast the night before on the riverbank hadn't been triggered, so Sarah was confident that the Lazars had not yet arrived in New Orleans.

Perhaps the rain had forced the Lazars to ground.

Sarah sat in the bishop's tiny study, in one of its three wooden slat-backed chairs. The bishop objected to wealth, which she could understand and respect, but she felt no sympathy for his apparent dislike of simple physical comfort.

Cathy Filmer sat in another chair. Thalanes and the bishop stood, browsing among books as they talked, waiting until it was late enough to go to the pawnbroker's and redeem William Lee's guns. The bishop sucked slowly at a small clay pipe, filling the room with the sweet odor of burning tobacco leaf.

Cal sat by the window, putting a fine edge with his whetstone on the silver letter opener, looking out into the gray flood falling from the sky. He had his face turned away from the rest of the party; was he being vigilant, or was he turning his back to her as punishment?

"Death is in some ways the heart of my craft and calling," the bishop said with a kindly smile, "but I confess that I am unaccustomed to *walking* dead men. Perhaps my more thaumaturgically gifted colleague, Father Thalanes of the Order of St. Cetes, can illuminate us."

"I wish I could." Thalanes arched his eyebrows. "Robert Hooke was called the *Sorcerer* even in his mortal life, of course—"

"That's somethin' different from a wizard, I reckon?" Cal said from his perch in the curtains. So he was listening, at least.

"It's all the same thing," Thalanes said, "hexing, wizardry, gramarye, all terms for the same magic practiced by the children of Adam. People just use different names for practitioners to indicate approval or disapproval, or sometimes to denote a specialization."

"Like *illusionist* or *summoner*," Cathy offered by way of illustration.

"Or *necromancer*," the bishop said. "Or *warlock*."

"What d'you got to do to git called a *sorcerer*, then?" Cal asked.

"It has the connotation of someone who dabbles in dark arts," Thalanes said, "someone who deals with demons, for instance, or specializes in curses, or works death magic."

"What's that say about Hooke?" Sarah asked. "Anythin' in particular I maybe should ought to know about?"

Thalanes smiled. "Robert Hooke was famous in his mortal life for insatiable curiosity. He experimented with summoning, and his lectures at Cambridge apparently inspired young Oliver Cromwell."

"I didn't know Cromwell was a university feller." Calvin scoured at the little blade. "It figures."

"So was Hooke," Sarah pointed out.

"What did he inspire Cromwell to do?" Cathy Filmer asked. "I wasn't aware Hooke was a political man."

"He wasn't," the monk said. "He was a wizard, in practice and in theory. And it was something in his lectures that moved Cromwell to the execution of Jock of Cripplegate."

"Never heard of him," Sarah admitted.

"There's no reason you should have," Thalanes said. "Jock was a pickpocket and a cutpurse and a second-story man who was sentenced to hang. The only thing noteworthy about him was that it just so happened that Jock's father was Firstborn, a refugee from the Serpentwars that were just beginning in Bohemia and the Palatinate at that time.

"Cromwell was a gentlemen, with some connections in Parliament, and he convinced the king's justices to let him carry out Jock's execution. And he used Jock's death as an experiment. He captured the energy released at Jock's death, and used it to perform a magic spell."

"Poor Jock," Sarah remembered the explosions of light she'd seen on the Natchez Trace.

"Poor Jock, nothing," Thalanes said. "Jock was a criminal and a low character and he probably deserved execution. None of that makes what Cromwell did right."

"So that was the beginning for the Necromancer," Cathy said. "He learned he could exploit the deaths of Firstborn and he did.

He overthrew King Charles Stuart, he knocked over half the kingdoms of Europe before John Churchill finally stopped him. What was it all for? What did he do with the magic?"

"Create his New Model Army, for one thing," the bishop puffed at his pipe. "Marching wooden men and corpses, creatures of sorcery and evil."

"Of course," Cathy Filmer agreed. "He killed Firstborn to create his army to kill more Firstborn to create an ever larger army. But that's just a circle that never goes anywhere. Was he actually doing anything?"

"Yes, that is a circle," Thalanes agreed. "I don't know what his plan was, other than to establish the Eternal Commonwealth. I don't know whether John Churchill cared enough to ask that question, or if he was happy just to cast the Necromancer out of England. And Cromwell appears to have achieved his own immortality."

"The Death Wind," Cathy said.

Thalanes nodded.

"What about Hooke?" Sarah asked. "He was Cromwell's teacher, and I know he was called Sir Isaac Newton's Shadow . . . what else? Why is he called the *Sorcerer*?"

"I don't know," Thalanes admitted. "We should assume that Hooke is dangerous, and that he means to destroy us."

"Ain't they a piece of the story missin' here?" Cal wanted to know. "How in tarnation is Hooke still walkin' around, and chasin' after Sarah? Is they some story in which he gits raised from the dead?"

"This is very dark talk," the bishop said with mild disapproval.

"That's the Death Wind," Cathy said. What could she possibly be thinking about this conversation? She sang two lines:

> Come with me, my servant fair, onto the holy floor
> The Death Wind soon shall catch me up, if you go
>   on before

Sarah shot the other woman a curious look.

"I listen to songs all night at *Grissot's*," Cathy explained. "There are ballads about Robert Hooke and Black Tom Fairfax."

"Hooke mentioned the Necromancer," Sarah said in a monotone, and she felt like her voice was the voice of someone speaking far away. "He said my screams would feed the Necromancer, or something like that. So should we assume that Oliver Cromwell is also on my trail?"

"This jest gits worse and worse," Cal muttered gloomily.

"I do not know why you would expect Robert Hooke to tell you the strict truth," Bishop Ukwu objected, "or even any truth at all. He was a sorcerer, a heretic, and a murderer in life, and I see no reason to think that death has made an honest man of him."

"Nor I," Thalanes hastened to agree. "That he can talk at all surprises me, as I thought—in my admitted absence of experience— that Lazars were mute. But you say he didn't move his lips, that he seemed to send his thoughts to you directly, so it must have been some sort of spell."

"Which brings me back to the original question," Sarah observed archly. "How can he do magic? When I do magic, I draw on my life energy, unless some other source is available, like a ley. How can Hooke cast spells at all? Isn't he *dead*? Is he tapping into a ley line all the time?"

Thalanes shrugged. "He must be drawing power from some source. It might be simply the Mississippi."

"What else might it be?" Sarah asked, feeling a chill shiver in her bones.

Thalanes shrugged and shook his head.

"Beware," the bishop said. "Be very, very careful."

Ezekiel eventually opened the door to Captain Berkeley's bedchamber himself, after repeated knocking beyond the bounds of decency and any reasonable allowance for a hangover failed to produce the captain. Berkeley was gone, as were his clothing and weapons, and the only sign of him, on a small table beside his bed, were his Tarocks.

The cards sat beside an empty liquor bottle, mute testimony of an all-night vigil and a wrestle with some dilemma. Berkeley had dealt three cards face up on the table and had left them there, so Ezekiel examined them. He didn't know the Tarocks, but the cards bore both pictures and, underneath, neatly lettered titles.

The first of the three cards Berkeley had left was the Horseman, a soldier with sword and pistol, mounted on a white horse and wearing a long red coat and a tricorner hat. Ezekiel frowned, noticing that the painted figure strongly resembled Captain

Berkeley. Coincidence, but the captain might think otherwise. The second was Simon Sword, and it depicted a blond boy swinging a two-handed sword. The third card was the Priest, a Spanish friar-looking character with a cross on top of a tall walking stick and a bag in his hand. No, on a closer look, Ezekiel saw that it wasn't a bag that the cleric held in his hand, but a letter, folded and sealed.

Ezekiel cursed himself for not speaking privately with Berkeley the night before, for not pursuing the subject of the bishop's visit. What was it that Berkeley knew? Some dark secret troubled the captain. Did he just want to defend Thomas from the accusations of the bishop?

Or did he want to defend Thomas from the blackmailing the chevalier?

Ezekiel was puzzled. Berkeley's absence irritated him, too—this morning, they were to have split up to comb the city for Witchy Eye, pairing each Dragoon with one of the chevalier's gendarmes so as best to combine local knowledge and Imperial authority. For Berkeley to disappear now was a dereliction of duty.

Or had he left the Tarocks as an explanation?

Obadiah edged into the door behind Ezekiel. He'd come to the Palais with the message that the Blues were ready to search, as ordered, and that a contingent of gendarmes of the same number of men was likewise at alert.

"Where be the captain?" Obadiah asked.

"How should I know?" Ezekiel snapped, and instantly regretted it. "I . . ." he couldn't bring himself to apologize to the pagan Obadiah, no matter how much time the man had spent recently digging into his Bible. "I don't know."

"Aye, Father." Obadiah hesitated. "Ought I . . . ?"

"Get out," Ezekiel commanded him. "Just *get out*. Go join the Blues and the chevalier's men and wait for me."

Obadiah *clopped* away without another word.

The Horseman, Simon Sword, and the Priest.

Franklin's Tarock was rank superstition of the worst kind, worse than astrology or hedge-witch hokey-pokery, which at least had some root in God's created order. The Tarock had no basis but the fevered imagination of Benjamin Franklin and the lascivious whispering of gypsy soothsayers. It made a mockery of God's election, His grace and His love, and His true gift of prophecy. Ezekiel sneered at the cards.

Devilish gibberish though they were, it was possible that Berkeley had used the cards to leave Ezekiel a message.

The Priest could be him, Ezekiel. Or it could be the bishop. And Berkeley was definitely a horseman, even if the card hadn't looked so much like him.

Simon Sword? What was the mythical folk-bugbear of the Mississippi supposed to mean? This was a card Berkeley had been rattling on and on about back in Nashville, when it had seemed to the captain that he drew Simon Sword in every reading.

Simon Sword. Ezekiel racked his brain to try to recall the Poor Richard Sermons he had memorized in his first year at Harvard. Simon Sword was a bringer of change, and chaos, and war. Judgment, Berkeley had said.

Simon Sword meant judgment.

Ezekiel gathered up the cards to take them with him.

They trooped out into the rain under Thalanes's *facies muto* incantation. Sarah still felt the drag on her soul of her Mississippi River alarm spell, so she was glad it was Thalanes casting the disguise enchantments, and not her.

"I'm glad you're with us," Thalanes told Cathy.

"I'm pleased you find me charming," she said. "A disproportionate number of my friends are priests. I think they enjoy my elevated conversational style."

"Oh?"

"That's one of the things they enjoy, in any case."

She winked at the little man.

"I didn't mean that," he said, reddening. "I don't . . . I don't know what you . . . look, my order is a chaste one, Mrs. Filmer. I only meant that changing the composition of our group will help reinforce my illusions."

"Of course you did, Father." She fixed him with an eagle eye. "I expect you to find my friend Sir William. If you have to make me look like someone else with your gramarye to find him, I'm perfectly happy to cooperate. It won't be the first time I've dressed up for a priest."

Thalanes coughed, and Sarah wanted to laugh. Since she'd known him, she'd never seen the priest so off-guard and disarmed, and Sarah had certainly tried.

The rain had let up from its earlier downpour, so Sarah

eschewed her heavy coat for her purple-and-suns shawl, which
had always been a favorite. She carried the sharpened silver letter
opener tucked into her belt. She was careful not to let it touch
her skin, so it wouldn't interfere with the watchfulness spell she'd
cast on the Mississippi.

Thalanes went first, looking like a gaunt little Igbo monk with
his illusory curly black hair and dark brown complexion; then
followed Sarah and Cathy Filmer, whose glamour-spun façade was
of two dark-eyed hidalgo dames; and Cal brought up the rear,
looking heavier than himself, grizzled and paunchy, with bright
white hair and a long scar up one side of his face.

The Place d'Armes was nearly empty, and Sarah was silently
grateful for the cobblestones as she trekked under the warning
stare of King Andy Jackson—the puddles of cold water were
better than puddles of mud. The Quarter was calm, the lights
all out in the inns, taverns, and dancing halls, and most of the
residents drunk or asleep.

But Hackett's was open for business, its shining glass windows
and front door thrown wide.

"I'll honor the ticket," Hackett said when Calvin presented
it, along with the nine Louis d'or indicated on the ticket's face,
"though it troubles me it isn't Captain Lee himself to redeem
his pledge. Is the captain well? I heard there was some trouble
with the gendarmerie."

As he spoke, Hackett retrieved from behind the counter
a brace of long, large-bore horse pistols and laid them on his
countertop, then dug out and set beside them a heavy cavalry
saber. Sarah hoped she could work the spell she imagined she
could, and find William Lee.

"I hope he's well, too, Mr. Hackett," Cathy agreed, and her
smile put old Hackett at his ease.

"We're all Will's friends here," Thalanes said. "We're collecting
his weapons for him and expect to meet up with him later today."

"You're absolutely sure these are Captain Lee's guns?" Sarah
confirmed.

Hackett nodded.

Sarah let Thalanes take his old comrade's sword, but she
took the heavy guns in her hands and led the way out of the
pawnbroker's. The street outside was empty, but she saw no sense
in taking any chances, so she turned down a small alley to get

behind Hackett's. This was close enough; for all practical purposes, she was standing where Bill had stood. When she was sure no one was watching, she squatted in a patch of mud.

Should she walk to the river to take advantage of the ley's energy? The arrival of the Lazars was imminent, and Sarah chose haste over access to the river's power.

WILLIAM LEE, she scrawled in the mud with her finger, and scratched out the rough outline of a man around the name, head, body, arms, and legs. Rather than wiping her finger clean, she smeared that mud around the open mouth of each gun, tracing two circles of dark wet earth on the steel. Sympathy and Contagion, Sir Isaac's two laws. Things that appear to be connected, and things that were once connected. She stood, her feet on Lee's names, and held the pistols by their grips.

She closed her eyes. "*Ducem bellorum quaeso*," she incanted, the same words she'd tried the night before over the claim ticket, and she poured her spirit into the guns.

Instantly, the weapons bucked in her hands, twisting and pointing so that she had to clutch them tightly and turn with them in order not to lose her grip, as if guiding a plow pulled by a particularly aggressive mule.

"Ha!" She opened her eyes.

"Congratulations," Cal drawled, a proud and gently mocking gleam in his eye, "I reckon you've jest created the only two possessed pistols in all of New Orleans."

She pressed them into his hands. "Jest for that, you git to hold 'em."

"Whoa!" he called to the pistols as they pulled him to one side. "Now what?"

"They's jest like dowsing…" Sarah caught Thalanes looking at her with a raised eyebrow and clamped down on her glee. "They should work just like a dowsing rod, Calvin. If you let them pull you, I think they'll take you to Captain Lee."

"You should go back to the bishop's apartment," Thalanes told Sarah. "We don't know where Lee is, and it could be dangerous."

Sarah felt nettled at being given such a strong suggestion, though the monk had a point. She bit back a fiercer retort in favor of a mild objection. "It's dangerous for me everywhere."

"You can disguise both your appearances as well as I can, and we'll meet you back at Bishop Ukwu's home shortly." He smiled. "I hope. I only worry that we might find Sir William in a gendarmes' jail, or someplace worse. If we get trapped, I don't want it to become worse because you're stuck with us, and we get overtaken by the Lazars."

"Have you forgotten the slaver on the Natchez Trace?" Sarah asked. "You sure you want me going off alone?"

"I haven't forgotten how well you handled him," Thalanes said, "and I think this is the safer thing to do."

His efforts to make his suggestion sound reasonable only irritated Sarah, as did his flattery. She steeled herself to reply with a blanket assertion of her authority.

"Please," the monk added, his voice soft. "I can't tell you what to do, Sarah, I'm just asking. I really think you'll be safer."

Once again, the monk was talking to her as if she were a child!

Sarah gritted her teeth and was winding up to let out a shout when Cathy cut in. "I would like to go to my room and change clothing, if I could. Sarah, would you mind terribly accompanying me?"

All the wind spilled out of Sarah's sails. She nodded. "Only I ain't sure I got enough mojo to cast me a *facies muto* jest now," she said in Appalachee, a final gesture of defiance.

"Take this," Thalanes offered, unpinning his moon-shaped brooch from the front of his habit and handing it to her. Unable to think of any reason not to, she glumly took the offered bauble and was impressed that at the slightest touch, merely holding the jewelry in her palm, she could feel it throb with energy.

"It will work as well for you as for me," Thalanes predicted. "I fill it with a little of my own energy every day, and then I have a reservoir to draw on when I need it. You should be able to use it, too, since you can draw from the leys. You'll have to touch it during casting, but otherwise it works just the same."

Sarah pinned the brooch to the shawl, somewhat mollified. "*Facies muto*," she said, touching the brooch, and she shaped her own face into the likeness of a craggy old woman, turning Cathy into a similar crone. She could feel power coming out of the brooch. It made her tingle to have the energy flow through her, but it didn't leave her exhausted.

Thalanes smiled. "Grand old ladies. You both sort of resemble the Elector Calhoun."

"After a terrible drunk, the fall-down kind where you wake

up and best no questions asked why you're wearin' what you're wearin'," Cal agreed. "Honestly, you look more like Granny Clay."

Then Cal was off, struggling with the bucking dowsing rod-guns. Thalanes followed close behind him, walking fast.

Cathy offered an elbow to Sarah. "Shall we go?"

Sarah cheerfully locked arms with the older woman. "You're always so calm. Please tell me how you do it."

"It isn't terribly complicated," Cathy said. "But it requires a lot of practice, Sarah Carpenter. Or should I say, Your Majesty?"

Obadiah was looking for an opportunity to leave. His employer hated him. All the things he had formerly seen as the great benefits of his job as the chaplain's factotum—travel, food, women—had become tiresome and empty. He would have preferred to hole up and read his Bible, or look for a good puppet show. He wanted to go home.

He wanted to see Sarah.

Duty had gotten him out of his cot that morning, and had kept him working with the gendarme lieutenant to arrange the gendarmes and Blues into paired teams he jokingly referred to as "yokes," to their blank incomprehension. The chevalier's man du Plessis had observed at his shoulder, and du Plessis followed him through the enormous Palais du Chevalier as well, when Obadiah went to report.

Angleton had dismissed him curtly, angrily, indifferently.

There was a higher life, and it would not come from Ezekiel Angleton.

Obadiah believed Sarah could show it to him. Even if she couldn't love him, and of course she would never love him, not the way he loved her, he could be in love with her. He would follow her home.

He would have left the Blues already, except that sticking with the Blues was his best chance of finding Sarah.

Captain Berkeley still hadn't appeared by the time they all mustered in the large courtyard of the Perdido Street gendarme station, and Obadiah was a little surprised that the Blues still formed in ranks in the rain and took orders not only from Father Angleton, but also from Obadiah.

Under his watchful eye the Blues matched up each with his assigned gendarme, and took a printed city map with their assigned patrol area indicated on it with pinpricks. Then the Blues and gendarmes assigned to the first watch exited the station's courtyard and those assigned to the second watch returned to their bunks or to the predictable leisure activities of soldiers and constables everywhere: gambling, eating, drinking, and thinking about, talking about, and looking for available women.

Obadiah turned his back on them with a great sense of relief.

Ezekiel Angleton said nothing to Obadiah and assigned himself to a search yoke ad hoc, simply joining the first pair of men to leave the yard. Obadiah joined another by the same expedient, and found himself trotting toward the Quarter behind two grim men in nonmatching blue uniforms.

He was on patrol, and he had a plan.

"En cette direction ici," the gendarme said to the dragoon. He led and the dragoon followed, Obadiah bringing up the rear.

He almost missed Sarah when they passed her.

He had been dreaming of Sarah Calhoun for weeks, replaying in his mind's eye every moment he'd spent with her and lovingly revisiting every detail of her dress and manner. So he might have missed the fact that one of the pair of crones stumping down the boardwalk by his side had the walk and bearing of his beloved, but even deep in emotional turmoil, he didn't miss the fact that the crone was wearing Sarah's purple shawl with golden suns.

His mind processed the shawl over a couple of seconds' time, so that he realized he had seen it only after he had passed the old women. A mighty impulse washed over him and he fought back the urge to turn his horse, jump down, and plead his case to her. Instead, he discreetly drew a pistol from his belt and thumbed back the hammer.

Did he really want to throw away his position with the Philadelphia Blues for this girl? Sarah didn't love him, and he was being treated with respect by the dragoons.

But the respect he was getting now was surely temporary, and would vanish with Berkeley's return. And Father Angleton was still treating Obadiah like a bad dog, to be snapped at and whipped. Once, that had been an acceptable burden to bear for a decent wage. Now, Obadiah longed for a life of meaning and love.

Whichever it was to be, he had to get Sarah.

He wheeled his horse, barking to his search yoke. "She be 'ere!"

But she wasn't there. The only person on the boardwalk was a little boy, sweeping the detritus of the prior night's carousing from the boardwalk with a rough straw broom.

"Lad!" barked Obadiah. "'Ave you seen a girl wiff a caitiff eye this mornink, all red and swole up?" Pushing a thumb into his purse, he threw a copper bit at the boy.

The boy caught the copper, but only stared back at him. "Je ne comprend pas."

Obadiah sighed and looked at the building. *Grissot's*, its signboard said. There was nowhere else they could have gone. "Keep the bit," he told the boy, and dropped from his horse. The search yoke stopped and looked puzzled, but Obadiah didn't wait—beckoning them to follow, he entered the tavern.

A hunchback vigorously working the bar raised his polishing rags above his head as he saw Obadiah enter. "Look ye," he said, "we've no desire for trouble on us." Obadiah ignored him and stepped across the disarrayed common room, toes only onto the stairs on the other side, at the top of which he'd seen a flash of purple and gold.

What would Obadiah do once he had her? Could he go through with his plan? Would he submit again to Father Angleton, and his life of safe satisfaction of bodily lusts, safe but grown stale?

He didn't know.

He turned just long enough to shush the search yoke, following a few steps behind him, with a finger over his lips—and how he would love to feel Sarah's finger on his lips—and then crept up the stairs, gun first.

He heard two women's voices talking and recognized one of them as Sarah's. He couldn't make them out on the staircase, but as he reached the hall of the upper floor, he caught a few words: "Penn," "Lee," and "Mad Hannah" were among them. Whoever the other woman was, Sarah was recruiting her.

Obadiah peered down the hall and saw the two crones shut a door behind them. Perfect. He walked slowly, not wanting to alarm them, and when he reached the door they had entered, he threw his shoulder into it, smashing it open.

Inside sat the two old women, one on a small bed and the other on a chair beside, their hands clasped together in intimate woman-talk. They pulled apart and jumped to their feet as Obadiah drew his second pistol, leveling both guns at the women.

"Sarah Calhoun." He locked eyes with the crone in the purple shawl.

"I don't know what you're talking about," she insisted in a creaky imitation of an old woman's voice.

Obadiah shook his head. "Nay, you'll not fool me wiff that old phiz, poppet." He swiveled one pistol to point at the other crone's face. "An' if you try again, I'll 'ave to blast your friend 'ere to kingdom come."

The crone Sarah blinked, and then the illusion disappeared, and Obadiah saw his love, Sarah Calhoun, with her eye covered by a patch made of a long strip of cloth, and a tall, brown-haired woman he didn't know.

"Fank you, love." He tucked his guns back into his belt and turned, just in time to meet his search yoke in the door and block their view. "Gents," he said, digging discreetly into his purse as he talked, "it ben't 'er, but I definitely 'ave somefink 'ere. Stand watch whilst I palaver wiff these 'ere informants." He shut the door in their faces and turned back to the ladies.

"Sarah, my poppet." He opened his arms wide to show his harmless, affectionate intentions. "Can we 'ave a wee chat?"

Suddenly, Sarah yelled, and Obadiah leaped back. She slapped at her own face, scratching her cheek in her eagerness to tear the patch away, and then she was digging her fingers into her eye, and scooping something out of it, something that might be . . . mud?

"No, no, no!" she gasped.

"Poppet, what is it?" He felt genuine concern.

She looked up at him. Her eye, though it seemed to be smeared with mud, was no longer inflamed. Nor was it shut—it was open, and it stared at him with an iris as white as snow and full of horror.

"They're here," Sarah whispered. "They're here!"

"I was unaware that we had differences,
Lieutenant Berkeley."

⟐

CHAPTER EIGHTEEN

Down in the crypt beneath the St. Louis Cathedral, surrounded
by the shelved bones of hundreds of priests and other grandees,
Bill realized he didn't want to kill the bishop.

He tightened his grip on the hidalgo's pistols.

Just because the bishop had a son and hadn't personally
wronged Bill, he shouldn't get off the hook. The bishop's death
wasn't a matter of merit, it was a matter of Bill's duty to his
new master, the Chevalier of New Orleans. After years in exile,
Bill had a lord again, a position, a master who was a gentleman.

But was he? Was this all it was to be a gentleman? Or to be a
soldier? Merely taking orders? Bill remembered something more,
facing Spanish lances on the walls of Mobile and riding with the
Lion of Missouri. Honor in defense of innocence.

Bill's mouth tasted sour.

But he could regain all that. He had agreed with the chevalier
to kill the bishop in exchange for his freedom, and the honorable
man kept his bargains. Bill could kill the bishop, take his place
in the chevalier's service, and from then on live a higher law,
fight with all his honor as a gentleman to protect the innocent,
as he once had.

He only had to do this one dirty deed first.

And it wasn't all *that* dirty. The bishop was a moneylender
and a gangster. Those who live by the sword die by it, though

he couldn't remember whether that was in the Good Book or the sermons of old Ben Franklin.

He wished he had a bottle of whisky.

"Bill," Jacob Hop asked, pausing from a minute inspection of a complete human skeleton, folded neatly into a mass of cobwebs within a cubbyhole six inches wide and tall, "do your people do this with their own bones?"

"Do you mean in the Chesapeake, Jake?" Bill asked.

Hop shrugged.

"We bury our dead. Those who are wealthy enough have a family mausoleum."

"Do you have a family mausoleum?" Hop asked.

"Yes." In his mind's eye Bill saw the stone building in the cemetery on the hill, there in northern Johnsland. He hadn't been to his family's cemetery in . . . twenty years? Twenty-five? "We Christians, I mean. My pagan neighbors burn their dead. I don't know how they treat their dead in the Cherokee towns. How do the Dutch do it?"

"I don't know how the Dutch do it," Hop said. "One moment." He paused. "They bury their dead in the earth. Singly. In little plots of land, with stones to mark the location. Stones with writing on them."

My deaf-mute protégé is a madman. "That's common enough. It's we mausoleum people, and the crypt folk, that are unusual. Though we're not as odd as those who expose their dead to wild animals, or throw them into the sea, or shrink their heads, or eat them."

"We burned my father." Jacob Hop's voice was unemotional. "I shall be burned someday by my son."

"What, no headstone for the good old Dutchman? What was your father's name?"

"Peter," Hop said.

"Dearly beloved," Bill intoned, "we are gathered here to pay our respects to that good old meneer, Peter Hop. Shall we give your father the ceremony he deserves, Jake?"

"Go ahead," Hop said. His facial expression looked curious and amused, but not mocking.

Bill stood up and shuffled over to a bone-filled niche. He selected a skull, blowing the dust off it and propping it up in the opening of the cubby, where it glared into the greater crypt.

"Dearly beloved," Bill began again. "I give you Peter Hop, nation: Dutch, homeland: Hudson River Republic, profession... what was your father's profession, Jake?"

"King," Hop said.

Bill laughed. "Profession: king. Jake, will you give the eulogy?"

Hop looked perplexed. "What is a eulogy?"

"Tell us—" Bill gestured at the walls full of bones to indicate who the audience was, "about your old father."

Jacob Hop considered. "As always, he was a man of peace, law, stasis, and prosperity. His subjects were fat and happy."

"Hear, hear!"

"I despise him and his works," the deaf-mute continued, "as my son in turn shall despise me. I seek to overthrow his peace with war, his law with chaos, and his stasis with the colossal wheel of change."

Bill snorted. "That's the funniest eulogy I ever heard, Jake."

The Dutchman considered. "Ought a eulogy to be funny?"

"The best ones always are." Bill crossed himself sloppily in the direction of the skull, then shoved it back into the cubby. *"Requiescat in pace."*

They waited awhile, the dark lantern shuttered. Bill drifted into a light sleep. In his dreams he ran back and forth between two giant specters, the bishop and the chevalier. The two Electors of New Orleans were puppets swinging enormous stick clubs at each other, and in his dream Bill threw himself flat to the ground or cringed behind gnarled oak trees. Dream-Bill feared both combatants, and loved neither, and couldn't choose between them, sprinting to and fro in a space that continuously narrowed as the giants charged each other. The chevalier swung his club one final time—

Bill couldn't evade, he was doomed—

tantara-tantara-tantaraaaa!

Horns blew, and a choir of angels burst from the heavens with voices and instruments ringing—

Bill awoke.

The choir was singing, and he fumbled to find and open the shutter of the lantern, stinging his fingers on the hot metal. The light snapped open on Jacob Hop, sitting quietly.

"Has Mass begun?" Bill nearly choked in consternation.

Hop shrugged. "I was waiting for you to wake up."

"Dammit, Jake, I know you're the apprentice in this relation-ship, but you've got to show a little more initiative!" Bill took a pistol in his hand and scrambled up the staircase.

If it was the bishop officiating, he could simply wait until afterward and kill the man. Or, if attendance was low enough, he might take the open shot when the man was defenseless and count on his ability to get away in the confusion. This was New Orleans; the bishop wouldn't be the first priest assassinated in the middle of Mass.

The staircase door (the staircase went both down by spirals into the crypt and up by spirals, Bill presumed to the roof) was well behind the rood screen, hidden from the congregation and giving Bill an easy route to slip behind the choir's high wooden benches. From there he could watch the bishop's movements at and around the altar.

Hop stuck close behind Bill in the shadow.

The priest had finished at the altar and was climbing the short stairs to the pulpit, his movements followed closely by the choir as well as by the attendees sitting on the other side of the rood. This must be the homily; Bill focused on the back of the priest's head. The man had short, tight, curly white hair, and the nape of his neck was dark brown.

It was the bishop.

Bill cocked his pistol slowly, muffling its *click* inside his long red coat. *One dirty task.*

Just one.

Bill stepped to his side, gaining a clear line of sight at the bishop's back. He didn't like shooting the man from behind. It stank.

The bishop was a usurer and a gangster.

Bill raised Don Sandoval's large-bored pistol and sighted along it at the bishop's curly white hair. At this range, he couldn't miss.

"My children," the bishop began in a loud voice, "my text today is from the twentieth chapter of the book of Exodus. The Ten Commandments." The crowd was large; the cathedral was nearly full to capacity.

Bill felt a knot in his stomach.

He owed this act to his lord, the chevalier. He had promised. To be a man of honor again, he had to keep his promise.

"Thou shalt not steal!" the bishop shouted.

Bill touched the trigger with his finger...but he couldn't pull it.

He lowered the gun again, feeling both shame and relief. He would serve the chevalier if he could. If not, he might have to leave New Orleans.

But he would be again the man who had ridden with the Lion of Missouri.

"Thou shalt not bear false witness against thy neighbor!"

Bill eased his hammer back into place. Would he see Cathy again? What about Sally? What would the chevalier do?

He slipped the pistol into his coat pocket and enjoyed a long, deep breath.

"My children, there is a liar and a thief in New Orleans today." This seemed like a strange thing for the bishop, of all people, to say, and the congregation laughed. Oddly, though, they seemed to be laughing *with* the bishop, rather than *at* him.

At the far end of the nave, the great front door of the cathedral swung open, rain gusting through and a flash of lightning crackling on the other side. Two figures staggered in from the storm. The one in front lurched up the aisle between the pews, reeling as if in some grotesque dance toward the altar, hands held out before him; his companion followed a few steps behind.

The bishop plunged ahead. "More than just the one, you might say, and you would be right. But today I wish to speak to you about the one."

The dancer held a pistol in each hand, and was headed for the bishop.

Some portion of the crowd reached this realization at the same moment as Bill, and there was a general gasp. Bill knew what he had to do—he had decided that the bishop did not deserve to die because the bishop was, at least with respect to Bill, an innocent man; therefore, the bishop deserved his protection.

Bill rushed past the surprised Jacob Hop, sprinting at the rood screen and vaulting over a small door that cut through it. He landed in a crouch in the broad open space at the center of the cathedral.

The members of the congregation sitting nearest Bill gasped, but no one stood to stop him. Good, that would keep things simple.

"The liar that I care about!... the thief I must reveal!... the corpse in the temple of New Orleans!" The bishop was shouting again.

Bill stood to see that a third man had arisen in the congregation, holding a pistol. To his shock, Bill knew him—it was his former aide in the Blues and fellow gentleman of the Chesapeake, Daniel Berkeley. The crowd burst from its seats in a sudden hubbub.

"... is the Chevalier of New Orleans, Gaspard Le Moyne!" the Bishop of New Orleans howled.

"Berkeley! Help me!" Bill gestured at the lurching man and his companion. Berkeley had been an able lieutenant. The fellow was a skilled horseman and fighter, especially with his sword.

Bill saw the man lurching forward more clearly now; he was tall and rangy, with long red hair tied back on his shoulders, and he wore the breeches, moccasins, and long hunter's shirt of an Appalachee. He was soaked, and he seemed to be holding on to the two pistols in his hands by main force, being dragged forward by them as if by horses he was breaking.

Stranger still was the fact that Bill thought he recognized the guns—he would have sworn, even from twice as far away, they were his own long horse pistols.

The lurching man's companion was smaller, pale and dark-haired, and dressed in a gray monk's robe. His shock continuing to mount, Bill realized he knew this man, too. He was Thalanes, Firstborn, itinerant mage, Cetean monk, chaplain to the Philadelphia Blues when Sir William Lee had been their captain, and Bill's fellow conspirator in the concealment of the Empress Hannah's children.

Thalanes carried a sword.

Bill's sword.

Sweet merciful Heaven, now I'm the one who has gone mad. Bang!

Bill jerked his eyes back to the Appalachee spastic, but no smoke poured from those long familiar guns. He spun to look at Berkeley, and saw that his old comrade in the Blues had his gun pointed at the bishop—

smoke billowing out—

and the bishop was collapsing sideways, toppling over the railing of the pulpit, crashing on top of the altar, bloodying its covering cloths and dragging them with him in his slow tumble to the floor.

The crowd exploded like a flock of pigeons at the shot.

"Berkeley!" Bill shouted again.

Berkeley turned to face Bill, and time slowed. Berkeley tossed aside his spent pistol, wheeled on the ball of his foot and charged at Bill, sweeping his sword free of its scabbard.

Bill yanked his own pistol from his pocket, raised it, and fired—

click!

"Hell's Bells!" Bill was a fool to have rushed out of the damp crypt without refreshing the firing pans of his guns, or at least checking them. And then Berkeley was upon him, with his first murderous, disemboweling swing aimed at Bill's stomach.

Sarah fought a boiling wave of panic. The first Lazar foot that slapped onto the dock had triggered her spell and her witchy eye had filled with a view of the Mississippi Gate. The sudden inpouring of greenish light almost blinded her.

At the same moment, her mind had echoed with a shout in the groaning rumble of Grungle's voice. *Beware, Your Majesty! The Lazars arrive!*

His voice sounded only in her head, and yet it seemed to be coming from the small disk of tortoise shell in her pocket. Instinctively, Sarah wrapped her hand around the bit of shell and squeezed it.

"Grungle!" she cried out.

Her eye grew accustomed to the light of the Mississippi ley, and she saw she had a river's-eye view, looking up at boats, wharves, and the shoreline. She saw the tattered brown backs of the Lazars' coats as they disembarked. Their boat bobbed as they stepped onto the wharf, and the last one to come off the vessel held a long straight blade in his hands, something like an Arkansas Toothpick.

Black Tom Fairfax, wielding the knife that had taken its owner's life and damned him to Cromwell's service. Blood dripped from the weapon, and the sails of the Lazars' hijacked ship were spattered with the blood of its crew.

Untied, the little yacht drifted out of her vision.

Run away, disengage! Sarah's mind screamed, but a need to know the outcome kept her pinned. The Lazars padded toward the bank, Hooke and Tom Long-Knife striding quietly in front and the others clustering behind, hunched, gangrel things, rancid and festering.

She wondered what horrible services the other Lazars had done Cromwell, or what outrages they had perpetrated against him, that had led them to this end.

People on the shore pointed, stared, or ran away, and someone shouted for gendarmes. A thick-chested harbormaster with
a blue cap bearing a gold fleur-de-lis stood with feet apart and
a truncheon in his hand in the middle of the dock.

"Arrêtez-vous! Stop right there!" he barked.

Black Tom swung his long knife once, lightning-fast, and
the harbormaster crumpled to the ground in a fountain of his
own blood.

Splash!

His head landed separately, in the water.

Picaw and Grungle blocked the end of the dock to keep the
Lazars from dry land. "No further, death-slaves!" Grungle croaked,
and he produced from beneath his robes a pair of sharply curved
blades. He swung them left and right and advanced upon the
walking corpses, a thresher of men.

His forward motion halted in mid-flourish. His body slumped,
but his eyes stayed fixed forward, and Sarah felt cold fear; the
Heron King's tortoise-headed servant had been snared by the
Sorcerer Hooke. Whatever trap Hooke had been trying to lure
Sarah into when their minds had touched on the Mississippi, had
instead seized the beastman.

"Don't look at his eyes!" she shouted.

Picaw cried something in a tongue Sarah didn't recognize, and
an array of knives, like a crescent of green-streaked steel, whipped
from her hands. The weapons flashed and bit into the Lazars—

and they kept coming forward, knife hilts protruding from
their cold chests.

Grungle seemed to be shriveling. His black eyes no longer
glittered, his mouth hung open, and Sarah saw a green glowing
vapor rising from him. The beastman's aura faded and Robert
Hooke sucked the bright mist into his own body.

"No!" Sarah shouted.

Black Tom Fairfax stepped past Grungle and lunged at his
companion. Picaw, too, produced a scimitar from under her
robe and gamely parried several quick stabs at her torso. When
she counterattacked, though, Black Tom ignored it, and even as
her blade bit into his ribs, cutting a deep slice into the tattered
brown coat—but otherwise having no visible effect—Tom Long-
Knife plunged his long dagger into her neck.

Picaw dropped her blade and as her blood jetted down the

front of her robe, Black Tom jerked out his weapon. Seizing the beastwife by the tip of her beak, he dragged her to her knees and raised his blade over his head like a cleaver.

He's going to chop off her beak! Sarah felt sick, and she jerked her vision away from Picaw and back to Grungle.

Thwack!

Grungle was gone, his aura snuffed. His body collapsed forward onto the planks beside the dead harbormaster. Further up the slope, gendarmes and the customs toughs backed off, making way for the wrath of the Sorcerer Robert Hooke and Black Tom Fairfax.

She wanted to scream.

I believe we are being spied upon. The Sorcerer began to turn back in the direction of the river, in Sarah's direction, and she saw his pallid forehead over his shoulder, then his eyebrow, then—

Sarah yanked herself out of the vision.

"Sarah!" Cathy was shaking her. "Sarah, are you all right?"

They were not half a mile away; she had no time.

And now Obadiah Dogsbody wanted a wee chat.

Sarah pried herself from Cathy's grip and faced the Englishman. He held a pistol in his hand, cocked and pointed at her.

"Obadiah," she gasped, "terrible evil men're not ten minutes from this here room, men as'll jest as soon kill you as me. We gotta git outta here!" She hoped the truthful plea might soften the Englishman up.

"Oh, aye?"

"*Liberate nos!*" She willed all the energy she could from Thalanes's moon brooch through her words at the smiling Obadiah, commanding him to set her and Cathy free.

Obadiah stopped, cocked an ear, and seemed to think a moment. "What was that, poppet? I ain't ever 'ad mickle of an 'ead for Latin."

He slowly, melodramatically turned his free hand around, and then suddenly uncurled his fingers to show her his palm. Obadiah Dogsbody held a tarnished silver coin.

"Hell," Sarah said.

"It be a bit 'arder when a chap ben't taken by surprise, ben't it?" His face tightened into an expression that hung between sweetness and a snarl.

"What do you want, Obadiah? If we don't leave now, we're dead, all three of us."

"I want to come wiff you, poppet," he said. "An' I want you to forgive me."

"What?" she and Cathy asked together.

"I fink I might love you," he explained. "I ben't right sure 'ow to explain myself, it's been a confusing few weeks. But I definitely want to come wiff you."

Sarah had no time to argue. "I might jest be able to agree, iffen you can git us outta here!"

Obadiah eased the hammer of his pistol back down, turned it around and offered its grip to her. "You take it, pet. Token of good faiff."

Cathy Filmer leaped to her feet. "Let me get my things." She knelt to pull up a loose floorboard, hoisting out from beneath it a stitched leather shoulderbag.

Should Sarah take the Englishman's gun and then shoot him? Or just leave him?

But she might need him to get past the soldiers out in the hall.

And besides, astonishingly, he seemed sincere.

She waved the offer of the pistol away, and Obadiah tucked it back into his belt beside its mate. "Can you git us outta here?" she asked him.

Obadiah smiled. "Of course I can, poppet."

Berkeley's blow was rushed, trying to take advantage of the fact that Bill had no sword. It was unlike the Daniel Berkeley Bill had known, who was a cool and efficient swordsman.

Bill deflected the attack with the metal barrel of the hidalgo's pistol and then stepped inside Berkeley's lunge to headbutt Berkeley in the nose.

Except that Berkeley slithered under Bill's blow and the two men collided, shoulder to chest, neither very well balanced. Bill hopped back and drew the other pistol, leveling it at his former comrade-in-arms. People ran for the exits, swarming all around the combatants, but it was a close shot and Bill wouldn't miss.

"Put down—" Bill started to demand Berkeley's surrender, but the younger man regained his balance and flicked the tip of his sword, jostling the gun, so that Bill fired—the *bang!* was loud in the hollow drum of the church, with its people noises receding—and missed, the bullet gouging a bite out of the rood screen.

Berkeley's backhanded return swing of the blade came for Bill's face, but Bill was already in motion, retreating. "I would say it's a pleasure to see you, suh," he commented, "if you weren't whole-heartedly engaged in seeking my death. Was it something I said?"

Berkeley made several neat slashes and pokes at Bill, never exposing himself to counterattack and forcing Bill back.

"Are you the bishop's man, Lee?" Berkeley asked. "Is that how he knew? Blazes, did *you* tell him?"

Lucifer's codpiece, what was Berkeley nattering on about?

Thalanes hovered at the outer ring of the fight, but as Bill sidestepped another series of jabs, the red-headed man came barging toward Bill, through a knot of frightened women and past Berkeley, catching the dragoon in the elbow.

Bill saw his chance and hurled a spent pistol at Berkeley, but the red-haired man was moving faster than he had thought—

the pistol clubbed the stranger in his head—

and he collapsed, Bill's long pistols falling at Berkeley's feet. Bill lunged for them, but was deterred by a length of sharp steel he suddenly found at his throat.

"These look like *your* pistols, Captain Lee," Berkeley drawled. "You were once a famous shot. Are you still any good?"

Bill nodded warily.

Berkeley was breathing hard from the exertion, but Bill was breathing harder.

"Naturally, you're hoping I will test you," Berkeley ruminated. "You're hoping we can resolve our differences with a pistol duel, which you believe will give you an edge, and remove my advantages of youth, strength, speed, stamina, and superior swordsmanship."

"I was unaware that we had differences, Lieutenant Berkeley," Bill said, as placatingly as he could through the huffing of his old man's lungs. "I only hoped for an explanation as to why you've killed the bishop, especially in this manner. It is a surprising act for a man who once fought for the credo *honor in defense of innocence.*"

"It's *Captain* Berkeley. I'm Captain of the Blues, now."

"Someone has to do the job."

"What are you up to, Lee?" Berkeley knelt, his sword still between them, and scooped up one of Bill's guns.

To both their surprise the gun jerked forward, pulling Berkeley off balance. He stumbled over the unconscious Appalachee man and fell to his knees.

"Will!" Thalanes yelled.

Bill turned in time to catch the saber, *his* heavy cavalry saber, that the little monk had tossed to him, hilt-first and still in its scabbard.

Bill whipped the scabbard off and held it in his left hand.

The crowd was dissipating. Would the gendarmes show up? If they did, would they recognize him as a colleague, or would he find himself in chains and bound for the Pontchartrain again? Would the chevalier be upset that someone other than Bill had killed the bishop? Did Bill even *want* to serve the man?

Bill sighed. Life had once been so simple.

Berkeley regained his feet. "Who told you, Lee?" He leaped to the attack. Bill retreated, turning aside Berkeley's attacks with a curtain of defensive steel.

Behind Berkeley, Thalanes chanted some hocus-pocus and then rushed over to the fallen man.

Why had Lieutenant Berkeley—*Captain* Berkeley—killed the Bishop of New Orleans, and why was he now attacking Bill? Could it possibly be coincidence that Thalanes had reappeared at the same moment as Berkeley, and carrying Bill's weapons?

"*Captain* Berkeley," he said in his most polite tone, barely parrying a blade that whistled at his throat. Berkeley was right; he was a better swordsman than Bill was, and he was younger and stronger. "I congratulate you on your preferment. I regret I was unable to attend the ceremony."

"You left the court." Berkeley pressed his attack. "You became a deserter."

That stung. "Captain Berkeley, suh, that's hardly..."

"What were you thinking, Lee?" Berkeley pushed Bill hard. Bill retreated back at a ninety-degree angle around a cluster of pews, forcing Berkeley to come around the long way and gaining precious seconds.

"I had my reasons, suh," Bill muttered.

"Where did you go, old man?" That jab hurt, and the anger almost distracted Bill from the attack that immediately followed. Berkeley lunged and Bill danced sideways between two pews. Berkeley chopped at him again and he skittered back further, slashing at Berkeley to keep the pursuit from being too eager.

"I bear you... no ill-will, Captain... but I insist that you... account to me for this death."

"You have no authority to insist upon anything!"

Slash, duck, slash, and Bill stepped back again.

He and Berkeley had once been friends and fellow soldiers, and he had to believe Berkeley was attacking him now, somehow, by mistake. Maybe he'd also killed the bishop for mistaken reasons.

"A request, then," Bill puffed. "If I lay down my blade, suh... will you do likewise... that we may converse?"

The bishop's congregation had all emptied out, other than a lone woman who bent over the bishop's body. She wore a white nun's habit with a red cross on it over a stylized heart—a Harvite, a Bleeding Heart, a Circulator; one of the Sisters of St. William Harvey, and for a moment hope sparked within him that the bishop might yet survive.

"What have you been doing in this pit of whores?" Berkeley's eyes boiled. "And does Sally know?"

Bill leaped forward with an attack that caught his opponent by surprise.

"I was minding—"

He slashed at Berkeley's face, and the man parried, trapped between pews—

"my own—"

Bill whipped Berkeley across the head with his scabbard—

Berkeley crouched, trying to avoid the blow, but still took it in the ear, and yelped—

"damned business!"

Bill planted his boot in the dragoon's teeth, sending Berkeley tumbling back, almost losing his grip on his weapon and falling out from between the pews onto the broad flagstones of the aisle.

With the kick Bill had lost his own balance, and he fell onto one knee on the seat of a pew. Berkeley spat blood and leaped to his feet, firming up his grip on his sword hilt.

"Hell's Bells, Dan," Bill growled. "What is this *about*?"

The dragoon drew his second pistol, pointed it at Bill, and fired.

Bang!

Berkeley had fired from a distance of scarcely fifteen feet, but the bullet went wide. That had to be Thalanes with his sly wizardry.

"Hellfire!" Berkeley cursed, and Bill flung his scabbard at the other man's face.

Berkeley bounded away. Bill lurched after him, around the pews and toward the altar. "It's no good, Dan! Honor—"

He stopped himself—where was his old lieutenant going?

Berkeley hopped the gate in the rood screen, swooped low and pulled the Bleeding Heart away from her work with his free hand. Bill stopped at the screen as Berkeley put his sword's blade to the nun's throat.

"In defense of innocence?" Berkeley snarled.

"Stay your hand!" Bill hollered.

"You're right, Will," Berkeley called, "it's no good. I have no choice. I've done what I've done, and now I'm leaving. If you try to stop me, I'll kill you...after I've killed *her*."

The Bleeding Heart's face was young and frightened, her hands and white habit bloodied from efforts to save the bishop.

"That's fine, Dan. I'm not your judge. Take your guns and go." Bill felt tired. Daniel Berkeley began edging his way to the exit. As the other man moved slowly out of the chancel and into the nave, Bill did him the courtesy of gathering up his pistols and presenting them to him.

Thalanes continued to bend over the Appalachee, who seemed to be stirring, and Jacob Hop sat on a pew, observing mutely.

Berkeley nodded, took his pistols and spat blood again onto the floor. "I'm leaving, Will." He backed away with his hostage, his eyes darting constantly between Bill and Thalanes. Bill kept his position.

Finally, Berkeley released the nun and darted out the front doors.

Bill scratched his scalp. He didn't like letting Berkeley go after he'd committed a murder, but, after all, it was a crime that Bill had come very close to committing himself, so he wasn't in a position to judge. He brushed aside the unanswered questions.

Bill also set aside for later a sharp word to his apprentice, who had sat out the entire fight.

For now, he had an old friend to catch up with. Hopefully this one wouldn't try to skewer him. Bill collected his pistols and headed for the altar.

As Bill approached, Thalanes and the redhead finished straightening the bishop's robes and folded the dead man's hands over his chest, then stood. In death, at least, the bishop didn't *look* like a gangster; he looked like a nice old man.

Bill was glad he hadn't killed him. He was sorry the bishop was dead.

"Thalanes, you little addict!" he called to his friend. "Hasn't your gut thoroughly percolated yet?" He extended a hand in greeting, but Thalanes didn't take it. There were tears in his eyes.

Bill cleared his throat uncomfortably.

"I'm Calvin Calhoun," the red-haired man offered, and shook Bill's hand. His eyes, too, were red with sorrow. "Jest plain Cal, you can call me."

"William Lee," Bill said. "Bill."

"I reckoned so," Cal said. "We come down from Nashville a-lookin' for you."

"Berkeley murdered Bishop Ukwu." Thalanes spoke like a medium in a trance.

"Yes, he did," Bill agreed. "I thought Berkeley might be with you, but I gather from your choice of verb that you disapprove of the man's action."

Thalanes glared at Bill with a distraught eye. "Why would I kill Chinwe Ukwu? He was my friend, and he was a saint!"

Bill shrugged and looked at his feet awkwardly. A saint? Was it possible he had been mistaken about the bishop? "I'm sorry, I didn't know. This has...this has been a terribly strange time for me, old friend."

Thalanes grabbed Bill by his shoulder. "There's no time for this. We have to get Sarah, and get out of here."

"Who's Sarah? Hell's Bells, Thalanes, what's going on?"

Thalanes dug his fingers into Bill's flesh and looked him in the eye. "Sarah is Hannah's oldest child, the one I hid. Her life's in danger. Berkeley and the Blues, among others, are pursuing her. She's an innocent girl in danger, Will, and she needs your help."

Honor in defense of innocence.

Bill smiled.

Sarah could hear Obadiah's men in the hall outside, asking about the screaming. He sent them away with the curt disclosure that his 'informants' had known nothing after all, and then, Sarah's urgency setting their pace at a gallop, the three of them ran downstairs and outside.

"I've got an 'orse!" Obadiah grunted, but Sarah ignored him, hitching her skirt up and running. Visions of the black worms in the corners of the Sorcerer Hooke's eyes flooded her mind. Obadiah and Cathy followed, stumbling and cursing.

Fear cracked a loud whip behind her.

At the Place d'Armes she hesitated. People streamed out of the cathedral's doors, frightened and yelling for the gendarmes.

King Andy Jackson grinned at her from his cage above the scattering mob.

Sarah steeled herself for the worst.

"He's dead! They shot the bishop!" a heavy man in an apron yelled as he rushed past, and her blood curdled in her veins. She imagined cheerful, charming, generous Bishop Ukwu, wounded or maybe even dead, and she broke into a run.

Obadiah grabbed her elbow and held her still. "Bide, poppet. We wot not what 'appened, an' it ben't safe for you. Let's 'ide a minute, bide an' see."

She knew he was right, though it galled her. "*Facies muto,*" she muttered, and though she felt it drain her strength to its dregs, she was satisfied to see Obadiah's and Cathy's faces change, and then Obadiah chuckled.

"You be sharpish, sure enough," he said. "No wonder we ain't ever found you."

"I ain't waitin' long," she warned him. "Jest a minute, and then I'm a-goin' in. Devil's on my tail, Obadiah Dogsbody, and iffen you look behind you, you jest might see he's on yours, too."

"Aye, poppet."

They waited just a minute, as she'd sworn, but that minute lasted forever, and Sarah felt an itch between her shoulderblades the entire time, as if the Sorcerer Hooke and Black Tom Fairfax were standing behind her.

What was happening inside? The wait was rewarded when the cathedral's front doors opened and spewed out one of the Philadelphia Blues, naked sword in his hand.

"'Erne's blood and damn me," the Englishman muttered.

"He's one of Angleton's men? The Philadelphia Blues?" Sarah asked.

"'E be Daniel Berkeley," Obadiah whispered. "'E be the bloody *Captain* of the Blues. 'E'd gone missink this mornink. What be 'e doink 'ere, then?"

Sarah waited until Berkeley had passed and then she charged for the cathedral's front doors.

She crashed through a few steps ahead of Obadiah and Cathy, pushing past a bloody white apparition who shoved her way out the doors at the same moment, and whose gory nun's habit threw fuel onto Sarah's already blazing bonfire of fear.

She hesitated halfway down the nave of the cathedral. The bishop lay on the floor, straight and stiff, smeared in blood, at the foot of the altar like some completed sacrifice.

Thalanes and Cal stood above him, talking with a third person she didn't recognize, a large, big-chested man in a red coat, with long black hair flowing out from under a battered black hat, armed with a sword and pistols. Off to one side lounged a small blond man; he, too, was armed, with a long blade belted over his shoulder.

She didn't mean to, but found she was weeping as she ran up, crossed the rood screen at a small gate, and threw herself on the body of the bishop.

"He's dead, Sarah," she heard Cal say, and he tried to pull her away.

Bishop Ukwu was bloodied, but could they be sure he was dead? Sarah raised her eye patch and turned her Second Sight on the bishop, hoping to see a glimmer of white light in him.

He was cold and dark.

"Berkeley killed him," Thalanes said, kneeling to help her up. "It was murder, and I don't know the sense of it, but it's done. We need to get you out of here. This is Sir William Lee."

Thalanes was presenting the big-chested man, but Sarah looked beyond him in astonishment at the other stranger. Through her normal eye, he was a plain, tousle-haired, blond man, disheveled and dirty in knickerbockers and buckled shoes, with a sword hanging incongruously on his back.

With her Second Sight, on the other hand, she saw something completely different. A white figure, a normal man, a son of Eve, sat crouched in the blond man's place, but the white figure's hands and mouth were bound with glimmering green, and his eyes were wide with wonder and fear. Above him, around him, towering over him, was a completely different being. It was green, it shone and throbbed like the Mississippi, and though it was humanoid, its head was the head of a gigantic crested bird.

"Satan on a stick," she heard Lee mutter, and she couldn't have agreed more. "Cathy?"

"Sir William," Cathy Filmer said, "I'm so pleased to see you well. Your stick aside, I hope I have not just heard you refer to me as *Satan*."

Sarah forced herself to act as if she hadn't seen the mysterious green figure. She slipped her eye patch back on, returning to the conversation before the altar.

Sir William smiled. "Never, ma'am." He bowed to Cathy Filmer. "I beg you to pardon an old soldier his rough expressions of surprise."

"Why's *he* here?" Cal jabbed a figure at Obadiah, who shambled up to the rood screen looking bashful, his travel-stained black tricorner hat held by the fingertips of both his hands.

"I'll explain," she said, "but not right now. We have to get out of here this very minute—the beastfolk have been killed, and the Lazars are in New Orleans." As she spoke, she heard the distant *click* of the cathedral's front doors swinging shut.

"Too late," Thalanes said darkly.

Sarah spun and looked—at the far end of the nave stood two men whose names she had heard as history and folk tales all her life, men who had died and been raised by a fell power to pursue her.

The Sorcerer Robert Hooke and Black Tom Fairfax.

Undead slaves of Oliver Cromwell, the Necromancer.

The Lazars.

"Jerusalem, Sarah, is they any feller I don't
have to compete with for your attention?"

———⊰•⊱———

CHAPTER NINETEEN

"Father!" Ezekiel heard Captain Berkeley shout, and it snapped him out of his thoughts. He turned from the fetid alley down which he had been peering to see Berkeley, mounted on a skittish horse in the middle of the street. The downpour spouting off the front of the dragoon's tricorner hat made him look like a gargoyle.

"I found her!" Berkeley shouted.

"Where have you been?" Ezekiel resented Berkeley's disappearance without notice, or least without decent, intelligible notice.

Berkeley and pointed down the street. "Your Witchy Eye, Father! Fate favors us this morning—I saw her little monk at the cathedral, the St. Louis on the Place d'Armes!"

Ezekiel wheeled his own horse around, directing it the way Berkeley indicated. "Why didn't you take him?"

"He wasn't alone, Parson," Berkeley spat out. "Gather any men you can and get to the cathedral! I ride for the barracks!"

Ezekiel wanted to object that he didn't take orders from Berkeley, but he knew Berkeley was right, and before he could think of anything else to say, the captain had plunged off into the rain.

"Beware, Will," Thalanes said. "They're Lazars. Walking dead. One of them is a sorcerer. And you should know that I'm almost drained already, and am unlikely to be very much use to you."

"I'm out, too, or near enough that I won't be throwing Franklin

361

bolts around." Sarah grinned, trying to communicate a confidence she didn't quite feel.

Sir William seemed to be taking control of the tactical situation, which eased some of the weight off her shoulders. And though she'd only just met the man, he gave the impression of having enough blunt courage for the entire party.

"I got silver bullets," Sarah heard Calvin offer, and that reminded her of the knife in her own belt. She gripped its hilt for comfort, careful not to touch the silver.

"How many?" Sir William asked, holding out a hand, and Cal passed him the lot.

"Jest the seven. I made eight, but kept one loaded in the Elector's rifle."

"Seven is a lucky number, suh," Sir William observed. "Not that I wouldn't rather have one more."

Sarah could see Hooke and Black Tom pacing slowly up the nave and two more Lazars standing by the door in one transept. They must be moving slowly so as to coordinate their attack. There had to be two others, somewhere. She made out now a detail she had missed in her visions, that all the Lazars' feet were bare and that long gnarly nails grew forward from each white toe.

"I count four of 'em," she called, "and they oughtta be six."

"There be two more in the apse, poppet," Obadiah responded.

"*Poppet?*" Cal asked.

"These are half-inch balls," Sir William noted regretfully, "too small for any of my pistols. What did you cast them for, Cal, a hunting rifle?" He set the bullets down on the altar.

"The Elector's rifle's got a half-inch bore," Cal answered, squinting suspiciously at Obadiah out of the corner of his eye, "only it's at the bishop's, and I find I can't run a-gittin' it jest now."

I would not shed unnecessary blood, the Sorcerer Hooke said-thought. *Surrender the Penn child to me, and in return I shall give the rest of you your lives.* Sarah could tell by the looks on the others' faces that they all heard him. He and Black Tom Fairfax strode up the aisle in the center of the nave, shoulder to shoulder in quiet menace.

"You, suh, can go straight back to Hell!" Sir William drew his sword. Sarah wished she could radiate that kind of charisma.

But what could one aging soldier do against the Necromancer's pet sorcerer and his entire undead gang?

Black Tom drew his famous short sword.

Sarah saw Cal staring at the altar; what was he looking at?

"I have a different proposal," the small blond man said quietly, and in an unfamiliar accent. The Lazars stopped in their tracks.

"Jake," said Sir William, "if you have a minor cantrip up your sleeve that's effective for banishing the walking dead, now's the right time."

"I will do better than that." The man he called *Jake* stood and faced Sarah.

Sarah tried not to look at him. "What do you want, Jake?"

"Sarah Elytharias Penn," he addressed her, "I will incinerate these troublesome Lazars, I will strike dead your Captain Berkeley and all his men, and I will take you away to my hall, where you will be safe and worshipped as the queen you are.

"In return, you must marry me."

Stunned silence filled the cathedral.

Sarah considered the man's two auras, and the great crested heron-headed creature she knew him to be. She remembered the worms swarming in the eyes of the Sorcerer Hooke and the groping hands of the spell he had unleashed upon her. This man—this *being*—might save her, might save them all, and he even seemed to want to save her as a queen.

But as *his* queen.

Could she surrender her freedom? Any man she married would become a factor in her decisions, but to agree to marry someone—some*thing*—this powerful was a devil's bargain, and might mean the complete surrender of her autonomy.

Was the devil worse than Robert Hooke and Black Tom Fairfax, and the Necromancer who must lurk behind them?

"Jerusalem, Sarah," Cal muttered, "is they any feller I *don't* have to compete with for your attention?"

She laughed at Cal's wisecrack. "You're the Heron King," she said to the blond man. "Your servants Grungle and Picaw died for me, fighting these creatures, and I am grateful."

The blond man shrugged. "They died for *me*, as others have, and as many others yet will. You have guessed who I am, or almost."

"Almost?" Sarah asked.

"I am Simon Sword," the man said. "Together with my father, I *was* the Heron King, as together with my son, who was my father, I *will be* the Heron King."

Sarah let this information sink in. It resisted easy analysis, but it sounded like reincarnation to her, and the dynastic politics of gods. It didn't make her any more interested in marrying the creature.

She considered her words carefully.

"I am flattered by your offer," she told him, "and I look forward to further entertaining the possibility when I am come into my kingdom."

Simon Sword laughed. "You have a keen mind, Sarah Elytharias Penn. I hope you survive long enough for me to propose again."

He sat back down.

"Jake!" Sir William snapped peevishly. "Your treatment of my queen is unbecoming of a gentleman."

"Is it?" Jake asked.

"I am amused by your oddities, suh," the cavalier growled, "but now is not the time—I *demand* your assistance!"

The man who had identified himself as Simon Sword smiled gently. "Friend Bill, you should not mistake me for a child of Adam, with human affections and loyalties. Do not force me to kill you."

Sir William looked stunned.

The Lazars resumed their advance.

"Ain't they supposed to be guns here?" Cal asked. He was looking at the altar again.

"What guns?" Cathy asked him.

"The Lafitte pistols, the ones as drove old Andy Jackson out of town back in eighteen and ten. I heard tell over and over about guns on the altar, only they ain't here."

The Lazars moved closer. The four nameless undead drew pistols, as did Obadiah Dogsbody.

Cathy pointed above the altar, and Sarah saw two pistols, mounted on a gold frame.

"Ha!" Cal clambered up on top of the altar in his muddy moccasins. "Sorry 'bout your table, Lord," he muttered. "I know this ain't polite."

"Cal," Sarah called to him, drawing her silver letter opener, which suddenly felt small and useless. "What're you doin'? We need you!" Her companions backed with her into a loose circle around the altar, facing outward.

"Checkin' the bore of these here guns," he called back, "and hot *damn* if they ain't half inchers!" He dropped lightly to the floor and pressed the weapons into Cathy's hands.

"I'm not much of a shot, I fear," the tall woman said, "but I can certainly load them."

Cal drew his tomahawk.

Obadiah fired first, one gun and then the other. The reports of the shots were loud and echoed long, and the bullets bit into the flesh of the foremost of the Lazars advancing from the apse. They chewed open little black holes in the flesh of his face and chest, but no blood flowed and the impact only rocked him back, slowing his forward progress a moment.

Sarah saw in her mind's eye the coming return fire, and she reached deep into her being for energy. She found a tiny handful and she molded it quickly into a defensive spell Thalanes had taught her, one of his favorites. She thought for a moment about material components and wished she carried a few bullets in her pocket.

"*Pallottolas averto,*" she whispered, brushing away the bullets with her hand before any of them had left the barrel.

She felt woozy as the spell's energy flowed out of her, and took a deep breath. Turning to check on the progress of her enemies, she caught, ever so slightly and far away, the gaze of the Sorcerer Hooke.

A mind-presence crushed down upon her, and in her weakness she almost fell over. *Die thou, die, die*, she heard Hooke's rattling whisper in her mind's ear, and she felt a cold hand wrapping its clawed fingers about her heart to squeeze it. Other hands seemed to grope her; the cathedral wavered and faded from view, as if a sheet of water had fallen over it.

She had no strength to resist, and breathing became difficult.

Gunfire erupted in the church. Sarah wished she could see the results, but her vision was blurring. Hands closed in around her and pulled her slowly from her friends.

"Thalanes!" She fell to her knees, dropping the knife.

Die thou! Die! Die!

Then Thalanes was there, and his gentle hand that smelled reassuringly of coffee was prying the cold talons from Sarah's soul. Sarah took a deep breath. Her vision became crisp again.

One of the Lazars was bearing down on her.

Cal reached out to try to grab him as he barreled past, but

Calvin and Obadiah were engaged in a fight with the other three Lazars—his grab missed, and the Lazar rushed at Sarah with a dull grin on his white lips and a knife in his hand.

Sarah held up the white ash staff to ward him off—

bang!

The Lazar fell back to the floor. He shrieked and howled, clutching at his hip where the bullet had struck him, and thick black ichor gushed from the wound. He rolled back to his feet again and lunged forward topsy-turvy, knife first.

Sarah looked up and saw Sir William looming over her, holding one of the Lafitte pistols in his hand—

bang!—

he fired again, and this second shot hit the wounded Lazar in the face, bowling him over in a shower of black liquid and leaving him still on the floor.

"Again, Mrs. Filmer!" Sir William's voice was incongruously merry. He handed the woman the smoking pistol and took up his saber to meet the charge of Black Tom Fairfax.

Sarah shot a look at Thalanes; strain was visible in the contorting muscles of his face, but she no longer felt the Sorcerer Hooke in her spirit, and the hands were gone, so the monk was at least fending off the attack, if not doing more than that. She considered rushing Hooke in a physical counterattack, but he was still far down the nave, and her other friends were in mortal peril right beside her.

She dropped her staff and picked up the silver knife.

Black Tom came in low and fast, the tip of his long knife pointing up and a fierce leer exposing yellow teeth, bright against the white skin of his face. Bill would have liked to take his time, playing to his advantage of a longer reach, but there were enemies at his back too, attacking his queen.

Bill swung for the head.

Black Tom didn't slow down to defend, he only hunched his shoulder slightly, to take the blow there rather than in the neck. Bill's saber bit into the dead flesh reluctantly, as if into hard wood, and then twisted out, and the Lazar was unfazed.

Fortunately, Bill's blow knocked the dead man slightly aside, so his knife thrust missed Bill's heart and instead the blade skidded along his ribs, slicing coat and skin with its razor edge.

Bill gasped and clamped his arm down over the Lazar's elbow, grabbing him by his lank hair and pinning the dead man.

If the advantage of reach was gone, Bill would play to size and strength.

The Lazar reeked of decay, and Bill looked into his eyes to find them white and milky, but writhing with small black worms. Corruption tainted his foul breath.

Bill battered Tom Long-Knife uselessly in the jaw with the basket hilt of his saber, then hacked again at the dead man's neck, pounding the base of his sword-blade at the bunched muscle. He scored the skin but barely bit into the flesh, and after a second, similarly futile blow, and a third, he stopped.

He needed a better weapon.

He punched Black Tom in the face again and pulled his hair back at a more extreme angle to keep the Lazar distracted. What else could Bill attack with? He looked around desperately. Shouldn't there be some silver on the altar? The dead man's feet kicked at the stones below him as Bill hit him again in the temple.

Bill was stronger than the dead man, but soon he would tire, the pain in his ribs would bleed away his strength, and then the calculus would shift to Bill's distinct disadvantage.

There *was* something on the altar, toppled and plaintive among the Appalachee lad's muddy moccasin prints. It looked like a little pyramidal box, and it had a dull gleam that might be silver. He punched Tom again. The box wasn't sharp, but it was pointed on top.

He punched the Lazar in the throat, then looked down—

and found himself looking into the barrel of a pistol.

Damn.

Bang!

For a split second, Bill knew it was over, and he was going to die, his skull blown into fragments by a low-down snake, failed rebel, and traitor who had died, throat slit with his own knife, over a hundred years earlier.

But Black Tom missed.

Astonishment registered on the dead man's face, but Bill didn't stop to check the horse's teeth. He tossed his saber in the direction of the altar and whipped off his trusty hat with his free hand.

Tom pummeled him twice in the shoulder with his empty pistol, and then Bill crammed the hat down over the dead face, smashing it on as completely as he could and grimacing at the pain that lanced into his injured arm and side.

He dropped the dead man and sprang out of reach of his darting knife, leaping toward the silver object on the altar.

No doubt Black Tom had missed him because of his lucky hat. Every soldier needed a good lucky hat.

Cal kicked himself for not going with the lariat.

He could have at least roped one of these rotting white bandits into immobility, which would have evened the odds. Instead, he parried the attack of one and then the other with his tomahawk, circling and dodging to avoid being caught between them. It was like playing at Indian Fighter with the Calhoun younguns, and Cal was the only Indian against a large troop of John Smiths and Daniel Boones. Only these Daniel Boones weren't just armed with withies, and Cal desperately wanted to smash their brains in.

But all he could really do was dodge. He didn't dare put away the war axe now, and he was pressed too hard to have any opportunity for counterattack.

He'd hoped briefly that the Englishman—what in tarnation Sarah was thinking bringing along Father Angleton's pit bull, he couldn't imagine, but Dogsbody did seem to be fighting on their side—might somehow dispense with the single Lazar he was facing and help Calvin, but Obadiah grunted and swore a stream of bitter curses Calvin didn't recognize as he struggled with the dead man, arms locking and blades flashing in an off-kilter dance about the choir's seats.

Cal would tire, he would slip, he would put a foot wrong, and it would be over. He needed to get one of them down, now, or he was a dead man.

One Lazar overextended himself in stabbing for Cal's stomach, and Cal took his chance. He clubbed that corpse aside with the handle of his tomahawk, knocking away his knife in the process, and whirled, swinging with all his might for the center of the other Lazar's chest.

Thwack!

The sharp war axe struck home, sinking a couple of inches into the cold flesh of the dead man. The Lazar stumbled back, then lurched forward, stabbing at Cal's head. Cal caught the attacking knife arm by the wrist with his hand, stopping the blow with an effort, and smashed his elbow into the Lazar's face. The dead fellow grinned, and with his free hand clawed at Cal's eyes. Calvin caught the incoming claw and now held the Lazar by both his wrists, struggling to throw the dead man to the ground, but feeling himself forced inexorably down.

He couldn't take this much time, he knew he was vulnerable.

When would the pistols be loaded again?

Cold fingers closed around Cal's throat and teeth sank into his shoulder.

Bill scooped up his saber and grabbed the silver object on the altar. A *pyx*, he thought it might be called, and up close the peaked roof of the thing was disappointingly blunt.

He wheeled to face Black Tom Fairfax and blinked hard as his own hat struck him in the face. Bill threw himself back to avoid the blow he knew must be coming. The altar struck him in the kidneys and then he felt Black Tom's knife bite into his upper thigh, on the outside.

The pain seared him, but it was a wound he could live and fight with.

He could see again, his traitor hat out of his face, and he swung the pyx up just in time to deflect Tom's knife. This wasn't what he'd wanted the pyx for, though, so he punched with his saber at the dead man's weapon hand, attempting to move the blade aside and make room for a bludgeoning with the pyx.

He made contact; it felt like an awkward blow to Bill, but, to his surprise and satisfaction, Black Tom dropped the knife.

Bill swung with the pyx, and Tom stepped back from the arc of silver. His right arm hung still at his side as he dodged Bill's attack, hissing.

Bill stepped forward to press his advantage—*crunch*—his boots crushed something long and brittle.

Bugs. They've let bugs infest the cathedral. Bill didn't look down.

Calvin hollered as the Lazar bit into his flesh; Sarah felt terrible guilt.

He'd come all this way, had evaded Imperial officers, had fought demons in clay vessels, and now he was being killed by two walking corpses. And he'd done it all for her; he loved her, and she had refused to take his feelings seriously. She owed him better than that.

Whether his love had some origin in her hexing of him hardly seemed relevant now.

Sarah tightened her grip on the tiny silver dagger and leaped in. A better fighter than her might have made a tactical decision about which Lazar to attack based on position and relative strength. Sarah simply knifed the dead man closest to her.

It turned out to be the one in front of Cal. She stabbed with all her anger, plunging the sharpened letter opener through the rotten fabric of his jacket and into his back. Cold, wet, black ichor gushed out onto her hands and moccasins, and the Lazar broke his silence to howl wordlessly.

Wraaaaarooooooghh!

He spasmed, he twitched, and he sank to the floor, tangling up Sarah's feet and giving her a close look at the other Lazar's face, yellow teeth sunk into the flesh of Cal's shoulder, white eyes staring at her, black worms squirming and dropping in an obscene, wiggling dance onto Calvin's skin and into his loose shirt.

The white knuckles of the Lazar's hands writhed as he choked Cal; Cal threw an elbow back, but couldn't free himself, and his struggles were slowing.

Sarah strained to roll the downed Lazar over and recover her knife, but he was too heavy.

Cal gasped and choked, fingers pawing at the Lazar's hair and ears.

Sarah reached inside herself for power to try to cast a spell and found the well dry.

Cal was doomed.

Bang!

The Lazar choking Cal released him, hissing in anger and spinning to face a new threat. The shot had come from Cathy Filmer, who now calmly laid down one Lafitte pistol and took up the other.

"Are you well, Mr. Calhoun?" she called.

Cal sank to his knees and gasped, scrabbling to remove his tomahawk from the dead man Sarah had destroyed. It squeaked as it came out, like the sound an axe head makes when it's pulled out from being deeply embedded a log.

The remaining Lazar, black blood streaming down his side, jumped at Cathy.

Bang!

Cathy coolly fired her second shot. She hit the Lazar square in the chest, knocking him prone in gouts of his own dark ichor.

As Calvin staggered to his feet and recovered his breath, Sarah managed to extract her knife from the dead man. The twice-holed Lazar flailed in his own black, mephitic mess, and Sarah crawled over to him with dagger in hand. He stared up at her with white eyes, wormlets streaming down his cheeks and into his hair. He had once been a man. What had made him hate so much that he had turned to murder? What was worth so much to him that he'd been willing to make a pact with dark powers, to return from beyond the grave and attack her?

Or had he been forced into it? Was he a slave, like Tom Fairfax?

Or a willing accomplice, like Robert Hooke?

The dead man grinned at her mutely, and she shoved her dagger into his throat. Cold liquid spurted out, spraying Sarah and covering her hands. His eyes filmed over and went dark as his body spasmed, shook, and finally grew still. The worms twitched and wiggled around him and dried up before her eyes into crispy, twisted threads.

Sarah clambered to her knees and surveyed the scene.

Sir William dueled Black Tom Fairfax. He was wounded but seemed to have the upper hand. Obadiah wrestled with a Lazar, cursing obscurely; they had both lost their knives, and were reduced to battering each other, so the Englishman's face was bruised and bloody.

Were they winning? Was it possible they were winning? But where was Thalanes? She found him slumped against a column.

Thalanes looked bad. His eyes fluttered and sweat streamed down his face, though the church was chilly. He murmured, and she couldn't make out the words, but it sounded like an incantation. He was still fighting Hooke, and Sarah was filled with gratitude—this could have been her, and she would have been long dead by now.

She wanted to help him, but how?

Sarah tightened her grip on her silver knife and bent over. She shook the blade to clean it of the black ichor of the Lazars, rolled up the gray sleeve of his cassock, then pressed the flat of the knife to Thalanes's arms.

He groaned, and a red welt appeared where she had touched him, but he didn't open his eyes.

She pushed harder. The welt turned to blisters and he groaned louder.

Sarah rotated the knife blade and cut into his skin. Red blood flowed and Thalanes gasped, but he didn't open his eyes.

What, then?

Sarah stood. She looked down the long nave at the Sorcerer Robert Hooke, and she knew. Shaking Thalanes's blood from the silver dagger, she propelled herself, awkward and uncomfortable though it was, into a sprint.

Bill didn't know whether he could bludgeon the Lazar to death, but he was game to try. He smashed the pyx into the dead man's skull with a satisfying *crack*.

Tom Long-Knife hissed. He slashed with his blade, a blow Bill managed to turn aside, but only by a hair.

The Lazar still favored his right arm, leaving it hanging limp by his side. Bill saw no blood, even of that ugly black variety the Lazars had, and he wondered whether the Lazar suffered from some previous injury.

Bill hilt-punched Tom in the jaw to keep him guessing, then jabbed with the pyx. The Lazar hurled himself sideways to the floor, rolling and coming up with the knife in his left hand, stabbing again. Bill dodged with a slight shuffling backstep. His breath came in ragged gasps. How many more times would he be able to avoid the bite of Black Tom's famous blade?

Dying impaled on a weapon of historical significance was not an end to which Bill had ever aspired.

Truly ambidextrous men were rare, but a good fighter trained himself to be dangerous with both hands. That was especially true, in Bill's experience, of knife fighters, and Black Tom Fairfax was proving to be no exception. Setting his jaw, Bill closed in.

His feet stepped on something crunchy again, and he decided he should know what it was. He swiped at the dead man with his sword to create space between them, then drew back half a pace to throw a quick glance at the floor.

It was strewn with fingernails.

They were the long, yellow nails of the Lazar, neatly snapped off. *It sheds*, Bill thought in disgust. *Like a dog.*

"I find, suh," he said, "that the name Tom Long-*Knife* does not suit you so well as Tom Long-*Nail*. You, suh, are unkempt."

Black Tom hissed and lunged.

Bill stepped forward again to answer the attack, ignoring the *crunch* of the Lazar's fingernails underfoot as he parried Tom's short sword and checked the undead's body with his own.

Someone rushed past them, behind the Lazar, springing up the aisle of the nave.

It was his queen.

Bill glanced toward the end of the nave to ascertain where she was going, and saw one more Lazar, one that hadn't joined the fight and had instead hung back, fingers flickering.

Hell's Bells, had she been trapped in some bit of arcane jiggery?

Black Tom stabbed him. The knife took him in the forearm and Bill dropped the pyx, shouting in startled pain, but when he slashed with his saber Tom was gone, turned and already running after Sarah up the aisle.

The young red-haired Appalachee, Calvin, came sprinting after the Lazar, a coiled leather rope flapping in his fist.

The dead man ran surprisingly fast, given the long toenails that clicked on the stone floor as he moved.

Nails.

Bill looked down at the floor again at the scattered fingernails, and up at the running Lazar, seeing now that the inert arm was nailless. He must have cut them off with his sword, when he'd hit Tom Long-Knife in the hand.

He could cut the nails off the Lazar's other hand, too.

He broke into a run.

Sarah charged the Lazar as if the Devil was on her heels.

Hooke saw her and raised his hand, pointing a gaunt finger at her. He hissed and Sarah tripped and fell, losing her grip on the knife and seeing it clatter away across the floor.

Curses and death magic, Thalanes had warned her. But the knife was silver; how had he been able to affect her with any spell?

She had been holding it by its wrapped hilt. She should have been holding it by the naked metal—it would have irritated her skin, but might have given her some degree of warding against Hooke's hex.

Or maybe not. He'd hexed her feet, after all, not her hands. Besides, she'd tried to free Thalanes from the hex that trapped him with her silver knife, and to no avail. Maybe the Sorcerer's spell was too powerful. Maybe she needed a bigger piece of the metal. Maybe the connection between Thalanes and Robert Hooke was localized somewhere in particular, and to terminate the gramarye she would need to identify a precise place on the monk's body to touch with silver.

Sarah still had a lot to learn.

She scrambled to her feet, and then heard the running footsteps behind her. She turned, just in time to see the Lazar Tom Fairfax raise his knife hand over his head—

and Black Tom fell backward to the floor and skidded past. He was carried by his own forward momentum, but his body was no longer under his own control. She saw the lariat looped around the dead man's neck, saw Calvin pulling on it, and realized he had again saved her life.

She scrambled after her knife, pushing a hand down under pews and feeling around on cold stone to try to find the weapon.

Black Tom groped after her with an empty hand, nails scratching on the floor and fetid air hissing through his lips. The nails scratched at her leg and Sarah pulled away.

A heavy boot came down on the Lazar's wrist, putting a sudden end to the groping.

Sarah looked up and saw Sir William, saber raised above his head. "I wonder, suh," the Cavalier said to the dead English rebel, "how you cared for your appearance in life."

The Lazar twisted but the boot and the lariat held him firm.

"Did your mother not teach you that a gentleman trims his nails?"

The sword flashed as Sir William swung it, and brought up a stream of blue sparks as it crashed to the stone, not chopping off the Lazar's hand, but slicing neatly through all his nails.

Tom Long-Knife hissed and tried again to roll away, but Sir William kept his weight on the dead man's now-limp arm. Calvin tightened the slack in the lariat and pulled it in the opposite direction, and together the two men effectively anchored their foe.

"Now, Calvin," Sir William said in his slow drawl, "I believe we may deal with this last piece of carrion at our leisure."

Beyond them, at the front of the nave, Sarah saw the main doors to the cathedral abruptly swing open. To her dismay, Ezekiel Angleton stepped in, followed by a contingent of the Philadelphia Blues.

"Haven't we all?"

———⟫•⟪———

CHAPTER TWENTY

Obadiah was getting tired. The bare-knuckle boxing matches of his youth and the wrestling polls at county fairs he attended in the New World produced plenty of hard men to fight, but they were still *men*; if you broke a man's nose, or his finger, he stopped the match and, like as not, you won the purse.

This walking corpse just kept coming.

Obadiah had early on ripped the knife from the corpse's hand, but hadn't counted on losing his own broadsword when the Lazar smashed his fingers against a fluted stone column. Since then it had been brutish, animal combat, no quarter given and no dirty trick omitted, while guns went off and swords flashed around them.

The Lazar had smashed out one of Obadiah's teeth on the floor.

Obadiah had put a knee in the Lazar's crotch with all his weight behind it.

The Lazar had pulled two of Obadiah's fingers so far back they had broken.

Obadiah had gouged out one of the Lazar's eyes with his thumb.

It was during this last operation that Obadiah realized he couldn't win. Any Sunday Fair wrestler would have surrendered at the mere suggestion that a thumb was about to go into his eye, but the Lazar didn't flinch. Lying prone with the dead man's arms about his waist and squeezing, Obadiah dug one callused,

375

horn-nailed thumb into the writhing mass of black worms at the corner of the Lazar's eye, slid it under the blank, white, iris-less eyeball and popped the eye out. No fiber held the eye in place. It fell on the floor and splattered into a viscous gray puddle.

Still the Lazar squeezed.

"Wayland's petticoats," Obadiah grunted, "'ow in the 'Ell am I meant to put you down, you rottink bugger?"

The Lazar hissed, spraying the stench of death into Obadiah's face.

Obadiah grabbed a spent pistol and bashed the Lazar repeatedly in the face with its butt, cursing all the while, until the Lazar released him to grab the gun.

Obadiah rolled away and climbed to his knees. Sarah was running from him now, toward the front of the church. The Appalachee redhead was in motion too, and the big gunfighter, but he had no time to try to see what the commotion was. He launched himself at his foe, knocking the other man forward and wrapping his arms around his neck and shoulders.

"Time to give over, you wee manky git!" Obadiah swung the Lazar's forehead against the stone floor with all his weight and strength.

Smack!

The Lazar grunted and pulled his leg in, getting one knee on the ground under him. This feat would have caused any ordinary man serious pain from Obadiah's hold, but the Lazar did it, snorting like a boar.

"I wot not what you be, mate," Obadiah grunted, still casting about for some kind of effective weapon, "but I 'ope I never see your like again."

His eye landed on one of the row of oil lanterns lighting the chancel from white-painted hooks set in the stone walls. Springing from his knees, Obadiah cracked the Lazar's head against the stone floor again—*smack!*—and then jumped to his feet, leaping for the lantern.

The Lazar was up instantly after him, and yanked Obadiah back with hands at his shoulders and then a cold forearm about his throat. The Lazar had him by the windpipe and was cutting off his air.

Obadiah leaned forward, picking the Lazar off his feet and then running backward into a column, but to no effect.

His vision began to swim; Obadiah had only seconds left. Staggering forward, he grabbed a lantern off its hook.

The Lazar squeezed tighter, and Obadiah felt himself begin to slide into unconsciousness. He swung the lantern backward in a wide arc, smashing it toward his own back—

shattering the glass and spreading liquid fire on the Lazar.

Gwaaaraaaaraaaaraaaarghhh!

The ungodly howl pierced Obadiah's skull. The Lazar released him.

He tripped. His vision went black but air rushed into his lungs again, and he crashed to the floor.

Obadiah floated with no sensation for some time, and then he felt a searing, stinging pain on his back.

Roll over.

A woman's voice. Gentle.

Was it his angel, Sarah?

He rolled. As he did, the angel threw her wings about him like a great white shroud, and patted him with her hands, and he was comforted and floated, on the billowing clouds of heaven.

His eyes snapped into sudden focus with the realization that his back and shoulders and neck *hurt*. "Wayland's bloody balls!"

He lay on his back, in pain. His body was swathed loosely in the white altar cloth, stained dark red with the bishop's blood and now also splotched black here and there by the ichorous spray of the Lazars' wounds. Smoke rose from the cloth, and the stench of scorched flesh filled his nostrils.

A woman knelt over him. "You lit yourself on fire to kill that thing."

"Eh," said Obadiah, unable to force any more complex thought through his lips. To his disappointment, the angel of his delirium was not Sarah, but the woman he'd captured her with, the tall brunette Cathy.

Graaaaaaaraaaaaaaaagh!

He could still hear the Lazar's shriek, and light bounced off the chancel's columns like the glow of a dozen dancing torches. He struggled to stand, wincing.

"I've loaded the pistols again," she said, and he saw that she held one of the Lafitte guns in each hand. "But I don't see any of them left to shoot."

Had they won, then? Obadiah surveyed the cathedral.

The Lazar Obadiah had been wrestling was staggering away down the long nave of the cathedral, a twisting column of flame throwing great orange sheets of light against the walls. Sarah and the two men—the Appalachee and the Cavalier, he couldn't remember their names—both ran back toward him. The front doors of the cathedral were open, and Obadiah saw a familiar party coming in. His heart sank.

Ezekiel Angleton stood in the doors, at the head of a squad of the Imperial House Light Dragoons.

"You'll 'ave summat to shoot at soon enow, dearie," he promised Cathy.

"Pardon me, Mr. Dogsbody?"

"You keep those pistols, love." He threw off the shroud and collected his own weapons from the floor. "You'll want 'em by an' by."

"Why, Mr. Dogsbody," Cathy said, "you call me *dearie* and *love*. Are you playing the flirt with me?"

"Nay, ma'am," he said, fighting back tears from the pain scoring his back, "I be just playink the Englishman."

The sea above his head was infinite. The sea below his feet was infinite. All around him, infinite undulating sea of bile, and he died of drowning every second.

At least, Thalanes thought, *I'm the one dying, and not Sarah.*

Elsewhere, Thalanes felt other things. He felt a burning on his arm and he knew it was Sarah, trying to help him. He called to her and she couldn't hear, not through all the hands.

Cold hands scrabbled at his throat. Cold hands groped at his heart. Cold hands clutched at his face, his limbs, his torso. Everywhere, cold dead hands. They were the hands, the spirit-hands, the mana-hands, of the dead man, the Sorcerer Robert Hooke.

The hands had once belonged to others, and Thalanes caught wisps that hinted at faces behind the hands. Their expressions were sorrowful and angry, bitter and surprised. They were the faces of stolen souls, lives damned and converted into power to be consumed by the Sorcerer. Many of those faces must belong to Firstborn, but he couldn't tell those from the children of Eve. There were beastkind muzzles behind the hands, too, and those stood out, badger snouts and women with fox's ears and things that had human faces but glittering black, impenetrable eyes, like animals.

You won't have my life, he vowed, and he pushed back. His

heart strained and he heaved with all his soul, and he threw the hands off, at least for a moment. In that moment, he looked into a thousand eyes and saw their deaths, the great gulfs that separated them from their loved ones, even from their beloved dead, saw their permanent sense of betrayal and their undying grudge.

He didn't have a name for what he was seeing. Robert Hooke was some sort of soul-thief. This was damnable magic, malign craft worthy of the name *sorcery*, and the sort of engine in which Jock of Cripplegate must have ended.

If he succumbed to it, if he died this way, he would only add to the power of the Sorcerer and his master, the Necromancer, and put Sarah at even greater risk. It could be *his* face staring at her from the wall of lost souls, and *his* hands grabbing to pull her in and destroy her.

He must not succumb. He thrashed about, striking back with all his limbs and pushing with the energy of his heart, fighting to keep a small space about him free of the grabbing hands. He didn't have the strength to resist, so he tried to be clever, ducking around the hands instead of wrestling with them.

But there were too many, and he had nowhere to run.

Yield thou, Serpentspawn, Hooke spoke into his mind, and there, through the writhing hedge of hands, Thalanes saw him. Robert Hooke floated in the amber-colored infinite sea, long, curling red hair drifting about his head like a halo and a devilish beatific smile on his pale face. *Thou canst not win, Cahokian. Waste not the effort.*

Behind Robert Hooke loomed another presence, darker than him, and larger, but something that seemed only half-formed. A stink of decay permeated the infinite sea.

You keep bad company, Hooke, Thalanes told him. *I can win, and I will. Your master's heart is rotten and evil, and I'll see his schemes all spoiled.*

He fought to move his lips, to speak. He had a very important message he had to give Sarah, the last he would ever give.

The nave of the St. Louis Cathedral was a warm respite from the storm. Ezekiel blinked while his eyes adjusted, and then he realized that he was seeing the backs of people.

There was the back of someone wearing a long brown coat that fell all the way to the floor and a broad hat.

There was the back of someone rising to his feet, arms queerly hanging at his sides, also in a brown coat.

Beyond them, running away and therefore also showing him their backs were three more people, and one of them was a young woman who might be Sarah Calhoun.

Ezekiel would have liked to investigate carefully, and to act with great discrimination shown as to the different fates of innocent and guilty parties. That would have been consistent with the Covenant Tract's long history of careful and wise adjudication, and also with the dignity and legitimacy of the Penn family's place on the Imperial throne. But he had been wrestling for weeks, with the Witchy Eye, with Obadiah, with Berkeley, with his dreams, with the chevalier, and with the bishop. He was tired.

"Shoot them all," he said to Captain Berkeley.

Berkeley nodded. "Two rows!"

Waaaaraaararaaararghh!

A shrill howl erupted from the bowels of the church and an orange light flared. A flailing, running pillar of flame, a fire with a man inside it, rushed up the aisle of the nave in Ezekiel's direction. The fleeing figures broke past it and disappeared behind the veil of its brilliance into the vault of the church.

The Blues didn't hesitate. The eight dragoons at the front door (eight more had been sent to the apse and the remaining eight to one of the transepts, thus covering all three doors that the Imperial party had identified in its scouting) formed into two rows of four.

The front row took aim with their carbines and fired.

Bang!

The report boomed loud in Ezekiel's ears and stung his eyes with its acrid smoke. The shooters repeated the process twice more, each with his two pistols, then they knelt to reload and the row behind them began to fire.

Bang! Bang!

Ezekiel looked out into the rain and saw twenty-four gendarmes, the chevalier's men who had participated in the search for Witchy Eye. They had mustered in neat order and stood with the chevalier's harsh-faced and laconic Creole du Plessis at their head, maintaining formation and watching.

Fine, let them watch. Let them learn to respect Imperial discipline and power. Maybe that would make the chevalier think twice about his blackmail scheme.

The Creole left his men and walked up to join Ezekiel, standing by the open cathedral door. He said nothing, and watched.

Ezekiel turned again and looked into the cathedral, and was stunned to see the brown-coated man walking purposefully through the bullet fire in his direction. The man's appearance was shocking—he had pale skin, like an albino or even a corpse, his eyes were white and his fingernails were long and twisted. Under the rotting coat, his clothing looked a hundred years old, at least; he had a billowing cravat that had once been white, and was now a sort of putrid yellow, and a waistcoat and breeches that might have fit well into a country ball during the reign of King Charles Stuart.

He didn't react as bullets plowed into his body, only occasionally stumbling from the impact. Ezekiel was looking death itself in the face, and he took a step back.

The apparition stopped a few feet from Ezekiel and met his gaze with strange eyes, white, black around the edges. The black writhed, like a mass of bees on their hive. Ezekiel shuddered.

He pictured the face of his youthful love, Lucy Winthrop, with this undead specter's pallor upon it and such twitching orbs. He felt nauseated. This was foul magic indeed, and he despised Witchy Eye for having deployed such a fearsome agent.

"*Ani gibbor*," he murmured, quickly deploying his favorite all-purpose magic for rough situations, a spell that enhanced his own speed, strength, and toughness. He couldn't maintain it for long, but combat seemed imminent.

Ezekiel touched the hilt of his father's sword to cast his spell, and he heard as if in an echo the marching songs of the Order of St. Martin.

Words entered his mind in a voice Ezekiel didn't recognize, a voice like dry leaves rustling in the wind. *My lord instructs me to give thee passage*, the strange voice said, and Ezekiel knew somehow that it came from the corpselike man, though his pale lips were still. *Be thou grateful, Roundhead; today I am not required to kill thee.*

Did Ezekiel's face show the horror and confusion he felt? Why would Witchy Eye instruct her creature to let him past?

Was it *possible* this apparition was not in the service of Witchy Eye? The phrase *my lord* didn't seem to fit the Appalachee girl, even in the mouth of one of her creatures. Ezekiel shuddered.

I lose patience, priest, the mind-voice growled. *Thou art a distraction. Move thou, before I break my oath and kill thee.* Behind him came the man with arms hanging at his sides; he too was pale as a corpse, and had the same repulsive eyes.

"Let's go, Captain," Ezekiel said to Berkeley, and the albino and the numb-armed man both stepped aside to let the Imperials advance.

The third creature, the column of flame, thrashed limply about on the ground in a corner, the fire slowly dying.

The Creole and the chevalier's men stayed behind.

As he and Berkeley rushed down the aisle, Ezekiel felt the power of his spell course through him, and he longed for battle. Urgently. "Where are they? I saw them, but I was distracted. Where did the Witchy Eye go?"

Ahead, other contingents of dragoons entered by the side and from behind the chancel.

"This is a cathedral, Parson," Berkeley drawled, "so the only two likely possibilities are that they went down into the crypt or that they went up onto the roof."

Suddenly, Robert Hooke was gone, and so was the presence behind him.

The hands hesitated, and Thalanes took his chance. He pressed against a wall of inert fingers, cold and deathly, wiggled, and, having made a hole, he swam through it. Above him he saw light, a shimmering ball like the sun on the surface of the water—the infinite sea was abruptly finite above him.

He scissor-kicked his way toward the light—

and felt hands grab at his ankles.

Bill sent the ladies up first.

He didn't think there would be anything on the roof of the cathedral to attack them, and if there were, Cathy at least had the two Lafitte pistols, primed and loaded with silver shot. Even a gargoyle would have to beware the lady from Virginia.

Then Cal backed up the stairs, hunching his lanky frame over but never enough to avoid banging his head against the stone ceiling of the narrow staircase. He shuffled backward, kicking each foot heel-first up over the next high stone step, because he had his arms under Thalanes's shoulders to carry him, the monk's head slumped to one side in semi-consciousness, lips moving but no sound audible.

The burly Englishman came next, carrying the Cetean's feet, and he mumbled curses involving the anatomy of Wayland Smith, Herne the Hunter, and other members of the English pantheon too obscure for Bill to recognize them. As his ankles disappeared up the stairs, Bill saw that his neck and the back of his skull were burnt from ear to ear, and his coat was charred.

Bill respected the toughness of the man.

After the Englishman, Jacob Hop marched up the stairs without a comment and without an invitation. He smiled at Bill, and Bill glared back; Hop wasn't a Dutchman, Bill reminded himself, or maybe he wasn't *only* a Dutchman, he was *also* the Heron King.

Hell's Bells, Bill was living in a fairy tale.

It wouldn't have mattered who Hop was if Bill had remained alone. But Bill had responsibilities once more, he had a mistress and a position, and it mattered very much that Hop couldn't be relied upon and might betray them.

Though Hop wasn't helping their enemies and he wasn't interfering. He was deliberately refraining from doing anything at all.

Bill scowled.

And Bill's position wasn't Captain of the Blues. On the contrary, the Blues were marching in his direction with hostility, coming at him from three sides.

Bill would go last. He wasn't idling as the others went up, he was reloading and priming the four pistols now in his possession, his two long horse pistols and the hidalgo's brace of large bore mankillers, as fast as he possibly could. Which was very, very fast.

He couldn't defeat all twenty-four of the Philadelphia Blues, but he could put a little fear of God in them. Fear of God, and fear of Captain Sir William Johnston Lee.

Looking down at his feet, he saw drops of his own blood on the white stone floor, and he remembered the wounds Tom Long-Knife had inflicted on him. The pain in his ribs and his thigh flared sharply, and he felt old.

Eight Blues marched down the nave toward the altar in the wake of Daniel Berkeley. Bill's old lieutenant walked beside a tall man in a Martinite tabard and a black Yankee hat with a naked sword in his hand.

More dragoons came in through the transept door, and more

still picked their way through the devotional chapel in the apse. Bill stood out of sight near the altar, at the tight spiral staircase that descended into the crypt and climbed toward the ceiling, his guns all ready. He squinted at the Blues in the nave and recognized a few faces, men he had known as young, idealistic soldiers, and who were now grizzled veterans.

They might similarly recognize him.

He stepped out beside the altar and into sight, a pistol in each long pocket of his coat and another in each hand. The carved wood of the rood screen still separated him from Berkeley and his party, but it didn't impede visibility and he doubted it would give him adequate protection from flying pistol balls, either.

Bill wished, not for the first time that day, that he had a bottle of whisky.

"Atten-*shun!*" he bellowed in his best parade ground voice. Despite themselves, several of the Blues straightened, and they all stopped.

"What are *you* doing here?" the Martinite demanded in a shrill Yankee whine.

Berkeley looked wary. "Get out of the way, Will. This affair needn't concern you."

"Oh, but it does, suh." Bill wondered how much the man knew. And the Martinite—times had changed, indeed, for the Imperial House Light Dragoons to have a devotee of St. Martin Luther for a chaplain. "This affair and I have a long history together."

"Do you understand that I am on the emperor's errand?" Berkeley demanded. "Do you remember, *Captain*, what it was like to serve the empire? I will not be deterred or further delayed! Stand aside!"

"I think I know what it must be like to hold up the skirts of little Tommy Penn," Bill granted. "Do you know whom you are pursuing?"

"Kill him," snarled the priest, but none of the dragoons raised a weapon.

The Martinite resumed walking forward, though none of the other Imperials followed his lead.

"Yes," Berkeley said. "Do you? Do you know she is a pretender, that the emperor wants her apprehended so she can't raise a rebel flag against him?"

"She has a valid claim to the Penn land, suh," Bill said, "and if there is a Penn usurper, it isn't she." His eyes searched the

Blues, trying to discern how much of this information was new to them. They were an elite unit, but they were soldiers, and he guessed they had no idea whom they were hunting.

"That's a lie, Lee!" Berkeley shouted.

"I'm no liar, Dan. She's the Empress Hannah's daughter." The dragoons were too disciplined to gasp or cry out, but Bill saw looks of astonishment on several of their faces, and not just the old men who had served Kyres. "I stood outside the door at her birth with pistols in my hands to protect her and her mother. I'd have killed any man who dared attack her then, and I'll do the same today."

"Mad Hannah's daughter by whom?" The Martinite sneered.

Bill remembered the rain, fifteen years earlier, a storm much like the one that now dumped water on New Orleans. He remembered the three acorns lying in Thalanes's palm, then the chaplain of the Blues and soon to become Hannah's confessor in her confinement. He remembered the blood on them, Kyres's blood, which Kyres himself had smeared on the acorns with his dying breath.

He remembered Hannah's secret pregnancy, possible to keep secret because virtually no one was allowed to see her, shut out of the Palace as she was and hidden away in the old Slate Roof House above the Delaware River. He remembered three disfigured babies, smuggled out of her apartments in a warming pan. He thought of young Nathaniel, the boy with the puckered red ear folded to the side of his head, whom Bill had taken to hide, and Margaret, with the grotesque scabs on her scalp.

He'd ridden, alone and hard, to Johnsland, to deliver little Nathaniel to the earl because the earl was the empress's friend and at the time had not been fallen into madness. Bill remembered feeding the boy with the oozing milky rag that Thalanes had enchanted, singing soldiers' songs and campfire ballads to him on the road. He had only seen the other two children once, briefly, and Thalanes had taken the one with the disfigured eye to hide her.

That child was Sarah.

"By her husband, King Kyres Elytharias, suh," Bill said firmly. "Which makes her also the rightful Queen of Cahokia. If there is a God in Heaven, I'll see her restored to her family lands and the upstart Thomas Penn kicked to the gutters of Philadelphia to shake a begging bowl."

"Silence!"

The Martinite roared and jumped, and Bill was astonished to see him fly into the air and crash through the rood screen. He plummeted earthward again with sword raised, exploding toward Bill in a cloud of flying splinters.

Bill was surprised, but not taken flat-flooted. As the Martinite rushed through the air, Bill raised both the hidalgo's pistols and squeezed their triggers.

BANG!

Both shots blasted the flying priest in the chest. The simultaneous explosions shivered Bill's arms; the priest landed off-balance, and slipped.

Bill didn't wait to see what happened next. Spinning on the balls of his feet, he sprinted for the door of the staircase.

"Fire!" Berkeley yelled. A ragged volley of bullets plowed into the stone wall about the doorway, several pinging through the open door and ricocheting briefly inside the staircase.

Bill was already on the stairs, and though lead whizzed around him through the air, none of the balls hit him, and then he slammed the door shut behind him. He wished he had something to bar the door with.

Tucking one pistol into his belt and reloading the other, Bill began his slow backward climb up the stairs. The years of experience it took to reload a pistol under these circumstances, measuring quantities by feel alone, tamping in patch and ball without needing to look at them, were unbearable to think about. Bill felt *ancient*. The tightness of the passage made it easy for him to stay upright, and he had one of the pistols reloaded by the time the door below— now barely in Bill's sight around the curve of the spiral—opened.

Bang!

Bill shot at the head that peered through, hoping it was the Martinite, or one of the Blues he didn't know. The shot resounded gigantically inside the stairwell, and Bill didn't stick around to see who owned the head and whether he'd hit it—shoving the empty gun into his belt alongside its mate, he turned and charged up the stairs.

At any moment the door below would be thrown open, and guns would be fired after him up the stairs. In this spiral tube, even bullets that missed would ricochet and continue to be deadly, though with each impact with the wall, a bullet would lose some of its force; he needed to get far enough around the stairs that the coming fusillade would not tear him to pieces.

He'd gone three or four times around, these calculations pounding through his brain as his feet pounded on the white stone steps, each worn down into a deep rut in the center, when the attack came.

B-B-BANG!!!

The guns' explosion resolved into a single crashing boom that left Bill's ears. He felt the ricochet; bullets struck him in the back of the neck, and the calf, and the buttock, each feeling like a sharp stinging punch rather than a bite that tore flesh.

Bill stumbled, but didn't fall.

The stairs were built with sconces for candles to light them, but the sconces were empty, and the little light by which Bill made his way came filtering from above or streamed through slits in the wall that periodically opened into the main vault of the cathedral. Bill heard booted feet on the steps below him, but risked stopping a moment to peer through one narrow window.

Below, a group of the Blues crowded the chancel around the dead body of the bishop and pushed one at a time into the staircase. Other Blues jogged for the exits; they would be looking for a way up the outside of the church, or blocking off escape routes.

He turned and kept running.

Bang! Bang!

The occasional bullet sped past him or pounded into his back as he ran, and Bill was grateful for the slimming effect his stay in the *Incroyable* had had—two weeks earlier, he would not have been able to run up the steps. As it was, he reached the top bruised in the head (from the low ceiling), back (from the occasional flying bullet), and toes (from the stone steps) and very happy to see daylight, even if it was the gray light of a rainstorm.

He exploded onto the roof of the cathedral, rain blown sideways cooling the flushed skin of his face. The others must have reached the rooftop only moments before him; the Appalachee and the Englishman were laying Thalanes down under eaves, while the two ladies ran to the edge and looked down. Cathy held her skirt hitched up as if it were wrapped about something to protect it from the elements.

Bill stood in a small courtyard that covered the roof of one transept, ending in two steep shingled towers with slat-barred windows at the far corners. Stone-flagged paths led up around the edge of the roof of the nave, and down similarly around the edge of the apse.

"Find a way down!" Bill barked to Calvin, and was pleased to see that his command was unnecessary—the young man was already sprinting for the edge.

The Englishman joined Bill in the opening of the doorway where, sheltering from the wet, they both reloaded pistols. The sound of boots pounding on stone echoed up the staircase to Bill's still-ringing ears.

"My name be Obadiah Dogsbody," the Englishman said. "I should tell you I 'ave been a very bad man."

"I'm Bill, suh," Bill offered in exchange. "Haven't we all?"

The first face to charge up the stairwell belonged to a young dragoon Bill didn't know, and he and Obadiah fired at the same time, sending the soldier falling back into his comrades. Then they both stepped aside to avoid the inevitable response of a burst of whizzing lead.

Another dragoon, two more shots, and then Calvin was at Bill's shoulder, reporting that he didn't see a way down. "Lessen you're a pigeon," he grimaced, holding up a handful of gray feathers.

"What about that rope you carry on your belt?" Bill asked.

Cal shook his head. "It ain't long enough, not by half."

"Get down to the front of the nave, gentlemen," Bill told the other men, reloading. "Find some defensible spot, and *find a way down*, even if it means jumping or climbing down St. Louis's face. I'll hold them here as long as I can."

Cal and Obadiah ran to pick up Thalanes. "And wake the monk up!" Bill yelled after them.

Thalanes was their best hope. Without him, they couldn't hold out for long.

Another volley rocketed out of the stairwell and then, to Bill's surprise, the Martinite came scrambling up the stairs, sword in hand. He didn't know how the man was still moving, having taken two bullets to the chest. Maybe he was wearing armor under that tabard, or maybe he'd protected himself somehow with magic—his jump through the rood screen stank of combat wizardry.

Bill raised the hidalgo's loaded pistol and pulled the trigger.

Click! The gun misfired.

Behind the Martinite he saw the Lazar sorcerer.

"Hell's Bells," Bill muttered, hurling the pistol at his attacker and ripping his sword from its scabbard.

Thalanes was trying to say something.

Cold rain poured into his face as Cal and Obadiah slung him along the roof of the cathedral nave between them. Sarah didn't know if the motion had pricked Thalanes from his stupor, but he was formulating words.

Her heart pounded with panic, but she was still able to feel concern for the monk. He'd been a sort of father to her, at least for a little while. Besides, she didn't see how they could possibly escape the trap they were in without him.

Simon Sword seated himself on the cathedral rooftop's southern parapet, overlooking the Place d'Armes. Through Sarah's mundane eye, he looked like a wet, unassuming little Dutchman in brown knickerbockers and buckled shoes, incongruous sword on his back.

Should she have accepted his offer?

"Sarah," Thalanes croaked.

"Talk to me," she said. They reached the front of the nave and the walkway became another small courtyard between the higher nave, with narrow iron-latticed windows, and a shingled steeple tower rising at the very front of the church. The men set Thalanes down against the nave and Sarah took his hand.

His skin was cold.

"Kill me," Thalanes said, and her heart froze. He was delirious. His eyes were shut, he might be sleeping.

He couldn't mean what he said.

"I hate to do this," she heard Cal say, and she turned in time to see him bring his tomahawk down hard into the wooden slats covering the tower's windows. Pigeons exploded out from under the blow with a squeak.

"Listen," the monk murmured, his eyes fluttering faintly. "I'm a dead man. You can't let Robert Hooke take my soul."

Tears welled into Sarah's eyes. She remembered her vision of Hooke at the prow of the little ship sailing down the Mississippi, the hands that clutched at her, and her distinct sense that her soul had been in peril.

"I'll free you," she insisted.

Calvin smashed the slats again with a loud *crunch!*

Thalanes shook his head feebly. His body twitched and shivered on its bed of pigeon droppings and feathers. "Your father left you many gifts. You have his courage and his charisma and his gift for gramarye." He squeezed her hand as he said *gramarye*, and Sarah thought of the acorn she carried hidden on her person.

"It ain't over," she objected.

"You aren't strong enough to save me, Sarah," the monk mumbled. "I'm not strong enough to save myself. You must... you must kill me. For your sake, and for mine."

"I'll jest kill Hooke."

"No time." His voice sounded distant, and receding further away every moment.

"I don't think I can do it," Sarah said.

"Now, while he's distracted. Use... the silver... knife..." The Monk's lips stilled. He was white as chalk. White as a Lazar.

"Jerusalem." Cal peered through the hole he had smashed. "Iffen we had wings, I'd be havin' a much better day."

Sarah began to weep.

Clang! Clang!

She heard the clash of steel on steel and looked back along the path down which they'd come. She saw Sir William's red-coated back as he retreated slowly in her direction, sword flashing before him as he fended off some foe.

"They be on this side over 'ere, too," Obadiah called from where he stood looking up the far side of the nave's rooftop. He drew his sword and Calvin crossed the little courtyard to join him, war axe in his hand.

Sarah armed herself with the little silver knife and looked at the monk, shivering beneath her. The cross of leadership had fallen on her. She wanted to be the person who had the stomach, who was decisive enough to do this horrible, necessary thing, but she cringed from the task.

She wanted Sir William to take away the burden, but he was busy. So were Calvin and Obadiah.

Would it matter, anyway?

Would it make a difference if she did what he asked? However Thalanes died, he would be dead, and without him, Sarah didn't see how they could escape. Thalanes had always been clever, and he would know some spell that would get them off this rain-blasted rooftop, but Sarah was out of ideas, and she had no strength left for magic, in any case.

But by killing him, she might save his soul. She remembered the short moments she had had under the influence of the Sorcerer Hooke's baleful magic, the hands grasping her, the infinite uncrossable space around her, and the sense that she was in damnation's own clutches. She tightened her grip on the knife.

"I'll do it." She thought he smiled. She held the blade up to his exposed throat...

And still she couldn't bring herself to kill him.

The clashing steel and stomping boot sounds of Sir William retreating before the onslaught were close now, and Sarah trembled. On the other side of the rooftop, Calvin and Obadiah scuffled with someone she couldn't see. She heard all the noises, the yelling, but could make out no words. She floated in a tiny bubble that contained just her, the dying monk, and the silver knife.

She couldn't do it, it was just too brutal.

They would all die, and Thalanes would lose his soul to the Sorcerer Hooke.

Poor Thalanes. He had served her parents and saved her life, time and again from the moment of her birth until now, and she didn't have the strength to do this tiny thing that would save his soul.

"It is not too late," Simon Sword said in his strangely accented English. She turned to look at him, sitting calmly on the stone parapet, water running out of his hair in rivers. "I can save him, too. I can save you all. I will turn your enemies to dust and take you all from here. Only say that you will marry me."

He looked calm and human, almost handsome, and Sarah was sorely tempted. He could save them. She valued her freedom, she valued her independence, but did she value them more than she did Thalanes's life?

She hesitated, the knife trembling, and the sounds of combat closed in on both sides of her.

Why had she resisted Simon's offer in the first place? She didn't remember now. It must have been her own vile selfishness. Her personal freedom was not worth the death of any of her friends.

Ffffft.

Sarah heard the sound of tearing cloth.

But there was something else, she remembered. Something... something about Simon.

Something about the way he looked.

She pushed the eye patch out of the way and looked at the Dutchman, and the shreds of fog and fear bedeviling her mind fell away. Through her witchy eye she saw him loom tall, green, and dangerous over the imprisoned white soul of the little Dutchman. His heron-crested head leered down at her through piercing eyes, waiting for her answer, expecting a yes. Behind those eyes, though, was no human compassion, no human mind or heart. She couldn't trust Simon Sword; she feared him immensely.

"No," she whispered.

"Try this." The woman's voice seemed wildly out of place, until Sarah realized that she was still on the church rooftop, and Cathy Filmer, tall and glowing white in her Second Sight, was talking to her.

Talking to her and holding out to her a loaded pistol, covered in a strip of torn white cloth. One of the Lafitte pistols.

She took the gun and the little cloth that shielded it from the rain.

"It's loaded with silver," Cathy said.

Sir William backed into view, ducking a swing of his opponent's sword, and Sarah saw that he dueled Father Angleton. The priest moved fiendishly quickly, and where his long iron sword crashed into the walkway's balustrade or the wall of the nave it threw up stone chips. The Cavalier resisted his opponent with economy of movement, slipping back only as much as he had to, deflecting rather than catching blows with his saber. Sarah could see Angleton had been cut deeply several times and bled great red gushes, but still he came on in unstoppable rage. Sir William might be the better fighter, but he was injured too, bleeding from his side and his leg, and his breath came hard and fast.

Beyond the dancing white glows of Lee and Angleton she saw the dull dead aura of the Sorcerer Hooke. He showed concentration in his face, and he walked slowly, and she knew he was sucking the life out of her friend.

On the other side of the nave, Cal and Obadiah skidded back, forced onto their heels by several dragoons that crashed out onto the little courtyard, sabers weaving.

Thalanes jerked, his body quivering down its entire length, and she looked at him through her witchy eye. He was blue and, as she had told him, looked younger and more handsome to Second Sight than he did to her normal vision. Now, though, he lay wrapped in a cloud of black, a sinuous, serpentine coil of darkness that nearly enveloped him—only the lower half of his face was free of it. Within the coil, Sarah saw a multitude of crawling, pricking, stroking movements.

It had been Thalanes who had intervened, had saved her from the Sorcerer Hooke. Both times. She owed him this.

"Goodbye," she said, and then her voice caught in her throat. "I love you."

She snatched his satchel with its precious little sack of roasted coffee beans, slinging it over her own shoulder. Then Sarah Elytharias Penn pressed the muzzle of the pistol against Thalanes's temple.

"It ain't over," she said.

And pulled the trigger.

"My conscience may be less
metaphysical than yours, suh."

———⊷◦⊶———

CHAPTER TWENTY-ONE

The black coils looped around Thalanes's soul vanished, dissolving
in the rain. He kicked once, with both feet, and he was still. Just
for a moment, Sarah thought she saw a smile on the handsome
blue face of the aural Thalanes.

He smiled, and he exploded.

She knew the explosion would come and at the last moment
she had the presence of mind to open herself up. A blue ring of
mana-fire rolled out from his body and most of it flowed directly
into Sarah. The experience was like drawing energy from the ley
lines, only mixed in with the tingling power was something that
felt like love.

She was an empty cistern, and the heavens suddenly opened and
dropped a flood upon the land. The flood filled her, warmed her,
made her skin dance. She channeled energy into Thalanes's moon-
brooch as well, filling it. Still the flood came on, and she sucked
it in. She felt like a waterskin pumped too full. Her hair stood on
end, her skin prickled, her Second Sight focused into crisp clarity.

She dropped the pistol.

Angleton hesitated, perhaps feeling Thalanes's death, and Sir
William beat him back a pace or two.

Robert Hooke stood behind Angleton; he raised his hands
and closed his eyes. The blue light of Thalanes's aura blackened
as it touched Hooke, swirling tightly around the Sorcerer.

"Hooke," Sarah gasped, "stop him." She was trying to call to Sir William, but her voice was drowned out by the constant hammering of the rain. William didn't hear her.

But Cathy did.

The tall woman strode over behind Sir William, unheeding of the blades that flashed near her and the ringing of steel on steel across the roof. Just as the Sorcerer Hooke raised his hands to shape his spell, Cathy pulled the trigger of the second Lafitte pistol—

bang!—

and Hooke went stumbling back down the walkway, black blood spraying from his chest. Sarah saw the murk that had been his building spell wink out like a snuffed candle.

Cathy stooped beside Sarah to pick up the second Lafitte pistol. "Waste not, want not."

The wave of energy exploding from Thalanes's death was gone, and Sarah felt the crackle of surplus power within her. Her limbs twitched like autumn leaves in the wind. She needed something to do with it, before it hurt her. She looked at Angleton; could she get rid of her persistent pursuer? She saw Hooke, climbing to his feet, and several of the Blues behind.

She should get herself and her friends off the roof.

Sarah scraped up a handful of pigeon feathers in a wet plaster of gray excrement from the stones beside Thalanes and she spun in a circle, hurling them at her friends.

"*In aves mutamur!*" She willed together all the excess power playing on her skin and through her hair and lurking in the rain about her, channeling it through the pigeon mess and her words and into her companions.

With a cooing and a fluttering of wings, Sarah sprang up from the rooftop.

She was disoriented by the change, and the struggle in her brain translated into the frantic flapping of wings. The flapping pulled her away from the sea of slick gray stone, and the raging men.

Other pigeons rose with her. What would happen if the pigeons separated? What would happen to poor Calvin if the spell ended and he was two hundred feet off the ground above the Place d'Armes?

But the other pigeons followed Sarah.

Sarah's wings weren't the same as arms, but if she concentrated and focused on controlling her movements, she could fly.

Her flock struggled as she did, and they collided more than once in mid-air, but none of them fell.

They left behind the still, cold, smiling body of the Cetean monk.

They also left the blond Dutchman, but Sarah watched with a round, sharp eye as she beat away into the rain, and she saw the little man shimmer and disappear. A great crested heron rose in his place, lifting itself from the roof of the cathedral and swooping south over the Place d'Armes, heading for the Mississippi River.

Behind it, the heron left a sword clattering on the stones of the rooftop.

Shots were fired by the shrinking men on the cathedral, but they hit nothing.

And then the soldiers and the Lazars were gone, whipped away as Sarah and the other pigeons slipped into the gray cloak of the storm.

Ezekiel stumbled back down the steps. He was soaked and bleeding, but the injuries were minor. His combat magic had given him strength, speed, and resistance to bullet and blade, but the exertion left him so tired that now, with the fight over, he could barely walk.

He had lost the girl.

Who had transformed her and her companions into birds? Thalanes might have done it, the Cetean heretic had always been a better wizard than Ezekiel, but Thalanes was dead. He was fairly sure that Thalanes died before the flock of pigeons appeared and took flight. The girl herself had shot the monk, for reasons Ezekiel did not understand.

The girl must have done it. She must be a more powerful thaumaturge than he had realized.

Had Thalanes taught her?

And what about the blond man in knickerbockers who had gone off alone afterward, in bird shape—who was he, and what power did he serve?

Obadiah Dogsbody was now fighting for the little witch. Obadiah, with whose lack of faith and many mistakes he had been so patient, and on whom he had showered so much beneficence, had shown himself to be an ingrate.

Well, for every Judas there was a potter's field.

Ezekiel stopped in the chancel. He leaned to rest against the shattered remains of the rood screen—he expected to be forgiven for that damage, as he'd only done it in pursuit of the Witchy Eye. The light was diffuse and tinted, coming through large and elaborate panels of stained glass.

Ezekiel preferred the more austere Roundhead churches of his native Boston. Not that his people eschewed images, but they were more restrained, and a cathedral this size was likely to contain only some central image of the Savior, and maybe a painting or a statue of a single patron saint, like St. John Wycliffe of the Book or St. Cotton Mather, the great Matthean of the northeast.

But he had to admit that the images carved, painted, or glazed into church architecture served a useful teaching function.

Ezekiel looked up, and his breath was taken away.

It was as if he was instantly transported into the first chapters of Genesis and the glories of God's creation. From where Ezekiel stood he could see and interpret the whole story in the stained glass.

Here in the windows, for those who couldn't read or wouldn't listen to a homily, was painted a sermon about God's creation of the world, the wreckage that sinful Adam had made of it, and the central and eternal salvage work of the great Second Adam, the Messiah. Imagery from Job, Isaiah, and the Psalms had been worked in, so that on the First Day, Jehovah on his great white-winged charger smote the dragon Rahab in the watery abyss. Allegorical, of course, but it was in the Bible. And when God divided the waters from the land, Ezekiel saw the great four-legged Behemoth grazing beneath snow-capped mountains while its aquatic counterpart, nine-headed Leviathan, dove beneath frothy waves.

Thinking of Adam, he turned in the chancel to regard the stained glass depiction of the Fall. Adam and Eve were both portrayed as young people, which was right and proper—an older Adam might remind viewers of the wife of his youth, whom God disfavored. Eve had eaten her bite of the apple and looked mournful; Adam was reaching out, his white teeth showing in a smile, unaware of the sorrow that was about to be his. It was a good picture because it was a true picture.

Without warning, Ezekiel's vision spun out of control and he fell to his knees.

Was this fatigue?

But Ezekiel felt as if he were being called.

"Yaas?" He swallowed as much cold air as he could, but the world refused to stop turning. With an effort, he reached out to the naked altar, meaning to climb it like a ladder, but his legs wouldn't cooperate.

Then, suddenly, someone was there in the chancel with him.

Ezekiel found he could not look above the knees of the personage. Feet paced up to Ezekiel and stopped, feet clad in tall black riding boots. Ezekiel saw the boots and the mail above them, but couldn't lift his eyes any higher.

"Ezekiel Angleton," said the personage. The voice was sharp and unmusical and impossible not to hear, and it rang with authority. "Ezekiel Angleton, behold thou the Fall of Man."

Ezekiel looked to the windows, and again saw Adam reaching for the apple that had already slain Eve. Eve and Adam looked different, though, subtly. He thought he saw in the tall, long-haired Adam a reflection of himself.

And Eve was absolutely the perfect image of his lost Lucy Winthrop. Ezekiel choked back a sob.

Then he blinked, for the image was changing. Adam bit into the apple before Ezekiel's eyes, and then dropped it, and Ezekiel saw the head of a worm protrude from the fallen fruit. Now Adam had a saddened mien, and Ezekiel, astonished, wondered what would happen next.

And who was this giving him this vision? Was it the same source that had given him the dreams that had led him to New Orleans?

The worm succumbed first, shriveling and fallen from the apple to be lost on the garden floor. As the worm died, the apple was already rotting, and Ezekiel thought he could actually smell the pungent cidery tang of the withering fruit. That odor thickened and darkened, until Ezekiel was assailed all about by the cloying stench of decay. The green leaves of the trees in the Garden turned red, yellow, and brown, and the whole scene was suddenly autumnal and tinged blue with a chilly wind, harbinger of a bad winter.

"Stop this," Ezekiel muttered.

There was no answer.

"Please," he begged. "I know what happens."

Eve-Lucy and Adam-Ezekiel went together. His nose and ears grew longer in a bearded face, his chest sank and became hollow, his belly bulged out and fell, the fine muscles of his arms and legs died to nothing. Her breasts withered and drooped, the flesh around her eyes collapsed and became dark; Ezekiel whimpered. Both lost their teeth and their hair and the gleam in their eyes.

"Stop this, I implore you," Ezekiel said, louder this time. His own years weighed on him and he felt death approaching inexorably on the road, a dark presence growing closer by the moment. Lucy's loss rose above and behind him black and furious, an implacable angel of pain. He tried to turn his head to look at his merciless instructor, to learn who would want to pierce his soul with such withering knowledge and memories, but he could not move.

Green returned to the leaves in the Garden, and then autumn again, and then spring, and Adam-Ezekiel and Eve-Lucy still aged. Eve-Lucy succumbed first, but only by a hair's breadth, and both the first parents of mankind died in the same horrible way under Ezekiel's flinching gaze; they shrank and shriveled and the flesh fell from their bones until they collapsed, dead puddles of bone and corruption in a grove that flashed repeatedly from green to orange and back again.

"Stop!" Ezekiel saw in his mind's eye his own form, already beginning to lengthen in tooth and lose muscle, rotting into the ground like Adam's. He was horrified, though he knew he had no right to be.

Death was merely death; it was the common lot of mankind, and it was acceptable to grieve for the Fall, but nothing could be done about it, so one grieved while one was young and then learned to accept the world as it was.

Still, there it was, in his heart: fear.

As if responding to his secret thoughts, the sharp voice spoke to him. "Man dies by Adam's fall," it said, "but it was not ever thus, and it need not be."

Ezekiel felt cold.

He strained again to look at his interlocutor and could not; after wrestling against the impossible for long seconds, he let his gaze fall back to the floor.

"Are you an angel?" he asked, drained and weak.

"God sends angels," the voice answered, "but I am my own messenger, and the message is this: death is not necessary. It may be avoided, it may be ended, it is a curse that may be lifted. I have escaped death, Ezekiel Angleton, as may thou and, by the grace of God and through thine efforts, all the children of Eve."

The ambition and arrogance in the voice—Ezekiel could not

tell them apart—thrilled him. *Death is unnecessary* . . . could it possibly be true? He wanted to weep and he wanted to sing.

Wasn't it blasphemy?

"Christ . . ." he struggled to regain control of himself. "Christ is the resurrection and the life."

"Yes," the speaker agreed. "God has wrought a salvation that is glorious. I am but the finisher, seeking to work a more glorious salvation still."

More glorious? The finisher of God's work? Who was this person, who spoke in riddles that were both blasphemous and divine?

"I do not require thee to love thy fellow servant Robert Hooke," the voice shrilled, "but accept him, and thou shalt be rewarded."

Hooke? Ezekiel felt his eye drawn up and he craned his neck to see again the stained glass windows from his dog-like posture. The windows now bore a different image, a vision of the corpse-like albino wizard Ezekiel had encountered at the cathedral doors, and who had been on Ezekiel's heels in pursuing Witchy Eye up to the roof.

"Fellow servant?" Ezekiel croaked. "Is that why you give me these terrifying visions, sir? Would you have me for a servant? But I already serve the Order of St. Martin Luther, and His Imperial Majesty Thomas Penn."

The voice laughed, a harsh sound like bells being slammed against a stone wall. "Rest assured, Ezekiel Angleton, that a man may serve many masters. And thou, good fellow, hast long been in my service."

Ezekiel struggled. "In your service?" He thought again of the horrific apparition that had greeted him at the cathedral door. The Sorcerer Robert Hooke. "How can you employ such fiends, when you say you serve Heaven's ends?"

There was silence in response, and Ezekiel was left to answer his own question: death. Was not any means worth employing that would overthrow the grim specter of death hanging over every child of Adam from the moment of his or her birth? Was that not *the* great evil, to be defeated at all costs?

He nodded in submission.

"I do not claim to serve Heaven's ends," said the voice of Ezekiel's teacher. "I serve the ends that Heaven *should* have served."

"I . . ." Ezekiel felt slow of thought and of tongue, drained in his soul and shattered in his body. "I would serve those ends, too."

The discordant voice spoke again. "Then look now, and behold thy master!"

Ezekiel tried to rise from his groveling posture but could not. He turned his head to see the person to whom he had been speaking, the source of his visions. He saw a rather ordinary-looking man with a high forehead, long hair, and a tuft of beard below his lower lip. He wore black plate armor from neck to toe, the monotony broken only by his riding boots and a white neckcloth.

As Ezekiel recognized the man, though, it seemed to him that he saw, glowing dimly through skin that seemed almost translucent, a death's head in the speaker's face.

The source of his vision—and, Ezekiel now understood, the source of all his visions—was Oliver Cromwell. The Regicide. The Lord Protector of the Eternal Commonwealth.

The Necromancer.

Ezekiel groveled. "But I don't understand. How can you end death? And what do you want with the Witchy Eye?"

The Sorcerer Hooke dumped Thalanes's corpse beside the bishop's on the floor of the chancel, where Ezekiel sat in dumb contemplation. Berkeley and his men had secured all the cathedral's doors, probably with the collusion of the chevalier's Creole and his gendarmes.

Who had killed the bishop?

In the confusion, he must have been shot on accident, though Ezekiel didn't remember seeing it happen. The little monk's corpse and robe were soaked, and he fell into a sloshing puddle that reminded Ezekiel of his vision of the death of Adam and Eve. He winced.

"I know you now," Ezekiel said to the Lazar. "You're Robert Hooke, the Sorcerer."

I am the disciple who did not wish to see death until his master came again. Hooke's voice rattled in Ezekiel's mind. The bullet hole in his chest was no longer bleeding, but the long black stain down the front of his moldering shirt gave him a gory, nauseating appearance. *Thou hast spoken with our master, then?*

"You serve Oliver Cromwell," Ezekiel continued.

Yes, Hooke answered, *thou and I both. Now, wilt thou join me in making inquiries of this Serpentborn monk?*

Ezekiel looked at the body of Thalanes, wet and cold and

pathetic. He had never liked the heretic, but it still seemed impious to manhandle his body about like a sack of grain.

As it seemed impious to be working with Lazars.

But if Cromwell really could eradicate death, what then? Was that not a fine end to serve, to restore God's creation to what it had been before man's great mistake? Was that, after all, what Cromwell had been after, with his Eternal Commonwealth and his wars against the Firstborn? If Cromwell had his way, then all men would live eternally from birth, as God had always intended.

All would be saved.

And Lucy...wouldn't he see Lucy again?

But...the Necromancer? He had always been taught to loathe and fear Oliver Cromwell. And Ezekiel despised black magic.

And, despite Ezekiel's questions, Cromwell had not explained himself or his plans.

Two other Lazars joined them, a silent man whose arms hung at his waist and a man whose white skin had been burnt a crisp black, like badly overdone roasted chicken; he stank of sizzled flesh and rot at the same time, and he lacked one eyeball. Hooke nodded to them, and the two Lazars with working arms hoisted Thalanes's body up and shoved him against the bloodied altar, in a sitting position with his chin slumped onto his chest.

He did not need to serve the Necromancer.

At least, he didn't need to make a decision one way or the other, not yet. He could work with Cromwell's creatures to serve the ends of St. Martin and the Penn family. He could walk away from an alliance with the Necromancer whenever he wanted.

It is time, Hooke said. *Come here and join us, or get thee hence.*

Ezekiel steeled himself and stepped closer to the altar. He would be like Saul, consulting with the Witch of Endor when he could get no answer from the prophets, and speaking with the shade of the prophet Samuel. That biblical touchstone quelled the disquiet in his bowels, though the thought crept through his mind that the comparison was rather more flattering to Thalanes, in the shoes of the dead Samuel, than it was to him.

We need blood. Hooke turned abruptly to Ezekiel, holding out a knife and a gold chalice.

"I don't have any blood," Ezekiel demurred, feeling this was asking too much of him. He had thought to be only a witness.

The weak-armed Lazar looked at him skeptically, eyes squirming.

Dost thou not? Hooke again pressed the tools upon him.

It was only for the moment. He would work with Cromwell and his disconcerting agents for now, until he could recover the Witchy Eye. Recover or kill, if he had to. Then he would wash his hands of them and ride back to Philadelphia.

He took the knife and chalice.

"Where should I...?" He gestured vaguely at his body with the blade.

Thou mayest find it convenient to mark the palm of thy hand, though it makes no odds to me.

Trembling, Ezekiel cut a line into the flesh of his left palm, letting the thin trickle of blood well up and then drip modestly into the chalice. He stared at the red beads that slid down the inside of the gold vessel, smearing it crimson and then pooling in the bottom. Had he gone too far already?

More. Hooke seized Ezekiel by the wrist and the burned Lazar grabbed his hand with surprising mobility and strength, squeezing the flesh of his palm and tearing it, bringing a torrent of bright red blood down into the cup. The red was shocking against the gold, an insult, a blasphemy, a wound.

Ezekiel gasped in pain and anger and tried to pull away; Hooke looked down into the cup with his dead white eyes.

That will do, he finally said, and the Lazars released Ezekiel.

Then the Sorcerer Hooke dipped his fingers into Ezekiel's blood and daubed it on Thalanes's face, anointing the corpse's eyes, ears, and tongue, and smearing a great red line across his pale wet forehead. Ezekiel's palm ached at the sight of his own blood being used this way.

Robert Hooke handed the chalice to Ezekiel. A small clot of drying blood remained in the bottom of the cup.

It will be safest for thee to destroy this, the Lazar said.

"Destroy it?" Obviously, if the Witchy Eye had Ezekiel's blood, she could use it to ensorcel him.

It is safest of all to drink it.

Ezekiel imagined himself licking his own blood from the sacramental chalice and felt ill.

Then the Sorcerer was still a moment; he must be incanting a spell in his mind-speech, but one that Ezekiel couldn't hear. Ezekiel felt even more vitality leach from him, and he nearly swooned.

Thalanes's eyes opened and his chin snapped up off his chest.

For a moment, Ezekiel thought Hooke had made a mistake, that Thalanes was still alive, but then he saw the all-white eyes in the monk's head and he knew he was in the presence of necromancy. He shuddered and took a step back, but not so far away that he couldn't see and hear the interrogation.

Thalanes, Hooke intoned, crouching beside the corpse. *Thou owest me three answers.*

"I owe you nothing," Thalanes replied. It was not in his natural, living voice, but in a basso mockery of it, a deep, rumbling grunt that seemed larger than the chest it came out of. "But I am compelled. Speak."

Compelled to tell me the truth, mind thou. No tricks, Ophidian.

"Compelled to answer three questions only," the dead monk countered. "Speak."

Ezekiel had never seen such magic firsthand, and only read about it in Mather's *Denunciations*. This was vile necromancy. Ezekiel clenched his wounded hand into a fist; he would cut ties with the Necromancer as soon as he'd found Witchy Eye.

Robert Hooke sneered. *Where has Sarah Penn slept in the City of New Orleans?*

Ezekiel thought he understood why Hooke had asked the odd question—this interrogation was a contest between the two dead men. The shade of Thalanes would answer three queries truthfully, but would not volunteer information or make up the weaknesses in defectively-phrased questions.

If the Sorcerer could find something of Witchy Eye's, including, ideally, some small part of her body or her intimate toilette, he could use that to cast a spell to find her again. How had the Lazar followed the girl thus far? Ezekiel frowned.

Thalanes lay still for long seconds. "In the palace of the Bishop of New Orleans," he finally groaned. A trickle of blood slipped from the bullet hole in his temple and onto his shoulder, as if from the mental effort.

Hooke grinned humorlessly at Ezekiel. *Knowledge always begins with the asking of the correct question.*

"Are you looking for material for a finding spell?" Ezekiel asked.

Hooke spat clotted black phlegm onto the floor. He turned his attention again to the interrogation. *For what purpose didst thou bring Sarah Penn to New Orleans?*

Thalanes was slow to answer again. "To find Captain Sir William Johnston Lee."

"They found him," Ezekiel confirmed. "He's the big man in a red coat who was here in the cathedral today."

What did Thalanes and Witchy Eye want with Lee? Lee was the former Captain of the Imperial House Light Dragoons, the one who had served under Kyres Elytharias. Could he have something of her father's for the girl?

Or was the girl gathering her father's retainers about her to aid her in a rush at the throne? Lee had almost said as much, standing beside the altar with guns in his hands and defying the emperor.

Hooke nodded and the weak-armed Lazar hissed, his breath a cloud of decay.

Hooke considered his third and last question at length. *The last time thou hadst knowledge of her intentions, what did Sarah Penn plan to do when she left New Orleans?*

Ezekiel nodded. Maybe they could get out ahead of the Witchy Eye, instead of always being a step behind. He leaned in closer to hear the answer; this information would justify the black magic taint.

"She intended to find her brother," Thalanes said in his rumbling death rattle voice.

Ezekiel's ears pricked up. "Her brother? Where's the brother?"

The dead monk slumped, still and cold.

"Is that it? He must know more, make him tell us more!" Ezekiel demanded, almost yelling.

Robert Hooke shook his head. *Thou art no necromancer, art thou, priest? We have finished here. Let us go see what we can find at the Bishop's Palace.*

Ezekiel looked down at the sacramental chalice in his hands, with the clotting lump of his blood in the bottom, and felt sick and foul.

It was cold inside the crypt. The heavy marble roof shielded them from the direct blows of the storm, but wind-flung spray still slicked and chilled their hands and faces.

At least, Bill thought with some wonder, they were mostly dry. After winging down to a landing among the glaring angels, sad-eyed gargoyles, off-centered stone memorials, and tall weeds that comprised the cemetery, they had shaken the water off. Pigeons must be water-resistant, being feathered and oily like ducks. And when he had suddenly found himself a man and clothed again, he had been a dry man in dry clothing.

Sarah and Cathy had tended to various injuries, Sarah with incantations and Cathy with bandages, and then they had begun to take counsel. Sarah told her story, and then Obadiah.

The storm-battered above-ground crypt had to be the strangest place Bill had ever held a council of war. The chiseled names of the dead to whom the crypt belonged stared at him from all sides, reminding him of his conversations earlier that morning with Jacob Hop.

Simon Sword. There is no such person as Jacob Hop, or if there is, he is a stranger to me.

Bill was chilled and wounded. He had betrayed his employer the chevalier, he'd been insulted by a former subordinate, and he'd watched two innocent men in a row killed, both of them priests, but Bill felt better than he had in years. He kept looking from Sarah to Cathy and back again, and trying to do more than just grin.

Bill did feel shock about Thalanes; after years of not seeing each other, he and his old friend, the little monk, had exchanged scarcely a handful of words, and now Thalanes was dead. The echo of the gunshot that killed the Cetean would be with him a long time.

It was Bill's turn. He told his companions what he had to say, starting with the night the Lion of Missouri was murdered, fifteen years ago. He told about the storm at the junction of the great rivers, rain not unlike the rain from which they now huddled in shelter, about Kyres's insistence on standing his turn at watch with Bayard Prideux, about Bayard's foul murder and Bill's subsequent pursuit into the rain, ending in Bayard's escape.

He told of Kyres's death under the oak tree, of the three bloodied acorns. He told of burying his master's body in secret, as he had instructed them to do, along with Thalanes, then the Chaplain of the Blues, and of looking for, but not finding, the regalia of Cahokia—the sword, the crown, and the orb. He told of returning to Philadelphia to deliver the acorns, of the empress's grief and terrible whispered suspicions, suspicions that were fully validated when Thomas had had his sister shut away, claiming she'd been driven mad.

"Thomas must have put Bayard up to the murder," Bill concluded. "Bayard said there was another man involved, too. 'Ze ozer,' he kept saying, frog that he was."

"Who is this other man?" Sarah asked.

"He deserves death, whoever he is, Your Majesty," Bill said.

"Revenge?" Calvin asked, looking dubious. "I ain't sure how I feel about that. Turn the other cheek, Jesus said. Seven time seventy."

"My conscience may be less metaphysical than yours, suh," Bill shot back. "Revenge is what the other fellow is after; what *I* want is *justice*. Besides, Cal, I saw how you turned the other cheek to the Lazars back there. I'm not fooled."

Cal's face colored. "That wasn't revenge, though. That was jest self-defense."

"He *does* deserve death, and we'll *return* to it." Sarah said.

Bill bowed, deferring.

He told them of the three babies born and smuggled out of Hannah's prison chambers in a warming pan. He told what he remembered of Sarah, which was mostly that she was a perfectly beautiful baby with a swollen red eye, but he had more to say about Nathaniel, the infant he had nurtured, concealed, carried, and delivered to—

"Don't tell me!" Sarah interrupted him.

"I beg your pardon, Your Majesty," Bill said, "but I was under the impression that this was the information you came to New Orleans to seek."

Sarah looked lost in a maze of thought, huddling into her purple shawl in the corner of the crypt. "It is. Only now I ain't so certain my mind's a safe place for the information, with that damned Sorcerer Hooke on the loose. Best you keep it to yourself for now."

He resumed his story with circumlocutions to conceal the people and places. He told them he'd hidden the boy Nathaniel with a great man and friend of the empress, he told them of the great man's son, who threatened to turn Bill and the child over to the emperor, of Bill's duel with the young man that had led to his death, of the great man's subsequent madness and Bill's exile and flight.

He left out his tearful goodbyes with Sally, her grief and anger and suggestions that he was choosing his dead lord over his living children. He'd promised to write, and he had kept that promise for years, much as he disliked putting pen to paper. She had sworn never to write back, and she had kept her oath, too.

Bill swallowed back that irrelevant detail and continued.

He told them of his life in New Orleans, hiding nothing and fearing condemnation for it, but no one spoke against him. He

told them of his night at Bishopsbridge and the improbable message of the two beastfolk. He told them of his imprisonment on
the *Incroyable*, of meeting Bayard, of their conversations, and of
beating the Frenchman to death.

"Thank you," Sarah said simply, when she heard of the traitor's end.

Bill bowed his head and said nothing. He burned to tell Sarah
that he'd find the mysterious other man as well, and beat him
to death, and that he would ride into the throat of Hell itself, if
he had to, to bring justice to Thomas Penn.

"Have you seen this confession letter Bayard spoke of?" she
asked. "In which he identified his co-conspirator, and hinted to
the chevalier where he'd hidden the regalia?"

Bill shook his head. "The chevalier must have it, I presume."

She nodded. "Go on."

He explained the letter Jacob Hop—Simon Sword—had helped
him write, his strange release and dark errand, and finally his
decision not to kill the Bishop of New Orleans.

"Your letter must have provoked the chevalier," Sarah thought
out loud.

"Might Bayard a wrote to the bishop?" Cal asked. "I didn't git
nothin' from it at the time, but I recollect a conversation between
Thalanes and the bishop about bees, and in hindsight it sounds
an awful lot like Bayard might a wrote the bishop, and then the
bishop might a confronted the chevalier..."

"And then the chevalier commissioned me to kill the bishop,"
Bill said. "Bayard may have, or maybe the little Dutchman...
pardon me, ma'am, I mean Simon Sword, perhaps Simon Sword
wrote a second letter without telling me."

"Why would the chevalier only give you a saber, though?"
Cathy asked.

Bill scratched his head. "I'm beginning to think it likely that
the chevalier intended to have me killed after I had accomplished
his errand, ma'am," he said. "No blood would then be on anyone's
hands but mine, and I'm the sort of person the citizens of New
Orleans are perfectly content to see executed by their chevalier.
A sword would have been enough to kill the bishop, being a
defenseless old man, but would have left me hard pressed to
defend myself against the chevalier's gendarmes. What puzzles
me is why Daniel Berkeley should have killed the bishop instead."

Bill looked to the Englishman for an explanation, but the Martinite's servant only shrugged. "'E be stayink at the Palais," Obadiah offered. "Mayhap the chevalier put 'im up to it. Mayhap it were the price of the chevalier's cooperation in lookink for Sarah."

"Speakin' of the chevalier's place," Sarah said, "how do you reckon we can find that letter Bayard wrote?"

Bill nodded. "I don't know, Your Majesty, and I fear we may have to ask the chevalier himself. But I'm pleased to serve you in the distribution of long-overdue justice." He nodded deferentially to Calvin. "Or revenge, if you prefer."

"Justice will come," Sarah said, "but it's not our errand today. We're weak, Sir William, out of power and on the run. Our errand is to recover my regalia, so I can regain my throne. When we have wealth, power, and safety, we'll be able to worry a little more about justice."

"Yes, Your Majesty," Bill acknowledged.

"How do we find out where Bayard hid them?" she asked.

Bill considered. "Bayard's gone, so he can't tell us anything helpful, and the only people he regularly consorted with to my knowledge are a gang of deaf-mutes who are all now dead at the bottom of the Pontchartrain, a Dutchman who turns out to be the Heron King, and a tongueless Choctaw whore. *She* may be alive, of course, but finding a particular whore in New Orleans is like finding a particular flea on a dog."

"Kinta Jane Embry," Cathy said.

"I beg your pardon?" Bill was caught off guard. "Do you know her?"

"New Orleans is a large city," she answered him with a look that might have been amused, "but not *that* large. If there were a tongueless Choctaw duelist in New Orleans, Sir William, do you imagine you wouldn't know his name?"

Bill blushed. Had he insulted Cathy? "Bayard claimed his... companion... was related to someone important in the chevalier's house," Bill said. "I suppose that makes some sense—the chevalier didn't want anyone seeing his prisoner who couldn't be trusted."

"I don't know anything about that," Cathy said coolly, "but I know where we can find Kinta Jane. Provided Your Majesty is willing to go to the rougher parts of New Orleans."

"Rougher than we already been?" Cal muttered. "Jerusalem."

"I'm the Prince of Shreveport, damn your eyes!"

—◦—

CHAPTER TWENTY-TWO

The war was coming, but Kinta Jane Embry still had to eat. She had had to hand the Heron King's coin over to René, because there were important people who needed more to convince them than just Kinta Jane's word at second hand. But would she have been able to spend such a coin, in any case?

On evenings like this, when she had no standing client appointments, she walked the street. The rain didn't deter her, but it did keep her close to her rented room, slowly circling her own block on the edge of the Faubourg Marigny.

Deeper into the shabby maze of the Faubourg, closer to the Franklin Gate on the east side of the city, were the strange fires, the dark alleys where chickens and cats lost their lives to houngans seeking to know the future or to mambos who wished to placate the mystères. If rumor was true, the loa themselves sometimes crawled the alleys deep in the Faubourg Marigny, in search of entertainment, worship, or blood.

The mystères didn't generally walk Kinta Jane's neighborhood, which made it not nearly so spiritually powerful, though also considerably less dangerous. She was close enough to the trees of the Esplanade that decent clients came her way, and when the clients weren't so decent, well, she didn't mind the occasional Irishman or Portugee, especially if he was clean.

The tall red-headed man looked clean enough. He also looked like a chawbacon, a total Reuben, a hick, with his hair long and loosely tied back on his neck and his frayed wool coat with the long-sleeved hunter's shirt beneath. He had a bony Appalachee face that could be charitably described as *homely*, but the look in his clear eyes was gentle, and even nervous.

"Evenin', ma'am," he squeaked in a thick mountain twang, shaking water onto the boardwalk.

Kinta Jane smiled her best sultry smile and twisted her shoulders in a way that emphasized her curves. She slapped her thigh, pumped her hip in his direction and winked.

He chuckled. "I reckon I know what that means. Might could I git jest an hour of your time?"

She smiled and took his elbow, leading the bony young man around the corner and up the iron steps to the third floor of the boarding house. He smiled at her and kept looking around, nervous as a cat. The young man's uncomfortable innocence was refreshing; in this town, she'd become used to men who were too hard, too worn, or too cold to feel any embarrassment at all.

Kinta Jane turned the key in the lock and opened the door. Suddenly, the Appalachee shoved her into her bedroom. She stumbled, reaching as she fell for a stiletto in her long sleeve. Before she could draw it, other hands were seizing her wrists and pinning her, and then the door slammed.

Others were in her room. How many?

She couldn't see in the dark. She bucked and twisted but could not escape, realizing that there were at least two men, two *large, strong* men, holding her down. This might be an assault, which was horrifying enough, since her pander, Elbows Pritchard, was a useless drunkard and as likely to beat her for the cash deficit as to take any meaningful action against her assailants, but they could also be black magic men, after her hair or her heart or other parts for some wicked ceremony.

Worse still—they could be servants of the Heron King.

Had the Appalachee had some beastkind feature, and she had missed it?

A Lucifer *scritched* and sputtered into flame, and then the oil lantern beside her bed was carefully lit and replaced on the cheap three-legged table, and Kinta Jane could finally see her attackers.

The Appalachee stood in the door, and he twisted open the wooden slats of the blinds with their control rod ever so slightly to peer out. "They ain't nobody followin'."

The two men pinning Kinta Jane were rougher than the Appalachee, with none of his backcountry innocence. One was heavy, with a thick head, neck, and torso, but bony legs; he wore a ratty black coat, smelled sour and badly needed a shave. The other was tall and more muscular, though showing his age in the iron gray of his long mustache; he wore a red coat, and a black perruque under a battered, broad-brimmed hat. This last man seemed vaguely familiar.

All three men were armed, with swords, pistols, and, in the case of the redhead, a tomahawk and a lariat that he now picked up from Kinta Jane's own bed.

There were two women, too; so this was not a simple assault. They didn't look like Vodun people, either—mostly, they gave the impression of being from out of town.

Kinta Jane steeled herself to say nothing to the Heron King's agents, but then she had another shock—she recognized one of the women. It was Long Cathy, a very high-class girl who worked in a French tavern called *Grissot's* in the Quarter and tended to see rich men. Cathy sat on a stool to one side holding two pistols, not exactly aimed at Kinta Jane, but nearly enough and with hammers cocked so that she could effortlessly shoot the Choctaw if she wanted.

The last person in the room was another woman, and she now shoved herself into Kinta Jane's view. She was young and thin, with dark hair, pale skin, and a bandage hanging loose over one eye. She looked Kinta Jane in the face, studying her for long moments while the two big men hoisted her and flung her onto the bed, never letting go of her arms.

This was to be her interrogator, then. Kinta Jane wondered whether they would torture her, and began taking slow, deep breaths to prepare.

"I know you ain't got no tongue," the eye-patched girl said, "but I reckon you can still tell us *yes* and *no* by noddin', can't you?"

Kinta Jane refused to answer even this question. Every question she answered would make the question following it harder to duck.

Instead, she smiled coldly, slapped one thigh and cocked her hip to the side.

The redhead laughed, in an embarrassed-sounding way, but the scrawny girl didn't look amused.

Instead, she removed her bandage.

Kinta Jane shivered, profoundly unsettled by the sight of the girl's unmasked face. She had one eye that was a normal, human blue, and the other that was the color of ice, like a bird's eye, or the eye of some other proud animal. What beastkind was this? The girl blinked, and Kinta Jane felt drawn in and *known* by her piercing gaze.

"Can you read and write?" the girl asked.

Kinta Jane only smiled, controlling her breathing. Of course she could write. And of course she wasn't going to tell this beast-wife witch. *Answer no questions at all*, she told herself.

"She can," the beast-eyed girl said to her companions, and Kinta Jane's heart sank.

That might be a bluff.

Calm. Breathe.

"Is it true you're sister, or half-sister, to the chevalier's man, René du Plessis?" the witch continued.

Kinta Jane tried to force from her mind all thoughts of René and his kindness to her over the years, how he'd fed her when she couldn't feed herself, or given her clothing discarded by ladies of the chevalier's household, or even arranged clients for her when the chevalier needed services such as she provided. René had told her of Franklin's vision, too, and brought her into the Conventicle, and trained her in the ways of secrecy, patience, and watchfulness.

Good René, kind René, she would not betray him.

"Yes, she is," the witchy-eyed girl said.

The beastwife was reading her mind!

Kinta Jane felt despair. She knew now that she would give up all her secrets and then be killed, killed and not missed by this cold city. At least she couldn't give away anyone else in the Conventicle beyond her little cell. Thank Heaven for the wisdom of old Ben Franklin.

"Now," the girl said, and her ice-white eye pounded into Kinta Jane's soul like a sledgehammer, "you're going to help us meet your brother."

Kinta Jane's mind spun.

Who were these captors? Was the Conventicle already betrayed, and was the Heron King hunting down its servants? Did they already know René was her cell leader? She looked again to

Cathy, but the other woman sat calm and impassive, with loaded pistols ready.

Kinta Jane wouldn't betray René. Nor would she even shake her head to dignify the order with a response. She couldn't bear to meet the gaze of those eyes any longer, and just stared at the dirty white ceiling, trying to calm her racing heart.

"Ought I 'it 'er?" asked the thick-headed man, and Kinta Jane recognized his accent as London English.

"A gentleman doesn't hit a woman, suh," the mustached man told his companion, "even if she's a whore."

"Why, Sir William," Long Cathy drawled, teeth of steel audible in her voice, "you are a true cavalier."

The tall man blanched and fell silent. What kind of interrogation was this? Kinta Jane expected to be tortured or beaten or at least shouted at. And could the witch not read her mind after all?

"You're gonna take us to your brother," the cracker witch insisted, "or you're gonna write us how to find him." She shoved a scrap of paper and a bit of charcoal in Kinta Jane's face, and the Choctaw turned away.

"All right, then," the witch said, retracting the writing implements, "we're gonna have to do this the hard way. Cal—"

The redhead pulled a knife.

Kinta Jane braced herself. Would it be an eye or an ear, or maybe her nose?

The Appalachee Cal stooped and cut off a lock of her hair. Without a word, he handed it to the beastwife sorceress and resheathed his knife.

"Tarnation, Cal," she said. "You cut me enough to braid a rope."

"Jerusalem, Sarah," he answered, "how'm I supposed to know how much you need? I couldn't hex away a wart iffen my life depended on it and I had a whole forest of stumps full of rain water."

"Where's my little Dutchman when I need him?" the mustached man asked, then looked suddenly crestfallen.

The witch, Sarah, laughed, but in a surprisingly kindly way. "I think we can do this without the help of Simon Sword. Best tie up the Choctaw, though."

Simon Sword!

The two big men tore her carefully laundered sheet to strips and then proceeded to bind Kinta Jane hand and foot. *Without the help of Simon Sword*, she had said, and for Kinta Jane the mystery of the encounter deepened and became more ominous.

"Are you sure this will work?" Cathy asked.

"No," Sarah answered, "and I sure as shootin' wish youins could git a better magician than me to give it a try, and one as wasn't already tuckered out, but I reckon it ought to do the trick, and I'm all we got."

"You can do it, Sarah," Cal told her.

"Huh," she answered. "We got anything else, anything... stringy, like a bit of ribbon, mebbe?"

Kinta Jane watched helplessly as the invaders of her very small private space ransacked her drawers and cracked armoire and came up with a faux pearl necklace. The witch Sarah knotted the long hank of Kinta Jane's hair around the pearls and then balled the necklace up into her two hands and closed her eyes in concentration.

"*Fratrem quaeso*," she said. Kinta Jane didn't know what it meant. Was it Latin? This might be no hedge witch, then, this but a classically trained wizard, and dangerous.

She wasn't wearing Polite red, though, and New Orleans didn't have another college for gramarye. Philadelphia did, and New Amsterdam and Memphis, and Kinta Jane wondered which of them had accepted this whippet of an Appalachee girl.

Maybe the girl maybe wasn't what she seemed. Maybe her appearance was an illusion. The mystères, the loa, did that sort of thing all the time.

Did the Heron King appear in disguise?

She still had no idea who these people were.

Sarah then opened her hand and let the pearls dangle from her fingers, the hair knot at the bottom. For a moment nothing happened, the necklace hanging perfectly still, and then the hair knot twitched and rose, dragging the pearls a few degrees to one side, looking like a tiny hairball dog straining on a very expensive leash.

"Thank you, Miss Kinta Jane Embry," the witch Sarah said. "I reckon that'll do."

"A bit more of the *amo, amas, amat* might could be in order here," Cal volunteered. Cal's Latin litany reminded Sarah of every incantation she'd ever heard Thalanes say. She was barely able to choke back tears.

Mercifully, the rain had stopped. Sarah had handed the pearl-and-hairball compass off to Cathy, who had calmly accepted it and then led them with long, confident strides through the darkening evening and the thickening crowd in whichever direction the hairball indicated.

That had turned out to be back across the Quarter, and Sarah wanted to disguise their faces. She was just too conscious of the low level of her remaining reserves of energy to expend any of it unnecessarily. Instead, she suffered with the uneasy foreboding that the Sorcerer Hooke must inevitably catch up to her, and that when he did, he would know her from a mile away.

"Keep an eye out for gendarmes and Imperials both," she'd reminded her friends, huddling deeper into her shawl. She was cold and wet, and part of her wanted to just run away, burrow into the warm earth somewhere, and hide.

But she couldn't give up. It wasn't just her life, it was the lives of her brother and sister she didn't know, and justice for her murdered parents, that kept her marching through the storm, into the teeth of her almost-paralyzing fear of the Sorcerer Hooke.

Hooke had found her before, somehow. It had to be sorcery. What would she do if she had to face him another time?

She wouldn't meet his gaze, for starters. She would keep moving, and hope that by the time he caught up to her next, she was powerful enough to handle him.

The compass had led them out of the Quarter again at its other end, across a wide avenue that was all light and vibrant carousing on the near side, a staccato screen of tall oaks down the middle, and dark-windowed commercial establishments on the other. Sarah had hunkered down in the knot made by her three male companions to hide.

Beyond the storefronts, they had moved into neighborhoods of free-standing homes with wrought iron fences, street lanterns on poles, and flickering tapers just beginning to show in their parlors and dining rooms.

"We be movink toward the Palais," Obadiah had observed. "I trow that be as should be, an' the 'ex be in effect."

They had passed some larger buildings that looked as if they had government functions, with legends like *City of New Orleans* written above their doors in iron letters and contingents of gendarmes providing security. Sarah had thought of the sole building with any kind of government function she had ever seen in all of the Calhoun lands—the Elector's Thinkin' Shed—and almost laughed out loud.

Among the government buildings, Sarah had begun to see more and more people on the street, principally riders in large coaches, pulled by two, four, and even six horses in matched teams. At her request, Cathy had slowed the pace to give them all an opportunity to assess what was happening around them, and it had been Cathy herself who had made the key discovery.

"Look in that red and white carriage there," she had said. "They're holding Venetian masks."

In all her relentless drilling by the Elector, Sarah had never heard of a Venetian mask, but she had seen that the passengers in the carriage held little masks on sticks up to their faces as they rode laughing by, looking out through the windows of their coaches, and she had inferred that must be what Cathy meant.

"It's a ball," Sir William had said.

When they had finally gotten close enough to see the Palais, it had taken Sarah's breath away. It was the largest building she had ever seen, by far, and it sparkled with the light of a thousand lanterns, torches, and braziers, and a thousand glass windows to further reflect and shine. Dozens of masked footmen walked about the cobbled courtyard before the front door of the Palais, white-wigged, -gloved, and -stockinged, and dressed in blue and gold coattails. A line of coaches crawled one at a time up the wide street, each examined by footmen and gendarmes within the large gatehouse, and then admitted within the courtyard to deposit its occupants before the open doors.

"Impressive, is it not?" Sir William murmured. "Count Galvéz of New Spain destroyed the old one in the war, so the father of the current chevalier built this replacement. One hears the quip in the salons of New Orleans that when Andy Jackson developed his famous interest in the real property of the city five years ago, it was principally because he wanted to own this particular lot."

"Did you fight in the battle?" Sarah asked him.

Sir William shrugged modestly. "I threw a few bullets in the direction of King Jackson. Not as part of any organized unit, you understand."

The hairball strained on its leash all the while, suggesting that René du Plessis was at the ball.

"I jest don't see any other way in," Cal said. "Iffen it was quieter, we might could climb the fence, but no way we can do that tonight without gittin' seen, they's far too many people."

Sarah hesitated. She saw the logic of Cal's suggestion, but she didn't know whether she could do it. She could jump them all over the fence, but that would be exhausting, even with the handful of pigeon dropping paste and feathers she had kept and secreted away in Thalanes's pack, and once inside, they'd stick out like sore thumbs in their tattered clothes. She could use some variant of a *facies muto* spell, but it wasn't just a matter of changed faces—they had to have *specific* faces to be on the guest list, and she would have to provide illusory clothing and masks.

And even once inside, she'd still have to maintain all the illusions.

She was already carrying the hairball compass spell and had kept it up for their entire march across town. She already felt weak, and she didn't want to be completely drained if and when the Sorcerer Hooke showed up.

"I don't know," she said slowly. "It would be . . . difficult."

"I have a suggestion, ma'am," said Sir William, "if you're able to make bodies invisible, even briefly."

"I can." Sarah hoped she was right.

"It will only be for a few moments," Sir William told her.

"I can do it," she repeated.

"Well, then," he said, "it's only a matter of choosing the coach that suits us best and inconveniencing its occupants. Allow me to reconnoiter first, if you will."

Sir William left them in their shadowed observation post down the street, across from the Palais, and strolled casually along the line of coaches, looking into the window of each and occasionally tipping his hat as passengers greeted him. Well before he reached the gatehouse, he turned and ambled back.

"The white coach pulled by six horses, with the lion and griffin rampant," Sir William told his waiting companions, "will do very well."

"What is your plan, Sir William?" Sarah asked.

"In my experience," he said, "the best plans are simple. If you will now render us invisible, Your Majesty, we'll open the door to that coach, take it at gunpoint, and ride it through the front gate in the costumes of its current passengers."

"Its current passengers likely include the Prince of Shreveport," Cathy observed, "or someone in his household, since those are his arms."

"One of the Cotton Princes." Sir William smiled. "Then I dare to hope that our borrowed costumes will be comfortable to wear. I suppose we should hold hands, so that we can stay together when unseen." He bowed to Cathy Filmer, as if he were asking her to dance. "Might I have the honor of holding yours, Mrs. Filmer?"

They formed a chain, Sarah in the middle and Sir William in the lead, a long pistol in his free hand. She was glad for the hand-holding, because, per the Law of Contagion, she could run her spell through the physical contact of all its targets and ease the drain it imposed.

She had seen Thalanes perform exactly this spell before. Reaching down to the edge of the street, she collected a blob of mud on two fingers and smeared a little on each person's cheeks, then took Calvin's hand again. "*Oculos obscuro.*" She blinked.

When she opened her eyes, she still felt Cathy's hand in her own right and Calvin's in her left (they locked fingers around the Elector's ash staff), but she could no longer see any of her companions or even her own limbs.

"Well done, ma'am," she heard Sir William say. "I'll walk slow. Stay together, and don't bump into anyone. When I signal you, Your Majesty, release me from your spell."

A couple of minutes later—dazzling minutes in which Sarah watched through coach windows a sitting parade of finery such as she'd never witnessed in her life, and kept reminding herself not to drop her friends' hands—they stood at the side of the white coach.

The two coachmen perched stoically on top were armed, each with a well-polished blunderbuss and short sword, but their attention was elsewhere, at the line ahead of them and the approaching gatehouse.

The coach waited its turn several lengths from the gatehouse, and Sarah stood in its shadow, looking into the carriage filled with light from the Palais.

Its passengers looked Bantu, three men and two women, their complexions blue-black in the artificial light. The men had shaved heads and the women wore their hair long and bound in wire. Their clothing took Sarah's breath away, all white with gold thread and buttons. All of them, men and women alike, had hands thick with gold bands and heavy hoops of gold through each ear. The passengers held large furs across their laps, and each bore a little mask on a stick, designed to cover the upper part of the face only, concealing it behind a bird-like nose and a spray of feathers shooting back over one's hairline. One of the younger men stroked a plump white cat in his lap. It was a family. The prince, the princess, and three children; she was charmed by the domesticity of the scene. The Bantu had all been pirates, not too many generations ago, and in all the gold of the prince's finery, she imagined she could see an echo of that heritage.

The near carriage door opened—it must be Sir William—and then Sarah's heart stopped.

Inside the doorframe of the carriage, hammered into the wood all around, ran a thin, dully gleaming bit of filigree.

Silver.

Inside the door, it was hidden except when the door was open, so its purpose could only be to intercept malignant hexing.

Sir William winked into view, in the moment of climbing into the carriage door, a pistol in each hand, both of them pointed at the oldest of the men.

The Prince of Shreveport looked up, startled.

"Drop the spell now!" Sir William hissed, not realizing it was too late.

The Bantu stared, but said nothing, and Sir William smiled.

He sat on the broad back seat of the coach, across from the prince, and continued to hold both his guns pointed at the man. "Shhh!" Sir William quieted the astonished family, and pulled back the hammers of both pistols to make his point.

"This is outrageous!" the Prince of Shreveport whispered, eyes flashing.

"It is indeed, suh," Sir William nodded, "and I hope it works. Now take off your clothing before I feel myself compelled to pull the trigger and spoil everyone's evening."

The carriage had paper blinds that could be pulled down over each window for privacy, so once Sarah's entire party had crept inside, each popping into view as he or she climbed over the thin line of silver, they pulled down the blinds. Sarah noticed thin filigrees of silver inside the windows, too.

All the people entering made the carriage jostle.

Tap, tap, tap. The sound came from the roof of the carriage, and then it was followed by some words that might be in Bantu, and sounded like a question.

Sir William pressed his pistols into the prince's chest and raised both his eyebrows. "Everything is just fine in here, thank you very much," he prompted his prisoner.

The Prince of Shreveport flared his nostrils in anger, but when he called back to the coachmen his voice sounded efficient and calm. "We're fine, thank you, Sergeant."

"Well done, suh." Bill eased the hammers of his pistols down. "Now undress."

"You can't get away with this for long!" the prince warned them, handing his coat to Sir William and reaching for his belt.

"You're probably, right, suh," Sir William agreed genially, "and I certainly hope I don't have to. Please cooperate, and no one will be harmed. I expect that it's no great consolation, but know that I hold you, your office, and your family in the highest respect."

The Prince of Shreveport snorted his derision and pulled off his breeches.

Sir William stood watch with his long guns while the prince and his family stripped down to underthings and Calvin hog-tied them all with strips of improvised rope torn from clothing.

The coachmen didn't interrupt again.

Then Sarah and her companions changed, all at the same time, elbowing each other in the face and stepping on each other's feet as they did so—the carriage was large, but intended to seat six capaciously, not ten.

The cramped space slowed the process, as did the occasional gentle jerk as the carriage rolled forward. Sarah's own progress was further slowed by her simultaneous close examination of the faces of the prince's party, so they had barely finished changing into the white formal clothing (all more or less fitting, though Obadiah burst a button in his collar and had to hide the damage with his neckcloth, and Cal's wrists jutted out of his borrowed sleeves nearly two inches), covered the prince and his family awkwardly under the furs—their cat looked on placidly without objection—and picked up the masks when the coach pulled forward and there was a knock at the door.

"*Facies muto.*" Sarah willed mana through the mask in her

hands and replaced all their faces with images of the prince's and his family's. "*Captivos occulto*," she added, almost as an afterthought, touching the furs and hiding the prince and his family from sight. She felt a flush of pride in her work for both the idea and its execution, but also a strain from casting so many spells in quick succession. How long would she be able to hold out?

She felt lightheaded and a little feverish.

Sir William, in the prince's clothing, opened his blind; they were stopped inside the gatehouse. "Yes, gentlemen?" he drawled to a paper-bearing footman and two gendarmes. Sarah heard his unmistakably Chesapeake tones and wondered whether she should have done something to disguise all their voices.

Too late.

"Are you 'ere for ze ball?" asked the footman blandly, holding a quill pen black with ink up to the paper.

"No, I'm here for the kidnapping." Sir William held his bird mask up to his face. "Have you not heard? We batheads are all pirates in our deepest hearts, as we are in our family trees."

"Yes, sir," the footman smiled a completely perfunctory smile. "I just need to check you against ze list. Name, please?"

From her drill sessions with the Elector, Sarah knew that the Princedom of Shreveport was held by the Machogu family, and she thought the prince's own name was Kimoni. How much did Sir William know?

"Dammit, man, can you not read?" the Cavalier thundered, and he reached an arm outside the coach to thump it against the heraldic lion and griffin.

Sarah nearly fainted. The moment that Sir William reached outside the carriage, his disguise fell away. From inside the carriage she saw his black perruque reappear, and she knew they were doomed.

Sir William, though, didn't notice. He swelled to his full height, even sitting down, until his shoulders blocked the window and he loomed over the French footman. "I'm the Prince of Shreveport, damn your eyes! Party of five!"

"Yes, sir, ze Prince of Shreveport," The footman notated his sheet and stepping away.

Sir William brought his arm back inside the window, pulled down its paper blind, and dropped his mask. He looked at Sarah and must have seen an expression of fear. "Don't worry, Your

Majesty. There is an art to dealing with men who are accustomed to taking orders."

The coach rolled forward, and Sarah felt her heart start beating again.

Cathy pulled out the hairball-and-pearls compass. It hung inert, the spell dead from crossing the carriage's silver threshold.

Sir William turned to face Cathy, again lifting up his mask. "I find I rather enjoy being a prince."

Ezekiel went alone, first, to the Bishop's Palace, and there he learned to appreciate the cunning of the dead heretic Thalanes. Berkeley, after the riotous action at the cathedral, had fallen into some reverie from which he could barely shake himself to give orders to the dragoons. And even with the rain and Hooke's scarf, hat, and long hair to mask his pale face, Ezekiel preferred not to be seen much with the Lazars.

He limped, tired from his spellcasting and wounded. The Sorcerer Hooke had offered to heal him, and Ezekiel had declined.

The palace was mostly given over to an association of red-robed Polites, and Ezekiel imagined with horror a showdown with himself and the Sorcerer Hooke on one side and an entire squad of thaumaturgical monks on the other. Thalanes, from beyond the grave, had almost led him into that trap.

Ezekiel inquired of the Polite doorkeeper about a party from Appalachee that he was to meet at the Bishop's Palace.

The Polite, a fat, cinnamon-colored Amhara man with tight buttons for eyes, scratched his bald head. "I keep the door both for the sisters and brothers of the Humble Order of St. Reginald Pole," he said chirpily, "as well as for the Johnnies. I can tell you none of us has any guests at the moment, nor has had any for more than a week."

Ezekiel was perplexed; Thalanes and Hooke had both seemed to enter their battle of wits with the expectation that Thalanes would be unable to lie. "I was told to meet them at the Bishop's Palace. Does the Bishop of New Orleans keep more than one palace?"

"As to that," the Amhara grunted, raising his eyebrows and turning down the corners of his mouth, "he can barely be said to keep this one. If you're looking for the bishop himself, you may find him around the side, in the servants' quarters that face the cathedral. That's where he lives. Though there's been some commotion at the cathedral this afternoon, and I have heard the bishop himself may have been involved."

Ezekiel knocked at the indicated door. As he waited for an answer that never came, the Lazars and several of the Blues, including Berkeley, joined him. "*Ani poteach et hadelet.*" He opened the locked door with a very simple spell (cast with his fingers touching on old iron key hanging around his neck) that nevertheless nearly knocked him unconscious, and then Hooke entered. Ezekiel hadn't the stomach to join him in breaking into the bishop's home, and Berkeley wasn't able to rouse himself from his slump.

"Wake up, man!" Ezekiel said to the captain of the Blues as they stood on the doorstep in the rain.

"Bad luck, Parson," Berkeley ground out his words through gritted teeth. "A man does what he must do, but killing a bishop..." He trailed off, staring out into the gray, wet afternoon. "Bad luck."

Ezekiel shivered. Had *Berkeley* killed the bishop? Before he could ask, the Sorcerer exited the bishop's apartments, coming away with a bundle of clothing and a clump of dark hair. *The female of the species is entirely predictable,* he said. *I found it in a bathing tub, and I can tell it is hers. It only goes to show the wisdom of the Royal Society's advice against too frequent immersion in water.*

Ezekiel heaved a sigh of relief to get away from the Bishop's Palace and the cathedral; the chevalier's Creole had withdrawn with his gendarmes much earlier. As the dragoons rode across the Place d'Armes in double file, he looked back and saw the first intrepid onlookers brave the cathedral doors. Soon the rumors would be confirmed as fact, and New Orleans would know it no longer had a bishop.

However uncomfortable he felt with breaking into the dead priest's home or witnessing black magic performed on his altar, Ezekiel found he just didn't think the bishop's death was his problem. Even if it had been Berkeley who had shot him.

The Lazars rode, too, on spare horses belonging to the Blues; their long-nailed bare feet looked strange in the stirrups, though they sat like practiced horsemen. The party rode west, then north, then circled east again, all in the wet, frothy tail end of the storm, Hooke ignoring repeated queries other than to say *I follow where the evidence conducts us, priest. A man of reason cannot do otherwise. She is on the move. Be thou patient.*

Hooke seemed to follow the Witchy Eye by sense of smell, sniffing at the hair in his hand and then at the air of New Orleans like a hound given the scent of a fox or a raccoon.

Ezekiel disliked riding with the dead, but between the thick weather and Robert Hooke's scarf, he didn't think anyone noticed the Lazar for what he was.

As afternoon turned into evening, the rain stopped, and Ezekiel found himself riding west again, with the Sorcerer Hooke and a morose Captain Berkeley, exposed at the head of a restless column of dragoons, hoping night came soon. They skirted the edge of the Quarter, headed back toward the Palais du Chevalier. They passed fine homes and streets lit by lantern poles.

Then they turned a corner and the Palais itself was in sight, hurling its shafts of light into all directions. A line of ornate coaches beetled its way one at a time through the gatehouse, each disgorging passengers at the front door and then trundling to a stop within the cobbled courtyard. A second gatehouse, further down the street, would permit exit later.

She must be inside. Hooke held the clotted ball of damp black hair in his hand, alternating sniffing it and nosing the air. *She is near.*

"I can get us in," Ezekiel said.

Hooke wrapped his scarf more closely about his face and Tom Long-Knife followed suit. The burnt, one-eyed Lazar could do nothing about his appearance and simply fell back slightly, hovering between his fellow undead and the first of the dragoons. Berkeley and the other Imperial soldiers kept impassive faces, but the presence of the Lazars made all the horses skittish.

Ezekiel ignored glares and teeth-clenched curses from the drivers and guards on the foremost coaches and rode up to the gatehouse. After hours of riding around in the dark and wet, to feel the air only damp about his face and to stand in the blazing light of the thousand lamps and torches of the Palais's exterior made him feel warm, dry, and exposed to view.

He hoped no one noticed the strangeness of his companions.

The gatehouse crawled with gendarmes; two stood in the gate itself, with a list-toting footman, in the act as Ezekiel approached of signing off a carriage and sending it on through to the front door. They glared at him.

"Good even," Ezekiel called. "May we enter?" Out of the corner of his eye he watched the Lazars, who hung a little behind.

"You don't look like invitees to ze ball," the footman sniffed.

Tom Long-Knife reached for his weapon and Hooke held up a restraining hand.

"We're not," Ezekiel agreed. "I'm staying here as a guest of the chevalier."

The footman shook his head. "Only invitees to ze ball are to be admitted at zis time."

Now Robert Hooke hissed, his rancid exhalations drifting into Ezekiel's nostrils like the stink of a dead skunk. Ezekiel shot him a pleading look.

"There must be a mistake," he protested, "please contact the chevalier. Or perhaps his seneschal, Mr. du Plessis."

The footman looked bored but he waved another gendarme to his side and sent the man into the house. Ezekiel and his company stepped back from the gate while the footman processed several more coaches. *She is here, I am certain of it*, Hooke whispered into Ezekiel's mind. In this light, no scarf would hide the Lazar's peculiarity, and Ezekiel imagined stares of disapproval and fear boring into his back from each passing coach.

Finally the chevalier came out the front doors of the Palais, accompanied by another half dozen of his men. They were prepared for combat, wearing blue-stained leathers and festooned with weapons, but he wore an elegant blue and gold coat, waistcoat, and breeches, cut tight to display his trim physique, and an enormous white cravat. He strode directly through the gate to Ezekiel, and his gendarmes drew up into a disciplined line behind him.

Elsewhere about the gatehouse and the courtyard, the chevalier's presence made his men snap to even tighter focus, and Ezekiel felt watched by a thousand eyes.

"My Lord—" Ezekiel began, and the chevalier immediately cut him off with a wave.

"You gentlemen will have to bunk in the station with your men tonight," he said, nodding to Berkeley and Ezekiel. "I appreciate your patience. Your things will be brought out to you."

"But, My Lord..." Ezekiel began, but didn't know how much to say. "There are other..."

"Yes," the chevalier cut him off again. "I had suspected your pretender might have reason to try to enter my home. Your presence here with these—" he indicated the three Lazars with a twist of his wrist, "these *things* confirms my guess."

"My Lord?" Ezekiel could think of no better answer.

A flicker of a smile crossed the chevalier's lips. "How much do you think Thomas will be willing to pay me to keep her hidden? Annually, I mean."

Tom Long-Knife and the burnt Lazar hissed and lunged forward at the same moment, pushing past Ezekiel but pulling up short of the chevalier as a bristling hedge of steel sprang into the fists of his men, forcing them back.

No, not steel, Ezekiel realized, recognizing the gleam of the weapons: *silver.*

The chevalier had armed all his men with long silver daggers. It was a shocking display of wealth.

Ezekiel and the Sorcerer Hooke shared a brief glance; the sorcerer's cold face was unreadable, but Ezekiel knew he was broadcasting confusion and alarm from his own. He looked about the courtyard and the gatehouse and saw dozens of well-armed men, all now brandishing silver daggers. Bewigged heads stared shamelessly from the line of ornate coaches.

"We expected you might not wish to cooperate." The chevalier turned his gaze to the Lazar. "Now the sorcerer will want to try some arcane attack, but I advise against it."

Robert Hooke squinted, and Ezekiel involuntarily stepped back a pace. He worried Hooke *was* trying something, incanting in his silent mindspeech, and if his incantation exploded, Ezekiel didn't want to be caught in it. There were no explosions, though, and then Hooke said-thought sardonically, *I am not generally in the habit of taking advice from men in frippery. Still, tonight I shall heed the Lord Protector's counsel and keep my powder dry.*

The chevalier laughed. "The wisdom of the ancients. Good night, gentlemen." Then he turned and walked back into his mansion, leaving his silver-armed men behind to reinforce the gate.

"The chevalier may be that wealthy,
but he is not that generous."

———⊰•⊱———

CHAPTER TWENTY-THREE

The transition from the carriage into the Palais was tricky. Sarah stepped out first, mask held to her face, and as her foot touched the ground her thin, lanky, short black hair became thick, curled, and bound in wire, and her chalky white neck and shoulders assumed a dark, burnished hue. Bill came next, and then the others, and as each touched the ground he or she became a Bantu noble.

Obadiah Dogsbody came last, holding his mask and a bundle of their weapons. The others stood around the door at his exit to camouflage what he held in his arms, and as he touched the smooth stones of the ground, the bundle became a fat white cat.

"Miaow," purred the weapons.

They left the paper blinds pulled down.

Bill led the way, ignoring the footmen other than to hand the real prince's visiting card to a man at the door.

"His Serene Highness," the man announced to a crowd of indifferent ball attendees, "Kimoni Machogu, Prince of Shreveport. Her Serene Highness, Princess Jwahir Machogu..."

Bill kept moving.

A minute or two later, as the five of them drifted across a marble floor beneath a mural that ridiculously showed the Chevalier of New Orleans, Gaspard Le Moyne, defeating both Count Galvéz of New Spain and King Andy Jackson in a single battle, Bill became himself again.

He knew when it happened because his companions abruptly became themselves as well. He felt an itch to drag his hat out from where it was folded inside his waistcoat, but he knew it was too battered to make an appearance in this company, and with a twinge of misgiving he left it stowed away and kept the little mask over his face.

When the spell ended, Sarah's shoulders slumped. How much spellcasting did she have left in her?

Bill's pistols were inaccessible, wrapped in a bundle of his coat with the party's other weapons. Obadiah carried the bundle, and as he noted the illusions on the party's faces falling away, Bill turned to look at Obadiah, and was amused to see that he still appeared to be carrying a fat white cat. "Miaow," said the bundle of pistols, tomahawk, lariat, and so on.

So that bit of gramarye, unfortunately, she would have to continue. And, for the moment, the hair-and-pearls lodestone spell.

At least Bill was wearing his own sword.

Bill looked for the seneschal. He knew René du Plessis by sight, though they had never met—he was always about town on his master's business, public, private and, if any of the rumors was true, *very* private, indeed, for du Plessis was the most trusted servant of a man who kept many secrets.

Including, Bill hoped, a certain letter.

But in the thick crush of people in which Bill found himself now, he could see no faces. Once through the great front doors, Bill and the others had entered a swirling pool of New Orleans aristocracy. Most would be frenchies and Spaniards, though the scummy whirlpool of New Orleans threw up enough rough and tumble entrepreneurs, smugglers and gamblers and bawdy house owners and much, much worse, that there would be the occasional Anglo, Yonkerman, Memphite, Gullah, Texian, or whatnot.

Not that Bill could tell one from the other. They wouldn't stop moving, and their faces hid behind demonic masks.

The light fell about him like blinding diamonds, the punch bowls squatted on their long tables calling Bill's name, and the grotesque faces streamed tauntingly about him. Bill moved from one ballroom to the other following Cathy's indications; she held the hairball guide discreetly in hands folded on her stomach.

How much time did they have before the Prince of Shreveport wiggled out of his bonds and escaped?

They needed to find du Plessis, get the letter, and leave. If they separated, they ran the risk of not being able to find each other again. Once they had found the letter, they had no escape plan. Bill hoped they could simply walk out, but it might not turn out to be that simple.

He looked closely at the hair and jawline of the woman walking next to him to be certain she was Catherine Filmer, and took her arm in his.

"I seen him," Cal whispered. "Dark-skinned feller with a hard face, like you said, Bill, o'er there talkin' to the banjer picker. That him?"

Bill looked, and there stood du Plessis, conveying instructions from a sheet of paper to a quartet of Igbo minstrels, who respectfully held their banjo, guitar, bass fiddle, and lapharp still while they listened.

"That's him." Bill released Cathy's arm. "Follow me, and look natural."

With his companions trailing behind, Bill glided across the floor, evading would-be dancers as gracefully as he could. As du Plessis turned to leave the room, Bill swooped upon him and caught his bicep. "Stay calm, suh, and you'll not be hurt." Du Plessis let himself be guided from the room.

"You're making a serious mistake," he told Bill, but his face was pleasant.

Outside the room, Bill found himself again in one of the wide halls that made up the skeleton of the building. Guests chattered away gaily, scintillating glasses of punch in their free hands. Punch probably spiked with rum, and somewhere in the palace there would be good whisky. Barrels of Elijah Pepper's finest.

Bill forced his mind back to his task.

"Where's a quiet place where we may speak undisturbed, suh?" he asked the seneschal.

"Upstairs," du Plessis said immediately, and Bill turned to maneuver the smaller man toward a staircase—

but stopped.

Du Plessis wasn't resisting at all, and Bill hadn't so much as brandished a weapon.

"I'm hungry," he growled. *And thirsty.* "Take me to the kitchens first."

As the two of them walked, Bill forced du Plessis into a chat.

Bill had no natural small talk to make, so he forced his face into a frivolous smile and asked du Plessis question after question about the endless parade of martyrs' portraits that decorated all the walls; du Plessis obliged.

"And that one?"

"St. Edward the Martyr, stabbed in the back at the order of his stepmother."

"And this gruesome fellow?"

"St. Bartholomew, skinned alive by the wild men of Armenia. That cloak is his own skin."

"And her?"

"St. Anne Hutchinson, nailed to a cross by the Haudenosaunee for her preaching."

As they walked, Bill noted a couple of grand staircases moving up, but once they had passed out of the front of the Palais with its complex of ballrooms and into servants' territory, the halls and staircases (including a staircase that climbed up from right inside the main kitchen) became narrower. The saints disappeared, too, in favor of simple dark wood panelling.

"A quiet pantry," Bill muttered, "and look cheerful." A glance over his shoulder and a quick count told him that the right number of white-clad partygoers was following him.

He hoped all the right faces were lurking under the Venetian masks.

Du Plessis indicated a long hall off the main kitchen—servants rattled in and out and a master chef stood at the center of a storm of underlings, howling, tasting, and throwing rejected food, sparing only a glance for the outsiders passing through their midst—and at the end Bill found a small room full of linens and china.

"These are the second-best settings," the Creole said. "They won't be used tonight, so no one should have any business to bring them in here, unless some servant girl wants to get a foot-man alone for a few minutes."

"I'll take the risk." Bill shepherded in his companions before grabbing a taper from a sconce in the hall and shutting the door. They all fit, but only standing. Instantly the cat illusion disap-peared and Bill saw the butts of his pistols protruding from the folds of his red coat.

Sarah sucked in air, as if she'd been holding her breath.

"The rest of you, please stay here," he directed, and then he set his own Venetian mask on a linen shelf, drawing one of his long pistols. "You, du Plessis, are going to help me." Bill cocked his pistol and pressed it against the Creole's cheek.

Du Plessis threw his hands up, palms forward, on either side of his head. He looked slightly comical. "O Lord," he said, slowly, and almost as if it were a joke, "is there no help for the widow's son?"

Bill frowned at the pantomime. "Hell's Bells, man," he said, "let us leave our mothers out of this affair."

"That might have worked on me," Sarah told the prisoner, "only you Freemasons don't admit girls, do you?"

The Creole nodded. "Tell me what you want."

"Years ago, a Frenchman named Bayard Prideux wrote the chevalier a letter. I want to see it." As Bill made the demand, he realized it might be ridiculous. The chevalier must have voluminous correspondence, and the idea that this servant would know the location of one particular letter was absurd. "His private correspondence files."

"I know the letter," the Creole said modestly, "though I haven't read it. It's in the chevalier's study, upstairs. I can take you all directly to it."

This was all wrong. Du Plessis was cooperating much too easily. Hell if it wasn't a trap. "How far away?"

The Creole shrugged. "Two minutes' walk."

"What we waitin' for?" Cal asked. He had let his mask drop, showing a look of consternation on his face, like a man who felt intense belly-pain. Bill patted him on his shoulder.

Still, even a mousetrap was baited with real cheese.

Bill forced the engine of his brain to grind over the thought that just outside the door and down a short hall, underlings to the chevalier's master chef were liberally pouring sherry into soups and sauces.

Bill could go alone.

"Your Majesty," he asked, "I have another plan. Could you render me invisible again, for perhaps a quarter of an hour, and this fellow as well? I'll need him as a guide, but I think the two of us alone can retrieve the letter as easily as all of us together, and at less risk. I fear trouble. I ask in the full awareness that we have already called upon your resources in a profligate manner today."

She nodded, after a little hesitation.

"Do I ask too much, ma'am?"

"I reckon that ain't a problem," she said. "Only I have a different idea, something that'd be a little easier for me, and probably ought to do the trick."

Bill nodded his acquiescence and shoved the Creole toward Obadiah and Cal. "Gag him and tie his wrists. I am in your hands, Your Majesty."

"Forgive me." Sarah plucked a long hair from Bill's mustache and one from the Creole's head and she picked up two soup spoons from one of the shelves.

Bill rubbed his face.

"Pewter," she said, and she looked at her own reflection in the back of one spoon. "Good thing these're the second-best settings." Then she wrapped Bill's plucked mustachio around one spoon and the Creole's hair around the other.

"These are impressive preparations," Bill said.

"Good components means the spell is less…costly…for me," she explained. "Also, it will be easier if you swap wigs with the prisoner. I'm going to make you two trade faces, and being able to leave out the wigs'll be a small mercy."

The others gagged and bound du Plessis in the meanwhile, and he exchanged perruques with the seneschal. Then for good measure he extracted his lucky hat from inside his waistcoat, cramming it down over the little man's head. The hat was too big, like a man's hat on a child's head.

Sarah rubbed the Bill-hair-spoon against Bill's cheek and tucked it into the seneschal's pocket and then repeated the operation the other way around. Bill acquiesced with all the grace he could muster.

Finally, she mumbled some *hic, haec, hoc* Latin, and suddenly Bill was looking at himself, bound and gagged, under his own hat brim.

"Your Majesty," he said. "I beg you to stay here. I'll take this man upstairs and retrieve the letter, then meet you here again. If he's telling the truth, I should be back directly, so if I'm not, it may be necessary to flee."

She nodded; she understood. Did she, too, fear a trap? "Be careful, Sir William," she said. "I'll keep up your illusion until I see you again. Your life's much more important to me than the letter."

His queen called him *Sir William*. Bill almost forgot to hear the voices of the whisky calling. Bill grabbed his second pistol from the bundle, refreshed the firing pans of both guns, and stuck one in his belt.

"Move," he said, prodding the other man out into the hall.

Now du Plessis walked slower, and Bill guessed at the direction of the other man's thoughts. If this was a trap, the seneschal would try to lead Bill into it. Bill pressed his gun firmly into the Creole's ribs. "If you run, suh, I'll shoot you."

In the kitchen, du Plessis turned to head back toward the light and movement of the ball, but Bill forced him by main strength straight across, past the maelstrom of cooks fussing over exotic dishes and up the narrow servants' stairs on the other side. This time, no doubt due to the gun in Bill's hand, they spared a little more attention, but they all quickly saw their master's chief servant in charge and went back about their tasks.

"I can't believe the basilisk etouffé is genuine, suh," Bill joked to du Plessis as they climbed to the second story. "The chevalier may be that wealthy, but he is not that generous." The shorter man glared at him.

Two stories up (the second story was quiet, and its narrow halls suggested servants' sleeping quarters and maybe storerooms), du Plessis turned to a large doorway that led out of the dark servants' wing and back into the golden-lit, saint-plastered main portion of the Palais.

Bill reined his prisoner in.

"Understand very clearly, suh," he said, "that at this moment you look like me just as much as I look like you. If anything goes wrong, I will simply shoot you dead and walk away, and none of your fellow-servants will be any the wiser for a good long time. You hold your life in your own hands, and much more precariously than you hold mine."

The seneschal nodded, eyes downcast, and then he led Bill down a long hall to a closed door. Gloomy-faced saints stared down at him from the walls (Bill only recognized Robert Rogers, the famed white devil Wobomagonda, rangy and sharp-eyed and leaning on a notched walking stick), and the hall was otherwise empty.

"Where are the guards?"

The Creole nodded twice to indicate direction, once at each door adjacent to the one by which they stood, up and down the hall.

"Any particular signal?" Bill stared into the other man's eyes. He felt he was staring into his own eyes, underneath the brim of his own hat, which was unnerving, but he kept his snarl tight and angry.

Du Plessis shook his head *no*. Bill took a deep breath, then pulled open the door, dragging his prisoner inside.

Behind the door was a spacious office. After the parade of the sanctified Bill had endured, he was relieved to find the walls of this room bare, other than doors leading to adjoining rooms right and left. A modest table stood in one corner of the room and bookshelves in another, and near the shuttered windows squatted a solid wood desk bearing writing implements and paper.

"The chevalier is a more modest and practical man than I'd imagined, suh," Bill whispered to his prisoner. "Unless...this is your office, isn't it, and not his at all?"

The Creole nodded and Bill snorted a short, suppressed laugh. "Where's the letter?"

Du Plessis nodded at the desk and then, when Bill had maneuvered him behind it, touched one drawer with his knee. Bill opened the drawer and found a single sheet of paper, folded and yellowed with age, on top of a stack of ledgers. He tucked his pistol into his belt, took the letter and unfolded it for a quick look.

French. Of course it was in French.

Dammit.

"Arrêtez-vous!" barked a harsh voice.

Bill started to raise his hands before he remembered that as they saw him, *he* was the seneschal. With a forced calm, he looked up and saw a squad of soldiers filing in through each of the three doors to the room. They were the chevalier's men, in blue and gold, and half of them held up pistols but the other half held knives—knives that, if Bill was not mistaken, looked to be made of silver.

Not only had it been a trap, but the chevalier had known Sarah was a magician. He almost shook his head in appreciation, but had the presence of mind to look to the bottom of the letter, where at least he could read the large signature: *Bayard Prideux*, in a frilly hand.

Bill tucked the letter inside his waistcoat.

Silver, he suddenly thought...magic...

Bill took a step back into the corner of the room, dragging

du Plessis with him. The spoon in his pocket felt conspicuous and heavy. If those daggers got too close to him, his disguise might suddenly fall away, and at fifteen or twenty to one, he didn't like his odds.

He needed to get out the door, fast.

The soldiers lowered their weapons and relaxed, a strong contrast to the tension Bill felt in his own limbs. One of them was talking to him, some kind of sergeant, by the extra gold on his uniform, and Bill concentrated to listen. "Voulez-vous homina homina avec le frou frou prisonnier wah wah doo wop au chevalier?"

Bill's heart sank; that had been a question. If he ran, he might surprise these gendarmes and slip through them, but he'd never get out of the Palais alive. Worse, they'd raise the alarm and his queen would be trapped. As would Cathy.

But what else could he do?

De Plessis, beside him, fidgeted.

"Monsieur?" the sergeant prompted him.

"Oui," Bill said decisively, growling to disguise his voice.

Then he drew his pistol and clubbed du Plessis on the back of the skull. The Creole collapsed. Bill stepped over his body and made for the exit, not looking back and navigating to pass through a cluster of soldiers armed with pistols, rather than silver knives.

He was across the room, marching resolutely, the gendarmes he passed nodding informal salutes.

He was out and into the hall. He patted his waistcoat and heard the reassuring *crinkle* of paper. He hoped the letter was genuine. He hoped Bayard had told him the truth, and the letter identified the other man who had participated in the murder of Kyres Elytharias, the *ozer* man whom Bayard had so feared.

He hoped that René du Plessis was unconscious, or if not, that the gendarmes would leave the seneschal bound and gagged at least until Bill could get down to the pantry and tell Sarah she needed to extend her illusion.

His hat had stayed behind.

He hoped the sacrifice was worth it.

Cal reeled.

The chevalier's seneschal had made the great sign of distress, had done it clearly and deliberately, and Cal had ignored it. Cal had already betrayed the trust his grandfather had put in him by inducting him into masonry and raising him, in a single night, to the degree of Master Mason. Cal had lain awake at nights watching the stars and reviewing in his mind the signs and tokens and passwords and due-guards, anxious not to forget them. The Elector had told him he could use them to call on fellow Masons for help.

And then a fellow Mason had called on Cal, and Cal had ignored him.

Even Sarah had recognized the sign of distress. And of course, she was right; she wasn't a Mason, and she had no obligation to assist the man.

How had the seneschal known Cal was a Mason, though? Cal didn't carry any visible sign, like the square and compass and letter G. Had his induction been published, somehow? Had word been carried to New Orleans?

No, that was ridiculous. Obviously, the fellow had needed help and had made the sign of distress in the hope that someone in the party would recognize it and come to his aid.

And Cal had let him down. Jerusalem, he didn't think the Elector had made him a Mason to get him to work against Sarah, but he still felt bad.

"Mrs. Filmer," he said, "I'm right glad we found your friend Bill." He wanted to distract himself from his own thoughts about Freemasonry, but he also meant his words as a peacemaking gesture. Cathy's presence made him uncomfortable, and she probably knew it.

"Why thank you, Calvin. I'm glad, too ... mostly." She laughed softly, a sound too feminine to be a chuckle and too mature to be a giggle. "He *can* be a handful. And I must admit that I didn't expect to spend the evening standing in a closet. I'd much rather be outside dancing. Are you a dancer, Calvin?"

"Cal dances," Sarah interjected. "He does a rain dance, the dance with death, the song and dance, and, on a rare occasion, if he really has to go and is holding it in, he can shake a leg in a truly impressive pee-pee dance."

Cal was caught off guard and groped for a response, but nothing came to him. Obadiah laughed, and Cal balled his fists. Sarah might trust the Englishman, but Cal hadn't forgotten that he'd once punched her in the face.

Without a warning knock, the door swung open. Everyone threw their masks back up, and Cal nearly jumped out of his skin at the sight of René du Plessis, white powdered wig askew and pistols in his belt.

He grabbed for his tomahawk, but Obadiah caught his hand.

"Your Majesty," du Plessis said to Sarah in the voice of William Lee, bowing slightly, "I have the letter." Cal nodded a grudging thanks to the Englishman, who shrugged and nodded back.

Bill's face again became his own. He produced a folded paper and gave it to Sarah, then handed his pistols to Obadiah, who tucked them back into the bundle of equipment.

"Thank you," Sarah said.

"I'm afraid I can't tell you its contents," Bill apologized, "as it is completely written in Frog, which was Bayard's native ribbit, and in the deciphering of which I have no art. I suggest that we examine the letter when we have a little more leisure, and that now we make a straight line for our borrowed carriage. I fear our discovery is imminent, and I suggest you maintain the illusion on du Plessis as long as you can—it may buy us precious time."

Sarah took the letter, her face a slab of stone, and tucked it inside her shirt. "Agreed." She marched past Bill and into the hall, mask rising as she exited the closet, leaving Cal wondering about the pee-pee dance comment. Did *he* have grounds to be mad at *her* . . . or was *she* mad at *him*?

"If we're detained, Your Majesty," Cal heard Bill say as they passed back through the servants' quarters, "your escape is our *only* priority."

The ball continued as before while Cal followed Sarah and Bill back through the ballrooms toward the exit. The wait inside the china closet had felt eternal, but they had only been in the building an hour or so, and the evening was still young. He saw both Sarah's and Bill's heads shift and become unfamiliar, strangers' heads on his friends' bodies, and the bundle in Obadiah's arms again became a fat, yawning feline.

Could they really just walk out?

Cal wished he were holding his tomahawk.

The ballrooms made Cal feel like a poor, dumb hick. Light sprang from lamps and sconces on all the walls and glittered off gold, silver, and bronze everywhere. Huge paintings hung on all the walls in polished frames, and Cal had no idea who and what they were paintings of. Even the people shone with jewelry and fine cloth, and Calvin reckoned there wasn't a person at the ball who wasn't wearing more wealth on his or her body than Cal had handled in his entire life. Windows glared down at him, windows two stories tall, taller than any house on Calhoun Mountain and tall as most of the trees, shouting at Calvin that he was unwelcome.

Cal shook off his feeling of unease. Sarah needed him.

They passed beside the Igbo quartet leading a room full of New Orleans's good and great in some sort of courtly jig. In a second ballroom, a hurdy-gurdy and pipes played a rousing tune that sounded almost, though not quite, Appalachee, and the Venetian-masked notables galloped a vigorous reel familiar enough that Cal could have joined in. The third ballroom they crossed swayed back and forth to the elegant triple-time rhythms of a small orchestra, and the dancers waltzed so scandalously close to each other that Cal blushed.

They reached the front door. Footmen were still welcoming in guests, announcing each to the attendees who drank and chatted in the front hallway.

This is it, Cal thought, *we made it*. Now they would just walk out the door and disappear into the night.

Only Sarah and Bill had stopped. They stood in a slightly awkward spot, impeding entrance to the hallway, which awkwardness was only made worse by Cal's joining them. A footman hissed through a forced smile to urge them to move on.

"What is it?" Cal still felt stung, and he tried to keep that feeling out of his voice.

Sarah turned and walked back into the ballroom, Bill at her shoulder. Before he wheeled and followed in their wake Cal got a good look out the front door, across the courtyard, and past the gatehouse. Massed in front of the Palais were the Imperial House Light Dragoons, and Cal thought he saw the rotting brown coat of one of the Lazars.

Sarah led them back into the orchestra chamber, where the waltz had ended, a round of clapping was dying out, and the dancers were moving back to clear a large space in the center of the room. Without warning, Cal found himself standing at the edge of the clearing; he felt exposed. He looked back to see if they could retrace their steps, and saw Obadiah and Cathy crammed up behind him, with more guests packing the room behind, making inconspicuous retreat impossible.

He caught Sarah's gaze (Sarah now wore the face of a blond-haired girl with a strong jaw and a German complexion); even through the illusion he could see she was tired. She pushed to try to get through the crowd, but the crowd pushed back, and she stopped.

Another round of applause started, louder this time, and Sarah joined in, turning with the rest of the crowd to face into the empty space. Cal followed her lead. They couldn't break through this throng without being obvious, so best to fit in and lie low.

A man stood alone in the center of the room. He was tall and thin, with dark hair beginning to go gray, and his clothing looked like the ornate, dazzling original of which the gendarmes' uniforms were pale copies—blue and gold, with the stylized three-pointed flower in the detail of it, and a very complicated necktie. He must be the chevalier.

The applause ended, but before the chevalier could speak, there was a commotion at the far entrance to the ballroom. Someone cried something in French, the crowd writhed and jostled and then coughed up a harsh-faced man in a blue and gold uniform.

René du Plessis, the chevalier's seneschal, wigless, bald, and wearing his own face.

Jumpin' Jerusalem.

Cal resisted an impulse to turn and slam his way through the crowd—even if he got through, the footmen and soldiers at the door would stop him cold. His best bet was to continue to play it cool and try to stay hidden. He looked at Sarah to confirm her illusion was still in place, and it was. She also stood still, watching the scene unfold.

Did her insides feel like a mass of seething worms, as Cal's did?

The Creole bowed to his master, approached and whispered something; the chevalier's face grew cold and hard. As they spoke, du Plessis turned, scanning the crowd.

Could he detect them? Might the seneschal have something that let him see through Sarah's illusions? Might he recognize their clothes?

A cold rivulet of sweat trickled down Cal's spine.

"Voilà!" du Plessis shouted, pointing at Cal, and then followed up with some more French.

The crowd exploded.

Jerusalem.

Well, he'd failed to help a fellow Mason when he'd been in trouble, but Cal would be damned before he'd fail to help Sarah. At least he could provide cover for the others to get away.

He turned and saw Obadiah at his shoulder (he knew him by the cat) and, gritting his teeth against the visual strangeness of what he was doing, Cal dropped his mask and shoved his hand into the feline's chest. He planted his fingers in a mass of wood and steel and found his war axe. Pushing Obadiah back into the crowd, he yanked free the tomahawk and spun to face the chevalier.

Lord hates a man as won't stand up for his friends.

"Oh Lord, is there no help for the widow's son?" he cried.

And he charged.

Cal got nowhere.

Bill, standing next to the brave young Appalachee, watched him thrown to the ground in a shower of discarded Venetian masks. Gendarmes shoved guests aside at the entrances, struggling to get into the room, but it was the crowd itself, the assembled eminences of New Orleans, that grabbed Calvin.

Say what you will of New Orleans, but even its gentlefolk were hard as nails.

As was Cal, who thrashed with fists and feet and gave as good as he got.

Bill grabbed Sarah's arm to whisper into her ear. "Run! Calvin's distracting them!"

But even as he said it, he knew the crowd surging around them was too thick, and too many gendarmes pushed their way. Sarah regained her own face, eye patch and all, and Bill ducked, hoping the chevalier hadn't seen his head protruding above the crowd.

Sarah mumbled something that included the word *"serpentes"* and flung her fingers at Cal where he wrestled on the floor. A black hairball landed on Calvin's chest.

Cal, having regained his own features, was buried in a sudden avalanche of snakes. They were striped orange, white, and black, and they wound all about him about the hands and arms of those that fought him down.

"Serpientes!" a fat man shouted, and jumped away.

With many-pitched gasps and more than one shriek of surprise, the rest of the crowd dropped Calvin and took a startled step back.

"Emmenez-les!" shouted the chevalier. *To hell with it*, Bill thought, and he straightened his posture.

The cat was gone, and Obadiah held the bundle toward Bill, wrestling with his elbow against two bewigged Frenchmen in livery Bill didn't recognize. It was a good thing the Englishman was burly.

Bill batted aside a bony man who tried to bite him and regretfully restrained a claw-flailing matron with his forearm on her chest, yanking both guns from Obadiah and spinning to meet the nearest gendarmes.

Out of the corner of his eye, Bill saw Cal standing up free of the tangle of snakes, tomahawk sweeping a wide space around him that the ballgoers hesitated to enter. Obadiah had a broadsword out, Cathy held two pistols, and Sarah gripped her staff like a club. They would not surrender without a fight, at least.

"Emmenez-les!" the chevalier yelled.

Bill clubbed down an overenthusiastic footman with the butt of one horse pistol. He was understanding more French, and felt a small surge of pride.

"Cet homme la, il a assassiné mon fils!" the chevalier cried.

Bill had been spotted. He tossed a short gendarme aside. At least the ambiguity of his employment situation had been resolved.

The dancers were flushing out of the way.

Half a dozen blue-and-gold uniforms advanced on Bill. Bill raised both pistols and pulled the hammers back.

"Arrêtez-vous!" shouted a voice Bill thought he recognized. He ignored it, bound and determined not to *arrête* anything until they pried his guns from his cold, dead fingers, but the gendarmes facing him stopped, looking startled and uncertain.

Bill risked a glance over his shoulder.

The chevalier stood in the center of a cleared piece of floor, even his seneschal having stepped away. Someone stood beside him in an elegant black suit, pressing a knife into the billowing cravat at the chevalier's throat.

Someone Bill knew, though it took him a moment to realize it. An old man, with rouge on his cheeks, a thin mustache grease-penciled onto his upper lip, and a mad gleam in his eye.

Don Sandoval.

Hell's Bells.

"Iffen anybody as ain't William Lee or Obadiah Dogsbody
sticks his head in, you knock it clean to Baton Rouge."

CHAPTER TWENTY-FOUR

The crowd pressed itself against the walls of the ballroom, and
Sarah drifted with them. The gendarmes shouldered past her to
surround the old Spaniard with his knife to the chevalier's neck;
in the urgency of the sudden threat to their master's life, they
had forgotten entirely about Sarah's party.

"*Facies muto.*" She willed herself and her companions to again
resemble the Prince of Shreveport and his family.

Her own reservoir of magical energy was at a very low ebb,
a sensation which felt a lot like exhaustion and fatigue and a
little bit like being hungry and thirsty. She still had Thalanes's
moon-shaped brooch, pinned now to the white dress she had
borrowed from one of the Machogu women. She hadn't tapped
any of its energy yet, out of a sense that the energy humming
within the monk's bauble was the last piece that remained of
the man himself, his *pneuma* or his *psyche*, his *spiritus* or his
anima, and once she used it up, he would be irrevocably gone.

Sir William was distracted by the spectacle in the center of
the room. "Sir William," she hissed at him, "let's go!"

He didn't seem to hear her.

"Non!" The chevalier raised an arm to direct his men, but
his captor cut him off.

"Je le fis!" shouted the old man, and pressed his knife tighter
into the chevalier's cravat. He drew a thin trickle of blood, a

shocking crimson flower in the bed of white. "Je suis moi qui l'assassinais!"

"Hell's Bells," Sir William muttered. "The old fool will kill himself."

Sarah thought she saw the Spaniard wink at Sir William, and Sir William tip his head in a slight deferential bow, and then she pulled his elbow and drew him back with her into the hall. "We gotta leave while they're distracted, out the front door."

Sir William shook himself like a dog coming out of water and focused on the exit. Calvin, Cathy, and Obadiah fell in behind them. "You're my queen, ma'am. I will only observe that the Blues and the Lazars remain outside, and if we're detected we're likely to face combat."

"We're between a rock and a hard place, Captain," Sarah said. "It's my choice, and I choose the rock."

Sir William tucked his pistols into his belt, crooking an elbow toward Sarah. "In that case, Your Majesty, the Prince of Shreveport offers you his arm."

Sarah took the proffered elbow and followed him out the door.

She and Sir William both inclined their heads to the footmen at the door, ignoring their sour looks in return, and passed into the cool evening air. Behind them she heard cries and blows.

Twenty-odd Blues, the Right Reverend Father Ezekiel Angleton, and several of the rot-coated Lazars stood mounted beyond the front gate. She ignored them and turned right along the face of the Palais, strolling at a casual pace past clumps of magnolia and cherub-festooned fountains toward the white and gold coach they'd left an hour earlier.

"Jerusalem," Cal whispered. "I ain't ne'er felt more nekkid in all my life."

Could Sarah's enemies see through her disguise? She resisted a strong desire to turn her head and look to see whether she was being watched, and instead focused on the coach. The smooth cobblestones before her stretched like an endless sea to the white and gold wheeled lighthouse on the distant shore, calling her on, guiding her through the shoals of footmen and fountains.

There was a commotion behind her, at the door of the Palais. Sarah willed herself to keep walking.

Closer.

Footmen bowed, and Sarah and Sir William nodded in return.

She heard shouting behind her in French.

Almost there. One of the two coachmen stepped down to hold the door open, while the other mounted the front of the coach to take the reins.

The shouting suddenly got louder. "Emmenez-les!"

"Sarah, they spotted us!" Cal cried.

Sir William dropped Sarah's arm and pulled both pistols, leveling them at the two servants. "Get away from the carriage, gentlemen, or I shall release you from my service in a fashion you will find most abrupt."

The coachmen stumbled away in terror and Obadiah climbed, quite spryly for his size, up to the coachman's seat. "Get in, poppet." He took the whip and reins. "I can 'andle this well enow."

They jumped into the carriage and the party's disguises dropped. Cal tossed the real prince and his family, still tied and squirming, to the ground. As he shut the door again, Sarah heard the *clop* of horses' hooves and the coach rolled forward into action.

Sarah finally risked a glance out the window, and her heart sank. From the Palais swarmed gendarmes, armed and barking. The Blues beyond the gatehouse turned their horses to move in the same direction as Sarah's carriage, following a course convergent with her own down the street, with Angleton and Hooke at their head, both staring at her.

She snapped her gaze away, remembering with an icicle through her heart the groping hands and endless amniotic sea of Robert Hooke's spell; she could not afford to meet his eyes again, at least not until she was stronger. She looked ahead.

There was a second gatehouse at the end of the cobbled yard, and the carriages were organized to exit through it. The night still being young, there was no queue ahead of them, but a dozen gendarmes were forming themselves into a line across the gate, drawing pistols and yelling at Obadiah in French to stop.

"Froggez-vous!" Obadiah yelled gleefully back at them.

"Pardon me, Your Majesty," Sir William said to Sarah, "but would you please keep your head inside the carriage? I believe we're about to exchange pleasantries."

"I see them," she said.

To Cathy, who was loading the Lafitte pistols, the Cavalier added, "Save your powder, ma'am, until they try to board us."

Then Sarah pulled herself inside and ducked, pressing her body against the heavy back of the coach, while Sir William leaned out the window in her place.

"The portcullis!" Obadiah shouted. "'It that fellow ere he brings the gate down on our 'eads, Bill!"

Bang!

"Drive!" Sir William shouted.

Then the gunfire began in earnest.

The glass windowpanes of the carriage shattered and the wood of its frame spat splinters as lead balls punched their way through. Sarah hunched low with Cathy and Calvin and hoped Sir William could avoid being shot, hanging as he was out the window.

The carriage rattled across the cobblestones. Sarah ventured a glance out the window and saw the Blues, galloping behind Angleton and Hooke; they were behind, but gaining, and Sarah racked her brain for a spell. She didn't think she had the energy to turn the entire carriage and its teams of horses invisible, not for long enough to make a difference; she knew she hadn't the strength to turn them into birds; disguises at this point would be useless.

Bang! Bang!

Wheels thundered across stone; bullets ripped the air to dangerous shreds. They must be almost to the gate now. Sarah peeked again across the tall iron fence—she could see Hooke's pale face and white, worm-seething eyes framed by his flapping scarf, and she ducked.

"Here they come, Mrs. Filmer!" Sir William shouted, and fired.

There was a *thud!* of colliding bodies as gendarmes threw themselves against the front and side of the carriage. Sarah thought she heard a cry from the roof of the carriage, but gave it no thought in the general ruckus of shots, blades, and flailing limbs.

Bang!

Sir William dispatched a gendarme with an efficiently-aimed pistol ball to the sternum, then drew his sword and swung out the door of the coach to attack someone at the coachman's seat.

Bang!

Cathy shot one assailant in the forehead, knocking him off the side of the vehicle, then calmly switched pistols and fired into another man's shoulder. The second man cried out in surprise, and had no strength to resist when Cathy pistol-whipped him in the jaw, sending him tumbling to the ground. Acrid smoke from the pistols filled the coach.

The Imperials clattered through the gatehouse and into the street, and the coach swerved to put the dragoons directly behind them. Sarah still rummaged through her imagination for a good spell. She wanted the horses to go faster, and she remembered Thalanes's morning coffee spell, and the little sack of beans nestled in the monk's satchel. The Latin, though . . . it had been more complicated. What was it Thalanes had incanted? Pedes *something, though of course* pedes *is feet, and horses don't have feet.*

But could she even cast a spell at all, through the silver filigree in the doors and windows of the coach?

Cal, meanwhile, needed help.

He had smashed one attacker away from the door with his tomahawk, but the blow left him open and another gendarme was dragging him slowly out the window by his long hair. Cal's left hand fought for a grip strong enough to keep him from being tossed overboard, and he couldn't bring the ax in his right hand to bear. One begrudged inch at a time, the young Calhoun slid closer to a hard fall.

Sarah drew the silver letter opener and moved toward the gendarme. His eyes widened, but he couldn't free up a hand, either, and so he made no effective resistance when she stabbed him in his stomach. For good measure, Cathy punched him in the temple with the butt of a pistol. Crying out wordlessly, the gendarme let go and fell.

"Thanks," Cal said to both of them.

Sarah regretted snapping at him in the china closet. Scuffling and thumping sounds continued on the roof, but there were no more gendarmes actually trying to climb inside the coach, so Sarah pulled out Thalanes's sack of beans.

She poured a handful into her palm and looked at them, wondering how best to use them in an act of gramarye. She wanted to build a conduit for the transmission of power, because that made the transmission efficient, and it cost her less to cast a spell that way. Ideally, she'd like to boil a pot of coffee and give it to the horses, but in the circumstances that was impractical.

She'd use the least power if she could somehow get up onto the top of the carriage and get the beans into physical contact with the horses, but that seemed impossible. If she didn't simply fall off from all the rattling, she'd get shot.

Looking at Cal, craning his neck to peer out the carriage window as he hefted his long-handled tomahawk, she had an idea.

"Calvin!" she called to him, and he immediately gave her his attention. "I need you to smash open a hole in the front of the coach here." She had meant to request his help, but it came out sounding like an order.

She pointed at the front wall of the carriage, low and just above the front seat, and drew a little square in the air with her finger. She felt reasonably sure that would be well below where Obadiah sat, holding the reins.

"Big enough for what?" Cal didn't quite meet her gaze. "You fixin' to climb through?"

"No," she told him. "I jest gotta be able to spit through it."

He shot one last look out the window and then set to the work, hacking at the carriage wall and grunting. The workmanship was solid, but Cal's axe was sharp and he was an old hand at chopping wood.

Whack! Whack! Whack!

But what was the Latin she needed?

Ungula, that was a hoof, she remembered. Were accelero *and* augeo *the verbs Thalanes had used?* Of course, really, she could use any words she wanted. Any that fit.

Calvin had chopped open the hole. It was square, splintered around the edges and about the size of Sarah's face. The *cloppety-cloppety-cloppety* rattle of hooves on cobblestones filled the coach, and Sarah could see indistinct brushes of movement through the opening.

He stepped aside to show his handiwork, she nodded, and he went back to the window.

Bang! Bang!

Sarah heard shots from the top of the carriage, and then felt the coach jerk sideways as something hit it from behind. It must be one of the Blues, jumping aboard—they were overtaken.

She lost her hesitation and found her vocabulary.

"*Ungulas accelero crures augeoque!*" She touched the brooch at her chest and threw coffee beans into her mouth.

She bit into them hard as she willed vitality and speed out of Thalanes's moon brooch and into the beans. She pressed her face to the hole and spat, spraying chewed coffee beans onto the hindmost pairs of hooves and the pole that ran up between them, and the soul energy of the monk Thalanes flowed through Sarah's mouth, through her spittle and the ground coffee beans, and into the carriage horses of the Prince of Shreveport.

The coach leaped forward, throwing its three occupants to the floor.

A rooftop *thump!* made Sarah fear she might have dislodged Obadiah or Sir William, but it was followed close on by a *snap!* and then a cry of pain, and then Sir William poked his head in the window, his body apparently lying flat on the carriage roof.

"Heaven's curtain, Your Majesty," he drawled, the seneschal's white powdered perruque dangling upside down off his bald skull and making him look completely ridiculous, "you've lit quite a fire under the horses' hindquarters."

Sarah nodded, feeling weak. "It won't last, unfortunately. Please take us to the river, Sir William."

"Yes, ma'am," he agreed. "Do we have a plan?"

She shook her head. "Not yet, but I hope to by the time we get there." She needed to get to the river and its great ley line, where at least she could become magically effective again. Even if it killed her, she'd be able to cast some big spell of escape, or defense, or attack.

"Yes, ma'am," Sir William acknowledged. "The Englishman has been hit, but I have some experience with carriages myself, and I believe we'll have no difficulty making the Mississippi." He pulled his head back in and disappeared.

All the power Sarah had collected at the death of Thalanes was gone.

He was gone, however many parts it was that really made him up.

"Good-bye," she murmured.

Then she chuckled, softly. The little Cetean would probably have been amused to know that when he finally went, the last of him had gone in a spurt of coffee.

"I'm sorry, do you want me up top?" Calvin asked.

"No," she said. "I's jest ... I wasn't talking to you."

"Shall I stay here, then, Your Majesty?" Cal's eyes were down-cast, and his miserable expression stabbed Sarah in the heart.

"Calvin Calhoun, you vex me," she said. "One minute, I

want to kiss you—" here his eyes lit up, "and the next I almost can't help but whack you upside the head. First of all, you don't call me *Your Majesty*, leastways not in private. Second, yes, stay here, iffen we get attacked again, I'll want more'n this here toy pigsticker to ward off my uncle's thugs." She waved Chigozie Ukwu's silver letter opener.

Cal nodded.

"Third, you and I got to have us a long talk about important things like feelin's, only it ain't gonna happen today, so I need you to hold your horses. For now, I reckon I ought to say that there ain't any feller on earth I like more'n you. Any problems with that?"

Cal shook his head, looking almost hopeful. "No, Sarah, I ain't got no problems with any of that." He paused a moment, then continued slowly. "I don't reckon you believe me yet, but I'm jest crazy about you. Even if I weren't, though, you're my friend and my granddaddy loves you like his own child. I promised the Elector I'd keep you safe, and Jerusalem iffen I don't aim to do jest that."

"Fine," Sarah said. "Then for right now, your job is jest to watch the windows, and iffen anybody as ain't William Lee or Obadiah Dogsbody sticks his head in, you knock it clean to Baton Rouge."

"I reckon I can do that."

"I know you can," Sarah said, "so I'll git to cogitatin' about what to do when we git to the Mississippi."

And for good measure, she kissed him.

Daniel Berkeley felt a cold ball of fear in his stomach. His hand was steady, his eye fierce, his men would never have detected his uncertainty, but there it was, lodged deep in his bowels.

Why had the Witchy Eye gone back to the Palais? Why had the chevalier excluded him and the parson? Was it, as the chevalier had implied, merely for money?

Daniel Berkeley feared he was about to be exposed.

He didn't know for certain what would happen if he was unmasked, or if Thomas Penn's guilt was known. The emperor might lose his throne, but then again, he might not. The Cahokians might want to withdraw from the empire, and that was a potential nest of vipers—it seemed to him, not being a political man—but then, Cahokia had no king, had not had one for fifteen years. Would the other Ohioans withdraw over the death of one of their fellows? Could the Ohioans do anything at all, really, with the Pacification troops encamped in their lands and all their commerce in the hands of the Imperial Ohio Company?

Would the Electors be so offended at the murder of one of *their* number that they would call a new election and replace Thomas? Would Thomas simply lose prestige and therefore power and be vulnerable to some rebel upstart, some minor figure in the Penn family or even some outsider? Berkeley didn't know, but he knew Thomas would want his secrets kept. For the same reason that he wanted the girl captured.

So he had had to kill the bishop. He hadn't wanted to do it, but the priest was threatening to expose Thomas Penn and Daniel Berkeley, and that had forced Daniel's hand.

Surely, the fact that he had had no choice must mitigate the bad luck, mustn't it?

But a little bad luck might be worth it. If Daniel Berkeley could continue to keep the stain on the Penn family shield hidden, all would be well—he would remain Captain of the Imperial House Light Dragoons, his own secrets would stay hidden, he would prosper. But if he failed, he would not survive the ensuing storm. He might finish at the bottom of a rope, or at the wrong end of a revenge drama, or even as his master's scapegoat in front of a firing squad, but, short of turning and running right now into Texia, his death was certain.

And Daniel Berkeley was not a man to turn tail and flee.

He itched to cast the Tarock—the parson had returned his cards to him with a haughty sniff. Addicted to card-reading like some gypsy crone, but as the Andalusian gray beneath him surged through the dark New Orleans streets, and the heavy carriage ahead somehow pulled away, Daniel Berkeley felt the heavy hand of fate closing about him.

He had sins to pay for, and his Tarock these days seemed to contain nothing but Simon Sword. Judgment, judgment, judgment.

"Gee yap!" he shouted, spurring his horse harder.

He'd seen the Andalusian foaled and raised it himself, on his family lands. They were too high above the Chesapeake to be any good for farming, but they had plenty of good pasturage for horses, and as horse people the Berkeleys had thrived. Their horses had thrived, too, and were prized by discerning riders from Champlain's Acadia to Igbo Montgomery. Now this animal responded magnificently, straining and accelerating.

But Berkeley could see it would not be enough.

"Can you do nothing, then?" he turned to shout over his shoulder at his two spell-wielding companions.

Father Angleton shook his head and shouted back. "I am spent!"

"Blazes!" Berkeley shouted, wishing the Blues rode with a real combat wizard.

The witch will tire, the Lazar reassured them both in his mindspeech. *Do not fret, she cannot last. All the same . . .* The white-skinned dead man seemed to focus his mind for a moment, and then two horses, the mounts of his two dead companions, burst forward ahead of the pack, closing the gap with the coach.

The Englishman didn't look well.

Several fingers were splinted, making his grip on the reins awkward. He bled from at least two wounds Bill could see, one in his thigh and a more disturbing one in his chest. Blood soaked his waistcoat and breeches and he sat in a sticky pool, giving *hee-ya!* to the horses as vigorously as a man in perfect health, though pallor crept into his face under all the stubble.

The man had animal qualities. He'd have been a good soldier.

Bill himself had been lucky not to be shot. Surely, this luck could not last.

Not hatless as he was.

He finished loading both pistols and tucked them into his belt, then looked back at the pursuit. The Blues had fallen behind but were still visible, a spectral *posse comitatus* slipping in and out of pools of light in the distance.

For a moment, Bill entertained the notion of trying to hide the carriage somewhere, perhaps turn a sharp corner and plunge into the thick trees of a park, or into some alleyway. Maybe Sarah could disguise their coach, make it appear to be some other wagon.

He dismissed the idea. It would be a gamble on a single throw of the dice, and if they were caught, they were doomed; no, their best hope lay in flight. They were outnumbered five to one, not even taking into account the Lazars.

As if his train of thought had brought it on, Bill noticed that two of the horses following them were drawing nearer, and that their two riders were Lazars: the burnt one missing an eye and Tom Long-Knife. Bill shuddered. Only hours earlier he'd chopped the fingernails off Black Tom and left him incapacitated, and now the undead rebel was riding again.

"We're about to receive visitors, suh," he informed Obadiah. "Are your pistols loaded?"

"Aye, an' primed." The Englishman laughed a death-defying chuckle.

Bill watched the two undead edge closer; as they splashed through a pool of yellow light he saw the white of their three eyes between rotting hat brims and moldering scarves. He hated to risk a bullet on any shot from such an unstable platform, but the thought of fighting two of the Lazars simultaneously soured his stomach. Bill knelt, bracing himself on the coach roof, and fired.

Bang!

Some irregularity in the street's paving jostled the carriage at the wrong moment, throwing off his aim.

"Damn," Bill muttered.

The Lazars grinned and leaned lower over their mounts.

Bill looked over his shoulder at the inky road ahead. "Try to avoid the potholes, suh." Obadiah laughed in answer and cracked the reins. Bill took aim again, carefully. The Lazars were closer now, twenty feet behind the carriage's rear wheels, fifteen, ten—

Bang!

Bill hit his target between the eyes. The recipient of his attention—the horse of the burned Lazar—plowed into the stone of the street, throwing its rider to the ground.

Bill tucked both pistols into his belt and drew his sword as Tom Long-Knife jumped, flying through the air like a grasshopper and alighting on the coach roof.

Bill slashed at the Lazar's knees. Tom shuffled back and drew his famous long knife, and Bill pressed his attack, leaping onto the roof to swing again. The Lazar took the blow on the shoulder with a grin, then slashed repeatedly at Bill, Bill barely managing to parry the hard, swinging blows. Then Bill battered the long knife aside and plunged his own blade deep into the Lazar's chest.

The wound would have instantly killed a living man, but in the moment he inflicted it, Bill knew he'd made a mistake. His face inches from Tom's, he saw in stomach-unsettling detail the pallid flesh of the creature's face, his bulging white eyes, and the worms boiling in his eyesockets. Death-reek hung like a cloud about him, and where Bill expected gushing blood, there was none.

There was only a yellow-toothed, humorless smile, and then the Lazar swung his knife again.

Bill stepped in closer to the dead man to make his attack ineffective. He yanked on his sword's hilt to no avail—he had buried his own Excalibur in a stone of necromantic flesh.

He stepped too close; Black Tom bit Bill's ear.

Bill yelled, punching the undead and separating the two fighters. They both tottered, a long pace apart, each struggling to regain his balance. Spanish moss-hung oaks flew by in the darkness like half-seen trolls and the cool, damp air of the night whipped away Bill's stolen perruque.

Beelzebub's topknot. Where's my hat when I need it?

He saw Calvin's red head peeping out from the window of the coach. "Stay inside, Cal!" Bill yelled. "Watch the queen! There's no room up here!"

Black Tom lurched forward, stabbing at Bill's stomach.

Bill narrowly managed to step aside, his heels slipping at the edge of the coach roof but not quite losing their grip. He grabbed the Lazar's knife hand in both his own, stepping with his left foot inside the dead man's stance. They grappled for control of the blade, the hilt of Bill's own weapon teasingly poking against his shoulder.

He felt the long sharp fingernails of the dead man; how had they grown back so fast? That was what he needed to do, ideally, chop off the thing's nails off again. On the top of a rolling coach, though, was not a great location to attempt such precise maneuvers.

Worms dropped from Black Tom's eyes onto his arm, and Bill felt faint from breathing in the grave-like exhalations.

Bang!

The Lazar staggered from the bullet's impact and Bill took the opportunity to kick his foot out from under him. He dropped the Lazar bodily to the rooftop.

"I've done for you now, you rotten bugger!" Obadiah roared, and laid his empty pistol beside him on the seat.

The dead man had fallen back with the point of Bill's sword aimed down at the rooftop, pushing the weapon out of his chest.

Bill took the hilt and jerked it clean, staggering to his feet and slashing hard at Black Tom, aiming for the right hand of the walking corpse.

The Lazar sprang to his feet, avoiding the blow and raising his guard again. No blood, no black ichor dripped from the gaping hole in his chest where he'd been impaled, nor from the bullet wound Obadiah had put in his cheek.

How to kill such a monster?

More trees whizzed by, and Bill looked at the dark ground. He smelled the river and knew they were getting close. He didn't know what Sarah planned to do when they arrived, but he was sure her plans couldn't include having a Lazar aboard.

He engaged with Tom again, parrying a flurry of attacks, and in the repeated clash of steel Bill let himself be backed into a corner. He carefully felt out his footing on the rumbling, jittery coach rooftop, preparing to grapple his enemy again, careful not to back too close to Obadiah, who had enough to do with handling the horses, and didn't need Black Tom Fairfax falling on top of him.

When he was ready, Bill feigned an overextension and dropped to one knee—

the Lazar stabbed for Bill's exposed head—

Bill twisted, parried, and got his basket hilt and his free hand pinched around Tom's sword hand. He threw his body back toward his own shoulder and pulled, meaning to yank the Lazar over his own back and throw him to the street.

But Tom Long-Knife was more cunning than Bill had planned, and had kept his center of gravity low. When Bill yanked, the Lazar dropped to one knee himself and jammed a sharp elbow into Bill's throat, knocking Bill onto his back, gasping, vision spinning, and perilously close to falling off the top of the coach.

The Lazar raised his blade overhead to deliver a killing blow. Bill held his own weapon up to parry, but his arm was weak and his fingers nerveless, and he felt himself staring into the rotten white eyes of death. Hell's Bells, just when life was beginning to get interesting again.

Someone had said those words to him. Who was it?

Something crashed into the Lazar, grabbing the dead man and dragging him by sheer impetus away from Bill. He felt the carriage slow and drift, and Bill realized semi-consciously that

Obadiah had left the reins to attack the dead man. He choked and coughed, trying to gasp out words of encouragement and warning, but could say nothing other than "O . . . badi . . . ah!"

"Now I'll finish the job, you bloody stinkink 'eathen!" Obadiah headbutted Tom Long-Knife in the nose. The Lazar punched him back and then bit the Englishman in the shoulder.

Bill struggled to sit up, his breath coming in gasps, and faced an immediate choice. Obadiah Dogsbody might or might not be able to handle the Lazar by himself. On the other hand, the horses, left to their own devices, would either run amok or stop, neither of which was acceptable.

Bill looked past Obadiah to see their pursuers. Did he have the time to split the difference by helping Obadiah and then taking control of the horses? He saw the Blues, less than half a mile behind, and he knew he had no time to spare.

He sheathed his sword and slid awkwardly down off the front of the rooftop and into the coachman's seat, where Obadiah had left the guiding lines wrapped around the seat rail. Bill took the reins.

But on the blood-smeared seat, wedged between its leather cushions, he saw Obadiah's two pistols.

Bill snapped the reins to get the horses back to speed, though it seemed to him that they weren't going as fast as they had been. Maybe Sarah's magical burst of speed was exhausted. Sitting at the front of the coach, he now knew where they were—coming down Canal, with a left turn onto Decatur just ahead.

The quickest route to the river would be down Decatur and to the docks.

Fortunately, Canal had a variety of light traffic, foot and the occasional horse but no other vehicles. "Scatter!" Bill roared at the pedestrians in his path. He took the turn onto Decatur wide, cutting through the traffic and sending strollers flying in all directions.

The horses neighed in objection—
the coach creaked and lifted briefly onto two wheels—
Bill made the turn without slowing down—
crash!—
the raised wheels of the carriage slammed down again onto the ground, and Bill found himself staring down the straight shot of Decatur at the Mississippi Gate.

Bill wrapped the reins around his left fist, grabbed one of Obadiah's pistols in his right (one of them, he knew, had already been fired, and he hoped he'd grabbed the loaded gun), stood, turned, and looked for a shot.

Obadiah grunted and swayed, locked in a mortal embrace with the decaying Tom Fairfax. Blood pooled on the rooftop, and one of the dead man's thumbs lay twitching in the pool. Blood poured down the Englishman's chest, and from his mouth, where he seemed to have lost teeth, and out of one gaping eye socket, but he looked indomitable in his rage, shouting obscenities as he pushed his dead foe's neck back with both hands.

The dead man struggled to bring his knife down in a chop on Obadiah's neck, but could not quite do it.

Bill took careful aim at Black Tom's knee and pulled the trigger. *Click.*

Damn gun. Bill shoved the pistol into his belt and cast a glance forward as he picked up the other.

Decatur Street, being the southern border of the Quarter, was thick with evening traffic, traffic that leaped and skidded out of the way of Bill's six rampaging white horses. The Mississippi Gate loomed nearby; it was recessed from the street, creating a plaza, and Bill intended to try to turn his carriage and race through the gate without stopping. If any gendarmes expected to stop him and exact a toll, so much the worse for them.

The Blues were gaining ground, his old lieutenant Berkeley in front, beside the Martinite and the third Lazar. The Prince of Shreveport's teams were tired and their magical enhancement had definitely ended. The Blues might be only a quarter mile behind. He had to take the gate at a run, and he hoped Sarah had a good plan, because the only idea Bill had was to commandeer a boat and flee on the river, and he didn't think he had the time or the firepower to pull it off.

Obadiah was hunched down, now, with his hands around Tom's wrists and his head pounding into his foe's chest, so Bill had a clear shot at the Lazar's face, and almost took it. At the last moment, though, he remembered Tom's nails, lowered his aim and pulled the trigger.

Bang!

Bill's bullet tore through the walking corpse's long, gnarled toenails, breaking them and scattering them to the dark night winds. Black Tom stumbled, spinning awkwardly on one suddenly useless leg—

but as he staggered away, Obadiah lost his grip, too, and slipped forward—

and the Lazar rammed his knife into the Englishman's chest.

Obadiah roared as the tip of the blade poked out between his shoulderblades. "You miserable nuffink!" He lurched forward to headbutt the Lazar one last time.

Crack!

Tom lost his grip on his knife and fell off the back end of the carriage. He hit the cobblestones at a bad angle with a sickening *crunch!* and lay in a heap. Obadiah collapsed to the rooftop of the coach, blood gouting from his chest.

"Hold on, suh!" Bill tucked the fourth pistol into his belt and turned to pay all his attention to the team of horses and the Mississippi Gate.

The pistol shot had helped scatter the crowd. Also, the gendarmes didn't have the heart to get in Bill's way, maybe because he wore the Prince of Shreveport's clothing and drove his coach. For all the chevalier's men knew, he was some servant of the cotton prince on an urgent errand, and they stood away as he turned the horses in the direction of the gate.

The horses were tired, and didn't respond as quickly as he'd like. Bill hauled on the reins with all the strength of his upper body, the horses whinnied, they turned, the coach rose up onto two wheels, Bill pulled, and the lead left horse barely, just barely, missed the stone wall of the gate and made it inside.

But the wheels of the coach were not gripping the wet stone, and as Bill turned into the short tunnel that was the Mississippi Gate, the carriage slid left.

Crash!

The left side of the coach smashed against the wall, and Bill felt both the left wheels shredded instantly into toothpicks. "Hell's Bells!"

The axles *screeched* against the stone and kept the coach upright on two wheels as it plunged through the gate, but this was the end. Once out of the tunnel, the carriage would collapse, and within seconds they would be overtaken.

He looked back at Obadiah. The Englishman had pulled the blade that killed him out of his chest and lay in a pool of his own gore, breath rattling thick and hard in his throat. He caught Bill's gaze with his bloody, one-eyed stare and managed something that was almost a jaunty grin. "Tell my poppet," he wheezed, "I mean, tell *'Er Majesty*, I was a brave man in 'er service, at the end. Please."

Bill nodded. "You were indeed, suh."

Obadiah closed his remaining eye and breathed deeply. "An' tell Peg I always loved 'er," he added, and then expired.

Peg?

The end of the gate loomed before Bill, the horses emerging from the tunnel to pound down the gravel slope toward the river and its wharves. He tightened his grip on the reins and prepared to battle with the animals against the coach's collapse.

Instead, to his utter astonishment, the lead horses lifted off the ground and into the air.

And then the second team followed, and the third.

And then the coach burst from the outer mouth of the Mississippi Gate and took flight, rising into the cool night air. The reins hung slack in Bill's hands. The carriage ascended and turned and above the Mississippi River it climbed, as if the river itself were a great black highway on which it alone of all coaches knew how to travel.

Bill reached back to grab Obadiah's body, to keep him from falling off the carriage. He looked down, thankful he'd never been afraid of heights, and both amused and slightly disturbed to see Berkeley and the other Blues, pouring en masse down onto the Mississippi wharves and pointing up in his direction.

Shots were fired, but it was too late. Even as its horses realized they were no longer pulling any burden and stopped moving their legs, the Prince of Shreveport's coach rose, picked up speed, and slid away into the night, shedding its other two wheels with faint splashes into the water below.

Hell's Bells, Bill thought. *I could really use a shot of whisky.*

"I's ugly afore, remember, Cal?
Now I'm jest ugly and bald."

—➤◦◄—

CHAPTER TWENTY-FIVE

Sarah felt as if the river itself were flowing through her. She lay across one of the seats of the ruined carriage, her muscles taut, and she thought she might even be weeping, but her body seemed far away.

And on fire, and floating in a sea of ice.

Her soul (or was it her spirit? her *psyche*, or her *pneuma*?) she held stretched open, like a funnel, and the green light of the Mississippi ley line poured through her, lifting her and her entourage. She did not feel the passage of time, but she was aware of distance. She knew it not as riders or walkers know it, the stretching of the road to the horizon, the fields and woods connecting one hamlet to the next, nor even as sailors, landmark and star, astrolabe and compass, but as the river itself knew it. She sensed the thick sheets of mud slide about her as she flew, and catfish, alligators, snakes, and darker, unknown things crawled over her soul and left her feeling slimy and wet.

She could not keep this up long, and was determined to get as far from New Orleans as she could before the Mississippi burned her out. She turned with the bends of the river. She knew it was cold, and she was aware that Calvin and Cathy covered her with one of the prince's furs. She tried to grasp Cal's hand in gratitude, but in her power-whelmed and distracted state, she barely managed a scratching claw at his thigh.

Finally, her body and heart on the verge of being torn into shreds by the raw power of the experience, Sarah brought the coach down. She remembered her physical surroundings as she did so, and realized she needed to see.

"The window," she croaked. "Help me to the window."

Cal and Cathy bore her gently, and Sarah looked outside. Under a thick blanket of stars, both banks of the river were dotted with the evening lights of human habitation, which helped clear her head and give her a more distinct sense of the distance she had come—since the west bank was not swallowed yet by the Great Green Wood, they must still be somewhere over the Cotton Princedoms.

That could even be Shreveport off to the left, though Monroe might be closer—the dizzying heights gave her vertigo, and she couldn't clearly remember the Elector's maps.

"Lord hates a man as won't try new things from time to time," she heard Cal say, "but I think this flyin' is like to make me sick."

"Sir William and Obadiah?" Sarah asked. "Are they with us?"

"Yeah," Cal said. "Bill's got the both of 'em strapped to the coachman's seat."

Below and to the right Sarah saw cultivated fields. Inhaling deeply, she willed the coach to slow, to fall, to turn to the side—

"Hold on!" Cal shouted—

and the carriage plowed to rest into neat rows of yellow cotton stubble. Her insides felt liquefied and hot and the air around her froze her at the touch. Sarah lurched to the carriage door, battering it open and throwing herself onto her belly, just before she started to vomit.

She threw up again, blind from tears and exhaustion, while Cal sat and tried to hold her. As she retched for the third time bringing up nothing but bile, and noticed that the bile tasted of blood, mercy claimed her and she passed out.

Bill and Cal threw stones over Obadiah Dogsbody to make a rough grave. He lay in a natural depression beside Long Tom Fairfax's dagger, which Bill had placed there as a trophy, and with a shawl from one of the Bantu ladies wrapped around his face to hide the loss of his eye.

Sarah lay face down in the reeds at the edge of the Mississippi, both hands dangling in the water. Occasionally she splashed her own arms or face, and Cal kept interrupting his share of the labor to look over at her.

Cathy sat on a fallen tree and read, translating the letter from French as she went, leaving Bill as much in awe of her culture and sophistication as he was enraged by the letter's contents.

"To Monsieur Gaspard Le Moyne," she read, "Chevalier of New Orleans, et cetera. Dear Sir."

"What does 'et cetera' mean?" Cal asked.

"It means Bayard knows the man has other titles," Bill grunted, settling a long, flat stone over Obadiah's chest. "That's not the important part. Listen."

Cathy continued. "I write this, at your request and for your records, to confirm what I've already told you in person. A few weeks ago, on the borders of the Ohio, I killed with my own hand Kyres Elytharias, the Imperial Consort and King of Cahokia. I was able to do this because I was in his service as a soldier of the Imperial House Light Dragoons."

"Traitor," Bill growled.

Cathy kept translating. "I didn't act alone. In killing Elytharias, I acted under the orders of my superior officer, Lieutenant Sir Daniel Berkeley, and he acted under the orders of Colonel Lord Thomas Penn, younger brother of the empress herself."

"Son of a bitch!" Bill yelled.

"Which one?" Cal asked.

"Berkeley!" Bill spat. "That's what he was on and on about in the cathedral. Had I been the one who told the bishop, he wanted to know. I had no idea what he was talking about. If I'd known, I'd have killed him then and there."

He kicked the nearest tree.

"May I continue?" Cathy asked.

"Go on." Bill crossed his arms over his chest.

"I give you this letter, sir, with some fear. I don't wish you to think that you can now dispose of me, because you have my testimony in writing. Know, then, that I have yet another secret. After I had slain the King of Cahokia, I took his famous regalia— the crown, the orb and the sword, all three—and I buried them where only the moon can see, in a location known only to me. Yours, Bayard Prideux."

"Hell's Bells," Bill swore. "Miserable rotten murderous traitor

Berkeley. Melodramatic little frog Bayard. Thought he was so damned clever."

He spat and threw the last stone on Obadiah Dogsbody's grave.

"I reckon you must a drunk enough for Gideon and all three hundred of his men by now, Sarah," Cal called. "They's only so much water in that river, you know."

In reply, she groaned.

"Bayard kept winking at me." Bill tried to explain his train of thought to Calvin. "He was lonely and perhaps losing his mind, and when he told me he'd stolen the regalia—which ought not to have been any great surprise, since there had been no one else there to steal it, though when I caught him in the woods, I didn't see any sign he had it—he winked at me, over and over."

"Like he was sharin' a secret?"

"I think he *was*." In Bill's mind, he reenacted the events of the night of the murder, and the geography of the place where they happened. "The spot where Kyres was murdered, you see, it has a . . . well, what might be a giant eye. I think Bayard was hinting to me that that's where he buried the regalia. Under the eye."

Cal squinted. "It's a moon's eye? Only the moon can see it?"

Bill wiped sweat from his forehead. "Well, no, it's a big snake that has the eye. But I think the snake and the moon are the same."

Cal scratched his head. "I can't say as I see how."

Bill struggled. "This is out of my area of expertise," he said finally, "but I understand that the serpent and the moon are both important totems to the Firstborn. They were important to Kyres, anyway."

"The moon changes its phases like the snake changes its skin," offered Cathy, who had been listening intently. "Like trees that shed their leaves in the winter and then bud again, they are icons of changeful life. They're all womanly images, symbols of Wisdom, of Adam's first wife. As told by the Firstborn, anyway."

"Why, Mrs. Filmer," Bill said to her, smiling, "I knew you to be a woman of many gifts, but I confess I didn't know you for a scholar."

"Why, Sir William," she answered with an arched eyebrow, "though I esteem you above all men, I'm not surprised you see this matter only as through a glass, darkly. Some things are best understood by women."

"I have no doubt, ma'am." Bill chuckled. "Let us hope the

chevalier is as impaired as I am in this matter, and less familiar with the geography of the Ohio."

"I do not believe the site of the King's death is general knowledge," Cathy said. "Your personal experience is our advantage, Sir William."

"You hearin' all this?" Calvin called to Sarah again.

Sarah levered herself up slowly on the palms of her hands and turned to face them. She looked exhausted, small, and frail. Like a woman grown old before her time, like a corn husk doll.

And Bill thought *he* felt tired.

"I heard." Her voice rattled in her throat, and she fingered a small, moon-shaped brooch pinned to her shirt. Bill hadn't noticed the brooch before, but observing it now, he recognized it as Thalanes's.

"Moons and trees and mysterious lady things," Cal said.

"Berkeley," she rasped. "The serpent's eye that is also the eye of the moon. And it ain't the *water* I'm drinkin'."

"Berkeley," Bill agreed, "and the eye of the serpent."

He was ready to act as soon as she was. They would have to abandon the carriage, but Bill had unhitched the six horses and tethered them to the trees. He had expected the animals to be exhausted from their ride, but once they got over their panic they seemed weirdly exhilarated. The party would have to ride bareback, but they could ride tonight, as soon as they had formulated a plan.

"What are your directions, Your Majesty?" Bill asked. "I apologize if the question is abrupt, but whatever head start you've given us is almost certainly already being eroded."

"Obadiah Dogsbody deserves a prayer." Sarah tried to climb to her feet, wobbled, and then sank back to the ground. She coughed and spat a thin stream of blood into the reeds.

"Jerusalem, Sarah," Cal muttered.

"Is any of us able to say one?" she insisted.

There followed an awkward silence.

Bill scratched his bare, stubbly scalp—he hadn't said any kind of prayer in years, unless you counted swearing. Indeed, Obadiah had been the sort of fellow who might not mind a good hard cursing and drinking session over his grave, but that didn't seem to be what Sarah was suggesting.

"For that matter," Sarah added, "we've said no prayer for Father Thalanes, or for Bishop Ukwu."

"Amen," Bill said, but that wasn't a prayer, it was just agreement that there ought to be one.

"We have many losses to grieve," Sarah finished quietly.

She tried to stand again and this time Bill rushed to her side to help. Her skin burned at his touch, and felt crisp, like paper, or like the skin on a roasted fowl. He smiled at her.

"I ain't got much gift for talkin'. What about a song?" Cal offered, and Sarah nodded. Bowing their heads, Sarah, Cathy, and Bill all gathered around the pathetic barrow of stones. They stood quietly and, after a moment, Calvin lifted his voice and in a clear, certain tenor, sang. Bill was pleased to hear Cathy join in after the first measures, singing a close harmony over the Appalachee's melody.

> *Alas! and did my Savior bleed*
> *And did my Sovereign die?*
> *Would He devote that sacred head*
> *For such a worm as I?*
>
> *At the cross, at the cross where I first saw the light,*
> *And the burden of my heart rolled away,*
> *It was there by faith I received my sight,*
> *And now I am happy all the day!*

Sarah limped over to the cairn, leaning on Bill and Calvin both. She tied her purple shawl to a stick and shoved its butt end deep into Obadiah's pile of stones.

"Justice will come to Daniel Berkeley." She trembled on her feet, but she stayed upright. "But we're in no shape to see to him tonight. We ride north, to the junction of the great rivers."

"You can't ride," Cathy objected. "A doctor would never let you out of bed."

"Jest watch me!" Sarah snapped. She pulled away from Bill and Calvin and took two tottering steps toward the nearest horse.

"The regalia?" Bill's first choice would have been to kill Daniel Berkeley, but he understood Sarah's decision, and in any case, he respected it.

"The regalia." Her eyes glittered. "As Sarah Calhoun, Berkeley may be beyond my grasp. As the Queen of Cahokia, I shall have him."

✧   ✧   ✧

Sarah hadn't managed to refill her own energy reserves from the Mississippi (she had to let the power seep in slowly, because it hurt her if she let it in any faster), but she shared Sir William's suspicion that pursuit was imminent. She let herself get bundled up onto a large white horse and they rode into the night, mounted bareback, wearing a motley assortment of their own clothing and the ball attire of the princely family of Shreveport.

They found a worn wagon road and Sarah dozed as they plodded along it, the chill of the night warning her of the coming winter. When daylight came and Sir William proposed to make camp off the road, Sarah reached inside herself and found she'd recovered enough to take a different tack. They had no fire to boil water, so she recited the coffee endurance spell, passed each member of the party a few beans to chew, and then used the power she had to fill all their legs, including the horses', with renewed strength.

Not much, because of her exhaustion.

She couldn't make them go any faster, but she kept them going.

And she herself felt worse for the effort.

They rode that day up along the Mississippi, seeing Igbo merchants (in their round brimless caps and long embroidered tunics) and Bantu farmers (with shaved heads, earrings, and stubbornly undecorative straight shirts and trousers, sometimes under wide-brimmed straw hats) on the road and in small villages. Near a crossroads they met an Indian wearing a buffalo-felt hat with horns and leading three ponies laden with buffalo hides. Behind him rode three Indian women who stared proudly and said nothing.

"Comanche," Bill said when they had passed. "Fierce fighters. Their constant warfare leaves them few men, so their women share."

"I can think of worse things," Cathy murmured in response.

At a chinked-log trading post late in the afternoon, Cathy produced a few gold coins from her stitched leather shoulder bag, which turned out to be enough (with some haggling by Cal) to buy saddles, blankets, and other basic supplies, including a couple of long-handled shovels and a half-inch bore hunting rifle. At Sarah's urging, they rode late into the night. Sarah dozed, Cal repeatedly catching her and holding her on her saddle, until they made camp in a grove of trees on the bank of the river.

"*Hostes video*," Sarah murmured, huddled in a blanket by a

tiny fire. She drew energy from the Mississippi's ley and sent her vision down along it, wincing from the stinging of her eye and the crackling burn throughout her entire body; in the short moments of sight she permitted herself, she saw the Blues, haggard and hard-ridden, but bedded down to camp on the road north of New Orleans. At the fringes of their fire stalked the Sorcerer Hooke, and she instantly shut down her vision before she could see any more, and before he could see her.

The Faubourg Marigny was full of fire and stalked by the mystères.

Kinta Jane saw the torches first. A dozen men marched in two lines, holding high torches that blazed an unnatural red, a bright red with white and pink in it, more like a firework than a fire. With and around them came men and women drinking and tearing their clothing. The torchbearers and the drinkers alike wailed and beat their chests.

The Bishop of New Orleans was dead.

Behind the torches there was an empty space, and in it staggered Etienne Ukwu, the bishop's son. Etienne was ordinarily an immaculate man, but tonight he looked as if he'd been savaged by wild dogs. His black and silver waistcoat was torn open, buttons ripped off. His red sash, marking his loyalty to the great mystère of the crossroads, the keyholder Papa Legba, was knotted around his neck like a cravat. His black trousers were torn, white lining sprouted out the ruined pockets, and his white shirt was stained with blood.

"Mon père!" He cut at his own chest with a small knife.

One of Etienne's men, unmistakable in the simple black waistcoat and white sleeves, pressed along the boardwalk where Kinta Jane stood watching, recruiting participation in the procession.

"Sou pour qui porte le deuil," he whispered, loud enough to be heard on the boardwalk but not loud enough to distract those in the funeral parade. "Penny for a mourner."

Kinta Jane shook her head, refusing the money. Then she stepped off the boardwalk, wrapping her shawl around herself and joining the procession anyway. The bishop had been a good man. And anyway, these mourners were her people.

Behind Etienne came the black coffin, carried by six of Etienne's men.

Musicians followed the pallbearers. There were fiddles, banjos, horns, and men with drums slung from their shoulders, and they played music that was slow and sweet and a little cacophonous, all following the same modal melody, but only more or less. Singers joined them, wordless and howling, and Kinta Jane opened her mouth and found that, for the first time in years, she could join the choir.

Behind the musicians came mourners, and they were legion. Some marched in small cadres behind cross-hung, forward-facing banners showing that they marched for the Veterans of the Spanish War, the Stevedores Guild of New Orleans, or the Grand Lodge of Louisiana. Most of the marchers wore red sashes around their waists or from shoulder to hip, but some wore other colors.

These people were not the great and good of New Orleans, but they were the many.

And beyond them, and behind them, came the shadows. Dark things that moved in darkness and that Kinta Jane couldn't clearly see flitted from rooftop to rooftop, or crowded out of the mouths of the alleys, following behind and shuddering along parallel to the marchers and sometimes seeming to rise directly out of the wet earth of New Orleans.

The mystères. Even the loa mourned the death of the saintly bishop.

The Faubourg sloshed up against the eastern wall of the city of New Orleans, cluttering the space around the Franklin Gate. At this late hour, the gate should be shut and guarded, but it lay wide open.

The night air was warm and heady. The torches filled the air with a strange perfume, a stink of smoke and life and death at the same time. Some of the mourners, broken by the singing and by the thick incense, collapsed before they ever got out of the city.

Kinta Jane picked up a tambourine from a fallen ululatrix and walked through the Franklin Gate. Gendarmes in the uniform of the chevalier stood on the parapet with lowered guns and bowed heads as the bishop's coffin passed.

Beyond the gate lay a few farming villages, nestled among thick groves of oak heavy with silvery-green Spanish moss and hemmed in by the bayous, with their sluggish, fetid water, their alligators and their cottonmouth snakes. And there was a cemetery.

The cemetery was formally named after St. Vincent de Paul.

St. Vincent had been a great preacher to the poor in his life and the Congregation of the Mission continued his work. When the Vincentians had approached Count Galvéz, at the time sole ruler in Louisiana, about setting aside land for the burial of the poor of New Orleans, the count had happily given them a plot... outside the city.

Upon their return to power, the Le Moyne family had made no move to relocate the funeral, and so St. Vincent de Paul looked to the burial of the poor in a large field on a low hill outside the eastern wall of New Orleans, mostly marked with temporary grave identifiers of wood, cloth, or even paper. Burial cost only a copper penny, payable to the Congregation, and when the family of the deceased couldn't afford it, the Bishop of New Orleans paid instead.

The penny for the burial of an executed criminal was almost always paid by the bishop. And now, in death, he was going to join the men for whom he had performed this final act of charity.

St. Vincent and his Congregation of the Mission looked to the poor, but the poor didn't look only to St. Vincent. They also looked to the mystères.

The men with torches and the weeping women moved between two pylons with defaced images of St. Vincent and out into the moonlit meadow of the cemetery. A square pit had been dug, in a corner of the field away from other burials, beside a mound of excavated dirt and several long-handled shovels. The procession formed a ring around it, waving torches, wailing, and tearing clothing.

Kinta Jane smelled the sweet rotting fecund stink of the bayou below.

Etienne stood beside the pit while his men lowered the black coffin into the ground. When the coffin was down the others stepped away, leaving him alone by the grave. He shrugged out of his silver-embroidered vest and let it fall to the earth.

Could that really be the bishop's body in the black coffin? Would the bishop's other son have permitted such a burial? Would the bishopric?

Had Etienne stolen his father's corpse?

The wailing did not diminish, other than by the absence of Etienne's own voice. If anything, it got louder, and Kinta Jane wailed along.

Etienne took two things handed to him by a follower. Kinta

Jane was close enough to see that they were a short-necked bottle, of the sort usually filled with rum, and a powderhorn. Etienne Ukwu uncorked the bottle of rum, tipped gunpowder into it, corked the bottle again, and shook it up.

His motions were slow and deliberate, and when he had finished he threw the powderhorn to the ground.

Stepping to one of his twelve torch-bearers, he took the light from the man and moved to the edge of the open grave.

"Papa Legba! Here I stand at the last great crossroads, and I invoke you!" His words were in French, and shouted loud enough to be heard over the crowd.

He passed the torch once over the open grave. Kinta Jane saw dark shapes, faceless and impossible to pin down with the eye, writhing in the cemetery beyond the crowd.

"Baron Samedi!" he continued. "Here I stand in the palace of the dead, and I invoke you!"

He passed the torch again over his father's grave in a swoosh of red flame. Kinta Jane thought she heard a new note join and mingle with the howling of the human throats, something different, animal, alien, wild.

"Maitre Carrefour!" Etienne shouted, and now his face twisted into a mask of fury. "Here I stand where a wrong has been committed, and I am in need of vengeance! Maitre Carrefour, I invoke you!"

He waved the torch a third time over the grave, and all the torches flared.

Aaaaaaaaaaaaaaaagh!

With a collective shriek, the women mourners nearest the center of the circle fell to the ground. The torch-bearing men, other than Etienne, staggered as if they had been hit by unseen hammers and sank to their knees.

The wailing hushed.

Behind the mourners, the shadow things towered tall and black, blotting out the stars and hanging a veil of darkness through which Kinta Jane could scarcely see the oak trees surrounding the field. They emitted a low, wailing moan that made her bones ache.

She cowered and raised a hand to protect her face. *Papa Legba have mercy upon me*, she thought. *Eleggua hide me, and get me out of here.*

The mystères.

Etienne uncorked his bottle of gunpowder-infused rum and raised it in one hand. He looked over the mourners, at the groaning shadows.

"This I swear!" he shouted. "I will know the men who slew my father!"

He filled his mouth with the rum-and-gunpowder mixture and spat it into the grave. The mystères trembled and wailed.

"This I swear: I will have them in my power!"

He filled his mouth and spat again. The shadows spun, agitated. Kinta Jane shrank even lower to the cold earth.

"And this I swear: I will destroy them!"

Etienne filled his mouth a third time, and this time he spat into the torch. Flame gouted from his mouth and rose to the sky in a bright red column. The shadows rose with the fire, until they covered the entire meadow with a thick dome of darkness that blotted out the night sky, moon and all.

Etienne threw the uncorked bottle down into the grave pit, and the torch after it.

Above the red flames that rose out of his father's grave, Etienne Ukwu took his small knife and cut the palm of his own hand. The flames showed no signs of dying down as he dripped his red blood into them.

"This I swear!" he shouted one last time, and the mourners exploded into howling.

The shadows still surrounded the funeral procession, writhing and groaning, when Etienne took a long-handled shovel in his bloody hand and dropped the first dirt onto his father's coffin.

The next morning Sarah woke up in seven kinds of pain. She was tempted to say "*dolores mitigo*" to ease her saddle-soreness, but saddle-soreness was a lesser evil than the husklike, burnt feeling she got as she prepared to enact even that modest bit of gramarye. She waited until the others were ready, then dragged herself into the saddle.

As they traveled parallel to the river, Sarah began to see Memphites. Both Amhara and Oromo inhabited the Kingdom of Memphis, and Sarah thought she saw both the long faces of the latter and the pointed chins of the former (also notable for their fairer coloring) on the road. Memphis was rich, and those of its citizens who were personally wealthy or important enough to travel showed it in their silk dress, gold ornaments, and elaborate face painting. Above all, they showed it in their slaves. The wealthy of Memphis were carried on litters, or rode in chariots or carriages pulled by Draft Men, or sailed the rivers on galleys that overcame missing or unfavorable winds by multiple banks of chained rowers.

The Memphites spoke Amharic, so Sarah and her party could only bow as they passed. In return, they occasionally got hand waves but more often got nothing.

When she could do so without slowing their progress, Sarah began to fill Thalanes's satchel. Another confrontation with her enemies loomed, and she was determined to be prepared. She exercised her imagination, looking for objects that she could carry that would be effective material components for interesting magic. She gathered feathers, pine gum, poison ivy leaves (carefully wrapped in a swatch of cloth), a small rodent's skull and—her prize find—a tangled robin's nest, complete with three eggs. Eventually, she took the acorn from inside her clothing and slipped it, too, into the satchel.

Increasingly, Sir William and Cathy Filmer rode side by side, chatting, while she rode with Calvin. Cal again proved his worth as a hunter and a woodsman, killing game to supplement their purchased stores, preparing it on small fires, and locating discreet, defensible, reasonably comfortable campsites.

Though the two of them were often sufficiently alone for private conversation, and though Sarah knew that Calvin longed to be told that she loved him, she found she couldn't say it. She smiled at him as often as she could remember to do so, and got many shy, sometimes slightly rueful, grins in return.

Sarah rode with her ash staff across the bow of her horse's saddle, a charm against evil spirits and a weapon if they were attacked. The feel of the carved wood reassured her. She imagined *she* was the Elector's carved knight now, making good time by leaping over her enemies.

At night, Sarah peeped in again on her enemies—for a moment only—and found them drawing nearer. Would she reach the great junction, and then Cahokia, ahead of her foes? Would the regalia be weapons she could turn against her pursuers?

Before falling asleep, Calvin sang. Sarah figured he was trying to cheer her up. It worked, partly because his enthusiasm and affection came through in the music, and partly because of the songs he chose. Among other things, he sang about Sarah's father.

> *The wild beasts of the Great Green Wood*
> *The bison, the sloth, and the wolf*
> *Learned to hear his footstep and light out in a hurry*
> *His blade was sharp, his arm was strong*
> *His eye was keen and his shot was long*
> *The Lion of Missouri*
>
> *St. John's Knights and the Viceroy's men*
> *The Hessian, the Greek, and the Turk*
> *Felt the white-hot fire of the young Cahokian's fury*
> *His word, his heart and his aim were true*
> *His iron will and his soldiers, too*
> *The Lion of Missouri*
>
> *Against sorcerers and highwaymen*
> *Lawyers, land agents, and banks*
> *He rode as hangman, circuit judge, and jury*
> *His horse was fear, his cloak was awe*
> *His look was death and his word was law*
> *The Lion of Missouri*

After another morning of riding, fueled by coffee and gramarye, they were within the bounds of the kingdom proper, and all the farmers they passed were Memphite serfs. These did not dress as richly as their overlords, and their only cosmetic was dirt. The great cotton, corn, and tobacco fields along both sides of the road had already been harvested, so the serfs Sarah saw tended vegetables in truck-patches or cared for cattle, chicken, or goats. They wore rough cotton clothing, with corte-du-roi jackets against the evening's chill, and they kept their heads down. The buildings that housed the serfs and made up their villages were built of mud brick. Such royal buildings as Sarah and her companions saw, toll houses that waved them past because they weren't merchants and carried no goods for sale, were carved of stone.

That night, Sarah got too confident and very nearly made eye contact with the Sorcerer Hooke. The sight of his face, bone-white and grinning, chilled her, and she decided not to scry again, at least not for the time being. The Blues were gaining on her party, and might catch her before she reached the junction.

Above all the others, Hooke terrified her. She had to do something about Robert Hooke.

Sarah began to scheme.

On the fourth day, they passed through the city of Memphis. It took all day, because the city was large, because it was built within concentric rings of immense stone walls, and also because they walked, leading the horses rather than riding them. They stopped with bowed heads every time a wealthy Memphite passed in his or her litter, which was a frequent occurrence. They did this together with the mass of ordinary Memphites and most outsiders, and at Cathy's insistence.

"But Sarah's a *queen*," Cal objected. "I been bowin' to Memphites for days now, and it ain't ever got us nothin'. It ain't like they ever show any gratitude for it."

"A Memphite of noble blood," Cathy explained, "believes himself to be of the line of King Solomon and the Queen of Sheba, and also descended from the Pharaohs of Egypt. This is divine ancestry and it makes him chosen, very special indeed, and much superior to ordinary mortals, including queens."

"Superiority does beg to be humbled," Sarah said.

"Lord *hates* a man as is superior," Cal agreed.

"In the interest of speed, Your Majesty," Cathy pleaded, "I suggest that we not try to humble the Kingdom of Memphis today."

"Isn't your husband buried somewhere here, ma'am?" Sir William asked, looking about the crowded square of carpet-sellers where they stood as if just behind one of their striped and awning-fronted tents might lie one of Memphis's fabled necropolises. The crowd was a jumble of nationalities, and Sarah wondered what a man might look like who was strong enough to be married to Cathy Filmer. "The schoolteacher? Also, the Beguine cloister that took you in for a while?"

"I had to choose the Beguines or the Pitchers," Cathy said. "And the emperor's lady artillerists have such a fame for being slatterns."

On the north side of Memphis they camped on the shores of a large ox-bow lake made and abandoned by the river, and in the morning they again found themselves on a dirt road, trotting north.

"I don't understand," Sarah complained to Calvin. "We're ridin' the line of some major cities—New Orleans, Memphis, Cahokia, the German Duchies—and the roads ain't any better than the Natchez Trace, and they ain't half so good as the Charlotte Pike."

Calvin nodded slowly. "Yeah, I's a bit wondered about that, too, but next time we git the river in sight, try countin' the boats on it."

Sarah felt foolish. "The traders go by the river."

"Yeah. Soldiers too, I reckon, and anyone else as has to move a lot of people or a lot of things. I b'lieve these roads we're ridin' are mostly traveled by the locals. I reckon that's why we keep seein' so many farmers and small traders."

"I should have known that," Sarah said. "I reckon the Elector taught me more politics than he did trade."

"I reckon so," Cal agreed with a smile, "though often enough, those two can be the same thing. You're Queen of Cahokia, Sarah. That there river—" he gestured vaguely off the west, over forest and a low hill that blocked the Mississippi from their view, "belongs to you."

Sarah laughed. "To me, the Chevalier of New Orleans, the King of Memphis, the Hansa towns, Catalan and Igbo smugglers, the Bantu princes, the Wallenstein family, and maybe Simon Sword!" The thought had seemed funny in her head, but when she heard the words coming out of her mouth she felt daunted.

Calvin laughed, too, but weakly, and Sarah spent the rest of the morning brooding, hoping the Cahokian regalia were indeed things of power, praying her enemies continued to follow her by road and hadn't taken to the river, and asking herself whether she could possibly survive to claim her throne and rescue her brother and sister.

She thought of her siblings, wondering whether they were well and where they were, knowing she could ask Sir William and he would tell her, but fearing even her own mind might not be safe. Like her, they had been disfigured infants; were they mutilated now? Had those disfigurations given them any usual gifts, as hers had given to her? The acorn in her pouch felt very heavy, and she doubted she could carry it as far as she needed to.

Not with Hooke chasing her.

"Stop here." She'd made her mind up. "Follow me," she told the others, and she stalked off the side of the road toward a grove of weeping willow trees on the edge of the river.

She got to the trees first, dismounted and started stripping off her clothing. "Calvin," she snapped at him when he arrived, "stop starin' and git to choppin'."

He dropped off his horse, keeping his wide-eyed head turned awkwardly away from her. "I don't understand. Choppin' what? You want a fire?"

"I want the best likeness of me as you can make," Sarah told him, "chopped out of wood, jest like the Elector'd do it. Don't worry so much about the hair, I'll git that part. Time to show me you got the Calhoun gift for woodwork."

Cal nodded and scratched his scalp. "I ain't the Elector, but I reckon I can make you a person-shaped hunk of wood."

"I need it soon as you can do it," she added. "Fifteen minutes'd be soon enough."

He pulled his tomahawk from his belt and wandered in search of a log, keeping his back carefully turned to Sarah.

"Life-sized!" she called after him.

Sir William also kept his eyes averted. "Your Majesty," he began, and then trailed off awkwardly. "I . . ."

He needed a task. "Stand watch!" Sarah directed him. "Iffen anyone takes us by surprise and I'm nekkid, it ain't gonna go well for me."

Sir William bowed, checked his pistols and took a position a few paces away with his back turned.

"Are you well, Sarah?" Cathy asked.

"Better'n I been in days, thank you very much. You got Circulator training, don't you? Ain't you the one as pulled bullets out of Sir William?"

Cathy nodded, a worried look on her face.

"Perfect," Sarah said. "I'm gonna need you to bleed me, as much as you can without killin' me."

"It can be hard to know how much bleeding is safe," Cathy pointed out softly.

"Err on the side of more blood spilt," Sarah directed. "Only that's gonna be the last thing. First, the hair."

She pulled out Chigozie Ukwu's silver blade and then thought better of it. "You got a knife I can borrow?"

By the time Calvin returned, Sarah was totally naked and had shaved off her hair, setting it in clumps on top of the puddle of her clothing, along with the bit of his shell that Grungle had given her. The earth of the little grove was low near the river and marshy, and she stood with wet feet in a cold afternoon breeze and shivered, her bare skin prickly with gooseflesh. She was sheltered from the sky and the river under the drooping green arms of one of the trees, but whatever sliver of modesty it might have provided her, it didn't keep out the cold at all.

"That's a fine doll, Calvin," she said, "and jest the right size for what I need. Now help me git it dressed, and then we'll need some withies cut, and I got a piece of tortoiseshell I need chopped in two. I reckon you're the feller to do the job, so I'm promoting you to apprentice gramarist. Apprentice to an apprentice, I know that ain't grand, but we all gotta start somewhere."

"I can help with the clothing." Cathy promptly began dressing the log doll.

Cal tried hard not to look.

"I's ugly afore, remember, Cal?" she prodded him. "Now I'm jest ugly and bald."

He shook his head. "You ain't ugly, Sarah," was all he managed to say. "You ain't e'er been ugly."

"Please," she said to him. "Help me."

"It is time I revealed to thee my plan."

The harsh, jangling-metal voice tore Ezekiel from uneasy sleep, and he found himself lying on his back, staring into the night sky. He froze; in the night he'd kicked his own blanket off—for a week, his dreams had tortured him—and as bleary sleep pooled and slipped from his eyes, the stars above looked like a glittering skull, with cavernous eye sockets black as the void and a vast swinging jawbone of fire.

"Cromwell," Ezekiel murmured.

His vision cleared and the skull dissolved into the shining veil of an ordinary autumn night, but Ezekiel still felt a presence, a shadow in his heart. He tried to sit up and could not.

"I am accustomed to being addressed as *My Lord*," the cacophonous voice asserted placidly. "Manners are important, Father."

Ezekiel strained again to sit, and then to roll, but could not move a muscle. His heart beat violently. What did the Necromancer want with him? He heard the crunch of heavy boots in sand and then a shadow fell across him, and he saw again the man in plate armor and white neck cloth, looming over him like judgment.

"Yaas, My Lord," Ezekiel whispered. The stone of his limbs became flesh again and he sat up.

Cromwell regarded him without expression. "Walk thou with me in the garden." The Lord Protector turned and paced slowly out of the camp, and Ezekiel rose and followed.

Ezekiel was used to waking from his tormented sleep several times a night, always finding some dragoon alert and tending the fire, or men talking, playing at cards, or cleaning and polishing weapons. Now they all lay still, breathing deep and regular breaths, faces innocent under the waning moon.

The Lazars did not sleep, but sat at the edge of camp unmoving, paralyzed.

The sentries slept, too; the sleep must be Cromwell's doing. From the orange-lit and slightly fire-warmed camp, he passed in the Necromancer's wake into a bone forest of denuded cottonwoods. Dried branches leaped to claw at Ezekiel's face; he batted them away with his hands and struggled to keep pace with the armored specter.

"Thou servest thine emperor," Cromwell asserted, turning slightly to speak to Ezekiel. He slowed his step, apparently to let the mortal catch up to him. "Thou huntest the Witchy Eye at his bidding, to bring her to Philadelphia in chains, and if thou cannot, then to kill her."

"Yaas," Ezekiel acknowledged.

"I commend thee for this," the Lord Protector nodded. "Also, thou hast no great love for the Ophidians. Thou art a follower of St. Martin, who refuses them all rites and ordination."

"They simply have no souls," Ezekiel explained. "I bear them no ill will. One might as well baptize a fish."

"Nor do I bear them evil will," agreed Oliver Cromwell. "Indeed, I am grateful for them. They are a gift of God to us."

"I wouldn't go that far."

The Lord Protector smiled and nodded. "Know thou that Thomas Penn is also my servant, though he may not always fully understand as much."

Ezekiel stumbled and nearly fell. "Penn serves you?"

Cromwell nodded serenely. "Many serve me. More than are aware of their service." He stopped walking. They stood in a clearing. Bone-dry trees menaced them in a circle around the patch of sandy soil, and in the center squatted a thick stump, waist high and stripped of all bark and branches. Ezekiel had seen judicial beheadings carried out on stumps just such as this in the Covenant Tract, and he shuddered.

"What do you want from me?" he asked.

"Understanding." Cromwell reached a hand out to touch the stump. He murmured something that Ezekiel didn't hear, as if talking to the wood, and then faced Ezekiel again. "Man must die, because Adam fell."

Ezekiel gasped. As if its outer layer were a swarm of ants, previously sleeping and now suddenly pricked into motion, the stump began in his vision to *crawl*. Its skin writhed, and then cracked into ridges that rose, grew, thickened, and became hard— the dead stump was growing bark before his eyes.

"God's Eldest has worked a great salvation, it is true," Cromwell conceded. "But only some men are saved, and even they are only redeemed after great suffering and distress, and after facing the blind horror of death."

"The elect." Ezekiel's theology sounded useless and dwarfed in his own ears.

The stump was stretching now, inching upward as Ezekiel watched it. Cromwell ignored the tree and continued to talk to Ezekiel Angleton.

"Another sacrifice is wanted," he continued in his grating crash of a voice, "a more perfect act. Know thou this, my servant Ezekiel—death can be overcome. In my body, it is overcome already. I am no haunt, touch me."

Cromwell pulled his right hand from its mailed glove and held it to Ezekiel, palm up. Fearfully, Ezekiel took the Lord Protector's hand in his own and touched it. It felt like flesh, living, though perhaps slightly cool. Ezekiel trembled and fell to his knees, still clutching Cromwell's hand. He looked to the stump and saw it was as tall as a man now, and branches began to shoot out its sides.

"There is no mumbo-jumbo here, no wonder, no ineffable mystery." Cromwell turned his hand palm down and gripped Ezekiel's fingers tightly. His eyes were calm and rational, Ezekiel thought, not at all the eyes of a madman. "I can end death for every son and daughter of Eve alive today. It is mere gramarye, magic worked according to the laws God Himself established. The limitation, the challenge, is simply power."

Ezekiel's mind raced. Cromwell's aspirations were vast, his

vision out of reach and bordering on madness. This must have something to do with the Witchy Eye and Ezekiel's pursuit of her, but he couldn't imagine what. Buds were forming on the branches of the tree beside him.

"God in His wisdom, however, gives us no challenge which he does not also give us the means to overcome. Here, on the shores of the great Mississippi River, He has given us the solution to this problem, the source of power I need to be able to undo Adam's Folly, and give instant and painless eternal life to every child of Eve."

"The . . . the ley?" Ezekiel asked, hesitantly. Above him, the sprouting tree had hit its full height, and now it shot its branches out into a bud-covered canopy.

The Lord Protector shook his head. "Sanctify unto me all the firstborn, both of man and of beast: it is mine."

Ezekiel knew the quotation instantly, and the implications spun his head around. "Exodus?"

"In whom we have redemption through blood, even the first-born of every creature," Cromwell continued.

"The Epistle to the Colossians," Ezekiel said. "The serpentspawn, they . . . they have a magical energy about them. It is what they possess in place of a soul, and it's released when they die, because they are not permitted into Heaven. Is that . . . ?" An idea of what the Lord Protector's plan might be, grand and horrible, coalesced in his head. The branches above him rustled with newly-sprung leaves.

"Thou shalt not delay to offer the first of thy ripe fruits," Cromwell answered. "The firstborn of thy sons shalt thou give unto me."

"Exodus again." Ezekiel felt that he had to be the one to say it out loud, that his statement committed him. "You would kill the serpentspawn. You would kill some number of them because you could use their deaths to fuel your gramarye."

Blossoms burst forth upon the tree's many limbs.

Cromwell pulled Ezekiel to his feet. "Not mine. Ours. All of ours. God has given us all the gift of the death of the Firstborn. We will undo Adam's Fall. Thou, Ezekiel Angleton, shalt never die."

Ezekiel's knees shook and his breath was quick and shallow; he could barely stand the immensity of the thoughts that burned through him. "How . . . how many?"

A family? No, that was too small a scale entirely. A city? A kingdom?

"All of them," the Necromancer said, his eyes clear and free of doubt.

Ezekiel was stunned almost beyond speech. So many deaths... but then, the end of death... Finally, he mustered one more question. "And the Witchy Eye?"

"I would," the Lord Protector said slowly, "that the Cahokians not have a queen to lead them."

Ezekiel could only nod, seeing the terrible logic in all its cold beauty. He tried hard not to think of her, but before his mind's eye he kept finding the smiling face of Lucy Winthrop.

"My good servant Ezekiel," Cromwell broke him out of his reverie. "I have a gift to give thee."

Ezekiel bowed his head, unable to think of any other appropriate reaction. The Lord Protector reached down and touched him. With one hand Cromwell pinched Ezekiel's earlobe, and with the other he pulled down the Martinite's chin, opening his mouth, and then gripped Ezekiel's tongue.

Cromwell's hands were cold.

And then he squeezed with his fingers, and they burned.

"These images are all quite barocco, Your Majesty."

⟫•⟪

CHAPTER TWENTY-SIX

The Sorcerer Hooke spurred his horse on ahead and Angleton followed. Daniel Berkeley kept up with them as a point of honor, which was easy on the Andalusian gray, but he kept one hand near his pistols.

Hooke sniffed his little bird's nest of hair and then the breeze over and over again. Berkeley didn't trust the Lazars—he had only Hooke's words and the word of the Martinite priest that the Lazars served Thomas Penn as he did, and besides, they seemed like the personification of the evil fortune that had overtaken Daniel Berkeley and threatened to sweep him away.

Also, he was unimpressed by the hairball. He didn't need magic to tell him where the renegade Will Lee was taking the girl, it was obvious. They were making a beeline for the Serpent Mound.

The pre-morning gloom was dissipating into sunshine when the three men reined their mounts in on top of a low rise and looked down on a grove of weeping willows. The trees grew right down to the water's edge on a shelf of land that was more than half surrounded by the Mississippi River.

Among the trees were low, snarled bushes and Berkeley saw a snatch of something, sheltered under a willow, that might be dirty white fabric.

There! Hooke jumped forward at a trot.

Berkeley grabbed Angleton's arm and stopped him from doing the same.

The priest stared at him. He must not be sleeping well. He he was sweating far too much given the cool temperature of the morning and he had one ear blackened as if by soot. For that matter, the inside of his mouth was black, as if he'd eaten charcoal. Had the Martinite rolled too near the campfire in the night?

"Don't touch me," Angleton snarled.

"Patience, Father." Berkeley adopted a conciliatory tone. He owed the dead man nothing, but Angleton was a fellow servant of the emperor, and Berkeley didn't want to have to account to Thomas Penn for any mishaps.

Something about the situation smelled wrong.

"Don't you see? She's down there!" Angleton pointed frantically.

Berkeley wanted to cast his Tarock. "Then she'll still be there in a minute, Father, and unless Robert Hooke plans to devour her whole, I'm sure you'll be able to get a piece."

"I hadn't taken you for a coward," the priest said.

"And I am not one," Berkeley agreed. "Nor am I a fool."

Ezekiel Angleton nodded slowly. "Yaas."

Berkeley sent his men to set up a cordon around the low-lying grove, and then he and the Martinite rode down, the other two Lazars and the Philadelphia Blues at their backs.

Hooke's horse splashed into shallow water yards ahead of them, an ankle-high flood submerging the little grove, and something caught Berkeley's eye, something at the level of the animal's hooves. Berkeley raised a hand to stop his men and this time the company's chaplain cooperated without complaint. Black Tom Fairfax and the third Lazar also stopped to watch.

Berkeley dismounted to look at the ground with a soft splash.

It's not her! Hooke shrieked in rage.

A chain of withies, each forked and splinted and wrapped to the next with strips of green bark, lay low in the water and the wild grass. The water moved; the ground was low enough and the river high enough that the willows stood in running water, in the river itself, though in a shallow edge.

Berkeley paced alongside the withies, to see how long the chain was. They formed a loop all around the landward side of the willow grove.

He looked up and called to Hooke. "You'd better come back

out. I don't know what this grove is, but something has been
done here by craft, and the place isn't what it appears."

The Lazar stood over a log that lay underneath one of the
willows. Curiously, the log wore a white dress. Also, it appeared
to have black hair pasted to the head end of it, and it was spattered in something dark and brown that might have been blood.

They have thrown us off the track, Hooke called back in his
crackling leaf voice. *But we shall find her again.*

He scraped a clump of the hair off the big, clumsy doll and
sniffed it. Then he bent to the dressed log and picked something
else up. Berkeley couldn't see what the object was, but it was
small and brown and shiny, like a river-polished bit of stone.

"Come back!" Berkeley took two steps back himself.

Stop that! Robert Hooke suddenly shouted, and slapped at
the air.

His horse neighed and reared beside him, splashing down
hard with its hooves in the shallow current.

"Get back!" Berkeley shouted to his men.

He didn't care what the Lazars did at this point, but he sloshed
through the water, grabbed the reins of Ezekiel Angleton's horse,
and dragged it with him a few paces out of the flood, to where
the ground was higher and dry. Angleton didn't stop staring at
Hooke. Berkeley mounted his own horse, then drew and cocked
one pistol. He scanned the higher ground around them for signs
of an ambush, but saw nothing.

The other Lazars stared at Hooke too, but didn't cross the
withy chain.

Unhand me! Hooke danced a strange sort of jig, swatting at
nothing with both his hands and kicking the air with his feet.

Berkeley withdrew another twenty feet, and the Blues with him.

Hooke's horse whinnied again, reared back, and this time it
fell into the water with its entire body.

Berkeley cared nothing for the Lazar Robert Hooke, but he
did feel bad about the horse.

The wind picked up.

No, it wasn't the wind. But something...something else...
was moving through the air, following the current of running
water from the sluggish primary mass of the Mississippi, over
the grove of willows and back into the river again.

Obey me, damn you! You cannot rebel against your lord and

master! Hooke broke out of his dance and ran toward the other Lazars. He reached forward with his white hands—

Black Tom Fairfax and the third dead man stood impassive, watching—

and then Hooke ran into the withy.

He might as well have charged a stone wall. Without a sound, he collided into an invisible impediment, a force that threw him backward and into the water, stretched at full length.

The log, and everything on it, burst into flame. The handful of black hair Hooke held exploded into fire and smoke also, and he dropped it.

And then the Sorcerer Hooke's body began to move through the grass.

He flailed and thrashed about him, but something unseen pulled him steadily away. *Maybe it's the running water,* Berkeley told himself, knowing it wasn't. *Maybe it's the strange current blowing through the air of the grove.*

Berkeley drew his sword and held it defensively between his own body and the trees.

Smoke filled the grove. The log and the hair burned at an unnatural speed, not like wood at all, but like oil, evaporating into the flames.

Ezekiel Angleton gasped.

He slapped at his pockets, looking for something.

Hooke's coat plucked out at points, as if there were hands dragging him.

No! he shrieked. *Do as I tell you! You are my creatures, obey me!*

The fires snuffed out, their fuel all consumed and nothing left behind but greasy circles of ash, drifting on the water.

"*Ani ozer!*" Angleton babbled, turning his pockets inside out and coming up with nothing. "*Ani matzil otakh! Qumi!*"

Whatever spell he was attempting, it had no effect. Berkeley snorted.

The unseen thing or things Hooke was talking to paid the sorcerer no heed. Berkeley, the Philadelphia Blues, Ezekiel Angleton, and the other Lazars stood and watched as the flailing dead man drifted through the grove—

and out into the waters of the Mississippi—

where he sank like a stone.

"Great God of Heaven," Ezekiel murmured.

"He followed where the evidence conducted him," Berkeley said.

They stood awhile without saying anything further, and then Berkeley sheathed his sword, put away his pistol, gathered up the Blues, and directed them northward again. He knew where the Witchy Eye was going.

He wanted to tell himself that whatever bad luck had been earned by the bishop's death had been paid for in the destruction of the Lazar Hooke.

But he didn't believe it.

After carefully setting her trap, spattering the mock-up of herself with as much of her own blood as Cathy Filmer was willing to shed, setting the bit of Grungle's shell down in the center of the mess, and then tying the whole thing to the river's current with gramarye, Sarah had taken a swim.

She had been exhausted to the point of trembling, her whole being emptied in the trap, so she hadn't had the strength to do it alone. At her instruction, Cal had looped his lariat under her bare arms and had held her to his saddlehorn with it, riding his horse into the river until the animal was submerged to its shoulders.

Cal had turned upstream, paralleling Sir William and Cathy Filmer on the river's bank, and ridden nearly a mile. Sarah had mostly just hung on the saddlehorn, trying to let the Mississippi hide and obliterate her aura in its mighty stream. From time to time, she'd dunked her own head under the water as well and held it as long as she could, feeling the strong legs of Calvin's horse churn up water and mud beside her.

Finally she had staggered back onto the river's bank, naked, exhausted, and chilled to the bone, wet and filthy as a sow.

The next morning she had held the other half of Grungle's piece of shell and watched through the beastman's eyes as he and the other soul-prisoners of the Sorcerer Hooke, empowered by the resistless flow of the Mississippi ley, had dragged him away screaming. She'd seen tortoiselike clawed fingers as if they were her own, grabbing fistfuls of Robert Hooke's mold-eaten coat and plunging him into the cold, green depths of the Mississippi River.

Afterward, head throbbing and skin on fire, Sarah had lost contact with the trapped souls. She was disappointed her spell didn't free the prisoners. She was even more disappointed it didn't destroy the Lazar, but only swept him away, somewhere downriver.

But he was gone for the time being.

She said a short, mostly wordless, prayer over the other half of Grungle's bit of shell and threw it into the river. She didn't know whether the beastkind had either a *psyche* or a *pneuma*, but they had an aura. Grungle had done her good service, and he deserved whatever rest the river could give him.

Two days later, at evening, Sarah rode through a skeletal gazebo of cottonwood trees and swallowed hard against the feeling of her own smallness. Before her two mighty rivers oozed sluggishly together, brown waters mingling and crawling, bigger than any lake, big as an inland sea—the rivers pooled together and continued to flow.

"Behold, the Mississippi!" Sir William gestured grandly with one arm, sweeping at the westernmost of the two tributaries, flowing down from the north. Then he turned and pointed east, along the other inflowing river. "And her sister, Your Majesty, the Ohio!"

Cal whistled low.

West of the Mississippi, the Great Green Wood snarled in close to the shore, impenetrable and lightless. Beyond the wall of trees lay Missouri, where beastkind roamed and small farmers battled to carve fruitful fields and modest livings out of the wilderness. Sarah's father had been called the Lion of Missouri. Could Sir William tell her, beyond the stories and the folk songs, what that name meant?

Across the Ohio from her, in the triangular elbow-crook of land where the rivers joined, rose a high stone bluff. Its gray cliffs loomed above her; it ought to look forbidding, but instead it called to her.

"What is that place, Sir William?"

"That, Your Majesty," he told her, "is the beginning of your kingdom. That is the southernmost point of Cahokia, called the Serpent's Mound or Wisdom's Bluff..."

He hesitated.

"It's where my father died, isn't it?" she asked.

He nodded.

Sarah slipped her eye patch off her head and looked at it all again. The rivers were immense glimmering ribbons, green and iridescent with light and life. The vast gray cliffs still stared without expression, but the hill was now in her vision crowned with light, blue and white and astral, as if the mountain had reached up to the heavens and brought down stars.

Was her father up there, in all that blue and white?

She missed him, which was odd, since she had never known him, and she found that sensation mingled in with a feeling of missing the Elector, and of missing Thalanes, and a pang of guilt shook her. Not an hour passed that she hadn't thought about the little monk who had trained her to do effective magic, and remembered the moment of his death at her own hands. The Elector had saved her life, had hidden her for fifteen years from a vengeful and murderous emperor, and taught her almost everything she knew.

What could the Lion of the Missouri give her that would compare?

She looked at her companions, and saw from their auras they were as tired as she felt. "Come on, let's boil water for a cup of coffee. We're all exhausted, but if we cross the river tonight we'll gain at least that much protection from Ezekiel Angleton and his boys."

Cal grinned. "I've always had an idea as it might be kind of fun to walk on water."

"That's hilarious, Calvin," she answered, "'cause I always thought you were jest the feller as had enough faith to try it."

They crossed the river swimming alongside their horses, with their belongings tied down on a raft Calvin lashed together. They spent the night at the foot of Wisdom's Bluff, huddling around a small fire screened all about by tall red oaks.

By morning, they had all dried out and they climbed the hill.

The bluff was wedge-shaped and climbed to a high, flat, narrow plateau above the junction of the rivers. On two sides, the bluff rose from muddy water in sheer gray rock faces that Calvin judged could be climbed, but only slowly, in small numbers, and by unburdened climbers. Practically speaking, defenders of a position on top of the bluff would only have to worry about the third side, the side sloping inland, between the two rivers.

He thought it possible they might be overtaken while they were up on the bluff, looking for the Cahokian regalia, and Calvin judged it prudent to consider in advance how a battle might go. Lord hates a man as doesn't look after his own interests, and didn't the Savior himself tell his disciples to be wise as serpents?

The sloping approach up the bluff was by no means easy. There was a road, and though it looked old—old and alien, made of rounded stones perfectly flat and smooth, like river rocks sawn in half—it was solid, clear, and easy on the feet. To ascend the bluff, though, it zigged and zagged up the steep slope, among red oaks and gnawed, fanglike columns that might have been boulders or might have been ruins older than time itself, and through the cheerfully splashing rivulets of a small stream that trickled down from above. The climb looked easy on the feet, but hell on the legs, and Cal patted the neck of his big white horse in gratitude.

They left their camp before the sun peeked over the horizon, for once foregoing the shot of hot coffee that was becoming habitual for Calvin. In less than an hour they were cresting the hill and Cal saw the tail of the Serpent herself.

At first, the Serpent just looked like a low, grass-overgrown ridge, three feet high, in a long narrow clearing surrounded by leafless red oaks. The road paralleled the low ridge, though, and Cal soon realized the ridge and its clearing were long and narrow and stretched to the tip of the bluff, twisting like a snake.

The road ended in a paved square, a courtyard surrounded by the oak trees, in which were embedded long stones, above knee height, worn smooth like the pavers beneath them so that they resembled nothing so much as benches. Cal turned to look back over his shoulder—from the edge of the plaza he could still see down the length of the slope.

"I suggest we dismount," Bill said, leading by example. "Heaven knows I have no art in sacred things, but I think it would be a sign of respect to Lady Wisdom if we were to enter her temple on foot. Kyres, at least, always did so. We might also remove our hats," he grumbled, running fingers through the short white hair that grew close to the back of his skull. "That is, if we had any."

They all followed him in dismounting.

"That ridge over there." Cal pointed, though he felt pointing was impolite, or maybe irreverent, as if the ridge were not only a person, but a person who merited special respect. "It's a serpent, ain't it? When they call this place the Serpent Mound, they really mean it, don't they?"

Bill nodded, gravely. "The Serpent is a quarter mile long. Its head and its . . . eye . . . lie up at the tip of the bluff."

Sarah said nothing and avoided Calvin's gaze.

"Where did you bury the king?" Cal asked. "In the Serpent?"

Bill shook his head. "I wanted to, but Thalanes objected."

"Why?" Sarah asked.

Bill sighed. "As I recall, he said that would be both sacrilege, burying a dead body in a holy place, and also impiety, burying a dead body where there was already a burial. He could be pedantic at times, and I say that with affection for the little fellow. I deferred to the professional in the matter, but I did persuade him that we could bury Kyres elsewhere on the bluff. Would you like to see your father's grave, Your Majesty? It overlooks the Mississippi."

"Take me to the eye," Sarah told him. "We can walk."

Bill led them through the oaks to the edge of the clearing, and then they followed the line of the Serpent itself, to the side. Halfway along its length, the forest ended and they walked forward along the height of the bluff, only sixty or seventy feet wide. To either side of the grassy shelf, the ground fell away sheerly into the great waters below.

"They's some cover to hide behind back in the trees," Cal observed to Bill, feeling an uncomfortable prickling between his shoulder blades, "but iffen we git surprised out here, we're gonna have to lie down behind the Serpent itself or git shot to pieces."

Bill nodded. "Good eye, Calvin."

The wiggling body of the Serpent Mound ended in the point of a long triangle, the other two points of which curved forward and slightly in. Within those points of the triangle was another mound, three feet high and ring-shaped, with a depression in its center. Beyond the ring lay a third low mound, a semicircle that did not quite touch either of the other two shapes, but enclosed the great ring between it and the triangle. Beyond the semicircle, the ground disappeared, and Cal saw muddy water and forest, hundreds of feet below. He felt an electric tingle, the kind of sensation he only felt occasionally, in a tent where tongues were being spoken, or during the hymns at a riverside baptism.

Bill called them to a halt at the edge of this exotic geometry.

"I am uncomfortably out of my depth, Your Majesty," the Cavalier admitted, "but Thalanes and your father told me this was a place of visions, hallowed secrets, and mighty miracles, very sacred to the...your father's people. The ring is generally thought to represent the eye of the Serpent, and thus you have the visionary connection."

"It's very abstract, isn't it?" Cathy observed. "It could just as easily be a serpent swallowing something."

"Or a serpent disgorging something from its head." Sarah stared, lost in some secret reverie.

Bill looked perplexed. "These images are all quite barocco, Your Majesty, and I don't pretend to be able to choose among them. Nevertheless, that ring is known as the Serpent's eye, and I believe it must be the eye of the moon beneath which the murderer Prideux buried your father's ... buried *your* regalia."

Sarah nodded.

"With your permission," Bill continued, "Mr. Calhoun and I will enter the ring and dig, as it were, for buried treasure."

Sarah nodded her agreement again.

What must she be thinking?

"I don't know how to measure the piety of digging into Lady Wisdom's head with a pair of long-handled shovels," Bill said. "Given the possibility that lightning may strike us down for temerity, perhaps you ladies should remove yourselves further down the mound and wait for us. You may easily find the spring in the trees; its waters are sweet, and you may rest at the plaza."

"You might should oughtta keep an eye on the road," Cal offered. "Lessen they fly, anybody as is gonna catch us up'll have to git themselves up that hill."

Sarah nodded. Her eyes were unfocused.

"A wise suggestion, Calvin." Cathy took Sarah gently by the hand and led her, horses both following on short lead ropes, back the way they had come.

"Check the priming on your pistols, Mrs. Filmer," Bill called. "And if you see anyone in an Imperial uniform, shoot first!"

Cathy waved acknowledgement and the ladies disappeared into the trees.

"Well, Calvin," Bill said, grabbing the two shovels off the pack horse, "I know from personal observation that you can fight, hunt, trap, shoot, throw, trade, cook, and fly, and I suppose that makes you, as they say in Appalachee, a hell of a fellow. Are you also able to dig?"

From the very first push of his shovel Bill was grateful for the touch of his wizardly queen that had closed his wounds, and for the week's ride during which his former aches and pains had had time to heal.

Without any further discussion of the fact, both he and Calvin treated the site as sacred. They cut up the turf with their shovels and laid it out in careful squares on the ring, and then began to dig into the dark soil beneath.

"You see any signs of diggin' in the Serpent's eye that night?" Cal asked the older man. "I mean, the night of the murder?"

Bill threw a shovelful of dirt up onto the mound. "Not on the ring itself, no, and I believe I would have, if he'd buried anything in the ring. But it was raining hard, and this depression we're standing in now was quite muddy. Bayard could easily have dug a shallow hole to hide the regalia, expecting no one else would ever dare dig here to look, and planning to return."

"Dirty thief," Cal said.

"Amen." Bill looked at the dirt beneath his feet and snorted. "It's been a long time since I farmed, and I confess I was never much good at it to begin with, but does this earth look like highland dirt to you, Calvin?"

Cal shook his head. "No, it don't. I'm a cattle man and no sodbuster, but it looks like pure river bottom to me, rich and dark. Queer." He kept digging.

"This is a strange place all together," Bill agreed. "Full of wonders."

They dug awhile in silence.

"Do you love Cathy?" Cal asked.

Bill laughed. "Do I have a rival in you, Calvin?" They had dug the depression about a foot deeper, all around.

Cal blushed. "No, I...I's jest makin' conversation. She's smart and elegant and pretty. Jerusalem, Bill, I reckon iffen you *don't* love her, they might be somethin' wrong with you. She sure has her eye on *you.*"

Bill leaned on his shovel. "I'm a married man, Calvin. Or at least, I *was* a married man, when I was thrown out of my home fifteen years ago by the earl. But I haven't heard from my wife since. I don't know whether she's alive, or what happened to Charles—my boy, my oldest—and the other children."

"That's hard," Cal said.

They both slung dirt for a minute.

Bill stopped digging and drew a deep breath. "Hell's Bells,

Calvin, yes!" he bellowed. "Yes, I do love Cathy Filmer! I love her, and I have no damn idea what I'm going to do about it." He returned to digging, feeling like a fool.

"You're lucky," Cal said.

Bill laughed. He laughed hard, and once he started, he couldn't stop, laughing until he dropped his shovel and had to throw himself down on the ring-shaped mound and let the guffaws roll out so he could regain control.

Calvin looked self-conscious and dug faster. "What you laughin' about?"

"Calvin Calhoun, you're an honest man, and no doubt God loves you for it. I only laugh because I haven't been called 'lucky' in a long, long time." The last of Bill's laughter gusted out as a heavy sigh. "On the other hand, I must say that I believe you're right."

Cal stopped digging as Bill stood up. The trench was two feet deep.

"You reckon the women're all right?" the younger man asked.

Bill struggled to regain his composure.

"Believe me," Bill reassured him, "if anyone had tried to join us on this hill, we'd have heard the sound of Catherine Filmer shooting him by now." The two men laughed together now, and then Bill looked uneasily at his shovel. "On the other hand," he said, "I have a hard time imagining that Bayard can possibly have dug this deep. We should rejoin the ladies and discuss how to proceed."

"I don't know how to be queen," Sarah said.

Cathy sat with the girl on a stone at the top of the slope, watching the road. The horses were hidden in the trees and Cathy had refilled all the waterskins and made sure the Lafitte pistols were loaded and primed before perching in this natural vantage point.

Sarah had been mostly silent, and Cathy didn't begrudge her the time with her own thoughts. It seemed to her that they were all in a pivotal moment of their lives, but especially the Appalachee girl, all tangled up in thrones and destiny. When Sarah finally broke her silence, she sounded lonely and afraid.

"You seem to be doing very well to me." Cathy answered.

Having located Bill, she had also burned her bridges pretty

thoroughly in New Orleans, and she would have liked nothing better than to leave alone with him, go somewhere quiet and become Mrs. Catherine Lee. *Become Mrs. Lee and find my child*, she thought, and the stitched leather shoulder bag against her body burned.

But Bill still thought of himself as married to another woman, and his first loyalty was to this girl-queen. Cathy would stay with him and continue to be patient.

Patient and calm.

"Thalanes told me I had to become the one to make all the decisions," Sarah said, looking down at her feet, "and right or wrong, I'm makin' 'em. It's one thing for me to call the shots and have Cal go along—he's been doin' that all his life, b'lievin' I's his auntie, and besides, he more or less promised the Elector he would—and I don't rightly know why Sir William follows me, but he does. I guess because he loved my father. But if I'm really gonna go try to convince a bunch of Cahokians I'm their queen, I reckon I'm gonna need a sight more'n an old crown and the claim that I'm Kyres's daughter. They're gonna git one look at me and laugh me out of town for the scared little girl I am."

Cathy let the cool silence of the oak trees settle on Sarah's words a while before she said anything.

"Anybody," she finally began, "*any* child of Adam who had suffered what you've gone through in the last three weeks would feel tired, frightened, and inadequate, Your Majesty. But if I may be so bold, I would like to offer a small piece of counsel."

"Tell me."

"When you ride into Cahokia wearing its crown," Cathy continued, "you ride in as the returning and triumphant queen. No one will know you feel like a scared little girl—though I would have said *young woman*, rather than *girl*—unless you tell them. So don't. Keep your feelings to yourself generally, but always, *always* keep hidden any feelings you have of weakness or inadequacy."

Sarah shot her a curious look.

"May I offer you further unsolicited advice, Your Majesty?" Cathy asked.

Sarah nodded.

"*Do* nothing unless and until you have to. *Say* nothing unless and until you must. You keep your hand free thus, you protect your dignity, and you preserve your image as queen. People around you will assume you're deeply thinking, planning, and waiting for the proper moment. They'll judge you calculating and wise. Nothing will lower people's opinion of you so fast as unconsidered speech or rash action."

"Do nothing?" Sarah asked.

Cathy saw that it was not the advice she had been expecting. "Ask questions. Make comments, if they commit you to nothing. Engage, entertain, discuss, flirt. But take no action until you *must*, and until you're sure that you're doing the right thing for the right reason with the right likely consequence. Think of it as taking your time. Cultivate mystery. Master your eyes, Your Majesty, and your hands. They are the parts that will give away your uncertainty. Cool eyes and steady hands will make inaction seem like mastery, rather than hesitation."

Sarah gazed out over the oak forest below. "I'm told my father was a good king, a warrior brave and true, and loved by his people. I wish I had those gifts."

"What makes you believe you don't?" Cathy asked. "Do you really think Calvin Calhoun *ever* followed you *just* because he thought you were his aunt, or because he promised his grand-father? Do you believe Sir William would have given you his loyalty, whatever his feelings for your father, if he found you inconstant, a coward, or a fool? What do you think *I'm* doing here, Your Majesty?"

The implication of this last question was mildly dishonest, but it was true that Cathy found the girl impressive and com-pelling, and thought she would someday be as good a queen as anyone else could.

"You're very kind," Sarah answered, looking down at her feet, "too kind. You attribute to me the virtues of others."

"That's exactly what it is to be queen." Cathy paused to let her words sink in. "You have many gifts from your father, Sarah Elytharias Penn. I'm sure you have more gifts from him than you know."

Sarah thought quietly, fidgeting with the satchel that hung on her shoulder, and eventually smiled. "I'm glad to have you with me, Catherine Filmer."

"The pleasure's mine, Your Majesty." Cathy smiled. "I grew tired of New Orleans in any case, and without Sir William, I believe I would have found it completely intolerable."

With a slow swish of legs cutting through tall grass, the two men rejoined them.

"The regalia?" Sarah asked.

After a moment's wait, Bill spoke up. "They're not there, Your Majesty. I believe we've dug as deep as Bayard possibly could have buried anything, and we've seen no sign."

As they walked back along the bluff to the Serpent's eye, Sarah pondered. She thought of the acorn in her satchel, anointed with her father's blood and blessed with his final breath. The acorn was her father's gift. It was a witness and a wanderer, it had given Sarah life and traveled the land with her, and now she'd brought it back, carrying it in her eyesocket itself, on her body, and in her pouch of magical spell components, to where it had participated in the terrible events of fifteen years earlier.

Sarah took the eyepatch from her head and the acorn from her satchel. It lay in her palm and she gazed on it as she walked, seeing it gleam blue, a color similar to that of her own aura. Acorns and other plants didn't generally have a blue aura, so the light of this acorn must be her father's own light.

Would his regalia be similarly imbued with his aura? Or would they have their own, being things of power, things handed down and wielded by great thaumaturges since time immemorial?

She closed her fingers around the acorn and left the patch off her eye. The Serpent Mound thundered and crackled an electric blue beside her, so vivid and alive that she half-expected it to move. On impulse, she stepped up onto the Serpent's back. She could feel its power *thrum* though her feet, tight and tingling like a ley line.

And the Serpent welcomed her.

No one spoke, and Sarah walked all along the length of the Serpent to its head. Again she looked at the triangular head with the ring in its prongs. Was it a great serpent's head, with its single eye showing? Was it a serpent—a woman—swallowing an acorn? Was it rather a serpent, a woman, ejecting that acorn from her eye socket?

Her whole life seemed carved into the earth atop this ancient bluff, and Sarah suddenly felt tiny and thoroughly *known* to the universe.

She stepped to the top of the ring—the acorn eye of the Serpent, beside the downturned flaps of turf and piles of excavated soil. The hole was an open wound in the Serpent's eye. "I'm sorry," she whispered, and then she looked down into the earth.

And saw them.

"They're here," she announced.

Calvin and Sir William scrambled to pick up their shovels again and joined her, dropping into the depression. "Where should we oughtta dig?" Cal asked, and Sarah pointed to the center of the ring, where she could clearly see, blazing through the dark dirt like a bonfire shining through smoke, the glorious blue light of a crown and orb, and a bright green brilliance in the shape of a sword.

"Old Bayard must have dug deeper than I'd given him credit," Sir William said as they attacked the earth with their shovels.

"Or dirt might a filled in these fifteen years," Cal suggested.

They dug another foot, and then another, and then a third, piling the dirt about them in the depression.

"You sure you can see 'em, Sarah?" Cal asked.

She nodded, and they dug more.

Sarah focused her vision on the aural regalia as Cal and Sir William dug. The regalia never moved or disappeared, but at every new shovelful of earth dragged out of the pit, the crown, orb, and sword seemed to be just one more shovelful away, just out of reach.

"Stop," she finally told them, and they did, straightening their backs and setting shovels aside. They were dirty and sweat-streaked, standing in the pit up to their shoulders, and both men looked as if they were fighting to keep doubt from their faces.

Sarah considered. There was magic here. Someone or some-thing was protecting the regalia. Who?

Bayard? That seemed impossible on its face.

The Serpent? Was the Serpent somehow, for some reason, keeping the Cahokian regalia hidden in the grip of its jaws? But she had felt it welcome her, and if it welcomed her, why would it not give her what was, after all, supposed to be her own?

Was it perhaps her father who was protecting the regalia? Had he in his dying moments sealed them into the earth for safekeeping? Bayard had stolen them and buried them, but maybe her father saw the burial, or knew it had happened, and acted to keep Bayard from ever enjoying the fruits of his theft. But why would he want to keep his regalia from *her*?

Or had he locked them away, and given her a key?

She opened her fist and looked again at the acorn, and at the regalia. The blue of the acorn and the blue of the crown and orb were exactly identical—the three auras might have belonged to one body.

"We're going about it the wrong way," she said. "I know what to do now. Please replace the dirt."

She would not have begrudged resistance by either man, but was pleased when they only nodded, clambered out of the hole, and began shoveling dirt back into it. Within a few minutes, they had filled the pit, leaving the turves where they lay.

"I think you'd best step back," Sarah suggested.

They did so, and she entered the depression.

The acorn pulsed in her palm, winking blue light at her. The crown and orb pulsed at the same moment, and then pulsed again, and then the three objects began to beat together like a single, three-part heart. She knelt, scooped aside a handful of cool, loose earth from the refilled pit, kissed the acorn, and laid it in the ground.

"I need a knife." She had Father Chigozie's silver letter opener in her belt, but didn't want to risk it interfering with the magic she hoped was about to happen. When Cal handed her the hunter's knife from his boot, she gave him the silver blade in return. "Step out of the ring," she ordered her companions, and they complied.

With a swift motion, she cut the palm of her hand.

Bright red blood welled up and she let it flow, warm and sticky, down onto the acorn. With the same bleeding hand, she pulled dirt over the acorn and patted it down, then laid her hand on the earth over the acorn, palm down and gently pressing.

She thought of her father dying, his murderer fleeing, his regalia hidden, delivered unwittingly into the custody of the great Serpent, his blood sent to her, sent to *become* her, in the little acorn of the red oak tree. She willed her blood back to her father now, she willed him a message of gratitude, and she willed the Serpent to open its jaws and deliver to her what was hers.

"*Arborem crescere facio.*" Strength flowed from her into the acorn.

Shoots leapt from the rich earth under her hand, rising skyward between her fingers. The shoots swelled, quickly gaining finger-thickness themselves, then the thickness of Sarah's wrist. She stumbled to her feet and backward to avoid the sapling that strained and wrestled as it broke from the soil.

The air crackled with power and the ground hummed; some of the energy came from her, and she felt her limbs grow weak. She scrambled up to the top of the ring, suddenly fearing the drain on her might be too much. She turned to look again at the sapling, and it was a tree ten feet tall and as big around as her leg.

Branches arched up and out from its trees, sprouting before her eyes into a treetop even as the trunk continued to expand and to shoot up. Soon it was as thick as both her legs, and then as big around as her waist, then bigger. Bark coagulated like a gray scab, roughened, swirled into knots and bumps under Sarah's gaze. Buds popped into view all along the tree's branches, buds that extended and unfurled like green banners into scallop-edged leaves.

It was an oak tree, of course.

She staggered. The tree towered above her now, twenty feet tall, thirty feet, and its branches spread wide, casting a pool of shade all over the ring from the center of which it sprouted, as well as the triangular serpent's head and the semicircle containing the ring. The bright green leaves were incongruous enough in the autumn air, a vivid splash of spring at the top of a hill of autumn, but then blossoms—three barrel-sized blossoms, pale blue and orchid-like, alien to the tree from which they sprang—exploded on limbs high over Sarah's head, their brilliant blue outdoing even the surprising green of the leaves.

The tree had stopped growing; its leaves rustled in the breeze. She looked at the tree with her Second Sight and saw, unsurprised, that it had the same aura as the acorn, the same exact hue to its blue glow as the crown's and orb's auras she had seen through the earth.

Sarah's heart pounded in her chest as she stumbled back down inside the ring. Trembling, she wrapped her arms around the tree. "Father," she whispered softly into its bark. She held the tree in a tight embrace and felt tears run down her cheeks to water it, feeling, beyond all reason or self-consciousness, that the tree embraced her as well, and kept her from collapsing.

"Jumpin' Jerusalem." Calvin's mild oath brought her back to

herself, and she stepped away from the tree, tottering out of the depression and looking to see what he saw.

The three great blossoms had opened into long blue flowers. Within their petals, high in the branches of the tree, were nestled the Sevenfold Crown, the Orb of Etyles, and the golden sword of Kyres Elytharias.

All her strength was gone, but Sarah felt triumphant. She had recovered the regalia of her father's kingdom.

As, she knew, her father had intended.

Calvin climbed the tree for her, plucked the regalia from its branches one at a time, and brought the three items back down. She didn't tell him she felt that her father was somehow inside the tree, but it warmed her heart, as she lay on the triangle of the Serpent's head, to see Cal climbing among her father's branches.

It felt like the symbol of a family scene she would like to have seen, but never would.

She was exhausted of all her magical power.

As Cal climbed down to hand her the second of the three items of her inheritance, the Orb of Etyles (the Sevenfold Crown had been first), she touched Thalanes's moon-shaped brooch experimentally, and found it also inert. She didn't feel burned, dried out, and sick the way she had casting other large spells, but she felt drained.

Sarah set aside the crown and orb and sat up in the grass while Cal went shinning his way up the oak tree a third time. She had dealt with the Sorcerer Hooke, at least for the time being. But if Ezekiel Angleton and the Imperial House Light Dragoons came upon her now, she would be defenseless.

The Serpent glowed and felt like a ley line, blue and sizzling beneath her—could she draw energy from it? She relaxed, closed her eyes, and reached out. She could feel the Serpent's aura just as she could see it, but when she tried to reach into it and draw from it, she found she couldn't. When she tried to take the Serpent's energy, it no longer felt like a ley. It felt like . . . like . . .

It felt like a soul. Like a person.

She shivered in the excitement of discovery and veiled mystery at the same time. Whatever the Serpent was, it wasn't a ley line. She didn't let herself wonder; she urgently needed to refresh her reservoirs.

How far behind were her enemies?

The Mississippi and Ohio Rivers flowed beneath her, only a few hundred feet away. She strained her spirit to reach out to the rivers, to dip into their green well of energy and fill the tired, aching void within her.

Nothing. She was too far and couldn't reach.

"Your Majesty!" Sir William's voice cut into the disappointed fog shrouding her will. "We must flee!"

Cal dropped to the earth. When he straightened from his landing crouch, he handed her the third and last item of the regalia, a glittering golden-hued sword. She stood, gathering all three objects in her arms as Sir William and Cathy ran around the great ring, waving and shouting.

"Is it the Blues?" Sarah asked.

Cathy and Sir William both shook their heads. "The chevalier's men," Cathy explained.

Sir William rushed past Sarah and dragged her along in his wake, back toward to the horses and the slope down. "Two small vessels are moored below, Your Majesty, flying the chevalier's colors and disembarking gendarmes. If we run, we may yet descend the bluff and escape before they have a chance to organize themselves."

They pelted through the Serpent's clearing without talking, and Sarah looked as closely as she could at the three precious objects in her hands. The crown was unlike any crown she had ever imagined; it bore no gems, no inscriptions, no elaborate inlay or fine filigree. It was a gray iron circlet with seven spikes rising from its brow, the center spike being the tallest and the others decreasing in height progressively to the right and left. The orb was even simpler; it was a perfect gray iron sphere, without mark.

The Sevenfold Crown and the Orb of Etyles were mates, sharing also the blue aura of the acorn and the oak tree, while the sword looked utterly foreign. It had the appearance of gold, but its edge was sharp, to a degree impossible in true gold. The whole thing was of one piece, with no visible seams or joints, as if it had been cast in a single perfect mold. Carved into the side of the hilt nearest Sarah's face was a blocky image, somewhat abstract, and it took her a few moments to realize that it was a simple picture of a plowshare.

As the clearing ended, she twisted the sword in her grip to

get a look at the other side of the hilt; she expected to see the mirror image on the reverse, and was surprised to see instead that the other side bore the carved image of the head of a crested bird. The weapon's aura glowed green like the Mississippi River's.

Sarah bounced to a stop at the tethered horses, the stone courtyard, and the top of the long slope. She looked past her companions and felt her heart sink; there were no gendarmes at the bottom of the slope yet, but instead she saw two other clots of massed soldiers.

The first group was the Philadelphia Blues. They were mounted and mustered in two lines behind Captain Berkeley and Ezekiel Angleton.

Two Lazars sat astride horses to one side, and Sarah's heart skipped a beat. Even after she realized that they were Black Tom Fairfax and another, and not Robert Hooke, she was still reluctant to let her gaze linger on them.

Angleton and Berkeley faced a contingent of warriors as numerous as the Blues, and maybe even slightly more so—it was hard to count from this distance, and the men shifted and moved about as she tried to count them. These were men she had never seen before—*creatures* she had not seen before, beastfolk—their auras the green beast-and-man double auras Picaw and Grungle had possessed. They were dressed and armored like medieval warriors, in chainmail, greaves, and helmets, and they carried long spears and swords. A few had bows or crossbows slung across their shoulders. They stood on their own feet—or, in many cases, hooves or paws—in all manner of body shapes; Sarah saw goat-men, horse-men, lion-men, wolf-men, and more. She could hear a low, growling, snuffling animal rumble rising from the beastkind mob.

At their head, also unmounted and calmly conversing with the Imperial officers, stood a little blond man she recognized immediately, the man whose white aura's mouth was bound with green and who stood under the shadow of an immense being of shimmering green light, a monster with the head of a gigantic crested bird.

"The calendar is with us, at least, Your Majesty," Sir William observed mysteriously.

"Oh?" Was this some astrological point?

"It's St. Crispin's day, ma'am," he explained. "Patron of those who fight against long odds. And, I believe, shoemakers."

Sarah would have liked to hear the conversation that was being had at the foot of the bluff. "Sir William, what tactical options do you see?"

As she asked the question, the gendarmes arrived from the Ohio below. They rode on horseback in double file, with pistols, rifles, and swords, all in blue-stained leather and marked with the chevalier's fleur-de-lis. She guessed their number at fifty, and at their head rode the Creole René du Plessis, and the chevalier himself.

"Hell's Bells," Sir William muttered.

"Yes," Sarah agreed. "That's exactly what I was thinking."

"To hell with your Code Duello, suh, there is no honor between snakes. Texian rules, draw and shoot!"

———◦◦◦———

CHAPTER TWENTY-SEVEN

The Serpent, the Horseman, and Simon Sword.

Berkeley shivered though the day was only cool and he was fully dressed in waistcoat and coat, with a warm horse beneath him. He had cast the Tarock an hour earlier, standing in a commandeered keelboat, being ferried across the Ohio River by grumbling Germans. He knew well the place where he was headed; he recognized Wisdom's Bluff towering above him and he remembered clearly the events of fifteen years earlier.

He had only given the order for the kill, of course, promising to make Bayard a sergeant for his success as well as to pay him cash, knowing the Frenchman was always in debt and forever pestering his fellow Blues for loans. Berkeley had given the order and he had stood by, prepared to intervene and kill Kyres Elytharias if necessary.

And it had been his job to intercept Bayard after the deed and eliminate the Frenchman. He'd waited in the rain with saber drawn, planning to impale the murderer without warning.

But Bayard had come upon him craftily from behind, seen his drawn sword and escaped, and then fought and escaped William Lee as well, and then disappeared. Berkeley had been duly promoted, and Thomas had in time become emperor, all without suspicion. At least, without meaningful suspicion, without any suspicions that had threatened to unhorse the conspirators. All as

507

the cards had promised, because of course, when Thomas Penn had put the scheme to him, Lieutenant Daniel Berkeley had cast his Tarock before he'd taken any action at all.

The Serpent, the Horseman, and Simon Sword.

Standing on the keelboat, he'd just stared at the cards numbly. He hadn't drawn any of the Minor Arcana since...since before he'd left Philadelphia. It could not be a coincidence. It was impossible.

For weeks, the cards had been speaking to him. Personally.

And who was speaking through them? God in His Heaven? The Necromancer? The dead Lion of Missouri, Kyres Elytharias, manipulating Berkeley from beyond the grave? Berkeley was willing to believe each of those was a possible actor. He was unwilling to surrender his soul to any of them.

Maybe the cards spoke with the pure voice of Fate. Maybe surrender was the only option.

Now the Tarock had brought him here, again, to the bluff. Thomas feared discovery or a challenge from Kyres's child, and Berkeley feared the mailed fist of Fate. The Serpent depicted a bronze-colored reptile, winged and mounted on a forked stick, spitting fire from its jaws with a crescent moon behind it, and he saw at once it could only mean this place; he remembered the long, low mound on the height.

There was something wrong with the Horseman card, and Berkeley had stared at it long and hard before he realized what it was. The Horseman must be him, Daniel Berkeley, he'd known that as soon as he'd seen the horse and rider turn face up, but still something had caught his eye and tickled the back of his brain and he'd stared until he'd realized what it was.

In the Tarock that Daniel Berkeley owned, and had owned for years, the Horseman was a soldier in a red coat, riding a white horse.

But the card he had turned up on this day, identical in all other respects, showed a man whose horse was gray and whose long coat was blue.

Berkeley had shivered and stared. He'd checked the back of the card to be certain it was his, and examined the image again.

And again.

Something had happened to the card. Someone, some *power*, had altered it.

Fate. Was he to suffer violence on the bluff?

And Simon Sword—judgment, again, the blond boy with the sword.

The Serpent, the Horseman, and Simon Sword.

Blazes!

Berkeley had thrown the Tarock into the water, watching the cards float apart in the keelboat's wake. He'd shuddered to gaze upon them, imagining that he could see their images spreading apart in the choppy flow, and that each and every card was now printed with the grinning image of Simon Sword, long blades swinging back and forth in the water, an army of judgment and death.

The beastkind had been waiting for them at the foot of the bluff. Not attacking, but looming menacingly. They looked as fitting an instrument of judgment as any. As soon as Berkeley had reassembled the Blues on dry land, he'd given the order to fix bayonets.

If Fate came for him today, by Hell's teeth, she'd have a fight on her hands.

Now he sat tall in the saddle, the parson and the surviving Lazars at his side, facing two different mobs of fighting men, standing at right angles to each other like three sides of a square, with the fourth side occupied by the long, boulder-strewn slope up to the top of Wisdom's Bluff.

Fate was a fickle and vengeful mistress.

The gendarmes sat still on their horses, too, armed and armored like the Blues. But for the gold fleurs-de-lis they bore on their chests and livery and the absence of the tricorner hats, they might have been a companion unit of Imperial troops. The chevalier stared back at Berkeley, puffing on a long cigar. His Creole seneschal rode calm and inscrutable at his side. Berkeley found the chevalier formidable, but he could talk to the Frenchman, understand his reasons, and perhaps negotiate with him, if necessary.

The beastkind, on the other hand, were alien. He'd killed plenty of feral beastmen and beastwives in his time, and had occasional conversations with their more lucid kin, but he'd never faced a large number in the field. And these beastkind, for all their pawing, stamping, slobbering, and wild-eyed stares, were not feral; they were armed and armored like knights and they stood in ordered ranks.

Beyond any strangeness Berkeley could have imagined, at their head stood a short blond man in buckled shoes, brown coat, and knickerbockers. Berkeley remembered the little man from the cathedral and assumed he must be a wizard, or some kind of beastman whose animal nature was occulted. He'd flown away from the cathedral's rooftop, after all, in the shape of a bird.

"May we assume," Father Angleton called out to the chevalier, "that our interests are aligned? Or that they may become aligned? We wish to return this child, Sarah, to her uncle." His tongue and ear were still black, which gave him a queer appearance, partaking something of the beggar and something of the corpse.

"Do you, now?" the chevalier called back.

"Yaas. We serve the emperor. This is our only errand. We have no quarrel with you, My Lord. Will you help us?"

"A week ago she was a pretender." Le Moyne blew a cloud of smoke their way. "I'm impressed she has managed to matriculate into the Penn family."

Angleton looked abashed, so Berkeley stepped in. "Are we then at an impasse, My Lord Chevalier?"

The chevalier laughed harshly. "In New Orleans we prefer the term *Texian standoff*, in honor of our neighbors. And I don't know yet." He turned in his saddle to face the blond man. "Who are you then, and whom do you serve?"

The two Lazars shifted restlessly, looking at each other.

"I know the man's face." Du Plessis frowned slightly. "His name is Jacob Hop, he's a Dutchman and a deaf-mute, and until the *Incroyable* burned down in that terrible accident, he served *you*, My Lord. He was an assistant to the man Prideux. I am surprised to see him here."

Prideux! Could the Creole possibly mean Bayard? Or was the better question whether he could possibly mean anyone else? The air around the bluff was thick with ghosts, and Berkeley half expected to see Kyres Elytharias himself rise from the tall grass. Perhaps he should not have thrown away the Tarock.

The chevalier regarded the Dutchman.

"It pleases me that you managed to escape the accident," he said. "I find it peculiar that you're at the head of a column of beastkind, but I welcome you back into my service. I welcome the beasts as well, if they're willing. Do you speak for the beastkind? You may nod to acknowledge me again as your master."

"The beastmen are mine," the little Dutchman agreed. Once Berkeley got over the astonishment of hearing a man described as deaf and mute speak, he found his accent not at all Dutch. It sounded musical and enchanting, like some stage actor's invented elocution. "I will not serve you, Chevalier Le Moyne, and nor will I throw in my lot with Thomas Penn, or with any of the weak and benighted children of Eve. I have business of my own with the Queen of Cahokia, and you are well advised to stay out from under my feet."

Berkeley saw the chevalier's Creole stiffen in his saddle. Did he dislike beastkind? Was he, too, shocked to hear words coming from the mouth of a deaf-mute?

Bang!

Berkeley twisted in the saddle, thinking for a moment that the shot must have come from one of his men; the dragoons all sat on their horses, tautly disciplined, weapons undrawn.

The shot had been fired from the hill. Two hundred eyes swiveled at the same moment as Berkeley's, turning to see who had pulled the trigger.

It was a woman, who had ridden two thirds of the way down the hill unnoticed during the confrontation. She was tall and beautiful and had long dark hair. She wore a white and gold dress that had been elegant once, but was now filthy with the dirt and stains of hard travel. Her saddle was plain and poor, not matching her dress at all, and she rode a large white horse that looked, to Berkeley's eye, more like a coach horse than a lady's palfrey. She held in the crook of one arm a long stick, at the end of which fluttered a tattered square of white cloth.

She lowered one smoking pistol (fired straight up into the blue sky), but she had a second gun in her lap. "My name is Catherine Filmer, and I come as herald of the Queen of Cahokia," she called. "The queen invites you to a conference. She bids you send a delegation of two men each." She surveyed them all with cool eyes. "By *men*, Her Majesty does not mean *Lazars*. She bids you identify your envoys to me before we ascend."

The chevalier recovered first. "I'm Gaspard Le Moyne, Chevalier of New Orleans. I'll join you, and I'll bring my aide, René du Plessis." He nodded to indicate the Creole.

"Very good," Catherine Filmer said.

Angleton had regained his power of speech, and jumped in.

"I'm Father Ezekiel Angleton of the Order of St. Martin Luther, and with me will come Captain Sir Daniel Berkeley, representing His Imperial Majesty, the Emperor Thomas Penn."

Berkeley looked up at the top of the bluff and felt the burden of fate on his shoulders.

The Serpent, the Horseman, and Simon Sword.

"Agreed," Filmer said, and Berkeley thought her eyes lingered on him a little longer than they did on the others. He might have enjoyed that thought in another moment, but here and now it made him nervous.

Long Tom Fairfax made a sour face and looked at Ezekiel Angleton.

"Silence, Lazar!" Angleton barked.

Then the Martinite turned pale, stared at the two Lazars, and scratched at his own blackened ear. Had the priest gone mad, rolling around in the fire and now hearing voices?

"Yes," the blond man said, staring down the white-eyed ghoul. "Keep your place, or I will blast you into the void whence you came." He turned to address Catherine Filmer. "I will come. As your mistress well knows, I am two men."

What in Blazes? Berkeley felt gooseflesh on his arms and back at the odd declaration of the little fellow, and the chevalier's man looked positively stricken. The lady herald, though, didn't question it.

"Understood." She turned to make her way back up the slope. "Follow me."

The sky overhead was a brilliant pale blue, a cool breeze furred its way through the short hair of his head, and Bill was armed to the teeth. His own horse pistols (loaded and primed) hung in the long pockets of his battered red coat. Obadiah's smaller-bore guns (loaded and primed) were tucked into his belt. Various powder horns hung around his neck, along with picks and powder measures. At his left hip hung his heavy cavalry saber (sharp enough to shave with), and in his boot he carried a knife.

A fight seemed unavoidable now, and as Cathy turned and headed back up the slope, with a handful of men in her wake, Bill itched to take the initiative. Sarah wanted to confer, and he hoped she was successful, but there were three small armies at the foot of the hill, and she couldn't talk all three out of wanting to capture them . . . or worse. He didn't think talking her way out of it could possibly be her plan, in any case. Surely, Sarah must be seeking to play all the forces off each other until she could convert one of her pursuers into an ally.

Maybe she thought they could take a hostage.

One of the men drifting up the hill behind Cathy Filmer was Daniel Berkeley. Bill had known and respected the younger Berkeley, but now he was a traitor and he deserved to die. Bill would like to ambush Berkeley, simply kill him out of hand in a surprise attack; he'd given Kyres no more warning than that. He refrained, though—his queen had called for a truce and a parley, and he would honor it.

Calvin Calhoun was armed too, with rifle loaded, war axe in his belt and lariat carefully coiled beside it, and a hunter's knife in his boot. The Appalachee prowled the stone plaza like a mountain lion sniffing for prey. He also carried a silver knife that belonged to Sarah, which she hadn't wanted to touch—maybe she was expecting to have to cast spells, and didn't want the silver on her person.

Hopefully.

What she did have was the Sevenfold Crown on her head and the golden sword of Cahokia thrust through the shoulder straps of her satchel. She had the Orb of Etyles in the pouch, along with other oddments Bill had only glimpsed that looked like hexing paraphernalia, such as bird feathers and twigs. She was dirty and tired, but her eyes were defiant—defiant and alien, or maybe *divine*, with their piercing look and unmatched colors. She leaned on her burnt wooden walking staff but she looked, Bill thought, like a queen.

His queen.

She had a lot of sand, to be standing so coolly in the face of all the assembled men who wanted her captured or dead. Kyres would be proud.

Cathy regained the top of the hill, tossed her white flag of truce into the trees, tied up her horse, and took her place behind Sarah and to one side, where she reloaded her fired pistol. Her guns were the Lafitte weapons, and she had carefully loaded one of them with their last silver bullet, the only one not fired in the melee at the St. Louis Cathedral.

Bill and Cal stationed themselves each a couple of paces to either side of Sarah, hands free and weapons in easy reach.

The chevalier and his man du Plessis arrived at the plaza next. They dismounted and du Plessis hitched their animals to a tree. The chevalier waited, finishing the last of a sweet-smelling cigar and then grinding its stub out with his heel on the smooth stones of the plaza. The smear of ash looked like a cancer on the white stone.

Then the Imperial officers arrived, the Martinite and Berkeley. Bill reminded himself as their boots clicked onto the stones of the plaza that the Martinite could work magic, and that Berkeley deserved to die. The priest looked determined, but stricken; he was frightened of something.

Berkeley looked resigned.

As well he should. Bill marked the man for death in his mind's eye.

Finally, on foot, but not any slower than the horses he followed, came Jacob Hop. *Simon Sword*, Bill told himself, *there is no Jacob Hop*. Or the Heron King . . . Bill still didn't quite understand the relationship between those two names. Simon Sword winked and Bill bristled.

The chevalier and du Plessis faced Bill; Angleton and Berkeley faced Cal; Simon Sword stood between them, facing Sarah.

"We have—" the chevalier began, but Simon Sword upstaged him, stepping forward and executing a deep, elaborate bow.

"Your Majesty, you have my unalloyed respect," intoned the blond man. "You have come so far."

Sarah slightly inclined her head. "You are kind, sir."

The chevalier moved swiftly to regain the ground he had lost, bowing deeply himself, and followed in an even deeper bow by the Creole du Plessis. "Your Majesty, we are pleased to be invited to this conference. We have a gift, and an offer to make you."

"A gift," Sarah repeated neutrally.

"For your man, really," the chevalier explained, rising from his bow, and he signaled with his hand to du Plessis.

The Creole reached slowly into his jacket (Bill casually inched his hands closer to the grips of Obadiah's pistols while the man made his move) and brought out an unruly mass that untangled in his hands and became . . . Bill's black perruque and hat.

"I believe," the seneschal said, "you left these in my master's home inadvertently."

Bill looked to Sarah for direction and she nodded. "I did." He stepped forward to take back his property. The perruque didn't fit as well over his short hair as it had over a bare scalp, but the hat felt good on his head.

The hat felt *right*.

"I thank you kindly for the return of my hat, suh," he said to the Creole. "I regard it as a signal personal favor."

The Creole nodded.

"You'll understand, of course, that if my queen so desires, I shall still be obligated to put a bullet between your eyes."

Du Plessis nodded and laughed. "Likewise, Sir William."

"This is a farce." The Martinite's face was pale and lined, and he had ashes smeared on his tongue and on one ear.

"You forget your place, Father!" Bill barked. He pointedly put his hands on Obadiah's pistols.

"Indeed," the chevalier agreed.

Simon Sword raised his eyebrows to show impatience.

The chaplain gritted his teeth and then executed a quick, forced bow. In a more leisurely, determined fashion, Berkeley joined him.

"If we have satisfied the ludicrous protocol of this nonexistent court," the Yankee continued, his face red with frustration, "your uncle commands you to come with me."

Bill drew both small pistols in one quick motion, pointing them at the Imperial officers. The other armed men jumped, startled by his move, but no one tried to draw, to Bill's mild disappointment—in particular, he had gone for his guns half-hoping it would give him the pretext to shoot Berkeley.

"I'm afraid you have *not* satisfied protocol, suh," he snarled. "You may not address Her Majesty in such tones. Perhaps you should try again. I recommend you start with another bow. *Both* of you."

The chevalier looked amused; the priest looked infuriated, but forced himself into another bow, Berkeley doing the same. "*Your Majesty*," Angleton said, choking out the title, "your uncle—"

"Are you an Elector?" Bill asked, pulling back the hammers of his pistols. "A king? A count, perhaps? Do you even *own land*, Yankee?"

"Your Majesty—" the Roundhead ventured.

"*Bow again!*" Bill had a hard time not grinning, especially when he saw the black look of rage on Berkeley's face as the two Imperials bowed another time. "Court Speech, you dog!" He shot a quick glance over Angleton's shoulder down the hill, to reassure himself that the three small armies at the foot of the bluff were staying put.

"Yaas. Your Majesty," the priest said again, "thine uncle—" he looked irritably at Bill to be sure he'd be permitted to continue, "hath sent us to return thee to Philadelphia."

"Did he?" Sarah's voice was flat and unemotional.

"We have come a long way, Your Majesty." The Martinite looked as if he were spitting out his own teeth.

"I see that you have," Sarah agreed. "Was this thy purpose, Father, when thou didst come to Nashville to shake thy Yankee pistol at me? I confess it seemed less an invitation from a beloved uncle and more a kidnapping."

The Martinite paled further, his face twisted.

"I have a better offer to make, Your Majesty," the chevalier reminded her.

"Yes, My Lord Chevalier," she acknowledged, "I am interested to hear it. I expect we are all interested."

"Come back to New Orleans with me," he suggested. "Be my guest. Avail yourself of all my wealth and power in pursuit of restoring yourself to your *lands* and your *thrones*." The Frenchman looked sideways at the Imperials as he made this last insinuation; the Martinite blanched, but Berkeley just looked irritated.

"I wonder if I would be safe in New Orleans," Sarah mused. "It's a rough place, as I've learned for myself."

The chevalier nodded deferentially. "I understand that the emperor's officers threatened your person very impolitely in Nashville. I assure Your Majesty that they do not have the power to be so impudent in my New Orleans."

"No," sneered Bill, "in New Orleans they're reduced to murdering defenseless old clerics. But then, suh, in New Orleans they are men of low character and cowards."

He immediately worried he'd gone too far. Sarah's expression, though, continued to be cool. Maybe she expected him to go after Berkeley. Maybe she wanted him to.

Maybe that was part of her plan.

Berkeley glared at him and Bill arched a cold eyebrow.

Sarah stepped smoothly back into her dialog with the chevalier. "You might keep me safe from *them*, My Lord Chevalier," she said, "but who would keep me safe from *you*?"

The chevalier smiled wolfishly. "Your Majesty would not wish me to be harmless, I believe. You would instead wish me to be dangerous and powerful, and tied to you by strong shared interests."

Sarah pursed her lips. "Shared interests such as blackmailing my uncle?"

The Imperials fidgeted.

"Yes," the chevalier agreed. "He's our common enemy. Your Majesty should not discount the strength of having a common enemy as a unifying bond. It's a much better bond than love, or family ties."

"I must say, Your Majesty," Bill drawled, "that I don't feel much pity for Thomas Penn in the matter of this extortion. He's a snake and a vile murderer, and deserves nothing but contempt and a painful death. As do his accomplices."

Bill let his pistols slowly drift sideways as he spoke, until they both pointed at Berkeley. The captain of the Blues was lobster-red in the face.

Sarah nodded and continued. "Do we have other common interests, My Lord Chevalier? Surely, the unifying effect of a common enemy can last only until that enemy is defeated."

"We share the Mississippi," the chevalier pointed out. "You and I together could pinch the Memphites between us and cut the Germans off entirely. We would control all the river's traffic, which would bring, I assure you, great wealth."

"Or you could control it alone," Sarah countered, "if you had the management of my inheritance. Then all that wealth would flow into your coffers in New Orleans. Surely, that would be even better for you."

"We share a proximity to the Great Green Wood," he added. "That is a common danger to us and to all civilization and an enemy that will not go away. And, Your Majesty, you could marry one of my sons."

"I need not be an enemy," Simon Sword objected. "Indeed, I have only ever tried to befriend Her Majesty. And Her Majesty has other marriage options she may yet wish to pursue."

"I reckon she could do a sight better'n marry the son of a jumped-up mayor," Cal growled.

"You have just finished lecturing me on the weakness of family ties," Sarah pointed out, "and New Orleans has not always been safe even for the sons of the chevalier." She ruminated. "Yes, My Lord Chevalier. I can think of many reasons why you might wish to control me and my *lands* and *thrones*. I cannot think of even one reason why I would wish to be controlled."

Berkeley spat. "Blazes! This is too much!"

"Silence, you pox-ridden whoreson traitor!" Bill roared.

"Have you something to say to me?" Berkeley raged, spinning on Bill. His veins bulged at his temples.

"What, suh, are you surprised to hear yourself called 'traitor' and 'murderer'?" Bill snapped back. "Are these not the traditional names for a man who stabs his lord in the back? Or do you object merely to the *adjectives*?"

"Stop!" the Martinite yelled, but Berkeley stepped past him.

"It's easy to talk tall with guns in your hands, Will!" he shouted.

Bill wore a condescending sneer on his face, but he felt grim satisfaction. His chance had come almost without coaxing. "Your Majesty," he said, keeping Obadiah's pistols trained on the other man, "I'm in your service and subject to your command. May I have the honor of disposing of this traitor for you?"

Bill thought he saw Sarah's hands shake, ever so slightly. "Please do, Sir William," she said. "But I insist that you survive. I shall continue to require your services for some time to come."

"Your Majesty," Bill protested mildly, "I'm wearing my lucky hat."

"You are the challenged," Berkeley growled, "name your weapons."

"To hell with your Code Duello, suh," Bill shouted back at him, "there is no honor between snakes. Texian rules, draw and shoot!"

Berkeley's eyes widened in surprise, but he nodded, and Bill tucked Obadiah's pistols back into his belt. He held out his elbow as he had at the chevalier's ball and escorted Sarah to one side of the stone plaza, seating her with Cathy on a stone bench.

"Fear not, Your Majesty," he said, "I am in my element."

Sarah nodded. "I need you alive, Sir William," she reiterated.

"I share your preference." He smiled.

"So do I," Cathy said.

Bill sighed. "Mrs. Filmer, you're a conundrum to me. I don't know what can possibly be between us, and I may yet have a living wife. Still, I believe I am deeply in love with you."

Cathy rose to her feet and kissed him with the sweet, wise, tender kiss of a woman who knew herself and absolutely knew what she wanted. "We'll have time, Sir William." She rejoined Sarah on the stone seat.

Bill looked Calvin Calhoun closely in the eye as he gripped him by the hand. "Cal, if I fall, it's your job to kill the son of a bitch. Absolutely no matter what."

"Fair enough," agreed Cal. "I'll tomahawk the skunk and hang his pretty scalp over my fireplace. Jest don't fall."

"The hair is a wig." Bill grinned. "And don't worry, I won't."

Bill moved back to the center of the plaza. It had become a short stone lane, with Sarah and her companions on one side and her assorted pursuers on the other—aside from Berkeley, who faced Bill down the center of the aisle. He had his two horse pistols in his belt. The sun was overhead and the brim of Bill's hat shaded his face.

"You look like a fish, suh," Bill called, making a show of stretching his fingers, "surprised to find himself suddenly thrown upon the shore. But then I shouldn't be shocked. While I have spent recent years killing men in the Quarter, you have been prancing about the ballrooms of the great houses of Philadelphia, dining out on your dishonor."

Berkeley only squinted, which was not enough. Bill wanted him angrier. Angry and rash and anxious. Bill was fairly confident that he was a better shot than Berkeley, but Berkeley was more than good enough to put two big holes in Bill.

"Your long horse pistols will be slow to draw, tucked as they are into your belt." Bill eased his hands nearer the grips of Obadiah's guns. "If you choose to make a career of violence, young man, you may consider acquiring a pair of holsters such as the Texians use, that hold your gun low on the hip."

Berkeley said nothing.

"Mind you," Bill continued, "speed is rarely a factor if you have the luxury of shooting your man in the back."

"Shut your mouth!" Berkeley sprayed spittle from his lips.

That was better.

"Make your shot count, you verminous weasel," Bill further counseled. "I intend to leave your body for the beasts. And you will have noticed that I am carefully facing you, so as to render you impotent."

Berkeley drew. As the other man jerked his pistols quickly from his belt, Bill pulled out his borrowed guns at a more deliberate pace.

Berkeley leveled one pistol at Bill—

Bill stepped to his left, quickly, falling into a sudden dash, left because if he was going to draw Berkeley's shot wild, he preferred it to go wild away from Sarah and Cathy, rather than in their direction.

Bang!

Bill felt the first shot punch through his thick red coat with a *pfft!* and tear his flesh under one arm, along his ribs. The wound burned. He gasped and held his fire, still running left, secretly pleased to know he'd only been grazed.

Behind him he heard surprised shouts and the crashing sounds of men throwing themselves aside as Sarah's pursuers came under the stern glare of Berkeley's other gun.

Bang!

Berkeley's second shot hit Bill in the flesh of his upper left arm, and he dropped the gun in that hand. Judas fortune, that wound had just finished healing. Bill staggered back, rocked on his feet by the impact of the big gun's bullet. His vision blurred for a moment.

Hell's Bells, maybe he'd made a mistake.

Bill regained his balance and his sight in time to see Daniel Berkeley bearing down on him, raising his naked saber in his hand and yelling incoherently. Bill took careful aim, exhaled smoothly, and pulled the trigger. *Bang!*

Berkeley staggered, a crimson fountain spouting in the blue field of his waistcoat. He was too good a soldier, though, to stop and meditate upon his injury, and he rushed forward again, mad fury in his eyes.

Bang!

Bill shot him with Obadiah's other pistol, snatched up from the smooth stones. He shot a little too quickly and the bullet went a bit astray, burying itself with a *thunk!* in Daniel Berkeley's thigh. Berkeley fell to one knee. Bill dropped both of Obadiah's guns and slipped his right hand into the pocket of his coat.

Berkeley laughed, rising unsteadily to one knee, and then, with an effort, to his feet. "You'll have to fight me hand to hand now, old man." He coughed, spattering blood on his lips, chin and sleeve. "Draw your sword!" The captain of the Blues lunged forward in an off-balance attack.

"No, suh, I will not." Bill raised the horse pistol, still shrouded in its long pocket, aimed it at the center of Berkeley's chest, and squeezed the trigger.

Bang!

Berkeley crashed backward onto a stone bench. He lost his grip on its hilt and his sword rattled away across the plaza. His blood spurted out on the white stones.

With some awkwardness, Bill reached with his right hand into his left pocket and pulled out his last loaded pistol. He looked carefully at the clutch of Sarah's pursuers (the Martinite registered shock and dismay in his smudged face, but the other men were unperturbed, and the chevalier looked pleased) and then at Sarah (her face was darkly satisfied, and she nodded) and then stepped close to stand above the fallen man, a pistolero angel of death.

"I won't insult you by inquiring whether you wish quarter, suh," he said. The captain of the Blues stared at him wild-eyed. "You won't insult me with a confession or an apology."

Berkeley's breath rattled in his throat. He hacked and coughed, and spit a small string of defiant bloody phlegm, mostly onto his own chest.

Bill nodded, pointed his last loaded gun at Daniel Berkeley's forehead, and pulled the trigger. Bill's final shot echoed off the surrounding trees and died away into silence.

No one spoke.

As the sound dissipated, a wave of exhaustion swept over him. Berkeley was dead, which was some measure of justice, but Sarah was still surrounded by dangerous foes. By an act of will, Bill forced himself to scoop up Obadiah's guns and begin reloading the long horse pistols.

"I'm afraid I've lost a member of my delegation," the Martinite priest said.

Bill kept reloading.

"Your choice of companion was your own, Father," Cathy told the man.

"Yaas." He was pale, sweaty, and trembling despite the cool afternoon. He looked ill. Had the fool been eating charcoal? "And nevertheless, I have summoned reinforcements."

Bill heard footfalls in the leaves. He finished priming and

looked up, pointing his one loaded gun. Standing at the edge of the plaza were the two remaining Lazars, both grinning thin-lipped, humorless grins. Their tattered, rotting brown coats flapped in the breeze.

"It falls to me. Very well, then, I shall see that the Emperor Thomas's interests are adequately represented," Ezekiel Angleton said.

Sarah stiffened.

Bill wasn't sure, but he thought that as he heard the man's voice with his ears, he simultaneously heard it in his mind. The mind-voice was dry and crackling and it sounded vaguely familiar to Bill.

It sounded a lot like the voice of Robert Hooke.

"We'll be a delegation of three now."

The Lazars grinned.

"Don't speak to me of sentiment.
This is a thing of power."

———→•◦•←———

CHAPTER TWENTY-EIGHT

Sarah cursed mentally. She had no fully-formed plan, but the ideas she did have (stall, try to stalemate the parties chasing her against each other, gain time so her reservoir of magical strength could be replenished, and look for an escape route) were jeopardized by the Lazars' presence. They were impatient, aggressive and imbalancing.

At least Hooke was gone.

But what was happening to the Martinite?

Until the moment when the Lazars had reappeared, she'd felt satisfied with the course of events. She had recovered the regalia. Sir William had avenged her father's murder upon the body of the dragoon Berkeley (though Thomas had yet to pay his due). Enemies loomed, but they had kept each other in check, and she had felt confident that with time, she would be able to prevail.

If nothing else, with time she would recover enough mana to fly her party down from the top of the bluff and make an escape. She imagined them all leaping off the head of the Serpent Mound, and herself drawing energy from the ley as she got close enough, and at the last second, catching them all in mid-air.

But the presence of the Lazars, and the possible transformation of Ezekiel Angleton into...something else...were oil thrown onto the coals. What would he do? She trembled at the memory of Hooke's deathly magic, of herself pointing a gun at Thalanes's head and pulling the trigger.

Ezekiel Angleton stepped closer to the Lazars, nodding a welcome.

They nodded back.

Angleton nodded again. Was unspoken communication passing between them?

The Martinite looked pale, tired, nervous, and sick. There was something wrong with his aura; black spots dotted it, almost as if it were dirty. His face was filthy, too. The Yankee priest stepped forward and knelt beside Berkeley's body, fouling his boots and trousers in the captain's gore, and then his sleeves as well as he laid both his hands on the dead dragoon's bloody skull.

"I suppose this ends the pretense of a kind invitation from my loving relative." Sarah said. Sir William and Cal had both drawn closer to her, and Sir William had reloaded his pistols.

"*My* invitation, however, remains," the chevalier reminded her. He stood with his arms crossed; did that reveal impatience or discomfort? "Tell me, Your Majesty, what you would require in order to find my proposition attractive?"

Was there any condition under which Sarah would submit herself to the chevalier's control? Of course there was. If the alternative were death, or capture and carting off to Philadelphia, she'd surrender to the chevalier.

Otherwise, though...

Besides, however collected and commanding the chevalier might appear to her normal sight, when she looked at his aura she saw shiftiness, deceit, malice, and greed. She didn't trust him at all.

She had the regalia. She had her rights to vindicate.

And she had her brother and sister to protect.

"I'm considering the question," she said.

What was Angleton doing? He still knelt by the dead Cavalier's body, cradling Berkeley in his arms. And talking to him. Her heart beat quicker as she noticed with her Second Sight that wisps of black smoke coiled up from Ezekiel's mouth.

Sir William couldn't see the smoke, but he must have shared her sudden unease. "Get up from the body, Father. It's too late for last rites."

Sarah looked again at Sir William's wounds and saw the dark red trickling down his trousers from his chest. Could the regalia help them? The Orb of Etyles—it was magically powerful, Thalanes had said. No, that wasn't quite right.

He'd said it was *a thing of magical power.*

But what did it do? Might it be a reservoir, like Thalanes's brooch? She slipped a hand into the satchel and brushed the cool metallic sphere with her fingertips, willing it to surrender its power to her, to open its secrets.

Nothing happened.

"*Yaas, he accepts.*" Angleton looked over his shoulder to the Lazars. They grinned.

"That's enough, suh," Sir William ordered the priest. "Stand back."

Angleton leaned closer over the body and kissed its mouth, breathing into its lungs. "*Ani mekim otakh mehakever.*"

A voice in Sarah's head screamed.

The black smoke curling from Angleton's mouth plunged into Berkeley's body, filling it from head to toe.

Sir William pointed his pistol at the Blues' chaplain and cocked it. "*Now,* damn you!"

Ezekiel Angleton stood. His mouth was twisted into an obscure, devious smile, and he had blood on his lips and chin, smearing the charcoal mark underneath. "*Too late.*" The priest staggered and nearly fell.

A long, slow *hiss* escaped the lips of Daniel Berkeley, pulling with it thin tendrils of the black necromantic fog. As Sarah stared, the dragoon captain twitched and his eyes rolled slowly back into his head, leaving him with bloodshot white orbs. The Cavalier's wounds blackened and clotted over, his skin grew pale and a curled rictus seized his lips. His nails and hair lengthened.

Slowly, as if testing new muscles, Daniel Berkeley the Lazar rose to his full height. He stepped across the still-drying slick of blood left by Berkeley the man, and stooped to gather his pistols.

"Hell's Bells!" Sir William growled.

Sarah wanted to scream.

"*Now, child, I believe it's my turn.*" Ezekiel Angleton stepped forward, as did the three Lazars, all reaching for weapons on their belts.

"Stop!" Simon Sword cried. A shimmering curtain of green fell across the plaza in the sight of Sarah's witchy eye, and the Martinite and his Lazars all froze.

"*Let me go!*" Angleton shrieked, but the little blond man ignored him and faced Sarah.

"Your Majesty." Both the blond man and the great heron-headed spirit bowed, together, as they spoke together, mouths synchronized like a puppeteer and his doll. "You impress me with your resolve and your knack for survival."

"I'm Appalachee." She shrugged as nonchalantly as she could manage. "We're tough." Simon Sword was about to propose marriage to her again. Could she accept? And on what terms? On the same terms on which she could accept the chevalier—if there were no other choice. But didn't she have to come to some sort of agreement with him, or face the imminent attack of the Lazars, not to mention the gendarmes and the beastkind?

And what did the mysterious Heron King really want from her? Was it, after all, marriage? Or was it *only* marriage? The golden sword of her great-grandfather, with its crested bird's head on one side of the hilt and plowshare on the other, came to mind.

"I admire toughness," Simon Sword said. "My friend Bill is tough."

Bill snorted.

"Do you have a proposal?" Sarah asked, instantly regretting her choice of words.

"My proposal remains the same. Marry me, Sarah Elytharias Penn. Marry me and I will destroy your enemies. Marry me and you and I together will rule the Mississippi, and the Ohio, and all the lands between the saguaro deserts and the polar ice. In Cahokia you will be a queen, east of the Mississippi I can make you empress, and in Pueblo and the Great Green Wood, we will be worshipped together as gods!"

"I expect that would be a wedding that would make the social calendar," she mused.

The blond man and giant green thing nodded together. "Wouldn't you say that is a more appropriate mating than with a...how did your friend Calvin say it?... a jumped-up mayor's son?"

"If you wish to marry a beast, Your Majesty," the chevalier said, sniffing, "I have the finest stables and kennels west of Philadelphia. I believe I can still offer you the better match."

"You're generous," Sarah said to Simon Sword.

Cal ground his teeth so hard Sarah feared he'd shatter them.

"But you don't really want to marry me," she finished.

"I don't?" The blond man smiled.

"You want *this*," she said, and drew the golden sword from its improvised hanger. It glittered in the air in the center of the plaza, surprisingly light in her hand and pulsing green in her Second Sight.

"Careful," Cal cautioned her under his breath.

Simon Sword's eyes gleamed and his smile became stiff.

She was right.

"You can't have the sword by marriage," she told him, "but I might be willing to make a trade."

The Frenchman's aide suddenly became very agitated. "Don't do it, Your Majesty."

The chevalier looked sharply at his seneschal. "Is there some reason I should care about the sword, René?"

The Creole shook his head and averted his eyes.

"I know that blade," Simon Sword admitted. "It belonged to me, before my father gave it away. I would like to have it back, for sentimental reasons."

"Don't speak to me of sentiment," Sarah said. "This is a thing of power."

"It is."

"This is a thing of *your* power," she continued, "and you want it back. What is it worth to you?"

"Yes, it's a thing of my power, as you have your crown of oaths and your ley magnet." Simon Sword considered. "Very well, let us bargain. I have already offered to make you a queen, an empress, and a goddess, and you have rejected these things. Perhaps you should tell me what you desire."

Du Plessis strangled back a cry.

"Silence!" his master ordered him.

"Make him pay," Cal counseled her in a whisper. "Iffen he's chased you all around and done all he's done because of that there sword, then he really wants it. The advantage is yours, and you shouldn't ought to git less'n jest about everything."

She nodded. Ley magnet? Did Simon Sword know what the Orb of Etyles did, and had he just told her? No time to explore now, and she didn't want to expose her own ignorance by asking questions. She needed to get off the mountain.

"Three things," she said finally. "First, my enemies. I want the Lazars obliterated."

"Easy," said the Heron King.

Ezekiel Angleton scowled.

"I want the Imperial officers returned to Penn lands and the chevalier and his men to New Orleans."

"That can be done," the Heron King agreed, "also easily." The Creole looked pale and the chevalier uneasy. "Do you intend this all as *one* of your three requests? By my count, you have asked for three things already."

"I'm not done asking," Sarah told him. "Besides, you've already told me the things I've asked so far can be done easily."

Simon Sword was quiet a moment, then laughed. The little man's chuckle was modest and soft, but the great green spirit behind and above him threw back its head and roared in hilarity. "Well done, Sarah Elytharias Penn. Very well, I would like to hear the rest of your requests."

"Second, I want all the beastfolk you brought with you today to swear an oath of loyalty to me. A binding oath on the Sevenfold Crown." Sarah was continuing to guess, and from the look of surprise and interest on Simon Sword's face, she thought she was guessing right. Thalanes had described the crown as a thing of power, and Sarah had a hard time believing its power was purely symbolic, that the mere absence of a *symbol* of unity could result in fifteen years of strife among Cahokia's nobles. The crown must have some less symbolic power, and that power must have to do with oaths and binding.

She thought ahead in time to the step beyond Wisdom's Bluff. Escaping her immediate enemies would do her little good if it left her defenseless. She wanted a force, an escort, protection; she wanted to ride into her father's kingdom at the head of an army.

"That is no small request." Simon Sword's faces were solemn. "But it may be possible, provided they are willing. I may use strong persuasion, but I must respect the free will of my subjects."

"Of course," Sarah agreed. Was he telling the truth?

"And there is a final thing you desire," the Heron King prompted her.

Sarah took a calming breath and made her wildest guess of all. "The sword has a complement. A plowshare, stamped with the image of a heron's head and a sword. You have it, and I want that as well. In exchange for all those things, yes, I will give you the sword." She wasn't sure such a plowshare existed, and she didn't know what power it would have if it did, but it seemed like it must exist, and if she was going to surrender the power of the Heron King's sword—whatever that was—she should at least get its counterpart.

Simon Sword was quiet.

Sarah turned to the chevalier. "And as to you, My Lord Chevalier, I must respectfully decline your offer at this time. However, I would like to be at peace with your land, and I welcome future embassies, including any future emissaries carrying more articulated proposals of marriage."

"What?" Cal gasped. The chevalier's facial expression looked perplexed, but Sarah thought that his aura had an *angry* tone to it.

Simon Sword broke his silence with a loud and hearty laugh. "You are bold, Sarah Elytharias Penn! I admire that, too. You ask too much, however. The plowshare you refer to is part of my own regalia, one of my things of power. Why would I ever give it to you?"

Bull's eye.

"Because," Sarah said, "you want the sword more. You are Simon *Sword*, not Peter *Plowshare*, and whatever bargain my forefathers made with yours . . . or, perhaps, with *you*, it has stripped you of power. Maybe that was the purpose of the bargain, to contain your might on the day when the reign of Peter Plowshare ended and the reign of Simon Sword recommenced. Very well then, I will help restore you to power. I will give you the sword. For the price named." If she was right, she was unleashing a dark power on the world. So be it.

It fell to her to decide, and decide she would.

The blond man smiled, but the specter of Simon Sword frowned. "I will give you everything but the plowshare. That is generous on my part."

"Hold out, Sarah," Cal whispered. "You got him."

"It's not enough," she said. "I need it all." She couldn't possibly get everything she asked for; what did she need most? If she asked for the removal of her foes, could she ride alone into Cahokia? If she asked for the loyalty of the beastkind soldiers, would that be enough to help her defeat the Lazars, the Blues, and the gendarmes? Or might she get the chevalier on her side? And could she, after all, figure out how to use the Orb of Etyles, not at some future moment, but now, today, here on the bluff, and in time to use it against her enemies?

"You can't have it all, Your Majesty," the Heron King said. "I'm not a giving man, and the price you ask is too dear. If you insist on having the plowshare, very well, you may, but you will have it and nothing else."

That wasn't enough. The plowshare was as large an unknown to her as the sword, and at least if she had the sword she could poke it into one of the Lazars and see if it did anything. "The plowshare and one of my other requests," she countered.

Simon Sword smiled on both his faces. "Very well," he said slowly, "I will give you the plowshare and one of your other requests. *Not* one of your other *two*, but one of your other *four*. Do you need reminding of what they were?"

"I remember." Destroy the Lazars, get rid of the Imperials, get rid of the chevalier and his men, receive the loyalty of the beast-men. Sarah pondered. The Orb of Etyles was a thing of power. Simon Sword had described it as a "ley magnet," and it seemed he ought to know what he was talking about—the more she heard, the more Sarah found her family was entangled with the Heron King.

She opened her satchel and took out the Orb. She looked into it, and with her witchy eye she focused on the blue glow of the Orb's aura, trying to see into it, through it, not looking for a vision, but a hint at the device—

there it was. Now that she knew what she was looking for, she saw it. *Magnet* was not a good description; the Orb was a connection, a *tunnel*, and looking through that tunnel Sarah saw chambers of light, rooms pulsating with the green of the great rivers below. The Orb was a conduit, and she knew that with it she could draw power from distant leys. Might she also be able to draw out power in a larger stream?

The plain gray iron ball was quite literally a *thing of power*.

If only Thalanes were here, he could use such a tool to work mighty magic.

Could she simply now fly away? She looked at the angry faces of the Lazars and Ezekiel Angleton, the anticipating look in the eyes of the Heron King, and the cool façade of the chevalier. They all wanted her, and they would not willingly surrender.

The time had come for resolution. No more running.

She looked at the chevalier, and he met her gaze with guarded eyes. She thought she could get him to ally with her, or at least persuade him to stand down. The Creole twitched, which gave her pause, but she addressed the Frenchman anyway.

"My Lord Chevalier," she said, "shall I expect your embassies?"

He held his face impassive for long moments, then turned to look carefully at Simon Sword and at the frozen Lazars. Finally, he nodded. "I will send them, Your Majesty." His aura glowed with a tone as guarded as his expression.

"I agree to your terms," Sarah said, turning again to the Heron King. "I want the loyalty of the beastfolk."

"No!" The Creole pulled a pistol from his belt.

"René!" the chevalier shouted, spinning on his own man and grabbing for the wrist of his gun hand.

The seneschal pointed his gun at her—

Bang!

Acrid smoke stung her eyes and Sarah flinched, but no bullet touched her flesh.

Bang!

A second shot shattered the air, and this time Sarah saw gray plumes from the Creole's pistol, firing pan, and muzzle, but he was toppling over backward, his aim was high and his bullet disappeared into the afternoon sky.

Sarah looked to her side and saw Sir William standing with one of his pistols calmly extended at du Plessis, smoke drifting from its mouth. "I regret to say it, suh," he called to the fallen man, "but I warned you."

"Thank you, Sir William," Sarah said. "I seem to fall deeper into your debt."

"Not at all, Your Majesty." He raised his hat with his injured arm. "It is I who continue to fall deeper into your service. I find it satisfying, though not without its moments of piquancy."

He took bone measure and powder horn in hand and began reloading the fired weapon.

The chevalier knelt beside his aide, listened to his breathing, and felt his pulse at his throat. "He lives, but not for very long."

Sarah looked at the Creole. Sir William's bullet had hit him in the chest, and had probably entered his lung. Why had the man attacked her, apparently against his lord's wishes?

"Shall we make the exchange now?" the Heron King asked.

Sarah looked at the Lazars, frozen dead-white and enraged in the middle of a forward stride, along with their companion, and possibly new leader, Ezekiel Angleton. Father Angleton, hater of the Firstborn and Christian priest, who had proven himself a practitioner of black magic.

Behind them, as if they cast a great collective shadow, she fancied she saw the unassuming English country gentleman whose face she had seen in a dozen portraits—Oliver Cromwell, the Necromancer.

"Yes," she said.

The trees and the plaza vanished. With them went the Lazars, Angleton, the chevalier, and his dying man.

Sarah stood in a columned hall. The pillars were towering conifers, with reddish-barked boles bigger around than the supports of the St. Louis Cathedral, but running off into visual indistinctness in stately rows. Under her feet was a carpet of emerald green moss; shafts of white daylight pierced the shade from high in the forest canopy above.

With her stood her companions and Simon Sword. The Heron King had left his borrowed human body on the Serpent Mound, and stood before her now in his full majesty. He towered above her like a giant, not a mere aura now, but a hulking, fear-instilling, trollish thing of flesh and bone, with the great crested head of a heron. His aura was the same sparkling green, but his physical person was covered in fine white feathers, iridescent when struck directly by the light. His black eyes were all pupil, and infinitely deep.

"Sweet wounds of Heaven." Sir William retreated half a step.

You see I am handsome in my own person, the Heron King said. Sarah heard his voice like Hooke's, in her head. *It is not too late to reconsider our bargain. This*—he turned to gather all the trees and shadow about them with a sweep of his arm—*would be one of your palaces.*

Sarah looked closer, and saw that the columned forest hall sparkled in many colors with berries, vines, and wildflowers. The air was crisp and sweet, and she was tempted to lay down her cares and be done, surrender to the importunings of Simon Sword and become his queen. She might not be free, but could she not be safe and happy without freedom?

But then she saw the stricken look on Calvin's face.

"Send your embassies later," she said. "For now, let's keep the bargain we've made."

The Heron King laughed again, and waved his arm. Suddenly the forest hall before Sarah was filled with a crowd of beastfolk warriors. They snorted and shrieked in surprise, but held their ranks. Perhaps they were accustomed to such strange goings-on.

And were they really there in person? Or was this some sort of shared vision?

Sarah scrutinized the beastkind. They were all man-shaped, bipeds standing mostly on their hind legs, but she spotted among them the faces of wolves, eagles, bears, stags, bison, and even fish. She saw ape arms, immense folded wings, furred legs terminating in all manner of hooves, and even one creature that looked like a forest sloth, though shrunken to the height of a man. They wore a motley assortment of armor, chain and plate, and carried an equally picaresque array of swords, spears, hammers, and axes. A few had bows or crossbows slung over their backs. They had the collective musk of a farm, and savage stares.

Could Sarah really lead such a regiment?

She turned to look at Sir William and saw that he stared back at the beastkind, meeting their fierce stares with his own unflinching green gaze. If she couldn't do it, Sir William could.

The Heron King addressed them in a shout that boomed loud in Sarah's mind. *Warriors of the Mississippi! You served my father brave and true, as you have served me! I am warmed by your affection, strengthened by your loyalty, and proud to be in your company! Never has this hall seen a worthier band!*

A general snorting and stamping of hooves seemed to indicate a pleased reaction.

Simon Sword turned and bowed his head to Sarah. *Now I must ask of you a great sacrifice! Some of you will die today and be gathered again into the earth, but that is not the sacrifice I mean.* More pleased and rowdy tumult. *This woman is Ophidian, the daughter of Kyres Elytharias, called the Lion of Missouri, and rightful Queen of Cahokia. She has agreed to return to me the Heronblade, so that I may rage against the kingdoms of men as is my true and only destiny.*

Sarah swallowed back an uneasy feeling.

In return, I have sworn I will give her your service. Sarah expected at this point that the excited noises would turn to outrage, or at least die down, but they continued. *Understand clearly what I ask, my warriors. Those of you who agree to my request will enter her service by an oath upon the famous Sevenfold Crown, which she bears. This is an oath you will not be able to break, and you will serve her to the end of your days. If necessary, you will serve her even against me.*

The noise quieted slightly, but the beastkind still champed and snarled in approval. As the Heron King paused, the beastfolk turned their heads and Sarah felt dozens of animal eyes upon her. She stood as straight and tall as she could and gazed back, trying to broadcast confidence.

I can only ask, Simon Sword continued, *in this matter I cannot command obedience. I will turn my back, and any who wish to continue in my service may leave the hall, with no shame or punishment. All who accede to my request by staying will then take their oaths and will return to the rivers with their new queen.*

He turned his back.

Sarah looked at the beastkind, challenging them with her eyes. They looked back and did not look away.

None of the beast-shaped fighters left the hall.

Simon Sword pivoted to face the warriors again and smiled. *Thank you, my sons and daughters. In these, the last moments of your service to me, know that it is you who have brought me back to my throne.*

Then the Heron King stepped aside, leaving Sarah and her companions with a crowd of expectant beastkind soldiers.

"Sir William," she said, "I have no experience with military oaths. Can you devise one appropriate to the occasion and administer it for me?"

Sir William nodded thoughtfully and stepped forward, facing the beastmen but not obscuring their view of Sarah. Sarah replaced the golden sword in its hanger and took the Orb of Etyles in both hands. She looked into it and saw through it, within easy reach, the mighty green mana-currents of the Mississippi River.

She reached out with her spirit and seized hold of that power, drawing it to her. She felt her own reservoir and Thalanes's brooch fill instantly, and the overflow was enormous, so great that it felt like it might burn her out and leave her a husk if she handled it for very long at all; for the moment, she held it ready and extended her soul into the Sevenfold Crown, examining it and trying to determine how it worked.

"Raise your right hand...or foreleg," Sir William barked to the rows of beastmen, "and repeat after me."

The crown shivered, and Sarah sensed within it conduits

going out much as the orb presented to her conduits *coming in.* As Sir William began the oath, pausing every few words to let the dozens of animal-rough voices follow, she drew power from the Mississippi through the Orb of Etyles into her own body, feeling it like an electric tingle, and pushed it back out again through the Sevenfold Crown.

In the vision of her witchy eye, she saw green light flow into her body, and blue light stream back out of her, through the seven points of the crown, spreading in a wide arc to strike each of the swearing beastmen in the eyes.

"I," Sir William began, "say your name—" here there was a confusion of barking, snuffling and hooting noises, "hereby swear upon the Sevenfold Crown of Cahokia my faithful allegiance to Her Majesty, Sarah Elytharias Penn, rightful Queen of Cahokia and heir to the Penn lands. I swear to uphold her rights against all challenge, to defend her person and her honor against all threats, and to do her will in all things, not sparing my own blood or life. So help me God and all the powers that be!"

Sarah let go of the stream of power with relief.

The oath echoed with a growling buzz. Sir William turned to face Sarah again, and executed a deep bow; the beastkind followed his example. The Cavalier was bloody and tired, but his expression was one of pure exultation.

"Your Majesty," he said.

"My warriors!" Sarah called, stepping forward to face the crowd. "I thank you for your oaths and for your loyalty. This is your commander, Captain Sir William Johnston Lee. You will follow his orders in the execution of your promise."

Sir William bowed to Sarah again, as did all the beastfolk.

Simon Sword presented himself with a short bow, holding in his hands (feathered on their backs; a wing-like membrane hung from his arms and shoulders) a small plowshare. It had the same glittering golden appearance as the sword, glowing similarly green in her Second Sight, and the Heron King showed her both sides, so that she could see the heron head carved into one side of the plowshare's blade and the image of a sword carved into the other. *The Heronplow,* he told her. *Your foundations will be solid, your boundaries known, your fields fruitful, and your people at peace with each other.*

He held it out to her.

Sarah slid the Heronsword from the satchel strings where it rested. It felt heavy in her hands. "Do you not wish for peace, solid foundations, and fruitful fields?"

He shook his great crested head. *Those are the works of my father, and I despise them. I am the bringer of change, the avenger of time, the harbinger of justice and war.*

What horrors was Sarah unchaining? But she had made her choice already.

Sarah exchanged the sword for the plow.

The Heronplow was light, as the sword had been, and she placed it in her satchel, nestling it down below the bird's nest and other items. In Simon Sword's hands, the Heronsword seemed to grow, until it was as long as Sarah was tall.

"Do you still seek a bride?" Sarah asked.

The bird face smiled. *It is my imperative to find a queen and mate. I believe you will be a mighty ruler of your country, Sarah Elytharias Penn, and would be an excellent queen of my own.*

"Send your embassies." Sarah forced a smile. She feared this strange demigod, and had no desire to be his mate, but as long as he had intention to court her, he might withhold his judgment, change, and war from her and her kingdom.

The Heron King nodded. *I will return you now to Wisdom's Bluff. As it happens, it is not far from here. I will not come with you, so this is farewell.* He bent, like an adult kneeling down to a child, and kissed Sarah's hand. *You understand,* were his last words to her, *that you receive no more help from me.*

Sarah nodded calmly, controlling her eyes and her hands though her heart galloped like a runaway horse. She had a flash of terror thinking that the beastmen might not, after all, be loyal to her, and that she might have traded away the Heronsword for nothing, but then she thought of the Sevenfold Crown and the oath Sir William had administered, and the panic passed.

Simon Sword turned to Sir William, who wore a steely expression on his grizzled, weary face. *You are my friend, Bill, whether you like it or not.* He held out a crescent-shaped ivory horn, yellowed with age, trimmed with battered golden bands and fixed with a thin leather strap. *These warriors I am giving into your care are my Household Guard, and no ordinary soldiers. I rejoice at handing them over because I know they have not had a more able commander. You will, however, want this.*

Sir William nodded stiffly, took the offered horn and slung it over his shoulder. "It has been an adventure, suh."

It has, the Heron King agreed, and, just as suddenly as it had appeared, the hall of forest pillars was gone.

The redwoods were gone and Cal found himself again in the stone plaza on Wisdom's Bluff, at Sarah's side and looking down the slope, at two different armies charging up it.

He didn't glance long enough to tell one from the other, but just saw a wave of mounted men in blue uniforms riding up the hill toward him. Beyond them, at the foot of the hill, Simon Sword's beastmen soldiers—*Sarah's* beastmen—held their position.

But he had no time to worry about the soldiers. Straight ahead, across the plaza, three of the Lazars came sprinting at Sarah. Tom Long-Knife rushed first, pulling a dagger from its sheath. The one-eyed Lazar and Berkeley were one step behind Tom Fairfax and on his flanks, also drawing out blades.

"Bill!" Cal shouted, "git ready, they're a-comin' up the slope!"

Then he raised his rifle against his shoulder and shot Black Tom Fairfax.

Tom took the ball in his shoulder, spun away, and dropped.

A hunting call sounded just outside Calvin's vision—Bill, blowing the Heron King's horn. Cal gripped his musket like a club and stepped forward, lowering his shoulders to charge; Lord hates a man as won't get his hands dirty. Sarah had a blank look on her face, and Cal couldn't risk either of the Lazars getting past him. He braced himself to hit Berkeley with his rifle and throw his body at One-Eye—

Bang!

Berkeley crashed over backward, a shower of black ichor spraying out of his chest, his hat and perruque flying. The last of the Elector's silver bullets, and good shot, Cathy Filmer.

The abrupt disappearance of his target left him off balance and slightly stumbling, but Cal managed to come in under One-Eye's swinging knife blade, musket first, held sideways like a bar, and he crashed to the ground on top of the Lazar. He trapped the dead man's knife hand under his musket and one knee, freeing his right hand to grope at his belt for Chigozie Ukwu's silver dagger.

Jumpin' Jerusalem, but as bad as the empty socket was, the white eye was worse.

✧　　✧　　✧

Bill blew the horn with one eye on the beastmen at the foot of the hill and the other on the chevalier and Jacob Hop, who were crouched over the body of the dead Creole. Sarah's new soldiers responded to the horn's call, and broke into a tight charge up the slope, howling an animal war cry.

But the mounted men didn't slow in their ascent, and Bill faced a dilemma—deal with the soldiers charging up the hill, or deal with the Lazars? He cast a quick glance about the plaza and decided that the Chevalier of New Orleans, however much he was a selfish, ruthless man, would be forced to fight against the Lazars, too.

Sheathing his saber, Bill ran down the hill.

Ezekiel Angleton hung back at the edge of the plaza, mumbling. Sarah had more immediate problems; the Lazars were going to cut her friends to pieces.

"Help, damn you!" she yelled to the chevalier, who hadn't joined the fray.

Tom Fairfax rolled silently to his feet, knife in his hand—

Sarah felt in her satchel and her fist closed over the robin's nest she had stored there—

"*Labyrinthum facio!*" she shouted, and hurled the nest at the Tom Fairfax. Black Tom reared back, the small tangle of twigs and grass hitting him in the chest and falling to his feet. She willed energy into her spell, drawing a tiny stream of the ley-flow of the Mississippi through the Orb of Etyles and pouring it into the nest to effect her desire.

Her entire body burned.

Tom stopped his charge. He dropped his chin, stared down at the nest and shuffled his feet aimlessly. The knife fell from his hands to the stone of the plaza.

And then Sarah felt something push back against her, through the tangle of twigs and the maze she had turned it into. Angleton.

Sarah furrowed her brow and poured in more power.

Cal shoved the little silver knife into One-Eye's throat, afraid that any moment the undead Berkeley would stab him in the back.

A gout of cold, black fluid that spurted out. The Lazar kicked and twitched and finally lay still, his eyes glazing over with a dark film and his eye worms finally stilling their dance.

The captain's shadow crossed him.

Bang!

Cathy Filmer's silver bullets were gone, but the force of her lead ball was enough to knock the Cavalier off balance. Cal yanked the blade free and rolled to his feet. Then he heard a hard *crunch*.

"Stop where you are or I'll shoot her!" he heard, and he froze.

The Chevalier of New Orleans stood behind Sarah, two pistols pointed at the back of her head. Sarah had one hand in Thalanes's satchel, which Cal didn't think the chevalier had noticed, but she looked lost in concentration. Cathy hung to one side, the Lafitte pistols on the ground before her, tangled hair and blood at the corner of her mouth testimony to a failed resistance.

Berkeley recovered his balance and came charging back, sword raised high.

"I *can't!*" Cal jumped forward to meet the undead dragoon.

"Fine," the chevalier conceded. "I'm happy to kill the victor."

"You sure know how to motivate a feller." Cal sidestepped a thrust, falling back. He wasn't used to fighting swordsmen, and his preferred weapon, when he had to fight hand to hand, was the tomahawk. He tightened his grip on the knife and attacked with a series of controlled stabs.

Berkeley was unimpressed, calmly parrying with progressively shorter, tighter strokes. Then Cal was chest to chest with the dead man.

But Cal had fought the Lazars once before. He bumped the other man back with his chest, then dropped, as if he'd tripped.

Berkeley swung for his head, missing for the suddenness of Cal's fall—

and Cal sliced with the silver knife through the protruding toenails of the Lazar's lead foot.

The sword came down again, Cal rolled away away, and Berkeley stumbled, his front foot suddenly refusing to move in response to his will.

Berkeley's attack became awkward, and it caught Cal only lightly across the shoulder as he moved, not cutting through his coat. The Lazar looked astonished and Cal jumped to his feet, twisting to curl the fingers of his wounded arm into the dead man's long, ragged hair.

Berkeley pulled away and turned, tripping as he moved, pummeling Cal with the hilt of his sword in the chest and arm.

The blows hurt and Cal cried out, but he held tight to Berkeley's mane. The chevalier might kill him afterward, but he couldn't risk that the Lazar Berkeley would hurt Sarah.

Raising the little silver letter opener, he punched in one quick motion—

slicing all the way through Daniel Berkeley's hair.

Berkeley dropped like a slaughtered hog.

Cal slipped sideways and almost fell over. He was breathing hard and his muscles ached, but mostly he felt relief.

"Stop right there, boy," the chevalier commanded him.

Cal winced, tossed aside the handful of greasy hair.

"Well done," the chevalier said. "Really, I'd much rather deal with you than the Lazars. Dead men can be so irrational."

"What are you doin'?" Cal asked. Now that Berkeley was down, he had a hard time taking his gaze from Sarah's face. She looked as if she were concentrating.

Ezekiel Angleton, standing across the plaza, had a similar expression. What in tarnation were they doing?

"Consider this my embassy." The chevalier took long steps around Cathy and stood on the other side of Sarah to look her in the face, holding his two pistols steady on her the entire time. "How am I received, Your Majesty?"

Sarah said nothing.

The chevalier laughed and looked back to Cal. "Now, you kill the Lazars."

Cal took a closer look at Tom Long-Knife. The Lazar still stood staring at his feet, mumbling without words and aimlessly scratching the stones of the plaza with his long toenails. Sarah must have done something to the dead man.

Calvin hadn't yet killed a man, he realized, thinking back to his last private conversation with the Elector, at least not that he was sure, though he'd knocked a few of those gendarmes pretty hard, and it was possible they might have died of it. But he had for certain dispatched a fair number of things that *looked* like men, and he reckoned the Elector would give him credit.

He raised the silver letter opener.

Sarah had miscalculated. The chevalier had not swallowed his frustration and peacefully ridden away as she'd hoped. She struggled against Angleton, feeling as if she were pushing with her entire body against a stone wall. There was something behind Angleton, something pushing through him and giving him strength.

She hoped—desperately—she had enough power to intervene against the chevalier, too.

Her hand in the satchel closed around the sticky wad of pine resin and an egg. They would do just fine; she crushed them together and, with only half her conscious mind, put together a final piece of magic.

Pistolas viscosas facio, she spoke in her mind, and she turned a rivulet of power with her will, directing it to gum up the chevalier's weapons.

Sparks filled her mind. A hammer blow pounded into her, over the entire length of her body all at once and deep into her soul. She cried out and dropped to her knees.

She let go of the flow of the Mississippi's power.

What was that?

Her spell had failed. Far away, she saw the chevalier laughing as she fell forward onto the ground.

Sarah crumpled to the dirt.

In that instant, Tom Long-Knife looked up from his feet.

"Jerusalem," Cal swore, but the Lazar hesitated and Cal plunged the silver knife into his throat.

Black Tom Fairfax's eyes trembled and jumped in their black-jellied sockets, raining worms down his rotting clothing. The Lazar collapsed in a shower of cold black gore, and when he hit the ground, Cal thought the look on his face was one of relief.

"No!" Ezekiel Angleton cried.

The chevalier laughed mirthlessly and looked down at Sarah. "Some people are born with magical talent. Others hire it." His body seemed to be covered in a shimmering field of white.

"Some of us jest do without," Cal said sourly.

The little Dutchman had stood up from where he watched over the dying Creole and now moved over to stand by the chevalier. He looked nervous, an expression Cal hadn't seen on that face before. If he wasn't Simon Sword anymore, who was he? Hop held something in his hand, hidden against his wrist and in the end of his sleeve so Cal couldn't get a good look at it. The chevalier gave him a look of contempt and then returned his attention to his targets.

"Drop the knife," the chevalier said to Cal.

Jacob Hop attacked.

The thing hidden in his sleeve glinted strangely as he pulled it out and spun it around, and Cal just had time before the little Dutchman stabbed the object into the chevalier's side to see that it was a knife.

A silver knife, from the shine of it.

Sparks and blood showered from the wound and the chevalier roared. He jerked away from the blond man and turned, aiming his pistols—

and Cal jumped, crashing into him from the side, bowling him over—

and knocking the aim of his two pistols awry.

Bang! Bang!

The chevalier's guns went off, and the Dutchman fell back, dropping his knife; he'd been hit.

"Cathy!" Cal shouted. He tossed her the silver letter opener and yanked his tomahawk from his belt.

Bill pulled a long pistol from the pocket of his coat as he ran down the hill. He would go out fighting.

Honor in defense of innocence!

The first of the Blues were only a hundred feet away. They saw him and didn't slow, spurring their horses to gallop faster up the stone road. They had fixed bayonets to their Paget carbines, which could be devastating in a foot battle, but here worked to Bill's advantage. The riders had no good way to carry the carbines with the bayonets attached (the blades would slice through the long holsters that ordinarily held the guns on the horses' shoulders), other than to hold them in their hands. So the Blues could shoot at Bill with their carbines (less than ideal; a dragoon rode to the battle, but dismounted to shoot), or use them like short lances (also not very effective), but they couldn't draw their pistols or sabers to get at him without abandoning their carbines.

It would at least buy him a few precious seconds while his enemies switched weapons. It wasn't much, but given that he was charging a line of twenty-four mounted soldiers, Bill was happy for any edge he could get.

He hoped some of the dragoons might remember him and feel loyalty, or might have taken to heart what they'd seen and heard in the St. Louis Cathedral. Every soldier who peeled away and left the fight was one less soldier who could make it to the top of the bluff.

Or one less Bill would have to kill.

Also, the sun was on Bill's shoulder; maybe it would get in the eyes of the dragoons.

And he was certainly glad he had his hat back.

Behind the Blues, Bill saw the beastmen had overtaken the chevalier's men and were routing them. Guns still fired, and there were wounded beastkind, perhaps even dead ones, but the gendarmes were decimated and in retreat.

Bill skidded to a halt. If he could only slow down the Blues long enough for the beastmen to catch them, together they might stop the dragoons from reaching Sarah. He raised his pistol and shot at the first dragoon.

Bang!

Or at least, at his horse. The bullet hit the animal in the chest and at its next bound its legs failed, and the great beast crashed cheek-first to the stones. Its rider was crushed beneath it, trapped by a leg that was mangled in the fall, but Bill had no time for his howls.

His first gun discharged, Bill tossed it aside—there would be no reloading in this brawl—and yanked the other horse pistol from his pocket. The second dragoon had his carbine raised in one hand, clamping the stock under his arm to try to steady the ungainly weapon.

Bang! The musketball went wide, plunking into the earth and throwing up tufts of grass.

Bang! Bill's shot was true. He tossed his second pistol aside, too, as the second horse shuddered to the earth, its blood spilling out.

The first wounded soldier struggled to reach his carbine, which had fallen just out of his grasp. Bill would have liked to save a shot and use his saber, but he had no time, and Obadiah's pistol, drawn and aimed at the dragoon's head, was quicker.

Bang! Bill dropped Obadiah's pistol and picked up the carbine. He regretted killing the man, but it was unavoidable, and then he had no more time for regret.

The second dragoon had landed better than his comrade, rolling away from his collapsed mount, and raced at Bill now, saber in his hand. Behind him, two mounted men had reached the unnatural bank now blocking the road, formed of the corpses of two horses, and they split. One rode uphill to get around the horseflesh blockade and come at Bill from his left, and the other skirted the corpses on the downhill side to come at Bill's right. Guns boomed downhill, but the advantage of being surrounded by his enemy was that Bill had become a very difficult target to see, much less hit.

The beastmen had almost overtaken the hindmost of the Blues.

Bill raised the carbine to his shoulder and fired into the saber-wielding man's chest, dropping his assailant in his tracks. Without missing a beat he turned and hurled the weapon at the attacker to his right; it was too heavy to throw like a javelin, but Bill managed a sort of caber toss that sent the bladed gun whirling like a pinwheel at its target.

Then he dove to the body of the first dragoon, scrabbling for the man's pistols. He came up with guns in both hands, just in time to see that his uphill attacker had tossed aside his bayonet-carbine in favor of his long sword, which he now sent slashing down at Bill's head—

Bill swung at the blade with the pistol in his left hand; he caught the sword with a wooden-metallic *chink!* and knocked the attack slightly, just slightly, to the side—

the saber bit into Bill's already-wounded shoulder and he fell back, crying out in pain.

"Damn your eyes!" *Bang!*

Bill's shot caught the man under his chin, knocking him out of the saddle. The dragoon's horse reared riderless over Bill, hooves lashing out in all directions. Bill's downhill attacker cursed, his way blocked by the panicked horse, and sheathed his saber, reaching instead for one of his pistols.

Bill pulled the trigger on his second gun—

nothing happened. Bill risked a quick look at the weapon and saw that in parrying the saber blow, its hammer had been sheared off. Bill lurched forward to his knees and threw himself at another dead soldier, grabbing for guns.

Bang!

The downhill attacker's pistol shot bit Bill in the thigh. Bill grunted in pain and silently thanked Heaven for the distraction of the rearing stallion, knowing the ball could easily have hit him between the shoulderblades instead. He jerked a long handgun clean of its holster and turned to take a careful shot, blowing his assailant out of his saddle and stone cold dead while the man struggled to draw his second pistol.

A volley of gunfire downhill told Bill the beastmen had overtaken the Blues. He drew another dead man's pistol and rolled onto his back, facing down the road at the charging Blues.

Bang!

A pistol ball hit Bill in the chest like a hammer, knocking the air out of him. Bill held his fire and sucked wind back into his lungs for a few doubtful seconds until his vision stopped swimming and he could see his new attacker, an older dragoon who was drawing a bead on Bill with a second pistol. Behind the man, the other dragoons were turning back, and a growling, snarling wall of beast-headed death was swallowing up the unit.

BANG!

The two guns fired simultaneously.

Bill smiled as the soldier's ball took him in his unwounded right arm, and he lost consciousness.

His last waking thought was how much he'd like just one shot of whisky.

He deserved it.

Hitting the chevalier hurt Cal, but it knocked the other man off balance.

The chevalier staggered away, dropping his pistols and fumbling at the sword hanging at his belt; Cal leaped forward again with his tomahawk in motion, bringing the war axe down on the chevalier's arm.

The tomahawk struck the shimmering, glowing chevalier and snapped back. A shock that burned like fire and tingled in his bones jolted through Cal's arm and into his shoulder, and in its bouncing back, he narrowly avoided being brained by his own weapon. The axe sprang across the plaza and clattered onto the stones.

Cal had given away the silver knife too soon.

"Jerusalem!" He grabbed at the braided leather lariat. He'd roped that Mocker on the Natchez Trace, so why not the Chevalier of New Orleans?

Cal slipped open the loop just as the chevalier's blade cleared its scabbard and jumped to a defensive position. "I'll gut you, *boy*," the nobleman snarled.

"Mebbe." Cal circled left, trying to get outside the man's guard.

The little Dutchman struggled for breath on his knees, and Cathy seemed to be helping him. There were all the silver daggers.

The chevalier slashed and slashed again. Calvin fell back, feeling the inadequacy of his weapon. "Do you seriously intend to *rope* me?" the chevalier asked, an amused and incredulous smile on his face. "As if I were *cattle*?"

"Yessir, pretty much jest like that." Cal lacked the confidence of his words. He would need a lucky throw to get in over the chevalier's defense. He thought he might do it, if he could lure the chevalier into a miss, and then throw the loop while the man was extended. Of course, he'd still have his sword in his hand and he'd still be dangerous. And for all Calvin knew, the chevalier's defensive shield would repulse his lariat, too.

"Is this out of mercy," the chevalier mocked him, "or incompetence?" He stepped forward for another slash, and Cal almost took his chance, but the swordsman quickly pulled back and the moment passed. Cal saw then that the chevalier bled from his side, where the Dutchman had stabbed him.

"You might get mercy from young Calvin, My Lord." Cathy Filmer closed in on the chevalier too, to Cal's left, and in her hand she held Chigozie Ukwu's little silver letter opener. "I, on the other hand, will happily kill you if you don't lay down your arms." She wiped blood from the corner of her mouth with the back of her hand.

Cal could have kissed her.

Then the Dutchman climbed to his feet, behind the chevalier, and brandished his own silver weapon. "Ja," said the Dutchman Jacob Hop, startling the chevalier into a sideways stumble to avoid being completely encircled. "Ik ook, Mynheer Chevalier."

The chevalier snarled a fierce look of anger, and Cal braced himself for a fight. Instead, the chevalier suddenly turned on his heel to run—

Cal threw. His lariat settled over the nobleman's shoulders, pinned the man's arms to his sides and brought him to the ground as neatly as any calf. Jacob Hop rushed forward to thrust his silver knife in the chevalier's face, and tossed the Frenchman's weapon aside.

"Jest like a little bull calf." Cal dropped a second loop around the chevalier's ankles to hogtie him. As he worked, he cast a worried glance at Sarah. She lay unconscious, her crown upside down on the stones before her.

Behind her, the Martinite Ezekiel Angleton knelt over the body of the dead Creole. He leaned over the man, as if he were going to kiss him.

"Hey!" Cal looked around for his tomahawk.

"Merde!" the chevalier grumbled as Cal tightened the knot.

Cathy Filmer crossed the plaza, heading for Ezekiel Angleton.

"The odds were but twenty-four to one,
ma'am. They never had a chance."

⟢⟡⟣

CHAPTER TWENTY-NINE

Cathy Filmer shoved the silver knife into Ezekiel Angleton's thigh.
BOOM!
Light and noise threw her and the Martinite priest apart and knocked Calvin, on the other side of the plaza, to the ground.
He was blinded and deafened, and for a time only the feel of cold stone on his palms and knees reassured him he hadn't been killed. Eventually the coruscating whorls around his head resolved themselves into vision, blurry but serviceable, and Cal rose to his feet.
He staggered over to Sarah and knelt beside her. She was breathing, though her breaths came uneven and shallow. Her skin burned to the touch, and felt scaly; her lips were cracked, there was dried blood in her ears and at the corners of her eyes and under her fingernails.
But she lived. Cal carried her to the long grass and tried to make her comfortable, draping his coat over her.
He checked Cathy Filmer next, and found her conscious. "I'll live, Calvin." He helped her to sit up. "What about the Martinite?"
Angleton had disappeared.
By this time the Dutchman had regained his feet, and stood guard again over the chevalier, silver blade resolutely pointed at the Frenchman's throat. Cal offered his hand in friendship and they shook.

"How long've you...I dunno, been awake?" Cal asked.

"Ja," Jacob Hop said, "het's strange for you. Natuurlijk, het's all strange ook for me. Ik have been awake, as you say, all along. The other...Simon Sword...took my body after Ik first saw Bill, on the *Incroyable*, and he controlled me, but het left me able to see. And ook to *hear*."

"I see." Cal thought he'd most likely understood the Dutchman.

"Nee, maybe you see niet," Hop contradicted him. "Ik was a deaf-mute, from a long time ago. Since Simon Sword took me, Ik have been able, for the first time in many years, to hear and ook to speak. And not only did het open my mouth, het gave me ook the gift of speaking English, a thing which Ik never before have done het."

"*Sort of* he give you the gift of English." Cal laughed. "But you ain't Simon Sword now, right?"

"Nee, Ik ben hem niet," Hop agreed, and Cal nodded in relief.

"Well," Cal said, "I'm right glad to have you along."

"Dank je," Hop answered with a disheveled grin.

"If you two have finished plighting your troth to one another," the chevalier called, "free me. I've lost feeling in my legs."

"I can't free you jest yet," Cal answered, "but iffen you promise to be good, I reckon I could sit you up and tie you to a tree."

Sarah awoke to the feeling of arms around her. She started, panicking—

"Whoa!" Cal whispered. "Jest relax, Sarah, I got you!"

She lay wrapped in blankets and coats, propped against Calvin's chest, and he held her tightly. Before her blazed a small fire. Across the flames, Sir William sat on a fallen trunk wearing just breeches, boots, and his floppy black hat. Even half-naked, he looked formidable, his chest and arms heavily muscled, scarred, and covered with iron-gray hair. His right arm and chest were bandaged, and he held a bottle of whisky from which he sipped while Cathy Filmer dug a bullet out of his left shoulder.

"How's the frog?" Sir William called out, and then Sarah realized he was addressing the Dutchman. Sarah shuddered, but only for a moment—her witchy eye was unbound and she saw instantly that the Heron King was gone, and Jacob Hop's aura glowed bright, white, and healthy. He sat facing away from the fire at a right angle, a pistol in each hand, aiming them both at the Chevalier of New Orleans, tied to a tree.

"Ja, he's good," Hop answered cheerfully. Sarah was pleased to hear his thick Dutch accent.

"You awake?" Cal held her close, closer than he ever had, closer than anyone had ever held her. His nearness frightened her a little, but his presence also felt warm and comfortable.

Sarah felt her satchel around her waist and she pushed away her coverings to check it, reassuring herself that it held the Orb, the Crown, and the Heronplow; they were there, on a bed of fresh green grass.

"Yes," she said, "and I feel like hell."

Cal relaxed his grip.

"Your Majesty," Sir William greeted her, raising the bottle in salute. "I would rise and bow, but I fear doing so might cause my physician to stab me."

"It might indeed, Sir William," Cathy agreed, but she stopped her work to curtsy to Sarah, bloody knife in her hand. "Welcome back, Your Majesty."

"Thank you." Sarah felt like a corn doll lying too near the fire.

"You all right?" Cal wanted to know.

She nodded, though it was a lie. "What happened?" She gestured to the trussed up Chevalier. "Where are the others?"

"We killed the other Lazars." Cal shrugged.

"Good riddance," Sarah said.

"Your . . . men, your soldiers," Cal continued, "the beastfolk, they made short work of the gendarmes, and then Bill, well, he charged down the hill at the dragoons and he run 'em off."

"Alone?" Sarah asked.

Sir William saluted her with his bottle again. "The odds were but twenty-four to one, ma'am. They never had a chance." He took a modest sip. "And they were kind enough to leave us a store of supplies."

Sarah laughed; it hurt her to do so, from her scalp to her toes, but she was so happy and relieved to be alive that she almost enjoyed the pain. She sat up, carefully not disentangling herself from Calvin or pushing him away.

"What about Father Angleton?" she pressed.

"Gone," Cal told her. "He run hisself off without any help. And Cathy knifed him, in the bargain."

"He was trying to resurrect the Creole, I think." Cathy finally pried the ball from Sir William's shoulder and tossed it into the fire. "A bit of well-placed silver changed his plan."

Sarah was sorry she'd missed it. "We need to set a watch, to make sure he doesn't creep back in the night."

"Yes, ma'am," Sir William agreed, "it's done. In the morning, when you've rested, I'll introduce you to your new guard."

Sarah shivered.

"In the morning, as well, you can give us direction," the old soldier added. "Whether we ride for Cahokia, for instance, or whether you wish some or all of us to ride . . . elsewhere."

"Thank you for keeping my brother's location from me, Sir William," Sarah managed to say, with an effort. She took one of Calvin's hands in her own. "Please continue to do so. We'll ride north tomorrow morning."

"They's beans iffen you want 'em." Cal pointed with his free hand to a pot hunkered into the coals of the fire. "And hard bread and bacon."

Sarah shook her head. "I doubt my stomach'd handle 'em right now, Cal," she said, "but you're sweet to offer. Is there water?"

Cal had water to hand. He brought her a plate of beans, too, despite her reservations, and Sarah managed to get down a couple of spoonfuls.

Ezekiel's leg hurt where the woman had stabbed him. He'd wrapped the wound, but he hadn't had time to apply any healing gramarye. He ran, staggering through bony woods as the air grew chill.

He had walked away from his vision of the Lord Protector the night before feeling strong, healthy, full of tingling, smoky power. It was part of Cromwell's gift, along with the specific magic the Necromancer had taught him. His raising of Daniel Berkeley as a Lazar (like Elijah raising the widow's son, like Jesus calling Lazarus from the tomb—Cromwell's words) had cost him, and he'd spent the rest of his strength in the battle.

The battle he'd lost.

Ezekiel stumbled north and east, thrashing his way through the trees and wiry thickets of brush on the high ground overlooking the Ohio River. If he kept the Ohio on his right, he'd eventually reach Free Imperial Youngstown. Of course, that was hundreds of miles away; he would hit towns long before that, and likely a Company stockade, or some Imperial outpost.

This was the Ohio. Pacification garrisons should be easy to find.

He stopped, standing on crisp dry leaves in a small clearing. Did he really want to find an Imperial garrison? Habit made him think of himself as an Imperial servant, as chaplain to the Philadelphia Blues. But the Blues were shattered and Ezekiel had failed Thomas Penn.

Ezekiel had also failed the Lord Protector.

Did he have a master now?

Ezekiel stared up at the night sky, a splotch of darkness overhead glittering with distant stars. Could he still be God's servant? He had been, once, but for a long time he had had earthly business to attend to. And in the furthering of that earthly business, Ezekiel had done things men might see as crimes.

He collapsed to his knees. He must still be a servant of God, he *must*. He had only ever wanted to do good. He served the Lord Protector, and Cromwell's designs were godly, righteous, perfect. He sought to end *death*. He would undo the Fall of Adam, like a second Christ, a greater Savior, the author of a more perfect work of salvation.

And Ezekiel had failed him.

"Help me!" Ezekiel croaked, and fell sobbing to the hard earth.

"I am here, Father," the harsh voice of the Lord Protector honked, and Ezekiel realized that he sobbed upon a pair of riding boots.

Ezekiel looked up into a gaze that was kind and imperious at the same time. "I've failed, My Lord." He wept.

"Hush," the Lord Protector calmed him. "Thou hast fought a brave battle. The long war yet stretches ahead of thee."

"But . . . but, My Lord, the Witchy Eye lives." Some part of him yearned to be chastised.

"Yes," Cromwell agreed, "and I wished her dead. Still, the soldiers of my servant Thomas Penn yet occupy the Ohio, and it is a good thing that Sarah Elytharias Penn has been forced into taking up her father's banner so soon."

"My Lord?"

"Yes," Cromwell mused. "She is young and unready, yet she thrusts herself into the cockpit of power like a starving dog into a stewpot. Chaos must result. Thomas will have to increase his efforts in the Pacification, more troops must be sent to the Ohio. All thy work, my servant Ezekiel, redounds to the greater good."

The Lord Protector made it sound almost as if he had planned for Sarah to survive.

"My Lord." Ezekiel bowed his head. "Should I . . . ? Should I then rejoin Thomas Penn in Philadelphia, and serve him again as chaplain?"

"I think not," the Lord Protector replied. "There is work for thee in the Crown Lands."

"The Crown Lands?" Ezekiel was puzzled.

Cromwell nodded solemnly. "Dost thou not recall what the monk Thalanes told thee?"

Ezekiel thought back. Thalanes had been slippery, had truthfully told Robert Hooke that the Witchy Eye had slept under the roof of the Bishop of New Orleans, but had omitted to mention that most of the bishop's palace was occupied by a cloister of wizard-priests. Ezekiel had managed to avoid falling into that trap, but he couldn't remember the other two answers Thalanes had been forced to give.

"Lee," he finally recalled. "Thalanes said that he had come to New Orleans to find the man William Lee."

"Correct," Cromwell said. "Dost thou know William Lee?"

"Yaas." Ezekiel tried to put together the pieces of a puzzle he sensed the Lord Protector had already solved. "Not well. I know him by his fame. He was captain of the Blues before Daniel Berkeley. He left Philadelphia shortly after I arrived. I'd heard he'd gone back home, to Johnsland, but I suppose after that he went to New Orleans."

Cromwell nodded again, smiling. Ezekiel shivered in the cold, wishing he had his cloak; in his haste he had left it with all his things at the foot of Wisdom's Bluff. "What else?"

Ezekiel shook his head. "I don't remember."

"My servant Robert Hooke asked about the Witchy Eye's plans after she left New Orleans."

A thunderbolt struck Ezekiel Angleton in the back of his head. "Her brother. She was going to go get her brother."

"Yes."

"If she came to New Orleans to get William Lee, it was because Lee knew where to find her brother." He felt like a fool for not having made this connection earlier.

"It seemeth likely."

"Lee hid her brother fifteen years ago, in the same way that Thalanes hid her."

"I believe so," Cromwell agreed. He was smiling, and Ezekiel basked in the approval.

"In Johnsland."

"Perhaps," Cromwell said, "and perhaps not. But a badly disfigured fifteen-year-old boy is not an easy thing to hide."

"And then the boy can be used against his sister."

"In many ways," Cromwell agreed. "But I must send someone to Johnsland I can trust."

"Send me, My Lord," Ezekiel begged.

"But I cannot allow thee to freeze to death on the Ohio." Cromwell had a bundle Ezekiel hadn't noticed, and he now shook it out. It was a coat, a long, tattered brown coat that smelled of mildew and the grave. Cromwell draped it over Ezekiel's shoulders and Ezekiel shuddered into the moldering fabric, repulsed by the Lazar stink but grateful for the warmth.

"Get thee to Johnsland, my servant Ezekiel," the Lord Protector said. "Find thou the Witchy Eye's brother."

Ezekiel nodded; he had no more words.

He waited, expecting more direction, but there was only silence.

Ezekiel looked up, and found that he was alone.

"Lucy," he croaked. There was no answer.

Finally, with heavy legs but determination in his heart, he lifted his feet and began again to make his way along the river.

The whisky (consumed only in moderate doses) dulled Bill's pain enough to help him sleep, but old habits of command he had thought long dead woke him, and sent him hobbling to the perimeter to check his sentries.

He had never commanded beastfolk before, but it didn't make him uncomfortable; he had seen too many beasts with men's faces to be bothered by one that had the face of a coyote. Frankly, after exchanging passwords with the warriors on guard and ascertaining that all was in good order, he felt Sarah's beastmen were less foreign to him than, say, the French. They were fierce and they did their duty, and Bill looked forward them to drilling them.

Would they ever be able to use firearms effectively, though? Many of the beastmen had eyes on opposite sides of their heads, which must limit their ability to estimate range. Perhaps he could divide them, and arm with pistols only the ones whose eyes faced forward, and who had fingers and thumbs.

Bill had not known what to make of the little Dutchman now, and had spent the evening avoiding too much conversation with the man. One part of him wanted to call the fellow *Jake* and tell him war stories, but another part felt like a wolf with its paw mangled from a trap, wary at scenting what he thought might be another.

Standing outside the firelight at the edge of the stone plaza, looking along the steep slope down which earlier in the day he'd charged to a likely death, Bill heard a sound. Turning, he saw Long Cathy, and on impulse he put his arm around her.

"I'm afraid the better view is on the other side, ma'am," he apologized. "From here all one can see is the forest."

"That's the Ohio," she said. "It must be full of Imperial soldiers."

"I expect it is," he agreed. "And traders, of the Imperial Ohio Company and the Dutch Ohio Company both. Also Firstborn, and beastkind, and bandits, and wild animals, and even a few ordinary people." Her body melted into his.

His wounds hurt him less when she was present.

They watched the darkness for a few minutes, listening to the slow chirping of crickets. "I've been told that you can ascertain the temperature by counting the speed of a cricket's chirp," Bill said eventually, "but I'm damned if I can remember how."

"That's a farmer's skill," Cathy observed.

"I've never been much of a farmer," Bill conceded, thinking of the perpetually chaotic state of his family lands, the spiraling debts and unkept ledgers, the shouting matches with his steward. "Mine are other gifts."

There was a long silence. "Bill," Cathy finally said, "I need to know there's a chance for us to be together."

Bill paid very careful attention to his breathing and did not let himself sigh. "I hope there is." He turned Cathy Filmer to face him and looked into her eyes. "I must follow my queen. For now that means my road lies north, into the Ohio. When she is safely on her throne, I must go to Johnsland and discover what has become of my...of my family. It pains me to say this, but my life will be much the simpler if I discover that Sally, my wife, has been silent these years because she is dead. I will not say that

I *hope* that she is dead; that would not be a desire fitting for a Christian man. But I do hope that my discoveries, whatever they may be, permit me to return and be with you."

Cathy looked up at him with blues eyes glistening. "I love you, William Lee." Bill felt jolts of electricity racing up his spine. "My road is with you."

"I love you too, Catherine Howard."

They kissed then, and it was a long time before they returned to the fire.

In the morning, they gave the Chevalier of New Orleans his pistols, sword, money, and a spare horse, and they bid him farewell.

He climbed slowly into his saddle, stiff from a night spent tied to a tree. Chafing his wrists, he bowed his head slightly to Sarah. "You're as gracious in victory as you are formidable in action, Your Majesty."

"Yes," Sarah agreed, "I am."

"I plan to send my embassies soon, notwithstanding our . . . recent misunderstandings."

She arched her eyebrow at him and said nothing.

The chevalier nodded and turned his horses, and Sarah and her companions watched him ride down the bluff and disappear into the forest. The instant he was out of sight, Jacob Hop cleared his throat.

"Your Majesty," he said, "Ik ook have something Ik moet discuss with you."

"Mr. Jacob Hop," she answered, "what am I to do with you?"

"Ja," he admitted, "Ik moet look very strange to you."

"No," she disagreed, gazing at his steady white aura with her witchy eye, "you look very normal."

"Ja," he said, "dat is good." He shifted from foot to foot for a moment while Sarah gazed at him, then cleared his throat again. "Your Majesty, Ik have a message."

"Ja?" Sarah asked, then corrected herself. "I mean, yes? Who from, Mr. Hop? From Simon Sword?"

"Nee," Hop said. "Ik have not seen him since you have. From the dead man. From René du Plessis, the chevalier's seneschal."

Sarah's interest was piqued. "What did Mr. du Plessis wish you to tell me?"

Hop dug into the pocket of his black breeches and pulled out a medallion, offering it to Sarah. She took it and examined it in the palm of her hand; it was a cheap disk, made of bronze, and it bore a cluster of the letters T, C, and B, with a stylized lightning bolt through them. There was dried blood on the medallion, crusted in and around the letters and the bolt, and it threw the carving into a higher relief. She thought she had seen the symbol somewhere before, but couldn't quite place it.

"What's this?" she asked.

Hop shrugged. "Ik know niet. He was dying, and the chevalier left him, and he put het into my hand. He told me two things. He said 'tell the Witchy Eye that she moet say to Franklin: the sword has gone back.'"

"Franklin?" Sarah didn't know any Franklin that she could think of. "Who is Franklin? Which Franklin?"

Hop shook his head.

"It's interesting that the message should mention the name Franklin, Your Majesty," Cathy offered. "That device is a sort of heraldic image of the Franklin family. It reminds the viewer of the four greatest accomplishments of Benjamin Franklin."

"The lightning bolt for electricity?" Cal asked.

Cathy nodded. "T is for the Tarock, C for the Compact of 1784, and B for the Bishopric of Philadelphia."

"I've been told by certain inveterate gamblers," Sir William interjected, "that the Shield is unlucky. Occult meanings."

Cathy frowned. "That may be, but Franklin's Shield is carved all over Philadelphia's great buildings. It's on all four exterior walls of the Lightning Cathedral, for instance."

"Why, Mrs. Filmer," Sir William said, "I was unaware you had ever been to Philadelphia."

Cathy Filmer winked at the Cavalier. "Why, Sir William, a lady must have her mysteries."

"And the second thing?" Sarah inquired.

"Ja, dat also did niet make much sense. He said 'het is niet help for the widow's son.'"

Freemasons. She turned and looked around at her companions, who all shook their shoulders and shrugged.

"Jerusalem," Calvin muttered. "He sounds crazy."

Cal was hiding something. Not something evil or treacherous. His aura looked ... embarrassed. Was Calvin Calhoun a Mason? It was the sort of thing you didn't talk about much on

Calhoun Mountain, but any man who wasn't no-account and got old enough, most likely got inducted. Cal seemed to care about the privacy of the thing.

"Did he say anything else?" Sarah asked Jacob Hop.

Hop shook his head. Sarah could tell from the tones of his aura that he was telling the truth. He was as confused as she was.

"Thank you, Mr. Hop," she said. "From here I ride north. I'm grateful for your services, and if you wish to ride your separate way, I'll send you with horses, food, money, and weapons."

"Ja, dank u. And if Ik wish to come with Your Majesty?" Hop stood straight and faced Sarah, but his eyes flickered to Sir William.

"I can use honest men in my service," Sarah conceded with a smile. "What skills do you have, Mr. Hop?"

"Ik have had many jobs, Your Majesty," Hop said, "including, recently, prison guard. Also, though Ik was under an enchantment at the time," he added shyly, "Sir William had begun to teach me soldiery."

Sir William looked astounded. "But you were Simon Sword, suh."

"Ja. And Ik was ook me." Hop looked at his shoe buckles. "Only Ik was in control niet. But Ik would graag like to be your squire again, Sir William, if dat is a possibility."

Sir William considered the request. "How do I know you're not Simon Sword? How will I know in the future you've not become Simon Sword again?"

Hop shrugged. "Ik know that Ik ben hem niet. How do Ik know that you are Simon Sword niet?"

The older man laughed. "Touché, as they would say in New Orleans."

"Neither one of you is Simon Sword," Sarah informed them. "I am confident. Mr. Hop, you are welcome into my service, if Sir William will have you, then as his squire, and if he will not, then as my quartermaster. I have recently come into possession of a herd of horses that needs management."

"Ja, Ik ben good with animals," Hop said, brightening.

Sir William laughed again. "Very well, suh, I'll have you as my protégé, and one of your duties shall be managing the horses. And between us, you may call me Bill."

Hop bowed. "Dank u wel! And you may call me Jake, graag." He rushed off down the hill, presumably to see to the animals.

"I'm going to have to teach that young man to speak English." Sir William sighed. "He keeps gargling in the middle of his sentences."

"Graag," Cal said cheerfully.

"Graag," Sarah agreed.

"Apparently what I had mistaken for Dutch is in fact a tonsil disease of some sort," Sir William growled. "I only pray I do not myself succumb."

"You're not likely to, Sir William," Cathy Filmer told him. "You of all men."

"It *is* Dutch," Sarah said. "It means a lot of things, but basically it's *please* or *gladly*."

"I see," Sir William nodded. "Well, then, would Your Majesty care to review her new household guard? Chraarch?"

"Now *that*, Sir William," Sarah told him, "sounds like a disease of the tonsils."

Sarah rode down the slope of Wisdom's Bluff with her four companions. Beside her rode Calvin, and as they clopped down the ancient road Sarah reached out unsteadily to touch his elbow.

"Careful, Sarah," he urged her.

"It ain't fair to you, Cal," she said. "I know you love me, and it ain't fair to you, but I gotta ask you to wait."

He nodded.

"I don't know where I'm a-goin' or what's gonna happen to me," she tried to explain, "and they's folks—well, you seen 'em, the chevalier and Simon Sword both—as seem to be interested in me or willin' to leave me alone, iffen only they reckon I might could marry 'em. That's an advantage, and I gotta preserve it as long as I can, but I know it ain't fair to you."

Cal nodded again. Sarah saw a single tear in his eye.

"Besides, I'm young yet," she added. "Even for an Appalachee I'm young to marry, and who knows what the Philadelphians and the Cahokians do? They's lots of time for you and me, Cal." She watched his face carefully.

"I promised the Elector I'd see you safe on this journey," Cal said slowly. "I reckon the journey ain't over yet." He turned to smile at her, and she felt relieved. "Besides, Lord hates a man as can't hold his horses."

At the foot of the hill waited her sworn guard of beastfolk. She held her head high as Sir William presented them.

"Their weapons and armor are mixed, Your Majesty," he told her, "and their tactics are quite direct. However, their discipline is impeccable and their individual valor is of a positively heroic scale. With Your Majesty's permission, I'll take time on our march to drill them."

"Of course, Sir William," she agreed.

"Also," he added, "there is this. One of our scouts, that coyote-headed fellow over there, I believe his name is Chikaak, found it on the trail ahead of us. I thought you might want to look at it, as a matter of setting your expectations for the days ahead."

He handed Sarah a crumpled broadsheet.

!! ~ Men of the Ohio ~ !!

Do not believe FILTHY LIES that are told by *seditioneers* and *regicides* lurking in dark corners. HIS IMPERIAL MAJESTY, THE EMPEROR THOMAS PENN is your Friend. His Heart is full of Love for the <u>bleeding people of the Ohio</u>, and he wants nothing better than *Peace for ALL Ohioans*.

The rebels and troublemakers are the Enemies of Peace. They <u>murdered the King of Cahokia</u>, and they plot against His Family! Help the King's Brother, THE EMPEROR THOMAS PENN, bring Peace. Show your Love for Your Emperor. Report troublemakers. Obey the Law. Assist Imperial officers. Trade with Company-approved merchants. Pay all requested exactions. Bring *Peace to the Ohio* at last.

Sarah finished reading the broadsheet and laughed. "Very well. We know what we're getting into."

She crumpled the paper and tossed it into the long grass.

"Let's go bring peace to the Ohio at last," she said, and she turned her horse north.